C000180331

KING PE...

THE FU...

James Hanley, novelist, short-story writer and playwright, was born in Dublin in 1901. Since 1930 he has published forty-eight books including one excursion into autobiography, *Broken Water* (1937), and one documentary on the situation of coal-miners in the thirties, *Grey Children* (1937). His work has received considerable critical acclaim: E. S. Duvall writing in the *Boston Globe* said of him, 'Referred to as one of "the ten most able and influential living writers in the English language" ... Hanley's work is unlike anyone else's ... [his] crystalline, rhythmic prose has a cumulative power that resonates deeper and deeper into the lives of his characters ... Hanley uncovers the terrifying but beautiful variations of the human heart ... He is quite literally a wonderful writer.' His novels include *The Hollow Sea* (1938), *The Ocean* (1941), *The Closed Harbour* (1952), *The Welsh Sonata* (1954, reissued 1978), *Levine* (1956), *Another World* (1972), *A Dream Journey* (1976), and *A Kingdom* (1978). He has recently completed a new novel, *Conversations in the Dark*, and in 1982 one of his earlier books, *Against the Stream* (originally published under the pseudonym Patrick Shone as *The House in the Valley*, 1951), was reissued.

JAMES HANLEY

THE FURYS

PENGUIN BOOKS

Penguin Books Ltd, Harmondsworth, Middlesex, England
Penguin Books, 625 Madison Avenue, New York, New York 10022, U.S.A.
Penguin Books Australia Ltd, Ringwood, Victoria, Australia
Penguin Books Canada Ltd, 2801 John Street, Markham, Ontario, Canada L 3 R 1 B 4
Penguin Books (N.Z.) Ltd, 182–190 Wairau Road, Auckland 10, New Zealand

First published by Chatto & Windus 1935
Published in Penguin Books 1983

Made and printed in Great Britain by
Richard Clay (The Chaucer Press) Ltd, Bungay, Suffolk
Filmset in Photina by
Northumberland Press Ltd,
Gateshead, Tyne and Wear

For Tim

PART ONE

CHAPTER I

I

As the woman approached the building she became aware of two things. First, that the wintry sun had appeared and was now shining on two great sheets of glass. Second, that an old woman was standing by the long flight of stone steps selling matches. She drew nearer. The two sheets of glass suddenly moved. The huge building opened its mouth and she passed inside. The uniformed attendant at the swing-doors stared after her. A rare visitor, he thought. At the bottom of the long marble staircase she stopped and her eyes sought the topmost stair. She sighed. She was a tall woman, between fifty and sixty years of age. Her faded straw hat seemed to sit uncomfortably upon her head, wisps of black hair peeped out. She had a long face, rather pale, with large brown eyes. There was a marked severity about her expression, the mouth seemed hard. She stood staring at the top stair. From time to time she turned her head round, furtively, as though on the watch for somebody, the while her hands kept going to her hat. No. The hat was not right. Then she sat down on the step. Some gentlemen came out of the lift, stared at her for a moment, then passed on. The attendant at the door had long ago forgotten her. She lowered her head, her eyes seemed to roam over the vast floor space. Once she coughed. It echoed through the building. She was mumbling to herself. 'From the mast on to his heels. Dear me!' Then she passed her hand across her face. 'Ah!' she exclaimed after a long silence. She rose to her feet. 'From the mast right on to his heels,' she kept repeating. She commenced to climb the stairs. These words appeared to have a strange effect upon her. She had been murmuring them all the morning. They circled round and round her brain. At times she seemed caught up in the very whirl of these words, to pass out of herself, to float in the air, carried along as it were in the flood of the expression which never left her lips. 'From the mast on to his heels. Dear me!' Now she paused again.

She was dressed in a long black coat and skirt. Her black shoes were too tight for her, and her ankles were much swollen. The shoes were worn down at the heel. She raised her head suddenly. Somebody was coming down the stairs. A middle-aged man, a clerk perhaps. Seeing the woman standing in the middle of this wilderness of marble, he stopped and

9

exclaimed: 'You ought to use the lift. You'll never climb that flight of stairs.' There was a kindness in the tone of his voice. He jerked his thumb behind him, indicating the eighty-eight stairs the woman had yet to climb. She smiled. It was the first time that morning that anybody had spoken to her. She rather liked the gentleman. It touched her deeply. 'You ought to use the lift.' She repeated the words aloud. 'Come this way,' he said, and he took her arm. Slowly they made their way down the stairs again. He conducted the woman to the lift. The lift attendant looked curiously at the ill-assorted pair. Which floor did she want to go to? This was different, she thought. The tone of the man's voice, everything was different. She looked round. The kind gentleman had already disappeared. She stared at the lift, hesitated a moment, a rather frightened expression upon her face, as though she were about to step into some sort of cage. The lift man coughed. Some girl typists came running up and entered. They stood in a group in the corner. They were giggling amongst themselves. The woman outside lowered her head. She still hesitated. This was worse. She had better rush back to the staircase and climb after all. She was really out of place amongst such an assembly. There was a pungent smell of powder about the lift. 'Hurry up,' the attendant said. She stepped inside. At that moment the clerk came hurrying back. The woman was sure he was a clerk. 'What floor do you want?' he asked.

'The top one, please,' she said.

'Put this lady out at the top floor,' the gentleman said, and went away again. He smiled. He was the Company's solicitor. He was just going out for his morning coffee. The lift ascended. At the third floor the giggling typists got out. The lift hummed once more. Then it stopped. 'Top floor,' the man said, and slid the gate back. The woman replied, 'Thank you,' and passed outside. Another wilderness. Great corridors, many doors, each door numbered. She looked up and down. Then she approached the nearest door. 'Engineering Secretary'. No, that wasn't it. It was the Marine Superintendent she wanted. She began to wander up and down the long corridors, her eyes scanning the names and numbers of each. Where this office was she did not know. How stupid of her. She ought to have asked the lift attendant. She was a little angry. It was simply stupid to be borne to the very top of this great building and then left in the middle of the desert as it were. Then she espied a boy hurrying towards her. She was certain he was going to speak to her, but he only whistled shrilly and went by. She called him. He came back to her. Where was Mr Lake's office? Did he know? Would he please show her to the door? They went off together, turned right, and at the end of a long brilliantly lighted passage they stopped. 'In there,' the boy said, and left her standing at the door. Yes, this was correct. 'Mr Lake. Marine Superintendent'.

She opened the door and went inside. She looked around. A shutter was suddenly shot up, and she jumped with fright. A girlish face pushed itself out and a voice said:

'Yes. Please.'

The woman went to the window. She shot a quick glance at this girl's face. Why of course. She had been in the lift with her. If only she had opened her mouth then, it would have saved all this trouble. But she had felt so ashamed. She did not know why. She experienced it again as she looked into the bright face of this colourfully dressed girl. Above her head a clock ticked. Instinctively her eyes wandered to its face. How late it was getting. Must hurry up. Denny would be coming home to dinner today. It would just happen on a day like this of course. The girl tapped on the desk with her fingers.

'I want to see Mr Lake, please,' said the woman. 'My name is Mrs Fury. It's about my son. I had a cable from New York to say that he had met with an accident. Thank you.' The woman drew back. The girl disappeared. The window shot down again. Mrs Fury sat down. 'Dear me!' she exclaimed under her breath. 'From the top of the mast on to his heels. Good God!' The door opened. The girl had come back. 'This way please,' she said, and led the woman towards an inner office. In the few moments of her crossing that highly polished floor Mrs Fury became conscious of her appearance. Her hand went to her hat again. She began to push the wisps of hair out of sight. She looked down at her dress, then lower. She felt this drabness cling to her like some sort of dirty skin. She was out of place in this office. The door ahead of her had opened now. A tall grey-haired gentleman stood facing her. The girl went away.

'Mrs Fury?' he said.

'Yes,' the woman replied. She passed inside. The door closed.

'Will you please take a chair?' said the grey-haired gentleman. Mrs Fury sat down. So this was Mr Lake. Lord! The number of times she had heard that name. And now here was the gentleman himself in flesh and blood. Mr Lake was indeed a name that had a certain significance for her family. Even Denny had spoken about him, trip after trip. She laid her hands in her lap and looked at this man. He was wearing pince-nez. Mrs Fury thought he looked a kind, benevolent old gentleman. Now she felt his eyes upon her. She sat up.

'It's about my son,' she said. Her whole body seemed to stiffen in the chair. 'I had a cable from New York. Is it very bad? How did it happen? Has he gone into hospital? I ...' she paused. The man lowered his eyes. He had been watching this woman and noticed how gradually she was losing control of herself. Her hands seemed to cross and recross her bosom. They appeared to him to be rather finely shaped hands. He rose from his chair and stood over her.

'Your son is a quartermaster on the *Turcoman?*'

'Yes.' She did not look up at him. The same aimless movements of her hands. 'How irritating it is,' thought the grey-haired man.

'The fact is, I am sorry to say,' continued the kind-looking gentleman, 'the fact is that your son fell from the cross-trees. He is not seriously hurt. He landed, fortunately enough, on his heels. I should think that with ...' Mrs Fury's head appeared to sag a little. 'From the mast on to his heels,' she said. Then she stood on her feet. 'Oh!' she said. The man put an arm about her shoulder. 'Sit here, Mrs Fury.' He drew up a chair. Then he flung up the window. He rang a bell on his desk. A young woman appeared. 'Bring this lady a glass of water,' he said. The woman opened her eyes and looked up at the window. The word 'lady' had a peculiar effect upon her. She smiled. How long ago was it, she wondered, how long ago since she was spoken to like that? She turned round in the chair. 'I'm sorry,' she said. The man smiled and sat down again.

'That's quite all right, Mrs Fury, I'm very sorry about this accident to your son. Unfortunately we have not full details from Captain Thomas. But the *Turcoman* is leaving New York for Gelton tonight. Your son is in hospital, and will eventually be sent home on another boat.' He began to tear some notes up and put them in the waste-paper basket. The woman got up from her chair, walked across to his desk, and leaning over said, 'Is that all? Or perhaps you could tell me how it happened?' Again he smiled. He did not know. As he had already told her, no details were available as yet, but as soon as he had them he would inform her. Meanwhile she was not to worry. Her son was having the best attention, and in a few weeks he would be on his feet again. Meanwhile she could continue to draw his allotment money from the ground-floor office. Mrs Fury realized at once that there was nothing more to be done. She turned towards the door. The man followed her.

'Could you please tell me which hospital my son is in?' she asked. The man hurried back to his desk and wrote the address on a sheet of paper. 'Anthony Fury, Riverside Hospital, West St., New York.' 'Thank you,' the woman said and passed out. She did not hear the door close, but when she half turned her head she discovered to her surprise that it *was* closed. The girl led her through the inquiry office. Another door. 'Thank you.' At last. She was in the corridor again. She stood there for some time, as though she were rooted to the very spot. Anthony fell from the mast. Good God! And she knew nothing. It was always the same. They never told you anything. Why, they hadn't even written to her from the office. She walked slowly down the corridor. At the end of it she stopped, and leaned against the wall. A weariness came over her. It had been so sudden. How strange it was too. She had only just looked up the movement of his ship in the *Journal of Commerce* that morning. And then the cable arrived. She now stood at the top of the stairs. Her eyes followed each stair until eventually they were focused upon the uniformed attendant at the bottom. What a frightful height she was. She drew back suddenly from where she stood. The man below appeared as a sort of insect to her. She turned round and half ran along the corridor. Where was the lift? She must go down that way. She simply could not face those stairs again. She was worried. The time was getting on. Before she knew where she was, Denny would be home. Yes, she could not waste time. A man and a girl came walking behind her. She moved aside to let them pass. Then she followed in their wake. They were going to the lift. Ah! There it was. One lost oneself entirely in buildings like this. She stepped into the lift. The attendant did not seem to notice her. She saw that he had one arm. The lift descended noiselessly. At the bottom she felt sick again. When she stepped out she looked up at the height from which she had come. It almost made her dizzy. At that moment doors opened and a stream of people came into the corridors. They hurried along towards the swing-doors. She tried to edge away from them, but they swept her on. Near the door itself she was carried away with this tide of hurrying bodies. After much confusion she found herself in the street again. She straightened her hat once more, brushed down her coat with a sweep of the hand, looked from right to left, then made to cross the road. She heard the clock of the near-by chapel strike. It was late.

She almost ran across the road and boarded a car. It started off with a jerk. She lay back in her seat. What a journey. What a place to have to go to. She turned her head round and looked out of the tram window. So that was the Shipping Company's office. That towering building on the water-front. And her son worked for that company, as once her husband had done. As once, indeed, that other son had done too. She made the sign of the Cross on her forehead. Poor John! He had never gone to sea, but had worked with the shore gang. That tall white building. Somebody on the seat in front of her opened the window. The wind came sailing in. Mrs Fury held on to her hat, inwardly cursing the woman for opening the window. Now the tram had cleared the water-front. It was on the long Harbour Road. Not far to go now. The road in front was almost bare of traffic. The tram careered madly along. Mrs Fury's head lay up against the window, but she saw nothing. Her mind was closed. It had shut out the sights and sounds outside, the shops, the many people passing to and fro, the tram itself, it carried her body only, for her spirit like her thoughts had suddenly taken flight and now hovered above the hospital where her son lay. She saw him lying in the bed, saw the changing expressions upon his face. The conductor called out 'Terminus', but she did not hear. Her thoughts were three thousand miles away. Now she shook herself suddenly, exclaiming under her breath, 'Good heavens, how late it is. The children are home from school.' She turned out of her seat and made a sudden dash on to the platform. 'Stop,' she said. The tram pulled up with a screeching sound. She got off and crossed the road. Twenty minutes to get her husband's dinner ready. She hurried along. When she reached the house a telegraph boy was standing at the door. The next door neighbour popped her head out. But Mrs Fury did not see the woman. She took the wire from the boy, tore it open and began to read. 'No answer,' she said to the boy, and went into the house.

2

As she passed upstairs, she glanced hurriedly at the silent figure of her father, sitting huddled in his chair. This high-backed chair stood on the right-hand side of the kitchen grate. Wound twice round the chair was a leather belt. Mrs Fury never left the house without strapping her father in his chair. It was 'father's' chair, and he himself had made it with his own hands. It had come over from Ireland with him eight years previously. The woman stood at the bedroom door, listening. The low murmurous noises that reached her ears came from beneath the kitchen grate. She must hurry down and take away the tin blower from the fire. She looked at herself in the glass, then suddenly turned away and began to change into her house clothes, a blue blouse and black skirt. As she drew off her long dress the telegram fell out from her dress-body. She had forgotten all about it. She sat down on the bed and looked at the message. When she read it her face grew pale. She put her blue blouse on and once more stuffed the telegram into it. The envelope she tore into shreds, stamping upon it. Her demeanour changed. She walked up and down the room, there was a sort of aimlessness in these agitated circlings of the bedroom. At that moment the clock downstairs struck. 'Oh!' she exclaimed, and hurried below to the back kitchen. As she went down the stairs she arranged her hair more tidily. She passed a hand across her face as she entered the kitchen. She put the kettle on the gas-stove, then busied herself with various pots and pans. She laid the kitchen table. She looked at the clock. A quarter to one. From kitchen to back kitchen she hurried, never once glancing at the silent figure cooped in his chair. Suddenly she stopped, gripping the table top with her two hands. Her expression changed. She felt a peculiar sickness at the pit of her stomach. She sat down on the sofa and lay back. The figure in the chair opposite did not move. Slowly Mrs Fury raised her head until her eyes were on a level with

14

her father's shoulders. Then she leaned forward and exclaimed – 'Father!'
Not a muscle of Mr Mangan's face moved. It seemed the word had not pene-
trated to his brain as yet. It was such a long time since he had heard the
word 'Father'. Mrs Fury rose from the sofa and crossed over to him. She put
a hand under the man's chin, and raised his face. There seemed no light of
recognition in those features, the face was expressionless. Once more she
said – 'Father.' How useless he seemed. How old. Her two hands now rested
on the belt. After a while she unbuckled it and took it away, folding it up and
flinging it into the lower kitchen cupboard. As she knelt down in front of him
her hair unloosened itself again, falling across her shoulders. Suddenly she
rose to her feet and began to walk up and down the kitchen, her pacings,
as in the room above, wild and aimless. Once more she looked at the clock.
Almost one. He would be in any moment now. She walked round and round,
her head held high in the air, one hand clutching at her blouse. These
restless pacings drove her to the window. She drew the curtains aside and
stared into the street. The clock struck. Strange! How late her husband
was today. It was raining heavily. She went to the sofa and sat down again.
Mr Mangan's head had lowered itself, the chin resting upon the waistcoat,
covered with grease spots. Perhaps he had fallen asleep. She called again,
'Father, Father.' The same silence as before. She sprang from the sofa, rushed
across the kitchen.

'Peter's coming home,' she cried, and struck Mr Mangan on the knee
with her clenched fist. 'Peter's coming home.' She went back to the sofa
again, and commenced drumming with her fingers on its mahogany back.
'Yes, he's coming home.' The old man in the chair gave a sort of grunt, but
did not move. Mrs Fury knelt in front of him once more, staring into the
blue eyes. Yes, this was her father. And he had been sitting in that chair
for years. They had hardly spoken to each other. He was now eighty-two
years of age. The head moved slightly so that the whole face was thrown
into the light. She could study every line and wrinkle of that wizened face.
It was like a mask. She took a large red handkerchief from her pocket and
wiped the old man's nose, turning away her head as she did so. She
leaned over and whispered into his ear, 'Father.' What a time he had sat
in that high chair. Ages, it seemed to her. Mr Mangan was dumb. The
chair appeared to have acted upon him as a sort of drug. She smiled now.
Calling him father, after that long silence. Again she thought, 'How old and
useless he is.' That corner was his world. He had never strayed from
it, excepting when in imagination he caught the Belfast boat. One time
the Belfast boat had occupied a significant place in his life. Now, like other
things, it had faded out as the years spun out their journey-work.

Once a week the old man went out. Each Friday the woman helped him down to the little Post Office at the bottom of the street. There he drew his old age pension, his daughter holding his trembling hand whilst he made the all-important X on the form. After pocketing this money she helped him back to the house. Then he would collapse into the chair. Going for his pension was indeed a great adventure for old Mr Mangan. But the chair was his prison. If his daughter maintained a sort of stubborn silence with him, her husband Dennis made it complete. Dennis Fury never spoke to his father-in-law. To him the old man had long since passed that stage. He was out of the world altogether. He was just something stuck in the corner, as much a part of the house as the chimney-corner in which he sat. Anthony Mangan was really dead. There was only this aged figure known as 'him'. This figure that sat in the corner through winter and summer, against the blazing fire which hardly ever went out. They carried him to bed and carried him down again. His daughter fed him. Sometimes as she held the slop to his mouth she would wonder if it was really her own father. The years seemed to have done something far more than their journey-work. One time it had been Anthony here and Anthony there with Mr Fury, whilst his wife invariably addressed him as 'Dad', but that was so long ago. After a time speech stopped. He was a fixture. The chair held him. The great black high-backed chair whose stout legs gripped the red-tiled floor so securely. Mrs Fury still kept her eyes upon her father's face. Perhaps she should not have called him by name. She ought to have shouted, 'Hey! Peter's coming home.' She began arranging her hair and smoothing down her blouse as she stared at him. 'Peter's coming home,' she screamed, jumped to her feet and ran upstairs. She sat down on the bed and burst into tears. Imagine. To have stood there like that, staring at him, that old mysterious man, her own father, that helpless figure, and to have said that. 'Peter's coming home.' Good God! As she sat there sobbing she heard the old man begin to cough. She ran downstairs. Yes. He was coughing and choking. She rushed to the chair and put her strong arms about him, and sat him up. He hung a dead weight in her arms. His eyes were partly closed. The woman held his head back. He had had these bouts before. He would soon get over it. How heavy he was. She bent her head and whispered into his ear, 'Peter's coming home.' But there was no response. She pulled the big handkerchief from her pocket once more. The man's nose was running water again. There were times when she wished this old man out of sight and mind, but always her feeling ran counter to her economic position. This figure in the chair was helpless, he was a nuisance, but whilst he sat there he remained for her a sort of gilt-edged security, and a security that could not go overboard at the behest of her feelings. The old man jerked suddenly and she sat him down again. That bout was over, thank heavens. But it was useless to stand there any longer, telling him that his grandson was coming home. She made him comfortable and went away into the back kitchen. It was nearly seven years now since she had seen Peter. Her father would never know him, nor Peter his grand-dad. Seven years, she said to herself. It seemed more like seventy. She put her head through the open door. Lord! Denny was late. Five past one. She became obsessed with the time, with the helplessness of her father, by the thoughts of her son in New York, by the shock of the telegram from her sister in Cork. Her whole face seemed suddenly illuminated by this agitation. She could not conceal it any longer. Why hadn't she cried out? Why hadn't she fainted? No. She had remained calm in face of the news. She had even overcome that physical disgust she experienced whenever occasion demanded attendance upon the old man. At that moment a key was heard being turned in the lock. 'Denny!' she exclaimed, and hurried to open the door for him. But the man was already in the hall. 'Oh, Denny,' she said. 'Peter's failed.'

'For Christ's sake!' replied the man and pushed past her. He went upstairs to his room. Mrs Fury watched his figure slowly mount the stairs. Then she went into the kitchen. Her father was coughing again. 'Heavens!' she cried and ran to him.

3

Mr Fury was standing by the window in the bedroom. He was a man of medium height, a little stooped about the shoulders. His hair was closely cropped, iron-grey in colour, that somehow contrasted strongly with his ashen-like face, the result of thirty years spent below the decks of ships. His face was covered with oil smears. His dungaree overalls were similarly splashed with grease. He was looking out of the window. The high wall opposite obstructed one's vision, but the man appeared to be gazing at some-thing beyond this wall. There were a number of children playing in the yard below. He could hear a barrel-organ grinding out its raucous tune. Somewhere a dog barked ceaselessly. His head leaned a little to one side as though he were meditating about something. There was a tiredness in the blue eyes that seemed only to stare into the empty air. He scratched his head. Funny. He had walked up the street and put his key in the lock and opened the door. Then the voice in the hall had cried out, 'Peter's failed.' It was a harsh rasping voice. He could still hear that voice. The words rang in his ears. 'He's failed, Denny. He's failed.' Suddenly he laughed and aimed a kick at the leg of the table. He could hear his wife moving about in the back kitchen. He yawned, stretched his arms in the air, then let them fall heavily to his side. He was tired. He didn't want to go downstairs at all. A voice saying, 'He's failed,' appeared to have acted upon him with all the potency of some powerful drug. He sat down on the edge of the bed. He noticed that the bed-clothes were ruffled. 'She must have been up here just before I came in,' he was saying to himself. Outside the barrel-organ suddenly changed its tune. The wild cries of the children continued, but the dog had ceased to bark. Then a voice called up the stairs:

'Dinner's ready, Denny.'

The man jumped with fright. How long had he been sitting on the bed? He must have dozed off to sleep. Confound it! Had to be back at the sheds again at two o'clock sharp. He pulled out the metal watch from his vest pocket. 'Damn!' he exclaimed, and put it back in his pocket. Dinner was ready. He gave an involuntary shudder and rose to his feet. Slowly he made his way down the rickety stairs. His eyes met those of his wife as he entered the kitchen. He was seized by a sudden furious hatred, became awkward and knocked over the chair on which he was trying to sit. She always stared like that. But why? Mysterious woman. He sat down, grumbling under his breath. The woman shot a questioning glance at him, then lowered her eyes until they rested on his plate. He was really tired. He didn't want any dinner. He had had a gruelling morning. He just wanted to sit quietly at the table, his head on his hands, thinking. But how could he do that with his wife staring at him across the table? His eyes wandered round until they came to rest upon the silent figure in the corner. Then he looked his wife closely in the face. It was indeed a question. Instinctively the woman nodded her head. Yes. Again this morning. He ought to have been in and seen what it was like. Mr Fury picked up his knife and fork, stared stupidly at his plate and commenced to eat. So the old man had had another bout. H'm! How long was this going to go on? Suddenly the silent figure stirred itself, and the exclamation 'Ah!' burst forth from the old man's lips. Husband and wife looked across in astonishment. At last, thought the woman. And after all that time. They watched him, waiting. But the figure lapsed back into its original state. Mrs Fury leaned across the table.

'He is getting very trying, Denny,' she said. The man nodded his head and went on with his meal.

They maintained a silence until the meal was over. Mr Fury followed his wife out into the back kitchen.

'I wish he'd go away,' he said. The woman frowned. Her husband went up to her and said again:

'Yes. I wish he'd go. Damn it all, it gets on a fellow's nerves. Why doesn't he go to his sister in Belfast? He used always to be talking about her.' He turned on the tap and let the water run into the wash-bowl. He rolled up his sleeves and started to wash.

'It's quite impossible,' replied Mrs Fury. 'One must put up with the inconvenience. Even the inconvenience of an old man like that. He's my father. And after all ...' She stopped. Her husband had not heard her. He was swilling his face under the water. She waited until he had dried himself. He seemed to have anticipated his wife's remark, for he suddenly asked: 'How is Anthony? What did they say at the office?' He began pulling at the roller towel.

'He's all right,' she said. 'He's in hospital. I saw Mr Lake this morning.'

'That swine?'

'Yes.' The woman was angry now. Why was he skirting round the other matter? 'Yes,' she repeated, 'that swine.' Then she pulled the telegram from her blouse and said, 'Look at that.' Mr Fury did not take it from her. His eyes ran along the form, then raised themselves slowly until they were on a level with Mrs Fury's face. 'Well?'

'Well!' she screamed out, 'is that all you have to say?' She was on the verge of tears now. The man rushed into the kitchen for his coat and cap.

'Talk about it tonight,' he growled. 'There's always something wrong in this confounded house. You never even opened your mouth about Anthony. No. It's this other pig in Cork you worry about. Look at the clock.' Mrs Fury did not look at the clock. Her eyes were on the floor. She saw nothing. A dizziness came over her. She heard the door bang. So he had gone. Tonight. When he came home. Suddenly she laughed. Imagine it. Fussing about her own father whilst that telegram lay in her blouse. And Anthony. 'God!' she cried in her mind. 'I ought to have stuck it in his face. Yes. I ought to have stuck it in his face.' Then she began to recite at the top of her voice: 'Peter's failed. Peter's failed.' Suddenly Peter disappeared and Anthony took his place. She could see the heavy swathes of bandages about her son's feet. 'From the mast on to his heels.' She went into the kitchen. That figure in the chair irritated her. 'You dumb fool,' she cried. 'You old fool. Your precious grandson is coming home.' She gave a high-pitched hysterical sort of laugh and ran upstairs to her room. She locked the door. She went across to the dressing-table and stared into the mirror. She brushed a strand of hair back from her face. Why, who was this woman staring into the mirror? Herself? Fanny Fury? Impossible. Only this morning she had dressed in front of it. What had happened? She burst into tears. She could no longer hold them back. Well, there was much to think about now. The old fear returned. The word 'Future' was imprinted upon her mind in letters of fire. Future. The future. She began walking up and down the room. The fear that had lain hidden so long suddenly took possession of her. She deluged the room with her violent movements. The indifference of her husband. The stupidity of the old man by the fire. She could talk about that tonight. Insulting enough. But what when the others heard about it too? She closed her eyes. It made her feel sick again just thinking about Peter. Her youngest son. She had idolized him. Denny had made so light of the matter. It was Anthony he worried about. She was angry with him about his remarks concerning her father. He had lived with them so long now. He was one of the family. And her husband all of a sudden wanted him out of the house. Where would he go? There was no place for him. His sister in Belfast? Poor Father. He imagined things. His brain was going. Eighty-two years of age and he wanted to go home to Belfast. That was a place she had never seen. No. It was impossible. He would just sit rooted in that chair until he finally passed out. It almost numbed her to think of Peter. The questions tonight. Why had he failed? As if she knew anything about it. And Anthony. Those two hours spent groping about the big shipping office, the meeting with the benevolent-looking gentleman, the climb up the stairs, the lift. She could not easily forget it.

She went downstairs again and began to clear away the dinner things. Her own meal lay uneaten on the table. How could she eat, worried as she was about her sons? God! Her husband knew nothing at all. Nothing at all. She could not help glancing across at her father. There was something peculiar about him, and she noticed it now. It was his huge head, completely bald. It seemed so out of place on those small shoulders. Anthony Mangan was five foot seven in height. His large hands, the skin of which was dry and yellow, lay idly in his lap. Mrs Fury said to herself, 'He's awake at last. He's really awake.' The old man had slowly stirred to life again. His pale watery eyes harboured a sort of suspicious dread. The expression upon his face changed. He could see this tall woman now. His daughter. Why was she staring at him like that? But now a faint smile crossed her face. 'Are you awake, Father?' she asked, and drew nearer to him. The man grunted like a pig. She knelt down in front of him. It seemed that with each movement he aggravated his daughter. She must now wipe his eyes. Again the large handkerchief appeared from Mrs Fury's capacious pocket. She wiped his eyes gently. She began to settle his coat and vest more comfortably. It was all crumpled, and stained with slobber and the remains of meals. His tie – it was a piece of string – was almost hidden behind his shirt. 'Straighten up now,' she was saying; 'your grandson's coming home soon.' At last he smiled. Mrs Fury said, 'Yes, he's coming home.' She drew back in fright as the old man suddenly opened his mouth, revealing the toothless cavern. Surely he was going to speak. She ran into the hall and stood there. What was her father going to say? The figure in the chair leaned forward, an idiotic smile upon the upturned face. Was he going to ask why? She tore the telegram from her blouse again. Yes. It was only too true. She laughed. That Denny should treat the matter so lightly, that 'he' should question. It was too ridiculous.

But the old man merely wanted a drink of water. The word 'Peter' had not crossed his mind. Mr Mangan was only thirsty. He tried to rise again, but fell back, gasping for breath. Where had she gone to? His eyes rested upon the door, waiting, watching. But Mrs Fury could not move. The blow had struck at last. Her head fell forward upon her breast, her two hands were entwined. She stared down at the much-faded carpet. First Anthony and then Peter. A sort of low screeching sound issued from the old man's mouth and she ran in to him. Ah! Of course. She ran to the tap and came back with a tumbler of water, which she held to his trembling lips. What a fright! And he had merely wanted a drink of water. How he slobbered. The old agitation returned, she lost patience with him. Why couldn't he hurry up, instead of spilling the water down his front? The telegram inside her blouse exasperated her. 'There now,' she said. In the back kitchen she took out the telegram and hid it behind the jars on the shelf. She went to her father and pushed him back roughly into the chair. 'Sit still.' Past two o'clock. She began to wash at the sink. She wrung out the clothes and flung them on top of the boiler. Then she rinsed them out under the clear running water. But her mind was not upon her task. Her mind floated elsewhere, her eyes saw nothing now save that helpless figure in the kitchen. She stopped and listened. There was no sound save the metallic tick of the alarm-clock. The time must be getting on. How it tied one down. Life was one continuous round of meal-getting. Then the neighbouring school bell rang. Four o'clock. Impossible. But when she looked out of the window she saw the children already on their way home from school. Another meal to get ready. She placed the last of the wrung clothes into the sink and set about getting the tea ready. She filled the kettle and placed it on the stove. Darkness was setting in. She went into the kitchen and lighted the gas. Mr Mangan's head had fallen forward upon his breast again. He was completely hidden once more. He was breathing heavily. She did not even look at him, but commenced to lay the table. It seemed but a few minutes ago that she had been laying it for the midday meal. She crossed to the chimney-piece to get the tea-caddy. As she did so her eyes came to rest on the top of her father's bald head. Why was it, she suddenly asked herself, why was it that she had been so full of feeling for him today? She did not know. She wanted to tell him again, to surprise him with the news. His grandson whom he had not seen for nearly seven years, he was really coming home. The future became suddenly black. She was filled with apprehension. Everything had seemed so perfect, easy running; she had had rough times, but she had overcome them. Now she was to sink into the mire again. Oh God! Why did these things happen? She closed her eyes, the tea-caddy still in her hand, whilst the heavy breathing of her father rose almost mournfully to her ears.

Mr Fury came into the kitchen. The woman swung round. Lord! Denny home. She rushed about the place, laying plates and cups, then she dashed outside to make the tea. Mr Fury took off his coat and cap and flung them over the back of the sofa. He sat down. He was black from head to foot. He heard the wash-bowl being filled outside, but did not move. His wife drew his chair to the table. She herself sat down. When he looked at her he noticed a strange expression upon her face. He had never seen it there before. He was filled with dread. He sat down opposite her. Probably waiting for him to say something, he was thinking. The clock ticked loudly. Promptly at half-past five the alarm rang.

'Confound it!' Mr Fury said, darting a vicious glance at his wife, 'confound it!' He got up and shut the alarm off. The woman smiled, a faint attempt at indifference. The man sat down again. How he hated the same old thing day after day. Going to work. Coming home again. Sitting in the kitchen. Her opposite to him. Mrs Fury put down her knife and fork. 'What a day I've had,' she exclaimed. The man did not reply. 'First it was Anthony. Falling from the mast. My Christ! And now it's Peter.' She watched her husband's face, but it conveyed nothing to her. It was impenetrable. A mask. She saw him digging furiously at the meat with his fork. He was going to say something. She could tell by his very attitude. She could read Denny like a book.

'How did it happen?' he asked suddenly, pushing his plate from him.

'Happen? God knows! I have only the wire here and . . .'

'I'm talking about Anthony,' he growled back at her. 'What's up with the lad? He fell from the mast. Wonder he wasn't killed. When's *he* coming home? Did Lake say?'

'No. He didn't say. I told you what happened at dinner-time, but you were in too much of a hurry to get out. Isn't Peter your son too? One might expect . . .' She stopped. What more was there to say? She had realized this impasse from the beginning. He wasn't interested in Peter. Didn't she know why. Only too well. But not to show a sign. Not to appear affected by the news. Heavens! She said coldly, 'After seven years he's failed. Have you no sympathy for anybody? What about the boy himself? Denny, what's the matter with you lately?' What a peculiar expression he was wearing. Of course, he was tired. Working all day. But to treat Peter's affair like that. It overwhelmed her. She was angry again. Why couldn't he open his mouth? Three times she had told him about the boy. And he had said nothing. If he hadn't any feeling, perhaps he had at least a little decency. She might well

22

have been talking to the floor-mat, on which her feet were now noise-lessly stamping. She thought – seven years' struggle. All gone. Like a flash. 'Denny!' Mrs Fury's voice softened a little as she uttered this single word. Her husband looked up at last. If only she did her talking when the family was at home. That wouldn't be so bad.

'Well?' he said. 'Well, what is it this time?' He saw her face darken with anger. She thumped the table with her clenched fist. She became agitated once more. She was working herself up into a frenzy. She thumped the table again with her fist. Her eyes flashed.

'I tell you the lad's failed. That's the fourth time. And you haven't a word to say. Not a word. All I have done for that boy. Denny! Denny! Please say something.' The man sat back in the chair as she cried out, 'Say something.' Her anger could hold itself no longer.

'Well, I told you,' said Mr Fury. He fidgeted in his chair. Comforting words, thought the woman. Mr Fury continued.

'I told you all along. Didn't I warn you? It will prove to you that you cannot drag a horse to drink if he isn't thirsty. Neither can you make a man go to the altar if he doesn't want to.'

'Denny! Denny!'

'Confound you! Why do you start these discussions every time I come home? It's been the same with every one in the family, and you know it. I'm tired of them. I've been working hard all day, and I tell you I'm in no mood for rows of any kind. I'm not going to sit here listening to what you have to say about Peter. I suppose the other lad might well freeze to death for all you care. Serve you right. Serve you right.' He got up and pushed his chair back to the wall. Then he asked suddenly, 'Do the others know?' When he looked across the kitchen, his wife was crying. He went up to her and laid a hand on her shoulder.

'Fanny,' he said. 'Listen to me. Don't you take on so about things. You gain nothing by it. The only thing to do now is to get the lad home. Right away.'

The woman jumped to her feet. What? She faced up to him. She thrust her face up against his own.

'Get him home. Heavens! That's all you have to say. Get him home. Can't you say something else? Try and think a little. Look at the disappointment to me. And is it the boy's fault? How do we know? We know nothing yet.' Mr Fury put an arm out and slowly pushed his wife back towards the sofa. She sat down, he looking down at her.

'No,' he said, with great bitterness. 'No. It's not the boy's fault. It's yours!' There. He had said it now. It had lain in his heart for so long. And now he had said it, and the bitterness had gone with it. He had carried this thing about with him for years, like an everlasting wound. And he knew it was the bitter truth. It had suffocated him. Well, it was said and over. Cruel. Yes. But what else could he have said? He looked down pityingly at the woman. She appeared to have grown smaller. She sat there, her face buried in her hands. The man looked at the other figure in the chair, then at his wife. 'Lord!' he exclaimed. 'Fanny! Fanny! You'll get over this. You'll overcome this bitter disappointment like you've overcome other things.' She answered him with sobs, and a periodic uttering of the word 'Peter'. Mr Fury sat down by her side.

'I told you,' he went on. 'Didn't I, Fanny? Tell the truth. Didn't I say you would never make a priest of him? A Fury a priest. Silly. Silly. Impossible. Now you know it.' He dug his hands into his pockets and stared at the inert figure of the old man in the chair. And now the lad had better come home at once. He could prepare to soil his fine hands too. He could roll up his sleeves with the rest of the children and get to work. The same as John had done, and Anthony, and Desmond. The woman laughed.

'Yes,' she said. 'Look at him! Look at his wife!'

'Look at them? Well, what about them?' asked Mr Fury.

'Will you get out and leave me alone. You have as much feeling as a stone. Good God! You're always tired. You're always fed up. No wonder the men on the ship led you a dog's life. Day in and day out you're always the same. Don't want to be worried. Don't want to be disturbed. Because you're tired. Oh!' She laid emphasis on the word 'tired'. She laughed again. Suddenly she turned round and struck him across the mouth with her open hand. The man drew back. He did not speak. He got off the sofa and stood in the middle of the kitchen, staring at her. He knew it all along. He had seen it coming. The difficulty with him was finding a way out. He had had these rows before. Once it started it went on and on interminably. He already felt himself entangled in the old web.

'Hang it all,' he said savagely. 'It's over and done with. Peter must come home and take his place with the rest of the family.' The woman broke in then. 'Yes,' she remarked coldly. 'You're satisfied now. You feel you've been right all along, don't you? You're all satisfied. Treated me like a dog. The lot of you. You've all done it ever since that child went to Ireland. Ah! Don't you deny it. You know it. Now you feel you've triumphed. You'll have him like the rest. Like Desmond perhaps – like Maureen. My God!'

Mr Fury was gradually losing hold on himself. It wasn't so much the thing said, as what grew out of it. And all these arguments seemed to him to be ringed round with a desperate maddening futility. They started anywhere and ended nowhere. He threw his hands into the air. 'Look here, Fanny. Why don't you try to see things from other angles besides your own? Whoever prevented the lad from going to college? I didn't, and you know it. I was away at the time. I never even heard a word about it until it was done. As for the others, they've been too busy to bother. Yes. Too busy to bother.'

'That's been the trouble all along,' replied his wife. 'The effort I had to make to keep him there. Did any of you help? Not a penny. Not even a kind word. The lad had simply ceased to exist for the lot of you. I know. You needn't think I am as blind as all that. The lad in Ireland is ruined.'

'Who ruined him?' growled Mr Fury. 'I say, who ruined him? Only yourself.' He went on, but now he could not hear his own words, for his wife was yelling like a child. He rushed into the hall, picked up his cap and went out. He saw the evening newspaper on the hat-rack and stuffed it in his pocket. The woman was talking to herself. The words rang sharply in his ears. The sound of her voice seemed to follow him up the street. He entered the public-house, ordered a pint of beer and sat down. 'What a woman!' he said. When he put his hand to his forehead he found it covered with sweat. 'Poor Anthony. Poor Anthony. A good lad that.' The barman placed the beer in front of him. 'Thanks,' Mr Fury said.

Damn it! He couldn't drive away the sound of that harsh rasping voice. 'Fanny is getting impossible,' he said. He picked up his glass and drank greedily.

CHAPTER II

The Furys had lived in Hatfields for thirty years. The row of houses, whose fronts faced the long King's Road, was counted to be the oldest property in that neighbourhood. Their rears faced the river. Those thirty back doors facing the sea were like so many dogs, barking out their defiance of time and change. They stood erect, solid as rock. Immune. Surrounding properties had been pulled down, new buildings erected, and these in turn had surrendered to the industrial flood, but Hatfields remained erect. The Furys were a large family. Their first child, Maureen, had been born in number three; Mr Fury was away at sea at the time. The last child, Peter, too, and again Mr Fury was at sea. Dennis Fury had come over from Dublin as a young man in order to find work in Gelton. He had been lodging with an Irish family for some months when he met his wife, Fanny Mangan. Mr Fury's tale was not exceptional. Indeed, he was only one of many thousands who left Ireland to earn his living. He was not without friends. Gelton was full of Irish people. The Irish tale of drift in his case meant the sea, as in Fanny Mangan's case it meant domestic service. For months Dennis Fury hung around the docks looking for a ship. It was on one of these hunting trips that he met his wife. She was a servant in the home of a wealthy Gelton cotton-broker. She herself had left County Cork at the age of twelve in order to make her way in the world. At least it showed her independence, and she was only two weeks in the city before she found herself the valued servant of this Protestant family. Her people were shocked. All communications with her mother ceased. In time her sisters and brothers adopted the same attitude, all excepting her youngest sister, Brigid Mangan. In spite of the horror which her action had inspired, she still continued to send money home to her mother, but no letters ever passed between them. Her leaving home was indeed the first glimmer of that independence and determination which was to carry her through the eventful years of her married life. Dennis Fury meanwhile floated about the city like a cork upon water, waiting and hoping for some release. Only a ship could deliver him. If Fanny Mangan's family had been shocked on hearing of her being employed by an English Protestant family, Mr Fury's people had betrayed no sign that their son's sudden departure from home had made any rift in their little world. He was

26

gone and forgotten. He had married Miss Mangan on the eve of his first voyage to sea. During all those years at sea Mr Fury had never forgotten the incident that had thrown this young girl in his path. It was on the deck of a pleasure steamer one summer's evening that Dennis Fury first met the woman who was to share his life. Fanny Mangan was accompanied by her employers, a Mr and Mrs Pettigrew, and their youngest child. The girl had her attention drawn to a Pierrot troupe who were performing on the open deck. Unseen, the child in her charge had slipped through the rail. There was a sudden scream. Without a moment's hesitation the girl flung herself into the river, and battling against the strong running current managed to reach the child. A second later a man jumped over the rail and swam to the woman and child. Willing hands hauled them to safety, the ship's boat was drawn up, and the rescued put to bed. Mr Fury always remembered how as he held the girl's head clear of the water she opened her eyes wide and looked at him. He had never seen such large brown eyes. In them he saw mirrored his own destiny. A month later they were married, and the following day Dennis made his first trip to sea. In this marriage Fanny Mangan found her goal. With it the silence between her family in Cork and herself was sealed. Then her youngest sister, Brigid, left home to work in one of the suburbs of that city. They corresponded regularly, a hidden bond of sympathy existed between them, an unbreakable bond that had been sealed from early childhood. Mrs Fury's leaving home had been necessitous. Originally destined for the priest's house at Forley, she had thrown up the work after only one day, and settled down with the Pettigrews. Without home, without friends, the meeting with Dennis Fury was a miracle. She became absorbed in her new life. They went to live in Hatfields. Maureen was born. The child became at once a barrier against the loneliness of her life, for her husband was away ten months in every year. She adored Maureen. The family increased. Now she watched them grow up. When Desmond was born the long silence between her family in Ireland and herself was broken, by the news of the death of her mother. This news came from her sister Brigid. Great changes, she learned, had taken place. Her two brothers had emigrated to America, and her father was now left alone. Brigid wrote of her inability to look after him. He was getting more awkward to live with in his advancing years. Fanny Mangan decided at once that she must bring her father over to Gelton. This was accomplished in the face of much opposition on her husband's part. He had never liked Mr Mangan. Asked his reason for this dislike, which appeared to grow stronger with the passing years, Dennis Fury could give no answer. It would be true to say that Mr Fury did not *know* why. The Fury family grew up. Desmond was followed by three more boys, John, Anthony, and Peter. With the addition of her father, Mrs Fury found her hands full. She was never idle. Desmond was working on the railway as a plate-layer; John had, until his death at work, been a stevedore at the docks; Anthony was a quartermaster at sea. Maureen, until the time of her marriage, had been working in a jute factory.

The last child, Peter, Mrs Fury adored. He seemed to her to be so different from the others. The woman, whose ambitions had long been thwarted by what she was wont to describe as her husband's 'lack of character', realized at once that Peter was something for her alone. Something to mould. Someone who would shine out differently from the rest of the family. The spirit within her, long buried, suddenly took fire. This son was going to be different. Peter must be a priest. At first Mr Fury protested. Why should this son be singled out for special favours denied to the others? Mrs Fury was equal to the occasion. Why had they been denied to the others? He himself knew best. Dennis Fury had nothing to say. He half believed that his wife was right, though his every word and deed only revealed the resentment against what he called his wife's 'crazy Irish idea'. The woman was determined. She broke down all opposition. Her ambitions had been buried too long. Her husband retired, he had nothing more to say. He ceased to take any interest in Peter. He watched the others, though indeed he saw little of them, being away at sea except for an occasional three-day holiday ashore whilst his ship was loading cargo or being overhauled in dry dock. But he saw a change in the other brothers. They alienated Peter from their affections. They looked down on him, at the same time secretly hating their mother for this sudden bestowal of favours never offered to themselves. Desmond said that it wasn't fair to the boy himself. Mrs Fury felt as though her eldest son had dealt her a blow. Wasn't fair to Peter? What on earth was he thinking about? But Anthony agreed with his brother. He said it was up to Peter. He knew best. Did he want to go away? Did he really want to go in for the Church? A veritable web spun itself about the mother. Only one person stood outside it. The silent figure of her father. He sat and watched. His ferret-like grey eyes studied each member of the household. He was the silent witness. The family took little notice of him. All excepting Mr Fury. He hated these ceaseless arguments in the old man's presence. He even fancied that Mr Mangan found a sort of malicious glee in this overpowering daughter of his as he watched her, day in and day out, weigh down all opposition. Arguments she wiped out with a single word. Suggestions were useless. Mr Fury would sit watching old Mr Mangan and say to himself: 'How much do you know, old devil? Aren't you laughing behind that sallow-looking face of yours?' He was certain that behind this mask, this skin which clothed his personality, Mr Mangan really smiled, really laughed, as he saw the ruthlessness of his daughter. This daughter who years ago had defied him. Now here she was, the mother of a large family. And that family had touched almost every part of the globe. 'Yes,' Mr Fury would repeat to himself, 'I'd like to know what you are thinking, you old devil.' Somehow he himself managed to steer clear of this great net. Her children were imprisoning her. She knew it, and her mind began to work. She made huge rents in this web they had spun about her. Her mind was imprisoned. If she didn't watch out she would be suffocated. Her children looked on, amused, indifferent. They tried to get Peter to themselves. Often they questioned him. Did he honestly want to go? Did he realize all that it would involve, the sacrifice, the isolation – did he understand? The boy said nothing.

They became more suspicious. Why didn't he speak his mind? It was impossible to understand him. He was like a drugged person. They could get nothing out of him. He maintained a stony silence. He had the stubbornness of his mother. Desmond accused him of hiding something. Why didn't he speak out? They weren't going to kill him. Mrs Fury witnessed these things, but she never betrayed her feelings. She remained calm and unruffled. Her spirit flamed. She would triumph. One day Anthony said straight out, 'He is only doing this to please you.' Mrs Fury lost her calm at once. She became angry. It was insulting. The others ceased to take any interest in Peter. His father ignored him. He was away at sea on the day that Mrs Fury saw her son off on the Cork boat. Then began the long series of humiliations. At first Mrs Fury only hinted, then cajoled, later still demanded. The children laughed in her face. And yet, they were responsive. There might be something in it after all, they thought to themselves, refusing to acknowledge their own weakness, for Mrs Fury had discovered the vulnerable in them. A sort of insane optimism prompted their actions. One never knew. The mother was winning. Those working contributed towards the boy's board and fees, when they were out of work they would be excused. They gave with unwilling hands. It was all a sop. Their ideas had changed again. They could see nothing in it. Mrs Fury secretly smiled. She could mow down these obstacles in her path. She became sympathetic, listened to them. It was silly, more than silly, they said. It was sheer madness. Besides, they couldn't remain in Hatfields for ever. The woman thought, 'Ah! That was it.' She had scented this. How long ago was it, she began to ask herself, since she had first heard this disturbing rumble? It was so close to her now. Almost deafening. She tried to gain their confidence. They withdrew, saying nothing. The eldest son was becoming restive. Then suddenly Maureen revealed her secret. She would be getting married soon. The mother remained calm. This was no crisis. H'm! She had seen worse than this. Yet she knew that the net was beginning to give under the weight. She could not deny it. How to prevent it? Maureen became expansive. Her husband was a young man from County Clare. He worked on the docks. Mrs Fury became inquisitive. Strange, she thought. Her suspicions of Desmond appeared to be correct. What hand had he had in this? A conspiracy? She thought they were together in the evenings for the purposes of their work. She had an idea it was something connected with politics, but she wasn't sure. This Kilkey fellow worked at the docks. John had known him too.

Desmond said nothing. He kept his silence. Marriage for him became freedom from the fetter. He called it a fetter. It goaded him to think that part of his hard-earned money should go to keep another in idleness. He was open and frank with his mother so far as Peter was concerned. His sister took his part. Her mother had no right to single out Peter like that. It was sheer folly. They all of them had to make their way without thinking of Peter. Mrs Fury saw with open eyes. The veil was torn away at last. The net she herself had flung out could hold them secure no longer. It wasn't Peter so much. It was herself. Had they no love or respect? Didn't they realize that it was her one great wish? Mr Fury could not be drawn in. If only he could – but he remained aloof. He was out of it all. One month in every twelve saw him home. He was a mere visitor to the house. He never mentioned Peter. He had sealed his whole soul against the boy, not because of any instinctive dislike of Peter, but merely out of the growing hatred of his wife. When he came home, Mrs Fury would ask, 'Well, have you written to Peter?' No. He hadn't written to Peter. What time had he for writing? His family were outside his interests now. Writing letters to his children! H'm! Too busy working, watch and watch, excepting for a couple of evenings off in port. Whenever he arrived home he always managed to go off with Desmond to a theatre. Mr Fury had a great passion for the theatre. They would talk together. 'Your mother is getting quite impossible lately,' he would remark to his son. 'Quite impossible. She's getting sillier as she grows older.' Yet he hated to have to say it. But there could be no barriers. There was no stopping of the tide where Fanny was concerned.

'The whole point, Dad,' Desmond would reply, 'the whole point is that Peter never wanted to go away. One of these days you'll see that I'm right. He only went to please Mother. That's all. And I don't think it was fair of Mother to influence him that way.' He would look straight into his father's eyes. Mr Fury would mutter under his breath. It was quite unintelligible. His father wondered if Desmond wasn't right after all. She had tried it once before with Maureen. Maureen ought to be a nurse. She was just cut out for it. Good Lord! Whatever was the woman thinking about, he would say to himself. He looked at his son. Aye. He seemed to know all about it. Then they would return home. She only wanted to mould Peter to her own liking. She was hungry for power. And now she had her way. The boy was gone.

Mrs Fury hated Desmond for going off like this. Denny and he must have long talks together. Her whole attitude changed. She became suspicious. What had they been talking about now? 'You're always talking together lately,' she would remark.

Mr Fury would watch the clock. He hated retiring. It was the same old thing, night after night. Dragging up the past. He had said to her one evening after they had retired, 'Of course, you think everything will sail along grandly, but where's the money to come from?' A real poser, he thought. But his wife remained silent. She ignored him. He was glad when sailing day came round again. Glad to get out of the house and back to sea again. It was paradise. On long voyages Mrs Fury wrote to him. All the letters were the same. Peter was mentioned in each one of them. 'Was he going to write to the boy, or not? Why didn't he say straight out? Be honest.' She knew he hated her for this, she would write, but she wasn't thinking of herself. When had she ever put herself first? Never. After all, he was the boy's father. Sometimes Mr Fury replied to these letters, sometimes he tore them up unopened and dropped them into the sea. But he never breathed Peter's name. How she hated her family for this miserable spirit. Or was it just spite? Jealousy? An insane determination to prevent anybody aiming a little higher than themselves? What curious natures they had. Thank God, she was not like them. She asked herself these questions many times. And how she loathed their help. If only she could do it unaided. Periodically Peter wrote home for money. A real struggle. She dared not ask her children. It would mean another row. More insults. Well, *she* would master all the difficulties. And it would not be the first time. She would sail through this. How strange. She was only beginning to know her family. Whenever Anthony arrived home from sea, she would say:

'Don't forget Peter.'

He would take some money from his pocket, fling it on the table, saying, 'There,' and that was the end of the matter so far as he was concerned. Like his father, he was glad to be at sea. What was it that drove them from the house? They did not know. Everything had seemed all right until Peter came along. From that time the change in Mrs Fury had been rapid. There was something in the woman, a kind of invisible and insidious poison, that drove her family from her. Desmond had often tried to find out the cause of this change in his mother. But, like the others, he was unsuccessful. As for Dennis Fury, he had given up that problem long ago. Sometimes, when she was alone in the house, she would take her chair over to the corner where her father sat. At times this old man seemed a godsend to her. She used to talk to him of her life, take him into her confidence. He sympathized with his daughter, though there remained with him always a sort of gentle

31

distrust of her, for he could never forgive her for her action of long ago. Thirty-one, nearly thirty-two years had passed since then, but he had not forgotten it. He listened to her day after day.

'Don't I do my best?' she would ask. 'Haven't I reared a large family as respectably as I could?'

Of course she had, he would reply. 'But, Fanny, some of your family are dirt.' Mrs Fury had never forgotten that remark. It remained imprinted on her mind. She was often puzzled by it. But she could not fathom its meaning. Mr Mangan, before he was finally afflicted, used to go out with her of an afternoon and sit in the park. This was a pleasure to him. He had long sensed his son-in-law's dislike of him, and he resented it. 'Fanny,' he would say, 'you're a good woman. But I should never have come here. The Furys are a strange family. So different from our own at home.' Tears would come into his eyes whenever he thought of his two sons far away in America. What a queer world it was. Families were born, grew up, and then were scattered over the earth. Mrs Fury would affect surprise, even anger. 'You mustn't talk like that, Dad,' she would say, though she knew how keenly the old man felt his obligations. He liked Peter. His grandson Peter was his favourite. This drew father and daughter closer together.

He had helped her too. When he had his little money he had given it unsparingly, unknown to the others. He rather enjoyed it. It gave him a certain satisfaction, as well as a kind of malicious glee in witnessing its effect upon the boy's brothers. They became inquisitive. Where was their mother getting the help from? Their own was a mere pittance. Who was helping? Instinctively they realized it could only be their grandfather. Mr Fury heard. But he made no mention of it to his wife. From that time he acquired a particular dislike for the old man. He was directly abetting Fanny. And all this was going on behind his back while he was at sea. Once the old man and he had had high words. Peter had just written home for money. Mr Fury himself took in the letter from the postman. Unknown to his wife, he opened it. When he read it he went white with rage. He ran upstairs with the open letter in his hand and flung it on the bed.

'Read that,' he said. The woman picked up the letter. But she did not read it. Instead she placed it inside her dress-body. Nothing more was heard of the incident until a wire came from the boy thanking his mother for the money received. Well, he thought, there could be no doubt about it. Her father was behind this. He openly accused the old man of backing up the boy against the rest of the family. Mr Mangan was equal to the occasion. He struggled from his chair, and facing up to his son-in-law remarked: 'What the hell kind of a man are you? You've got the heart of a louse. I gave the boy the money, and I shall continue to do so whilst I have it. You don't know what a good woman you have. That's what wrong with you. My God! I saw all this coming. And when, twenty-four years ago, you wrote home to Fanny and said you were "on the ice in New York", I knew, I knew then what a tragic mistake she had made. Why, man, the Furys are know all over Ireland, and, by God, so are the Mangans. Haven't you a heart at all? If you're incapable of ambitions, for Christ's sake don't think that everybody else is like yourself. I'm surprised, Denny, surprised and disgusted.' Only a month after Mr Fury sailed, the old man was seized with a stroke. From that day he had remained fast in his chair. He had come to live at his daughter's house, he had seen Peter go off. He had witnessed many things in the seven years since he had seen him go.

Mrs Fury felt a lump come into her throat as she looked at him now. He would never know the boy. How he had changed. He seemed to have grown smaller. His skin was the colour of old parchment, it was dry and leathery like that of a bird. The eyes set beneath the shaggy white brows appeared like two tiny beads. His huge hands wandered about the chair, as though the little life left in him had swum into these hands. They rose and fell, dragged themselves to one arm of the chair, then the other. 'No,' thought the woman, 'he will never recognize him, nor will Peter his grand-dad.' She tried to conjure up in her imagination the figure of her son as she had last seen him, with his small neat figure dressed in a stiff navy-blue suit, his round red face, his large eyes, brown as her own. She even remembered the design of the college cap he wore. And that little silver cross he wore in the lapel of his coat. But he must have grown. What would he look like? Perhaps he would be tall and erect, like her own mother had been. She could not imagine him stout. None of the Fury family affected obesity. Rather were they lean and wiry, like her own husband, whom thirty years of work down in the bowels of ships had not affected. He was fifty-eight now, and as good as any man half his age. The old man fell asleep. His heavy breathing filled the kitchen.

2

Mrs Fury went into the parlour and sat down. She wanted to collect herself. She laid the telegram on the table, reading its message over and over again. Strange! What could it mean? 'Peter failed. All my sympathy. Brigid.' But what could her sister know? Why had not she, the boy's mother, been informed? It sounded very mysterious. And the suddenness of it. How had her sister learned of this? She simply could not understand. And why had the boy failed? She leaned forward and drew the curtains aside. The street was deserted. Suddenly she exclaimed, 'I'll go up to Maureen.' She immediately got up and went back to the kitchen again. She fastened Mr

Mangan into his chair, and drew out the fender from the fire. Then she gave a last look round the kitchen. She had not far to go. Her daughter lived in the next street. She put on her coat and hat and went out the back way. She felt suddenly lonely – she must talk to somebody – she was utterly bewildered. She tormented herself with questions. Why hadn't Peter written? Perhaps there would be a letter in the next post. Again, the Principal ought to have informed her of this. No! She simply could not make it out. The boy had passed his other examinations brilliantly. Then why this sudden failure? When she reached her daughter's house she discovered Maureen was out. Should she wait? She looked up and down the street. What a nuisance. Why should Maureen be out the very moment she wanted her most? She knocked again, this time quite loudly. Perhaps she was lying down. Then the next door neighbour put her head out of the window – she looked questioningly at Mrs Fury. 'Maureen's gone to the city,' she said.

Mrs Fury looked up at the woman. 'To town? Today?' 'Yes,' the woman said. Then the window slammed down again. Mrs Fury retraced her steps. She felt disappointed, even a little hurt. Why should the girl have gone out? Everything seemed to be working the wrong way today. She, Peter's mother, knew nothing. Everything seemed vague. 'Well, there must be some explanation,' she said to herself as she unlocked the back door. 'Dear me!' she kept saying, 'dear me!' And now she must begin all over again. She stood in the middle of the kitchen, her two hands gripping the table. 'I don't believe it! I don't believe it!' she said, whilst her eyes fell upon the silent figure in the high chair. She had tried so hard, so hard. Her body became suddenly limp. Mr Mangan coughed. 'Soon be Friday,' she was thinking, 'and I shall have to take Dad down to the Office for his pension.' She sat down on the sofa. She wouldn't do anything now. Just sit and wait for the post. When the knock came to the door she made a sudden rush into the lobby. There was no letter there. When she opened the door she found Maureen on the step in animated conversation with Mrs Postlethwaite. 'Why, Maureen,' she exclaimed, and drew back into the lobby. Maureen came in. Mrs Fury gripped her daughter by the shoulders. 'Oh,' she said, 'I had a wire from your aunt today saying Peter has failed, and I don't understand.' Her voice broke.

'Oh, Mother!' said Maureen. They passed into the parlour and sat down. Maureen picked up the telegram. 'Oh!' Maureen exclaimed again. She looked up suddenly. 'Does Dad know?' The woman nodded her head. Somehow she could not find words to express what she felt at that moment. After a long silence she said: 'It's awful. I don't know anything. Not a line from Peter. Just that wire. I thought there might be a letter in the post this afternoon. When I talked to your father about it he got wild, and went out.'

She drew her hand across her forehead. Maureen looked at her mother. If it was true, then it was a real blow to her. She looked at the telegram again.

After a long silence Maureen rose. She folded the telegram up. 'Have you told anybody about it yet, Mother?' she asked.

Mrs Fury did not reply. She was studying her daughter. Was she going off again already? 'Sit down, Maureen! Sit down. I see little enough of you as it is,' she said. The young woman sat down again. 'I told nobody but your father,' continued Mrs Fury. 'And I don't want you to tell anybody, Maureen. Not even Joe.' She looked into Maureen's pale face. 'Not even Joe. I shall tell nobody.' She stamped her foot with a sudden burst of energy.

Maureen smiled. 'But everybody'll know in time, Mother.'

Mrs Fury caught her daughter's hand in a vice-like grip. 'Have you any respect left for me at all?' she asked loudly. 'Sometimes I think you haven't! Yes! That's what I think. You were in town today?'

'Yes, I was,' said Maureen.

'Have you seen Mr Sharples?' asked the mother.

'Not yet. Tomorrow afternoon,' replied Maureen.

Mrs Fury rose to her feet and began pacing the floor. 'So you are determined to go back to that factory, then?'

Maureen got up and stood in front of her mother. 'Yes,' Maureen said. 'I've quite made up my mind about that.'

'Oh,' the mother said. 'And what about this?' she remarked laconically, tapping her daughter's body.

Maureen laughed. 'I'll see to that too,' she said.

'Well, I just can't make you out, Maureen,' went on Mrs Fury. 'Here you are carrying that man's child, and now you want to go back to that factory.'

'Well, I don't want to talk any more about that, Mother,' Maureen said. The two women stood facing each other in the middle of the floor. Then Mrs Fury exclaimed savagely:

'I could never make out why you married that fellow. He's the laughing-stock of the neighbourhood.'

Maureen said slowly, and with great emphasis, 'You'll know why some day.'

Then she walked out to the kitchen. She looked down at her grandfather. Mrs Fury came in behind her. They both stood looking at Mr Mangan. Not a word was spoken. 'Of course,' thought Mrs Fury, 'she's not the least bit interested in Peter. I might have known.'

Then Maureen said she must be going. The mother looked at the clock.

'You aren't here five minutes yet,' she said coldly. 'I wanted to talk to you, Maureen. I wanted to talk to you about a good many things,' She paused.

'Joe'll be in in half an hour,' Maureen replied.

'Then you'd best get off,' said the mother. She stood with her back to Maureen, staring into the glowing coals of the fire. It seemed that in that glowing mass she could see mirrored Maureen's real thoughts. She heard her cross the kitchen, but did not move. Not until the door closed with a resounding bang did Mrs Fury turn round. She immediately lighted the gas. Well, she might have known. Yes, even she, Maureen, her only daughter, was unsympathetic. What were her children made of? She was glad now that she had not mentioned Anthony. No! Not if Anthony died that very day would she breathe a word to Maureen. The girl had completely changed. She seemed no longer her own daughter, her flesh and blood, but an utter stranger. For the first time that day Mrs Fury burst out laughing. Why on earth had a woman like Maureen married that fool of a man? Kilkey! Even the name sounded repulsive and ugly. Kilkey. She had met him once. She began to get her father's supper ready. This consisted of a boiled egg beaten up in milk, to which she added bread. Mrs Fury always tended her father. She fed him, washed and dressed him, and took him out occasionally. The rest of the family had no time for old Mr Mangan. Having made his meal ready, she produced a large spoon and towel. Then she drew a chair up to where he sat. She tucked the towel under the old man's chin and began to feed him. After a while her hand moved automatically from the plate to her father's mouth. Her thoughts kept taking excursionary flights. One moment Anthony loomed up largely, the next moment he disappeared and Peter took his place. What a peculiar family she had reared. More and more, so it seemed to her, they appeared to be taking after their father. When such thoughts took shape, she felt all the more keenly the bond that held her to her father. In moments of isolation and utter loneliness she clung to Mr Mangan as to a rock. He was a sort of refuge. Now she dare not think any more. She must drive Peter out of her mind. He was the last, the one in whom she imagined she had vested the best that was in herself. No. She must not think about it. She must just wait – wait for news. Of course, it might not be true. She contented herself with this. It might not be true. Mr Mangan having finished his supper, she wiped his mouth and took the towel from under his chin. Then she went into the back kitchen and returned a moment later with a tin bowl of water, a flannel, and a clean towel. She washed her father's face and hands. Then she cleared the things away and went upstairs. She made ready his bed. Mr Mangan was becoming more burdensome than ever. Mrs Fury came downstairs. She unwound the leather belt. Then she placed her hands under her father's shoulders. Hoisting the man over her shoulder, she carried him upstairs. She undressed Mr Mangan, tucked him safely in the bed, and picking up the lighted candle she held it aloft, at the same time bending over to look into his face. Mr Mangan's eyes were wide open, but they betrayed nothing. Not a muscle of his face moved. His breast rose and fell. 'Good-night, Father,' Mrs Fury said. Then she left the room. As she went slowly downstairs she sighed. That was done. What a relief. In the lobby she stood, hesitant, listening. The house was silent. Mrs Fury decided that she must go out. She could not sit in that kitchen another minute. She blew out the candle. Then she dressed herself in her outdoor clothes. She wrote a pencilled note to Mr Fury and left this pinned to the mantel-border, so that her husband would see it on his return. She closed the back door, and left by the front one. She stood on the step for a moment, looking up and down the street. It was quite dark. Then she slipped the door key into a hole in the wall, and walked quickly away. It began to rain. The woman hurried round the corner, just in time to see a tram coming down the road, its bell clanging loudly, whilst in front there galloped at break-neck speed a light horse and lorry. Mrs Fury boarded the tram.

'Carsholt Road,' she said as she handed the conductor her fare.

3

Mr Fury's head hung perilously near his glass. He had fallen asleep. The bar-room was empty. A big fire burned in the grate. The barman looked across at the sleeping man and smiled. The door opened. A tall, heavily built man came in and stood at the counter. He called for a drink. He turned round and looked at the man whose head was gradually drooping lower and lower. The man went across and drew the glass away. Suddenly he bent down and exclaimed, 'Why, if it isn't Denny Fury. Hey, Fury! What the hell! You're falling asleep, man. Wake up there!' The dozing man sat up with fright. He had been dreaming. As he opened his eyes he imagined the bar-room to be full of people, and that all these people were staring at him. The newcomer sat down beside him. Mr Fury stared stupidly at the froth now settling in his glass. He turned his head sharply and a flash of spit struck the open grate. The expression of bewilderment gradually wore off. He looked at his companion. Then he put out his hand, and a broad smile lighted up his face.

'Why, Devine! How are you? Haven't seen you for years.' 'I'm all right,' replied the man. 'What are you going to have?' Mr Fury said he would like a large Falstaff. They began to talk. They were old friends. Mr Devine asked after the children. How was the eldest lad getting on these times? Mr Fury groaned. Another of them, he thought.

'Desmond! Oh! He's all right. How's your missus?'

'She's none too well lately. This here rheumatism has got her again.'

37

'Sorry,' Fury said. 'Still on the same old packet?'

'Aye.' The man picked up his glass. 'Good health, Fury,' he said. 'Good health and good luck.' Mr Fury touched the man's glass with his own.

'Same to you, Dermod,' he said. They drank.

Dennis Fury endeavoured to look cheerful. He hadn't got that voice out of his ears yet. They were silent for some time. Then Fury said: 'I never see much of Desmond now. He hardly ever comes to the house, though it's only a stone's throw away, you might say. As a matter of fact, I heard a rumour . . .' He stopped suddenly. 'Well, Christ, one hears so many rumours. They say he's coming out on strike with the loco-men. How true it is I don't know. Strikes give me the pip.'

'Coming out in sympathy with the miners?' queried Devine. 'Aye.' Mr Devine had a sudden fit of coughing. Dennis Fury had sailed with this big raw-boned man from Dromod. He hadn't changed. The same shock head of red hair, the same straggling moustache. He looked at Fury.

'One swallows these rumours wholesale,' he said. Mr Fury merely nodded his head. His eyes were focused upon his glass once more. He pushed his half-glass of beer away from him. The man at his side ceased to exist. Damn and blast the woman! He wouldn't be sitting here at all but for her. Growling. Always growling. He wondered how long she would carry it on. Peter. H'm! Well, he had realized it all along. A blind plunge. Now she had been caught out. How she hated being caught out. Stubborn woman. Anybody taking a glance at Peter would know at once he wasn't cut out for the Church. *He* knew, though. The ease with which people talked of the tremendous possibilities that never existed excepting in their own minds. Of course, he was sorry for Fanny in a way. He admitted that. It was a blow for her. But to carry on like that. He wouldn't have cared so much if she hadn't left the other lad out of it. By heavens! Now he thought of it, he should have gone down to the offices himself. What would they tell her? The usual lies. He knew those people better than she did. The lad might be dead for all they knew. He could not get Anthony out of his head. But Peter would not be shut out. He kept creeping in. Fancy her making his failure an excuse for attacking Desmond. The pity of it was the woman didn't really know her own children. Not one of them. When would she really wake up? This continual conflict between stubbornness and common sense. Something jabbed at him. He looked up. Devine was poking him in the ribs with his long fingers. Mr Fury sat up as though struck.

'You're falling asleep again,' said Mr Devine. 'Why the hell don't you go home and turn in?' Fury smiled. It was a forced smile.

'Come on,' went on Devine. 'Drink up your beer. You've had a row with the missus, haven't you?' He looked into the other's wide-open eyes.

Dennis Fury had never credited his companion with any great powers of deduction. Now he had hit the mark. Suddenly he laughed. Having a row with Fanny was just like eating and sleeping and waking. It was part of the texture of their lives. Mr Fury drained his glass and got up. 'Well, see you again some time,' he said in an abrupt manner. 'So-long, Devine.' Then he sauntered out. The other stared after him, a surprised look upon his face. Going off like that! As Dennis Fury turned the corner, he suddenly remembered the newspaper. He pulled it from his pocket. Why, there was nothing in it. An idea had suddenly occurred to him. Why shouldn't he take a walk along and see Desmond? He hadn't seen him for quite a while. In fact, he had only seen him twice since his marriage. Better go. It was so easy to lose touch with one's own, thought Mr Fury. Fanny had felt that too. He himself did. He missed Desmond from the house. Yet he could not say anything against it. He could not blame the lad. When he reached the top of the road near the car terminus he stopped. He sat down on one of the wooden benches outside the tramwaymen's shelter. He pulled his cap off and began scratching his head. He was undecided. Should he go or not? Better think it over. One never knew. Fanny might hear about it. Then there would be another row. How she hated Desmond. A sort of poisonous weed. He could not understand the woman. He had tried, endeavoured to be helpful, and failed hopelessly. It was a mystery. She had *never* liked the eldest son. He had been a good son. Why shouldn't he go off and marry if he wanted to? Thinking of him brought the other children trailing in his wake. Maureen, Anthony, John. Aye. John had been a splendid lad. Mr Fury sighed. 'Better dead, perhaps,' were the words that slowly formed in his mind. And Peter. He jumped up from the bench. Damn Peter! He would walk a little further. He couldn't be very far from his son's house now. It was turned half-past seven by the tramway clock. He was certain to be in. He passed into Vulcan Street. When he came to the house he heard voices, punctuated by occasional bursts of laughter. Mr Fury stopped outside the window. The front room was full of people, the gas was lighted. They had not even drawn the curtains. People seemed to be holding animated conversations with his son. Desmond was still dressed in his workaday clothes. Just come home, thought his father. Hands were suddenly raised. Violent gestures were made. Above the noise he heard the word 'strike'. The father turned away from the window. That's how it was, then.

They were talking about the coming strike. Well, he had better go home now. How could a father talk to his son in the midst of such a crowd of agitated people? He hadn't seen Sheila either. He would have liked to have seen her. He rather liked her. By God! Desmond knew what was what. Mr Fury slowly retraced his steps home. A door a few yards from the house suddenly opened, and a woman came out and stood on the step. She cast a suspicious glance at Mr Fury and went in again. The door slammed. 'What a bloody street!' exclaimed the man under his breath. 'One can't move an inch without being watched.' He suddenly changed his direction and went back up the street. He would go home the back way. He would get there quick enough. She would still be there, of course. Probably sitting by the fire opposite her old father. What a pair. He went in by the back entrance. Mrs Fury was not there. He called up the stairs. No reply. 'Must have gone out, after all,' he said, and returned to the kitchen again. He sat down on the sofa and looked at Mr Mangan's chair. 'H'm!' She'd put 'him' to bed. Just like his wife to take offence. Like a spoilt child. It was simply amusing. Nearly eight o'clock. Looking up at the mantelshelf he espied a note pinned to the mantel-border. 'Gone across to Ferris's,' Mr Fury read. What good handwriting it was. Fanny was a good writer. He pulled the pin from the note and threw both into the fire. He sat staring at the empty chair. What a job Fanny had looking after that tailor's dummy. 'Now she's gone across there to cry her heart out as usual,' thought Mr Fury. It was always the same. Whenever they had a row she always went over to Mrs Ferris's. He sighed. Well! The woman would at least be consoling. Fanny and she were very good friends. Once he asked Mrs Fury her reasons for these periodical flights to the Ferrises' house. She replied: 'Because she understands me. That is something you can never do.' Now she had gone off again. For sympathy, he supposed. All over a failure. All over Peter. What a waste of money. All for nothing. The continual struggle. Sometimes to the extent of going without themselves. Now he was coming home again. They would hear everything then. Seven years. Seven long years. Mr Fury stretched himself and yawned. He went upstairs to his room. It was pitch-dark. He went and stood by the window, pressing his face against the glass. There was nothing he could see. He felt a sort of security standing in that corner, in the black darkness. There was a noise in the kitchen. She must have returned. He went down there again.

Mrs Fury was standing in the middle of the kitchen removing her coat and hat. Mr Fury said, 'So you got back, then?'

The woman muttered 'Aye,' and went into the hall to hang up her things. She came back and sat down on the black horse-hair sofa. After a long silence she exclaimed, 'I suppose you've had your supper, Denny?' No, he hadn't had his supper. He didn't want any. He felt like going to bed right away, he said. The woman sniggered.

'Why don't you go, then?' she demanded. Without replying, Mr Fury left the kitchen and went upstairs. Mrs Fury called out after him, 'And don't make a noise. Dad's in bed.' He lighted a candle and stood it on the table near the bed. He heard Mr Mangan snoring. 'Snores like a pig,' he said to himself. Below, Mrs Fury cleared the table of crumbs, and swept the kitchen. Then she backed up the fire with wet ash. This fire was never allowed to die out. It was continuously refuelled. Mr Fury undressed and climbed into bed. He lay there staring up at the ceiling for what seemed to him to be an eternity itself. What a long time she was coming up. Brooding over this boy again. He could not settle down. He got out of bed and went below in his drawers. His wife was seated with her back to him in the big chair just vacated by her father. There was something about her attitude that the man did not like. Was it indifference? Was it mere contempt? He went up to her and placed a hand on her shoulder. The woman did not move.

'Come on, Fanny,' he said. 'Don't sit mopsing there. Best get a wire off tomorrow to your sister and ask her to see the lad on the boat. He'd best get back and get started on something as soon as he can. He'll be at a bit of a loose end now. Bound to feel it pretty badly himself.' (Mr Fury was saying to himself 'though I doubt it very much'.) 'Maybe I could get him into the loco sheds.'

'Loco sheds! Oh, good heavens!'

She put a hand in her blouse and pulled out Anthony's letter. 'Here,' she said, 'this came by the last post.' The man took the letter from her and sat down. 'Where's my glasses?' he asked.

'Use these.' She pushed a pair of spectacles into his hand. Then she got up from the chair, pushed it back against the wall, and exclaimed:

'I'm going to bed.' Mr Fury did not reply. He was too occupied with the letter from Anthony. Not until he had finished reading it and had put it back in the envelope did he realize that he was alone in the kitchen. He rose to his feet. 'I'll be hanged,' he muttered. 'Fanny's a caution, sticks this in my hand and clears off.' He pulled out the jockey-bar and fender, saw to the locking of the doors, then went upstairs. He came down immediately, swearing loudly. He had forgotten the gas. He turned it out, then went upstairs again. His wife was already in bed. He climbed into bed and put out the light. There was something ominous about the silence that followed this action. Mr Fury lay waiting. It was inevitable. What use him trying to sleep? At that moment he struck a match to see if the alarm-clock was set for half-past four. He drew it nearer to the bed. Then he lay back again. He must say something. Get it over. Must have some sleep. Had to be out at half-five. He was conscious of Mrs Fury's violent movements in the bed. Nerves, he thought. The woman suddenly turned her face to the wall.

'I'm so glad to hear Anthony's all right,' he began. 'I was rather worried about him.' Mrs Fury made no reply. Another long silence. Mr Fury turned on his side and stretched out an arm.

'Look here, Fanny,' he said. 'You've got to show a better face than that. I

41

know it's a disappointment. I'm sorry about what happened today. It's hard, I know. It's rotten, disappointing, but best to forget about it. As things are, I should think he'll be better off working and living at home than sitting in a college half his life.' He paused, for Mrs Fury had turned round in the bed. Now he could see the large brown eyes. The blinds had not been let down, and the moonlight came streaming into the room. She turned again and lay on her back. He marvelled at her wealth of hair. Jet black yet, and she nearly sixty years of age. The outline of her features fascinated him, he could not take his eyes from her face.

'There you are,' she said suddenly. 'What a mean, begrudging spirit you have. Desmond was just the same. Maureen was not much better. Fine children! Wonderful!' She placed her hands behind her head. Mr Fury protested. He couldn't see anything wrong with them. After all, they were working for their living. They were at least independent. That itself was a great thing. She ought to realize it. The woman said, 'Good Lord!'

'Yes,' Mr Fury went on, raising his voice. 'You were talking about Desmond tonight. Damn it all. There's nothing wrong with that fellow. He is honest and upright. A good son. His only fault in your eyes was that he married too soon.' He saw her smile. 'His nightly glass,' she thought to herself. 'He'll get quite expansive just now.' She looked at him, and a kind of inward glow suffused her. Ah! All the things he didn't know! All the hidden things. She could feel them welling up in her, bursting to be free. But she held fast. One day she would have her say. Then she would reveal everything. What a story it would be. He wouldn't know where he was standing. He'd simply be swept off his feet. 'Poor Denny. Poor Denny,' she kept saying to herself. He knows nothing. A pity. But there you are. Peter was a history in himself. And what did her husband know of the boy, or of any of his children? Nothing. What had he known of John? Nothing. How could he know them, she asked herself, when half his lifetime was spent at sea? Only in the last two years had he seemed to realize that he was the father of a grown-up family. Too late, she thought. They were strangers to him. A man nearly sixty years of age, she wouldn't say old. No. Denny was far from being old. He was just well on in years. She would let him talk on. He would close up after a while. One day her turn would come too. She lowered her head.

'That's all,' Mr Fury broke in. 'Desmond married too soon for you. What about the others? I've nothing against them.' The woman sat up.

'What?' Why, he didn't even know them. He was talking through his hat. 'You don't know them like I do, Denny. I doubt if you ever will.'

'Ah! You make me sick.' He turned away from her. 'Did you lock up downstairs?' she asked, after a while. Of course. Did she take him for an absolute dullard? The woman laughed. 'Well, you are dull, and you know it. If you hadn't been so dull all your life we might never have been in this hole.'

'Oh Christ! Are you starting on that again?' Mr Fury swore under his breath. This was an old war-horse. How he hated it. The woman was insatiable. Give her a single opening and you were overwhelmed at once. You were caught up in the tidal flow, a flow that carried in its wake regrets, protests, insinuations, hints. Why had he ever mentioned Peter? He was a fool. He looked at her as she lay stretched out in the bed. His mind was torn with conflicting thoughts. He kept fidgeting about the bed. Mrs Fury stirred uneasily at his side. Whatever was wrong with him, moving about like that? How did he expect people to get to sleep? He couldn't hold himself back.

'I can't sleep,' he exclaimed almost savagely. 'I can't sleep.' Couldn't sleep. H'm! Well, she should just think he couldn't sleep. Whatever was he thinking about that it made him so restless? He didn't know. But she did. It was his bad conscience. Yes. That was what it was. Then she exclaimed in a loud domineering voice:

'I should think you wouldn't sleep. How do you think I feel? Do you think I am made of cast-iron? That I can stand every blow without saying something? That I shouldn't lose control sometimes?'

'You're off again,' The man spoke from beneath the bed-clothes. 'Yes. And I haven't said what I want to say. I know you, and I'll say it soon enough. I haven't lived with you all these years for nothing. You're the same old Denny Fury. You talk about Peter. What example was he ever set, what encouragement has he ever had from you, or any of your children? None. You showed a mean spirit all along, and the others took the cue from you. You begrudged me the boy. And when I told you today about the wire, about the shock it was to me, you never so much as opened your mouth. You never said, "I'm sorry," or "It's hard lines." Not a word. You were secretly elated. You know you were.' Mr Fury sat up in the bed.

'God! You could go on talking for ever. But *what* are you talking about? That's what I want to know. When I came in this evening I was dead tired. I wasn't in the mood for listening to groans about Peter. The other lad is just as much concern as he is. I'm tired now. But could a man get a decent sleep here? No. I say for the last time, I *am* sorry about Peter. I know it's disappointing after those years of struggle, doing without, hoping, hoping all the time. It can't be helped, Fanny.' There was real sympathy now. He put his hand on her shoulder.

'It doesn't matter, Denny,' she said. 'That's all too late. It's over and done with. It's not Peter, it's not so much that he's failed, but it's you . . .' She had risen in the bed and was facing him. They were so close together they felt each other's breath upon their faces. 'It's you and your indifference,' went on Mrs Fury. 'You are the living spit of your eldest son . . .'

'Will you give Desmond a rest? Are you going to argue about this the whole night through? I ask you? Isn't there a limit?' She began to cry. She felt weak, defeated. There was something she wanted to say and she could not express it. Each time she opened her mouth the desire was stifled, the power went. She couldn't say it. Once she had been full of courage. She felt that her whole soul had been crushed by Peter. Why had she hidden so many things from her husband? Why, why? she cried in her mind. Why had she allowed herself to be cheated? Why didn't she tell him everything? No! He had been away most of his life. She had spared him. He had only seen the nice part of everything. Fool! She cursed herself. She lay there thinking, thinking. And he had imagined her to be sleeping! If only he had known. If only he could have followed in the wake of her tormented spirit in those past few hours, as it flew, drew wing, and flew again, far out over the wide waters. To hover over Peter. Peter at his desk. Peter at the Mass. Peter at the dinner-table. Peter receiving the news of his failure. But how could Denny think? The man was too wrapped up in himself.

Mr Fury thought, 'It's like being penned in. Caged. The bitterness in her voice.' His hand fell away from her shoulder. 'Yes, it had always been like that,' he thought. Nothing but regrets. The past flung in his face like some soiled and faded garment. *His* past. If only he had done this. If only he had done that. Why hadn't he taken her advice years ago? There would never have been any trouble at all. And Peter. Had he been . . . Well, of course he would have passed through brilliantly. The man felt like a criminal. He was inured to it. This ceaseless round of nagging and regretting. Deep down in his heart he felt that sudden urge to be away again. It was like the sudden re-opening of a wound. Why had he ever left the sea? What did his family care about him? Yes! He ought to go to sea again. At least he would be free. No. His family were grown up now. They forgot him. He was a part of yesterday already. Their eyes already saw far beyond him. They were out of reach. He was only a fragment of the past. He didn't interest them any longer. Their father, of course, but nothing more than that. He closed his eyes. The silence of the room was broken only by the heavy breathing of his wife. She was fast asleep. He sat up and reached for the candle. No use his trying to sleep now. He placed the lighted candle on the table. The light from it fell upon the face of the sleeping woman. He could not help staring into her face. Nor could he conceal a sudden admiration for her as he noted her wonderful head of hair, that fell like two black clouds on either side of the pillow. Nearly the same age as himself, and not a grey hair. A remarkable woman, he thought. Her brow was as smooth as a child's. He wanted to read, but discovered he had left the evening paper in the kitchen. Should he go down for it? Hang it! She might wake up. No. He blew out the light and lay back again. What a day it had been. Suddenly he remembered Anthony's letter. He wanted to read it again. He got out of bed and silently left the room. He went down into the kitchen and lighted the gas. He drew Mr Mangan's big chair to the fire and sat down. He disturbed the slack with the poker and the flames roared. How warm and cheery the kitchen looked. He picked up Anthony's letter from the mantelshelf and sat down.

Then he drew on his spectacles and settled himself comfortably in the chair and began to read. Mr Fury noticed the date. 'Why! The lad must have written it before he had the accident.' He read on.

CHAPTER III

I

At six o'clock that morning, Mr Fury, having had a hurried breakfast, what he called 'a rush and a gulp', went out, banging the door so loudly behind him that the family next door were rudely awakened from their slumbers. The family's name was Postlethwaite.

'The Furys have had a row,' remarked Mr Postlethwaite, speaking loud enough for the family, scattered about in the three rooms, to hear. His wife agreed, yawned, turned over and fell asleep again. The man was hurriedly dressing himself. 'The Furys are always having rows lately,' he went on, as he sat down to pull on his heavy boots. 'They lead him a great dance since he stopped ashore.' Mr Postlethwaite went on talking to himself, for the rest of the family were sleeping too soundly to make any comment. He rose to his feet and looked down at his wife. 'A beauty,' he said in a low voice. 'And she could sleep for years if you let her.' He went downstairs. In the other houses in the same row men were already up and dressing for their work. The women folk in number five, having been so rudely disturbed by the alarm-clocks, vented their anger upon Mr Dennis Fury. He was always rowing. That was the general opinion in Hatfields. The street had never been the same since Mr Fury worked ashore. Mr Postlethwaite left the house and hurried down the street. At the bottom he bumped into Mr Fury, who was bent down by the wall fastening his bootlaces. He hailed him. Mr Fury stood up. 'Hello there!' he said. The two men went off down the road together. Mr Postlethwaite worked at the same sheds as Mr Fury. 'How annoying it all is,' said Mr Fury to himself, darting a furtive glance at the man beside him, 'one can never get rid of this fellow. He's everywhere. He's like a leech. He hangs on to you.' There seemed no way of dodging the man. If one turned a corner, one bumped into Mr Andrew Postlethwaite. He appeared from nowhere. And how the fellow talked. Almost as bad as Fanny herself. Mr Fury lighted his pipe. He remarked upon the coldness of the morning. 'Yes, it is bitter this morning. And I'll have that bitch of an engine to do as soon as I get in.' They walked on, maintaining a silence almost within reach of the sheds. Mr Postlethwaite was studying Mr Fury. He was preparing to put a question to him. He pulled out a handkerchief and blew his nose.

46

Mr Andrew Postlethwaite was older than Mr Fury by five years. He was a little bald-headed man, with a thin, elongated face. Mr Fury could never understand why his workmate and next-door neighbour should have brown eyes. They didn't seem to fit in somehow with the rest of his person. Mr Postlethwaite was nicknamed 'Sponger', and indeed this little man was a sort of human sponge, who spent the day absorbing as much rumour and information as he could safely hold, and then disgorging it when he reached home in the evening for the benefit of his wife and family. He had worked on the railway nearly forty years, in the same shed. Everybody knew 'Sponger'. Mr Postlethwaite beat the big drum for the local lodge band, and beat it to such perfection that the band felt proud of him. Mr Fury did not like the man. For one thing, Mr Postlethwaite was always asking questions. Now as he looked at the man he sensed at once that there was something coming. But the question was so sudden, and of so surprising a nature, that for once Mr Fury felt himself caught out. Mr Postlethwaite said: 'Don't you ever feel you let yourself down, Fury?' Mr Postlethwaite had not forgotten his broken sleep. Mr Fury wore a bewildered look.

'Let myself down!' exclaimed Mr Fury. 'What do you mean – let myself down? What the devil are you talking about?' He didn't understand. 'Hang it,' he was thinking, 'what is the fellow fishing for now?' Mrs Postlethwaite must surely be behind this. Curious people, those Postlethwaites. Of course, they were Billies. That accounted for it perhaps.

'How do you mean, let myself down?' Mr Fury repeated the question.

'Well, I mean this,' said Mr Postlethwaite. 'Don't you ever think you were a cod to give up the sea?' He laid great emphasis on the word 'sea'.

'No, I don't,' replied Mr Fury. He looked Mr Postlethwaite straight in the face. 'No, I don't! What made you get that silly idea into your head? Why should I be sorry? In fact, I'm glad.'

Mr Postlethwaite grinned broadly. Mr Fury felt awkward now. Somehow he always did feel awkward under the battery of Mr Postlethwaite's questionings. It seemed to be his chief duty in life to probe into the lives of other people. If Mr Fury had been fair to himself he would not have passed such a remark. It was not true. He knew it was not true. Ever since he had left the *Cardine* he had regretted it. He was wont to reflect in moments of bitterness that he had been a fool for ever leaving the ship. No use crying about it now. It was too late. Shipping companies weren't taking men like Mr Fury. There were too many young men walking about the docks. No, it would be nothing short of a miracle if he ever put a foot on ship again. The worst of it was – and each time he thought about it he felt angry – the worst of it was, that fellow Postlethwaite had actually got him the job on the railway. He, Mr Fury, had taken the job, just to please Fanny. Now he came to think over it, he had been a fool. 'Well! one of these fine days,' he said to himself, 'one of these fine days I'll just pack my bag and clear out.' Mr Fury's imagination carried him away. 'Aye, one of these days . . .'

Mr Fury took another glance at the little man from number five Hatfields. 'Imagine the likes of him beating a big drum,' he thought. The ludicrous side of Mr Postlethwaite seemed to become personified at that moment. Yes, and before he packed his bag he was going to see that that son of his packed his bag too. Wasn't going to have Postlethwaite getting Peter a job. One was enough. The very idea of being under an obligation to the Postlethwaites rankled in his mind. Yes, one obligation was enough. The high words he had had with Fanny were vividly recalled now. And the last word hadn't been said, he reflected. No doubt about it, Fanny had changed. But what had made her change? Mr Fury realized he had set himself an impossible question. Was it Desmond's marrying out of the chapel? Or was it Maureen marrying Kilkey? It was rather sudden, of course. Neither Desmond nor Maureen had breathed a word about their plans until the last minute. Perhaps Fanny thought her children were cheating her. He still felt resentful. There had been no need for that row last night. Sometimes Mr Fury even imagined that Mrs Fury was getting a little light-headed. There was a sudden pause in the thought. They had come in sight of the sheds. Ahead of them the little green door that led to the wooden bridge was wide open. They passed through. Mr Fury looked at his neighbour.

'Good-morning,' he said. 'See you again at clock-off.'

'Good-morning,' replied Mr Postlethwaite.

Later, more men came hurrying through the door. There were a series of 'Good-mornings', comments on the weather, a dirty joke. Mr Fury passed down the shed, his mind still full of the previous evening's bother – there wasn't the slightest doubt about it, the woman was beyond all comprehension. What was it that changed her? Rough times – the man laughed. But everybody had had rough times, sometime or other. Of course it could only have come to a point with a fellow like Peter. He had always been a strange child. The oddest relationship existed between mother and son. Quite different from the other children. Mr Fury was of opinion that this last child had been thoroughly spoiled. He hadn't seen much of Peter. Their relationship was somewhat distant and reserved. They weren't like father and son at all. He had been away in the Mediterranean when Peter had first gone to college in Cork. When he arrived home one trip the boy had gone. He had thought his wife's idea quite a ridiculous one, and he had told her so. He had felt hurt. Never to have breathed a word to him. As though he weren't his father at all. So his thoughts swung from his wife to his son.

Peter never even wrote to him. He was still thinking of Peter when the dinner-bell rang.

Mr Fury always went home for his midday meal. The house was only a few hundred yards from the shed. As he mounted the wooden stairs to the bridge a voice hailed him. He swung round. 'Hello,' he exclaimed, 'wanting me?' The tall broad-shouldered man who stood gripping a stanchion said, 'No. Nothing particular. Just happen to be going your way.'

'Oh!' Mr Fury said. Then after a long pause, 'I see.' The two men passed out into the street.

'See Desmond's gone foreman of that gang now,' he said.

'Foreman! Oh aye!' Mr Fury looked astonished. First he had heard about it.

'Yes. I was talking to him last night,' said the man. Mr Fury laughed. 'You're lucky,' he said. 'I've only seen my lad twice since he got skipped.' They halted at the bottom of Hatfields. Mr Fury looked at the man, the man at him. They both seemed a little embarrassed, as though the one were waiting his cue from the other. Then abruptly Mr Fury said, 'So long,' and started up the street. He disappeared into the entry. Mr Fury never went in by the front door. There was something about the front door that he did not like. And people were always at the doors, or sitting on their steps. And always talking. Mr Fury hated them. Once he had been a seaman. Now he felt he was nothing. He was unused to living ashore; a street was only another sort of monstrous stone cage, behind the brick bars of which the human monkeys chatted incessantly. Mrs Fury had fallen, quite unconsciously, into her husband's habit of using the rear entrance. Such habits, when formed in a street like Hatfields, naturally assumed a little of the mysterious. People talked, people whispered, flung out hints. Why did folk have to slink in by their back doors? Mr Fury hated the street. They had been arguing for some time as to whether they ought to change their abode. Mr Fury was full of the idea. But somehow Mrs Fury clung tenaciously to Hatfields.

Fanny Fury was standing at the back kitchen door as her husband came up the yard. The man knew at once that she had had news from Ireland. He could always tell when his wife had exciting news to communicate. Invariably he prefaced her breaking of such news with a laconical 'Well?' as he did so now.

'Well?' he said.

'Brigid has just wired me.' said Mrs Fury. 'She's crossing over tomorrow night, with Peter.'

Mr Fury put his hands in his pockets and stopped dead.

'Who? Brigid? What for?' Then before he could give Mrs Fury time to reply, he pushed past her into the kitchen. Dennis Fury had never liked his sister-in-law. Mrs Fury followed him, her temper rising. If anything served to rouse the woman's anger, it was her husband's laconical 'Well?' It smacked of indifference.

'For goodness sake, Denny!' she exclaimed; 'you can't think the boy can come over on one of *those* boats, and him just out of a seminary.'

The man laughed. He couldn't see anything to stop Peter coming, and he couldn't see anything wrong with the boats.

'Sorry,' he said. He took off his hat and flung it on to the sofa. His dinner was already laid out on the table. Mrs Fury went upstairs. The man sat down and commenced to eat. 'Thinks I've slighted her now,' he said to himself. 'Aye, Fanny's a queer'n all right.' The woman came downstairs again. Mr Fury drew her chair in to the table, but Mrs Fury went on through the lobby into the parlour. She felt her husband's remark was nothing less than a direct affront to her sister. Why shouldn't Brigid come over? Who else could come with Peter? Of course he had never liked her people. How well she understood the significance of her husband's 'sorry'. It simply meant 'Oh! shut your mouth.' That was generally the end of it. The man finished his dinner.

He went into the lobby. At the parlour door he stopped and called out, 'I say, Fanny, what time do you expect he'll arrive?' He could not enter the room. Somehow it had taken on a sort of sacred privacy that he could not invade. He stood outside the door.

'You know as well as I do,' she shouted back. 'You've met the Cork boat before this. What's wrong with you lately, Denny? You seem to be fishing for rows all the time. It gets on my nerves.' The man did not reply. There was nothing to say – well, yes, he had lots to say. He sighed. So useless.

'Ever since you gave up the sea you've been the same.'

Mr Fury stared at the door. In one minute she would dash out. Ah! So she had guessed. She had seen the truth for once. He became restless. What was he standing there for? Ought to be getting back to work.

'Well, I suppose we had better meet his boat at the Stage. It comes up about half-ten, doesn't it?' The door was thrown open. Mrs Fury appeared.

'Of course it does, you fool!' The door slammed in Mr Fury's face. He continued to stare at the door, as though it were a sort of mad dog. Then he shouted at the top of his voice: 'The whole trouble with you is that you're mad. Yes, you're mad about Peter, and now you want to take it out of me. That's solid truth and you know it. Good enough. I'll look for a ship and clear out of it. You can have your precious family all to yourself then. Anthony seems to be the lucky devil in this family. He's never home.' He went out, swearing loudly.

Family. His family. Christ! It made him laugh. Bloody fool he was ever leaving the *Cardine*. Yes, he thought, a bunch of strangers. Their father.

It made him laugh. Why, they already looked upon him as intrusion. They had grown up without him. When he retired from the sea they accepted it grudgingly. He was a sort of lodger in the house. He had tried to understand them, but their attitude, their indifference, had wounded him. He suspected his wife. She had known them more intimately, sharing all their days. He was jealous. Then Desmond had got married, and some while after Maureen had become independent too. He liked Desmond for no other reason than that his wife hated him. 'Well she might,' he thought. He was the only one in the family whom she had not been able to influence. That was the cause of most of the trouble. She wanted her own way in everything connected with the children. And he was seeing behind the scenes now. He went back to work and hardly spoke a word to anyone the whole afternoon. His wife was out again when he went home in the evening. He supposed she was to be found over at the Ferrises'. That was another thing Mr Fury hated. This continual going over to the Ferrises'. His meal was all ready on top of the hob. After tea he washed, shaved, and went out. Standing at the top of the street in the drizzle, he suddenly realized how miserable everything was. He couldn't even go up to Vulcan Street now, what with Desmond's latest activities, and the rumours he was hearing through Mr Postlethwaite. What a rotten world it seemed to be. Mr Fury hated this standing at the corner. He was always being hailed by somebody who knew him, but for the life of him he could not recollect half these acquaintances. Where else could he go? His life was divided between the house and the street corner. The house seemed to be broken up altogether since his daughter's departure. Often he wished he could go up and have a talk with her, but when the time came he always backed out. He was conscious of his loneliness. In the midst of these meditations a hand suddenly descended on his shoulder.

'Why, Mulcare!' he exclaimed, drawing back a little with the shock of this sudden meeting. What a time since he had seen the fellow. He looked at him a long time without moving. A broad smile covered the other's face. He was a young man about thirty years of age. He was dressed in a brown tweed suit, wore a sailor's jersey and a grey slouch hat. The clothes were not of English make. Mr Fury at once guessed where the young man had bought them. He continued to stare at Mulcare, hardly able to believe his own eyes. 'Hello!' he said, suddenly excited, 'and how are you getting along these times?' The young man smiled. 'Just back from Adelaide,' he said. 'Ah! I thought so,' Mr Fury remarked. 'I reckoned that was an Australian rig-out you got on. So you're still on the same old ship? I'll be damned. Well, you're looking grand, young man,' he concluded. Mulcare nodded his head. Yes. He was still on the same old ship. 'Come and have a drink,' he said. 'Just for old time's sake.' The older man brightened up at once. They walked slowly up to the Star and Garter and went inside, choosing seats near the brightly blazing fire in the snug back parlour. Mr Fury was still smiling. He looked casually, almost with in-difference, at the clock upon the wall. Time for a real good talk. Only seven o'clock. He took stock of Mulcare. The young fellow certainly looked fit and well. They made themselves comfortable. 'What are you having?' asked Mulcare. He sat back.

'I'll have a whisky,' said Mr Fury, 'but – no – a pint of Falstaff will suit me.' On reflection he had decided upon plain beer. He wasn't drinking much lately, he explained to Mulcare. Hardly at all. A drop of whisky might go to his head. The barman came over and served the drinks. They drank each other's health. The glasses clinked. Mulcare pulled a packet of Turkish cigarettes from his pocket and offered one to Mr Fury. The old man shook his head. 'Never smoke those things,' he remarked. 'Thanks all the same.'

'I have a bit of the real stuff here, then,' went on the young man. He pulled a plug of tobacco from his coat pocket and handed it to Mr Fury. 'Here you are. I know you like the hard stuff better.'

'Splendid. How thoughtful of you, Michael. Thanks.' He leaned back against the wall and surveyed Mulcare. 'Hardly changed,' he was saying to himself. 'Hardly changed.' He put the tobacco away.

'How is your father these days?' asked Mr Fury. 'Still the same old thing with him?' He recalled how he had first met this young man. It had been on a boat crossing over from Dublin. He had left home after some trouble with his family. He had made his first trip to sea with Mr Fury in a ship called the *Ballisa*. Mulcare laughed. 'Oh, I hear from him occasionally,' he said, 'but there's nothing to get excited about. Just the same. Hard as nails. Still sits in his office waiting for clients. I feel desperately sorry for him at times. He's living in the past. Can't keep up to scratch. And anyhow, the country is ruined. Poor Dad.'

'Oh!' exclaimed Mr Fury, and for some unaccountable reason he felt the young man's remark to apply to himself too. He felt suddenly old. Mulcare lighted another cigarette. 'How are you?' he asked.

'How am I?' Mr Fury grinned. 'Not so bad.'

'Out of a ship?'

'Yes. Gave it up two years ago. Left the *Cardine*. Sorry I ever did. Can't get used to the shore life at all. It takes it out of you, believe me. But I suppose, like all the other old-timers, I'll get used to it after a while. I'll fall into my groove.' He laughed loudly. Mulcare leaned across and said, 'Looking for a ship, then?' He watched Mr Fury's face, and noticed the sudden change in his expression. The old man shook himself like a dog.

'Looking for a ship!' Of course he was. Just the thing. 'Just the very thing I'm waiting for.' He was going to take his chance again. At that moment a pair of large brown eyes appeared to bear down upon him. Those eyes were Mrs Fury's. He sat up abruptly. He seemed embarrassed. He was lost for words. He dodged the other's persistent stare.

'No. I'm all right where I am, Michael,' he said. 'A chap named Postlethwaite got me a job in the loco sheds. Not a bad job. Better than nothing, anyhow.' The young man sitting opposite him said 'Oh!' in such a way that he could not help but feel a sort of sting in it. Oh yes. There was a sting in it. Why didn't he say right out, 'Sure! Are you any hands short aboard your ship?' But he could not say it. His mouth remained closed. He would not say a word. They sat looking at each other, each wondering what the other was going to say.

'Come along, Fury,' Mulcare said. 'Drink up.'

'Why!' exclaimed Mr Fury, and he half rose from his seat. 'The very thing!' Peter! Of course. Here was an excellent chance for him. He could not sit still. Mulcare ordered more drinks. Now he was speaking, but Mr Fury did not hear. He was too busy thinking. Then he said:

'I've got a son. A young lad, sixteen, in fact he's turned sixteen. Sixteen and a half. I was wondering . . .'

Mulcare finished Mr Fury's sentence. 'I could probably get him fixed up,' he said. 'Quicker than I could you. You mean you want your son to go to sea?' The older man became more excited than ever. 'Why, yes.' It was splendid. Things were bad. It wasn't easy to fall into jobs these days. He would have to talk it over with his wife first. Would he come up to the house one evening before he went away? How long was he going to be in port? Where was his ship lying? Peter. His son wasn't like other lads, of course, went on Mr Fury. Mulcare raised his eyes until they were on a level with Mr Fury's head. No. Peter was not like other lads. In fact, he had been in college for nearly seven years. He saw the young man smile. Mr Fury paused. Then the secret came out.

Yes. His wife had wanted this son to be a priest. He was their youngest. He had, however, failed. They had just heard about it from Ireland. It was extraordinary, he said, because Peter had passed all his other examinations with great brilliancy. Mulcare drew his hand across his mouth and looked up at the ceiling. Then his eyes returned to Mr Fury's level again, and he asked some questions. The man became more informative. Yes. It had been a great disappointment. Quite unexpected. Neither his wife nor himself could understand. Of course, he himself had never been a direct party to the business. Not that he didn't respect the religion. Nothing like that. But it had seemed rather fantastic to him. All right for people who could

53

afford it. But not of any use to people like themselves. A continual drain on their resources, a ceaseless struggle and no return for it. That was his own opinion, he concluded. He picked up his glass and drank.

'Yes,' the young man said. 'I quite understand. It's a weakness with the Irish, isn't it? Every family must have its priest. But the poor are as ambitious as popes. They must have two priests.'

'Quite right,' remarked Mr Fury. 'Though, as I said, I'm not against it entirely. But it's a different matter when you can't afford it.' Mulcare nodded his head. He tapped the bar-room table with his long fingers. 'Quite true,' he said. 'But what can one do with such people?' Mr Fury said. 'They're impossible. Look at Fanny. My wife. She's driven herself half crazy in order to realize her ambitions over that lad. Now he's failed her.' The young man turned a deaf ear to the remark. He wasn't interested in such things. He asked Mr Fury how long it was since he had left the *Cardine*. Mr Fury replied, 'A few years ago.' 'What a pity!' Mulcare leaned across the table. 'What a pity!'

He was talking now as though leaving a ship at his age was the most preposterous thing in the world.

'Can't carry on for ever,' Mr Fury said. A sadness came over him. The waters were rising. Soon he would let himself go. He could hear his wife talking now. Aye. There was Anthony and Peter now. He caught Mulcare's eye. 'I'm so glad to have met you,' he said. It was almost a whisper.

'I'm here for eight days,' said Mulcare. 'My ship is lying in the George V dock. We're shipping machinery across to the West Indies for the sugar people. I'll take a walk up to your place one evening.' They finished their drinks, got up and went outside. They stood with their elbows leaning against the long, brightly polished brass rail outside the window. Mr Fury's memory suddenly stirred itself. Thoughts shot up, faces appeared and vanished again. What a lot there was still to be talked about. Pity Mulcare was going off like that. He rather liked the young fellow. But the young man seemed impatient. He wanted to be off. Well, he would not deter him. He stood erect, shot out a thin horny hand and grasped that of Mulcare. He shook it warmly. Mulcare noticed the tattooed stars, one on each of Mr Fury's wrists.

'Well, so long, Michael. Just like old times seeing you again. Come up and see us before you go away. I'll have a talk with Fanny meanwhile. Don't forget now. So long.' He waved his hand in cheery farewell.

'Yes. I'll slip along one evening. Good-bye, Fury.' Mr Fury looked at the broad back of Mulcare as he vanished round the corner. He seemed rooted to the spot. He could not move. Confound it! He had been so glad to meet Mulcare again. He had even enjoyed the drink and talk. Yet he felt more miserable than ever now. It awakened the longing in him once more. Why didn't he get out instead of putting up with that kind of life? Swallowing the anchor. At his age. He wandered up the road, aimlessly, until a car came along. He boarded it and climbed up on top. He tendered twopence to the conductor, saying, 'Pier Head.' He settled himself down in a seat near the window. He hadn't seen the Pier Head for months. The blow would do him good. There was a strong breeze blowing in across the river. He thought, 'What luck meeting that fellow! It was simply splendid.' Then the wave of optimism broke against the breakwater of real fact. His wife would say 'NO' right away. Trust Fanny for that. Hang it! There must be some way of working this. When the car arrived at the Pier Head he remained on board. The conductor came up at the terminus. Mr Fury looked up. No. He wasn't getting out. He had only jumped on for the run down. The conductor handed him another ticket, muttering incoherently to himself as he went below. Mr Fury was returning home in a very different frame of mind. He even felt cheery about things. 'A good idea,' he said to himself. 'And the only obstacle is Fanny.' A stone wall. Well, he would see. How ridiculous he must have appeared to Mulcare. Why, as true as he was sitting on that tram-car, the fellow knew that he, Denny Fury, was simply longing to get to sea again. Yet he hadn't had the courage. He had just collapsed. He was losing hold on himself. He revolted against the whole thing. Him, a sailor, working with a lot of old women at the railway sheds. When the car eventually stopped at the bottom of Hatfields, Mr Fury's whole demeanour changed again. He went into the house by the rear entrance. His wife was there. And there in the corner sat Maureen. He could hear quite plainly what they were talking about. He entered the kitchen. Maureen smiled.

'Hello, Dad,' said Maureen. She thought she saw a frown on his face. But Mr Fury was not frowning. He was looking at Maureen with a peculiar expression upon his face. A sort of utter hopelessness had stamped itself there. He was looking at his daughter as one looks at a precious possession, which one has held all one's life, has touched, yet knows he can hold no more. Maureen. Mrs Fury was murmuring her name. He went into the back kitchen. How long had they been there? Talking all the evening, he supposed. She must have gone down to tell Maureen about Peter. The Ferrises' was a bad guess this time. Mrs Fury called. He went in, blowing his nose vigorously into his spotted handkerchief. 'Have you had your tea, Denny?' she asked. 'I was out. Maureen came up with me. Joe says there's rumour of a coming strike where he is. He'll strike, of course.' Mr Fury sat down. What a way she had of talking. She might as well have said, 'Joe is going out to commit suicide.' So he was going to strike! Oh! A stevedore at the docks. The thing was spreading, then? He looked across at his daughter. 'Who said they're coming out?' The young woman rose to her feet. 'Everybody's coming out,' she said, 'and so are you. If you don't, you ought to be ashamed of yourself.'

'Good God!' thought Mr Fury. Was this Maureen?

2

Mr Fury repeated his question. 'Who said the men were coming out? Forget it,' as though a strike were the most surprising thing in the world. Maureen was seated in the corner, her hands clutching the back of the cane chair.

'But everybody's coming out, Dad,' she said. 'Everybody.' Mr Fury laughed. 'Well, I'm not interested. Neither is your mother.' He got up and crossed the kitchen. He placed his hands on his wife's shoulders. He smiled at her. 'It's Lyric night, Fanny,' he said. 'You best get ready.' 'Oh!' exclaimed Mrs Fury, 'I'm not going.' Mr Fury took no notice of the remark. He turned to his daughter. 'Your mother and I are going to the Lyric,' he said. Then he faced Mrs Fury again. A smile came at last. She got up. 'All right,' she said. They went upstairs together. Maureen called after them that she was going.

'I'll slip round tomorrow, Mother,' she shouted up the stairs. 'I'll come before you go down to meet him.'

Then she left the house.

Mr and Mrs Fury were busy changing into their Sunday best. Mr Fury felt that he must not speak. He must not breathe a word. Fanny was such a contrary woman. One word and she would change her mind. He had an idea that she had had fresh news about Anthony from the shipping office, but he controlled himself. This was Lyric night, and everything else could go by the board. Even whilst he was at sea, they had always managed to see a show at the Lyric whenever he came home. The preparations on Lyric night had assumed almost ceremonial proportions. Mr Fury always put his blue suit on, and also his shiny hard hat came out of the box. Again, he wore a collar and tie. Mrs Fury always wore her grey skirt and a white silk blouse. Over this she drew on her long blue serge coat. Mr Fury had already changed. Mrs Fury was in the act of running the hatpin through her hat when Mr Fury lost control of himself.

'Fanny,' he said, 'if you'll come to Hobhouse's with me I'll buy you a hat. That one's a real veteran and it's nearly time you buried it.' Mrs Fury, quite indifferent, sent the pin through the black straw hat, and then drew back a pace, the more thoroughly to survey her figure. Mr Fury drove his hands into his pockets and stared at her. The way she clung to that hat. He couldn't make it out. As tenacious as an octopus. 'I'm not joking, Fanny,' he said, as he looked at her from head to heel. 'I'm not joking. If you'll get off the tram at Hobhouse's I'll get you a hat. A good hat. A real hat.' The woman laughed. 'Don't be silly, Denny,' she said. She turned round and faced him. Then her quick eye caught sight of his collar. She went up to him and rearranged his tie.

'You're a sloven, Denny.' She poked him in the ribs. Mr Fury caught her hands in his own and squeezed them. Somehow, as he looked her up and down his pride returned.

'Well, Fanny, I'll say this. That when you do dress, you look a real lady. No doubt about it.' He was filled with an admiration he could no longer conceal. He went over to the window again and looked out. He heard his wife sit down suddenly on the creaky bed. Mrs Fury was changing her shoes. The man fell into a contemplative attitude, resting his head against the window-pane. Well, they had been together a long long time, and in all those years he could not remember a single Lyric night that had been a failure. Yes, when he came to think it over, Fanny was a good 'un. A real good woman, Yes. He understood. He knew what it was like. Getting two disappointments on the same day. He turned round. Mrs Fury rose from the bed. She must see Dad was fixed up before she went. The man nodded his head. 'Of course,' he said, 'of course.' The woman left the room. Mr Fury walked across and surveyed himself in the mirror. 'I don't look so bad,' he said under his breath. He sat down on the bed. At length Mrs Fury called, 'Denny! Denny!' He went below.

The woman was standing at the front door, her hand on the knob. 'Ssh!' she said, 'Ssh!' 'This way,' Mr Fury said, and without another word led the way through the lobby. He wasn't going out through that front door. Not for any money. They passed out into the yard.

'What about the back door, Denny?' asked Mrs Fury. 'That's all right, Fanny,' he replied. 'You go ahead. I'll bolt the door after you, then come over the wall.'

A few minutes later he joined her at the bottom of the entry. They passed out into the neighbouring street. A mist was descending. The lamps shone dully through the haze. They arrived at the top of Dolan Street, and stood waiting for a tram. The light from a corner shop shone down on them. Once a man, passing by, called out, 'Night, Denny,' and Mr Fury, without turning round, replied, 'Night, Frisco.' He had recognized the voice. One of the things he most hated was waiting for a tram on the main road. People were always bumping into him. When an acquaintance bumped into Dennis Fury it inevitably meant two drinks at the Hangman's or the Pitch-pine. Mr Fury took drastic measures in view of his depleted pocket-money. He was rarely seen on the main road now. All right whilst he was at sea.

But railway wages didn't allow of him indulging his generous spirit. At last a tram came along. Mr Fury helped his wife to the platform. Slowly they pushed their way through and found a seat. They had not been seated a full minute before Mr Fury exclaimed, 'If we had caught a Great Comus Street tram we could have sat on top.' Mrs Fury said drily, 'Oh heavens, man! You won't die without your pipe for a few minutes.' But he could not catch her words. The tram had put on speed, and in addition its driver began stamping angrily on his foot-bell in a vain endeavour to clear the line of a pony and trap bowling along with a steady rhythm, its two wheels meeting the iron rails. Once or twice its driver, a red-faced youth, had turned round and shouted at the exasperated driver, 'Keep your shirt on, Dad! Keep your shirt on!'

This remark was not lost upon the passengers sitting at the front end of the tram, and there were occasional laughs and titters. But Mrs Fury seemed immune. She refused to be interested. She said under her breath, 'The lads nowadays are just devils. That fool will be killed one of these days.' Mr Fury said, 'Yes, yes.' His mind was occupied with something other than the tram and its angry driver. Suddenly the wheels of the trap skidded, with a loud grating noise. The tram had the road clear at last. When it pulled up at the top of Valley Street, nearly everybody descended, and Mrs Fury exclaimed, 'It must be a gala night, Denny.' 'Aye, perhaps so.' Mr Fury climbed down, then assisted his wife. The garish lights of the theatre shone down the full length of Valley Street. Outside the theatre itself stood a long queue of people. 'What a crowd, Denny!' said Mrs Fury. 'Best go into the pit,' remarked Mr Fury. They joined the tail-end of the queue. Everybody's attention seemed focused upon the huge man shouting, 'Gallery sixpence. Pit one and three.' He was dressed in a bright blue uniform, splendidly set off with brass epaulettes. Mrs Fury fidgeted. 'I hope we don't have to wait long,' she exclaimed.

Mr Fury was so absorbed in the antics of a tall lean individual who performed an amazing series of acrobatic feats in the street, that he did not hear Mrs Fury's remark. His eyes were fastened upon the acrobat. This gentleman's completely bald head looked like a great ivory ball. As he tossed and tumbled, he beat a most ecstatic accompaniment upon two large table-spoons. Mrs Fury leaned heavily upon her husband's arm. Her feet were paining her. She was now telling herself that she ought never to have put on those black shoes. They were too small. It was too late to change them now. 'What's the matter?' asked Mr Fury at last, turning round all of a sudden. The street acrobat had now finished his performance, and hat in hand was slowly making his way up the queue of people, most of whom regarded him with a curiosity giving rise almost to embarrassment on the

58

acrobat's part. They could see the man was old, and that he hadn't a tooth in his head. Then the head of the queue began to move. 'Oh! At last!' said Mrs Fury.

Mr Fury pressed inside. As they reached the corridor they could see through the open door that the first twenty rows of the pit were already filled. They glimpsed the orchestra tuning up. They passed through the door. After much pushing and struggling they found a seat. Mrs Fury had no sooner sat down than Mr Fury removed his hard hat and placed it on the seat beside his wife. 'Don't move, Fanny! and watch my place.' 'What's the matter with you, Denny? You always do this. Don't be so absurd.' She noticed the sudden change in her husband. His demeanour bespoke an urgency, a sudden restlessness. Whatever was wrong with him? At that very moment the orchestra struck up, to the accompaniment of loud chatter, swishing dresses, tearing paper, whilst the strong smell of tobacco and newly peeled oranges rose in the air. 'I'll be back in a tick, Fanny,' exclaimed Mr Fury. He was almost desperate. Mrs Fury clutched the tail of his coat. Her colour rose. 'You old fool!' she exclaimed under her breath. 'Are you ashamed to stand like everybody else ... ?' The remainder of her sentence was caught and overwhelmed in the first bars of the National Anthem. Mr Fury fled. He rushed straight to the lavatory. There he stood listening, and when the final note sounded he returned to his seat. Everybody stared at him. But now, to the sound of thunderous claps, the curtain rose. Mr Fury sat tight in his seat, staring at Fanny, but she looked straight ahead at the rising curtain. She couldn't understand such idiocy. Why Denny hated to stand for the Anthem she simply could not understand. A comedian came out from the wings. The theatre became silent, and the audience settled itself down for the evening.

Of course it simply meant that Anthony would come home on the first available boat. On crutches, she supposed. That meant she would have Peter and Anthony on her hands. A house full. Well, thank God it wasn't anything worse than an accident, and then Denny at least was working. That was a wonderful thing. Maureen's pound a week had been a great help. And Desmond's two pounds. Well – she'd see. Perhaps Anthony would write and say when he was coming. No! She wouldn't breathe a word to Maureen. Let her find out. Fool she was ever to have told her about Peter. The girl was utterly selfish. What a change in her since she married that fellow Kilkey. She laughed. Mr Fury said, 'That was a good joke, Fanny,' but Mrs Fury heard nothing. Indeed she had seen nothing. She had fallen into a reverie, almost unconsciously. She had been prepared to sit and enjoy the show with everybody else, but she could not pin her mind down to it. This meditative mood stole over like a cloud, completely overwhelming her. She became lost in it, whilst her husband gave vent to periodic bursts of laughter. Twice she looked at him, and each time thought, 'H'm! It is easy to see Denny has nothing on his mind.' The cool and collected way in which he had sat and listened to her recital of the visit to Mr Lake had not surprised Mrs Fury. To Dennis Fury the mere falling from a mast was nothing. Part of the day's work, so to speak. At one time this callousness had shocked the woman, now she had become used to his laconical 'Oh! Dear me! Bad, isn't it?' But what was going to happen when Peter arrived home? The lights went up. Everybody looked about. The curtain descended. Mr Fury looked at his wife. He knew then by the very expression upon her face that she had paid no attention to the show. 'Thinking again,' he thought. 'Thinking of those young beggars, I expect, and I don't suppose they care a toss.' He put his hand over her own, now lying idly in her lap. 'Come on, old girl! Let's have a wet.'

'No, Denny, you go,' Mrs Fury said. Mr Fury repeated, 'Come on! Come on!' People were pushing their way along the benches. Three times the Furys rose to their feet, and three times sat down again. Mr Fury was adamant. 'Come on, for heaven's sake, Fanny! Leave those lads out of your mind for a while, anyhow.' He paused suddenly. How awkward he was! At last the woman rose to her feet. He rose with her. She pushed against him. 'All right. Go on,' she said, and possessed by a furious burst of energy, pushed her husband all the way along the bench. They walked slowly up the foyer of the theatre. They found the bar-room crowded. 'Wait here, Fanny,' he said, and pushed and thrust until he reached the counter. Then he shouted, 'What are you having, Fanny?' He had forgotten to ask her. Mrs Fury lowered her head. That damned fool, she was thinking. Everybody in the bar-room stared in her direction as though waiting for the words to fall from her mouth. The barman looked impatiently at Mr Fury. Glasses were continually being banged on the counter, with urgent orders for refills. The barman said, 'Come on, old man. What is it?' He looked daggers at Mr Fury now. The man managed to stammer, 'Oh, a dash and a Bass.' He made his way back to where his wife stood. Nobody had moved, nobody had offered her a seat. She leaned against the wall. As Mr Fury handed her the glass and raised his own, saying, 'Here you are, Fanny,' the woman did not appear to see him, though her hand went out automatically for the glass. She saw, not her husband, but the gentleman at the shipping office. And the gentleman said, 'Put this lady out at the top floor.' Her eyes now took in the scene around her. She looked at the faces, thin and fat, red, blotched, coarse-looking faces, refined faces. The rows of faces seemed to swim about her. She drank, hearing Denny say, 'Well, I hope you enjoyed the show, Fanny.' Mr Fury was smiling. One could see at once with what pleasure the man was looking forward to the second half of the show. But suddenly Mrs Fury damped his enthusiasm. She wanted to go home. She looked almost pathetic now as she handed him back the glass. She had only drunk half her lemon dash. Mr Fury's face fell. The woman forced a smile.

'I'm sorry, Denny,' she said. 'It's my feet. I'll go. You stay on. It's all right. I don't want to spoil your night.'

Mr Fury merely said, 'Come!' They went out. His heart was full of tenderness for her. They passed out into the street.

They were silent for a good part of the journey from town. Mr Fury stared through the window at the brightly dressed windows, a long ribbon of light tapering up the long King's Road. He seemed to be fully absorbed. An idea had come into his head. When that tram reached Hobhouse's block he was getting off, and Fanny was going with him too. 'It's these shoes, Denny,' said the woman, breaking the silence at last. 'What's the matter with them?' he asked, still keeping his eyes on the passing shops. 'I think they're too small.' Dennis Fury looked round them. He did not look at his wife's shoes, rather did his eyes begin a minute survey of the black straw hat upon her head. He studied its lines and its angle, its brim and its crown. Then he said hurriedly, 'Getting off here.'

'Whatever for?' asked the woman. Didn't he know her feet were aching? Mr Fury stood up. The woman sat still in her seat. 'That's all right,' he said, 'but we're getting off here.'

There was something so domineering in the tone of her husband's voice that out of sheer astonishment she rose to her feet and followed him down the iron stairs.

'Here we are!' said Mr Fury. 'I'm sorry you didn't enjoy that show, Fanny. Look! There's Hobhouse's. We're going right in.' Mr Fury escorted his wife to the kerb. In absolute silence they entered the hat-shop. A smile broke out on the man's face, and he said to the assistant who came hurrying forward, 'My wife wants to buy a hat. And don't let her out of the shop without one.' He looked at his wife – 'I'll wait outside,' he said, and walked quickly to the door.

'This way, madam!' said the assistant, and Mrs Fury followed the girl into an adjoining room.

Five minutes later she joined her husband in the street.

'Well, Denny, you're a caution!' she exclaimed. 'A real caution.' 'That's all right,' said Mr Fury, 'but for heaven's sake, when you get home, burn that confounded hat.'

They boarded the next inward-bound tram for home.

Promptly at half-past five the next evening Maureen went round to Hatfields. Mr Fury had just finished his tea, and was sitting on the sofa reading the evening paper when his daughter came in.

'Hello!' she announced, with a sort of desperate enthusiasm, and sat herself down at her father's side. Mrs Fury was busy attending to her father. Mr Fury half turned his head and looked at his daughter. She was a rare visitor now. Since she had married Joseph Kilkey, he supposed she had been home twice in that twelve months. Mr Fury realized that there was something in Maureen he had lost sight of. It was the same with the other children. He had seen so little of them whilst at sea. Now they had grown up. Somehow they seemed beyond him. There was something about Maureen that he greatly admired, and he could not conceal it. Maureen Fury, like her mother, was tall and slim, and of graceful bearing. Their characteristics were almost identical. There was something imperious about her carriage, and even thirty years of married life had not wrested it from Mrs Fury. Maureen had a head of copper-coloured hair, whilst her eyes were deep grey in colour. Her face was long, the mouth was thin, like the mother's, and tended to give her a certain severity of expression, which her very nature at once belied. Mr Fury looked at her hands, and from her hands his eyes wandered to her face. His wife all over. Now at this very moment Mr Fury was puzzled. He had not forgotten his daughter's attitude when the question of sending Peter to Cork had first come up. Why this sudden change? He felt he wanted to talk to Maureen – but not there – not in the house. Perhaps he would go over to Kilkey's place and have a talk with her. Some night when Joe was working late. He had a faint suspicion that Maureen had changed her opinions, and was now taking her mother's part where Peter was concerned. The curious thing was that his wife had not breathed a word to Maureen about Anthony's accident. Mr Fury found a special place in his affections for Anthony. Anthony was looked upon as the simpleton of the family. He could not take his eyes from his daughter, even when his wife pushed Mr Mangan and his chair further back into the corner, and now turned round and faced them. He studied Maureen from the rear, frontally, and in profile. What was this something about his daughter that he specially admired? Was it her very youth, her freshness and enthusiasm? It certainly wasn't her interest in polemics. Mr Fury never associated women with polemics. Indeed, his daughter's sudden interest could only have arisen after contact with Mr Kilkey. Suddenly he patted Maureen on the back, and shouted, 'Well, Maureen, any fresh news?' Then he winked at his wife.

Mrs Fury had drawn up the cane chair, and was seated in it, looking at the fast-burning slack. Maureen assumed a quite serious expression, and facing her father, remarked, 'Yes, the tramwaymen are coming out too. They're going to support the miners.'

'Oh!' Mr Fury scratched his head with great vigour. Of course. He *had* heard something about it in the sheds. But he never wholly believed it. A mere rumour. And now they were talking about the police coming out as well. H'm! Next thing he'd probably hear about would be a war. A real War. What next! He looked up suddenly as Mrs Fury exclaimed:

'About Peter!'

About Peter? Mr Fury looked across at the bent figure of Mr Mangan.

'What's wrong now?' he asked.

'Wrong!' exclaimed his wife. 'Why, the lad will be stranded. That's what's wrong.'

Mr Fury burst out laughing. 'Get away! get away! To hear you people talking you'd imagine the whole world was coming out on strike this very minute.'

'There won't be any boats running,' continued Mrs Fury; 'you don't suppose the authorities at the college are going to keep him there for ever ...'

'Why?' interrupted Mr Fury. 'Have you heard, then?'

'I've heard *nothing*,' said Mrs Fury, '*Nothing*. All I know is, that his last fees were paid eleven weeks ago.' The word 'fees' remained in Mr Fury's mind for a long time. Maureen caught his eye.

'It's rather rotten about Peter,' she said.

Mr Fury made no reply. He took the plug of tobacco from his pocket, and began to cut at it with a large jack-knife. Then he said, 'Aye,' and began to rub up the tobacco in the palm of his hand. 'Aye,' he said again.

'Met somebody?' asked Mrs Fury.

It was a long time since Mrs Fury had smelt tobacco so strong. Not since her husband had left the ships. Mr Fury filled his pipe.

'Met a fellow name of Mulcare,' he said. 'A fine young chap. His father's in rather a big way in Dublin. But they don't get on very well together.' He saw his wife smile.

'How ridiculous!' she said, and changed the conversation back to Peter. Mr Fury was on the point of protesting. Very soon, he felt, they would be canonizing this young fellow. At that moment a wire came. It saved the situation. Peter was on his way, with Aunt Brigid. Mr Fury's face fell. So she was coming after all. Two of them now. Peter had left by an earlier boat. All eyes went to the clock. The woman jumped to her feet. 'Why!' she exclaimed, 'we've only got three-quarters of an hour to meet the boat. Get your coat on, Denny.' She half pushed her husband out of the chair. She rushed into the hall. A minute later she appeared, fully dressed, in the kitchen. She was wearing her new hat. Mr Fury beamed. 'You look a real toff, Fanny,' he said.

'Hurry up, Denny. You're so slow. And always behind time. Come along now. I half believe you don't want to meet the lad.' Her tone of voice suddenly changed. Mr Fury exclaimed, 'All right! All right!' It was a nuisance, but he did not want any scenes on the tramcar. Maureen got up and said she must be going too. Mrs Fury stopped her.

'A minute, child. We're all going your way.'

'What about "him"?' asked Mr Fury, pointing to the huddled figure of Mr Mangan. Ah! She hadn't thought of that. She looked appealingly at Maureen. Could she stay? Maureen was embarrassed. Well, Joe would be expecting her. She hadn't been in the whole evening. Perhaps . . .

'We'll take him with us,' said Mrs Fury.

'Good God, woman! That's impossible! It's impossible!' shouted Mr Fury. He looked savagely at his wife. Then he turned to Maureen.

'Look here,' he said. 'Why can't you oblige your mother for once? You know she wants to meet the lad, and so do I. Can't you stay with your grand-dad? We'll be back inside an hour.' Maureen remained adamant. No. She really couldn't. Besides, it didn't require two people to meet Peter, and Aunt Brigid knew her way. She had been in Gelton before. Mr Fury flung his cap on the table. 'To hell with it!' he said, and sat down. Mrs Fury swore under her breath. 'Maureen,' she said, then suddenly stopped. 'How could Joe go out and his wife like that? Expecting a child soon,' she was thinking. Mr Fury said, 'Well, what's it going to be, in or out? We're getting later every minute.' Maureen crossed over to the window. 'It's a filthy night,' she said. Mrs Fury shouted at the top of her voice, 'Off you go, Maureen. Get off home to your husband. Don't keep him waiting for you.' She turned to her husband. 'Denny, come here a minute.' She was bending over her father's chair. 'Give a hand here,' she said. Maureen slipped out into the back kitchen and left the house. Mr Fury went across to his wife. 'But heavens above!' he exclaimed; 'the man can't stand up!' Mrs Fury gnashed her teeth. 'How the devil do you think I manage him on a Friday? Of course he can stand. He's not as helpless as all that. Put your arm under his shoulder. There.'

They stood the old man up. 'Er – er –' he grunted. Mr Fury cursed inwardly at this turn in the situation. Why had he ever mentioned the old fool? Landed himself in this. He looked at his wife. 'You're crazy, Fanny; you're crazy! He can't walk. And the job we'll have with him on the car! It's madness. Besides which, the night is filthy. It'll kill him.'

'Come along,' Mrs Fury said. 'Get his hard hat from the rack. And his raincoat. Mangans won't lie down, Denny. Don't forget that.' Mr Fury went out for the old man's outdoor things. When he came into the kitchen, his wife was wiping her father's face with a wet flannel. Christ! What a stubborn bitch of a woman she was! 'Here.'

'Then give a hand,' she replied, as he held out the coat and hat. 'Take this away.' She almost flung the flannel into his face. But Mr Fury only said, 'You'll never do it, and in the end you'll miss this bloody boat, and serve you right.'

'Shut your mouth! Are you ready?'

Between them they half carried the old man to the door. After much confusion they managed to get off the step into the street. 'Go back and lock the place up,' Mrs Fury said. She held her father up against the wall until her husband came out. He put an arm around Mr Mangan. Half dragging, half carrying the old man between them, they made their way slowly down the street. A periodic grunting from this bent figure caused them to stop twice, whilst Mrs Fury wiped her father's eyes and nose. It was now pouring with rain. Some doors opened, a shaft of sickly yellowish light streamed out upon the murky pavements. The three figures stumbled into this light. A man came and stood at the door to watch them pass. He shouted into the kitchen, 'Look at this,' and he was joined by another man and a woman. All three stood on the step watching the snail-like progress of the Furys from number three. Mr Fury already felt this trio of eyes boring into the back of his head. Like the old man beside him, he was seized with a sudden longing for obscurity. He lowered his own head. Mrs Fury seemed oblivious of everything excepting the weight upon her right arm. They reached the bottom of the street.

'Did you put out the gas-stove in the back?' she asked.

A sort of low mumble was all the reply she received. Now they were approaching the main road. Mr Fury suddenly wished that the earth might open and swallow him up – if not himself, then this dragging helpless figure in the middle. How on earth did Fanny manage the fellow on a Friday? 'She wouldn't mind that,' he was saying to himself. 'It's a question of ten shillings every time with her. I suppose that went across to the beggar in Ireland too.' The rain was running down his neck. Once he set himself erect and glanced across at his wife. Her attitude was almost imperious. With her head erect she walked on, oblivious of the passers-by who stopped to stare at this quaint trio. At last they were nearing the tram-stop. Mr Fury heaved a sigh of relief. He didn't mind the rain. He was only concerned about hiding himself away from the light, from the curious eyes that looked into his own as he stumbled along. What a position to be in! Hang it, the fellow ought to be in his grave! Ought never to have come to the house. Mr Fury had never forgiven Mr Mangan for the remarks he had passed to him on the occasion of Peter's letter home for money. Now things would be worse. The lad home, Mr Mangan still in the chair, and worst of all, his sister-in-law. A hopeful prospect, he thought.

'By Christ!' he shouted. He had lost control of himself. Mrs Fury heard nothing. A tram was rushing down towards them, the driver clanging his bell. 'Hold him tight!' she shouted. The noise was deafening. Mr Fury hung on. The tram pulled up with a screeching sound. The driver looked astonished at the three figures as they stepped off the footpath, whilst the conductor, who had just shot down the stairs, exclaimed, 'What's this? A funeral?' He spat out on the road. 'Full up below,' he shouted, and looked down at the upturned faces of Mr and Mrs Fury. They looked yellow and ghastly beneath the light. The figure in the middle did not interest him. It possessed nothing, revealed nothing, to convince him that it was humanized. 'Full up below,' he repeated. This red-faced young man with an almost bovine expression upon his face began to get impatient. 'Hurry up now,' he said, and put out a hand to help them on. 'Best get on top, Denny,' Mrs Fury said.

'Oh God!' murmured Mr Fury. 'All right. Get on, for heaven's sake! I'll lift the old man on.' With the conductor's unwilling help they managed to get the old man on to the platform, Mrs Fury pushing him from behind, whilst her husband's one free hand gripped the brass rail. 'Strike me!' exclaimed the conductor. The woman shot him a vicious glance and exclaimed angrily, 'Can't you help? He's an old man. What are you standing there for?' She nudged her husband.

'Come on, Denny, for goodness sake. We won't get a seat at all in a minute.' She put a foot on the stairs. The conductor and Mr Fury followed, pushing the old man up in front of them. The woman held her father's hand. They reached the top stair. They held on desperately to the rails. The tram careered along. Through the open window the rain shot into Mr Mangan's face. 'At last!' They both breathed a sigh of relief. They found a vacant place on the long seat right in the front end of the car. More excitement and confusion as they threaded their way awkwardly through the seated passengers. A forest of murmurs. Everybody was staring. They sat down. Mr Fury put his hand at the back of Mr Mangan's head. The car seemed to sway from side to side. The old man's head bobbed up and down, backwards and forwards. Mrs Fury paid for their tickets. The conductor vanished again. Not a word was spoken, though the murmuring amongst the passengers had not yet died down. Mrs Fury was lost in thought. Her eyes saw nothing but her daughter Maureen, a sort of inner eye remained focused upon the young woman, and her change of form. What a time, she was thinking, for Joe to think of going out on strike! Maureen surprised her. Poor child! Did she think it was some kind of jolly holiday? She hadn't seen anything yet. Well, she would lose all her illusions soon. She kept staring through the window at the brilliantly lighted shop fronts. And the way the girl talked. She wasn't blind to her attitude towards her husband. No doubt Denny would think that she, Fanny, was behind all this. Joe was only a fool if he came out. Ridiculous that one man had to imperil his livelihood and that of his wife just because a number of other men said it was the only thing to do. Men were like children, and they hadn't half the imagination of children. H'm! She rubbed her hand on the glass, and looked across at her husband. 'What do you think about this business?'

'What business?' He spoke in undertones.

'The strike. Maureen will be in childbed soon.'

'I wouldn't offer any advice,' Mr Fury replied. 'Young people don't take advice these days. It's too old-fashioned.' He wasn't interested in Kilkey anyhow. He pulled out his pipe and struck a match. The woman changed the conversation. Between them the old man snored. He had fallen asleep. His bowler hat had slipped down over his eyes, the water kept dripping down his neck. The tram stopped. Some people got out. The atmosphere seemed a little clearer now.

'Well, Denny,' began Mrs Fury. 'I can hardly believe it. I've tried to imagine what he'll be like. Conjured up all sorts of pictures in my imagination. Seven years. It's a long time.' Mr Fury's pipe had gone out. 'Yes,' he said, and struck another match. He smoked contentedly until the car reached Wilson Street. 'How quiet he is!' thought the woman. She suddenly turned on him. 'I half believe you don't care a fig about the boy,' she declared vehemently. He did not reply, but the glance he threw his wife seemed enough. He looked out of the window. He was studying the gilt lettering on a draper's shop window. She was labouring under one of her usual illusions. 'I'm just as glad to see the boy coming home as you are,' he growled. 'He's mine as well as yours.' His voice rose. Mrs Fury said, 'I could see this coming.' People began to stare. 'The trouble with you,' went on Mr Fury, 'the trouble with you is that you want your children all to yourself. That's the living truth. I don't blame the others a bit for going off as suddenly as they did. You were simply asking for it.' His voice pitched even higher, his face had grown whiter than usual. Mrs Fury had never seen her husband so carried away as this. They were still arguing when the tram stopped at the Pier Head. Immediately the inert figure assumed an importance all its own. Even Peter was a secondary consideration. 'Best to wait until the others have got off,' said Mrs Fury. She could hardly conceal her rage at this affront in the eyes of a tramful of people. Mr Fury got up from his seat.

'You go ahead,' he said, almost authoritatively. 'I'll carry your father down myself.' He watched her go. When she passed out of sight he looked down at the figure. 'Strike me!' he said, and picked Mr Mangan up. Unable to carry him shoulder-high on account of the low roof, he dragged him along until they reached the steps. Then he placed him over his shoulder, and with one free hand clinging desperately to the stair rail made his way down to the platform. The conductor appeared much relieved at seeing the last of this ill-assorted family. He supposed they were a family. He stood watching Mr Fury carry the old man to the sidewalk. He put him gently down. Immediately Mr Mangan collapsed to the ground. Mr Fury barked savagely at his wife, 'There! I told you. Look at him! How in the name of the Lord are we going to get him along the floating bridge, never mind get him along to where the ship berths?' Mrs Fury, for the first time that day, felt that she had made a mistake. Ought she to admit it? What could they do with her father now? They daren't leave him alone. That would only bring the police interfering. Well, she had got him this far, and she was going to see that he reached the boat. Did Denny think that she was just going to lie down to whatever he ordered? 'Stand him up,' she said. Impatient, she went to the old man and stood him up herself. 'Dad,' she said. Her husband stared. This was the first time for years that he had heard her address Mr Mangan as 'Dad'. When the figure muttered, 'Well, – er,' Mr Fury felt he was witnessing a miracle. Mrs Fury stamped her foot. 'Put your arm under Dad, Denny,' she said. They started off again.

The sight of the Front awoke many memories in Mr Fury. It would have been an event, this walking along the Stage, in sight and sound of the river traffic. But now with Mr Mangan at his side he felt nothing. Yet he kept telling himself that he must go. His whole spirit cried out for the sea. To be free once again. Penned down like he was. Between four walls. And with a woman like Fanny. This, after spending practically the whole of his life on ships. They pulled up again. They had reached the bottom of the floating bridge. Here the brilliant arc lights shone down mercilessly upon them. More people stared. Mrs Fury ignored them. They moved on again. When they reached the Irish boat's berth, they discovered a large crowd already gathered there. Mr Fury thought this a little strange. Had it been the height of the summer he would have understood. But this. What was it all about? They drew nearer. Mrs Fury suggested they go up against the big chains. Mr Mangan would be able to rest against them. The man made no reply. They reached the chains. Now they could hear much talking amongst the broken-up groups of people. Mrs Fury became curious. She left her husband holding on to her father and moved a few yards further up the Stage. Then she heard words, clear and distinct, come to her out of the night air. 'Murderer,' caught her ears '... the fellow's from Arklow.'

'Good heavens!' she exclaimed, and ran to her husband. 'Why,' she said, 'Peter's on the same boat as the Arklow murderer. They've brought him over. Imagine! Peter on the same boat!'

'What about it?' growled Mr Fury; 'he won't eat the lad, will he?' He looked almost despairingly at the figure of Mr Mangan. 'You're the most excitable woman I ever met in my life,' he remarked. 'Now their eyes beheld the black shape of the ship looming up through the mist. Mrs Fury's hands gripped the chains. He noticed their whiteness. These chains ran the full length of the landing-stage. She swung round, exclaiming, 'Denny! Denny! Come here!' 'What a fuss she's making!' he thought. 'I can't leave *him*,' he said. People were watching Mrs Fury. 'What's wrong?' he asked. The woman almost flung herself at him. What was wrong? Why, his son was coming home. He was in that very boat. H'm! She tossed her head in the air. And wouldn't Peter be watching with the same anxious eyes as themselves? For his father and mother?

'Yes, yes. Of course.' Mr Fury put a hand on his wife's shoulder. Excitement and confusion. The slack of the hawsers was being paid out. Now they had the bight over the bitt. Soon the gangway would go up. They craned their necks. Figures moved about the decks, the white faces looking like so many splashing lights in the darkness. Mrs Fury was staring now at a tall figure standing against the saloon doorway. 'There he is!' she cried. She pinched her husband's arm. 'See! How tall he has grown.'

The person in question happened to be a King's Messenger. People were coming down the gangway. But where was Peter? Mr Fury strained anxious eyes towards the gangway. Would he know the lad? So long since he had seen him. Then there appeared at the top of the gangway a tall youth, carrying a suitcase, followed by a buxom woman of medium height. Tears came to Mrs Fury's eyes. 'He is there. There he is.' Mr Fury felt a weight on his arm, then it left him. There was a thud. 'Blast!' he said. Mr Mangan had collapsed again. He looked round despairingly for his wife, but Mrs Fury had already rushed to the foot of the gangway. He tried to lift the old man to his feet. How awkward he was! A little crowd gathered. Then a policeman hove in sight. 'Drunk?' he asked brusquely. Mr Fury looked at him, then at the gangway. 'Fanny!' he called out. 'Fanny!' Three people were rushing towards him now. Mr Fury imagined it to be three million. It was like an oncoming sea. Ah! Good heck! Was this his son? The buxom woman said, 'Oh, Denny!' and knelt down by her father. Mrs Fury said, 'One could not leave you alone for a single moment. How did that happen? Here's Peter.' Her husband looked at his son. Nearly six-foot high. 'Well!' he said.

'Well! I'm glad to see you home again.' He grasped the outstretched hand. The youth smiled. 'Hello, Dad,' he said.

'He'll be all right in a second,' Brigid Mangan was saying. She had an arm under her father's head. The policeman observed all this with consternation. He went across to Mr Fury. 'Best get a cab for the old man,' he said. For the first time Peter became aware of his grandfather's presence. He bent down and looked into the old man's face. How small he was, how thin his face was, and he hardly seemed to have eyes at all. Peter felt a sudden disgust grow upon him. His aunt was wiping Mr Mangan's eyes. 'Go and get a taxi,' Mrs Fury said.

Mr Fury went off to the taxi rank, glad of even a few minutes' respite. The silly woman! To bring an old man out on a night like this! He came back a few minutes later, standing on the step of the taxi. The driver got down to help Mr Mangan in. Mrs Fury was thinking, 'Will it hold five of us?' whilst Mr Fury stood staring at his son, hardly able to realize that this was the small boy he had known seven years ago. It made him feel suddenly old, as old as that man whom the driver had now caught hold of in his arms. 'Give a hand, Denny.'

'Yes.' Mr Fury went inside the taxi and helped the old man in. They sat him down in the corner. Mrs Fury touched her son on the shoulder. 'Sit 'longside your grand-dad,' she said. Peter got inside. He felt a repugnance to sitting by his grandfather. This was nothing like the man he had known seven years ago. What changes had taken place. He made himself comfortable. Mrs Fury and her sister climbed in. Mr Fury got in after them. They seated themselves after much fuss and bother. The driver stood holding the door, waiting for them. Mrs Fury looked across at her son. 'Hold your head up,' she said, a remark which made the man at the door smile. 'All set?' he asked. 'Yes,' said Mrs Fury, 'we're all set. Drive to the bottom of Hatfields.'

'Why the bottom, Fanny?' asked her husband from his corner. 'What's the matter with the door?' Mrs Fury said, 'Shut up,' and turned to the driver: 'Pull up at the bottom of Hatfields, driver,' she said. 'Right, ma'am.' The man climbed on to his seat. Nobody spoke. The engine tuned up. Mr Mangan still grunted like a pig. Mr Fury jammed his face against the window. Brigid Mangan kept fidgeting about, not comfortably settled. Mrs Fury sat back with folded arms, her eyes pinned upon her son. Peter coughed. Everybody began to move. The taxi started off. 'Shut the window,' Mrs Fury said. Mr Fury closed the window. He looked at his son again. 'Bless me,' he said to himself, 'he's a full-grown man!' His wife sat erect like a soldier.

CHAPTER IV

I

'Peter! Oh, Peter! How are you?' The youth felt himself caught in a pair of strong arms. He was overwhelmed, crushed against this body whose arms seemed to intensify their clutch upon him. A mouth sought his own. 'Oh, my dear boy!' Mrs Fury sat back in the taxi now, reflecting upon the animated scene at the bottom of the gangway. How he had grown! She had an idea that Peter had wanted to free himself from her grasp. She had loosened her hold upon him at the very moment when her husband had called out to her so frantically. The light from the powerful arc lamps had shone brightly upon them. Some people had laughed. He had looked splendid standing there. So strong and healthy-looking, a smile suffusing his tanned face.

'Hello, Dad,' he was saying. She remembered the astonishment with which her husband had met his son. She had known it all along. The man had never seen him for seven years. He hadn't appeared to recognize him at first. 'A bit of a whipper-snapper when I went away.' She could hear him saying that. She had smiled on seeing him grip her son's shoulders, saying, 'Well, Peter, I'm right glad to see you home again.' No more than that. Not a word about his failure. Not a word about his future. How old and wretched her sister was looking! Hardly as old as herself. She ought to have married, she was telling herself. She coughed loudly, but not a movement from the others in the taxi. Peter sat back, his head almost on the old man's shoulders. Mr Fury, on the same seat as his wife and sister, was jammed up against the window. Occasionally they caught glimpses of each other's faces, whenever the taxi passed a street lamp. They were well away from the Stage now, although to Mrs Fury the taxi appeared to be going at a crawling pace. From time to time she looked at her husband, then across at her son. She leaned forward once, certain that Peter had spoken to his father. But the stony silence was maintained. She sat back again. What a time the man was driving them to Hatfields! Mr Fury was still thinking of the great crowd they had left at the ship's berth, eager for a glimpse of the apprehended Arklow murderer. It seemed to him now that he had been the only one anyway concerned about his father-in-law. With Peter's sudden arrival his wife had ceased to pay any attention to the old man.

Suddenly Brigid Mangan broke the silence. She turned to her sister.

'What is this I hear, Fanny, about a general strike?' Mrs Fury laughed. 'Oh that!' She had heard about it. 'Why?' Brigid Mangan said, 'Well, if the boats are going to be held up I shall be in a fix. I have only a few shillings with me. Indeed, I hope I can catch the boat back at eight o'clock tomorrow night.'

Mr Fury said: 'You'll catch it all right. There won't be any strike. In any case, it wouldn't interfere with the running of the traffic for a day or two.'

'You think so, Denny?'

'Yes.' Mr Fury very much wanted to, but seated as he was, he could scarcely move an inch either way. 'Excuse me,' he said rather abruptly, and Miss Mangan moved away a little whilst he pulled out his pipe.

'Open the window, Peter,' called Mrs Fury. 'Your father's been presented with the most foul tobacco.' Her husband laughed. Peter laughed. He reached over and pulled down the window. He looked across at his father. This little old man with the grey hair was his father. He could only remember him as he was seven years ago. He was more robust then, his hair was fair and grew thick upon his head. How he had changed! There was a sudden jolt, and everybody was thrown towards the middle of the taxi. 'My heavens!' exclaimed Brigid Mangan. Then the taxi stopped altogether. The driver came to the door. 'Better get out, Missus,' he said, addressing himself to Mrs Fury. 'My taxi's broke down.' Mr Fury said, 'Well, I'll be hanged!'

'Did you ever see the like of it?' shouted Mrs Fury. 'Come along! We must get out. Have to get a tram after all.' Mr Fury knocked out the contents of his pipe and said, 'Good Christ Almighty!'

'Denny!' Mrs Fury pushed her face into that of her husband. 'Do you know where you are?' Peter had got out of the taxi. The man had already thrown up the car bonnet. Miss Mangan climbed out after Peter, ridiculing the driver for his vain efforts, whilst Mr Fury was left as sole guardian of the bundle in the corner. 'Peter,' he called, 'give me a hand with your grand-dad.'

They got the old man out. The bewildered group stood on the pavement. 'I won't pay you a penny,' stormed Mrs Fury at the driver. The man looked up from his engine. 'I don't want your money,' he said. 'Would you mind standing out of my light?' He stood watching the party edge away towards the car-lines. Peter was smiling. Mrs Fury said, 'Here's a car.'

The same commotion as before, the same searching for seats. Brigid Mangan was hanging on desperately to her brother-in-law as the tram started off. 'You never saw such a woman as Fanny,' he remarked to Miss Mangan. 'Creates such a fuss over nothing.' Brigid affected to be sympathetic. They went inside, leaving Mrs Fury with Peter and her father sitting at the furthest end of the car.

'I'd better go down,' he remarked to Brigid, and left her sitting by herself. In the brilliantly lighted car Mr Fury fell to studying his son. Peter began to talk excitedly about his journey across. The passengers looked at this youth. Mrs Fury was trembling now. It only required a word about his failure to start her husband off. Each time he sailed perilously near to the subject occupying both their minds the woman turned pale. She dreaded any mention of it. Peter turned to his father. At the the same moment Mrs Fury remarked icily: 'We get down here.'

She got up from her seat, saying to Mr Fury, 'Peter and you better get Father out,' and she sailed along to the platform. Her sister was already standing holding on to the brass rail. 'What a wild night, Fanny!' Miss Mangan exclaimed. The woman did not reply. She turned her head round, anxious to see what progress the others were making. She could not bear to have her son alone with his father, not for a single moment. Peter caught her eye then, and he wondered at the strange expression upon his mother's face. Mrs Fury's fear was that her son might suddenly expand. More than that. That he might confide in his father. There would be enough to talk about when they got home. She hoped the fire had not gone out. Peter and Mr Fury helped Mr Mangan down to the road when the tram pulled up at the bottom of Hatfields. Mrs Fury looked at Peter. She was glad to see him again. She loved her son, but that wasn't the end of the matter. There was a question to be asked and a question to be answered. She was to have her say, and there was plenty of time for that. The car moved on, leaving the party of five standing together in the middle of the road. The rain suddenly stopped. Peter went up to his mother. He was smiling at her now. But the mother turned her head away, saying to her sister, 'How I hate those trams!' – but she was really saying to herself, 'How could I? So soon.' Quite out of place. She had not failed to notice the little conversation that had gone on between the boy and his father. She resented this. The boy must learn to know his position. Peter was still standing at her elbow.

'Dad and I are going ahead with Grand-dad,' he said, but his mother replied, 'Not at all. We'll all go together, Peter.' A sudden frenzy seized her. She could not understand. She drew back from her son. This confrontation with her own flesh and blood after so many years rather frightened her. Gradually she would right herself. His coming home was, of course, associated with the other thing. It made her feel sick again just to think about it. Ahead she discerned her husband waving his free hand, the other was round her father. 'He's coming now,' she shouted, and at the same moment gave her son a violent push, saying, 'Go to your father.' She turned to her sister. 'Let them go ahead. Denny has the key.' The two sisters walked slowly behind. For some time no word was spoken. Then Brigid exclaimed, 'I say,

Denny looks awfully miserable. Isn't he well?' Mrs Fury replied, 'He's quite well, Brigid. What makes you think that?'

'He's so quiet,' went on Brigid. 'He's hardly spoken a word since we met.' The other woman laughed. Oh! That was an old habit of his. She wouldn't be surprised when she told her that Denny had never opened his mouth to her father for the past two years. Brigid Mangan said, 'They had a row, I suppose.'

'Yes.' Mrs Fury was not feeling expansive enough at that moment to continue any further. The row had been over Peter, of course.

'I hope you won't miss your boat,' Mrs Fury said. They were in the street now. 'What else could I say,' she was thinking, 'after that remark?' Quite out of place. She was always the same. 'Brigid,' she said, 'how long is Peter out of college?'

'Since last Monday.'

They reached the house. Denny and his son had already gone inside. When Mrs Fury and her sister entered the kitchen, they found Mr Mangan seated in his usual place. Mr Fury was standing by the window.

'It seems ten years since I saw you, Dad,' Peter was saying. 'I don't think you've changed much.' Mr Fury smiled. Mrs Fury looked from one to the other. How well Peter and his father seemed to be getting on, she was thinking. 'Denny,' she said quickly, 'will you take Brigid's things upstairs?' Mr Fury picked up Miss Mangan's bag. 'Will you go up with him, Brigid?' asked Mrs Fury. 'He'll show you the room.' Brigid crossed the kitchen and followed Mr Fury upstairs. No sooner had they gone than Mrs Fury swung round and demanded sharply of her son his reason for not replying to her last letter. Peter had seated himself on the sofa. He looked at his mother. He could not conceal his surprise at her sudden demanding tone.

'Why, I ...'

'Of course, the Principal will probably write to me,' his mother interrupted. She flushed a little. Somehow she had not liked the attitude of her husband. The word 'conspiracy' flashed across her mind. One only had to leave them for a single moment. What was the matter with her? Was she suspicious? Well, she would not blind herself to facts. Peter got up. 'Well Mother ...' but the woman immediately clapped a hand over his mouth. She could hear her husband and sister descending the stairs.

'Plenty of time tomorrow,' she said. The youth stared at her. To him she had suddenly grown huge, she overawed. *She* certainly had changed. He recalled the journey in the taxi. His mother had seemed to overawe everybody. Mrs Fury repeated the word, 'Tomorrow.' Her whole spirit thrilled to the word. Tomorrow. Judge and judged. A cross-examination. The whole truth. What she thought, felt, what she had hoped for and lost. She could feel the energy stirring in her. Tomorrow would settle everything. Besides, there was Brigid. She would hear what she had to say. How glad she was now that the woman had come over with Peter! She would not grumble at the temporary inconvenience. Brigid and Mr Fury came into the kitchen. Miss Mangan sat down beside Peter. She could not take her eyes from her father. There was something about his whole attitude that filled her with pity. Anthony Mangan did not even know his daughter had arrived. Mrs Fury started to prepare supper. Immediately Brigid got up and went to the back kitchen to help. Fanny Fury said:

'Just watch that pan, Brigid. I must show the boy his room. I completely forgot about it. Then Father must have some milk and be put to bed.' Mrs Fury felt that agitation growing. She called to Peter. 'Get your bag, Peter, and come upstairs.'

They left Mr Fury standing under the mantelshelf. He was looking at the old man, but he was thinking of the ride in the taxi. He could not forget that ride. The whole atmosphere seemed mysterious. His wife would do that, of course. But why the devil did she conceal things like she did? Why didn't she be open and say, 'I know why you failed'? No. She was content to skirt round the thing. Her whole attitude implied that she already knew everything. When was he going to get a chance to talk with his son? He wasn't blind. He knew what they would be talking about upstairs. Damn it! One would think the lad had committed murder. He joined Miss Mangan in the back kitchen. 'I can't make Fanny out,' he said, leaning against the sink, his eyes following the quick movements of her hands as she arranged plates and cups on a tray.

'No, I'm damned if I can. Do you know why the lad failed? I don't. It was all a surprise to me, because his mother wrote me a couple of years ago, when I was at sea, saying he had passed his preliminary examinations with great success.' Brigid Mangan said, 'I don't know, Denny. Fanny knows more than I do. All I can tell you is, that the boy came to me last Monday night and said he was finished at the college.' Mrs Fury came in. There he was again. 'Brigid.' Her sister looked up. 'Would you like a drink?' No. She did not want anything. Mr Fury said, 'I'll bring in a drink if you like.' 'Of course,' Mrs Fury said; 'go and bring some stout, Denny.' Mr Fury put his hat and coat on and left the house.

Upstairs, Peter was sitting on the bed. The same old room. The one he had left seven years ago. Hardly a thing altered. And there in the corner stood Desmond's fishing-tackle. He thought of all the fish he had caught at the strand in Cobh. He was still sitting there when his mother came up. A flood of memories swept across Peter's mind. 'I'm so glad to be home, Mother,' he said. His mother forced a smile. 'I'm so glad too.' They went downstairs together. Everything had turned out differently. But she must still smile. Mr Fury came back with three bottles of stout. The two sisters laid the table between them. Peter went up to his father. The man smiled at him but said nothing. He was lost in admiration for this son. Each time he looked up at him he smiled. He did not know whether it was his tall, splendidly proportioned figure, or whether it was the mop of hair, or even the enthusiastic light in Peter's eyes, but he was conscious of this admiration. He could not conceal it.

'Come along,' Mrs Fury said. They all sat down to table.

'What about Dad?' Brigid asked, turning round to look at her father. Mrs Fury said, 'Of course. Denny' – pause – 'Peter, just help your grand-dad upstairs. Father will put him to bed.' She dashed away from the table, filled a pan with milk and put it on the stove. She came into the kitchen again, and sat down. 'That's the first time I ever forgot Dad's supper,' she remarked to Brigid. They were alone in the kitchen now.

'Dad is looking awful,' said Brigid. 'How long has he been like that?'

'Some time now. My dear woman, you ought to have been here during the past three months. You would have seen things that would have opened your eyes pretty wide. Still, I don't mind. I always said I would stand by Father. But tell me, now that you're here, has he a sister in Belfast? It might seem silly asking such a question, but you know how uncommunicative a man Dad always was.' Brigid looked surprised.

'Of course,' she said. 'He has a sister just outside the city. Liam Doonan is in the dye business there.' Mrs Fury confessed her astonishment. 'I rather wondered,' she went on. 'At one time it was nothing but "Belfast, and the Belfast boat", until it began to get on my nerves. As for Denny, well ... Here, help yourself.' She handed her sister a plate of fish. 'Thanks.' Peter and his father came down again. Mrs Fury said, 'Before you sit down, Denny, will you see to that milk outside?' Mr Fury went out and brought the milk in. 'I must go to him now,' Mrs Fury said, 'Excuse me.' She got up from the table and took the pan from her husband. Father and son sat down. When Mrs Fury went upstairs, Mr Fury said, 'Hasn't he grown, Brigid?'

'Indeed he has. He's a fine young man now.' They looked at Peter. Mrs Fury joined them a few minutes later. Peter put a penny in the gas-meter.

'Now,' Mrs Fury began. She looked at her husband. 'You'd better sleep down here for tonight, Denny. Peter will have his own room. Brigid and I will sleep together.' Miss Mangan protested. With a wave of the hand Mrs Fury dismissed this. 'Father has to sleep by himself, Brigid, and besides, nobody could ever sleep with the snoring he does. Peter can't sleep down here. It wouldn't be fair to the boy. And I'm certainly not going to let you sleep in the kitchen. I can rig up a good bed for Denny.' Nobody spoke. They went on with the meal. Fanny's word was enough. There was a knock at the door.

'How late it is!' said Mrs Fury. 'Who can that be? Go and see, Denny.' But before Mr Fury could move, Peter had dashed to he door and opened it. 'It's somebody for Dad,' he called in to them.

'Hang it!' exclaimed Mr Fury. 'Who can it be this time of night?' He went outside. Peter came back. 'Who was it?' asked his mother. 'I don't know, Mother. Looked like a railway chap. He had a driver's clothes on.'

'Oh!' Everybody stopped eating. They could hear a conversation going on at the door. Then the door closed. Mr Fury came in. 'Well,' he said, 'there's no doubt about it; the miners and everybody are coming out now. Good Jesus!'

'Denny! Denny! Before the boy! What on earth are you thinking about?' She looked at her son. 'Peter, hurry up and finish your supper; look how late it is,' and her eye went to the clock again. The youth got up. 'All right. Goodnight, everybody,' he said. He went towards the door. His mother followed him. They stood in the hall for a moment, then went upstairs.

'It is true, then?' asked Brigid. Mr Fury smiled. 'Aye. It's only too bloody true, Brigid. It looks as though the whole country's going to come out.' Mr Fury was feeling so angry that he wanted very much to add, 'Aye, and it looks like you're going to be here for a pretty stay.' He pushed his chair back and got up from the table. Brigid followed. She seated herself in Mr Mangan's high-backed chair, remarking to herself how comfortable it was. 'Poor Father,' she was saying to herself, 'he looks a wreck and no doubt about it.' She stretched her feet out in front of the fire. Mr Fury fell to studying them. What a difference there was between this woman and his wife. Fanny was more wiry, had more energy. Brigid was always heavy and flabby, he was saying to himself. He wished his wife would come down. What on earth was she doing upstairs all this time? He never liked being alone with Brigid Mangan for long. He remembered too well the last occasion, when they had argued the whole night through about Parnell. Brigid was a real school-ma'am.

'Denny!' called Mrs Fury from the top of the stairs. Mr Fury went into the hall. Come upstairs.' He went up. Mrs Fury was standing in Peter's room. His son had partly stripped.

'You're quite a man now,' he said. 'You're even a fine-looking young man,' went on Mr Fury. 'You were only a nipper when I saw you last. Well, well.' He could not believe his eyes. He went across to where Peter was standing and gripped his hands. Mrs Fury looked on quite uninterested in this sudden display of filial devotion. For the first time Mr Fury kissed his son. 'Good-night, boy,' he said. He went downstairs again, his wife following with the bed-clothes. She cleared the sofa of cushions and laid his bed. She turned to her sister. 'You must be tired, Brigid.' It was a signal. Miss Mangan got up. 'I think I'll go up now, Fanny,' she said. She smiled at Mr Fury. 'Goodnight, Denny.' She went out. Mr Fury said, 'Good-night.'

'Don't forget to lock up and wind the clock,' said Mrs Fury. No. He wouldn't forget. Where was the evening paper? His wife picked it up from the dresser and threw it across to him. 'Good-night,' she called out, her hand on the kitchen door. Mr Fury made no reply. The door closed.

'At last!' he was thinking. 'At last!' He surveyed the deserted kitchen with a sort of triumphant air. All away. He was alone at last. He looked at the roughly made-up bed on the sofa, made a grimace, and drew out Mr Mangan's great chair. He settled it in front of the fire, and picking up the paper, he began to read. His eye fell upon the stop-press news, and remained there for some time as though glued to the spot. He could hear the moving about in the rooms above him. Suddenly he smiled. Did he mind sleeping downstairs? By heavens, no! He would miss Mangan's grunts for once, and Fanny would have somebody else to talk to. He stirred the fire. The paper fell from his hands. He closed his eyes and lay back. He lost himself in the past. What a change had taken place in his wife. He had traced this change right back to the time of Peter's going away. 'Confound the whole business!' he cried in his mind. One couldn't patch up anything now. Everything seemed to lie in pieces. Yes. There could be no doubt about it. Fanny was a changed woman. He had indeed probed a vital spot. And from it had flowed to waste all her respect, all her feeling, all her admiration and gratitude. But why should he suffer for her own folly? The stop-press of the evening paper suddenly blotted out these thoughts, and Mr Fury was muttering, 'Strike! Confound the damn strike! It would come now. And the house full of people.' He sat up. How could he sleep? No. He couldn't settle to anything until he heard all about Peter. What was she hiding? He had an idea, but he wasn't certain. Was it that she had realized her mistake? Or, on the other hand, was the real revelation to come from that young man upstairs? He got up and crept silently into the hall. He stood at the bottom of the stairs. Why, the light was still on in his son's room! And Fanny was talking away. 'Poor Brigid!' he was thinking. 'Devil of a bit of sleep she'll get!' He went back into the kitchen again and began pacing the floor. If only Fanny would say straight out, 'Well, it was a mistake, Denny, and now I realize it. Perhaps you had better get Peter fixed up.' But no. Stubborn woman. She wouldn't do it. A nice education Peter was getting. He wasn't blind to such tactics. Young people knew a hell of a lot more than she thought. He stopped by the door, hesitating. Then he exclaimed, 'Well, no. It's useless.' He went into the hall, put his coat and cap on, drew a woollen scarf round his neck, and went silently to the door. He opened the door and went into the street. How nice and fresh it was outside. He might as well go for a short walk. He heard the clock strike from the neighbouring chapel. He drew the door to, and jammed it with his handkerchief. Then he went off down the street. He did not know that Peter had seen him. Peter, like himself, had not turned in. He was standing looking out of the open window when his father passed down the street. Unable to conceal his astonishment, he called out, 'Dad! Hey, Dad!' A voice in the next room shouted, 'Who's that?' No reply. Peter left his room, crept downstairs, and hurried down the street after his father.

2

Brigid Mangan lived in an old-fashioned house on the Mall. When her mother died, it seemed that the house of the Mangan family had come to its appointed end. A month after Mrs Mangan's death, her two sons, Joseph and Terence Mangan, packed up their belongings and decided to seek their fortunes in New York, where an uncle of theirs already lived, and who had some sort of official position in the municipal offices of the city. Like their sister Brigid, they realized the end had come. Mrs Mangan lived to a ripe old age. She was some seven years senior to Anthony Mangan. But this fact did not prevent her children from attributing the cause of her sudden decease to their sister's brutal treatment. So Brigid called it. Why had Fanny ever decided to leave Ireland? It was all a mystery. When she left, it seemed the first rift had been made. When the brothers sailed for New York, leaving Brigid to look after her father, Miss Mangan decided at once that she could not stay in the house any longer. She shifted the furniture and family effects to the house on the Mall, taking Mr Mangan with her. Fortunately, Brigid Mangan was able to maintain her independence, partly from a small weekly pension left to her by her mother, partly from her own industry. Brigid Mangan was not an idle woman. Clever with the needle, she soon put this to good purpose, for, a few weeks after taking up her abode in the new house, she managed to get commissions to make altar cloths, surplices, and communion cloths. Always a pious woman, her interests were solely divided between the house and her father, and the near-by chapel of St Andrew's. She soon became known in the neighbourhood. She made arrangements with the local priest to put up and look after his visitors, so that in time her house was a sort of Open Sesame for passing students, brothers, priests, and even nuns. Her interests grew. She was getting older. Ambition served no purpose. She was content to spend her time in the service of her religion. She found her time taken up. When one summer she decided to put up five visiting missioners, it seemed to her that old Mr Mangan was an obstacle. She now began to regret her sudden generousness of spirit. Here she was, saddled with a man well on in years, and for whom she could do no more. She had even hinted to him that now was the time to consider going into retreat. The old man refused. He had felt somewhat shocked that but a year after his wife's death his daughter should want him out of the way. He knew why she wanted it. It was at this juncture that the old man realized that his daughter Brigid had been slowly alienating his affections from Fanny. Indeed, the nightly conversations, winter and summer, month after month, had seemed to centre round the woman in Gelton. Brigid Mangan impressed the old man at first. Yes. That had really been the first rift in their lives, their comfort, and their security. But when Brigid added that she considered Fanny's action monstrous, and the cause of her mother's death, the old man flung up his hands in horror. Impossible! Ridiculous! He would have none of it.

If Brigid Mangan did not openly express her dissatisfaction with the state of affairs, she did it secretly, and with great subtlety. Miss Mangan had suddenly decided to devote her whole life to service. More and more she found the work of her hands taking up her time, and now, with the extension of St Andrew's chapel and the installation of a new high altar, she was continually busy. For hours on end the old man was left alone. He felt miserable and lonely. He rarely went out, except when he struggled to the early Mass on a Sunday morning. He was silent. He made no protests. For a while his sons in America wrote to him. He treasured their letters. They served as a sort of barrier against his loneliness that had slowly grown upon him since the loss of his wife. One day his daughter Brigid arrived home very late. The old man, unable to fend for himself, had been left without food the whole day. He spoke to Brigid. She said she had had to stay and help serve dinner to the Brothers of the Cross, who had arrived that morning to conduct a mission at St Andrew's. The old man flamed up. 'And what about me? Don't I exist?' Brigid shouted, 'No! You don't!' burst into tears, and rushed off upstairs, where she remained for over an hour. She came down and made a meal for her father, but not before her anger had vented itself in a hastily written letter to her sister in Gelton. Mr Mangan never heard a word about the letter to his daughter Fanny. It was quite brief and to the point. 'I have so much to do,' she wrote. 'All my time is taken up with work at the chapel, and really I don't feel capable of looking after Father any longer.' She added with a sort of malicious glee: 'He still has a high regard for you, in spite of your action, and perhaps your taking him over will serve in some measure as an atonement for your brutal treatment of him.' Two days later Fanny Fury arrived from Gelton, and took her father away, as she remarked, 'from a most indifferent and unfeeling woman'. Brigid Mangan remained calm. She bid good-bye to her father, and saw the pair off at the pier that very afternoon. As the boat sailed out, she felt at last that she was free. Now she could devote her whole time to the church. The house in the Mall settled itself down to a sort of spiritual isolation. It became a kind of chapel itself. People living in the Mall were of the opinion that one day Brigid Mangan would go into a nunnery. Miss Mangan had no such ambition. She was content to carry on her embroidery work and her work at the chapel. Nothing ruffled the calm flow of her life until the sudden arrival on a stormy Monday night of her nephew, Peter Fury. She had never seen this boy but once, and was quite unaware of his being in Cork at all, and although she had once visited the very college where Peter stayed, she remained wholly ignorant of his presence.

Nobody was more astounded than Brigid Mangan when, one Monday night, returning from Benediction, she found a youth standing on her door-step. He was soaked through with the rain. The woman drew back with fright. It was quite dark. The very first thing she said to Peter was, 'Where's your cap?' The element of surprise lay not in his sudden appearance, but in his standing capless in the pouring rain. She looked at Peter. A stranger. Then the youth said, 'Don't you know me, Aunt Brigid?' The woman dropped the door key from her hand. Peter even smiled. 'I'm Peter,' he announced.

'What? Not Fanny's boy?' Miss Mangan drew nearer and looked him full in the face. Then, before he could make any reply, she had smothered him in her arms. They went into the house. Peter, as he followed his aunt upstairs to the bathroom, made a note of the house, its furniture, carpets, beds, even its peculiar musty smell. In a few minutes he was sitting in a bath. Brigid Mangan went downstairs to make a meal for him. She hung his wet clothes before the kitchen fire. 'Good heavens!' she was thinking. What was this? Amazing! Where had he come from? How? Why hadn't Fanny written to her? Just like her, of course. Aunt Brigid, quite capable of extending her hospitality to the religious orders, had other ideas when it came to taking in straying members of her sister's family. She reflected now, as she hurried from pantry to dining-room, that Fanny had only written twice since her father had gone to Gelton. When Peter came down, she was sitting at the dining-table waiting for him. Peter closed the door and sat down. She looked at him, not slow to notice the changing expressions upon the boy's face. Obviously he was embarrassed. H'm! A quite ridiculous thing. After all, he was her sister's child. Such nonsense. Putting on airs. The truth was, Peter was ashamed. He had a confession to make. Now, as he sat opposite his aunt, he saw the questioning look she gave him.

'Come, my boy,' she said. 'Eat your supper, we can talk afterwards.' Peter felt relieved at once. It was like a great weight taken off his shoulders. He was hungry. Soon he was doing justice to the cold ham and potatoes. Not once during the meal did he raise his head. The world seemed bounded by the huge plate in front of him. Nor indeed did Aunt Brigid take her eyes from him. She felt excited, the minutes seemed hours. There was such a lot to talk about. As soon as the meal was over they went into the back sitting-room. She made her nephew comfortable in the arm-chair, though Peter did not feel as comfortable as she thought. The horse-hair chair was old, its springs gone. From time to time Peter moved uneasily in the chair. Aunt Brigid did not seem to notice it.

She was sitting on the sofa opposite him, her head reclining on its arm, now covered with a clean antimacassar. Questions began. How long had he been in Ireland? Why had he arrived in such a state? She was glad he had not arrived in daylight. She was quite unused to such goings-on. Was his mother aware of his being in Ireland? Peter stared absent-mindedly into the fire. He was no longer conscious of the presence of Aunt Brigid, he was only aware of a certain insult to his mother. Damned fool! Why had he gone to her house? For the simple reason that there was no place else. At last she spoke. He had been in Ireland, in Cork to be precise, seven years ...

Miss Mangan threw her hands in the air. 'What? Seven years. My God!' And she didn't know! But what was he doing there? She leaned forward on the sofa and subjected her nephew to a stare so penetrating that Peter sat further back on the chair. He saw the blood rush to his aunt's cheeks.

'But your mother never told me!' Here she paused. There came vividly to her mind again the letter she had written to Fanny. Now she knew she had been justified. What a strange woman! Her own nephew at her very doorstep for seven years, and she had never known! Such treatment ... amazing ... that was Fanny all over. Now she rose to her feet, and began poking the fire. Suddenly she fired a question.

'But why have you come here?'

'Because I left the college. I failed. I'm through now.'

'Through!' What was all this about. 'Failed!'

'What college? What were you studying?'

'Studying for the priesthood,' said Peter slowly. Ah! Now the mist was clearing. Everything seemed crystal-clear. 'Why have you failed?' she asked; then, hardly waiting for his answer, she added, 'Have you told your mother yet?'

Peter shook his head. No. He hadn't told anybody yet.

'Who is your Principal?' she asked.

'Brother Geraghty,' replied Peter.

'Oh, I see! I know him well. I shall call and see him tomorrow.' She began pacing the room. Her mind worked swiftly. Something mysterious here. What was it? And that silence. That seven years' silence. She looked at the clock. 'I shall wire your mother at once, Peter,' she said. She felt the boy was hiding something from her. She had a right to know everything. Her sister's children could not drop in on her like this! She had had some of that before. Peter sat up in the chair. 'The Post Office is shut, Aunt,' he said.

'I'll send a *night*-wire,' remarked Miss Mangan with great emphasis. Peter lay back again. He watched her go to the window. She turned round.

'Have you had enough to eat?' she asked. 'Yes, Aunt.' He wondered if his clothes were yet dry. Miss Mangan seemed to divine his thoughts, for she said abruptly, 'Your clothes are far from dry. You must content yourself with sitting in that blanket. There is nothing in the house you could wear, and I'm certainly not going to give you clerical attire.'

Then she went out.

Her wire to Mrs Fury was brief and to the point.

'Peter failed. All my sympathy. Brigid.' Not a word more. As she walked home through the pouring rain she visualized the receipt of the wire in Gelton. But then she didn't know anything. Peter might have been telling some cock-and-bull story. At the same time she got some satisfaction from the sending of the wire. Nearly time Fanny had a shock of some kind. It might wake her up after that long silence. She was still too shocked to be able to comprehend anything beyond the presence of her nephew. Number thirty-seven the Mall had never suffered such a violent disturbance. Three days later she took Peter to the shipping office and that very afternoon they sailed together for Gelton. The house on the Mall was locked up, and the parish priest informed that she might be away for an indefinite period.

3

Miss Mangan moved restlessly in the bed as her sister suddenly sat up. Mrs Fury was certain she had heard somebody descending the stairs. 'Did you hear a noise on the stairs, Brigid?' she asked.

'No! Why?' Miss Mangan said. Mrs Fury lay down again.

'I thought I heard the boy go down,' she said. Brigid laughed. She wasn't interested in anybody on the stairs. This sudden startling exclamation from her sister had put a spoke into a most interesting conversation. She made herself more comfortable. 'Don't bother yourself, Fanny,' she remarked. Mrs Fury was staring up at the patchwork on the ceiling, now illuminated by the moonlight streaming into the room. Brigid Mangan's last question still remained in her mind. How had Desmond come to marry the woman?

'Well,' said Mrs Fury, 'it's always been a mystery to me, and I suppose it always will be. I knew nothing of their goings-on until I heard it from his own lips, that he was getting married. Yes. He was getting married almost immediately. It was a great surprise to me, Brigid, for Desmond never struck me as being of the marrying sort, and they say that when those kind of men do go off at last, they create the greatest surprises. I had been suspicious for a time. For instance, his last two annual holidays he spent in Ireland. Now, that *was* unusual. Do you know, Brigid, I have asked Desmond time and time again to spend his holidays there, either with his aunt at Ringsend or with you. But I could never get him to go. Sometimes he made me feel ashamed that I was Irish. Naturally I was bound to feel surprised when he suddenly decided to spend his holidays there. What part of Ireland he went to I don't know. He was always secretive, was Desmond. But there are some kinds of secrets that can't remain hidden for ever, Brigid.' The woman paused, and Miss Mangan said:

'Oh! How surprising!'

'Yes,' went on Mrs Fury, 'the next thing I knew was that he had set up house in . . . near here.'

'Where?' asked Brigid, her curiosity aroused by that sudden pause in the sentence.

'Oh, somewhere round here. I don't know where. I never go near them, Brigid. Nor will I ever allow them to enter my house. Of course, the biggest shock I got was when he married her out of the chapel. Even Denny was shocked, Brigid, and, as you know, he's pretty loose himself in such matters. Bitchery. That's what I call it, Brigid. Rank bitchery. One of these days he will find out his mistake. I've lived in this parish over forty years now, and then I had to suffer that disgrace. Yes. Take my word for it, nothing but evil can grow out of such actions. I shall *never, never* forget it. I had to keep away from the chapel myself. I felt too ashamed. And I couldn't stand the looks, the hints, the questions. It's blowing over now, and I am back there again, but for nearly thirteen months I attended to my duties at St James's in the city.' A silence came over the room.

Brigid Mangan thought, 'What a peculiar family!' Surely she had tapped a rich vein of history. She even began to feel glad she had crossed over with her nephew. She complimented herself now on her foresight. It seemed her stay would be for an indefinite period. As she lay there she went over slowly in her mind the events of the past three days. She had already sensed a kind of frenzied curiosity, a maddening impatience in her sister. She understood perfectly. Already she had collapsed, helpless, before the flow of Fanny's questions. For an hour and a half she had listened to it. If Fanny Fury maintained this expansiveness, then she could afford to feel sympathetic towards her brother-in-law, who had to sleep with her. The whole thing reminded her of a 'penny dreadful' story. Mrs Fury was speaking again. 'The whole house was upset, Brigid. Maureen had her own ideas about Desmond. I have always tried to do my best for them, but my husband does not seem to agree.' And once again she poured into her sister's unwilling ears the story of the last ten years of her life in Hatfields. Aunt Brigid almost sighed with relief when she changed her course. 'Up to now,' continued Fanny Fury, 'you have told me nothing of what has occurred beyond the fact that the boy went to your house saying he was through at the college. But he must have told you more than that. Surely! Did you do anything? Did you see his Principal, or anybody connected with the college?'

Again Miss Mangan had been thwarted, again Desmond's story was broken off. What a way her sister had of explaining things! She asked a question, and before one had time to answer she broke off and turned the point to something else. Miss Mangan had become tremendously interested in her nephew. She must see him before she went away, as she must indeed see this woman he had married. Mrs Fury became fidgety. Brigid said:

'What is there to say? Not much. I did not go to the college. I felt I ought not to interfere in such a matter. After all, he is your son, Fanny. When he came to me and told me he had left the college, I took him in. Naturally I wanted to know something about his sudden dismissal from the college. But Peter was not responsive in any way. He said he had left the college. No more than that. That he was going home. He said he had failed in his examination. But I didn't accept his excuse, as the examination results to which he was referring would not have been issued. I became suspicious at once. Indeed, this suspicion of mine increased after he had been with me only two days. He used to go out at night. Where to, heaven alone knows. One night he was out until midnight. I could get nothing from him at all, not a satisfactory word. He was dumb. I noticed the change in him at once.' Miss Mangan stopped. Mrs Fury had sat up again. 'I've half a mind to go down and make some tea,' she said, but her sister said: 'It's so late, Fanny, and you'll wake Denny too.'

'One would think,' began Mrs Fury, 'one would think that after thirty years one had had their fill of disappointments, that struggles would be a thing of the past, but it seems to me that they are only beginning. Desmond has put bad luck on this house, I tell you that.'

'Maureen seems to have been in league with him,' Brigid Mangan exclaimed. 'It's a complete surprise to me to arrive here and find Maureen married away too. You never said a word about it.' Mrs Fury replied, 'But I wrote you a letter as soon as Desmond went off.' Brigid Mangan said she had never received any letter. Where was Maureen living? Who was her husband? Was he Irish? Was he a Catholic? How long had she been married?

Mrs Fury remained silent. Why all these questions now, she was thinking. How useless dragging in all these uninteresting things. Desmond and Maureen were well out of it.

'Peter has ruined me,' she said suddenly, and burst into tears. The woman beside her sat up. It was the first time she had ever seen her sister lose control of herself. 'Why, Fanny,' she said, 'you're crying. I know how disappointing it must be to have this son come home like this. I know . . .'

'They're satisfied now,' went on the weeping woman. 'The whole damned lot of them are laughing up their sleeves. Can't you imagine the smile on Desmond's face when he hears about it? And who is going to keep it from him? Children! My God! They have kept me tied down like this for years. I never thought I would rear such a mean-spirited crew. Never! Never!' She buried her face in her hands.

'Fanny! Fanny! Don't cry. It's terrible, I know. But you take my advice and pack Peter off to work. Couldn't Denny get him away to sea?' The woman at her side fell back on the bed. She could not speak. Get him to sea. Was this all her sister had to say? Was this all the imagination she was capable of? Hardly different from the others. Could nobody see her point of view, could nobody assuage her feelings? Mrs Fury's mind was like a furnace. What was this about her son being out at midnight? 'Jesus, Mary, and Joseph.' She got out of bed. She could lie there no longer. How could she lie, knowing that in the very next room lay the answer to her questions, the relief to the doubts she harboured, the suspicions that seemed to choke? He knew. What use talking to this woman at her side any longer? She simply did not understand. 'Brigid,' she said, 'I'm going downstairs. I can't sleep. I'm thinking of this boy all the time. I am suspicious. I know I am. But it has been forced on me.'

Miss Mangan struck a match and lit the candle. She set it on the table at Mrs Fury's side of the bed, her eyes fastened upon her sister's face. This was not the Fanny she knew three years ago. This, Fanny? There was something almost hag-like about her; in the very expression upon her sister's face, in the lines about her mouth, she sensed the story of ambition and frustration, of striving and defeat. Yet, like her brother-in-law, she could not but marvel at her head of hair, at the smoothness of her brow. There was something fine about Fanny too. Brigid Mangan climbed out of bed and went round to her sister. 'Draw the blinds, Brigid,' Mrs Fury said. Miss Mangan crossed the room and drew the blinds. She came back to Mrs Fury. 'You get into bed at once,' she said in a commanding tone of voice. '*I'll* make the tea.' She threw her old dressing-gown over her shoulders and went to the door.

'Look here,' called Mrs Fury. 'Denny'll make the tea. Just call down to him.' Brigid Mangan was determined to have her own way. 'That's all right,' she replied, and opened the door. Mrs Fury lay back against the bed-rail. 'Ah!' she thought, 'even Brigid is hiding something! I never before realized what a vicious circle I was floundering in.' Get Peter to sea! After all she had done for him! He was to be like his father, like Anthony, like all the thousands of men who spent their lives between steel walls. It seemed willed that her children should desert her. 'Fool I was ever to breathe a word about Desmond! I won't see much of her now. She'll be off to see Mrs Sheila Fury first thing tomorrow.' She got out of bed and went and stood by the window. Looking out, she became conscious of a smell, a most disgusting odour, that seemed to rise from between two high walls that faced her window. Suspended in the air between these walls was a single electric bulb, that now blew this way and that with the wind. This light threw out a sickly illumination, it created rather than obliterated the darkness. Mrs Fury could also see a figure moving about this yard. It looked like a wraith to her. She pulled down the window. The people must be very busy to have started night operations, she was thinking, and her eyes remained pinned upon this figure that seemed to move furtively about the yard. Who could it be? She knew that the main gate was always open, for within the yard itself was yet another great gate that opened into the bone sheds. The man appeared to be going from one heap to another. She turned away from the window. Her sister came into the room. Mrs Fury said, 'You weren't long, Brigid.' The woman put down a jug of tea and two cups and saucers on the table. Then she climbed into bed again. 'Why, you've shut the window, Fanny,' said Miss Mangan. 'Don't you feel it stuffy in here?' Mrs Fury burst out laughing. 'Haven't you a nose, Brigid? Why, there's the most disgusting smell outside here. The bone yard appears to be very busy lately.' She got into bed and they took up their cups. Brigid Mangan remarked that she smelt nothing.

'Strange,' Mrs Fury said. She poured tea from the jug. 'I was thinking, Brigid,' she went on; 'what are you going to do if this strike comes off? It's going to be pretty awkward, isn't it?' Miss Mangan said, 'Yes. I suppose I'll have to remain here, Fanny. It will be most awkward for you. Poor Michael's dead, or I could have gone to his place.' 'Yes,' Mrs Fury replied. Her eyes sought the clock. Nearly four o'clock. Denny would be getting up in an hour and a half's time.

'I suppose we'll manage somehow,' she said. 'Really, I can manage anything. Father is the most trying. Lord! he irritates me sometimes. Yet I feel sorry for him too. He's so helpless. The job I have getting him down to the Office for his pension on a Friday!' She put her cup down. 'Finished, Brigid?' she asked, at the same time taking the cup from her sister's hand. Then she blew out the light and lay down. Miss Mangan was so surprised by this action that she did not follow suit for nearly half a minute, remaining erect in the bed, her mind torn between two conflicting thoughts. Peter and Desmond were like two huge pendulums that kept swinging to and fro across the room. She could see their faces quite clearly. Then she lay down. The woman was still under a spell; there was something astonishing about her arrival, about her lying here now, at her sister's side, about Peter hiding his secret in the next room, about Desmond hidden away some few streets off. What changes had taken place in her sister's family! The silence was broken by Mrs Fury asking, 'Was Denny asleep? Was he comfortable?' Miss Mangan gasped out, 'Why, I never noticed, Fanny, I went in by the other door.' Her whole soul hungered for Desmond's secret. 'I have a mind that I know these Downeys,' she said suddenly. She wanted to hear more about this woman. 'In fact, I half believe I met a Matthew Downey once at a Mission at St Mary's Cathedral.'

'Impossible, Brigid,' Mrs Fury replied.

'How strange!' Brigid said. 'I can't imagine how Desmond could have met this woman.'

'But haven't I just told you!' said Mrs Fury heatedly, 'haven't I just told you he met her in Ireland!' Miss Mangan's curiosity was aroused, and her sister seemed to have scented it, for she added, with an air of finality, 'He was bound to meet her anyway. Her family disowned her. She is nothing but a common prostitute. Worse than that, but I would not let the word cross my mouth.' Mrs Fury suddenly thrust her hand into the air, waved it excitedly in front of her sister's face, and shouted, 'It's true! It's too true! She is a bitch of the first water, beautiful, but all rottenness behind. My God! One only has to look at her face. Her whole character, her history, her very future shines there. The fool! He's madly in love with her. He can't help it. Carried away. Do I care? Not a bit. Do I worry? Not a bit. I only know that by his action he disgraced me. Then Denny wonders why I lose control of myself whenever his name is mentioned. I am glad he has gone. Glad in my very soul. Can you imagine anything worse than that boy in the room there and he living here, together? Impossible! Won't he laugh! The devil! As indeed he has laughed all along. Soon I won't be able to hold up my head at all. He's evil. They're a pair. Well met. Fate never was kinder. It had to be. Yet look at the difference in their upbringing. I know nothing of hers; I know that Desmond's was hard; well, God Almighty, wasn't the whole family's upbringing hard? Does it kill one? Look at me. I have had thirty-two years of it, but I haven't gone under. No Brigid, I don't want to hear a word more about Desmond, and if you have any respect for me as a sister, and for the sake of the old man in the back room, I ask you not to go seeking them out. I've had enough. Just enough. It made me sick. It wounded me. Let well alone.'

This was the most amazing piece of news Miss Mangan had heard for many years. Peter was an oracle no longer. Peter was only a schoolboy who had failed somehow or other and come home again. But this other thing. Desmond and Sheila. It was like a powerful magnet, a brilliant and blinding light. She could not drive it away, and every moment the fascination, the mystery, the curiosity was drawing her nearer and nearer to it. She vowed in her heart that she must see them. She must not go back to Cork having failed in her object. 'It's amazing,' she said, after a long silence. But Mrs Fury made no reply. She was sleeping the heavy sleep of a tired child. Brigid Mangan, on the other hand, did not feel tired. She experienced a fierce sort of restlessness. Morning seemed never to come, the hours were like eternities. What things she was yet to hear, yet to see! What a nest she had fallen into! The whole house seemed embedded in a mystery. She had not failed to notice Mr Fury's absence. It was only for her brother-in-law's sake that she had said nothing about it to her sister. But where had Denny Fury gone to? At that hour in the morning. Her mind throbbed. She wanted to get up, but dared not. It would wake Fanny. She could only lie there thinking of Desmond, of his wife, of Peter and Maureen, and not least, of Mr Fury's absence from the house. Yes, she was asking herself, 'Where has he gone to?' And Maureen was going to have a child by this husband of hers named Kilkey. Funny, she had never liked the name Kilkey. She turned over, her eyes towards the window. The moon had disappeared. The room was in darkness. As she looked through the window at the wall of the bone factory she could not repress a desire to see a little more of this wall.

Strange. Bone factories were foul places, yet never to have been conscious of the smell only made her more curious than ever. She slid silently from the bed and went and stood by the window. Where Mrs Fury had seen a single figure moving about the yard, Brigid Mangan now saw two men. They were standing in a corner, sheltered from the light, and near the main gateway. What could they be doing there, she wondered. They weren't workmen. She was sure of that. Also she noticed that one of the men had raised his head and was to all intents and purposes watching the white face of Brigid Mangan at the window. 'How peculiar!' she exclaimed under her breath, and went back to bed again. She covered her head with the clothes, as though she must keep intact every single thought, every impression. Her head beneath the clothes was a security at least. Her thoughts were like living beings, they swamped her, walked round and round her brain, guarded her pillow. Mrs Fury snored. But Miss Mangan, hidden beneath the bed-clothes, opened her eyes wide and peered into the cavity she made with her raised knees. Once – how strange that she should recall it now – once her father had said to her, she was still at school at the time, 'Your sister Fanny will be the only one amongst our family who will be remembered.' What had he meant by that? The passage of years had not robbed those words of their significance – indeed, to Miss Brigid Mangan they seemed rather to have intensified it. From time to time she looked out from the bed-clothes. Still dark. Then she thought of the alarm-clock. How silly of them! It should have been left below. How was Denny to wake up without it? Instinctively she put out her hand and picked it up, feeling for the bell switch with her fingers. Set, of course. She ought to take it downstairs. It would disturb her sister.

She got out of bed and stole silently to the door. She went on to the landing, closing the door softly behind her. At the top of the landing she suddenly stopped and put her hand to her mouth. Was that a voice she had heard? She put a foot on the stair. Yes. Somebody was talking in the hall. She became frightened now. Ought she to run in and wake Fanny up? No. On reflection she realized that would make matters more complicated than ever. Was it Denny coming back? Nobody else. She descended the stairs, and at the bottom drew the long green curtain around her. Yes. She recognized the voice now. 'You get up to bed at once,' she heard Mr Fury say. She clutched the curtain excitedly. It must be Peter. At that moment something brushed the curtain. It was her nephew climbing the stairs as noiselessly as a cat. Miss Mangan stepped out from the curtain and stood in the hall. A shaft of light from the kitchen splashed the dull red of the lobby wall. She went to the kitchen door and looked in. Mr Fury was sitting on the sofa taking off his boots. He had been out, then. But what was Peter doing out too? She hesitated, then something appeared to propel her forward. The next moment she was standing in the lighted kitchen, her old dressing-gown drawn tightly about her figure. In her outstretched hand she held the alarm-clock. Mr Fury looked up with astonishment. The whole house must be sleepwalking, he was thinking, staring at the pale-faced woman in front of him. 'Why, Brigid!' he said.

'It's the clock, Denny,' Miss Mangan said. She stammered; her nerves were on edge. Mr Fury stood up. 'Thanks,' he said. 'I clean forgot about it.' He sat down on the sofa. 'Is Fanny asleep?' he asked. Miss Mangan nodded her head stiffly. 'What is she doing up at this hour?' Mr Fury asked himself. He knew she was going to speak. He could even see her mouth moving, she was forming a question. He laughed.

'Damn it!' he said. 'I couldn't sleep down here. I don't know why. My head's a bit thick too. But you go off to bed, Brigid. Don't stand there like that. You'll get your death of cold.' He signified by his actions that he wanted to get undressed. Miss Mangan looked questioningly at the clock, as though at this very moment it was going to ring and proclaim in its strident voice the uselessness of such a proceeding. 'It's hardly worth while, Denny,' Miss Mangan remarked. She surprised him by sitting down on the sofa. 'Let me make you a cup of tea,' she went on. 'I don't mind at all. Fanny is tired out, and I don't feel sleepy myself.' Mr Fury replied, 'No. It's quite all right, Brigid, I always look after myself. Thanks all the same. You go back to bed. What on earth are you going to do with yourself till nine o'clock? Fanny rarely gets up before that time.' They looked at each other. Then they both laughed.

'All right,' Mr Fury said. 'You go ahead and make some tea, then. I'll go out and have a wash and shave. But I'll take my solemn oath that woman upstairs will make something extraordinary out of this, don't you forget. She's got such a mind.' But Brigid Mangan made no reply. She was conscious that she was in the midst of something exciting. She might even hear something, if she was patient. So far, he hadn't said a word about Peter. 'I'll sound him,' she thought. As they sat down at the table, Mr Fury with his toast in front of him, and Miss Mangan with her cup raised in the act of drinking, the silence was broken by the harsh voice of Mrs Fury.

'There! I told you,' exclaimed Mr Fury. He went out into the hall and listened. Miss Mangan put her cup down and waited. 'She's having a nightmare,' he said, as he came into the kitchen again. 'And no wonder. A woman like that could never be free from them.' Miss Mangan said, 'I heard Peter going downstairs about an hour ago. I wonder what he was doing?' She caught his eye, and knew at once that the boy had been out with his father. Well, well! There seemed to be no end of mysteries in number three Hatfields. Mr Fury went out to clean his boots. When he came into the kitchen Brigid Mangan had gone. He sat down on the sofa and exclaimed, 'Confound the woman! She came down here to spy. Aye. And she's caught the fellow upstairs too.' Yes. That son of his who had discovered him leaning against the wall behind the house. Even now she was telling his wife all about it. He went into the hall and put on his cap. Then he stood listening at the bottom of the stairs. Not a sound. He went out and banged the door loudly behind him. A minute or two later the alarm rang. Mrs Fury woke up. 'Why, Brigid!' she exclaimed, and sat up. Miss Mangan was standing by the window, staring down into the yard.

CHAPTER V

The bone factory, situated at the rear of Hatfields, was divided from the houses themselves by a huge wall. The inhabitants saw nothing beyond this great wall unless they happened to be in the attic part of the house, when they were able to see the yard, in the corners of which were deposited great heaps of bones. The yard itself was approached by a wooden gate. This gate, for some strange reason or other, was never locked. Another gate stood within the yard, and this in turn led to the shed where the bones passed through for crushing. If the occupants of the thirty houses called Hatfields had taken a certain pride in the knowledge that the street was indestructible, they were losing it now. The sense of security, of permanency, was wavering. The bone factory had been standing there five years. At first there were protests from property owners. The concern taking over the land offered to compensate to the landlord, but the people themselves, though conscious of the obnoxious approach being made upon their contentment, were the chief obstacles to the proposal. They preferred the smell to the trouble of finding alternative accommodation. In time the smell itself became a part of the place. It assumed the same permanency as the brickwork that had stood secure for so many years. But rumours were ever abroad that the houses would and must soon go. The factory people wished to extend, the health authorities decided that the matter was serious. When Mrs Fury heard about this she only laughed. But other people in the street had already realized that the collapse of Hatfields was inevitable.

When Mr Fury left the house, he walked slowly down the street. A walk in the night air would do him good. But he could not tell why his steps took him in the direction of this yard. Perhaps he did not want to be seen walking abroad at that late hour. The policeman who controlled the area round Hatfields might think it a poor excuse, that a man like Mr Fury should not be able to sleep. At the bottom of the street he turned sharp right, then stopped. He was practically facing the gateway. It had always seemed strange to him that this big gate on the road should be left open. The proprietor of the factory, however, felt that not even a tramp would care to take advantage of any sanctuary it might offer, for the most pungent and disgusting smell hung in the atmosphere. Mr Fury stood contemplating this gate. He had never been in the yard. At that moment he felt a tap on his shoulder, and a breathless voice exclaimed 'Dad!' Mr Fury jumped with fright. He turned round. Peter was standing in front of him. The boy had an overcoat over his underclothing, and was wearing slippers. 'Why! What the devil! What do you want?' asked the astonished man, staring fixedly at his son. Peter increased his astonishment by smiling and replying, 'What's the matter, Dad?' Mr Fury caught him roughly by the arm, saying, 'What's the matter? The matter is that if your mother finds you have come out here there'll be a holy row. Get back to bed at once, and don't come following me,' But the son did not move. His eyes roamed about the figure of his father. From the light of a single bulb that now swung aimlessly in the wind Peter was able to see his father's face. How ghastly and yellow it looked in that light! He moved a step. His father followed. 'Ah,' thought Peter, 'that's better.' The light no longer fell upon Mr Fury's face. 'Come along,' said his father, 'you get home. Do you hear me?'

'But why are you out here? Won't you tell me what the trouble is, Dad?' He had moved so close to his father that Mr Fury could feel the boy's breath upon his face. He could not longer conceal his surprise at this sudden development. How had the boy known where he was? 'Surely,' he thought, 'he isn't spying on me!' He would credit Fanny with even that. Peter took his father's arm. 'Come on home, Dad.'

'I can't sleep,' Mr Fury said. 'And I had a rotten day today.' Then he embraced his son, saying, 'Well, by God! I'm glad to see you home again.' There was something about Peter standing there like that, holding on to his arm that filled Mr Fury with admiration. Was this the little boy who went away seven years ago? He stroked his forehead. 'What's the matter?' asked Peter. He drew back a little. 'Oh, nothing,' Mr Fury replied. 'Nothing.' Ought he to say something? Ask that question? No. It might be dangerous. Fanny would hear all about it. He couldn't do that. He had been caught out once before over Anthony. Was he afraid? No, it wasn't that. But he was so weary, he just wanted to be quiet. The excitement of the last twenty-four hours had been enough. He didn't want any more. The incident with Anthony stood out clearly in his mind now. But this wasn't Anthony. This was the youngest of the large family, and he was different altogether. Perhaps the lad would say something. Christ! It was silly, standing there like that. They were like two shy children, looking at each other, saying nothing. How she had idolized Peter! He looked away towards the house. Peter said, 'It's cold, Dad. Come on home.' His father's hand fell suddenly on his arm. He began to push him slowly inside the gateway. Peter laughed, but his father said angrily:

'H'm, what's the matter with me? That's not the question, Peter. The question is, "What's the matter with you?" I told you to go home to bed. You have no right to be out this time in the morning. I'm your father. You had a right to go when I told you. But you didn't go.'

'Well, Dad ...'

'The question is, "What's wrong with you?" Yes, answer that. Stuck away for seven years, and now you just drop on us like a jack-in-the-box, and you haven't anything to say.' Mr Fury paused. What was this he was saying? Confound it! He meant to go home. What was he doing in this stinking yard? They were against the wall now, shielded from the light of the bulb swinging above their heads. Then Peter said:

'I'm sorry, Dad. I didn't ever want to go. I only went to please Mother.' The man fell back against the wall as though he had been struck a blow. He put his hands on the wall, he was like a drunken man. 'Ah!' he exclaimed. Then he spat on the ground. So the truth was out. Desmond had been right. *He* had been right. Everybody had been right. Excepting that stubborn woman. Yes. That stubborn woman. He looked at Peter.

'Your mother's sorely disappointed in you,' he said. Then he broke down. He could not help it. Peter went up to him.

'Dad!' he said. 'I'm sorry, I ...'

'Go away,' said his father. 'Go on. Go home at once. Don't stand there.' Then he yelled like a madman. 'Don't stay there, I tell you. D'you hear me?' He stamped his foot angrily. Peter walked away. Mr Fury turned his face to the wall. Whose fault? The boy's? Fanny's? He had never wanted to go away at all. Seven years. Thinking that over in his mind for seven years. God! He hated the lad now. He hated him. He was the cause of all the trouble. He had turned his own wife into a stubborn, powerful, indefatigable woman. He hated him for his silence. The word 'ruined' seemed to burst into flame in front of him. Peter looked well. 'And by heavens he ought to!' he cried in his mind. 'He ought to. The best of everything for seven years.' He shook himself like a dog and walked out of the yard.

Half-way up the street he saw Peter. When he went up to him he was crying. 'All right,' his father said, 'you get to bed. We'll talk about all this tomorrow.' They went to the door. Mr Fury pulled a key from his pocket. When they went into the lobby, the man caught his son by the arm, saying:

'Ssh! There's somebody moving about. You get up to bed at once.' He pushed his son forward. He was angry and confused. Then he went into the kitchen. A strange feeling overcame him. He sat down on the sofa. He felt old now. Really old. Peter was a failure. The rows they had had over him! Well, he knew what to do now. He had been silent for too long, he had never shown his hand. He got up from the sofa and began walking up and down the kitchen. He noticed that the clock was not in its accustomed place on the mantelshelf. 'Yes,' he was muttering, 'yes, I'll show them now. I'll have that fellow before the mast before he has time to say "Bah".' At that moment Miss Mangan came into the kitchen. He realized at once that she knew. She must have heard him going out. Had she seen Peter too? Must have done. His sister-in-law stood there holding out the clock. He saw how late it was. Not much use turning in now. Then he heard a rustling sound, and at the same time Miss Mangan caught his eye. Yes, she knew all along. They were indeed a pair. They must have been watching them all along. But this woman was no different to his wife. She never said a word. Her expression told its own tale. His anger grew. He said, 'Go to bed, Brigid.' But the woman stood there as though she were waiting for an earthquake to happen.

2

Peter had gone up to his room. He lay down on the bed. What had made him suddenly go to the window? He asked himself that question many times. It wasn't the smell that came to him. Of course he had pulled up the window when he heard the door opened. Here he was back again, and the secret was out. His father knew. He never wanted to go. Rain suddenly drove in through the half-open window, making a pattering noise on the bare wooden floor. The house was wrapped in silence. Had Aunt Brigid seen him? He could not drive out the sudden fit of restlessness that had seized him. He got up from the bed, already half-covered with books which he had flung out haphazard from his travelling-bag. He went over and stared into the dressing-mirror. The lamp, standing near, dimmed. He turned up the wick. He studied his expression in the mirror for a long time, allowing his long fingers to trace themselves over his eyes and mouth and nose. He stroked the film of down now growing on his chin. How old his father had looked when, unable to control his feelings, he had cried like a child. A little old man. His mother hardly looked a day older. The scene at the landing-stage lived again in his mind. He was like a stranger. He didn't know them. And his grandfather. How miserable, almost filthy, he looked now. What was Maureen like? And Desmond? He would see them soon. They were married now. He laughed. He was glad Maureen was gone. He had never liked her. She reminded him so much of his Aunt Brigid. Miss Mangan was the living image of his mother, though she lacked his mother's dignity and natural grace, he thought. Fancy Anthony having gone to sea too! He tried to imagine what he looked like. A quartermaster. What changes there had been! He picked up the lamp and looked more closely at the reflection of the figure staring into it. He had tried hard to remember. It was so difficult. Only seven years ago. It had seemed to him like twenty. No. He could not remember the little boy with the badge in the lapel of his serge coat. That was so, so long ago. A new person. A new Peter. He was seized with a sudden desire to look for old photographs of himself. He put the lamp down. Surely there must be some about the room. He had slept in this very room. His room. The bottom drawer of the dressing-table. Yes. Everybody had at one time or other used the same drawer. What a mine of information, what history lying there now! He went on his knees and pulled open the drawer.

It was tightly packed. He pulled the drawer out, and tossed its contents in a heap upon the bed. He buried his hands in them. Then he put the drawer on the floor. He put the lamp back on the table by the bed. He sat down, his eyes held by that great heap of papers with all the memories attaching to them. He rummaged with his hands amongst this pile of old letters, greeting cards, bills, certificates of birth and death, his mother's marriage lines, his father's old sea-book with its salt-stained and faded blue cover, John's Union cards. He held these cards in his hands for some time. Tears came into his eyes. Poor John! He had hardly known him, and now he was dead. Crushed to death at twenty years of age. It was terrible. He remembered the letter his mother had sent him on the day of his brother's tragic accident. He put the Union cards into an envelope. He could not bear to look at them any more. His hands dropped on a long envelope. There was something hard inside. A photograph. He pulled it out. Desmond and his wife. 'By heck!' he exclaimed under his breath. 'That's a beautiful face.' He drew nearer to the lamp. Desmond's wife. It was something of a shock at first. The most beautiful face he had ever seen. Beside it his brother looked quite ordinary. There was something fascinating about this face. He could not take his eyes from it. 'Fancy! Just fancy!' he was saying. His hand was shaking. Then, as though seized with a sudden inexplicable loathing, he flung the photograph down upon the bed. Where were those early photographs of his? He so much desired to see them now. Where could they be? Probably burned, perhaps thrown out with the rubbish long ago. At last! He found them between the covers of his father's sea-book. His father must have carried them about with him. He wanted to laugh. He held one of the photos near to the lamp. Himself at six years of age. Good Lord! It seemed outrageous. He spat at it, saying, 'Little fool!' But the face continued to stare at him from the hard glossy surface of the card. Peter at six. With those enormous eyes? Then he picked up another. It was a photograph of himself at two years of age, sitting on his mother's knee. He held it over the lamp until it caught fire. He flung the burning card into the grate. 'What a museum!' he said. 'What a museum!' He began to bundle the scattered papers together again. He put the drawer on the bed and emptied the papers and cards into it. As he was putting it back he heard the alarm go off below-stairs. He nearly let the drawer fall with fright, and he cursed the clock. Only a minute or two before it struck, his father had gone out and banged the door so loudly that his mother woke up, but Peter was so absorbed in going through the papers and photographs that he had not heard it.

'Dad's gone off to work,' he said to himself. He heard somebody climb the stairs. Then the climber coughed. His Aunt Brigid. He knew that cough so well. So she had been talking to his father. He got into bed and blew out the lamp. He could not rid himself of the feeling of shame. It clung to him. He shuddered when he remembered how he had left the college in Ireland. Like a thief, hardly lifting his head. He remembered the Brother at the college gate saying, 'Good-bye, Fury. Good luck.' He remembered the long walk to his aunt's house. Her questions. His own stubborn refusal to say a word. The journey to the boat. The Arklow murderer. The arrival at the Stage. The welcome his mother had given him. It had only heightened his sense of shame. But he couldn't help it. He had seen the thing coming. He put his head under the clothes and exclaimed passionately, 'No. It couldn't be helped.' Here he was back again. More of a stranger than ever. Tomorrow his mother would ask him everything. To-morrow. Why, it was six o'clock now. The paper in the grate still smouldered. The faces – there were three of them – still hovered about in the air above him. Once Peter, aged two, stuck out a tongue and grimaced. Then the beautiful woman standing beside his brother suddenly smiled, and he saw that she looked even more beautiful than the photograph. He closed his eyes. The figure of his grandfather appeared. Peter grimaced at the sallow leathery skin. How he hated that face! And his eyes were like little wax beads. He sat up in the bed. Why, his grandfather had never spoken a word. Not a word to anybody. And they had to carry him about everywhere. He could see his father now, as he half knelt, holding on to his grandfather, calling out frantically to his mother, 'Fanny! Fanny!' How funny it had all seemed. But now those figures vanished, and in their place came the little old man from the bone yard. This little man with the thin grey hair was his father. He would not believe it. Whom did he love the more, his father or his mother? He did not know.

He knew his mother more intimately than he did his father. He had hardly seen him. A lump came into his throat. He hated to go to sleep. Sleeping involved waking, waking meant morning and questions. Why had his mother liked him better than the rest of the family? The way she had clung to him at the landing-stage. Absence seemed to have intensified the bond, a sort of spiritual harmony that had held them together for years. Peter stretched himself in the bed. After a while he dozed off. Then a sharp knock came to the door. He shivered. Must have fallen asleep. How long had he been asleep? He looked up. His mother was standing in the middle of the room. The light from the gas below-stairs threw shadows upon the landing wall. Mrs Fury was fully dressed. She had even washed and combed her hair. 'Time to get up, Peter,' she said. 'It's a quarter past seven.'

'Yes, Mother.' He sat up in bed. He avoided her glance. He could not look her in the face. And she stared so. His mother went out. Yes. He was really back home again now. He jumped out of bed and began to dress. No. He hadn't been dreaming. He was really back home. He could hear his mother washing crockery in the back kitchen. He went downstairs. The kitchen fire blazed. The big chair which his grandfather occupied all day was empty. Mr Mangan did not rise until nine, when he was washed and dressed by his daughter and carried downstairs. Peter sat in this chair, his feet high up on the kitchen hob. He was fastening his bootlaces. His mother came in and laid the table. He looked across at her, but she avoided his glance. Then she went out again. 'Peter!' she called. 'Better come out and wash yourself before breakfast.'

'Yes, Mother,' replied Peter.

Somebody was coming downstairs. Aunt Brigid came through the back kitchen. Peter looked at her. How horrible she looked, he thought. Her hair hung down over her shoulders, her eyes were half closed. She coughed. She put her hand on the latch. 'Good-morning, Peter.' The boy did not reply. She went out to the yard.

Peter filled the wash-bowl with cold water and began to wash. As he wiped himself with the towel he stole occasional glances into the kitchen. It was empty. Mrs Fury had gone upstairs. There was a rap at the door. Peter dropped the towel, saying 'Post!' and ran out of the back kitchen. He stopped. Aunt Brigid was coming in, and already his mother had rushed downstairs to get the letter. He could even hear her slight exclamation as she picked it up from the floor. He went back again and started to dry himself. Aunt Brigid was standing by the big fire in the kitchen. She heard her sister pass upstairs. She sat down in her father's chair. Miss Mangan was so preoccupied with her own plan of campaign that she could hardly wait until breakfast was over. She must go upstairs immediately and dress. There was Maureen to see, and, of course, her eldest nephew. It would be mean of her to go away without seeing them, and she was still optimistic enough to believe that she would be safely on the ten o'clock boat the next night. She had brought Peter over. There was nothing more to do. She had not slept the whole night, and still looked tired. What with her sister and Denny and Peter, her imagination had run riot. Peter came into the kitchen and sat down opposite to her on the sofa. Miss Mangan said, 'Well, Peter,' paused, then got up and went out to the hall. She met Mrs Fury coming downstairs.

'Why, Fanny!' she exclaimed, 'are you ill?' The woman grinned. 'No, no,' she replied. 'Whatever put that idea into your head?' They went into the kitchen together. When Peter looked at his mother he knew the secret was out. There was no denying it now. She had had a letter from the Principal. The very expression upon her face was proof enough. They all three sat down. Aunt Brigid became talkative.

She had a busy day before her. She must see Maureen, and of course her husband. Then she might slip down to see Father Moynihan. He came from her parish in Cork. Mrs Fury poured out the tea. Her hand trembled, she spilt tea on the clean cloth. 'Fanny! my dear ...' Brigid hastened to her assistance. Mrs Fury said tartly, 'All right, sister. I can do this.' Then silence once more. Peter did not look at either of them. His face was almost hidden behind the tea-cosy. When Aunt Brigid picked this up to re-cover the teapot, he lowered his head still more. 'Now, Brigid,' Mrs Fury said, 'you're not eating. Peter, make your aunt a piece of toast.' Peter got up and went to the fire. He knelt down in front of it, holding the toasting-fork in his hand. 'Why, you fool!' cried his mother, 'you're burning the toast. Look!' Peter did not seem to hear. Mrs Fury rushed from the table and took the fork from him. 'What's the matter with you?' She returned to the table. 'I know,' she called out to him. Her son came back to the table. Aunt Brigid said, 'Good gracious, Fanny! You do get excited over little things. The child could not help that. Why, I never ...'

'Child! Child!' Mrs Fury burst out laughing. 'Oh Lord!' Miss Mangan now felt that she was only just beginning to know her sister. But really, and she had to admit it, she was not interested in Peter, or the toast, or the fact of her sister's strange manner. She had something else in mind which occupied her far more. She put down her cup, saying, 'Well, Fanny, I think I'll go up and change. Then I'll go down to Mass.' Mrs Fury said, 'Of course. Off you go, Brigid.' If she had only left out the word 'Mass', Mrs Fury was saying to herself, it would have been all right. But now she had given the whole show away. She knew what Brigid's Mass-going involved. Meeting the neighbours, old friends, and then, to crown everything, she would rush off to the children. The children! Mrs Fury wanted to get up and shout, 'Children! Children! She still thinks they're children. The fool! She's still living twenty years in the past.' Oh heavens! She pushed her chair away. Peter sat back. He was embarrassed. He did not know what to do. He ought to say, 'Well, I had better go to Mass too, Mother.' If he said nothing it would be just as bad. But Mrs Fury saved him the trouble. She cleared the table.

Then she went to the foot of the stairs and called out, 'Brigid, I want to see you before you go off.' Brigid appeared half-naked on the landing. 'Yes, of course. Whenever you are ready,' she called down. Then she vanished into the room again.

Peter was still sitting at the table. His mother took no notice of him. Peter felt more awkward than ever. Each time she returned to clear articles from the kitchen he went pale. He could feel this fear growing upon him. He turned round and stared at his grandfather's chair. Suddenly his mother was standing in front of him.

'Peter,' she said, 'I want to talk to you. Go into the other room.' Peter replied, 'Yes, Mother.' He went into the parlour and sat down. His mother followed. She went and stood by the window. Mrs Fury stood like a statue. She stared out of the window, looking at nothing in particular. She was thinking of how she had rushed down the stairs on hearing the rap at the door, and of the long, official-looking envelope that lay at her feet. She remembered that the Irish postmark was the first thing to catch her eye. Then she had picked up the letter and gone upstairs. She locked the door of her room and went and stood by the dressing-table. She put the business-like envelope on the table. She knew who it was from. She sat down on the bed. She was filled with fear now. What was she going to read? Perhaps they were his examination papers. She got up again. There was a decided air about that letter. It seemed to cry aloud to be opened, to proclaim its urgency and importance. She reached in the corner of the dressing-table drawer for an old knife. She slit open the letter and carried it to the bed. She sat down again. Her hands shook. She began to read. Then the letter fell to her knees.

'Regret ... out of bounds ... running counter to the strict rules of the college ... would advise control ...' the words began to dance before her eyes. 'Discovered after hours, Brother Twomey ...' The woman gave a low scream and collapsed on the bed. Almighty God! So this was the failure! This the examination he had failed to pass! This letter, those words! Liar! Beast! Her whole soul revolted. She could not cry. She lay there as though struck. Inert. Peter was whistling in the kitchen. she did not hear him. After a while she sat up. Her face became suffused with blood. She stood erect. Then she tore the letter into shreds. So that was it! Seven years of sacrifice, humiliation, and hardship for *this*. Oh! The last child. Words, disjointed phrases sprang to her lips. 'After eleven o'clock ... out of bounds ... regret ...' And he, Peter, was down there. Now. He was sitting at the table. What was he thinking about? She began to pace the room aimlessly; she walked round in half-circles, stopped suddenly, then crossed to the window. Then back to the bed again. She flung herself down.

She wanted to cry. Her mind was distraught. She could stand anything

but this. Then she rose to her feet and resumed her aimless pacing of the bedroom. If Denny knew! If Maureen knew! But they would laugh. She could
even hear them talking together. 'Well, there you are,' her husband would
say. 'So your mother got what was coming to her. It's a lesson.' And her
daughter's laconic, 'Serve Mother right.' Was this a child? A child of her own
that she had reared and suckled? Suddenly she pulled up sharply in front
of the dressing-mirror and began to hammer upon it furiously with her
clenched fists. She could not avoid seeing herself in the glass. Good heavens!
Must control herself. She went downstairs again. Peter was still sitting at the
table. Aunt Brigid was already suspicious. She was going up to dress. H'm!
She was off for the day. Lord! Her tongue would wag today. Titivating herself before the glass upstairs. She stood opposite her son now. Was it the
agitated woman now leaning against the kitchen dresser that sent the
message to Peter's brain? His mother had heard.

'I want to talk to you,' she said. He moved away from the table. He walked
into the parlour and sat down on the sofa. She followed and went up to the
window.

She was now standing with her long arms resting against the wainscoting. Peter, watching her, noticed how she continually drummed on the
wood with her fingers. He himself was pulling furiously at the sofa cushion,
and thinking of the many times he had played upon it as a child. The
same old horse-hair sofa. There was a vacant, almost helpless expression
upon Mrs Fury's face. She cried out, 'Close the door,' and heard him go over
and shut it. She did not move. She heard him sit down again. She knew
exactly how he sat, what he looked like, what he was doing. Fidgeting about,
his guilty conscience tormenting him, Peter sat quietly watching her. He
could not see her face, yet her very attitude struck him as terrifying. He had
never seen his mother like this before. He stared at her back, and even
studied the lines of her figure – how it broadened out at the hips, her long
arms, the thick bunch of hair resting against her thin neck. Then he
looked at her shoes. How firmly her feet held to the ground! It was like the
root of the determination in her. He knew it so well. His mother did not
stir. He heard her breathing. She was not thinking now. She had passed
beyond thought. Why think? A fly ran up the window-pane. Her eyes
followed it, then returned to the street. She watched a man filling coal into
a cellar.

Why didn't his mother speak? Why was she standing like that? His father
was different altogether. Had she gone mad? What was she looking at? What
was she thinking about? He could not keep still. A lump came into his throat.
Of course. Nothing else. Best to get it over and done with. Well, he was ready
as soon as she was. He opened his mouth to shout something to her, but the

words refused to come. Then Mrs Fury swung round and came across to him, dragging a cane chair behind her. She placed this in front of the sofa and sat down. They were facing each other. Peter felt his mother's knees against his own. How soft they were! They caught each other's eyes. No holding back now. The whole truth. The expression upon her face, her eyes, seemed to penetrate him. He lowered his head. He thought she grinned at him. What was she going to say? He looked up at her. She seemed cool, calm, collected, but her expression was grim. He could not conceal his agitation. Be cool. Mustn't show fear now. Then there came to his nostrils a most offensive smell. The circumstances of the occasion seemed to have heightened his nasal sense. Peter put a hand to his nose. Yes. He had smelt this before, but now it seemed one thousand times worse. 'Phew!' he exclaimed, and looked at his mother, a horrified expression upon his face. Mrs Fury was like solid rock. She suddenly swore to herself. A smell. H'm! Complaining like that! At such a time. Under the present circumstances. She leaned forward in her chair, gripped him by the arm, and hissed savagely into his ear, 'We've had that for *years*.' She laid emphasis upon the word 'years'. Then she shouted at the top of her voice '*YEARS.*' Peter drew back. It had begun. His mother drew her chair more closely. She gripped his other arm. Peter gasped. Her hands were like steel. He was imprisoned. She had pinned him down with a glance from her flashing eyes.

'Well,' she said … A long silence. He could not look into that face. He could not keep still. He kept moving from side to side. How strong her hands were! Nearly sixty years of age, and she was as strong as ever. 'Well!' The word shot from her lips. When he did not answer she released one of his arms. Then she struck him a violent blow in the face. 'The truth, Peter. The truth.' Why couldn't he open his mouth? He *must* open his mouth. Mrs Fury stood up. She had gripped him by the shoulders and was shaking him violently. She was unconscious of the ridiculous figure she now cut, shaking this son taller than herself. Rage, blind rage, stirred to life within her. He must speak. She would kill him. So many things had been held in leash. She had held them back. Hope, disappointment, misery, lies, deceit. They overwhelmed her now. They controlled her body and her spirit. She could feel this rage. It must soon run amok. 'Open your mouth!' she shouted. At that, Peter forced himself to his feet. He looked full into his mother's eyes. She turned her head away suddenly. His former expression had gone. Astonishment. She had never seen such an expression upon her son's face. Was this her son, her own child? Without knowing it, she had gripped him again and was shouting, 'Swine! Swine! Well, I want to talk to you. I want to *know*.' Her mind cried, 'I must and I *will* know.' She was like a hungry animal. She felt a numbing sort of pain. Those things. How they goaded her now, and laughed in her face. Misery, dirty hints, lies, and meanness. All for this. 'Tell me the truth,' she cried. 'I have had a letter from your Principal. Tell me everything. Everything.' She darted away and began the same wild pacing of the room, swinging her arms about. 'Oh Jesus Christ! I ...' She became so carried away on this wild tide that she could not complete her sentences. Peter shuddered. Never had he seen his mother in such a temper. She was like a wild beast. And he had imagined he knew her, knew her more intimately than his own father, than his sister and brothers. But he did not know her at all. How should he begin?

'Well!' she yelled at him from the middle of the room. 'Aren't you going to speak? Has your conscience struck you dumb?'

'I'm sorry, Mother!' At last he had spoken. 'I'm sorry, Mother,' he said again. He wanted to cry. He *was* sorry. He felt it in his heart. Sorry and ashamed. He went up to his mother. Mrs Fury suddenly drew her arms behind her back lest she might touch this son of hers. 'Go away! Don't you come near me. Beast! You've ruined me. Ruined my whole life.' She made a mad rush at her son, and carried on by her own impetus bore him back to the sofa. The two figures staggered about. Then Peter fell back upon the sofa. His mother sat down again. 'You've wounded me. Do you know that? Pig! I've done almost everything for you. But why should I start going into details? Yes, why should I? Now.' And she repeated the question in her own mind. Yes, why should she go through it all again, only to arrive at this muck-heap in the end? She couldn't do it.

'Seven years ago I sent you to Ireland, and I thought to myself, "Peter will do it. Peter will shine out above the lot of them." It wasn't easy to send you there. I was prepared for the battle. What a battle it was! I had to fight tooth and nail with your father. With Desmond, with Anthony, with Maureen. Excepting your grand-dad. And John. Poor John! He helped, and now he's dead. I am glad. You should be glad too.' She made the sign of the Cross upon her forehead and lips.

'Mother!' exclaimed Peter. 'Mother ...'

'Shut your mouth! Four pounds ten per month it cost to keep you there. Four pounds ten per month. I paid it. God! ... Yes, I paid it. Your father was away. What did he know? Nothing. Did he care?' She burst into a fit of hysterical laughter. 'Desmond helped.' She laughed again. 'Helped. Anthony helped. Maureen helped. Begrudging, a mite. One had to drag it from them. They hated it. Now they've gone. Good riddance, I say. Desmond is finished with me. I with him. He and his beautiful prostitute!' Peter suddenly said, 'Ah!' It was the first time he had heard the word cross his mother's lips. 'Yes,' she went on. 'Don't I know! And now it's all finished.' She kept her eyes fastened upon her son's face. How powerful filth was! What a magnet the gutter seemed to be! Low – just low. They could not climb. Her family. She laughed again.

'It was my great hope that you would do something. That you would be better than the others. Your father. Oh Lord! When I think of it! What an example! He threw up everything himself. For what? The gutter. He dragged me down with him. But you, you couldn't even fail honestly. You couldn't even leave with your head high in the air. Could you? Understand this. I'll hear everything. I've talked to your Aunt Brigid. I know lots of things already. You must crush me down. Crush me down. Do I deserve it? Has any action of mine justified it? Peter, what did you do?' Peter turned his head away. There was something almost repulsive in the expression upon Mrs Fury's face. She jerked his head back again. 'You won't say! Well, well!' Then she spat in his face.

'I never wanted to go. I never wanted to go. You fooled me yourself. You begged and begged of me to go. I went to please you. I went to please you. But I never liked it. It was like gaol. Worse than gaol. I hated it. And now I'm finished with it. It's silly. It's mad. Mother, I'm sorry, but . . .' He could say no more. He got up from the sofa, and as he moved away his mother's head fell forward. He did not look at her. He went and stood by the door, his hand upon the knob. His face was white. 'A dirty woman!' his mother exclaimed. Peter turned round and ran to her. When she looked at him he flung his hands into the air. He imagined she was going to throw herself upon him again. 'Mother, I . . .'

'Go away,' she said. She heard him walk across the room, heard the door open, close. A long silence. Then she began talking again. It was incoherent, a mere gabbling of words, confusion. What had she been saying at all? Good God! Great convulsive sobs broke from her. Her whole life seemed to be rooted up by a relentless hand. It lay before her now. In pieces. If only he had spoken. Only hinted. If he had straight out and told her, 'No, Mother, I don't want to go. I don't want to be a priest.' But that silence. It was foul, poisonous. That silence. All those years. Why had he stayed? Why hadn't he come home at once? Impossible question. But that lie. It was a great festering sore across her heart. If he had simply said, 'No.' Just that word. It would have been a disappointment. But this. It crushed one into the mud, into the earth. It debased. Her whole frame shook. They would every one of them laugh in her face. Even Denny. Her body slipped lower. Her head fell. 'Oh!' she said. 'Oh!' She dragged herself to her feet. She sat down, holding on to the back of the chair with her two hands. Her hair, now loosened, hung about her shoulders. In the struggle her comb had fallen to the floor. It lay in pieces at her feet. Peter had trodden it underfoot. She kept biting her lower lip. She looked round the room. She was alone. She went over and closed down the window. The smell from the yard had suddenly become repulsive to her. 'Well,' she said to herself, 'that's over.'

She left the room and went upstairs. She could hear her father snoring. She no sooner reached the landing than she turned and descended again. She stood in the hall staring at the hole in the lobby wall, at the little heap of plaster that lay on the oilcloth. Where had Peter gone? And she had quite forgotten her father. Tomorrow she would have all the old struggle again. She went upstairs again to her room. She stood by the window watching the men shovelling heaps of bones on to trucks, which in turn were pushed through into the mill. She had never before evinced an interest in this proceeding. Now, for some strange reason, she could not take her eyes off these men as they piled the bones into the filled trucks. Beyond this yard she could not see. If she looked higher she beheld a sea of roofs. A buzzer sounded, and she saw the men suddenly leave off their work. She must go downstairs. No matter how much one tried to think about these things, the clock forced its way in. Its monotonous tick accompanied her, sleeping and waking. As she passed her son's room she heard the sound of books being dusted. Then she went below. Good Lord! Denny was no sooner gone than he was back again. The clock glared at her from the mantelshelf. She could never escape from it. A sort of continuous threat. She picked it up and shut off the alarm-switch. She turned it face to the wall. Her father burst into a fit of coughing. She went out to the back kitchen.

She began to stir the broth in the pan. What was she going to do with this son now? He had proved her wrong. Her mind was confused. Where was Brigid? When Mr Fury turned the knob of the back door it seemed to turn in her own mind. She pulled off the pan quickly, exclaiming, 'Heavens! It's burning. Whatever can I be thinking about?' Her husband came into the back kitchen. 'Hello,' he said, then went out again. She heard him climbing the stairs, and shouted, 'Tell Peter to come down for his dinner.' Mr Fury called back, 'All right.'

Mrs Fury never approached the large wooden table in the middle of the kitchen floor without feeling the slave of it. It was like a huge magnet. Her whole life appeared to be centred around it. Nor could she escape it. As she spread the cloth upon it now she became conscious of its significance. What things had happened at that self-same table. What rows there had been, what words used. It was a fount of revelation. Her father stood outside of this. The magnet could not draw him. Peter and his father came down and took their places. Looking at her husband, she reflected upon the habit of which she had so long tried to cure him. Mr Fury's demeanour at table was always irritating to her. He never drew his chair right up, and only half sat in it. There was a take-or-leave-it attitude about his approach to meals. Peter sat at the further end, his head lowered, though had he cared to glance up he would have discovered that both his father and mother were ignoring him. Mr Fury concentrated upon his broth. The first ten minutes at the Fury table were always charged with a sort of electric undercurrent. After a long silence a sudden explosion. But to Mrs Fury's surprise her husband appeared most casual in his remarks. 'I met Kilkey going on,' he said. 'Brigid is down there.' Mrs Fury said, 'Oh! Well, what about it? Why shouldn't we expect that from a woman with such a large mouth as Brigid has? Before the day is out she will have interviewed Desmond and "the other one".' Mr Fury thought, 'It's funny, but I can't recollect a single instance where Fanny has used that woman's name.' He thought it rather silly this continual reference to Sheila as 'the other one'.

'I suppose so,' he replied. Then he looked at Peter. 'Well, so here you are, home again.' Peter said, 'Yes, Father,' and wanted to jump on the table and yell out, 'Of course I'm home. You pair of old fools! Of course I'm home.' Not a word about his reason for coming home. No. A dignified silence. Why didn't they say straight out, 'We know why. We know why'? No. They preferred to signify that they knew everything by mere glances. He wanted to get up from the table; he could not eat his dinner now. Mrs Fury turned round to look at her father. She must attend to the old man as soon as ever her husband went back to work. 'You can take it from me that the whole neighbourhood will know by now,' remarked Mrs Fury. She shot a glance at Peter, who lowered his head still further. 'What is going to come next?' he thought. 'Hold your head up, for Christ's sake,' shouted his father. Mr Fury then left the table, dragging the chair to the wall. He went out into the back kitchen to wash. 'Hurry up,' said Mrs Fury to her son. Peter tried to finish his meal, but it choked. He pushed the plate away. 'I'm finished,' he said. His father came in again. As he filled his pipe he exclaimed, 'Yes. You were wrong all along, Fanny. There is going to be trouble. Fellowes came down to our place today. There's going to be a real strike. No half-hearted affair. They want us to support the miners. Poor bastards! They always do it dirty on the miners.'

'Denny!' Mrs Fury looked from her husband to her son, turned her head further and looked at Mr Mangan. Then she said again, 'Denny! Denny!' Peter looked at the clock. Twenty minutes past one. His father was becoming expansive.

'Well, damn it, Fanny! A man can open his mouth.' Mrs Fury laughed. Mr Fury continued. 'Surely! What about it? Peter isn't a child now. Is he?' He stared open-mouthed at the expression upon his wife's face. 'I ... Fanny ...'

Mrs Fury seemed to shudder. She looked across at Peter. 'I'm not well.

That's what it is. Not well. I've felt like this for a long time. I'm really ill.' Then she screamed, 'I can't stand it.' Mr Fury caught her as she collapsed. He kicked the chair out of the way and exclaimed brusquely, 'Go for the doctor, you. Hurry up.' 'Yes, Dad.' Peter took his cap and fled from the house. 'Fanny!' Feeling her inert body against his own, he was suddenly filled with pity for her. Fanny could stand a lot. He knew what had struck her down now. Was it only in such moments as these that he was capable of realizing things? Mr Fury was asking himself. 'I hope I'm not going to be ill,' Mrs Fury said in a low voice. The door banged. Blast it! That lad had left it wide open. He looked down at his wife. He had laid her on the sofa by the fire. Why was she like this? Such a state to be in. And Fanny was always so particular about her appearance. He felt at the back of her head. She hadn't done up her hair. Where was her comb? He went to the mantelshelf and looked about. He must find that comb. He searched the dresser. Suddenly he ran to the sofa. He must be crazy. He picked his wife up and carried her upstairs to her room. He put her to bed. The woman opened her eyes. 'Denny!' she said. 'Denny!' Her arms fell to her side. Mr Fury ran downstairs to get a drop of brandy from the bottle hidden away in the cupboard. He rushed upstairs, muttering, 'Drink this. Drink this.' Mrs Fury's head fell back upon the pillow. He had to pour the spirit down the woman's throat. He drew a chair to the bed and sat down. At the same time he pulled out his gun-metal watch and stared at it. 'Confound it!' He hadn't much time. It *would* happen now. He held Mrs Fury's hand.

What had happened? Was it Peter? It must have been Peter. It couldn't be the ominous news of the coming strike. Fanny was too much of a veteran like himself. That could not be it. 'Then what is it?' he cried in his mind. He bent down and embraced the woman. 'Fanny!' he said in a low voice, 'Fanny! Tell me what's wrong.' But the woman did not appear to hear him. She lay like a log. Her eyes were closed, her mouth a little open. How white she was! She had never had a seizure like this before. He could not remember it. Well, well. The man got up and walked to the window. He looked at his watch again, became agitated, paced the room. Where had that boy got to? How long was this Dr Dunfrey going to be? He resumed his seat. He leaned his head on her pillow. What trials this woman had had! What obstacles she had overcome! Mr Fury's mind suddenly whirled back twenty-four years to the time he was on the ice in New York. Aye. That was the beginning. The beginning, the first paving of that hard road. Where had they arrived? Nowhere. A family, grown up, and she had reared them. He looked at the woman's face. 'A brick. That's what Fanny is. A brick.' That expression upon her face. It was like a mirror through which he could see the very workings of her heart and mind. He sat up. He wanted to go to the lavatory, but he dared not leave the woman. He would have to wait. 'Late, of course, hang it!' he growled savagely. At that moment she looked at him. He caught her eye. 'Fanny!' he said. 'What's wrong?'

'Nothing, Denny! I've been feeling like this for some time now. I suppose it's only natural. My strength has been taxed. I can't stand things like I used to, Denny.'

He put his hand on her head. He was filled with pity for her. 'I know! I know! I'm sorry, Fanny. I understand.' His watch came out again. 'Must go soon.'

Mrs Fury ignored the remark. She went on: 'I had a letter from the authorities this morning about Peter.' 'Oh!' Mr Fury forgot the time.

The woman leaned across to him and said, 'You could never imagine it, Denny! Nor could I. No, you could never imagine it, not if you lived to be a hundred.'

'But what did they say?' asked Mr Fury. 'Why did he get passed out?'

'I shall never tell you, Denny,' replied Mrs Fury. 'Never! Never!'

'But, Fanny . . .' stammered Mr Fury, 'I . . .'

Mrs Fury remained silent. This thing had come, had struck her, but the vision of it all was clouded out. 'It's happened, Denny,' she went on. 'It's over. That's all. There is nothing to inquire into, nothing to think about. Why should one think? I'll say no more,' she said. 'Get him out of it. Get him out of it.' Mr Fury got up from his chair and went to the door. That was how it was. He paused, thinking, 'It's terrible.' He went back to the bed, took hold of her hands, and said, 'All right. I understand. I understand, Fanny. It's opened my eyes. Aye. It's opened them at last. It's the children. We're getting further and further away from each other. Fanny, we must stick together.' He squeezed her hands. There was the sound of voices below. He jumped up. 'That's Dunfrey now,' he said. 'I must go now, Fanny. I'm late. So long.' He hastily kissed his wife and ran out of the room.

He met the big doctor coming up the stairs. 'Good-day, Fury. What's wrong? Which room?' Mr Fury jerked a thumb in the direction of the big front room. 'In there, Doctor,' he said. At the bottom of the stairs Mr Fury bumped into Peter. 'How awkward you are!' he exclaimed gruffly, stumbling towards the door. Peter looked up: 'Sorry, Dad.' The door banged. A great draught swept along the lobby. Peter went upstairs and stood listening outside his mother's door. He wanted to go in to her. He wanted to say how sorry he was. It was all his fault. Now his father had turned against him. He could hear the doctor talking to his mother. 'You'll have to look after yourself more, Mrs Fury. You must slow down a little.' He stood there, his hands gripping the panels of the door. A flood of memories swept through him. The door knob turned. Peter hurried downstairs again.

Aunt Brigid stood in front of the dressing-mirror. For some twenty minutes she had been contemplating. Should she put on the blue serge costume? No. The skirt was rather too full. She had better put on the green gown. Where was the green gown? The floor around her was already strewn with shoes, underwear, gloves and scarves, blouses of three different colours. She could not help admiring herself in the glass. What a difference between Fanny and herself! She undressed for the fifth time and put on the green gown. She found it a little tight about the waist. But she could not afford to change her ideas now. It was getting late. She simply could not miss the last Mass. At the last Mass one met everybody, one heard everything. The last Mass was an expedition from which one generally returned with new fauna and flora. Already she pictured the different people she would meet. She bent down and picked up the scent-bottle from the bag, and after applying a fair amount to the upper part of her person, felt she was completely groomed. She could not forget the incident of the burnt toast, nor her sister's remark. However . . . She heard Fanny calling 'Peter! Peter!' and realized too well the significance behind the call. Peter would have to unravel himself! A strange boy. 'Well now,' thought Aunt Brigid, as she surveyed herself in the glass for the last time, 'well now. You look quite well, in fact you look very well. That is as it should be.' She smiled and turned to her bag again. Every now and then a smile stole across her good-humoured face. It was a round red face, out of which two blue eyes gazed good-humouredly upon the world. She put back the scattered clothes, locked her bag, and placed it under the bed. Then she went across to the bedroom window and looked down into the street. What a dirty black place Hatfields was! She rather wondered why a woman like Fanny should ever elect to live in such a hole. 'There's no doubt about it now,' thought Miss Mangan, as she closed the room door behind her, 'Fanny's marriage has been disastrous.' Perhaps her father was right after all. 'Poor Dad!' she exclaimed. She had hardly spent a minute with him. But again those pictures came into her mind, and 'Dad's' importance was at once forgotten. This excursion down to the chapel was too exciting. The things she would see and hear, the changes that would confront her!

As she went downstairs Mrs Fury passed her. They smiled. Fanny Fury stood on the landing watching her sister go down the lobby. She smiled again as the door opened, and called down, 'Will you be out long, Brigid?' The woman at the door hesitated. What a silly question to ask! She called back, 'I really don't know, Fanny. I may be back about tea-time, but I won't promise. I have to go down to the shipping office after Mass, as I must see what arrangements can be made. I don't want to be stuck here.' The tone of her voice suddenly changed. 'I don't want to be held up by this strike, Fanny. Well, so long now.' The door closed. As the door of number three Hatfields closed, a half-dozen other doors opened, curtains were drawn back, bedroom blinds peered through. Mrs Postlethwaite herself, never an early riser, felt it incumbent upon herself to rise immediately on hearing the Furys' door close. This aunt from Ireland must be seen. As Miss Mangan walked sedately down the street, she was faintly suspicious that certain curtains upon whose dirtiness she had already formed opinions were moving, and once, as she approached number seven, she deliberately hesitated to hear a remark passed. 'Why, that's Fury's sister-in-law. Aye. Came over yesterday. Queer bloody lot.' Aunt Brigid went almost crimson, and heaved a sigh of relief when she reached the bottom of the street.

Yes, Fanny had ruined herself marrying that man. Dad had warned her. Now look where she was. Living next to a bone yard. Thank God she had kept by her resolution never to leave Ireland! It seemed to her that Irish people living in England always congregated in the worst quarters of the city. This harum-scarum fellow named Dennis Fury certainly had a lot to answer for. 'Denny hates me like poison. I know it.' She turned the corner and made her way to Hans Street, which she crossed, and passed through Ash Walk, and so arrived at the chapel. There were hardly a dozen people at the Mass. Following her usual custom, Aunt Brigid went straight up the middle aisle and took one of the front benches. She took out her Prayer Book and followed the Mass in Latin. She knew already that people were looking at her. Once she turned round and smiled at a woman in the bench behind her. A few minutes later the woman herself came into Miss Mangan's bench and knelt beside her. She whispered in her ear, 'Why, Brigid, I'm so surprised to see you ...' and would have gone on but that the ringing of the bell for the Elevation put a brake upon her effusions. Miss Mangan was not used to being interrupted during the saying of the Mass. She supposed it was a common thing in England. How quickly the Irish forgot themselves when once out of their own country! The woman at her side fidgeted about. It seemed she could hardly wait for the last gospel to be read. There was an impatience about her whole attitude to the Mass that shocked the older woman beside her. 'Obviously,' thought Brigid, 'this woman is very anxious to see me.' When the Mass was over they went out together. No sooner had they gained the door and street than the other woman began.

'Fancy! After all these years! And how are you, Brigid? You are looking well.' Miss Mangan had to smile. What a wretched-looking woman this was! Who was she? She didn't even know the person's name. 'Well, well. You mean to say you don't know Frances Sliney? I never!' 'Sliney. Sliney.' Aunt

Brigid ruffled her brows. 'Sliney. The Frances Sliney from Cove?' The woman nodded her head. 'My heavens!' exclaimed Brigid. 'I would never have known you. You've aged indeed.' Mrs Sliney, in answer to Miss Mangan's many questions, remarked that she had been a certified midwife for some seven years. When Brigid mentioned the word 'family' the woman laughed and replied, 'Yes. Eleven of them. And five of them dead. They're all gone now. You remember John?' Brigid Mangan shook her head. She didn't remember anybody of that name in the Sliney family. They walked slowly up Ash Walk. Suddenly a hand touched her shoulder. 'Well, this is gorgeous,' exclaimed Brigid. The old friends were just beginning to gather. 'How are you, Miss Pettigrew?' Miss Pettigrew, who admitted her age as eighty-two, smiled, and put out a hand that was so thin and white that Aunt Brigid felt a little afraid of taking hold of it. 'Still in the same place, Miss Pettigrew?' The old lady nodded her head, so that her poke-bonnet nodded too. The three stood on the edge of the side-walk. Miss Mangan was very anxious to know how far away Vulcan Street was, yet she did not wish to ask directly. She would be patient and wait. Perhaps if she waited long enough she would hear something very interesting. Miss Pettigrew said she must be going. 'I hope you will come and see me, Miss Mangan,' she said, revealing her toothless cavern of a mouth as she smiled. 'Don't forget now. I'm in the same old place. Good morning.' She bowed a little stiffly and walked away. 'Yes, yes, of course,' said Miss Mangan, though she realized at once the impossibility of it. There were too many things to be seen to already.

Mrs Sliney towered over Aunt Brigid. She kept leaning over and putting her face close to her as she went on animatedly telling the history of her years in Gelton, her marriage, her ambitions, her husband's recent promotion at sea. Miss Mangan felt rather bewildered with it all. Mrs Sliney suddenly stopped. Miss Mangan looked round and noted a row of five cottages alongside of which stood a small tin chapel. Miss Mangan's quick eye caught the words, 'Welsh Methodist'. Mrs Sliney was pointing at one of the cottages and saying, 'I live just over there. Won't you come and have a bite of breakfast with me?' She looked so appealingly at Miss Mangan that the woman hesitated before crossing the street. What time was it? Nearly ten. H'm! There wasn't much time to waste. The woman still held her with the same appealing glance.

'I'll slip in for a few minutes,' Aunt Brigid said. They crossed the street and entered the first of the five cottages. It was dark and stuffy inside. Mrs Sliney, like Mrs Fury, was very fond of huge fires, though, unlike Miss Mangan's sister, she rarely opened a window. 'Well now,' exclaimed Mrs Sliney, 'just drop your coat off, Brigid. You'll feel cold going out again.' She watched the woman take her coat off and stand resplendent in her bright green gown. Mrs Sliney felt that Miss Mangan dressed outrageously for a woman of her years.

'I have some tea ready,' she said. 'Won't you take a tot of rum in it?' Miss Mangan sat down as far away from the great fire as possible. She leaned her head to one side and replied, 'Hardly. Hardly, Frances.' Then, after a long pause, 'Oh, very well. Heaven knows when I'll see you again.' She watched the woman go outside. Then she let her eyes wander about the dark kitchen.

Mrs Sliney came back with two cups of tea and a small bottle. She sat down. She poured a little rum into each cup. 'There you are, Brigid,' she said, and began to stir her own tea. She kept looking at the woman in the green gown. Miss Mangan, looking up suddenly, caught the other's eye. This woman, she told herself, was envious of her. But why? Even Fanny had stared at her in the same queer way. Had marriage destroyed something in them that now shone triumphantly in her own person? 'There's something in it,' thought Aunt Brigid. She was looking in the mirror again. Of course, and she must admit it, she *was* looking extraordinarily well. That's what it was. She looked so well. Even a little prosperous. Mrs Sliney coughed.

'I hear you brought the boy over with you,' she said. 'How is he getting along these times?' Miss Mangan looked into the fire. She felt she ought to be wary at this stage. How was he getting on? In plain English it really meant: Why had he to leave the college so suddenly? 'How quickly things spread about,' she was thinking, oblivious of the fact that Mrs Sliney was re-filling her tea-cup. She expected this. She pushed the cup in on the table and assumed an attitude of imminent departure. 'Oh, well!' she exclaimed, half rising from the chair, 'now you are asking me a question.' She rose to her feet. 'I hardly know myself, and I'm certain his mother doesn't.'

Mrs Sliney said 'Oh!' and registered an expression of complete astonishment. This was interesting. 'How strange, Brigid!' she said. 'I suppose you're going up to see the daughter now, are you?'

'That's just where I'm going,' replied Aunt Brigid, drawing on her gloves. 'And then I'm going down to the shipping office to see about my journey back. I don't wish to be stranded here, what with all this talk of a strike.' She fastened her coat.

'Yes. She's having a child shortly, isn't she? As for this strike, Brigid, I think it's just a lot of guff. Just guff.'

'Indeed! I wish I could be as optimistic as that,' said Miss Mangan, moving towards the door. 'I was glancing at the headlines in the paper this morning. But then you never were one for reading much, were you, Frances?' and she smiled at Mrs Sliney.

112

'How long are you staying?' Aunt Brigid drew herself up at the front door. 'No longer than I can help, I assure you. It's a dirty place and no mistake.'

Mrs Sliney said, 'H'm!' and opened the door. 'It's a pity you going back so soon,' remarked Mrs Sliney. 'It would have been nice for you to have met some of the girls.'

Aunt Brigid was already in the street, feeling a little cleaner, filled with an earnest desire to be gone. There was something about the slatternly-looking woman on the doorstep that filled her with horror at the thought of ever being domiciled in Gelton. 'It's a dirty morning,' she remarked, looking away up the street. The woman nodded her head.

'God knows when we'll see you again,' she said, laughing.

'It's been nice to see you,' Aunt Brigid said, putting forth all the control she was capable of. 'Perhaps some day ...'

'Yes, yes. Of course ... well, bye-bye, Brigid.' They shook hands.

Mrs Sliney stood watching Miss Mangan's stately stride until she had turned the corner by the chapel. Then she went in and banged the door. Aunt Brigid, having passed the chapel, paused for a moment by a grocer's shop, looking into the window. She looked at nothing in particular. She was making up her mind. Her eye caught the clock on the wall inside the shop. Time was getting on. Ought she to go to Vulcan Street? She would certainly like to see Desmond. He had been her favourite, and, of course, that wife of his? She simply must see her. But she did not like to ask the direction to Vulcan Street. She turned away from the shop and walked on. 'How beastly people are!' she said to herself. A boy running towards her reminded her that she was not even sure of the number of the street where Maureen lived. She stopped the boy. 'Where is Price Street, sonny?' she asked, automatically putting her hand in her bag to get a penny for him. The boy turned away and pointed to a narrow street almost opposite them.

'Over there'm,' he said, taking the penny from Miss Mangan. 'Thank you'm.' Miss Mangan walked on. At last she was in the street. Number thirty-five. She mustn't forget it now. As she wandered slowly down, her observant eye scrutinized the various windows. Number twenty-five. Not far now. She stopped outside the house. The step had been newly scrubbed. 'My!' she exclaimed, as she noticed the bright yellow curtains of number thirty-seven, which appeared to throw out a challenge to Mrs Kilkey's bright green ones. She knocked at the door. When the young woman opened it, the recognition was not so spontaneous as Aunt Brigid had hoped. 'Well, Maureen,' she exclaimed, turning her head sharply to glance up the street, and thinking, 'What a place to have brought Maureen!' The young woman jumped down to the step and flung her arms about her aunt, exclaiming, 'Why, it's Aunt Brigid. How are you, Auntie?' Miss Mangan smiled. They went in together.

Maureen drew out a chair for her aunt, and Miss Mangan sat down.

'Oh!' Aunt Brigid said. 'I walked all the way here.'

'Let me help you, Auntie,' she said. The woman stood up, and Maureen took off her coat. 'Your gloves, Auntie.' Miss Mangan said, 'All right, child. Just hang the coat up anywhere. And how are you?' She turned and looked at her niece. There was something hard and penetrating in her glance. Maureen came forward, standing in front of the fire, her hands clasped behind her back.

'Is Peter home? How is he? What does he look like? I wanted to meet you last night, but I couldn't very well go, as Joe wasn't feeling too well.' Miss Mangan never slackened in her penetrating stare.

'Oh, Peter! Strange child. He's as big as an elephant now. But then you'll be going up there tonight, won't you?'

'Yes, Auntie.' Aunt Brigid put out a hand and caught her niece by the hem of her skirt. 'Come here.' Maureen took a chair and sat opposite her aunt. 'How are you? I heard the news from your mother. Tell me, are you happy, Maureen?' It seemed to the young woman that her aunt's eyes suddenly changed colour. There was a silence. Miss Mangan laid her hand on Maureen's knee, her eyes now taking in her niece's altered form. 'You are happy, then?' she repeated, and Maureen, as though just wakened from a long sleep, sat up suddenly and replied:

'Oh yes, Auntie. Oh yes. I like Joe. We are happy here.'

Aunt Brigid slowly drew off her right glove and laid it on the table. 'How did it happen, Maureen? I can tell you it was a great surprise to me. Your mother never dropped me a line about it. Your mother is a strange woman, child. Even with Desmond.' The same dignified silence. 'What is the use of it? I ask you. It's time your mother had a little common sense.' She tapped her foot upon the freshly scrubbed flags.

'But Mother wrote to you, Auntie,' replied Maureen, with some astonishment.

'Perhaps she did, but I didn't get it, Maureen,' replied Aunt Brigid coldly. Pause. 'What time will your husband be in for dinner?' She sat back in her chair, assuming her favourite position, head a little to one side, arms spread out upon her knees. Now that she was able to study her niece more closely, she realized how alike both mother and daughter were. The same head, the same eyes, nose, and mouth. The same self-assurance, the same tensity. But there was something else. A change in Maureen, and she had been quick to notice it. Yes. She had changed, but in what way? She could not take her eyes off the young woman.

'Joe will be here at twelve o'clock,' Maureen said. 'Will you stay for dinner with us, Auntie? Or are you going home?' Miss Mangan moved uneasily in her chair. Should she stay? Or should she just wait to meet Kilkey and then go off and see her eldest nephew? She looked at Maureen. She was smiling at her now. There was something quite charming, even genuinely affectionate, she felt, in the young woman's desire to have her stay. She could not very well disappoint the child. She drew off her other glove.

'It's so nice of you, Maureen,' she said. 'I should love to stay. Indeed, I'm rather anxious to meet Mr Kilkey. But won't I be in your way?'

Maureen laughed in her face. 'No,' she said, 'you won't.' She leaned across and said in a low voice, 'But what else have you brought back with you from Ireland, Auntie? Any secrets? Don't you know anything about Peter? Why he left so suddenly? Dad was awfully angry ...'

'Was your dad ever any different?' remarked Miss Mangan suddenly. 'One can well understand. Your mother asked me the same question this morning. I know nothing about him. He would tell me nothing. I was amazed when I saw him. Almost a man now, Maureen. You'll hardly know him. So your dad is angry about it! It's a pity. I can't remember a time when he wasn't angry over something. Don't you ever feel that you owed it to yourself to leave Hatfields? What a house it is! It seems they've lived there too long. Years and years. That's what gets your mother down, Maureen. I know it. It's like a prison.'

'H'm!' Maureen said. 'You don't know anything about Hatfields, Auntie.'

Miss Mangan threw her head back. 'You surprise me, Maureen,' she said. 'You must know by now that your mother has never had one ounce of luck since she went to live there. She's a changed woman since I saw her last. It seems to me that Anthony is wise to stay at sea. Poor boy!'

Maureen rose to her feet. 'Auntie,' she said, 'why bring Anthony into it? It's not Mother's fault if she's still in Hatfields.'

'Oh! Your mother tells me it's all through your father. Then your father says it's your mother's fault ...'

'Hello!' called out a voice suddenly from the back of the house.

'Why, it's Joe,' exclaimed Maureen, running into the back kitchen. 'Will you help me with the dinner, Auntie? It's your favourite,' she called out. 'Boiled bacon, cabbage, and potatoes.'

Mr Kilkey put his head inside the door. 'Visitors?' he asked, looking at Maureen. They both went into the kitchen.

'My Aunt Brigid from Cork,' said Maureen. She looked at her aunt. 'This is Joe, Auntie,' she said. She felt triumphant, as though she had waited all her life for this very occasion.

'How are you?' asked Mr Kilkey, putting forth a hand. Aunt Brigid hesitated. Her first thought was, 'What a repulsive-looking man!'; her first feeling one of physical revulsion. They shook hands.

'Now, Auntie,' Maureen said, laying a hand on Miss Mangan's arm. Mr Kilkey said, 'Excuse me,' and hurried outside to wash himself. He came in a few minutes later and went straight upstairs. Meanwhile the two women were busy getting the plates. Aunt Brigid laid the table, Maureen carried in the meal. Mr Kilkey came downstairs. He looked at his watch. 'A bit late,' he said. They all sat down. Mr Kilkey began his dinner, whilst Aunt Brigid drew her plate to her. She was seated at the top of the table. She could see both husband and wife in profile now. She found it difficult to conceal her surprise. It was something more than surprise. Twice Maureen looked her way, and she lowered her head quickly and began using her knife and fork with mock earnestness. It seemed to Aunt Brigid that wherever she turned, wherever her eyes wandered, the face of Mr Kilkey wandered too. And what a face, she was thinking. It was disgusting. To think that her only niece had married that man, with his bald patch at the back of his head, his dirty-looking skin – it reminded Aunt Brigid of wet leather – and his enormous hands. Surely the man must be old enough to be the girl's father.

'I hope you are enjoying it, Auntie,' said Maureen, looking up at her aunt, whilst she cut more bacon for her husband. Miss Mangan, from the other end of the table, smiled. 'It's beautiful, Maureen,' she said. 'You have your mother to thank for that.' At that moment Mr Kilkey looked up from his plate. Miss Mangan again lowered her head. 'What time does this fellow go back?' she was wondering. She positively hated him now. There must be something in all this. Why had Maureen flung herself at a man like Kilkey? It was disgusting. Maureen said, 'More, Auntie?'

'No, child, thanks,' she replied, and looked along at Maureen.

'Ah!' she exclaimed under her breath. 'I've got it now.' Why hadn't she noticed it before? It was staring her in the face. That young woman was coarsened. Yes. Coarsened. That was the change. 'My heavens!' she kept repeating in her mind. She looked at Maureen again, saying slowly to herself, 'Maureen is now in a jute factory. She rather likes it. The hours are long but the wages are good.' That was nearly three years – no, impossible, it was much longer than that, Miss Mangan was thinking. Her sister had written to her about it. 'Maureen has gone out to work. I didn't want her to go, but the girl was so restless, I let her go. It's in a jute factory. She seems to like it.' Yes, thought Aunt Brigid, she could read every one of those words on her niece's face. So that was the jute factory. The long hours. Maureen looked twenty years older. Mr Kilkey pushed his chair away, saying, 'Excuse me. I must go now.' He went to the mantelshelf for a cigarette, lit it, and went outside. Miss Mangan turned her head and looked out of the back window.

'What a peculiar street you live in!' she exclaimed. 'You have the railway at the back.' She supposed that Kilkey man had brought her here.

'Yes,' Maureen said. 'But it's quiet here, and handy for Joe's work.'

'Of course,' Aunt Brigid replied. She too got up, saying, 'Let me help you clear these off, child.' Mr Kilkey pushed his head round the door.

'So long,' he said. They heard the door bang.

They began to clear off the things from the table. Miss Mangan still felt a little bewildered. Now that Kilkey had gone, they might be able to sit in peace and talk about things. Looking at her niece, she could already imagine her framing the very question she so much dreaded to answer. Well, what could she say other than that Joseph Kilkey was disappointing? She kept looking at Maureen's swollen belly. They washed and dried the things. Suddenly Maureen said:

'When you come to think of it, Aunt Brigid, it's terrible the bad luck Mother has. Isn't it awful about Anthony?'

Miss Mangan hung up the towel on the rack. 'Yes,' continued Maureen, 'just think of it! But of course Mother told you all about it, didn't she?' Aunt Brigid nodded her head, saying, 'Yes, child. She told me. It's frightful. What a handful your mother has to look after! I suppose sometimes when you sit down and think it over you feel you are well out of it.' She looked at Maureen as if to say, 'That's solemn truth.' But the young woman made no reply. She emptied the basin and wiped it out. 'Let's go into the kitchen,' she said. They went in.

'I'll make a drink of tea later on,' Maureen said. They sat down.

'Your grand-dad seems to be quite helpless now,' remarked Aunt Brigid as she made herself comfortable in the chair. 'It nearly broke my heart to see him in such a pitiable condition.'

'Mother does her best. She can't do any more,' said Maureen sharply, at which remark Aunt Brigid sat up.

'Oh, I know, I know. Your mother does her best. But it is sad. One never imagines they will reach that stage, though. I remember when I saw him last he was a hale and hearty man.' The young woman rose in her chair. This surely was some reflection upon her mother.

'But he's old, Aunt. All old people are like that. Besides, it takes Mother all her time looking after the family and keeping the house over their heads.'

'Yes,' replied Miss Mangan, 'your mother seems to be fairly on her own now, what with yourself and Desmond out of the house. How is he getting on? That was another surprise. I hear he's on the permanent way, near your father.' Maureen sat silent. She realized the probable course her aunt's conversation would take.

'I don't know anything about Desmond,' Maureen said coldly. 'Nobody does. He's cut himself off from everybody, marrying that woman like he did. I never see him. I mind my own business and he minds his. Father is the only person who ever sees him, and then only because they practically work together. He's well left alone, as Mother says. He always was a bit of a suspicious character anyhow. But honestly, Auntie, don't you think Mother has much more to do than worry about him? She has Peter on her hands now, and Dad working ashore. And, before she knows where she is, Anthony will be home too. A cripple, I suppose. Don't you think that Mother doesn't realize things. She does. Only too well. Sometimes I think she's been a fool, but that's neither here nor there. I say again that you don't know Mother. You haven't lived with her in Hatfields for thirty years, have you? No. One would think that now two of us are gone she would get a little more air, a little more peace. But she never does.' Suddenly Aunt Brigid exclaimed:

'But why did you leave the house so suddenly, Maureen?'

'Well,' thought Maureen, 'that is a straight question, anyway.'

'Why did I leave? Why did I marry Kilkey? Not for a joke, Auntie.'

'I'm quite serious, child,' said Aunt Brigid.

'I married him because I loved him,' said Maureen. She stood up and pushed the chair away. 'Aunt Brigid,' she said, 'you don't understand things. That's the solemn truth, isn't it?' Aunt Brigid shifted her right leg on to the fender. She did not reply. She felt there was no reply to make. She had been working out a little theory of her own. Now it had turned out to be correct. Now she realized that change, that something that Maureen lacked, had lost. She wasn't happy. 'Like her mother,' thought Miss Mangan; 'she's made a bad job of it, and hides the mistake behind her stubbornness.' What was there to say? Nothing. She looked up at the clock. A quarter past two. Maureen looked at the clock now, as though she had seen mirrored in its face Aunt Brigid's secret thoughts. Then they met each other's glance. 'I suppose I'll see you up at the house, then?' Aunt Brigid said, after a long silence.

'If I have time,' Maureen said abruptly.

'But surely you'll want to see your brother,' remarked Miss Mangan.

'Oh, he'll be coming down,' she replied.

Maureen was thinking: 'She's come down here to get some information. She wants to see her favourite Desmond, but she doesn't like to ask me where he lives. Sly woman! All her talk gets nowhere. She doesn't like Joe. One can see that at a glance. She doesn't understand Mother. She never did. They never agreed. She's just an old matronly lady who ought never to be out after dark. She ought to go back to Ireland as soon as she can.' Miss Mangan casually remarked that she must get the tram directly to the Front.

'I should hate to be stranded here, child,' she said.

'Of course, Auntie,' Maureen replied. 'You can catch a tram at the bottom of the street.' Miss Mangan picked up her gloves. If that wasn't an ultimatum nothing ever was, she was telling herself. She looked curiously at her niece as she drew on her gloves. Maureen blushed. Why did she always stare at people like that? The young woman, conscious of these glances, these penetrating surveys of the lower part of her person, imagined that the citizen to come had suddenly moved. Aunt Brigid got up. 'My coat, Maureen,' she said. Maureen went out for her coat. 'Poor child!' thought Miss Mangan. 'And that's the factory for you! She would have done much better to have taken on a domestic job in a priest's house. The girl is ruined.' Maureen returned with the coat. Miss Mangan drew herself to her full height, as though to emphasize the splendour of her bright green gown. Maureen helped her on with the coat. 'I'm so glad you stayed for dinner, Auntie,' she said at last. It had been so embarrassing. Well, they both knew how they felt about each other. But why on earth had she come? Her mother didn't know. That was certain.

'Fancy that Miss Pettigrew being alive yet,' remarked Miss Mangan as she buttoned up her coat. 'I was talking to her this morning. It's amazing. She must be almost the same age as your grand-dad.'

'Yes,' Maureen said. They moved towards the door.

'It's been nice to see you,' Aunt Brigid said. She stood down on the step. 'A dirty little hole!' she said to herself as she surveyed the two rows of grey-looking houses. Maureen, as though divining her thought, suddenly exclaimed, 'You find it different here, don't you, Auntie? The King's Road is ...' But Miss Mangan, seeing the point, retreated skilfully. Observing a large number of men at the bottom of the street, she remarked with astonishment:

'Whatever are all those men doing there, Maureen?'

The young woman looked down the street and laughed. 'Oh! they're only from the sheds yonder. It's the dinner hour for them. It's like that every day, Auntie.'

'Don't you find the trains distracting? Especially at night-time?'

'Oh, no. We're used to that,' replied Maureen. 'One gets used to everything here in time. As soon as one realizes that it is impossible to get outside of it, the better one settles down,' she concluded.

'Now what can she mean by that?' thought Miss Mangan. She drew up the collar of her coat. 'I think it's going to rain again.'

'I don't think so,' said Maureen. 'Why, there's your tram now, Auntie,' she added with emphasis, as a car came slowly round the corner.

Aunt Brigid put out a hand and drew Maureen's face to her own. 'Good-bye, my child. Take care of yourself now. I may not see you again.'

'Good-bye,' Maureen said, confident that she would see her aunt again. The woman turned and began to run. Maureen stood on the step watching her, a smile slowly forming on her face as she watched the stout figure of Miss Mangan sail down the street, one hand holding her raised umbrella and waving frantically at the car-driver.

'Poor woman!' thought Maureen. 'Why she ever condescends to leave her little castle I really don't know.' Her aunt's one weakness was a ferret-like capacity for gathering in information from the family and carrying this information back to Ireland with something approaching the pride of an explorer who has returned with some rare fauna from secret places. The tram had stopped. She watched her aunt climb on, the conductor putting out a hand to help her. Then the car disappeared out of sight. Maureen went in and closed the door. She resumed her seat by the fire. And so Aunt Brigid had realized her ambitions. She had wormed that secret out. How? Maureen exclaimed aloud to the other empty chair, 'So you found out!' She felt as though something had been stolen from her, as though a relentless hand had torn the secret from her heart.

CHAPTER VI

I

Peter, on returning with Dr Dunfrey, had shown him upstairs to the front room. He had waited in the lobby until his father had gone out. Then he had gone and stood on the landing. Everything seemed confusing. At times he asked himself if he really was home again. Now he leaned against the wall, listening to the loud-voiced doctor in the next room. Was his mother very ill? He had been the cause of that. He felt his shame grow upon him. He could not escape it. It was like a sort of slimy skin clothing his person. Well, this was the end. It was all over. Everything had changed. His life at Hatfields before he went to Ireland was a complete blank. His parents were getting on in years. John was dead. Anthony at sea. Maureen and Desmond out of the house. He felt suddenly lonely. The old world and the old life were broken up. The companionship of his brothers and sister gone. Why had he been so foolish? He gripped the banisters, and exclaimed under his breath, 'No! That's wrong! That's wrong. Why did I go? Why did I stay? Why did I remain silent?' Those indeed were the questions. Each time he put these questions to himself the shame clung more and more to him. He was imprisoned by it. This shame was something he could feel, could touch with his hands. He stood erect. Well, as soon as that doctor had gone he would go into his mother's room. He was seized with an almost passionate longing to prostrate himself, to kneel down in front of his mother and to say how sorry he was. 'You fool!' he cried in his mind. 'You mad fool!' And what a time to break away! Here was his brother Anthony coming home very shortly. What was he to say? Do? What had he gained at their expense? An education. A good education. Suddenly he laughed, thinking, 'Even to whistle in one's room was a sin.' Well, he had escaped from all that. And yet he had to acknowledge that seven years ago it had been escape too. But the word was not so significant then. He was aware that he had passionately longed to go. Yes, he had wanted to leave Hatfields, that ocean of bricks and mortar, and go to Ireland. There, there had been airy rooms, good food, large fields, good companions, games. And now he was glad to be back. The green fields had seemed a greater prison. To Peter Fury, fresh from the college in Cork, the world was still a sort of huge forest, amok with chaotic growths. That seven years' isolation had filled his head with historical facts, a positive philosophy, some smattering of mathematics, and the principles of logic. He was well drilled in the articles of faith, of hope and charity. He knew his New Testament from cover to cover. He had been taught the essentials of truth, of clean living, of iron laws and strict obedience. He was well versed in geography, though his curiosity as to the exact position of Limbo had never been satisfied. That was part and parcel of another geographical system which steered clear of plain logic and reasoning, whilst proclaiming its infallibility. But Peter was soon to learn that this hotchpotch of knowledge, this seven years' isolation in the forge of learning, produced no weapon capable of hacking his way through a world beset with so many obstacles. There were philosophies both positive and negative, laws both good and bad, made sound and permanent only by the very paper on which they were limned. There was corruption, lies, deceit, and greed, as also there was beauty, nobility, and magnanimity. He was something new and strange in this industrialized ant-heap. What of his brothers and his sister? They had forged different weapons.

Peter was roused from his contemplations by hearing the loud-voiced Dr Dunfrey exclaiming, 'Good-bye, Mrs Fury! Stay in bed for the day. You can get up tomorrow.' Then the door banged. He heard his heavy, almost clumsy tread as he made his way slowly down the badly lighted stairs. Peter followed him down to the lobby. The six-foot man was putting on his overcoat. Peter took his hat from the rack and handed it to him. The huge man looked hard at Peter, then exclaimed, 'Why? When did you come back, young man?' He put on his hat. 'H'm! He knows too,' thought Peter. 'Why doesn't he shout out – "*I know too*"?' Standing there staring at him like that!

'I came home yesterday,' Peter said.

Dr Dunfrey moved to the door. He handed Peter a note. 'Take that to the chemist's, young man,' he said. He opened the door and went out. His car was humming at the kerb. Peter stood at the door until the car started off. Then he went upstairs again. He stood outside his mother's door. He could hear the rustling of paper. His mother must be reading. Then he knocked, and waited for her to call. But Mrs Fury did not answer his knock. He stood there, hesitant:

'Can I come in, Mother?' he called out; at the same time he turned the knob of the door and partly opened it. He could see his mother sitting up in the bed, propped up by pillows. The green-backed magazine she was reading dropped to the floor.

'Is that you?'

'Yes, Mother.'

'What is it?'

Peter was silent. A lump came into his throat. He coughed. 'I want to speak to you, Mother,' he said. There was something pleading and urgent in his utterance.

'Well?' called Mrs Fury, and Peter went into the room. He did not look at the woman in the bed, but stood with his back turned, one hand holding the door, the attitude of a person who has to make a quick decision. Then he closed the door silently and crossed over to the bed. He stood at its foot, staring abstractedly at the patchwork quilt.

'Well?' said his mother once more. Peter looked up. 'Mother!' he said, then paused. He seemed to be collecting himself for the next effort. 'Mother! Please forgive me! I am sorry. I know I have disappointed you. I could not help it. But please forgive me. I know how much you have done for me.' He stopped suddenly, and looked straight into his mother's eyes. Mrs Fury avoided his glance at once. She moved uneasily in the bed.

'The others said that too,' she said coldly. 'You see where you have put me.' Now she raised her head and looked at him.

'I'll do anything you ask, Mother,' said Peter.

She saw tears coming into the boy's eyes. But she was not affected by them. 'It is so easy to cry,' she thought. Peter's hands, suddenly endowed with a life of their own as apart from his body, began to move up and down the iron rail of the bed. They seemed a clue to his thoughts. After a while Mrs Fury shouted, 'Stop that! Stop it!'

He dropped his hands to his sides. 'Come here,' she said. Peter went up to her. The woman moved the chair at the side of the bed. She motioned to him. 'Sit down,' she said. There was silence for almost half a minute. Mrs Fury leaned forward and looked at her son. He had disappointed her, wounded her, he had lied. And yet she loved him. No matter what he had done, he was different from the others. And he was her son, he was still Peter. How tall he was! How well, even beautiful, he looked! She sat back.

'It's too late now,' she said. 'From today you had best look to your father.'

Peter's expression changed at once. He burst into tears. She watched his head lower itself until it was almost on a level with her own shoulder. Peter sobbed, his whole frame shook. He sat up, brushed his face with the sleeve of his coat, and exclaimed almost savagely, 'I *am* sorry, Mother. I *am* sorry. I *am* sorry.'

The woman was quite unmoved. 'But don't I tell you it's too late, or are you growing dull? What's the matter with you? I've told you to look to your father. He's the one. And it'll be quite a change for him to look to his children. It'll even be an education. No, Peter! You must go to your father. I want a little peace now. I've had my share.'

Peter put a hand over that of his mother. Neither of them spoke. They were like two figures carved in stone. 'Please, Mother,' exclaimed Peter. 'I'll do anything for you.' For the first time Mrs Fury smiled. Well, he had done that filthy thing, and yet, here it was, all-revealing, before her very eyes – that thing she had thought lost. It was still with him.

'You must go to Confession tonight, Peter,' she said at last.

'Yes, Mother.'

'You'd better go down now,' she said, 'and keep an eye on your grand-dad until your father comes home from work.'

'Yes, Mother.' He closed the door softly behind him and went downstairs. There seemed something almost symbolic in the closing of that door, as though he had shut out his past, shut out that helplessness, that burning sense of shame, that bewilderment and torment. Now he felt free. He had flung off that slimy skin. He knew where he was. He would go to his father. He would get work. He would make a solemn vow that very night. He would work hard, help his mother. He would win back her affection and respect. He would forget all that he had ever learnt. It was all waste, all fungus. He must start at the beginning again. The positive philosophy must be a belief in his mother. That was what it must be. He felt so suddenly happy that he wanted to shout, to sing. He went into the kitchen and sat down on the sofa. He was sitting there for nearly ten minutes before he became aware of the figure in front of him. Old Mr Mangan seemed to be staring at something. There was something fierce, almost frenzied, in his stare. Peter suddenly turned round and looked out of the kitchen window. At what was his grandfather staring?

'What is he staring at?' thought Peter. Why didn't his grandfather talk, say something? Sitting there like a dummy the whole day long! As the light fell away, old Mr Mangan's eyes appeared to take on an unusual brightness. In the fast darkening kitchen they seemed to him like two pinpoints of white fire. He got up from the sofa and took down the tin blower from the fire, and the murmurous noises beneath the grate suddenly ceased. He heard his mother cough. At that moment he exclaimed aloud, as though he were talking to the old man, 'I wish I could get away to sea too.' Mr Mangan seemed to be looking directly at Peter now. The boy got up and drew a chair nearer to his grandfather. He stared into the old man's face. There was something vacant and idiotic in that persistent stare, the way he sat there so limp and helpless, his mouth half open, continually snuffing up his nose. Mr Mangan was already on the threshold of a long journey, memory was reined in, his spirit was rising in that very chair. Suddenly his expression changed. Peter sat back in his chair. It was as though a sort of impotent rage had flashed itself there, imprisoning him, so that he could not start off on that long journey. All the power in him seemed to have rushed to the eyes, so intensifying their almost frenzied stare.

'Sits there slobbering all the time,' thought Peter, as he watched the saliva trickle down the old man's chin. He put a hand on the old man's knee. At once, as though there was hidden in that touch a kind of magic essence, the expression changed again, the vacant idiotic stare returned. It was as if Peter's hand had suddenly turned a sort of key, had freed his grandfather from this prison in which he sat. When Peter touched Mr Mangan's knee, he thought he had touched a slab of stone. He wanted to shout, 'What on earth are you staring at, Grand-dad? What are you staring like that for?' He turned round and looked out of the window again. Yes, what was his grand-dad continually staring at? Always staring, staring. Not a word from him. Had the stroke stricken him dumb? He remembered his mother writing and telling him the old man had had a stroke.

2

Mr Mangan could see Peter as clearly as he could see the window through which he stared. But he never thought of the boy. His thoughts were very far away now. Each day he had stared so, each day he had thought. It was as though his mind were imprisoned by clay; that with each throb of thought, which had to be dug out with pain and labour, the clay gradually crumbled away. And as the clay crumbled, so the light slowly filtered in. He was like a man working at a great bank, under which is hidden something he has long lost, and has suddenly remembered. So Mr Mangan's mind worked slowly, and as the world of the past slowly took shape, took the breath of life, the warmth of blood and flesh, so the world of the present slowly descended lower and lower. Peter watched his eyes. 'How bright they are!' he thought. 'Like a cat's when the darkness comes.' He could see into his grandfather's mouth. He heard his slow breathing. Suddenly he exclaimed, 'Grand-dad!' but Mr Mangan was seventy years away in the flesh, breathing his youth, leaving behind him in the high-backed chair a crumpled heap from which life had fled, something that had finished its journey-work, a small, yellowish face, the years clearly traced in its many lines and wrinkles, the huge and helpless hands, the dangling legs. Once he coughed, and Peter drew his chair back to escape the expectoration that came from his mouth. He took the old man's big handkerchief from the arm of the chair and wiped his mouth. The mouth moved in a most peculiar way, as though expressing a thanks of its own. Peter got up. He stood with his back to the fire watching the slow movement of Mr Mangan's right hand. He stared down at his big skull. 'How old he is!' he said, half aloud. 'No wonder Mother is fed up. And

Dad too. Having to take him down there every Friday slobbering like he does.'
He laughed. Could his grandfather hear him? Mr Mangan's eyes seemed to
change from white fire to red. In the darkness they appeared to have
assumed a liquidity, and Peter imagined them to be two little pools of red
water.

*Anthony Mangan was sitting by his father in the doorway of their stone
cottage. His father was telling him that it were best for him to be up and off
out of it, because he remembered that his wife had died on the roadside, and it
were best, he went on, that Anthony should get up and go away. Right out of the
country. Anthony was crying and saying he could not go. He could not leave his
mother, even though she were dead and now lying on that deal table in the little
front room. His father stroked his head, hearkening to him, saying there was
nothing else to do. Above their heads they could see the hot July sun. He watched
his father wipe the sweat from his forehead. A great weariness seemed to come
upon him as he sat there, outside the house he had built with his own strong
hands. 'You must up and go because times are bad now and it is not right that
a strong healthy boy should sit around here where there is nothing to see, nor
do, and what can I do? Bury your good mother as is right and just. No more.'*

A drop fell from Mr Mangan's eye, but Peter did not see it. He was busy
poking the fire. The kitchen was now in complete darkness excepting for the
sort of mad light that danced on the opposite wall as the fire took hold and
the flames roared up the chimney. He stood listening to the tick of the
clock. Soon his father would be home from work. He would tell him about
everything that had happened. Yes. He would tell him everything. Even about
Hanrahan, and Brother Twomey. His dad was kind. He had said, 'Well,
it happens and that's all. Now you best get settled down and help here a bit.'
Mr Mangan dribbled again, the white slobber hanging to his lower lip.
'Grand-dad!' Peter said with disgust, knowing the old man did not hear, did
not care. He breathed slowly, heavily, like a horse.

*'What can one do now, Anthony? Nothing. Look at me.' And he had looked
into his father's eyes. The eyes of an honest man. They were blue and as clear as
spring water. His father had a wart under his nose. 'I want to see my mother,'
he said to his father. They got up and entered the house. Anthony, seeing his mother,
cried, and his father thought, 'There! There lies the work of good men.' He
laughed then, so that Anthony turned round, tears running down his cheeks. His
mother lay between the sheets, like a wraith, her sunken cheek-bones made her
look as though she were grinning at him. Anthony touched her face with his
tiny hand. Touching it, he felt its coldness, and it seemed to him as though that
face had never been, had never existed within his memory. He could not remember. And his father said, 'That's how it was. You were away with Kelty in his
boat. You remember. That's how it was. And your good mother picked off that*

white road.' Anthony looked at his mother, then slowly he turned his head and said to his father, 'Was Mother taken ill that suddenly?' His father did not answer, but was thinking in his quiet mind. 'Yes. Taken ill like so many others with an illness that only evil blew out from its stinking nostrils. Your mother starved,' he said. 'We all starve. You up and away from here, my good son.'

The old man leaned forward in his chair, his mouth was wide open. 'Ah! Ah!' The sounds came from the back of his throat, and Peter stared at him. Then above there was a knocking upon the floor. He ran into the lobby and called up, 'Calling, Mother?' 'The post,' Mrs Fury cried. Peter went along the lobby. There was a letter lying there. He saw the American stamp, and the postmark – New York. He ran upstairs and dashed into his mother's room.

'A letter from New York,' he said. The draught swung the door to.

Mr Mangan slowly moved his right hand until it reached the edge of the arm of the chair. It slid off, falling heavily on to his knees.

'But leave my mother now, Father?' he said. 'How can I go? I love her.' He felt his father's strong hand upon the back of his neck. He was stroking the back of his head. He thought, looking at the still face, 'His hand is strong and warm.' The room was cold. It seemed as though life could not hold under that roof now. No place for either of them. 'You're shivering, Anthony,' his father said. They went into the kitchen. They sat down, watching the turf smoke curl up the chimney. Anthony was thinking. He could still see in his mind's eye the sunken jaws of his mother, as though she were grinning at him, as though she were saying behind her silence, behind her cold, ice-like frigidity, 'I am out of it. You are not. You are still tied to things.' As though behind that empty face some spark of life had yet remained, lying hidden, so that at the moment of his looking it had sprung forth, tracing that cool dead face into that of a grinning monkey. He could not shut out from his mind those sunken jaws. They seemed to mock him, mock his father. As if his mother had died still retaining some essence of her living spirit, harbouring it, so that when they looked down upon her and thinking her dead they were disarmed, and then it confronted them, seizing them in their loneliness, in their bitterness of soul. Anthony was certain his mother's jaws had slightly trembled even as he watched her. His father tapped his knee. 'I know it's hard,' he said. 'But it's the end. You pack your things and go. It is not fair. To your dead mother or to me.' He gripped his father's hands. 'And the rest of your life a barren wilderness. Think, Father, I am your son and I love you.' He was certain he heard his father sob of a sudden, though it may have been the rising wind outside.

Peter came downstairs. He went up to the mantelpiece to get a match. He lit the gas. As he turned round to look at his grandfather he was certain that the old man's face shuddered, like a leaf suddenly disturbed after long lying in the road, shuddered and seemed to change colour. 'Perhaps I only fancy it, though,' Peter thought. 'It's the light, that's what it is.' A quarter after five. His father would be here any minute now. Where was Aunt Brigid? If only she were here. He liked the house best when Aunt Brigid was there. He did not feel so embarrassed, so conscious of the secret shame which he could not efface from his mind. It lay there like a festering sore. He began to lay the table afresh for the evening meal, passing to and from the back kitchen with cloth and plates and knives and forks, making a great noise as he placed these on the table. There was no sound in the kitchen save the heavy breathing of his grandfather. 'Still staring,' he said, and rushed to the window. He pulled the blind down savagely, so that it tore at the side. 'Stop staring, you old fool!' he was crying in his mind. 'Now you can't stare any more.' The old man did not move.

'In the morning,' his father was saying. 'The roads are clear, the roads are good. Just after the rising. You can go on until you get to Heggerty's place, then stop for a while, but not too long. Our people are such a kind that they hate us to outstay our welcome. Make for Cromarstown, for well beyond it things are a little better than in these parts. Perhaps if you keep up your spirit and walk long enough you'll get sight of Cork city one fine morning. Keep a letter always in the box for me, my son. I think you'd best go tomorrow. Now it's late. Bed-time. You get some supper and go on up to your room.' Anthony got up from his chair, saying, 'Not hungry, Dad.' He remembered how his father had laughed, 'for it's the first time I ever heard anybody say they weren't hungry for many a bright day.' Anthony stood by the kitchen door, watching his father as he poked at the peat in the fire. His shoulder outraged the white wall against which he leaned, for it was milk-white. 'Lean off that wall,' his father said angrily. He went to bed, but he did not sleep. For hours he sat looking out of the window, feeling the wind upon his face, his mind far away, his eyes down in that room, staring into his mother's face. 'I can't go,' he said, 'I can't go,' and was seized by a sudden longing that swept upon him like a flood. He ran down to his father.

'Please,' he said. 'Please, I can't go. Let me stay here. My mother ... I ...' How his father changed! He stood up and caught him under his chin, slowly raising his face. 'Look at me! Are you my son? Is this the first time I have asked? Are you the only one? Or are there not many hundreds like you, their parents dead, their parents wounded, flung out on the roads like dogs? Must I tell you that you must go? As you love the mother in that room, I ask you, I beg you to go. You are young and strong. I am old. You have your whole life before you. Why stay? But remember this – remember it to your dying day. Your mother. Imprint it upon your mind, so that nothing shall ever wipe it out, your mother on that road, that white road. Dead, from hunger.' His voice rose to a high pitch. 'Oh Jesus Christ! From hunger.' Anthony knelt down and clutched his *father's legs, crying, 'Father, Father! Is that it? Is that Mother's illness? Oh, Father!'*

Peter ran from the back kitchen. He had heard a peculiar sound. 'Grandfather! Grand-dad!' Anthony Mangan was crying. It was the first time that Peter had ever seen him cry. What had he suddenly remembered? But could he remember? Could he even think? That old man with the idiotic face, the staring eyes that seemed to him like little balls of fire. 'Grand-dad! Grand-dad!' He clutched the old man by his arms, crying in his mind, 'I must tell Mother, I must tell Mother. Oh, Grand-dad!' He pulled out his own clean white handkerchief. He wiped Mr Mangan's face. 'Grand-dad!' he said again; but Mr Mangan evinced no sign, he did not stir. It was as if his mind hung, perilously suspended over the twin abysses of past and present, the one fighting against the other, all that represented his past seeking to tear away all that personified the present, from that high-backed chair, that prison in which he sat. 'Grand-dad!' 'I wonder if he is ill again,' Peter was thinking, for the old man was sweating . . .

'Hunger. Go to bed, Anthony,' his father commanded. His manner had changed. He had become stern. 'I'll call you just at daybreak tomorrow. Father Manion will look to you, him as will put your mother into the earth. Remember, Anthony, remember what sends you out, what leaves me alone, what puts your mother into the earth. Never forget it.'

'No, Father. No, Father. Good-night.'

The sun was riding high when he woke. Not a breath of wind. From his window he could see right across the rolling green plain that led to somewhere he had never known, would never know, for his direction would be direct south. His father was up before him, now stirring the oats in the black swinging pan. Anthony shivered as he went down the bare wooden stairs and so into the little room to steal a glance at his mother. He could hear a sort of low murmur in the kitchen now, it sounded to him like music, but music he had never heard before. His father was saying his morning prayers as he stirred the pot. Anthony drew away the sheet from his mother's face and looked at her. With her he had played, had said his morning and night prayers, with her he had wandered in the lanes on the warm summer evenings, in the cold afternoons of autumn and winter, sticking, and hunting for eggs whilst his mother broke the wood across her knee. With her he had walked with heavy sack and basket that often threatened to defeat his weak frame. Then his father would meet them on the road and take the sack on to his own back. With her he had eaten at table, taken milk and potatoes. 'Mother!' he said, 'Mother!' His father was behind him, a hand in the air; trembling, it gripped him. He was rushed into the kitchen. 'Father,' he said, and looked at him as they sat across the bench by the window. Why did his father seem in such a hurry to get him away?

Why had he such impatience, when he wished to look upon his mother's face for the last time? 'Eat now,' his father said. Anthony ate his porridge. They went and stood by the door. 'Your things,' his father said. 'Yes, Father!' He could not hold back his tears as he ran upstairs. He put on his heavy coat and woollen cap, and slung the black canvas bag over his shoulder. They stood looking at each other, the father saying, 'God take care of you now, Anthony,' but Anthony did not seem to hear the words, he was looking through and beyond his father at the cold dead face of his mother. There was something urgent and compelling in his glance, his eyes lighted up with a sort of frenzy.

'Mother! Mother!'

'Come,' his father said. They went into the room for the last time.

Anthony bent down and kissed the still mouth. He could feel his father's impatient hand upon his shoulder. He turned away, brushing his eyes with the sleeve of his coat. 'I'll walk with you a little way,' his father was saying into his ear. They left the house. As he stepped outside the door, Anthony was conscious of a change so sudden and so violent that he looked up with a pained expression into his father's face. He turned round and stood staring at the house. This thing about which his father talked, this thing that licked the land like a ravenous wolf. What did it mean? His eyes wandered up and down the white wall of the stone cottage. One took oneself away, he was thinking. His father said, 'Come now.' They walked slowly away. When one left one's home, one took with one breath and spirit, all the life that had spread itself about the house in years, one gathered it up, memories, faces, impressions, gestures, one gathered them up like one gathered one's clothes into a bag. They reached the top of the lane. The long white road was dusty. 'Here's the road,' his father said, with an expression almost amounting to horror upon his face as his eyes looked right and left. 'The road,' he said, and Anthony knew he was thinking of his mother, and how he had found her lying on that road, quite still, quite peaceful. 'And multiply it by ten thousand thousand,' his father shouted with great rage, as though some sort of poison lurked beneath its white surface. 'You take this way,' his father said. 'Yes, Father!' He held back. The road held him, his two feet seemed to cling, leech-like, to the stones. His head was turned south, his body inclined a little so that his father could see his bag well secured upon his shoulder. But his feet refused to move. They seemed endowed with a life of their own, separate from his living body. His father held out his two hands. Anthony gripped them. 'Good-bye.' He turned away. His father did not move. He walked on. Then he turned round. He shaded his eyes from the hot sun and looked back up the road. His father was still standing there. He put his two hands to his mouth, cupped them, and shouted, 'Good-bye, Father.' The other waved his hand. He was soon swallowed up in clouds of dust. He turned again. The figure had vanished. His father had gone into the house again. He went on. By a great open ditch he suddenly stopped, saying, 'Oh! Oh!'

'Grand-dad!' Peter said. The old man was sitting bolt upright. The expression upon his face changed again. Peter, looking at him, wondered why he had said 'Oh!' Mr Mangan's body began to resume with a painful gradualness its former position, shoulders bent, head low upon them, and a little to one side. Peter put his right arm back on to the arm of the chair. Mr Mangan, after that slow and painful excursion into the past, closed his eyes and sighed. Anthony Mangan had become 'him' once more. 'Him' that slobbered and suffered his helpless person to be carried from his bed to the kitchen, to be part carried and part dragged to the little Post Office at the bottom of Hatfields, so that his daughter, 'a splendid woman', might receive his pittance in order to further entrench against the hazards of the economic tides. Peter, after making him comfortable, wiped the sweat from his forehead.

3

Mrs Fury had fallen asleep, and her last thought had been 'I wonder where Brigid could have got to?' She had an idea that her sister would call on Maureen, and was sure she would visit the 'other pair'. What a fool she had been ever to say a word about Desmond! Then she reflected. No. Perhaps she had carried secrecy too far. She had not yet forgotten her sister's caustic remarks about her silence and her own complete ignorance of Peter's being in Cork, and within a stone's throw of her own house. No, this silence, this secrecy had taken its due toll. Then she fell asleep, utterly weary. She did not wake again until her husband came back from work. Mr Fury went straight upstairs, without changing. He sat down by the bed in his oil-smeared clothes.

'How are you, Fanny?' he asked.

The woman sat up in the bed. 'Oh! I'm all right!' she said. 'I'll be up tomorrow. Dr Dunfrey said I could get up tomorrow.'

'That soon? What was wrong?' he asked her.

She noticed the puzzled look he wore.

'Sometimes one takes to bed just to get a little peace,' she said.

'Oh!' The man got up, but Mrs Fury immediately said, 'Sit down.'

'I want to get these bloody things off,' growled Mr Fury, and he pulled at his greasy trousers. He sat down again.

'About Peter!' Mrs Fury said suddenly. Mr Fury looked at her.

'Well, what about him? Something else up now?'

'No. I talked to the boy this morning. I want you to look after him now,' she went on. 'I'm sick of it.'

'Oh aye!' exclaimed Mr Fury. So she had had a talk with him! And what was he to do with the lad? He said slowly, 'And what do you want me to do with him?'

'Get him to work, of course. Can't you get him to sea?' Mr Fury now looked really astonished. Here was a sudden change in the situation. Real capitulation. Get him a job.

'Haven't we had enough of the family at sea? There's one away now. Is that all he sat at the desk for seven years for? To go to sea?' Then he turned his head and looked away out of the window. He was thinking fast. Why, that fellow Mulcare. Of course, just the very thing. But . . . a sudden pause in the thought. He swung round again.

'I don't want Peter at sea,' exclaimed Mr Fury. 'Surely after the money that's been spent on him he ought to put up a better show than that. Besides, if I *did* get him a job, I could only get him below. I don't want that, Fanny. I've had thirty-odd years in the stokehold. On deck, that's different. But listen to me, can't we talk over this some other time? Why all this sudden haste?' Yes, why all this hurry? This was a climb down and no mistake. In fact, he was quite unable to understand it. Anyway, he hadn't heard a word about the reasons for the boy suddenly leaving the college. Why shouldn't he know? He was the lad's father. He had a right to know. He made as if to speak, then drew back. No. He couldn't ever ask her now. He would get it out of Peter himself. He knew she had heard from the Principal and had destroyed the letter. That was one of Fanny's failings. Keeping things to herself. She had been like that all her life. Hiding things. Now that he was working ashore he was beginning to find things out. Some were quite silly. Not even a child would conceal them. Well, it was just part and parcel of the woman. He supposed she would never alter.

'You know why I want him out of the house,' the woman said.

'Want him out of the house!' exclaimed Mr Fury.

'Yes. Look here, Denny, just think it over. Isn't it nearly time we had some peace? After all these years. Isn't it time we got to understand each other? All these years at sea I've hardly seen anything of you. I've tried; I can't do any more than that.'

'Well,' thought Mr Fury, 'that's honest, anyhow.' He took the sweat-rag out of his pocket and wiped his hands on it. Then he leaned over the bed and embraced his wife.

'All right, Fanny,' he said. 'Good enough! I know a chap who'll get Peter fixed up in a jiffy. Now I must go and get changed.' He crossed the room, opened the door, then suddenly stopped. 'I see you had a letter from Anthony,' he called across to her. 'How is the lad?'

'Oh, he's getting on well now. He hurt his heels. He'll be coming home on the next available boat, so he says. That will be one more landed on me.'

'Is that why you want Peter out of the house?'

'I don't know,' she said. The man stood there waiting, but Mrs Fury remained silent. Then he went downstairs. So she had heard from Anthony! He would never have known had not Peter told him about the letter. He had had to ask her even about that. 'Oh well! I'm glad he's not so badly off as I thought. Aye! Fanny's certainly surprised me. Fancy wanting Peter out of the way! The lad she has idolized. Well, well!' The thoughts remained with him. Even during his ablutions he kept thinking over his wife's remarks. After he had changed into his ordinary clothes he went into the kitchen. Peter had made the tea and laid the table.

'You get your tea, Peter,' he said. 'I'm taking up something to your mother.'

'Yes, Dad,' Peter said.

Mr Fury took the wooden tray from the cupboard, placed a cloth on it, then cups and saucers, a teapot, and some newly made toast. This was the first time he had ever carried up a meal to his wife. She had never been ill. It seemed strange to him that he should be carrying this tray upstairs, and that his youngest son should be eating alone at the table. A son head and shoulders over himself. He felt dwarfed, insignificant. He went upstairs, saying, 'Close the door, Peter, and watch the fire.'

'Yes, Dad.' He watched his father go upstairs.

'Well, Denny,' said Mrs Fury, 'this is unusual.' He put down the tray, saying, 'Yes, it is, isn't it?' He poured out tea.

'Here y'are, Fanny! Peter made the tea, and here's some toast.' He handed the cup to his wife and placed the plate of toast on the chair at her side.

'Dad must have his tea,' remarked Mrs Fury, as she stirred vigorously her own cup of tea.

Mr Fury nodded his head. Yes, certainly, they must not forget 'him'. He got up and went to the door.

'Peter!' he called. 'Peter!' The boy came to the foot of the stairs.

'Tell him it's in the oven,' said Mrs Fury.

'Peter!' called Mr Fury down the stairs. 'Your mother says to give your grand-dad his tea. It's in the oven.' Then he banged the door.

'That lad has grown into a fine fellow, hasn't he, Fanny?'

Mrs Fury supped her tea. 'Yes,' she said, between sups, 'he has.'

'Has Brigid been in?' asked Mr Fury.

'Haven't seen her yet.'

'Indeed!' Mr Fury put his cup down and took out his pipe. Immediately Mrs Fury said, 'The window, Denny.' 'All right.' He got up and opened the window.

'Well, Brigid's a caution,' he began. 'Out all day. Wonder when she'll be back?'

Mrs Fury said she didn't know.

'She's got a nose better than any fox,' exclaimed Mr Fury.

'I hope she won't be held up here, Denny,' Mrs Fury said.

Of course not. All those rumours were just silly. There was no more fear of a strike coming than there was of his dropping dead that very minute.

'Denny!' Mrs Fury stammered.

'It's right, Fanny,' he went on. 'It's all a lot of talk. By the way, that young fellow I was telling you about is coming along one evening. I hope you'll see him. Mulcare's a nice lad. He was with me on the *Ballisa*. His old father's a lawyer in Dublin.'

'A lawyer!'

'Aye, a lawyer. Quite a big chap, too, from what I heard about him. Seems they had a row.'

'Indeed! Is that the young man you had in mind when I mentioned Peter?'

'Yes, of course!'

'I'd like to see him,' said Mrs Fury. She put the cup and plate on the tray. 'I'm tired,' she said, and lay back.

'All right. You go to sleep. You'll be as right as rain tomorrow.' He gathered the things on to the tray, and went downstairs. As soon as he reached the kitchen he exclaimed, 'Why, Peter! What's wrong?'

'Nothing,' Peter said. 'It's the way Grand-dad slobbers and messes about. It made me vomit. I had to go outside.' The boy wiped his eyes. Mr Fury pushed Mr Mangan further into the corner.

'Your grand-dad's a bloody old nuisance,' Mr Fury said. He took the handkerchief that was pinned to the side of Mr Mangan's chair. He wiped the old man's face.

'How do, slobberer?' he said. Peter laughed. Mr Fury went into the lobby and came back with the evening paper. He got out his spectacles and settled himself down to read. Peter sat watching him turn the pages. 'Now is the time,' he thought. He went over to his father and pulled the paper away. 'Dad,' he said, 'I'm sorry about what happened at the college. Could you get me away to sea?'

'College! Sea! What are you talking about? Why, I don't even know why you left the college,' said Mr Fury. He gripped his son's hand and pulled him down on to the sofa beside him. 'I don't know a single thing,' he said once more.

'Mother knows.'

'But what's that got to do with it? Your mother never tells me anything.' Yes, why shouldn't he know? 'Well, haven't you got anything to say? Look how upset your mother is. I don't give a hang myself . . .'

'I can't tell you,' Peter said.

Mr Fury said, 'Oh!' he kicked the paper into the middle of the kitchen. And that was the result of Fanny's control! Couldn't get a word out of the lad. His face went suddenly red.

'Did your mother tell you not to say anything to me?'

'No, Dad!' Peter could not look into his father's face. There was a pained expression upon it. That shame stole upon him once again.

'Look here, Peter! I'm just a rough-and-ready man. I don't put on any airs. I don't ask questions. Not one of you children can say I ever had anything against you. Can you, now?' Peter looked him full in the face. 'No, Dad,' he said. There was something so earnest, so frank about the way in which he spoke, that Mr Fury got up and pulled Peter with him. They stood facing each other. Peter wanted to smile, but he controlled himself. What was his father going to say to him?

'Listen!' began Mr Fury. 'Your mother wants me to get you a job going to sea. But I have had enough experience of it to know that it's no good. It's no life at all. When I was the same age as you I made a mistake, just as you will be doing now if it's the sea you mean to follow. I tell you straight to your face that I don't want you to go to sea.' Suddenly, for some unexplainable reason, the man turned away and stared at Mr Mangan. Yes, he had made a mistake, and he had never forgotten it. It had followed him down all the years of his life. Fanny had never ceased to remind him of it. He turned to Peter again.

'I must talk to your mother about it. I'm not going to ask you any questions. I'm not even going to ask, as I have a right to do, why you left that college. If your mother had mentioned it to me, I would have put my foot down at once. It's absurd. Waste! That's what I say. Waste of time and money.' Mr Fury felt he had said enough. He sat down on the sofa and took up the evening paper. Peter still remained standing in the middle of the kitchen. Would he ever escape this sense of shame?

After a while, Mr Fury folded the newspaper up and threw it into the corner. 'Don't stand there like that!' he shouted, and Peter jumped as though with sudden fright. He went upstairs to his room. He called in to his mother:

'I'm going now!'

'Where?'

'To the chapel, Mother.'

'Very well. Don't you be late.'

'No, Mother! I'll be right back.' Mrs Fury put down the letter she was reading. She could hear her son moving about the room. What was he doing?

'Is your father downstairs?'

'Yes, Mother. He's reading the evening paper,' Peter called back.

'Come here.' He went to his mother's room. He saw the letter lying on the bed.

'When you go down. tell Father Moynihan that I'm coming to see him tomorrow.'

'Yes, Mother.' The boy stood hesitating.

'All right!' exclaimed the mother. 'You'd better go now. Have you got your Prayer Book?' Peter replied that he had.

'Tell your father to come up.' The woman lay down again and picked up the letter. She heard the street door close. Peter had gone out. She held the letter in her hand. She had read it three times. Now she began to read it again. It was a long letter from her son Anthony.

'Dear Mother, – Well, at last I'm out of hospital. But I'm on crutches. Can you imagine Anthony on crutches? If ever anybody had forecast this humiliating position for me I would have trounced them roundly. How are you, Mother? Well, I hope. I feel much better myself. though I can put neither foot to the floor, and the doctor says they'll take a pretty time healing. But I'm more than glad to be out again. I'll be coming home on the *Aurelia.* We should dock about the twenty-third of the month, providing the Atlantic is kind to her. She's an old boat. It seems funny; I'll actually be a passenger on this ship. Something new for me. I got your letter while I was in hospital. They sent it on from the ship. How is Dad? And Maureen? I often think Maureen was silly to go and marry that fellow Kilkey. He's . . .' the remainder of the sentence had been scratched out. 'Mike Nolan wrote telling me that Desmond has been made a foreman ganger. You never said anything about it in your letter. I suppose you still keep him out of the house. Honestly, Mother, I can't understand why you do this. In the end it will only recoil on you. However, I'm not going to start probing into the family history. Might do Aunt Brigid out of a job . . .' Mrs Fury laughed again. There was another long scrawly line after this which she could not make out. The writing was too illegible. She turned up the wick of the lamp, her curiosity aroused. What could it be? She put the page against the lamp globe. After a close examination she discovered it to be – 'Friday. Half-past ten p.m. I couldn't finish this letter last night. My feet began to pain badly. I won't be sorry when I am up and doing again, I can tell you. I just hate this going about on crutches. I used to laugh at Grand-dad when he had his four years ago, but I never thought I should be on them myself. By the way, how is Kilkey getting along? Is he still with the Porter company? How is old Possie from next door? Still wearing his Orange tie, I suppose. A funny family, aren't they?' Another scrawl. This was the beginning of a sentence scratched out, blotting the page. 'I've just come on board the *Aurelia*, straight from the hospital. I came on a stretcher. I was disappointed. I was hoping to see something of New York on the way down, but they wouldn't even let me sit up for a minute. This ship is sailing on Wednesday morning at half-past nine. As it takes an old tub like this about ten days to do the run from New York to Gelton, I reckon I should be docking at the Branston on Friday week. I won't be sorry. Oh! I never told you how it happened. It was rather funny, in a way.

'When we reached New York on the outward trip we had come through a three-day blizzard, and there wasn't a single man who wasn't glad to get the shelter of that harbour for a few days. But the cold only seemed to increase. They say it is the worst winter they've ever experienced in these parts. It was something below zero, I can't remember how much. But working on that deck was foul, I can tell you. Even the longshoremen, hardened to it as they are, even they began to feel it pinching after two days' work on the cargo. When sailing day came, the whole of the deck was coated with a thin film of ice. The ship really looked beautiful, but it wasn't beautiful to work on that deck. When the sun came out, it made things worse. We had to wash down fore and aft right away. We were supposed to be sailing at half-past five that evening for Baltimore.' ... Mrs Fury paused and looked up. 'What a bad writer Anthony is!' she was saying to herself. 'He must be the worst writer in the family.' She read on: 'I was sitting in my room when the bosun came along and called for two hands to work for'ard on the wireless. The men didn't respond. In fact, one of them said that he would only go up if he got a tot of rum. The bosun said he would arrange about that, but this man was stubborn and refused to budge from the fo'c'sle unless the rum was brought right away. "Think any man is going to go up that bloody mast in this weather?" The bosun was angry. He said, "Somebody's got to go up, we can't sail unless that wireless is rigged up, and that's all about it." Nobody said a word. Then from the corner bunk a man named Cash came. He said if another man volunteered he would go up. "All right," the bosun said, "there are already two men aft, they're waiting. They can't do anything until somebody moves out of here." Then he looked at me. "I'll go up, bosun," I said to him. He smiled. "Good, Fury," he said. "Good man." The three of us went out.'

Mrs Fury sighed. 'My heavens!' she exclaimed aloud. Of course he would. Just like his father! What a mad harum-scarum lot the Furys really are! And what's he got for it? A pair of smashed heels. 'It was just growing dusk. I started to shinny up the rigging, Cash following behind me. Suddenly I remembered that I had left one of my gloves in the fo'c'sle, but I couldn't go back, and I shouted to the bosun, "My glove! I've left it in my bunk."

'"Can't do that job with a glove, Fury," he said. "Impossible. It won't take you but a brace of shakes to shinny up there and get that job done." Then I climbed higher. It was bitterly cold. I remember I stopped to get my breath, as there was a wind bearing down on us, one of those icy east winds. I could hear Cash breathing under me. "Climb, man!" he was shouting, "climb! Can't stand here all the bloody day!" I went on. When I reached the cross-trees Cash shouted, "Hang on for a spell." I was glad to. I hung on like grim death, now feeling sorry I had gone up at all, as there were older and more experienced men sitting by that bogie in the fo'c'sle warming their own backsides. But the bosun is such a fine man, I hated to back out. By God! it was cold up on those cross-trees. I knew we would have to put a move on, for the light was going fast, and when I looked down I could only see the dim outlines of her deck, whilst the derricks seemed to have altered their shapes entirely. But I never looked down again.

'It was the first time I had ever been aloft in the *Turcoman.* You couldn't imagine what a ship looks like from her cross-trees, let alone her truck top, which was where I had to shinny, and quick too. I could hear the bosun shouting below, and a sort of ghostly voice aft. It must have been the man up the mainmast. Suddenly I screamed. I had reached the nest, and had gripped the iron ring at the back of the mast. I don't know why I screamed, I can't remember it clearly enough. But I did know that I could not move an inch higher, that Cash was bellowing just beneath me, that my right hand was kind of glued to this iron ring. I couldn't let go. I shouted them, "My hand's stuck. I can't move." Cash shouted up, "Christ, man!" That's all I know. Then I fell. I remember hitting Cash, one foot touching a derrick and glancing off it quickly like a bullet. But that's all. It was awful. I hit the deck, and I felt as though somebody had pushed red-hot spikes into my heels and right up into my whole body. I woke up in hospital. Later the doctor told me all about it. My hand had become frost-bitten, and he said another five minutes and I would have lost it. Honestly, Mother, it's impossible to imagine how cold it was that evening. It all happened in fifteen minutes. The bosun wrote to me before the ship sailed. He was awfully cut up about it. The doctor said if Cash had not been right underneath me I would have been killed outright, though how Cash broke my fall I don't know. Anyhow it's all over now.' ... The letter dropped to the floor. She sighed. 'Yes. Thank God, it's all over! Thank the great God!' She leaned out of the bed and retrieved the letter from the floor. She put it inside her nightgown, but a second later took it out again, holding it to her mouth, murmuring, 'Anthony! Off that mast! Oh! ...' She held the letter to her mouth, kissing it. This was the nearest thing to flesh and blood. The face of her son seemed to gaze upon her from its now crinkled pages. She could see his blue eyes, his laughing mouth, his weatherbeaten face. 'Anthony! Anthony!' she kept repeating under her breath. She lay back, picturing the accident in her mind. What a frightful fall! A mere lad, too! Now he was coming home. Another mouth to feed. She lay back again. Again she opened the letter, her eyes wandering over its pages. 'Why, there's something else!' she exclaimed, and sat upright. She hadn't read it properly. 'I only hope that I'm not going to be stuck on these crutches for life. I should simply hate that, Mother.' Mrs Fury's heart seemed to miss a beat – 'for life!' 'That's the only thing that worries me, Mother. By the way, I am bringing you some Indian embroidery work for your birthday. I am sure you'll like it. I bought it off a bum in Galveston. Now I think I've said all there is to say, so I close with love to all at home, and beg to remain, Your affectionate son, Anthony.

'P.S. – I think you had better see them at the Shipping Office, as I understand that the allotment money ceases from the day of the accident. I'm not sure, Mother, but think it best you should see about it right away. I dare say I'll get some compo out of this lot.' She crushed the letter into a ball and then let it fall to the floor. She could hear Mr Fury mounting the stairs. 'Imagine it!' thought the woman. 'Just imagine it.' She picked up the crumpled letter and clutched it tightly in her hand. 'To think that the boy met with that accident nearly three weeks ago, and I only heard about it a few days ago. I shall certainly have something to say to Mr Lake about this.'

CHAPTER VII

I

'Here's the evening paper,' Mr Fury said. He sat down on the bed and pulled the newspaper from his pocket.

'Has Brigid come back yet?' asked Mrs Fury.

'No. Not yet. 'Spect she's ferreting about somewhere,' replied Mr Fury. 'Here you are.' He handed the newspaper to his wife.

'Thank you,' Mrs Fury said. She laid the paper down and looked at her husband. Mr Fury was completely dressed for the street.

'Are you going out, Denny?' asked the woman.

There was something puzzling about his manner, about the expression on his face.

'Yes,' Mr Fury said. 'I'm going out! That is, as soon as that lad gets back.' He pulled out his watch. 'Gone seven now.'

Mrs Fury suddenly thought, 'I shall be up tomorrow.' The very expression upon her husband's face seemed to have engendered the thought.

'Where are you going?'

'It's Federation night, Fanny. I thought you knew. It's every month.'

'Oh!' exclaimed Mrs Fury, and she looked towards the window. 'I hope that boy won't be long, then,' she added.

'Aye,' Mr Fury said. He got up from the bed and commenced to walk up and down the room. Mr Fury was worried, he was growing impatient. Why the devil didn't Postlethwaite knock? Mrs Fury picked up the newspaper and opened it.

'Where's the rest of it, Denny?' she asked, and Mr Fury came to a sudden halt in the middle of the room.

'Isn't it there? I must have left it downstairs. Hang it! I'll go and get it.' He turned towards the door, but Mrs Fury said it didn't matter.

At that moment somebody knocked at the door. The man sighed. 'It's Possie,' he said. 'He said he'd knock for me on his way down.' He looked anxiously at his wife, thinking furiously, 'Where the devil has that lad got to?'

'You'd best wait, Denny,' Mrs Fury said. 'Peter will be back any minute now. I wonder where Brigid is?' The knocking was repeated. Mr Fury shouted, 'Brigid! I suppose she's busy collecting stuff for her family history.'

He went out. Mrs Fury heard him open the door, and Mr Postlethwaite said, 'Hello, Fury! Ready?'

'Aye. Just a minute!' said Mr Fury. He went upstairs again.

'Fancy that lad being out all this time!'

He called downstairs, 'Can you wait a few minutes, Possie?' Then, just when he was giving up hope, a welcome sound came to his ears.

'Here's Maureen!' he said.

Mrs Fury said, 'You'd better go, then, Denny. Don't keep that man waiting at the door.' Mr Fury said, 'All right.'

Maureen was already mounting the stairs. Mr Fury met her on the landing. 'Your mother's not very well,' he said. 'Will you stay with her a while? Peter'll be back any minute. And your Aunt Brigid won't be long now.' He rushed down the stairs. When he reached the lobby he turned round, filled with a sudden inspiration.

'Has she been to see you?' he called up the stairs. 'Yes,' shouted back Maureen as she opened the front room door.

'Ah! Thought so!' Mr Fury said under his breath. 'Coming, Possie,' he said. He went into the kitchen. He took the outer sheet of the evening newspaper from his pocket, rolled it into a ball, and flung it into the fire. As he did so, he looked at the figure in the chair. Mr Mangan's long hands gripped the sides of his chair. His breast rose and fell. But for its gentle rise and fall it seemed as though the life in that figure, imperiously alone and lonely, had suddenly been stilled.

'Aye, slobberer!' exclaimed Mr Fury, 'you don't know the bloody fun you're missing.' He waited until the bundle of paper had burnt out. Then he joined Mr Postlethwaite in the street.

'Better catch the next car that comes along,' exclaimed Mr Postlethwaite. They hurried down the street. Mr Fury remained silent. He knew by now how punctual Mr Postlethwaite was, how he hated to be kept waiting. They stood a moment at the bottom of the street.

'Did you see what the paper says?' remarked Mr Postlethwaite.

'Aye, I did that!' replied Mr Fury. 'Take it from me, nothing's going to stop those miners coming out. I don't blame them anyhow, they're always being shit on.' Yes, of course he'd read it. But he wasn't going to have Fanny reading it. He felt pleased now that he burned the sheet of newspaper. 'The missus isn't well,' he went on. 'I . . .'

'See that lad of yours is home,' interrupted Postlethwaite.

'Yes.' Mr Fury had been hoping all along that Peter would not be mentioned. He looked at Mr Postlethwaite now, as if to say, 'Your sponge must be pretty dry.'

'What are you going to do with him?' asked Postlethwaite.

'Oh! I don't know.' Mr Fury hated talking about him. Probably make him an ambassador.'

'Here's our car.' said Postlethwaite. They walked to the end of the line, and stood waiting for the passengers to descend. The tram would then reverse and go towards town again. As they stood together on the kerb, watching the people descend into the road, Mr Fury's eyes caught sight of a buxom and heavily laden figure coming down the stairs from the upper deck. 'It can't be!' he was thinking. 'It can't be Brigid. Surely!' He brushed the idea from his mind.

Mr Postlethwaite said, 'It's clear now.' They stepped off the kerb. Mr Fury said, 'D'you reckon if those miners come out they'll want support?'

'Why not?' asked Mr Postlethwaite. 'Why not?'

Mr Fury cursed himself for such a silly question. Then he swung round as a hand touched his shoulder.

'Why, Denny!' exclaimed a voice. Mr Fury did not move. He stood there as though rooted to the very earth. He knew that voice. He didn't want to turn round. But now Mr Postlethwaite looked at him, a penetrating sort of look, and he turned round to face Aunt Brigid, newly arrived from town. She seemed hot and flustered. She carried parcels in each hand. The little finger of her right hand was tightly clasped round her bag handle. Under her left arm she clutched an umbrella.

'Well, Denny!' she exclaimed again. 'This is a surprise.' Mr Fury looked confused. Somehow the figure of his sister-in-law appeared to swell. It seemed to move towards him like a great wave. In another minute he must be smothered beneath this wave of flesh and parcels. Yes. It was a surprise. Just when he and Postlethwaite were on their way to the Union meeting. And, confound it! Aunt Brigid's coat had blown open, so that her bright green gown shone resplendent for all the world to see. And Mr Postlethwaite hated the very sight of green, orange being his favourite colour. Mr Fury cried in his mind – 'Damn! Damn!' It *would* happen like that. Miss Mangan's breath came short and sharp. At that moment Mr Postlethwaite, to Mr Fury's great surprise, relieved Aunt Brigid of her parcels and placed them on the edge of the footpath. Mr Fury said, 'Here, Brigid,' and took the remaining parcels from her and placed them beside the others. 'We're just going to the Federation meeting,' remarked Mr Fury, after what seemed a long and ominous silence. 'Aye, we were just catching this tram.'

Mr Postlethwaite looked from Aunt Brigid to Mr Fury. 'A nice how-d'you-do,' Mr Fury was thinking. Aunt Brigid! Anywhere but there, on that kerb, her coat wide open. He felt sure the sight of the green gown must have been almost harrowing to a man like Mr Postlethwaite. 'Button your coat, Brigid,' he said. 'It's a dirty night.' Aunt Brigid looked over her brother-in-law's head towards the garish lights of the Star and Garter. On such a night as this those lights seemed to have an almost magnetic power. They beckoned to her. She buttoned up her coat and asked:

'Denny! Will you have something warm before you go?' Her eyes wandered to Mr Postlethwaite. They remained focused upon this little man, dressed in his loud brown suit, yellow shoes, and bright blue collar and white tie. 'What a funny little man,' thought Aunt Brigid. As though unconsciously obliging, Mr Postlethwaite at that very moment removed his shining hard hat, revealing to the now astonished Miss Mangan his completely egg-shaped bald head, as if to say, 'Why not complete the circuit?'

'Thanks all the same, Brigid,' said Mr Fury. He was angry now. He could not conceal his vexation, the more so since the man from next door exclaimed with perfect aplomb, 'Go ahead, Fury. I'll wait.' It was positively humiliating. 'No!' It was almost a growl. 'We have to go to this Union meeting, Brigid. We're late already. Another time. Sorry. But you see ...' Mr Postlethwaite looked at his watch. 'Go ahead, Fury,' he said again. 'No!' This was too much. Caught between two extremes. Seemed to Mr Fury as though they had specially designed this meeting. Making a fool of him! He looked almost savage now. 'Won't you have one, then?' he asked. He looked at Mr Postlethwaite, his tone was almost pleading.

'No. Thanks all the same. You go ahead. I'll wait,' he said.

'All right, then.' Mr Fury picked up the parcels and said, 'Come along, Brigid!' Mr Postlethwaite said, 'I'll be waiting here.' Dennis Fury could make no reply. He was full, really full. They crossed the road. Mr Fury pushed against the swinging doors, and almost fell into the public bar-room! 'Phew!' he said. The place was crowded. Aunt Brigid, immediately behind, had now recovered her somewhat scattered self. As she sailed through at Mr Fury's heels she assumed a carriage almost regal.

'Right through to the snug, Denny,' she exclaimed. The man growled back a reply quite unintelligible to Miss Mangan.

Miss Mangan sat down and leaned back in her seat. She surveyed the room. Mr Fury, having put down the parcels, took a chair and sat opposite Aunt Brigid. She could see at once that he was ill at ease. She smiled at him now. It was indeed her hour of triumph. Her foresight, she felt, had been almost prophetic. Here was her brother-in-law, however uncomfortable he might be, here he was sitting right in front of her. And this man had once vowed, she remembered the incident quite clearly, he had taken a vow that he would never sit in a public with her. She almost beamed – her triumph was mirrored there for him to see. She put out a gloved hand, and raising her finger pressed the bell. Then she drew off her gloves, laid them on the table, and opened her coat. Mr Fury looked at her expansive bosom. Where in heaven's name had she got such a gown? A brighter, more tantalizing, more provocative green he had never seen. And to come to Hatfields like that! Hatfields was full of 'Billies'. Mr Fury thought, 'The Postlethwaites will talk about this for a week.' He felt sure that if Aunt Brigid lived in Hatfields for one month she would agree with him. Miss Mangan roused him from his momentary meditation. 'What are you having, Denny?' she asked. Mr Fury paused. The moment for complete capitulation had arrived. But for Postlethwaite he would never have been in this humiliating position. He now evaded her glance, and replied, looking absently at the big mirror over her head:

'I'll have a glass of bitter, Brigid.'

There. It was done now. He had broken his vow.

Aunt Brigid looked at him, little short of astonished at his reply. 'A glass of bitter! Good heavens, man! A dirty night like this!' 'And on such an occasion as this,' she added to herself.

'Oh no! Have something really warm. A tonic, Denny?'

'No, Brigid. I never take that stuff now,' replied Mr Fury. If ever he hated his sister-in-law he hated her now. He was almost certain this business had been deliberately planned.

'Stuff and nonsense!' exclaimed Aunt Brigid. 'You want something warm on a night like this. And you look as though you wanted it.' If that wasn't a sharp thrust, nothing was. The barman came in.

'Two small Irish,' she said. 'No water in one.'

The barman went out. Aunt Brigid, beginning now to feel painfully sensitive to Mr Fury's embarrassment, allowed her eyes to wander aimlessly around the room. The shelf full of bottles was one splash of colour. In the grate the fire blazed merrily, its murmurous noises almost seemed like a song, inviting one and all to partake of its warmth and welcome. The barman returned with the glasses and put them down on the table. He stood waiting. He looked boldly at Mr Fury. He knew Mr Fury, but his glance at the buxom woman was almost furtive. It expressed the momentary bewilderment of a man who has bumped into something new in the human species. He had never seen anything like Aunt Brigid before. Hence his bewilderment. Miss Mangan withdrew some coins from her bag and paid for the drinks. 'Thank you,' she said. The barman went out.

'Well, Denny,' she exclaimed, as she pushed over his glass. 'Well, here's all the best to you!' As though the spirit in his glass did not contain sting enough, she added, almost indifferently, 'It will do you good. You need it.' A direct affront to her sister.

Mr Fury, hesitating at first, now picked up his glass. His mind was torn between two alternatives. Here was this woman whom he had never liked, and outside, just across the way, Mr Postlethwaite was patiently waiting. So he thought. But Mr Postlethwaite had already gone. He didn't know whether to drink or not. Then Miss Mangan hesitated, the glass almost at her lips.

'For God's sake, Denny, drink it, man! It won't poison you.' Mr Fury drained his glass at one gulp, and then banged it down on the table. He looked the woman full in the face. 'I know what you're thinking, Brigid,' he said.

The woman put down her half-empty glass. 'What?' she asked. 'That Joe Kilkey is the ugliest-looking man that ever set foot out of Country Clare?'

Mr Fury sat back. He had certainly not expected this. It was a complete surprise. For a moment he could say nothing. Then he managed to gasp out:

'So you saw Maureen, then?' He wondered if she had already been up to Vulcan Street.

'Oh yes,' said Aunt Brigid, 'I saw her this morning. Poor girl!' The man jumped to his feet. This was surely going too far.

'And what the hell's wrong with Kilkey?' he asked rudely. 'To hear you talk, you'd think the girl was a martyr or something.'

Aunt Brigid smiled.'What an excitable man he is!' A Fury all over.

'Now, Denny,' she said, 'Don't be so silly.' Unseen, she rang the bell again. 'Why get excited over nothing? I say quite truly that I think Mr Kilkey an ugly man – a repulsive-looking fellow. He must be years older than Maureen. How in the name of heaven did the child come to marry him? Why, the man's nearly bald!' Before Mr Fury could make a reply the barman returned.

'Same again!' said Miss Mangan, and pushed the glasses forward, without looking at the barman. Her eyes seemed to pin Mr Fury to his seat, to set a seal upon his mouth. Not until the barman had gone did Mr Fury find his tongue. 'Ah! a lot of blather,' he said. 'Kilkey's all right. A good, honest chap. He mightn't have brains, of course. He's straight, just the same. A good worker. Well respected. He treats Maureen all right. She's lucky.' He now lowered his head so that his eyes took in the bright green and white of the linoleum on the floor. It was a kind of preparatory manoeuvre, for Mr Fury was now expecting a real tidal flow to emanate from that large lady opposite him.

'What made her go?' asked Aunt Brigid. 'I never saw such a change in a girl. She's really coarsened. Looks older. What did Fanny say?'

Mr Fury slowly raised his head.

'I don't know what you're talking about,' he said. She watched him fumble for nearly a half-minute at his vest pocket, in an endeavour to extract from it his gun-metal watch, which was attached to a long bootlace woven into a form of chain. But somehow the watch refused to be brought out. At last he gave it up. Miss Mangan did not realize it, but the glass of neat whisky had gone to Mr Fury's head. It was such a time since he had tasted anything as strong.

'No, I don't know what you are talking about, Brigid,' Mr Fury repeated. 'The girl wasn't influenced by Fanny or by me. She cleared off on her own accord. And, by Christ!' – he paused, as though in the next effort he were giving up his very soul – 'and, by Christ, I don't blame her! Her mother is as ambitious as any Pope.' His voice rose, the colour was mounting to his cheeks.

'That's what's wrong with Fanny,' he went on. 'She had too many hoity-toity ideas. She drives her children away from her. She calls it in-difference; says they're mean-spirited. The truth is, she has dominated them all her life, and now two of them are married she hates it bitterly. She can't dominate them any more. She's got an almost insane ambition. Where she gets it from, I don't know.'

'She ought never to have left Ireland,' interrupted Miss Mangan.

'Oh!' Mr Fury stood up and leaned forward until his face almost touched that of Miss Mangan. He was conscious of her red face, her fat neck, her enormous breasts, and of the strong scent of cheap perfume that emanated from her bosom.

'That's insulting, Brigid. I know now that you planned this. Tell me this. What the devil was she going to do with her life, stuck in a bloody old fishing village? Fanny has brains, she has ambition. Those two things have plagued her, and me, and her own children.'

'I think you are very rude,' protested Brigid, 'very rude, and most un-sympathetic. I don't see eye to eye with Fanny myself, but at the same time, I must admit, I admire her. She is, after all, my sister. And I simply will not sit here and hear you say those things.' Mr Fury lowered his eyes. Miss Mangan's form seemed to swell, to move forward, to shrink, to ascend; in fact, Aunt Brigid appeared to be doing a series of acrobatic feats. If he kept on looking he would see her pirouetting about the bar-room. Mr Fury tossed off his second glass of whisky.

Aunt Brigid now began to feel more at her ease. Her brother-in-law was indeed becoming expansive, almost to the point of embarrassment. She sat back again, resting her head against the wall. The wallpaper was bright yellow in colour, and upon its surface there ran riot a number of birds, large and weird-looking. They hung upon the branches of trees not less weird-looking. The birds looked down upon Miss Mangan's head with respect and approval. Mr Fury's hands were stretched across the table. Glancing down, Aunt Brigid's eyes came to rest upon two bright blue stars, tattooed stars, on the back of Mr Fury's hands. What a passion sailors had for getting themselves tattooed, and the most awful-looking designs seemed to be favoured amongst them. Dennis Fury had completely forgotten Mr Postlethwaite's existence, as indeed Mr Postlethwaite had clean forgotten his, for he was now sitting enraptured in the back row of the Mechanic's Hall listening to a fiery speech from one of the Union delegates. Likewise Miss Mangan, leaning her head on the wall, had forgotten Mr Fury. Her gaze, aimless and vacant, seemed to be concentrated upon space, the space between the green curtain and the ceiling. Behind the curtain she heard many voices, mostly the voices of men, and over the top of the curtain itself there hung, as though caught in space itself and held, a great cloud of smoke, from pipes and cigarettes. Occasionally somebody spat heavily, or cleared his throat. There then followed a slow scraping sound, as a foot ground into the sawdust upon the floor. Here, however, it was quiet, cosy, and warm. Anything seemed possible – such a cheery, well-lighted room.

'Have you heard why that boy failed?' asked Miss Mangan suddenly, and her eyes pinned themselves upon her brother-in-law's hands. Mr Fury sat up as though struck.

'What?'

'Denny! You must be getting deaf. Have you heard why that boy left the college?'

'I expect,' growled Mr Fury, 'I expect he was running round after women in the Mall. Surprised me he never once ran into you.' All propriety was at an end.

'Disgraceful! Denny! Disgraceful!' Miss Mangan had indeed grown suddenly pale. So that was why! That perhaps revealed why Fanny was so silent. She had questioned her, but her sister had refused to be drawn out.

'Aye,' went on Mr Fury. 'That's the result of her ambitions. It's all a bloody cod.' He got up from the chair. Slowly his head was clearing. He could even see Aunt Brigid much more clearly. On the other hand, this sudden revelation had served its purpose. It was as though Miss Mangan herself had taken a drop too much. But her bewilderment and confusion were accompanied by a feeling of shame. Was this true? Her mind held on to the question leech-like. Was this true? My word! What was all this? Mr Fury said slowly, 'I'm going home.'

Aunt Brigid remained fast in her seat. There was still something left unsaid. She leaned across the table, gripped Mr Fury by the coat, and pushed him down again.

'Sit down, Denny! You're getting excited. That whisky has gone to your head.'

'Oh no!' he said. 'Oh no! it hasn't!' Suddenly the room seemed to shake, as a voice, bronze-like, roared out, 'Time, gentlemen! Time.'

2

When Peter left the chapel of St Sebastian he walked slowly down the gravel path. He was like a man who has at long last got over a very disagreeable task. Now that he had been to Father Moynihan he felt better. The ordeal was over. He had listened carefully to the priest's advice. He stood now looking to right and left. It was turned seven o'clock. Suddenly he exclaimed, 'I'll go and see Maureen.' He crossed Ash Walk, turned left, and eventually found himself at the bottom of Price Street. Price Street, like Hatfields, was old property. It belonged to the railway company. A high wall ran along the full length of the houses. The back yards of fifty-two houses faced it. It did not end there, for at the end of Price Street it crossed an open space, and continued its way behind two huge leather warehouses. He walked up Price Street until he came to number thirty-five. He stood looking at the door, then shifted his glance to the curtains. Perhaps Maureen was in the parlour. Would she know him? It was such a long time since he had seen her. There was something pleasurable in the anticipation. He knocked on the door.

Would Maureen recognize his old knock? Three short taps. He expected the door to be opened, expected Maureen to exclaim, 'Oh, Peter! How are you?' To his surprise the door did not open. Perhaps they were out. He knocked again. Then he stood in front of the window and looked through. There might be a light in the kitchen. As he stood there staring through the opening in the curtains the next door opened, and a slatternly-looking young woman came out on the step. Peter did not hear this door open. He was too engaged in watching for a light in the kitchen. Perhaps they really were out. He turned towards the door, and caught sight of the woman. He could see her face quite clearly, as there was a lamp lighted between numbers thirty-five and thirty-seven. There was something bold and questioning in the glance she gave him. Feeling like a thief, he knocked again, this time with great force. He knew the woman was looking at him. He was certain he had heard somebody talking in the lobby. Surely they weren't actually in, and refusing to open the door! He looked at the woman again.

'Is Mrs Kilkey in, could you tell me, please?' he asked.

'I don't know,' the woman replied. She went in and banged the door. It was as though she had banged it directly in his face. Peter scratched his head. 'What a funny woman!' he thought. Once more he knocked. He was growing impatient, he imagined that every door in Price Street had suddenly opened, and that the people had all come out on their steps to stare at him. He exclaimed angrily, 'Damn them! Damn them!' He looked through the curtains again. The house seemed in complete darkness. And yet he was certain he had heard somebody talking in the lobby. Could it be that Mr Kilkey ... no – impossible. He pushed the idea from his mind. He moved back to the kerb and stared up at the house. No! There was no light in the upper rooms. He said to himself, 'They must be out.' He walked away. He was suspicious. Could they have possibly shut him out? He could not believe it of his sister. Kilkey, yes. Of course, Maureen might be different now. She was married. She was going to have a child by Mr Kilkey. He had heard his father talking about it. Desmond never once crossed his mind. It was as if this brother was truly lost, severed from the family for ever. 'I'll go round the back way,' he thought. He walked down the street, and passed into the entry. Here the darkness seemed more intense. He struck a match and held it to the first back door. But it was unnumbered. He went further up. At last! Here was a door with a chalked number. Seven. 'Good!' He would easily find number thirty-five. He stood before the door now. Suddenly he told himself that this action was mean. It implied that he was suspicious, that he was now certain they had refused to open the door to him. When he climbed the wall and looked up the yard, he nearly loosed his hold from sheer astonishment. The whole yard was brightly illuminated, as the kitchen blinds had not been drawn. He could see everything in the kitchen quite clearly. Two people were sitting at the table. The man had just laid down his newspaper. He now stared through the kitchen window as though he were somehow conscious of the presence of a figure on the wall. But he could not see Peter, for the boy was lying flat upon the wall. The woman was sitting directly facing the window. She was wearing a brown woollen jumper. Her elbows were on the table, her hands, locked together, supported her chin. She too appeared to be looking down the yard. It was his sister Maureen. He knew her at once. She was sitting beneath the gas-light. She was rapt and concentrated in her gaze. 'And she wouldn't open the door! And she knew I was there!' Peter swore under his breath. Then he raised himself on the wall, and dropped into the darkened entry. For a moment he stood there, looking up and down. There was something furtive in his very demeanour. Suddenly he said, 'Oh, damn them!' and set off up the entry at a sharp pace. When he came out into the space in front of the warehouses he stopped again, listening. The sounds of hammering came to this ears. He looked up at the light above his head. It threw a sickly yellowish patch of light into the dark area. 'Damn them!' he said again.

Maureen Fury had seen her brother. She was sitting sewing when he knocked. Her husband was sitting in the opposite chair, his feet upon the kitchen fender. Maureen plied busily with her needle. Occasionally the silence was broken by Mr Kilkey remarking, as he looked up from his paper, that things weren't looking too good. When the knock came to the door, Joseph Kilkey put down his paper.

'Who's that, I wonder?' he asked, looking across at his wife. His face wore a peculiarly woeful expression. If there was anything Mr Kilkey hated, it was this invasion of his quiet hour by visitors. Seven to eight o'clock was Mr Kilkey's time for reading the newspaper. It was his hour for reflection from beginning to end, not even omitting the obituary notices. Maureen put down her sewing. 'I'll see,' she said, and got up from her chair. At once her husband's expression changed. There was something about Maureen that held his attention. Indeed, Mr Joseph Kilkey felt a peculiar pleasure at this momentary glimpse of Maureen's physical proportions. She went into the parlour and looked through the window. The action had a significance of its own. She never went direct to the door and opened it, but always spied through the window to see who the visitor might be. Nor was this habit confined to Mrs Kilkey. The inhabitants of Price Street all did the same thing. There were so many unwelcome visitors to the street. The parlour window was a sort of observation post. There decision was come to. Now, as she looked out through the chink in the curtains, she espied the tall youth. He was without a hat. Peter never wore any headwear. Yes. This was her brother. She could see him quite clearly by the light of the lamp. Had he seen her? she wondered, and drew back from the curtain. Yes. That was Peter. Her brother, whom she had not seen for seven years. He had changed, grown tremendously, broadened out, but she would have known him anywhere. Maureen tiptoed back into the kitchen, and sat down in the chair. Mr Kilkey looked at her, his lips framing a question. Maureen picked up her sewing as though nothing had happened. At that moment the knock came again.

'Who is it?' asked Mr Kilkey. He sat forward in his chair. 'Who is it?'

'Oh, somebody selling stuff, I think,' she replied. She flushed. Mr Kilkey thought this rather strange. Now the knocking was repeated. There was real determination and vehemence behind the knock this time.

'That's nobody selling stuff, Maureen,' Mr Kilkey said. He got up from his chair and made to go to the door, but at the same time Maureen also rose and barred his path.

'It's all right,' Maureen said. 'Sit down.' She pressed close to him. He could feel her body against his own. He saw her bosom rise and fall. Mr Kilkey suddenly embraced his wife. The visitor was forgotten. 'Sit down,' Maureen repeated. She pushed him back into the chair. The man laughed. 'Who is it?' he asked again. 'Somebody you don't want to see . . .'

'It's Peter. It's my brother Peter.' She sat down and took up her sewing. An expression of absolute astonishment passed swiftly, like a gust of wind, across Joseph Kilkey's face. He scratched his head. He was really astonished.

'And why don't you open the door, Maureen? Don't you want to see him? He's your brother. You haven't seen the lad for years.'

'No,' Maureen exclaimed, and the very tone of her voice seemed to spell finality. 'No,' she repeated with great emphasis. Mr Kilkey picked up the newspaper, and carefully folding it, placed it in the cupboard. Then he stretched out in the chair, looking up at the ceiling. He noticed then for the first time that the ceiling was badly stained. Probably the roof was leaking. The events of the day, the ways of the world, passed completely out of his mind. There was something else to reflect upon now. Something that was near, very near, to him. He was completely at a loss to understand his wife's attitude towards the boy. The visitor had evidently gone, probably having given it up as hopeless. The final knock seemed to ring in Mr Kilkey's ears. There was something demanding about it, as though the person had put into it his anger at such treatment. He lowered his head. he wanted to ask his wife a question. But, seeing the look upon Maureen's face, he reverted to his former position, and allowed his eyes to wander about the stained ceiling. He could see at once how determined Maureen was. 'Her mother all over,' he thought. Absolute determination. Ruthless. How positively ugly she looked now, with that thin set mouth of hers! No. She wouldn't see Peter. He knew it only too well. Not all the armed folks of the country would get Maureen out of that chair. It may have been the striking of the clock, or the sudden barking of a dog in a near-by yard, that made Mr Kilkey sit up suddenly and stare confusedly about him. His train of thought had been interrupted. Mrs Kilkey seemed to have forgotten her husband's existence. And yet she was thinking of nothing in particular excepting the task in hand. Occasionally she thought of her mother, and even told herself that she ought to go round and see her. Perhaps to-night. She had something to say when she went to Hatfields. She must think carefully about it. Mr Kilkey again looked at his wife. For some time his eyes focused themselves upon her hands. Against this restless, almost agitated play of her fingers the silence of the kitchen became irritating. Now Joseph Kilkey was a man who adored silence. There was nothing, indeed, that he liked better than to get his feet upon the fender. There was something grand, something magic, about the very action, as though as his feet gripped the fender he exclaimed to himself, 'There! Now I'm settled.' The world might be full of events great and small, happenings sad and joyous, but to Mr Kilkey there was something indeed above all this. It was holy and sacred, it was full of beauty. A man could always, by the very act of closing his door and putting his feet upon the fender, shut out the world and commune with himself. But this silence was different. It irritated, goaded one.

Something was hidden behind it. At last he cried out, 'I don't understand, Maureen, hanged if I do! Why didn't you want to see your brother?' The question was direct, there was such a demanding note about it, that for a moment Maureen Kilkey made no reply. This was a new Mr Kilkey, without a shadow of doubt. Marriage indeed must be one long educational process. She put down her sewing, closed the work-box, and pushed it on to the sewing-machine.

She looked at her husband. 'I don't want to see him,' she said slowly. 'I haven't the faintest intention of seeing him.' She turned round in her chair, so that she sat facing the kitchen window. She put her elbows on the table, and rested her chin in her cupped hands. It was then that Peter, climbing the wall, had first seen her.

'But it's ridiculous!' exclaimed Mr Kilkey. 'After *all*, he's your brother! What has he done?'

Maureen swung round. 'What has he done?' She laughed. 'He hasn't done anything to me. I wouldn't let him . . .'

'Well then . . .' went on Mr Kilkey. 'I don't see why you . . .' Maureen shut him up at once.

'I'll tell you what he's done!' she exclaimed. 'He's made my mother's life one long prison, that's what he's done. Sometimes I think she deserves it. She never takes advice. *Never.* It was silly. The amount of money that was expended on that fellow – what for?' She laughed again. 'Waste! waste!' She paused. She had been going to add, 'and no return,' but suddenly refrained. She respected her husband's ideas. Why should she offend Joseph Kilkey?

'All along Mother was told how useless it would be. It only tied her down. And now she's got her reward. She ought never to have sent him. The others got no such consideration. None at all. Mother has tried hard. But she's only a fool. A fool!' Maureen became quite passionate, the colour rose to her cheeks, she stood up now, one hand gripping the table. 'She thought she was doing her best. But she couldn't have done anything worse. I've told her time and time again. I've almost begged her, on my knees, to give it up. She'll get no thanks. No thanks. I've said, "Why don't you get out of the house – out of the street?" She won't. It's like a prison. She's been tied there years and years. And what does she say? She says, "If your father had been different." I think it's really silly. Dad has worked hard all his life. He has seen little of Mother, little of any of us. At her request he gave up going to sea, and took that job on the railway. But I knew he did it for

Mother's sake. In a way I was glad. At least, they would be with each other. But what has happened? He hates the job. Hates it like poison. He wants to go to sea again. I know it full well. Mother is seeing it now. This restlessness, this continual tugging at something he can never get. It's like a child trying to get a toy beyond his reach. But that isn't all. Mother began her campaign. "Thirty years of this," she said. Dad asked, "What?" Mother said, "This gaol. This gaol."' Again Maureen laughed. 'But she made it herself through her own foolishness, through her own insane idea of getting Peter into the Church.'

Mr Kilkey got up from the chair.

'Maureen,' he said, 'Maureen.' There was great tenderness in his voice – 'Maureen, I never thought you could talk like that of your mother.' Then he sat down, as though he had expended all effort. He could say no more. After a while he said, 'I'm surprised! I'm surprised!'

'You don't know anything,' exclaimed Maureen. She added heatedly, 'How *could* you be expected to know?' Then she went upstairs. Mr Kilkey remained rigid in his chair, as though the very words had bound him. Maureen stood by the bed in her room. 'Yes,' she thought, 'what does he know? What does anybody know? But I know! I know!' She had not lived at Hatfields all those years for nothing. She was neither blind nor dumb. She loved her father. All his life her mother had tormented him with his mistake. *His* mistake. And what was that? Dennis Fury at a most impressionable age had run away from home. He had left behind him security, comfort, money, a good home, and a chance of education. He had taken to the sea. And now her mother did nothing but taunt him with the errors he had made. She was in no way blind to her mother's struggles. She had seen them. In fact, she sometimes felt proud that she had a mother like Fanny Fury. But her actions, her ideas, her ambitions. Where had they taken root? What was this maddening thing that ringed her mother's life? Frustration? Suddenly she went across to the window and looked out. There was nothing to be seen but Price Street, dark and gloomy, a sort of black pit, over which there hung a cloud of smoke, of grease and steam. A sort of blessed trinity, the very essence of the world in which she lived. The thing was, her mother was not content. Well, why wasn't she content? What did she want to do? Maureen asked herself the questions. But there was no answer to them. It was like knocking at a door which will never be opened. 'Here,' she thought, 'here I had better stop.' She didn't want to think any more about it. Peter she could not forget. She had sensed the full measure of her mother's disappointment. Yes. It was a disappointment. No matter how mad the action, it was a cruel blow. The belief was there, the very essence of trust, almost childish. Yes. If Peter had succeeded and become a priest, the whole texture of her mother's life would have been changed. But he hadn't succeeded. On the contrary, he had failed. Well, she wasn't going to dwell upon why he had failed. That was best left alone. She sighed.

But what had his sudden return meant? This failure of her brother seemed to have opened a door, a sort of door in her mother's mind. And through it there now came in long processions the figures of the past, the deeds, the words, the hopes, the belief. One long panorama. Peter had opened this door. 'Sometimes when I think of that action I could kill him,' she exclaimed aloud. Then she went downstairs. Mr Kilkey had fallen asleep in his chair. She saw how late it was. She decided to put the kettle on. She began to lay the table for supper. Suddenly she thought, 'I wonder where he is now? I wonder what he's doing?'

3

Peter was standing in the open space. It had begun to rain. He turned up the collar of his coat, looking up and down the street. There was something about his demeanour that seemed charged with indecision. He kept looking from left to right. There seemed something fascinating about the patch of reddened sky, just above the loco sheds. He kept staring at this now. The dull glare appeared to throw sharply into focus the clouds of steam that hung like a sort of perpetual white pall over the sheds. Then he suddenly remembered hearing his father remark that they would be laying new lengths of rail that night. His brother Desmond might be there. He was a foreman ganger now. Why was his mother so afraid he would go to Vulcan Street? Why did his father always appear embarrassed when he mentioned his brother's name? These questions remained imprinted on Peter's mind. People kept hurrying past him, women with raised umbrellas, men grimed and talking loudly as they passed to and fro. These were men from the tramway sheds. Peter recognized them by their uniforms. A light flashed up as a train roared by. He hurried away, and did not stop until he had reached the bottom of the street. He stood again, still fascinated by that red glare in the sky. 'I'm going to watch them working,' he said, and walked on in the direction of the sheds. Outside the tramway sheds he stopped again, watching cars being stabled, hearing the voice of the watchman shouting. He could see the man standing far up in the shed, on the edge of the pit, along which men were walking with hammers on their shoulders. Then he heard a tram just behind him. It was empty. The conductor was sitting gazing bewilderedly out of the window, the driver muffled up so that Peter could hardly see the man's face. When this car turned into the shed he continued on his way. He knew the road to the embankment. He had played there as a child. Where the sheds ended he crossed a road, now in black darkness, and walked along until he came to a long low railing. Between this line of railing and the boarded embankment there ran a narrow path which, he remembered, was used only by the loco men going to and from their work. He stood leaning against the railings, looking down towards the sheds. In the far distance he could hear hammering. At the bottom of this lane he saw the light over the little green door. He had often been through that door. He could even remember how many times he had been chased away from it by angry loco men. He began to walk in the direction of the light, but again he stopped. He would not be able to get through. There was always somebody standing about. No. Best try the other way. He had been that way too. He turned back.

He climbed the railings and ran across a piece of waste ground. He climbed a fencing. He was now standing in the same small houseless street as before. There was a leather warehouse at the bottom of this street. Almost opposite he saw a light at the bottom of the entry. He ran across and stood at the corner. What time was it now? he asked himself. On one side of this entry there ran for over a quarter of a mile a wall almost twenty feet high. Standing there in the deserted street, he could almost feel the immensity of this wall. At the other side of the entry stood a public convenience. Its slate walls were begrimed, snotted, and much scrawled with chalk. The rain running down these walls gave them a glistening surface as the yellowish light caught them. Inside the convenience he could hear the harsh guttural noise of a running tap. He wondered why this tap was allowed to run. The air was rank, a pungent odour came from the leather warehouses. The whole atmosphere harboured a foulness. In the entry itself decaying vegetables, old tins, newspaper, and rags lay about. Peter could feel the rain trickling down his neck. He stared into the entry. He knew that in the middle of it there was a gas-light affixed to the top of the wall. He had once tried to climb its piping and had fallen. He kept looking round, furtively, as though somebody were watching him. Then he ran into the entry, and did not stop running until he stood under the light. He looked up. The darkness, broken only by this splash of spluttering gas-light, appeared to give the wall additional height. He felt the piping with his hands. He could hear men's voices quite clearly now. 'They must be working just behind here,' he was thinking. He put his foot in a niche in the wall and pulled himself up. Then he let go suddenly and dropped into the entry. The piping would not hold his weight. Ought he to go home? They would be waiting for him. No. He hadn't been out since he came home. He was going to climb that wall and watch the men working the rails. He tried again. This time he got a grip on an outjutting stone. He held on, his feet groping for a niche. Looking up again at the light, he noticed the slimy surface of the walls that, like the walls of the convenience, glistened under the rain. The wall itself seemed to ooze forth a peculiar rankness. Peter spat, the strange odours strong in his nostrils. There was something dead and beastly about the entry in which he stood. Now he could hear the noise of the oil-flares. A wagon shunted somewhere. Then a crashing sound as a load of rails were unshipped from the bogie. He raised his hands, catching hold of another stone, holding his breath, listening. He was certain somebody was climbing behind him. He looked down, but there was nothing, only the darkness. He had climbed nearly six feet now. The wall must be nearly twenty feet high, he was thinking as he pulled himself up higher. His right hand slipped, the wall appeared to be very greasy in parts, and Peter wondered where the grease could have come from. Would he ever get to the top? Somebody shouted, 'Hey there, Wooden-face!' He heard the voice quite distinctly. He laughed. He climbed again, as though the man's voice had given him an additional impetus. he was only half-way up. He clung tenaciously to the wall. Conscious of the rain running down his neck, he redoubled his efforts. When he reached the top, he flung himself flat upon the wall and exclaimed, 'Phew!' He shut his eyes, afraid to look down.

The depth to the permanent way was greater than that to the entry. He lay on his side. Then he opened his eyes and looked over, his two hands gripping tightly to the edge of the wall. He could now see the men right beneath him. There was something fantastic, almost grotesque, in their movements as they worked in the light of the oil-flares. To his left he could see an engine and tender, to his right a great mountain of sleepers. Further, another mound. A neat pile of new fish-plates. The ground about was littered with wedges. The men were engaged in fixing a new length of rail on one of the inner lines. Two lengths away the points gleamed white beneath the light. Peter began counting the men in the four-foot. Twelve, thirteen, twenty men. Peter supposed this was the main junction. The great network of lines gleamed like long silver ribbons. Straining his eyes and looking over the heads of the men he could discern another set of lines. He counted five sets. The plate-layers were relaying on the lines nearest to the wall on which he now lay. Beyond the black shape of the engine and tender, all was shrouded in a sort of black fog. Somebody shouted suddenly, 'Easy and over,' and Peter held his breath. The new rails slipped from the bogie with a low thunderous sound. He could see men picking up the long hammers. The concourse of sound deafened him. He put his fingers to his ears. Beyond this section of men he could see another group, seated about a brazier. They were drinking tea from cans, eating food from unwrapped newspaper parcels and red handkerchiefs. He could hear them talking about engines. A light engine. He began to feel cold, but dare not move. He pushed his head out still further. The height made him dizzy. He spat, following the spittle with his eyes as it fell through the darkness. He thought he saw it hit the rubble. Then he drew his head back again. 'What time is it now?' he was thinking. They would be waiting up for him at home. Supposing his brother Desmond was down there! Peter suddenly decided that it would be a rather good idea if he climbed over the wall and rolled slowly down to the embankment. Desmond might well be working with that gang. His brother worked on this very section. Somewhere in the distance he thought he heard the steady rhythmical roar of a train. Somebody shouted, 'Hey there, Wooden-face!' Again Peter laughed. Who was Wooden-face? Why did they call the man by that name? The men were now running another length of rail into position. As they bent down he could see the backs of their necks, their bared arms. The hammers flashed through the air. Again he put his fingers to his ears. Reaching over with his hand, he felt the other side of the wall. It was as smooth as glass. It ran sheer down to the high banking. Peter looked over and followed its line with his eyes. He would like to go down, to sit on the banking hidden in the darkness, and to watch them working.

Somewhere to the right a man began to sing, his deep baritone voice swelling into the night air with the clearness of a bell. Peter listened attentively. He was singing a popular song. Beyond where this man stood he could see the line of loco sheds, and thought, 'That's where Dad works. Funny to think of Dad working on the railway after being on ships nearly his whole life through. Desmond works somewhere in that section too.' Across the metals the engine and tender suddenly moved with a low hissing sound. 'You can dodge almost anything except a light engine,' his father had once remarked. That must be a light engine. It moved so silently along the metals, like a snake. Something came rumbling up the line. He saw the men from the brazier get up and move off in the direction of this rumbling sound. The darkness swallowed them up. Peter sat up now, clutching the wall. He felt a pain in his neck. If only he could get down that wall! He felt a sort of sliminess where he lay, the air itself seemed to secrete it, a dampness touched him, rottenness seemed to hang about. Then the clock at the tramway sheds struck the hour. But he did not hear it now. He looked up. The gas-light was directly above him. He peered into the entry. He could see nothing. A foul odour appeared to rise up from the depths. Tramps, rag-women, children used this entry. Peter remembered the many times his mother had warned him about going to it. People used it as a convenience. He heard the bogie coming up again, heard the men's voices biting on the night air. The bogie stopped. He heard the loud clanking of the coupling chain. Everybody appeared to be talking at once.

'They are going to drop the rails there,' he thought, just as the side of the bogie appeared to take fire, as the rails crashed to the ground. He watched a man picking fish-plates from the pile. Others were now gathering up the scattered wedges. Peter studied the man gathering the fish-plates. He was talking to himself. Then he saw him fling these plates one after the other into the length. Again that dull roar came to Peter's ears. Hearing it, his whole body stiffened. He stretched out his arms again and lay close to the edge. The smoke from the flares belched up, thick and black, roaring viciously as the wind caught them. Peter could feel this smoke in his nostrils. Again that roar, a low shuddering sound that seemed to swell and swell. It must be a train, he thought. It drew nearer now. Looking to his right he saw a dim glare, the reflection from the engine-fire. He could hear the hissing of steam. The man flinging the plates into the length drew his attention once more. He had walked back to the brazier. He saw the man pick up a can and drink from it. The stout little ganger shouted, 'Hurry up there, Wooden-face!' Why did they call him that? The man came back again. Right under Peter he stopped, looking about, as though he too were conscious of this approaching avalanche of sound. Peter shut his eyes again. The oncoming roar drowned the noise of the hammers. Peter shut his eyes tightly, opened them again. The steady rhythm of the train seemed almost upon him. The man was still standing in the four-foot. The little ganger was calling again. 'Hurry up there, will you? Wooden-face, hurry up!' The man came on, stepping over the metals. Suddenly a voice screamed, 'STAND BACK THERE! EXPRESS GOODS.' The voice was like bronze. It seemed to overwhelm all other sounds. 'They are shouting at *him*,' thought Peter. 'They are shouting at that man with the fish-plates. It must be him.' His whole body tensed itself, as though it had in that moment succumbed to the roar of the oncoming train. But he could not see it. He could see nothing beyond the flares, only the black shapes, the outlines of the loco sheds. Voices ceased, there was nothing save this low screeching sound. Then the long shape, like a monstrous snake, hissing steam and flame, seemed to spit itself into the light, as though the darkness itself had hurled it forth. 'STAND BACK THERE, WOODEN-FACE! EXPRESS GOODS. STAND BACK!'

Ugh! Peter closed his eyes again, murmuring, 'It's here! Now. It's on top of him! Ugh!' The tall man was still standing in the four-foot. His face was violent red under the flares. Peter thought he had red hair too, but the man's hair was as fair as flax. 'He must be deaf. Why doesn't he get out of the way?' Peter yelled.

The stout ganger waved his arms frantically. The man came on, heedless of the shouting, the wild gesticulations on the part of his workmates. The very pulse of the train seemed to beat in his ears. When the man saw the train coming he knew it was too late. He could not move. The train swept on. He could feel an intense heat, as though a flying furnace were shooting towards him. As the shape grew bigger he threw up his hands and pitched forward flat upon his face. His two hands pawed the earth. He tore at the earth, crying, 'JESUS CHRIST!' His body gripped the sleepers. A dull roar came to his ears, it seemed to swell. He tried to move his hand. He cried out, a terrific pain shooting through his head. The train roared on. He lay shivering in the four-foot. Men were shouting and running in his direction. But he could not move. His body seemed glued to the ground. Somebody shouted, 'Dobson! Dobson!' Then he rolled over on his back. His face was black with sweat. With his fingers he had made two holes in the earth. He saw a huge light above his head. It was the sky. More voices, running feet. 'My God!' he said. 'My God!' He felt himself picked up. They were carrying him. They stopped again. They were near the brazier. Somebody was pouring hot tea down his throat. 'All right, Dobson! Damn it, man! you must be deaf not to hear that. The whole of the north of England can hear that Goods!' They moved on again. He could hear the gentle hiss of the engine and tender. They were putting him on the tender now. 'Mary,' he said. Somebody was stroking his head. 'What a weight he is!' 'Aye.' The driver standing on the footplate of the light engine said, 'Hurt?'

Babble of voices, confusion. 'No. Stunned. Lucky devil!' A man wiped his face. 'Wooden-face'll get killed one of these days.' They laid the man on sacking in the tender.

'Easy there!' They were moving him further along.

'He's let go,' somebody said.

'Look out!' the driver said. He got up on the engine again.

'Half a minute! half a minute! Somebody running down the line.'

A silence came over the assembled men. The running figure came nearer. Then a voice shouted, 'Drop your tools, men! Drop your tools!'

'What the hell is this?'

The man came up then. He was a little man, wearing a porter's vest, hatless, a red scarf round his neck. 'Wire just come in from Shacklady. Everybody to come out.'

'Good!' the man on the engine said. 'Stand clear!' The steam shot out and a shower of spray descended upon the assembled men. Two men were standing in the tender, the man lying on the sacking between them. 'Pity they didn't send word before this,' one of the men said; 'this wouldn't have happened.'

'We'll scrounge a drink for him when we get to the sheds.' The engine moved away. Soon it was swallowed up in the darkness. The gang of men seemed to stand as though in contemplation. Then one of them kicked a flare, saying, 'Let the bastards have it this time, that's what I say.' He began to move away from the other men. 'Aye.' They set off in a body in the direction in which the light engine had gone.

'Funny Wooden-face couldn't hear that Goods!'

'Aye.'

'Mad bastard! That's what he is.'

The crowd fell silent again. Like Peter, they had suddenly become conscious of something, of something that was more than silence; a sort of unearthly hush appeared to have descended upon the whole city. They walked on. The drizzle still came down. In the light of the flares it appeared like a shower of fine white dust, shining silvery on their shoulders. The sheds loomed in sight. There was not a sound to be heard.

'Seems funny, doesn't it?' a man said, hearing for the first time the crunching of his hobnail boots on the ballast.

Nobody answered him. They passed on through the sheds. Coming out on to the streets, they saw even more men emerging from the tramway sheds. Once a car passed them, empty, dimly lighted. 'Last trip,' the driver shouted. Somebody called 'Hooray!' The tram vanished round the corner. The crowd of men passed into the King's Road. Most men from the sheds lived round Price Street, King's Road, Hatfields. They tailed off in little groups, arguing loudly. A policeman stood in the doorway of an emporium, silently observing them.

'They're the swine!' a man shouted. The policeman turned his head, staring after the crowd of men. They passed through Price Street. Other men were coming up from the docks. The streets seemed blocked with men. In Hatfields doors were opened. Women stood on the steps, while from the windows above half-dressed children stared into the street.

'They've come out.'

CHAPTER VIII

I

For the past fortnight Mr Fury had been telling his wife that things weren't looking too good. For one thing, the miners had threatened to strike. The issue at stake for Mr Fury was whether the railwaymen would be called out to support them. Mr Fury secretly hoped that they wouldn't. He hated strikes, for the very simple reason that he had never been engaged in one. Being a sailor, and most of his life afloat, he was wont to associate strikes only with those engaged in work ashore. Nobody was more surprised than Mr Fury when, promptly at midnight, all workers downed their tools. Indeed, it took his breath away. He had never expected it to come so suddenly. When with Aunt Brigid he had emerged, not too steadily, from the Star and Garter, he was surprised to find so many people abroad at that hour of the night. The streets were crowded with excited people. Crowds went off towards the tramway sheds, the loco sheds. Others veered off in the direction of the leather warehouses. Others towards the docks. Aunt Brigid, as much taken aback at this panorama as her brother-in-law, asked him what it meant. Dennis Fury was confused. His mind seemed blocked. He couldn't think. Mr Joseph Kilkey and his own wife appeared to bar the path.

'I don't know,' Mr Fury said. 'Looks like a gala night.' When he had been five minutes in the open air his brain began to clear. At the same time newsboys began to parade the streets with special editions of the local papers. Aunt Brigid fumbled in her bag, withdrew a penny, and asked Mr Fury to get one. Mr Fury did so. But there was nothing beyond a few words in the stop-press that made it any more significant than the evening edition of the paper, the front sheets of which he had burnt in the fire. With Mrs Fury in bed, he did not quite like the idea of her reading this news. He folded up the paper. Miss Mangan, with one stout arm through her brother-in-law's, asked him what all the fuss was about.

'There's some talk about a general stoppage at midnight,' Mr Fury said, and looked away up the street. He felt her arm relax. Aunt Brigid became excited at once.

'Oh, Denny!' she said. 'How awful! I do hope I can get a boat back home.' She looked almost despairingly into his face.

'Yes, so do I,' replied Mr Fury. 'Yes. By God!' he thought. 'I don't care how long this bloody strike lasts, so long as she catches the boat.' To have that woman marooned in the house was something he could not stand. The strike, so far as Mr Fury was concerned, could only be associated with one thing. His sister-in-law. Yes. By fair means or foul, it didn't matter which, Miss Mangan must be got on to a boat. Mr Fury was thinking furiously now. Yes. And it didn't even matter what kind of boat, so long as it was a boat, and, he told himself with a smile, 'a boat that could carry her without sinking'. She must be got away. He simply could not stand the woman in the house. Dennis Fury was more and more convinced that his sister-in-law's visits were planned, and not chance ones by any means, and that each occasion was used for the gathering in of more family history. He once mentioned this to Fanny, who straightaway told him not to be so ridiculous. But the idea remained imprinted upon his mind. Aunt Brigid came over for information, and nothing else. He had derived a certain amount of satisfaction at her disappointment over her father. Indeed, he was rather taken aback at the inability of Mr Mangan to recognize his daughter. That was another thing that had been occupying his mind for some time. Why had 'him' become silent all of a sudden? He dated this silence from the day they had had the row over his sending money to Peter. Was there some sort of maliciousness, some stubborn indifference behind it? Mr Fury had thought so. But now he had changed his mind. 'Old Mangan's on his last,' thought Mr Fury. Brigid Mangan almost wept when, on her first night in Hatfields, she knelt down in front of her father and exclaimed, 'Dad! Dad! Don't you know me? I'm Brigid.' Anthony Mangan did not seem to recognize the woman. Out of that incident Mr Fury drew satisfaction, even a certain amount of pleasure. He felt it had even been worth her travelling all that way just to be 'snubbed' by her dad. Mr Fury's theory was wrong. Aunt Brigid had come over because she was worried. Not about 'Dad', but about his little bit of money.

When Aunt Brigid and Mr Fury arrived back at Hatfields, they stood for a moment outside the door. A young woman had just hurried away. The door was still open. Perhaps it was this sudden return to Hatfields, to the dark and stuffy street, from the warm, comfortable, and cheery atmosphere of the Star and Garter, or it may have been pure imagination on Aunt Brigid's part, but she imagined her brother-in-law's arm to lie more heavily on her own. Indeed, Mr Fury was beginning to feel a little unsteady again. He may have been upset by this sudden vision of his wife standing in the doorway, when but a short while ago he had left her lying in bed. Or it may have been the air, or the unusual excitement of the crowded streets. He made a step forward, arm-in-arm with Miss Mangan, and suddenly lurched. Miss Mangan said, 'Denny! Denny, my boy! Be careful.' She gripped his arm more tightly. Mr Fury muttered something like 'Ah!' and moved forward again. Yes. Without a doubt, there was Fanny at the door, fully dressed. The woman must be mad after what Dr Dunfrey told her. Fanny Fury had got up and dressed, and gone below. She was attending to 'him' when the knock came to the door. Now Maureen had just gone. She stood at the end of the lobby, looking at the figures in front of her. As Miss Mangan mounted the step, Mr Fury following, Mrs Fury exclaimed, 'Denny! Brigid! I'm surprised.' It seemed to her that both her husband and her sister were none too steady upon their feet. 'I'm surprised,' she said. 'Don't be surprised, Fanny,' exclaimed Mr Fury jovially. 'Be jolly instead,' and followed the remark by a loud burst of laughter. The Postlethwaites' door suddenly opened, and Mrs Postlethwaite came out on to the step. That sudden burst of laughter she knew well. Only Mr Fury laughed like that, and then only when he was drunk. Mrs Fury observed the large lady. Mrs Postlethwaite was really so large that she put Miss Mangan to shame. She was a little woman, with a rotundness that had become the joke of Hatfields. Her husband, seeing her grow stouter day by day, had said, 'If that cooper at number thirty-seven ever sees you alone, he'll be greatly tempted.' This remark was quite beyond Mrs Postlethwaite's comprehension. But her husband was only too conscious of her proportions. Now as she stood at the door, watching Mr Fury and Miss Mangan ascend the step, she did look like a barrel, a very large barrel. Mrs Fury caught her sister by the arm and pulled her in. Then she gripped her husband and dragged him in too. The door closed. 'I'm surprised!' she kept saying. 'Surprised!' 'For Christ's sake,' shouted Mr Fury, 'don't be surprised! Be jolly instead.' The three made their way along the lobby. The Postlethwaites' door banged. Aunt Brigid sat down on the sofa immediately, gave a sigh, and lay back. She was completely out of breath. Mr Fury remained standing, hands in pockets, hat a little to one side. He was contemplating 'him'. The clock showed half-past ten. Mrs Fury looked at her sister. 'I hope you had a good day, Brigid,' she said. Miss Mangan now sat up. 'A very good day, Fanny! I met scores of old friends,' she said. She pulled a clean white handkerchief from her sleeve and wiped her face. 'A very good day,' she repeated, 'I never saw so many old friends.' 'Yes. I'm sure you did,' replied Mrs Fury. She looked across at her husband. 'Where did you *meet him*?' she asked.

Mr Fury was still contemplating. There was a vacant, stupid expression upon his face. He appeared to retain his balance only with the greatest effort. He had not even heard the remark passed. Aunt Brigid again wiped her face with her handkerchief. 'I met him as I was coming off the tram,' she said. 'He was with a peculiar-looking man. I can't remember his name.' She looked at Mr Fury. He, still balancing precariously, said, 'Postlethwaite from next door.'

'I hope you didn't prepare anything specially,' remarked Aunt Brigid, getting up from the sofa. Mrs Fury moved away from the table to allow her sister to pass. 'Oh no!' she said, following the woman with her eyes. The kitchen door closed. The sudden bang almost threw Mr Fury off his balance. Mrs Fury went to him, caught him by the arm and said angrily, 'You fool! You old fool!' She dragged him to the sofa and plumped him down. 'You fool!' she said. 'I like the way you kept your vow. Never to go into a public with Brigid.' She could hear her sister changing her shoes in the room directly overhead. After what seemed an interminable silence, Mr Fury looked up at his wife.

'I left you in bed!' he said. 'What are you doing up here now? You must be crazy, getting out of bed. Get on back.' Mrs Fury laughed.

'And where would you be if I stayed in bed? Where would Dad be? The whole lot of you? I have something else to think about besides staying in bed. You *fool*!' she shouted. Then she left him and went into the parlour. Yes. She had something to think about. How could she have lain in bed? She must make plans. First, Aunt Brigid must get the first boat back. She did not want her. Mrs Fury's great objection to a prolonged or enforced stay on Miss Mangan's part was occasioned by a certain suspicion. That suspicion was that Aunt Brigid would go to Desmond's house. And not only number seven Vulcan Street. Miss Mangan would go to her friends. From them she would learn many things. Mrs Fury did not wish this. She had her own good reasons for it. Aunt Brigid was curious, was suspicious. She had plagued her with questions. But Fanny Fury controlled herself. Her sister must be got back. That was the first thing. The next thing was Peter! Peter was like a wound. He too must go. If she had not paid much attention to her husband's remark about 'the nice young fellow who'll call', she intended to do so now. If this man could get Peter away to sea, it would be good. Good for Peter. Good for herself. His presence in the house was a continuous reminder of what had happened, a kind of mirror in which she saw reflected her aims, disappointment, and now humiliation. She had enough to do to look after Mr Mangan. Anthony would soon be home. Mrs Fury had dismissed her husband's hints about a strike with an emphatic 'Pshaw! – Rot!' Now it had come. It wasn't the first. Veteran-like, she had already visualized its end.

She thought, 'What a fool Denny is!' To have met that woman like that, and to have gone into a public with her! Truly he was a man easily influenced. She remembered the frightful row they had had four years ago. And he had vowed he would have nothing more to do with her. Heaven knows what they had been talking about! She heard her sister's door close. Miss Mangan went downstairs. Mr Fury was gradually recovering. He sat up now as she came into the kitchen.

'What about some supper, eh?' Then he called, 'Fanny! Fanny!' Mrs Fury came in, one hand over her mouth.

'What's the matter, Fanny?' he asked. Had she been crying? He looked at Aunt Brigid. 'It's the devil!' he said. 'Who would have thought this would have come about! I had heard rumours; but took no notice of them. Then, before you have time to get your breath, the whole country comes out.'

'It's perfectly disgraceful!' exclaimed Aunt Brigid. 'These men seem to have no consideration whatever. I do hope that I shall get a boat back tomorrow.' She looked over at her father. It seemed to her that everybody had suddenly replied, 'Yes! yes!' – even old Mr Mangan.

'What about supper?' asked Mr Fury. He got up from the sofa. 'Yes! What about it?' said Mrs Fury, and vanished into the back kitchen. 'Can I help?' asked Miss Mangan, rising from her chair and hurrying into the back kitchen. Mr Fury heard his wife say, 'No, no! Not at all! It's all right, Brigid!' He went out himself and carried back the bread, the cold meat, plates and knives.

'It's a pity we didn't bring in some Guinness,' he said. 'Tut tut!' exclaimed Mrs Fury. In a few minutes tea was made. All three sat at the table. Miss Mangan kept staring at her father. How long had that old man been sitting like that? Years. 'Ah!' thought Aunt Brigid, 'I'm sure he has seen much. And now one cannot get a word out of him.' What had he done with his 'little bit of money'? Was it already gone? Spent! She trembled at the very thought. Not that she wanted any of it, oh no! But to think that it might be spirited away by the Furys! Why didn't he speak? He was like a sphinx. If only she had a key to unlock that door in her father's mind, how much she might learn! As it was, she knew nothing. Fanny was as silent as the grave. Maureen no better. That girl was hiding something. She saw it at once. As for Desmond ...

'It's Peter!' said Mrs Fury, rising at once on hearing the knock. 'Peter!' said Mr Fury. 'But at this hour! I thought the lad was in bed.' He looked at Miss Mangan as if to say, 'Keep cool! Control yourself. There's nothing significant in Peter coming home at ten past eleven, you confounded fox!'

But Aunt Brigid was much too occupied with her own thoughts. Mr Fury had made to go to the door, but Mrs Fury was quicker. She seemed to have been waiting for it. They heard the front door open; a whispered conversation ensued, but they could not hear what was being said. Peter stood looking at his mother, one hand flat against the wall.

'Did you go?' she asked.

'The boy nodded his head, 'Yes.'

'Where have you been until now?' asked Mrs Fury.

'After I left the chapel I went round to see Maureen.'

'Oh! I see. Maureen was out; she came round to see me,' said his mother. She was totally unprepared for what followed.

'She wasn't out! She was in. It's a lie! It's a lie!' his voice rose. Mrs Fury clapped her hand over his mouth.

'Shut up! Shut up! Where have you been till now?'

'I told you, Mother, I went round to Maureen's place. She *was* in. I saw her. She wouldn't open the door. I went round the back way. I saw her plain as daylight sitting at the table. I saw her husband too.'

'Maureen was here, I tell you,' said his mother. 'Here – here with me.' Then she caught his arm. 'Come!'

They went into the kitchen. Only Aunt Brigid smiled. She smiled at Peter. She had heard the word 'lie'. It was intriguing.

'Well, so you got back, then?' remarked Mr Fury.

'Yes, Dad.' The boy sat down at the table. Everybody looked at him as though momentarily expecting a revelation. Mr Fury pushed away his plate. Then he took out his pipe.

'It's a b—,' he said.

'Denny, how many times have I to tell you about using that word?'

'Aw!' he growled. He went outside to the yard.

Mrs Fury looked at Brigid. 'Denny's awful.' Then she turned to Peter: 'You hurry up and get off to bed.' Then Mr Fury came back, trailing with him a great cloud of bluish-black smoke.

'Have you still got that old rope of yours?' asked Mrs Fury. 'Yes! And damned good tobacco it is,' he replied. Peter got up, said, 'Good-night everybody,' and went upstairs. Mrs Fury followed immediately – an action that quickened Aunt Brigid's curiosity. The secrecy, the whisperings, the looks and gestures – the house was really mysterious.

Miss Mangan took a chair and placed it beside that of her father. 'How awful Dad looks!' she thought. Mr Fury puffed away contentedly at his pipe. He was wondering how Mr Postlethwaite had got on.

'Dad looks terrible,' said Miss Mangan sharply. She placed her hand on the old man's head and stroked it.

'Does he?' said Mr Fury. 'Well, let me tell you, Brigid, that he's a rare handful. Fanny has her hands full. I suppose you wouldn't think of taking "him" back with you? I'm sure if you did he'd open that mouth of his. He used to be talking once about nothing else but Belfast. His sister in Belfast. Always hoping he would catch the boat. Now he just sits there with his mouth shut tight as a trap.'

'How could I take him back?' asked Aunt Brigid. 'How could I take him back – now?' It seemed almost an ultimatum.

'Why not?' continued Mr Fury. 'Why did he ever leave Ireland? Don't you think Fanny has enough on her hands without him?'

Miss Mangan replied loudly, loud enough for the whole house to hear: 'Nobody seemed more anxious to take Father than Fanny did. In any case, I think it was only right. He was always wanting to go to her. Her name never left his lips.'

Mr Fury blew a cloud of smoke into the air. He thought suddenly: 'What the hell is that woman doing upstairs?' 'You have only yourself, Brigid. I think it's only fair you should take your father back. It's time Fanny got a rest. She's reared a family. Now they're grown up, Mr Mangan won't get much show here. Fanny hasn't the time. He ties the woman down!' He put down his pipe, and folded his arms behind his head.

Brigid Mangan said, 'Well?'

'Yes, I'll tell you one or two things about old Mangan,' he said. Miss Mangan rose from the chair, and stood on the mat looking down at her brother-in-law. How thin his hair was getting, and grey too! His jaws were drawn up. She supposed that was due to working in a ship stokehold all his life. 'Aye,' Mr Fury began, 'I could tell you ...' 'Ssh!' Aunt Brigid put a finger over her mouth. At the same time Mrs Fury came into the kitchen.

'Dad must go to bed at once,' she announced. Mr Fury immediately got up.

'Can I help?' asked Brigid.

'No! It's all right. I can manage,' replied Mrs Fury.

Peter had no sooner entered his room than his mother stepped in behind him. She closed the door. She sat down beside him on the bed. 'Where were you until that time?' asked she. Peter saw at once that his mother was in no light mood.

'I went to see the men working on the railway,' he began. 'Then I came straight back here.'

'Railway! What railway?' asked Mrs Fury. She seemed to pin the boy to the bed with her cool, penetrating eyes.

'The railway sheds at the back of Maureen's street,' said Peter.

'Have you been to Vulcan Street?' asked the woman. Her expression changed at once. She rose to her feet and looked down at her son.

'No!' Peter said. 'I haven't been to Vulcan Street, Mother.'

'Are you sure?'

'Yes, Mother.'

'That's quite honest, then?'

'Yes, Mother. I only went to see Maureen. But she never opened the door to me.'

'That's a lie, Peter,' said Mrs Fury. 'A lie. Maureen was with me most of the evening. She only just went when your father arrived back with your Aunt Brigid. Did you meet your father and Aunt Brigid?' She walked up to the window and turned her back on him. Peter got up.

'No, Mother.'

The woman turned round. She went up to her son and said slowly, 'Did you give the priest my message?'

'Yes, Mother.' 'Why does she ask all these questions,' thought Peter.

'You are sure you're telling the truth?'

'Yes, Mother.'

Mrs Fury went to the door. She opened it. She held the handle tightly in her hands.

'Keep away from Vulcan Street,' she said. 'If I ever find out you have been there, I'll kill you.' She made a sudden rush back and whispered into his face, 'I'll kill you.' Peter fell back upon the bed from sheer astonishment. When he regained his composure she had gone. Why didn't she want him to go and see his brother? Why was she so afraid? He did not know. Nor could he find out anything. Maureen was no help there. Should he ask his father? Why couldn't he see his brother? What crime had he committed? Why did he never come to the house? Why did his mother hate this woman? None of those questions could be answered. Suddenly he said to himself, 'I'll go tomorrow. Yes. I'll go tomorrow.' With this sudden decision the questions became more urgent, there was something almost burning in the intensity they had created. Why? Why? Why? He crossed over to the window and opened it. A week ago he had stood at another window, and had looked out upon green fields, great open spaces, stately trees. Here one looked out and saw nothing but a black pit. And over this pit there hung a kind of miasma. Hearing somebody coming up the stairs, Peter closed the window and sat down again on the bed. At the top the climber paused. He knew then that it was Aunt Brigid. He sat listening. The door opened. Aunt Brigid had a parcel in her hand. 'Here, Peter,' she said. 'This is for you.' She flung the parcel to the bed. Peter, smiling, exclaimed, 'Oh, thank you, Aunt Brigid! Thank you!' The door closed again. When he opened the parcel he found a pair of pyjamas. 'Oh my!' he said. 'Oh my!' and immediately undressed. Just as he got one leg into the bright blue pyjamas, Mrs Fury called up, 'Are you in bed, Peter?'

'Not yet, Mother,' called back Peter, at the same time pushing his other leg in.

'Then come down and help your father get Grand-dad to bed.'

'Coming, Mother,' shouted Peter. He stood for a moment on the landing. Aunt Brigid was saying her night prayers.

2

'At last!' said Mr Fury. 'At last!' He lay down on the sofa and covered himself up. Mrs Fury had gone to bed. With Peter's help he had managed to get 'him' upstairs. He was still surprised at his sister-in-law's generosity. Peter had appeared in the kitchen like a sort of bright blue apparition. But she hadn't even thought of buying him, Mr Fury, a pipeful of tobacco. 'The skinflint!' he thought. 'And she has money too.' He stretched himself so that his legs came to rest on the arm of the sofa. He wasn't used to sleeping on sofas. Well, with the best of luck he would be back in his own bed tomorrow. He hadn't begrudged his sister-in-law the space. Not at all. On the contrary, the change had been welcome. He had escaped Fanny's nightly sermon, Fanny's harangue, Fanny's regrets. And although he would return to his own room tomorrow, there were compensations. He needn't set the alarm for half-past five. He would be able to lie in. But how long was this strike going to last? He thought Fanny seemed pretty cool about it all, but perhaps that was mere showing off before Aunt Brigid. Yes. That was the important question. How long was it going to last? Tomorrow he must go down to the Mechanics' Hall and see about his strike-pay from the Federation. There were a lot of things to be done tomorrow. Tomorrow was going to be a very busy day. Seemed like Fanny meant to have a holiday. There was only one thing he dreaded, though he had Peter to share it, and that was getting Mr Mangan down to the Post Office. What a job! He wondered how Fanny managed 'him' so well. Visualizing the scene, he almost regretted his promise. If only he could wake up to find Brigid gone. And 'him' too. But that was asking for a miracle. Then Miss Mangan had to be seen to the boat. Well, he didn't mind that. With this sudden thought he sat bolt upright upon the sofa. What boat? *Would* there be a boat? He doubted it. He lay down again. Then he had to call and see Mr Lake about Anthony's allotment money. 'Bloody old Lake!' exclaimed Mr Fury. 'Damned swine!' He could hear the two women talking excitedly over his head. Suddenly Mulcare came into his mind. Now if he came along he might be able to get Peter a job. Any job. Then Fanny and he would be on their own at last. He realized the truth of what she had said, again and again. Yes, at last they would have peace. He fell asleep seeing Anthony walking up Hatfields, his white canvas bag on his back.

Promptly at six o'clock he rose. He was astonished to see Aunt Brigid already up and dressed. She came bustling into the kitchen. Mr Fury pushed the sofa back to the wall.

'Good-morning, Denny,' Miss Mangan said, and passed into the back kitchen to wash herself. Well, she was going. But she was very disappointed. She hadn't seen anybody. And to have missed the pleasure of meeting her eldest nephew was more than disappointment. It seemed deliberate frustration. 'Good morning, Brigid,' called Mr Fury. 'Is Fanny up?' As he called, his wife came into the kitchen.

'Is everything ready, Denny?' she asked. Mrs Fury was fully dressed.

'Yes,' Mr Fury replied, 'everything's ready.'

'Will you come upstairs a minute,' she said in a whisper; 'I want to talk to you.'

The man followed his wife upstairs. Immediately the door closed, Mrs Fury said, 'D'you think there will be a boat, Denny?'

Mr Fury hesitated. He wasn't certain. He looked at his wife. 'I should think so,' he said. 'I wish I had a morning paper, we might know where we are. I'm just as keen to see her back as you are,' he concluded.

'Of course! of course! But will she get a boat?'

'Why not? Why shouldn't she? I'll see she catches it, anyhow.'

'All right. That's all I wanted to know. I do hope she goes off. I have enough to think about now.' She looked at herself in the mirror.

'I never heard a word about this,' went on Mrs Fury. 'Why did you burn the paper last night?'

'Paper?'

'Yes. The paper!'

'Well – you see, Fanny – I . . .'

Mrs Fury put a finger to her mouth. Miss Mangan was coming.

'Take the bag, Denny,' Mrs Fury said.

Mr Fury picked up his sister-in-law's bag. Then he went out. As he passed Peter's door he kicked at it. 'Seven bells,' he shouted. He heard a yawn as he went downstairs. At a quarter to seven all four were having breakfast. Mr Fury wanted to ask a question, and yet he dreaded to ask it. The woman was so contrary that she might well do exactly the opposite. No. He wouldn't ask the question. Just trust to luck. Then Miss Mangan obliged him.

'What about Dad?' she asked.

'Oh, I'll see about that,' replied Mrs Fury. All eyes were turned upon Fanny Fury. Each seemed to ask the same question: What will she do? Drag the old man all the way to the Stage again?

'Peter will stay with his grand-dad,' announced Mrs Fury. She sat back at the table, like some sort of general. This was a surprise. Mr Fury was relieved, Miss Mangan more so. The sight of her father lying on the landing-stage still remained vivid in her mind. A quarter past seven. Everybody rose from the table.

'What time does this boat go, Denny?' asked Aunt Brigid.

'That I don't know. Nobody knows. all you can do is, get down to the ship's berth and wait there. There may be a boat today, but there certainly won't be one tomorrow.'

'I see,' said Aunt Brigid. What a hole to be caught in! Mrs Fury turned to Peter. The boy was standing by the curtains that covered the kitchen door.

'There's nothing to do for your grand-dad, except to give him his porridge at half-past eight. But you must go up now and then and look at him. Sometimes he wants sitting up to help him clear his throat.'

'Yes, Mother,' Peter said. 'I won't forget it.' It made him feel sick again.

'All ready, then?' asked Mr Fury. He put on his hard hat and blue overcoat. Suddenly he called to Peter, 'Here, Peter. Just run over to the sheds and see what's doing there. There ought to be a special of some sort.' He looked almost despairingly at Miss Mangan. The boy went out.

'Surely there'll be a tram, Denny,' said Mrs Fury as she drew on her long blue serge coat. 'Surely! ...' Again the man looked at his sister-in-law, as though to say, 'It's all your fault.'

'I don't know,' he said. 'I don't know.'

Peter came back, almost breathless.

'There aren't any trams.'

'What?' Mrs Fury looked at her sister. Miss Mangan stared bewildered at Mr Fury.

'My heavens! This is awful. I don't know ...'

'Here,' cried Mrs Fury, 'run to Hollis's, Peter, and tell them to send a taxi at once.'

Mr Fury sat down. All this excitement and confusion! Why hadn't Miss Mangan made inquiries? Why hadn't she made better preparations? Too busy, he supposed. That nose of hers ferreting about.

'I thought you made inquiries yesterday,' said Mr Fury. It was almost a growl.

'I did,' said Miss Mangan. 'I did. Do you take me for a fool, Denny?'

'No.'

'Oh, don't start arguing now,' interrupted Mrs Fury. 'This isn't the time for arguments.'

'There aren't any taxis. Mr Hollis can't do anything.' The sudden shout as Peter entered the lobby seemed to strike the kitchen assembly dumb. Everybody stared at Peter when he came in.

'Peter!' said his mother.

'You can't get anything, Mother. Mr Hollis said so. Not even a taxi. Everybody's walking.'

'Disgraceful!' shouted Miss Mangan. She thumped the table. This was indeed a bitter blow. To have to walk three and a half miles, not knowing whether there was a boat! Well, it *was* disgraceful. She looked at her brother-in-law.

'Yes. I think it's disgraceful. The way these men go on strike. They haven't the slightest consideration for anybody. All for themselves. All for themselves.'

'Christ almighty!' shouted Mr Fury. 'The way you talk, one would think I caused the damned strike. Why . . .'

'Denny! Denny! What an excitable man you are! Here! Pick up that bag.' Mrs Fury put on her hat. Mr Fury picked up Miss Mangan's bag. Aunt Brigid said she must slip upstairs to see her father.

'Very well,' said Mrs Fury. Aunt Brigid went upstairs. 'Peter, don't forget what I told you.'

'No, Mother.'

Miss Mangan came down. She was wiping her eyes with a white handkerchief. Mr Fury gripped her bag.

'Well! all set?'

'Yes,' said Mrs Fury.

Mr Fury went towards the back kitchen door. Aunt Brigid hurriedly smothered Peter in an embrace.

'Good-bye, Peter, now. Be a good boy.'

Peter said, 'Yes, Auntie. Good-bye,' and freed himself from the embrace, the smell of perfume strong in his nostrils.

'Here!' cried Mrs Fury. 'This way,' and she opened the front door. Mr Fury was so surprised that he almost dropped the bag. As Miss Mangan stepped down into the street, followed by Mrs Fury and her husband with the bag, it seemed as though all Hatfields had turned out to see them go.

Mr Fury went on ahead. Mrs Fury and her sister walked behind. Not a word was spoken. Each was conscious of curtains pulled back, of people standing in doorways. Not until the bottom of Hatfields was reached did Miss Mangan explode. Dennis Fury was too far away to hear it. Indeed, Mr Fury might have been momentarily equipped with wings.

'Fanny!' exclaimed Aunt Brigid, as she swung round and surveyed the length of Hatfields. 'Fanny! What an awful street! The people at those doors, the eyes hidden behind the curtains. I don't know how you can live in such a place.' She pulled out her handkerchief and wiped her face. Miss Mangan felt she was wiping off Hatfields' grime. How on earth her sister had ever come to such a street she could not imagine, and that was the kind of den poor Dad was in!

Mrs Fury smiled. 'I've had thirty years of it, Brigid, and I'm quite used to it.'

'Don't you ever feel you want to get out of it?' asked Brigid.

Mrs Fury's eyes had a sudden far-away look in them. 'Sometimes,' she said, and her own voice sounded strange to her ears. 'Sometimes,' she repeated. They walked on. Mrs Fury kept her eyes upon her husband. He had now come to a sudden halt. The bag lay at his feet. He was looking at some men's underwear in a draper's shop window.

'I'm sure you must get tired of it sometimes,' remarked Aunt Brigid. She was genuinely sympathetic. 'Don't you ever want to go back home?'

'Home! Oh God!'

'I mean Ireland,' added Aunt Brigid.

Mrs Fury looked at her sister. She made no reply to the question. Aunt Brigid was diplomatic enough not to repeat it. There was something about her sister that moved her deeply. They caught up with Mr Fury.

'Listen, Denny,' said Mrs Fury, 'there must be some means of getting to the Stage. Can't we get a cab anywhere?' The man shook his head. Mr Fury had reached a stage in sheer desperation when he didn't care if a tram came along. He wouldn't do anything but walk. There was something almost spiteful in the look he gave Miss Mangan. 'No!' he said. 'You won't get a cab either. Even if there was one, it's too early.'

'Why not Hobhouse's? Surely there's a cab or car of some kind.'

'You won't get one, Fanny,' said Mr Fury. He picked up the bag again.

'Wait here,' said Mrs Fury. 'I'll run to Hobhouse's Yard. There might be one. You can't expect Brigid to walk that four miles.'

'What if she has to walk back?' Mr Fury said.

'Wait here, Brigid. I'll try to get you a conveyance of some kind,' and she rushed off, leaving Aunt Brigid and her brother-in-law gazing at each other, as though there was nothing else to do but gaze.

'She's a caution! That woman's a caution.' Mr Fury kept looking at his watch. Mrs Fury came back at last, flushed, out of breath, and defeated.

'I told you all along,' growled Mr Fury. 'We could have been half-way there.'

They set off once more, Mr Fury going ahead of them with the bag.

There was something almost ghostly about the early morning walk. The city seemed dead. The pavements were deserted. It was as though in the night the life of the whole city had suddenly fled, leaving behind it a desert, a ruin. The long Harbour Road seemed endless. Fortunately for Aunt Brigid, the journey was all downhill. Now, as they neared the entrance to the city itself, they came upon groups of men standing outside factory gates. Outside a large jute factory they saw about one hundred young women. All seemed to be talking excitedly. There was nothing about this early morning flight of Miss Mangan that aroused their curiosity. The procession of three, Mr Fury leading, aroused no interest in them. Miss Mangan focused her eyes upon this crowd of young women, remarking to her sister:

'It was in one of those places that Maureen worked, wasn't it?'

'Yes,' replied Mrs Fury, looking straight ahead.

'At last!' she was thinking. 'Here we are. Almost at the end of the journey.' The last few days had seemed like a nightmare. With Aunt Brigid gone, they might be able to settle down again. Mr Fury called back, 'This way.'

They turned down Salter Road. Miss Mangan could see the tall masts of ships. She looked reassuringly at Mrs Fury. 'Almost there,' she remarked. Again Mrs Fury's reply was 'Yes.' She was still looking ahead. Now they were on the dock road. They stood hesitating.

'It's the next gate,' said Mr Fury.

All three passed into the dock. Suddenly Aunt Brigid shouted, 'There is a boat, Fanny, after all!' She added, 'Thank God!' There was indeed a boat tied up at the quay. Mr Fury stood waiting for them. When they came up, he said, 'Yes.'

'Well, here we are,' exclaimed Mrs Fury. They looked up at the boat. Even then Mrs Fury was filled with apprehension. Yes. The boat was there. But the very atmosphere of the place suggested something else. Miss Mangan opened her mouth wide, and it remained open, like that of a fish, whilst Mr Fury looked up at the funnels of the ship.

There seemed nobody about. A silence like the grave itself seemed to hem them in, held them there speechless. Then a miracle happened. A man came out of a cabin and stood for a moment, his eyes upon the gangway, at the bottom of which Miss Mangan now stood. Mr Fury stood at her side, the bag locked between his legs. Behind Miss Mangan Mrs Fury stood, a sort of moral support in this fresh crisis now threatening. The man looked down at them, they looked up at the man. They were waiting, with something approaching dread itself, for this man to speak. Once they tensed themselves, for the man did look as though he were going to speak. But he only spat into the gutter.

'Any chance of this boat sailing, mate?' called up Mr Fury.

Miss Mangan gripped the gangway as though at the word 'Yes' she would spring forward. Mrs Fury said, 'Brigid! Brigid!'

'No.'

'Damn and blast!' shouted Mr Fury. He heard the man laugh. He did not look at the man, he could hardly control himself. 'Are you sure? Isn't there any kind of a bloody boat crossing to Cork today?' He would have liked to dash up the gangway and knock the man down. The fellow was actually grinning at them, as though revelling in their plight.

Miss Mangan drew back suddenly, so that she trod on her sister's foot. 'Sorry,' she said. 'Oh, Fanny!' Mr Fury had grown quite pale.

'There isn't a boat, then?' he called up.

'No! Haven't I told you there isn't any bloody boat sailing!' shouted the man.

'When will there be one?' asked Mr Fury.

'I don't know. Perhaps next year.' The man went into the cabin again, shutting the door with such a loud bang that Mr Fury cried, his anger having reached boiling-point, 'You insolent bastard – I'll . . .'

'Denny! Denny! Please control yourself. You fool!' Miss Mangan was speechless. She sat down on a large bacon box and surveyed the boat from stem to stern. After an almost unbearable silence Mr Fury exclaimed:

'Well! There isn't any boat. I told you, didn't I? There isn't any boat. It's useless.'

He picked up the bag.

'Come, Brigid,' said Mrs Fury. 'This is really disgraceful. To be caught out like this! We'll have to make plans.'

Yes. She would have to make plans.

They started off on the return journey. They were like three people stricken dumb. They left the dock behind them and turned up Salter Road. Miss Mangan was wondering whether she would even be able to walk back. When they came to the hill, for some strange reason they went into single file. And Brigid brought up the rear.

PART TWO

PART TWO

CHAPTER IX

I

Mr George Postlethwaite was a very happy man. Son of Mr Andrew Postlethwaite, next door neighbour of the Furys in Hatfields, he had now been married six months. George was a carter to Mr Dimmock, a shipping agent. Andrew Postlethwaite's son lived in number nine Vulcan Street, next door to Desmond Fury. It was Sunday morning. George was seated on the yard floor, his back against the wall, legs spread apart. Upon his knees there lay various chains and belts from his horse's harness. This he was now engaged in cleaning. As he applied spit and polish with energy and enthusiasm, the jingling of the chains rose into the air, so that the people in the neighbouring houses would say, 'That's George in the yard.' This continual jingle of the bright chains was accompanied by George's whistle. To whistle at his work seemed the right and proper thing to do for a man as happy as George was. Mr Postlethwaite junior was twenty-eight years of age, and though small like his father, was more thickly set. There was nothing extraordinary about George, except his perpetual smile. Nothing effaced this smile. He was wearing a sailor's jersey, the sleeves rolled up to the elbow. His head was bare. The hair was thick and curly, almost red in colour. His face was red, and it seemed that this continuous smile only served to enhance its natural colour. Mrs Postlethwaite was at that very moment frying her husband's breakfast. There was a lazy air about Vulcan Street on Sunday mornings, but George was wont to make a rift in this as soon as he appeared in the back yard, the harness dangling about his neck. If George was proud of his horse 'Nabob', the horse must have been equally proud of its master, for it seemed that no horse looked as well kept as Mr Dimmock's. Mr Dimmock's horses always took first prize in the annual horse parade. The back window of number nine shot up, and Mrs Postlethwaite called, 'George! Breakfast's ready.' 'Coming,' said George. He put down his cloth and went into the house.

In number seven a man and a woman were seated at the table. They had just finished breakfast. The strong smell of salted fish hung in the air. The woman's portion remained untouched. The small kitchen, like all the cellar kitchens in Vulcan Street, was dark, so that the light had to be

179

put on. With its cheery fire, and heavy curtains hanging over the door, it looked warm and comfortable. The man was dressed only in shirt and trousers. His arms were folded on his chest, and his head was turned towards the now open window. He appeared to be thinking deeply on some matter or other. He was obviously trying to come to a decision about something. The woman, on the other hand, looked straight in front of her. There was nothing upon the wall at which she looked, beyond the cheap red patterned paper that covered it, and a cheap oleograph depicting a Royal personage distributing Maundy money to poor people. But her gaze was so rapt, so intense, that it seemed as though her thoughts had taken flight beyond the wall, and the house itself. Not a word was spoken. Casually she pushed into the middle of the table her untouched portion of salt fish. At that moment the man looked round. 'Staring again?' he remarked, then resumed his former position. The expression upon his face changed. Then into the air there rose this jingling sound of chains. They looked at each other, as though to say, 'George is in the yard.'

A cloud of dust rose suddenly, and the man shot out his arm and closed down the window. He looked up at the clock. Almost half-past eleven. He swung round again, and without looking at his wife, exclaimed, 'I'll be late tonight.' He rose to his feet, pressed his large hands upon the table and looked down at the woman. The hands appeared to grow white beneath the pressure of the great body. As an afterthought he added, 'What will you do?'

Without raising her head, and still staring abstractedly before her, the woman replied, 'I'll go out.'

'Oh!' There was silence. The man looked at the clock again. Desmond Fury was tall and powerfully built. He looked like a butcher or a coal-heaver. His sheer physicalness seemed to dominate that little kitchen. His bullet-like head was closely cropped. He had fair hair. The eyes were of a steel-like blue, cupped and almost hidden by their shaggy brows, which, unlike his hair, were almost black. The nose was small, and seemed out of place on that powerful face, but the broad nostrils made up the deficiency. The shoulders were broad, the arms long. As he stood towering over the woman, she seemed puny and inconsequent. 'Oh!' he said again. Then he went out into the yard. The woman remained motionless.

She was of medium height, a little given to plumpness. Her hair, like her husband's, was fair. Under the light it appeared almost white. It now hung in two long plaits behind her back. Her face was white, oval in shape, crowned by a broad forehead. This forehead seemed to dominate all other characteristics. The chin was heavy and sensuous-looking. The eyes were set well apart, and of the colour of pitch, and had that luminosity that a tarred surface throws up under a film of water. As she stared at the wall the expression upon her face changed, coming and going like gusts of wind. She heard the noise of running water, and looking out of the window saw her husband coming up the yard. As she looked he stopped and said, 'Hello!' Then she heard George Postlethwaite's voice. Her husband had stopped to talk to the carter sitting in the yard. The woman got up from the chair and began to clear away the table, gathering the scraps of food into a pan. These she flung into the fire. She carried the dishes out to the back kitchen. As she washed them she sang. The conversation in the yard had now become animated. But Sheila Fury was hardly ever interested in the talk that went on between Mr Postlethwaite and her husband. Having placed the dishes on the shelf, she went upstairs and began to clean the rooms. Her husband's Sunday clothes were already laid out at the end of the bed. As she spread the bed-clothes she exclaimed under her breath, 'Where does he go? He's always out.' She now looked out through the bedroom window. She could see Mr George Postlethwaite polishing his horse's belly-band. Her husband was sitting on the low wall beside the lavatory. Mrs Fury threw up the window.

'What time are you going out?' she called down to her husband. 'Half-past one,' the man shouted back, without looking up.

'You won't want dinner, then?' said the woman. The man shouted 'No.' The woman closed down the window. She stood in front of the mirror of the oak dressing-table and began to unwind her hair. The jingling of the harness chain had ceased. Only the two voices rose into the air, the one a light tenor, the other a heavy bass.

Desmond Fury had not seen his family since his marriage. Although Hatfields was but a mile away, he had never ventured near, nor would he ever allow his wife to go there. Mrs Fury had been scandalized by his marriage in a Protestant church, and had closed her door upon him.

Thus the impasse seemed mutual. Only twice since his marriage had he approached his father. They worked near each other. Beyond a casual inquiry as to how the family was, to which Dennis Fury vaguely replied, 'Middling,' nothing much was said. Mr Fury senior asked how Sheila was; Desmond replied, 'Quite well.' Dennis Fury was never inclined to be communicative; Desmond seemed indifferent. But now, with Mr Andrew Postlethwaite's son as a next door neighbour, Desmond often received information about the goings-on at Hatfields.

This Sunday morning George Postlethwaite had a rare netful of news. 'Aye,' he said, as he polished vigorously at Nabob's belly-band. 'Aye, that brother of yours is home now. My old lady was telling me he's been home nearly a week. I reckon your old man's trying to get him away to sea ...'

'To sea?' said Desmond. 'You mean Peter?' George spat suddenly, as though the name Peter was distasteful to him. Funny how the Irish clung to Peter, he was thinking.

'Yes. Him as I used to play "tally-ho" with afore he went away.' Desmond Fury was looking over the back walls. Peter! The youngest brother! Going to sea! Then he laughed.

'It's a mistake, George,' he said. 'That young lad is going into the Church.'

'Church!' exclaimed George. 'He's going into no church. Your old man told me himself that he's going away to sea. Fellow name of Mulcare's taking him with him to London, soon's this strike's over.'

'I can't believe it,' remarked Desmond. George Postlethwaite made no reply. It is doubtful whether he would have made one. Mr Postlethwaite's thoughts were now centred round something else. This something was an animal named Nabob. Nabob must be seen to. George turned round and looked up at the man sitting on the wall.

'What do you think of all these silly blighters downing tools like this? Mugs! Bloody mugs! That's what I say. Now I got to walk two miles through crowds to get to that stable.'

Desmond Fury laughed. 'Yes, and I think it nearly time they downed tools too. A man wants his rights. Working men aren't greedy, George. Only want their rights.'

'But what about other people's?' asked George. 'Yes, what about other people's?' He had to walk two miles to that stable, pushing his way through crowds at every street corner.

'Are you going to the meeting this afternoon?' asked Mr Fury.

'Meeting! What meeting?' asked Mr Postlethwaite. He rose to his feet and flung the belly-band on the clothes-line.

'The meeting in Powell Square. Everybody'll be there – railways, trams, dockers, seamen, carters, labourers, everybody.'

'No, sir! I'm not going. Not me! I got Nabob. I'd sooner walk two miles to feed my horse than walk three to listen to a lot of gaff.'

'Don't be so damned thick,' said Desmond Fury warmly. 'Where would you be now but for the rights that working men have won in these last ten years? The Capitalists would have driven you into the gutter.'

It may have been pure habit, or it may have been instinctive, but George spat again. George was an affable fellow at any time, but to stand and listen to talk about working men's rights on a Sunday morning seemed to him to be beyond comprehension.

'Rights! What rights? Seems everybody's gassing about rights. What about other people's rights, Fury? What with all these rights that's been fought for and lost, and fought for and lost again, seems to me there's precious little rights left.'

'Don't be daft.' Desmond Fury's voice rose. 'Don't be daft.'

'Daft! Do I ever hear anybody shouting out for their right to be left alone? Do I hear anybody shouting out, "I claim the right to be left in peace – to be dirty, to have some different kinds of pox, to be left alone – alone ..."?'

George's sudden volubility was as surprising to Mr Fury as it was to Mrs Postlethwaite. That stout young lady shouted through the window:

'George! George! It's Sunday.'

'Course it is!' called back George. 'Course it's Sunday. But what about these fellers' rights?' He looked at Desmond Fury. 'What about Nabob's rights, eh? Who thinks of the animals? Nobody.' He strode into the house, exclaiming, 'Rights! Rights my bottom.'

Desmond Fury remained sitting on the wall. And young Peter was going to sea. 'H'm,' thought Desmond. 'George must know a great deal more than that.' Yes. He must talk to George again. What pride prevented him from getting from his own father he would get from George Postlethwaite next door. He jumped down from the wall and went into the house. As he passed into the kitchen, Sheila Fury came downstairs. He looked at her, his whole face mirroring his admiration, and he went forward, catching her hands in his own. 'You look lovely, Sheila,' he said. 'Where are you going?'

Her eyes suddenly lowered, and with one sweeping glance she surveyed her person as she replied, 'Out.'

'What else?' The man released her hands and sat down. As he leaned back in the chair his eyes wandered slowly from the woman's dainty feet to the crown of her head. Desmond Fury idolized this woman. As she passed over to the dresser to get her ear-rings from the drawer he followed her movements with his eyes. There was something in the mere sitting on the chair, of watching her body move, that imparted a sort of glow – a kind of thrill passed through his own body. The woman was never unconscious of this admiration. She always knew when his eyes were upon her. Now she turned and looked at him, her two hands busy affixing the ear-ring in her right ear. It seemed to him that, no matter which way this woman moved, he was caught up in that movement. Bending, rising, kneeling, walking, each one of these actions seemed to live for him, as though her body itself were speaking. Just to sit and look at her was ravishing. Now she was going out. He rose from the chair. 'I must get ready myself. I shall be late.' He passed upstairs, and began to dress. Something of the woman's presence appeared to remain in the room, the air was full of a cheap though delicate scent. As he put on collar and tie he noticed here and there powder smears. He dipped his finger into these and smelt it. This slight action seemed to alter his appearance at once. There was something repulsive about the huge man dipping his finger in the powder and smelling it. Completely dressed, he looked at himself in the glass. 'Look all right,' he said to himself. Then he went downstairs. The woman was now standing in the lobby. She appeared to be waiting for him. Having seen to the fire and made the doors secure, he joined her in the lobby.

'You're not going to that damned shore again?' he asked tentatively. 'No.' They went out.

As they passed down the street, neighbours on Sunday sentry duty remarked one to the other, 'There she goes. That actress woman.'

This remark had once come to Desmond's ears. Hearing it, he experienced a new pride in his wife, at the same time cursing the neighbours for the remark. Vulcan Street was intensely anxious about Mrs Sheila Fury. She was 'a cut above the ordinary', she was something alien in their midst. When the bottom of the street was reached, husband and wife parted company.

'I'll be out till about ten,' Desmond said, his hand in Sheila's.

'I won't be that late,' remarked Sheila.

Desmond Fury stood watching her go. When she had gone about one hundred yards she turned into a side street. The man followed. When he reached this street, his wife had already arrived at the end of it. He saw her turn left. He stopped, looking at the spot where he had last seen her, as though a hole had come suddenly into the earth and she had disappeared into it. 'Damn!' he exclaimed under his breath. 'Why did I follow her? What am I getting suspicious about?' No. It was surely mean to follow her like that. He turned round and retraced his steps. He had a four-mile walk in front of him. Well, the weather was fine, and it was a downhill journey. The city was bare of traffic. The streets were crowded. The people talked about the great strike. Desmond hurried on. The pavements were aflood with feet. Everybody seemed to be going towards town. It would be a grand meeting. They would show their bosses where they got off at. And before they knew where they were, they would have the police with them. Such were Desmond Fury's thoughts as he hurried towards town.

'Strange, isn't it?' remarked Mrs Postlethwaite, as she came out of the parlour of number nine. George was shaving in the back kitchen.

'Aye.' He paused, hand in the air, and looked round. 'Are you going to bed now?' The woman nodded her head. Mrs Postlethwaite was stout; indeed, her stoutness seemed on the increase, though this fact did not worry Mr Postlethwaite.

'Aye,' said George again. ' 'Tis funny. She goes off on her own quite a lot now. Must be something up.'

'H'm! Yes,' remarked his wife. She picked up the newspaper and went upstairs. Like George, Mrs Postlethwaite was pleased with the world. Sundays always found her very busy. She rose early, cooked the breakfast, laid dinner, and whilst that was cooking, proceeded to give number nine Vulcan Street a thorough clean down, whilst her husband spent most of his morning cleaning up Nabob's harness. Dinner over, she retired to read the Sunday paper, whilst George went off to Crocus Street to see to the horse. In the evening they went out, sometimes to the landing-stage to sit and watch the traffic on the river, or sometimes to the Park. The Postlethwaites did not go to church or chapel. They went to a mission once a month. The mission had a band. George beat the big drum in the band. Once a year the mission went on a treat, sometimes to the famous Correll Grounds, kindly lent by the Earl of Tolly. Sometimes they went on a cruise in the Channel.

Having shaved, George put on his Sunday best. He then went upstairs. His wife was lying on the bed. She was reading with great excitement about a divorce case held in the courts that week. The news about the industrial dispute was merely dull geography. George sat down. There was something rather delicious about Anne lying like that. She turned and looked at him. 'I'm going now,' he said. 'Give us a kiss.' They embraced. Only a stern sense of duty to Nabob prevented George from taking Mrs Postlethwaite there and then. There was something about Sunday that made him feel generous. The heavy dinner, the lazy, almost languorous atmosphere associated with their Sunday afternoons, aroused this feeling in him. Anne Postlethwaite turned a page, and began to read again. She had forgotten George. The man, standing at the bedroom door, was smiling down at her. Silently he closed it and went downstairs. 'Funny!' he said to himself. 'It wouldn't be Anne if she wasn't at that confounded window.' But now he reflected that the inhabitants of Vulcan Street made it part of the Sunday curriculum to sit looking out of the parlour window. He had watched his own mother do it many and many a time. She said she liked to see the different clothes people wore. Mr Postlethwaite now gathered up Nabob's harness, slung the chains round his neck, the belly-band over his shoulder, and going out through the back door, set off at a sharp pace down the entry. He followed the same route every Sunday, never diverting from this set course. And as he walked the chains jingled and sang a sort of song of their own. As George neared the stable, he began to whistle. Nabob always knew this whistle, and whinnied until the door was open. Having fed and watered the roan, patted and stilled her, George sat down on the bundle of hay and watched Nabob chumping enthusiastically. He hardly ever left the stable before tea-time. He then returned home by the same route. George's Sundays were all alike. Nothing save a revolution would alter them.

After tea, Mrs and Mrs Postlethwaite decided to go out. George maintained that a walk to the heath was the only possible walk.

'I'm fed up with that Park,' he said, 'and it's useless walking to town, seems everybody's gone down to that meeting in Powell Square. There'll be a few cracked heads tonight and serve them right.'

'All right,' remarked Anne, slipping on her grey dress with the scalloped sleeves. 'We'll go the shore.' The shore was three miles away from Vulcan Street. George put on his hard hat. He looked at Anne. It may have been the grey dress that suddenly accentuated Mrs Postlethwaite's plumpness, for George remarked upon it for the first time. 'My, you are getting fat,' he said.

The woman laughed, looked down at her body that threatened at any moment to burst through the tight dress, and remarked, 'Well, what about it?' She put her black toque on. Then her blue coat, which she buttoned up to the neck. They left the house.

'What was all the talk about this morning?' asked Anne as they turned out of the entry. She looked questioningly at George.

'Oh! It's Fury,' remarked George. 'Talking a lot of bosh about the damned strike and workers' rights. Trust the Irish! They're in the middle of everything. If there's a row of any kind you'll find them in it.'

'It wasn't that,' said Mrs Postlethwaite. They had reached the main road. Until the end of this road was reached they maintained a silence. There was something rather odd about the road, so it seemed to George. Then Anne exclaimed, 'How quiet it is, George!' The long main road, always crowded on Sundays, was practically deserted. With the absence of vehicular traffic it had the appearance of a desert.

'Aye,' said George. ' 'Tis funny, isn't it! Everybody's gone to town today. It's a change, anyhow. Nice and quiet.'

'Yes,' replied Anne. 'What was the conversation about this morning?' Again she looked at her husband as if to say, 'I'm very interested.'

'Oh! About that young brother of his who was going in for the priesthood. Yes. Desmond was surprised when I told him. The lad seems to have chucked it up. He's going to go away to sea.'

'Oh dear!' said Anne. 'That boy they were always talking about?'

'Yes,' continued George. 'They're not half upset about it either, so my old man was telling me.'

'But it's so silly,' said Mrs Postlethwaite. 'Serves the woman right, putting on airs like that. And they're no different to anybody else.'

'Quite right, Anne. They aren't! Though they think they are. Anyway, the old woman's getting it in the neck now. Thick and heavy. Suppose if she had had her way the whole bloody family would have been priests. But look what's happened. The girl cleared out. Desmond never goes near a chapel, and the old man's not much different. It's that fellow Moynihan at the chapel, I think. He's got Mrs Fury under his thumb.'

'Awful queer folk, Catholics,' Anne said.

'Yes,' said George. 'But even then they're still queer. They're always rowing about something. My people who live next door to them hear them at it night after night. When the lad came back some aunt came with him, and I believe she's a bloody tartar all right.'

'Does Desmond know?'

'No. He doesn't care a hang about them, anyway.' Suddenly George raised his head, took a deep breath, and exclaimed, 'Here we are! Here's the shore.' He stopped, looked round, and added, 'Aye! It's great, isn't it? Nice and peaceful.'

'It's lovely,' said Anne. They could now see the sea. To reach it they had to pass through a railway tunnel, down a houseless street, to the dock road, where they turned right. Then they walked down a long sandy lane, flanked on either side by great iron railings. At last they put foot upon the shore. Mr Postlethwaite stopped again, took another deep breath, and said 'It's great.' The woman was not so demonstrative. She walked quietly at his side. She felt happy. To be away from the kitchen, from its smells, from the street itself, that was something that Mrs Postlethwaite relished with a kind of secret joy. Nor were their outings confined to Sundays. When George came home in the evenings they went out. To escape from the kitchen, to get into the air, was almost a passion with Mrs Anne Postlethwaite. As they tramped slowly, lazily, along the deserted shore, they seemed lost in thoughts of their own. Something in the very atmosphere caught and held them. Such things as strikes never entered their heads. They were too happy. Half a mile ahead Mr Postlethwaite espied an old upturned ship's boat. Its bow had rotted. When one stepped into it the timbers creaked. This old boat was their rendezvous. In the summer season, to get a cosy place in the ship's boat was considered a great treat. Now not only the boat but the whole shore was at their command. As they drew nearer George exclaimed:

'Isn't that somebody paddling out there?' He pointed with his finger towards a black object at the edge of the water. Anne looked in the direction the finger pointed.

'Perhaps it is,' she remarked; she leaned against the old boat.

'But fancy paddling this time of year!' she added. She turned round. Mr Postlethwaite lifted her up. Then he followed himself and sat down by her side. The man and woman looked out over the foam-specked water. Here and there they saw a steamer, one bound seawards, one making for the port. Mr Postlethwaite looked up the beach again. The black object attracted him. At any other time Mr Postlethwaite would have ignored it. He was not a very observant person, but there was something about this object that did attract him. It stood out so clearly against the background of sand-hills. And it was the only moving object in sight.

'Funny!' said George. 'It looks like a woman to me.' At which remark Mrs Postlethwaite jumped, and exclaimed astonishedly:

'What woman?' Mrs Postlethwaite's thoughts had been very far away. Indeed, as her eyes fastened upon the distant horizon with a sort of rapt expression, she experienced a peculiar sensation: as though her thoughts and feelings, her very body had melted into the distant expanse of sky and water. She looked petulantly at George. The expression upon her face was like that of a child who has just been woken up.

'What woman?' she asked.

'Can't you see?' said George. 'I wish I hadn't smashed those glasses Mr Dimmock gave me last May Day. You could've seen perfect.' But now, looking at the distant object, which certainly seemed to be moving, she felt angry. There was nothing about it that could rouse her interest. It was quite insignificant. To be roused from a reverie to look at something black nearly half a mile away only increased her petulance.

'You seem very interested,' she remarked. The distant sky and water had lost their interest. She laid her hands on her knees.

'You're queer, George,' she said vexedly. 'You always interrupt at the wrong time.' George remained silent. As the silence grew, he became fidgety.

'Why on earth don't you go and see what it is?' said Anne. 'You seem greatly interested.' She pushed him with her elbows.

'I'm not!' protested George. 'Suppose you think I am, 'cause I said it looked like a woman. An ...' He climbed down from the boat.

'Come on, Anne,' he said. 'Let's go further along.' He helped his wife down and they walked further north. That particular part of the shore had lost all interest. As they drew nearer, even Mrs Postlethwaite failed to conceal her curiosity, now suddenly roused by the fact that the object at the water's edge was a woman. She made no comment. She wanted to hear what George had to say. Yes – it was a woman. She was sitting on a large stone, her head resting in her hands. She gazed out across the waters. Mr Postlethwaite said suddenly:

'There you are! What'd I tell you? It *is* a woman. She isn't paddling, though.

Just sitting there staring. Funny, isn't it?' Mrs Postlethwaite made no reply. She refused to go a step further.

'I'm not going any further, George,' she said. 'You go if you like. It isn't right to go and look at people in that way.'

'She might be going to chuck herself in,' said Mr Postlethwaite, and he laughed.

'Nonsense! She's a long time making up her mind.' Mrs Postlethwaite stood watching her husband. She saw him stop. Then he turned round and looked at her. The woman thought he was going to shout, but he went slowly on. George Postlethwaite's curiosity was now thoroughly roused. Why was she sitting like that? Was she asleep? What was she thinking about? Perhaps she was dead. He was almost within reach now. He slackened his pace. The figure on the stone did not move. The woman seemed unaware of Mr Postlethwaite's leisurely approach. 'Why should a woman sit like that for hours on a stone?' was the question that suddenly formed itself in Mr Postlethwaite's mind. Yes. Why? Now he stopped. He stared at the woman's back. Yes. She was alive. But what was she doing sitting there? The very idea that a woman might like to sit upon the shore on a Sunday afternoon and reflect never occurred to Mr Postlethwaite. George associated the shore with crowds – men, women, children, ice-cream carts, donkeys. But the seashore in winter seemed no place for any woman to sit. What had aroused Mr Postlethwaite's curiosity was the fact that the woman had been sitting there for quite a long time. Now she appeared to sense his presence, and she half turned her head. Mr Postlethwaite immediately turned his own. He felt like a thief caught in the act. Well, he had come all this way, so he didn't see any harm in looking at her. When he did so, his jaw dropped and he put a hand to his mouth; his face expressed both surprise and bewilderment. Then he turned and ran, and did not stop until he came up to Mrs Postlethwaite.

'Anne!'

'What? What's the matter? Is she dead?' Anne asked.

'No, no!' replied George excitedly. 'D'you know who it was? It's that Mrs Fury.'

Anne now revealed her astonishment. 'Mrs Fury? Which Mrs Fury?' She was holding on to George's arm.

'Desmond's wife,' said George. 'I was surprised – I . . .' Suddenly rain fell.

'Oh dear!' exclaimed Mrs Postlethwaite. 'Now we're caught, George!'

'Come on,' said Mr Postlethwaite. 'If we walk quickly we'll get in before it really comes down heavy.' Buttoning their coats tight up to their necks, they started off arm-in-arm, now running alternately with a fast walk. Once they both looked round. The woman was still there.

'Extraordinary!' blurted George, gripping Anne's arm more securely. Anne made no reply. Between the revelation on her husband's part, and the sudden fall of rain, she felt too bewildered to talk at all. In addition, Mr Postlethwaite was increasing his pace, and it was beginning to tell on her. She ought never to have put on that tight dress. 'Fancy that woman being there!' George gasped out. Anne said, 'Yes, it is strange,' and hung heavily on her husband's arm.

2

As Desmond Fury drew near to Mile Street the number of people seemed to increase. Never before had he seen so many people. He asked himself a question: Were all these people going to the meeting in Powell Square? 'No,' he thought, 'that's impossible. Powell Square would never hold them.' As he looked down the hill at the hundreds of people, he imagined that every room, every cellar and hole had yielded its quota to this human avalanche. It swelled before his very eyes. He stopped to look at his watch. It would soon be time. Desmond Fury was a railwayman's delegate. He was to act as steward at number eleven stand in the Square. The object of the mass meeting was to voice agreement with and support of the miners. Every trade was represented. It was a complete stoppage. Dockers, seamen, railwaymen, tramwaymen, transport workers, everybody who earned his living with his hands, had put down their tools in support of the miners. Desmond's astonishment remained. As he came up to the public-house called the Drums and Fifes he recognized a well-known figure. He stopped. This figure emerged from the swing-doors of the public-house, carrying with it the strong smell of beer and tobacco smoke, which later seemed to join forces with the sourish smell that emanated from the convenience right along-side the Drums and Fifes. The figure was dressed in a check suit, a suit quite unsuited to that period of the year, a white cut-away collar, red tie with white spots on it, and a pair of light-brown boots. Until he removed his hard hat in order to scratch his completely bald head nobody would have recognized in him Mr Andrew Postlethwaite. He looked more like a book-maker's clerk than a loco man. He was smoking a briar pipe. Mr Postle-thwaite's face was rather redder than usual. He looked quite pleased with himself. It was not often that Desmond met the little man from Hatfields. Whenever he saw him he always recalled the occasion when, one New Year's night, he had let the New Year in to number five Hatfields in such a boisterous way that Mr Postlethwaite, then in his prime, had promptly struck Desmond on the head with a brass rod. Desmond Fury still carried the marks of the stitches in his head. He hailed the man at once. Although he disliked Mr Postlethwaite the Billie, he had a great respect for that Mr Postlethwaite

190

who paid his subscriptions regularly to the Federation. Andrew Postlethwaite was a good man in that respect. He was never in arrears. Desmond knew that, having control of the books.

'Hello, Mr Postlethwaite!' he called. 'You going to the meeting?' The little man looked round. He had recognized the voice.

'Hello, Desmond!' he said, shooting forth a hand. 'How are you? Yes, I'm going down. I suppose you're speaking down there?'

'Oh no,' replied Desmond. 'Not yet. Stewarding for the railwaymen.'

He looked up and down the road. Then he smiled.

'Did you ever see such a crowd, Mr Postlethwaite?' he said. 'By Jove! I think this meeting will be good. I *never* saw so many people before.' He smiled again.

'Aye,' remarked Mr Postlethwaite. 'Fairish. No more'n fairish. Remember the time when I saw a crowd of eighty thousand watch the Villa beat Everton. That was a crowd.' He pulled out his pipe and spat in the gutter, as though in mock derision of Desmond Fury's astonishment and enthusiasm.

'Yes,' remarked Desmond. 'If one could get as many men to meetings as one gets at football matches, there would never be any strikes.'

Mr Postlethwaite changed the conversation at once. He pointed up the road.

'Hang on a minute,' he said. 'Your father's just up the road there. He'll be here in a tick.' Desmond followed Mr Postlethwaite's finger. Mr Postlethwaite appeared to look anxious now. Where on earth was the man?

'He's a heck of a time,' said Mr Postlethwaite.

'I'm rather surprised,' remarked Desmond. 'I never thought he would go to the meeting.'

'H'm!' muttered Mr Postlethwaite. 'You can't tell your father from one minute to another, Desmond. Pity you don't work alongside him.'

Suddenly out of a side street there appeared with the thunderous rush of water a crowd of men and women. It swung into the road, flooding the sidewalk, carrying everything in its wake, passing strangers, people coming home from church and chapel. It seemed to swell, to open fanwise, to draw everything to it. Where had it come from? It was making its way down the hill. Desmond Fury drew aside, Mr Postlethwaite jumped, flung his arm round the brass rail outside the window of the Drums and Fifes, and said to Desmond, 'What's this?' All Andrew Postlethwaite could see now was a mass of faces, a living map. Young and old, tall and short, fat and thin. Then this crowd began to sing. The noise was deafening. In a moment it had picked up both Desmond and Mr Postlethwaite in its stride. There was no escaping it. It was like an all-embracing octopus. Mr Postlethwaite shouted, 'Hey! Hey! What the hell . . . ?' but a woman's elbow seemed to jam itself in his mouth. Desmond hung on to the little man. Amongst this drab crowd, Andrew Postlethwaite's check suit seemed more out of place than ever.

'Stick to me!' Desmond Fury shouted in his ear.

The crowd seemed to have worked the two men into its midst. There was no time to think, no time to stand, to make a rush from it. It swung down the hill, increasing as it went. Before this tidal flow everything went down. Desmond Fury now with a single hand tried, as he was bowled along with the mass, to search his pockets for his delegate's ticket. Without that ticket he would not be allowed in the Square.

'Christ!' he growled under his breath. He was conscious of the warm, sourish, animal-like smell that seemed to rise from this fretted mass. Again and again he endeavoured to stop, to pull himself and Mr Postlethwaite aside. When they reached Upper Nile Street the miracle happened. To his right Desmond saw a public convenience. Now was his chance. He gripped tighter upon Mr Postlethwaite's arm. Then with a powerful lunge of his body he crushed his way through. A women fell. There were shouts, curses, screams.

'Aye! There! You swine! Knockin' a woman down. Hey, kick him!'

Desmond did not hear them. There was only one thing to do. To push through, to kick, to wrestle, to smash one's way free of this yelling mob. As he tore through what seemed to him like flying bodies, some of the crowd fell back. Carried on by his own impetus he fell, bringing Mr Postlethwaite on top of him. But they had reached their objective. Desmond dragged himself to his feet. He pulled his companion up. 'Quick! In here.' They rushed into the urinal.

All space was taken up by men who had just come out of a neigh-bouring public-house. Mr Postlethwaite leaned against the grey slate wall. 'Phew!' he exclaimed. 'Phew! That was a corker, that was.'

Desmond made no reply. He was listening to the passing feet. It sounded almost like thunder. There seemed to be no end to it.

'Well! This is a fix,' he remarked. Three men had left the urinal. There was elbow-room. He seemed unconscious of the sudden silence. Mr Postle-thwaite put his head out. Then he laughed. 'All clear,' he said. The road was indeed quite clear, save for a few groups of straggling people, and the usual collection of men standing outside each public-house window. These groups of men outside the pubs were generally old men, sailors, longshore-men. On Sundays they never failed to be in reminiscent mood.

'Well,' remarked Desmond, 'I've got to get down to that Square. And I have about twenty minutes to do it in. The police are drawn up at the bottom of the hill. A man would never get through with that crowd.'

'No,' replied Mr Postlethwaite. He smoothed his moustache. 'No. Those beggars are only out for mischief.'

'Of course. You can't keep them out of it. Looters out for some excitement.'

'I wonder where your Dad got to?' said Mr Postlethwaite, as though he had just recalled the fact that Dennis Fury and himself had left Hatfields together to attend the meeting.

'Heaven knows,' said Desmond. They set off down the hill. As they touched the crest of it, they paused for a moment to look down. What they looked down upon was a veritable forest of heads. This forest of heads represented one section only of the mass meeting. Above the heads, banners flew proudly in the wind. Desmond exclaimed excitedly, 'This is great, Mr Postlethwaite.'

'Is it? Indeed,' said the little man, 'if we get through those lines of police it will be very great.'

'Have you a card with you? You could come to the stand with me,' Desmond continued, 'and you might even be able to find a chair.'

'I don't want no chair,' replied Mr Postlethwaite; once more he began to smooth out his moustache. This action was a sort of signal that Mr Andrew Postlethwaite was now about to fall into reflective mood. At the moment he was asking himself a question. Should he continue? It was all right getting there; it was the getting back. And as for that ugly-looking crew from Hotspur Road, he certainly didn't like the look of them. He heard Desmond say, 'I saw George this morning. I tried to get him to come down. But nothing doing.' It made Andrew Postlethwaite laugh.

'No,' he said, 'you'll never get George to these meetings, Desmond.'

'No! He's got horse sense, hasn't he?'

'Well, I suppose a fellow can please himself. Sometimes I think it looks good to see a fellow who can stand outside all this kind of stuff.' Unconsciously he had raised Desmond Fury's ire.

'Of course, of course! They're the kind of people who do nothing,' said Desmond. 'They remain hidden in the background. But when the object fought for has been achieved, they come forward for their share. Don't they?'

'Aye,' Mr Postlethwaite said. 'Aye.'

'Here we are,' remarked Desmond. As he spoke, a policeman came up to them.

'You can't get past this barrier,' he said. Mr Postlethwaite seemed to shrink under the officer's glance, a glance that was at once suspicious. Perhaps it was Andrew's check suit. Desmond Fury pulled out his card.

'Stewards at number eleven,' he said curtly, and pushed past the policeman, dragging Mr Postlethwaite with him. It was now the officer's turn to quail before Mr Fury. He moved aside and they passed through the crowd. Every-

body stared at them. Not a few commented quite openly upon Mr Postlethwaite's suit. Andrew was not deaf to these comments. By the time he
reached number eleven stand he was almost crimson. Now men called out
to him – 'Hello, Postlethwaite!' At last, he thought, he was secure. Desmond
had worked his way to the foot of the platform, leaving Mr Andrew Postlethwaite talking excitedly to his workmates from the loco sheds.

'Hello, Fury!' called a voice. Desmond turned round. A tall thin man,
dressed in a black suit and wearing no hat, came pushing his way forward.
His name was Thompson. He was a paid official of the Federation.

'How do?' said Desmond, shaking hands. They turned their backs upon the
crowd and began an animated conversation.

'Williams and Power are late,' remarked Mr Thompson.

'Yes,' and Desmond looked across the thousands of heads towards the
Castle Hotel. All he could see was the upper windows, that led out to a
miniature veranda. One window had heavy curtains drawn across it.

'Well,' said Desmond, 'they can't be long. It's always awkward. Especially
when you have a crowd of men like that.' He swung his arm in the
direction of the mass.

'The authorities are well represented,' remarked Mr Thompson. He took a
pipe from his mouth and proceeded to fill it. Desmond nodded his head.

'That can make little or no difference to us,' said Desmond. 'I can tell
you that if these leaders stand by their word the authorities will have no
trouble.'

Mr Thompson commented upon field tactics. Every factory gate, every
station, shed, dock, warehouse, and foundry was picketed. As he mentioned
this to Desmond he smiled. Mr Thompson felt like a general on the eve of
battle who has just completed his plans. On less significant occasions the
difference of opinion between Desmond Fury and Mr Thompson would have
been ventilated. Mr Thompson was a man who liked to do his work quietly.
He liked to sit in the background and make plans. Not for him the rough-
and-tumble spade-work. This seemed to him more suited to a man of
Desmond's type. Desmond's opinion was that he had been doing spade-work
too long. He had ideas, and he was ambitious. The very sight of Mr Thompson
in his black suit, with his white linen collar and blue tie, was enough to
convince Desmond that he had done enough spade-work. Suddenly the
whole Square resounded to shouts, calls, cheers. They were coming at last.
The leaders were here. Mr Williams was a man much like Mr Postlethwaite both in build and manner. Mr Power, on the other hand, seemed
to have no affinity with the gathering. Mr Power looked like a bank
manager. He was faultlessly dressed. The crowd was not slow to make

comment about the differences between the two men. Shepherded by half a dozen policemen and an inspector, the two leaders were shown to the central platform. They climbed slowly up the wooden steps. The Square became silent. Only the police fringing the crowd seemed to be talking, whispering to each other. During the momentary silence the sound of horses' hoofs beat the air, and there appeared, suddenly and as though they had risen out of the earth itself, a company of mounted police. The horses were pulled up. They tossed their heads, stamped their feet. The restlessness of the animals served as a clue to the thoughts of the men mounted upon their backs. The men stared over the crowd. The crowd was something that did not exist. They were looking much further ahead than the crowd. Having reached the platform, Mr Power sat down. Mr Williams walked to the front of the platform and stood silent, surveying the assembly in front of him. Mr John Williams had addressed meetings before. He was quite used to crowds. He knew them like a book. Behind him sat Mr Power. Mr Power knew crowds too, and was even more thorough than Mr Williams. He had studied them psychologically. The Square seemed to shake beneath the boisterous cheering. Then a silence. Mr Williams raised his hand. 'Friends,' he said. It was like a sharp word of command. 'We are here today to demonstrate our solidarity ...' Cheers. That was Mr Williams' slogan. He now began his speech.

Desmond Fury listened attentively. 'Yes,' he thought, 'that gets to the heart of the problem.' He turned enthusiastically to Mr Postlethwaite.

"What do you think of that, Mr Postlethwaite?'

'Damned good,' replied the other. He puffed away contentedly at his pipe. 'What a sea of faces,' he was thinking. Where on earth had all these people come from? At last Desmond came and sat down by him.

'If we can get the men into the right mood, and I don't think Williams will have much trouble, I think the miners' case is as good as won.' He looked at Mr Postlethwaite, and for the first time he laughed. He had only just this minute noticed the texture of his friend's suit.

'Aye.' It was more of a growl than an expression of approval. 'Aye,' replied Mr Postlethwaite. 'That's easy, quite easy to say that. You don't know these sods of bosses like I do. You're only a bloody nipper, me lad. It could be as easy as all that. D'you think the bosses are going to be worried into submission by this?' Mr Postlethwaite waved his hand towards the crowd. 'Look!' he entreated. 'Just take a look. That's what they think.'

'But a lot of policemen might mean something else,' remarked Desmond. 'If they had a clear and honest case it wouldn't need an army of police to back it up.'

'Oh!' said Andrew. 'You've got it wrong again, Fury. Those fellows are no more interested than my backside. All they're out for is to take care of property, to see nobody steals a brick out of the Forester Hall.' He spat. 'Yes – and the damned theatre over there. A hive of inikity. They ought to pull it down. Nothing but leg shows week after week. The young fellers these days are really going off their onion, I seem to think.'

Desmond Fury didn't seem interested in this sudden burst of oratory on Andrew Postlethwaite's part. He now turned his attention to the speaker, and proceeded to ignore the man, finally to forget his very existence. Mr John Williams held his audience. Cheer after cheer followed every utterance. Once or twice he looked at Mr Power. Mr Power sat silent, a look of utter boredom upon his face as his eyes wandered slowly from end to end of the serried rows of faces. After a while they seemed to lose all human semblance. When Mr Power reached this stage he knew it was time for him to get up and address them. But Mr Williams seemed to be expanding, to be carried away on his own flow of speech. Desmond thought, 'Some day I'll be there too. And I'll be different.' He kept looking from Mr Williams to Mr Postlethwaite. He had decided to politely ignore Mr Power, that gentleman having ignored him, and not only him but the other half-dozen delegates who had assembled and now sat together on one corner of the platform. Looking at him now, Desmond recalled the occasion of his election to the Executive, and how keenly he, Desmond, had voted against his appointment. Desmond Fury felt it was all wrong. Why should men like Mr Power steal all the thunder whilst the working man had to do all the spade-work? Desmond had been doing spade-work. Tiring, unthankful tasks. And he had seen men like Mr Power welcomed with open arms. But what did these men know? He thought they knew nothing. After Mr Power had spoken at the Federation Conference he was certain of it.

'And all you have to do, my friends, is to stand fast, to be cool, to fold your arms. If you do that, the cause is won.'

Cheers! Mr John Williams wiped the sweat from his forehead. Now he stole a sly glance at the immaculately dressed Mr Power, and he chuckled inwardly. He had stolen his fire – his time – his thunder. With something amounting to pride, almost ecstasy, he stood erect and looked out at the gathered thousands. 'Hands up, then, in favour of that resolution.' More cheers. A forest of hands rose into the air.

'And now your duty lies at every dock-gate – at every railway station, yard, office, shed, factory, and foundry – at every quay, terminus, and depot.' The cheers were almost deafening.

Desmond Fury, carried away by this flow of oratory, clapped his hands, shouting, 'Hurrah! Hurrah!' The shout was taken up by the assembly. 'Hurrah! Hurrah! Three cheers for John Williams!'

'Hurrah! Hurrah! Hurrah!' Even Andrew Postlethwaite became infected. He knocked out his pipe, put it in his pocket, and joined in the clapping. He turned to Desmond.

'Looks as though Power will speak in the Park now. Are you going with the procession?' he asked.

'Yes. Why not?'

'Oh! Well, I'm going home,' said Mr Postlethwaite. 'I couldn't walk another five miles after this. Soon's this crowd has broke up, I'm off.' Desmond Fury was quite deaf to the remark. He was looking to the left of the assembly at a group of people wedged in between the stone lions. It seemed a policeman had had to push his way through this crowd. This he did without any by-your-leave. The people herded together resented it. It would not have been so bad had the officer in question said, 'Make way, please.' He had just barged through. An enthusiastic member of the crowd had had no compunction about withdrawing a pin from his coat and roughly prodding this thirteen stone of authoritative flesh and blood in the rear. At once the officer, sensing the culprit, struck out with his fist. Confusion immediately. Open curses and threats. 'Swine! Swine! For two pins they'd knock you flat, the bastards!' This ugly little interlude in the quiet, orderly meeting was most perturbing to Mr Williams. 'Order! Order there!' shouted the delegates. 'Order!'

Mr John Williams was speaking again. The incident closed. The policeman emerged with a very red face, and taking up his new position near the platform, scowled at Mr Williams, who politely ignored him. The crowd was all attention once more, though the atmosphere still seemed disturbed. That little tiff with the policeman had not been forgotten. It wasn't authority that was being questioned by the crowd, but the manners of authority.

Whilst Mr Williams was speaking, a new phenomenon had presented itself. This took the form of an elderly gentleman who, in full morning dress, came and stood at the open window of the Castle Hotel. He stood for a moment gazing indifferently down upon the sea of faces below him, then stepped out on to the veranda. As suddenly he withdrew. The gentleman gave the appearance of having dined well, even a little too well, for a hand shot out and grabbed him by the back of his coat. This sudden jerk seemed to have disarranged the pink bloom that he sported in the lapel of his coat. The waiter behind him smoothed down his ruffled coat and adjusted the flower. The sounds from below came through the open window. It may have been the voice of Mr John Williams, or the warm animal-like smell that rose from these packed bodies, or the whisperings in the various groups, but the gentleman, a little unsteadily, walked out to the veranda again, and again the ever-attentive waiter caught his coat: 'Careful, sir! Careful, sir!'

The gentleman, deaf to these entreaties, now looked down at the assembly. 'Profanum vulgus,' he said. 'Canaille.' Then he spat upon the veranda floor. But it was not this sudden remark that turned the key in the whole situation. Nobody had heard the words, few indeed in that assembly would have understood them. It wasn't the words, but the action. And as though to finish off with the requisite verve and polish, he once more pulled out his pink flower and readjusted it. Having done this, he patted his person almost affectionately. The waiter pulled him in again. At the same time somebody at the back of the crowd shouted, 'Look at 'im! Look at 'im!' and pointed with a hand that made wild aimless movements above the heads towards the window. Everybody looked. The man was obviously drunk.

'Look at 'im! Bloody Cap'list! Bloody Cap'list!' Even Mr Williams turned and looked up at the window. The crowd had caught sight of the rather bibulous gentleman. He seemed quite unaware of the extraordinary interest he had so suddenly created. Perhaps he had simply meant to get the air, or perhaps, like Mr Williams, he was interested in crowds. They now looked at him from every possible angle. They looked at him frontally, in profile; they studied him from head to foot. Mr Williams was a back number. The Cause – Solidarity – paled before this phenomenon. To add to the sudden interest there came murmurs from the crowd, whilst the hand in the distance still waved aimlessly in the air and its owner in a thick guttural voice beseeched the assembly to – 'Look at 'im!' 'Flower in his blinkin'–co–coat too. Hic!'

Mr Williams faced the crowd. 'Men! Men! Attention! Order! ...' To the speaker the crowd appeared to sway, to swell, to move forward, tremble, break forces, then gather as one again.

'I appeal ... Stand fast where you are. I ... I have seen this sort of thing before. I ...' He turned round and looked questioningly at Mr Power, as though to get the confirmation and support of that silent individual. But that gentleman did not respond. Mr Power was no longer interested. John Williams had arranged to speak for ten minutes and then let Mr Power do the rest. Instead of which, he had held the board for nearly an hour. Mr Power was bored. He was also a little jealous.

Desmond Fury caught John Williams' glance, and shouted across, as he pointed to the hotel window from which the bibulous gentleman had made a retreat, 'It's a trap. A police trap.' Mr Williams did not hear. It was too late to hear anything. The crowd had caught the words 'trap – police'. The spade-workers, the veterans of the movement, said to themselves, 'Spy! Agent provocateur!' The crowd's movements changed. As Mr Williams looked at the people in front they seemed to assume almost fantastic proportions. The gentleman who had so hurriedly disappeared from the window had not been entirely deaf to the sea of sounds that rose towards the window where he stood. Angry murmurs, obscene comments. It was indeed a whiff of the crowd's temper that came up to him this Sunday afternoon.

When John Williams first saw the man at the window he said to himself, 'Has the fellow no common sense? No decency? Is he not alive to the very obvious fact that his own person threatened danger? Or is he merely a repetition of another gentleman, French by birth, who during the Paris riots stood at an hotel window in just the same way? Why doesn't the fellow go away?' Such were Mr Williams' thoughts. He had travelled Saturday night and part of Sunday to address this meeting. Was it to be a failure? Was it to end up in bloodshed? A peaceful meeting? If anything was more fickle than a woman, it was a crowd. A crowd was a curious thing. Mr Williams had his own ideas about it. It was a monster without any aim or sense of proportion – a headless monster. Mr Williams shouted to a near-by inspector, 'If you don't want trouble, you will ask that gentleman up there to go away from the window.' The officer looked at Mr Williams. Then a loud crash of glass drowned his reply. Somebody had hurled a brick through the window. The cause of the commotion had tactfully made his exit from the rear of the hotel. This abutted on the railway station. The gentleman went into the toilet and carefully removed his flower, which he threw down the bowl. He then emerged on to the station platform; from there, after following various devious routes, he made his way to the street. A few minutes later he was lost in the crowd. The crash of glass was followed by yet another. Mr Williams now knew that the meeting was at an end. Any idea of controlling this angry mob seemed as remote as the moon. Well, he had been in such situations before. He knew his business too well. The crowd in front now began to shout, to yell. Mr Williams tried to drown them with his own voice. It was useless. He stood bewildered, powerless. His eyes wandered to the company of mounted men. The horses seemed more restless than ever. And what was the sudden movement at the back of the crowd? Mr Williams hammered on the table with his fists. 'Order! Quiet! Quiet! Keep cool!' A veritable shower of stones was now hurled at the hotel window. There was a sudden concerted rush for the platforms. At the same time the mounted police drew rein. The people shouted, 'Ah!' ... From the open window of the Forester Hall came a stentorian voice, calling through the megaphone, 'Clear the Square! Clear the Square!'

Mr Williams was almost in tears. He shouted himself red in the face. 'Stand fast! Stand fast! Don't move an inch.' But already he could see the ranks of mounted police widening. In the rear some scuffles were taking place. These holes, corners, and cellars had not yielded up their occupants for nothing. What had happened? The leaders' eyes searched the crowd. A concourse of ten thousand people were ringed in the Square. From the platforms men shouted at the top of their voices, 'Stand fast! Stand fast!' The police were already advancing. They intended to carry out their orders to clear the Square. Individuals appealed to individuals, banter was rife. The people stood fast. Why should they be cleared from the Square? Were they a herd of animals? Mr Williams was quite powerless now. This controllable crowd was beyond control. The people stood waiting. A volley of stones met the advancing police. Batons were drawn.

'Look out! Look out!' Before the rush Mr Williams went down. The platform collapsed. A hundred hands tore it down. People armed themselves with wooden staves. Pockets were filled with stones. Iron railings were pulled out. Now the police came forward at a run. The crowd broke. Shouts, screams, curses, laughter, the crash of glass, the breaking of wood. The mass of people swayed, held for a moment, rushed forward, scattered, gathered *en masse* again, and made a rush from the Square. At that moment the mounted police came forward at a gentle trot. Batons, now drawn, made a strange humming noise as they sang through the air and landed on heads with a sickly thud. Confusion and fear joined forces.

On number eleven stand Desmond Fury stood hemmed in by a group of men. Mr Andrew Postlethwaite was amongst this group. The difficulty with those on number eleven platform was that they could not move. The platform seemed to be encircled by a continuous procession of flying bodies. Mr Postlethwaite now realized that, like George, he should have stayed at home. Not so Desmond Fury. The situation was one in which he was quite capable of holding his own. Twice Mr Postlethwaite had watched for an opportunity of flinging himself into the Square. But now the slightest movement was fraught with disaster. A movement of any kind seemed a threat, an ultimatum. Already blood had been drawn.

Mr Postlethwaite was not deaf to the sickly thud of the batons. A section of the crowd had forced its way out of the Square. Whistles blew, bronze-like voices roared through megaphones, galloping hoofs struck fire from the stones. 'Look out!' shouted Desmond. The mounted police were coming towards number eleven platform at a gallop. Mr Postlethwaite spat and shouted, 'Bastards!' The horses came on. The man next to Mr Postlethwaite swayed, screamed, 'Oh Christ!' and proceeded to vomit over Mr Andrew Postlethwaite's new check suit. The owner of the suit was quite unaware of this. His attention had been drawn to a woman, a rather stout woman, wearing a black shawl over her head. She had been knocked down in a sudden rush. The horses advanced. They were almost upon her, and Andrew Postlethwaite was certain they would trample upon her. 'Bastards!' he screamed, and possessed of strength of which he never seemed aware until now, he broke free and flung himself, almost as if diving into water, over the platform to the Square. He fell in a heap. He was caught up into a group of men. All were struggling upon the ground, making frantic endeavours to get to their feet. In the midst of this lay the woman. As Mr Postlethwaite regained his breath he looked up and saw a long baton swinging downwards. 'My God!' He covered his eyes with his hands. He saw the horses upon him. Frantically he dragged himself to his knees and waited, arms outstretched. As he stood there, hemmed in by a yelling mass of bodies, he put his hand in his pocket and drew out his clasp-knife. He would, he vowed, slit the first horse. 'Ugh! Ugh!' he said, as the batons sang through the air.

'Hey! For Christ's sake! You swine! That's a woman! Take his number! Take his number!'

'Here's my bloody number!' roared the policeman, his horse's hot breath almost in Mr Postlethwaite's face, and crashed his baton down upon the man's head. As Mr Postlethwaite fell, a huge figure seemed to whirl into the air, landing upon horse and rider.

'Ah!' Desmond Fury screamed as he pulled down the man from his horse.

Behind the Forester Hall there had been assembled a dozen wagonettes. These wagonettes were full of women and children. Their destination was Corlton, where a concert was being given. But this assembly of happy and excited children had now been drawn into the conflict. Their destination was no longer Corlton. Their destination was Safety. On the first mad rush of the crowd the children had screamed. The mothers accompanying them made every endeavour to pacify them. This trip to Corlton was an annual affair. The children were cripples from the various charitable homes scattered about. It had been advisable to warn them. They must get clear as soon as possible. Now the convoy was wedged in, their occupants the unwilling witnesses of the fracas. A section of the crowd had streamed into Corys Street, where the assembled wagonettes stood. It was obvious that the children could not get any further than there. In the excitement they had one by one made their way out of the wagonettes. The moment their feet touched the ground they were caught up in the madness and confusion. Some of them had been carried headlong to Powell Square itself. The parents made vain efforts to find their offspring. All were swallowed up in the mob. In a sortie near the Court, some of these women and children had gone down before a rush of both mounted and foot police. A baton was something more than a piece of weighted wood. It was the symbol of authority, it had no respect for neutrality. The very hand that wielded it succumbed to its power. Its sickening hum, as it swung to and fro in the air, had taken the place of the indistinct hum. Its song had assumed control. It had taken the place of hooter and whistle, of all the concourse of sounds that usually came from out the industrial ant-heap. Trains, trams, ships, docks, cars, machines, were silent. On this Sunday afternoon there was only the yelling mob, the red-faced and sweating police, and the stiff wooden interrogator that sang ceaselessly through the air. The authorities took counsel. This was no peaceful meeting. This was open revolt. This was the mob getting its head. The twelve wagonettes seemed outside their thoughts and deliberations. That assembly of derelict vehicles gave the impression of some fugitive column that, caught in the tidal flows of mob anger and authoritative fury, had flung out its occupants and consolidated itself with a calm determination down one side of Corys Street. It took the drivers all their time to keep control of the frightened animals, from whose hoofs there periodically beat a veritable tattoo upon the stones, whilst they sent showers of sparks flying right and left. The drivers, all thought of Corlton having vanished from their minds, settled themselves down to a game of waiting. This was really a siege; some time in the evening, they hoped before dark, the mob would drift away, and they could proceed back to their repository. They did not expect the sudden change of programme.

At half-past four in the afternoon, Powell Square was like a battlefield. The crowd seemed to have renewed its determination. Its object was the storming of the Castle Hotel. Up the road the smashing of glass could still be heard. Ambulances began to make their appearance opposite the Forester Hall. About the Square lay men with bleeding heads, and terrified children clung frantically to pillars and posts. In the first charge there had been a maddening rush for safety. The stone lions were used as places of refuge, men and women climbing up to sit astride their backs. Holes and corners contained their quota too. If it had been possible to rip open the ground beneath them men would have done so, for they had been forced back and front by drawn batons. Mr Postlethwaite was lying in a pool of blood under the statue of the Earl of Breconsfield. A few yards away a mounted policeman lay on his face, which was bruised and swollen. Just at his feet lay his horse. It was dead. Somebody had driven an iron spike clean through its breast. Desmond Fury had disappeared. Andrew Postlethwaite's face was covered with blood. More ambulances, more police. Two ambulance men picked up Mr Postlethwaite and placed him on a stretcher. Outside the Forum Theatre an even more desperate situation had arisen. A section of the crowd, numbering some five hundred shouting men and women, were endeavouring to smash down the doors of the theatre. There was nothing inside that they wanted. They only wanted to escape. For the third time they had met a baton charge with sticks, bottles, and stones. Their supply of ammunition was used up. They only saw the raised batons, and beat against the doors, which at last gave way. The mass of frenzied people streamed into the theatre.

When Desmond Fury threw himself at the mounted policeman, he had one thought uppermost in his mind. He must kill this man. But the officer on the horse was equal to the occasion. He met Desmond's rush with a swing of the baton; Fury dodged it, clung to the horse, and seizing the reins with his hand shot out his powerful fist, throwing the officer, who had risen in the saddle, off his balance. The mounted man let go his baton and gripped Desmond about the waist. Beneath the horse's flying hoofs two men had already gone down. Desmond Fury, using every ounce of his strength, flung himself upwards until he was almost breast to breast with the policeman. At the same moment the horse reared, whinnied, and collapsed, blood pouring from its breast. Desmond Fury and the officer rolled over to the ground. The officer now discovered that the other man was no mean adversary. Desmond Fury worked his way over the body of the policeman, caught his raised fist in one hand, and without a moment's hesitation struck with the other. 'Swine! Swine!' Then he fled. He was now the centre of another yelling crowd at the corner of Horton Street. Desmond Fury had one idea. To get free. To be clear. If he could cross Horton Street he would find shelter – one of the shops. Then he would wait for a lull. When he got his chance he would run for it. If he could manage to reach the bottom of Mile Hill he would be as safe as houses. He did not know where Mr Postlethwaite had got to. He only realized that the baton had swung dangerously over the man's head and he had flung himself at the mounted policeman. Here one could not draw breath, one could not think. One was held, intoxicated by the very sights and sounds. He did not know what time it was. He only knew that the mass meeting had been a failure: that the police were ready, and had laid their plans well. He only knew that the great meeting had been turned into a kind of arena, packed with angry, shouting people: that a gentleman in morning dress had appeared at the window, complete with flower, and had roused the crowd's ire. Who had thrown the stone? No one would ever know. Desmond, watching the mob stream into the theatre, suddenly flung up his hands. 'Ha!' he thought. 'That's it,' and he began to beat his way through the bodies about him. For a single moment he stood alone in the cleared space. Then he ran. No policeman followed, only some people. Laughter and a shower of stones hurled after him. 'Coward, coward!' What was that? 'Coward!' Desmond

Fury flung himself through the door now torn off its hinges. The dark musty corner of a waiting-room seemed to beckon to him. He flung himself into it and lay down. 'Phew!' he said. 'Phew!' Then an arm moved. He was lying prone over a woman's body. 'Please, please,' a voice said.

3

Dennis Fury had changed his mind; as he left Mr Postlethwaite, telling him to 'walk on', he had practically come to a decision. When he came out into the street again, he stood for a moment on the kerb, looking in the direction of Andrew Postlethwaite. But the gentleman from next door was nowhere in sight. Mr Fury guessed at once. Andrew Postlethwaite had seized the opportunity to go in and have a wet whilst his friend delivered himself higher up the road. No use to curse Andrew for his miserliness. He, Mr Fury, had created the opportunity. Mr Postlethwaite never paid for other people's drinks. That was a new rule with him. He had refused Miss Mangan's invitation to the Star and Garter for the same reason. He couldn't see anything in it. In the end all such invitations turned out to be that one paid for other people's as well as one's own. Not seeing his friend on the road, Mr Fury immediately said to himself, 'Good enough! He's gone into the Drums and Fifes. Then he can bloody well stay there.' Mr Fury retraced his steps. Mr Postlethwaite could go to the devil. Damn mean, sliding into publics on the sly. From time to time Mr Fury looked round, not in the hope of seeing Andrew but of estimating the situation. From where he stood, he got a clear view of Mile Hill, and down it he saw crowds hurrying towards Powell Square. Yes, home was the best place on a Sunday afternoon. His stride was leisurely, the expression upon his face that of a peaceful and contented man. When Mr Fury was alone he certainly enjoyed his own company. From time to time he stopped and looked at the shops. Shops are entrancing, their windows full of lovely things. Here the road was not so crowded, and it narrowed considerably. It was flanked by equally narrow streets, each of which had its children playing about the gutters. The smell of roasting beef, of soup, of oranges, was in the air. It made Dennis Fury feel hungry, he had been out since eleven o'clock. He had gone to Mass, and from there right on to the Pitchpine, outside of which he had met Mr Postlethwaite by arrangement. He had asked Fanny to go to the late Mass, but she refused. Mr Fury was tired asking her. Mrs Fury always went to the earliest Mass. There were two reasons for this. One met nearly everybody in the parish at the eleven o'clock Mass. And again, Sunday in number three Hatfields was always a busy day; meals to cook, Mr Mangan to wash, dress and feed, house to be cleaned. When Dennis Fury returned about half-past twelve, armed with his Sunday paper, the house had been swept clean; Mr Mangan sat in his chair, with a clean shirt, collar, and tie; and the dinner was cooking. Today things were a little changed. The house had not got over Aunt Brigid's invasion, nor Peter's sudden return. It would be a while before the Fury household settled down to normal.

When Mr Fury reached the Prince's Theatre, he stopped to look at the contents bill for the coming week. 'H'm!' he exclaimed. 'Getting as bad as that Forum in the town.' He turned off the road and walked in the direction of the Lyric. Might as well see what was doing. It was too early for tea yet, and besides, Fanny was bound to be out. She always went to the chapel meeting on Sunday afternoon. The Lyric Theatre stood at the top of Valley Street; it was reputed to be the best variety theatre in the north end of the city. Mr Fury slowly climbed the hill. He was thinking of nothing in particular; his mind was wholly vacant. His eyes were already endeavouring to read the contents bill that was displayed on a huge hoarding at the top of the Valley. Strike or no strike, he and Fanny would go to the Lyric. Fanny always looked forward to it. And although she was not very demonstrative after the performance, he was convinced she enjoyed it. Dennis Fury now stood looking at the contents bill. 'Mac and Andrew – the Two Dancing Dolls. Ivano – the Master Juggler. The Five Tumblers. Anna Semple – Soprano.' 'Oh!' said Mr Fury. 'Looks good.' He walked away, making a mental note of the artistes, visioning them in their different parts. He looked at his watch. A quarter past twelve! Not much use going home before five. Fanny wouldn't be in. He walked further up the Valley, past the Lyric Theatre. Then he decided to go right to the top, and walk back through the Park. Mr Fury very rarely went to the Park. When he did go, he invariably met somebody he knew. He turned down Bolton Street, and entered the gates. The Park seemed deserted. Its atmosphere was cold and bleak. Mr Fury increased his pace. He looked at the miserable-looking trees with their coating of grime, the legacy of the industrial world, and once stopped to watch a sparrow, black as any chimney-sweep, peck frantically upon the gravel path, as though hidden beneath it were the choicest collection of worms and bread-crumbs. He stopped again to look at the deserted boat-house, badly wanting a new coat of paint, and the deserted boats drawn up on the slip-way. Passing the boat-house, he found himself in an open space, across which an easterly wind was now driving. Mr Fury increased his pace. Clouds of dust and sand blew into the air. It seemed to Mr Fury that nothing in the world was more miserable-looking on this Sunday morning than the Avon Park. He decided to make for the bandstand, a sort of oasis in the wilderness. When he arrived there it was empty. He took one look at the cold, dismal interior, and decided to sit on one of the benches surrounding it. He was sheltered from the driving wind, which was increasing in velocity. 'What a cold, miserable-looking place!' thought Mr Fury. He pulled out his pipe. Having filled it, he got it firm and snug between his teeth, lay back, and puffed away contentedly.

Mr Fury's eyes took in the surrounding scene. The bandstand was set right in the middle of the playing-fields. These fields were part grass and part sand, and bordered by trees, leafless and as bleak-looking as the stretch of wilderness they surrounded. The man leaned his head to one side. His attitude was contemplative, as his eyes followed the columns of thickish blue-black smoke that rose from the bowl of his pipe. His thoughts seemed to sail up after this column of smoke. He looked around him, thinking, 'Aye, what a difference there'd be if everybody was content! Peter working ashore and helping his mother. Brigid back in Ireland again, and "him" too. How nice it would be to see Desmond and Sheila coming round on a Sunday evening, and Maureen and Joe! A real happy gathering.' Ah! It was difficult. Everything was upset. It was a nuisance. Of course, the trouble was that children *would* grow up. And these children developed minds and ideas of their own. Yes, that was the cause of the trouble, that was the cause of the ceaseless arguments. That was why Fanny had changed, why Desmond and Maureen had married, why Peter had failed and he himself had given up going to sea. That was why Mr Postlethwaite secretly hated him, why George beat the big drum in the band. People had minds of their own.

'Aye, if only we could be a happy family.' There Mr Fury's thoughts stopped. It was really asking for the moon. 'To hell with it! Sometimes I wish I could just pick up my bag and clear out, right out.' He sighed, knocked out his pipe, and put it back in his pocket. Then he rose to his feet and began walking round the bandstand. He thought of his early years at sea. Round and round he walked, hands stuck in his pockets, as though he were chasing the very thoughts that had risen flood-like and taken possession of him. Sometimes he stopped suddenly and smiled, as though he were living again some moment of the past, catching and holding the memory of it with the frenzied passion of one who can live it no more. He thought of those sailings from the Hudson, from Maine, from Tilbury. He thought of that great hike from Baltimore to New York, of the rigging gang in Ohio and the rubber factory in Boston. 'Ah, those times are gone,' he thought. 'They can never come again.' Here he was, the same Dennis Fury as of old, but now washed up by the tide. Now there was no tide to catch, no ship to join, no tot of rum to share with mates on sailing day, no delight in fugitive excursions ashore, no yarns. There was nothing. Only that damned loco shed and the daily sight of Andrew Postlethwaite's miserable face. He stood by the door of the stand and began staring at the wooden sand-covered floor. When the wind grew stronger he went inside and sat down. Again he pulled out his pipe, not to light, only to look at, and to think of the years he had had it, the good times he had had, and here it was, the same old pipe. He looked at it almost affectionately as he put it back in his pocket. How nice it was to be alone, to be quiet just for a short space of time!

'Aye, in those days one could get a good show at the Lyric for tuppence.' How times were changing indeed! He began scratching a spot of grease from his trousers, and his thoughts were of his wife. 'Fanny got me this suit three years ago, and it's a good un yet.' Then he began to laugh. 'What would I like best?' he asked aloud. 'A holiday in Ireland with Fanny. She hasn't seen her home for thirty-one years, except that rush to Cork. Brigid is no good. She's no sister to that woman.' He pulled out his watch. Well, he had better go now. Mustn't be late. He brushed tobacco ash from his clothes and got up. Then he left the stand and started off at a sharp pace for the gate leading to Banfield Road. What a queer, lonely place a Park could be on a Sunday morning! Not a soul to be seen. A real miserable hole indeed. He reached the gate and turned round, to stand staring at the place he had lately left. From that distance it looked even more bleak. He leaned against a post and watched the wind send the sand along in waves, the bare branches of trees shake trembling in the wind, as though they sought to free themselves from the silent sentinel to which they belonged. In the summer they would be thick with foliage, and upon those desolated fields hundreds of children would play. Mr Fury fixed his hat firmly on his head and made his way home through Banfield Road. There was something splendid about the word 'home', there was something to look forward to, anyhow, after that wilderness of a Park. He even smiled at the thought of the big fire and the cosy sofa on which he would stretch himself. When he got back everything would be spick and span. Sunday was Fanny's day. 'That's the first time I've ever been in that Park,' said Mr Fury to himself as he turned into the Harbour Road, 'and it's the last.'

When Dennis Fury returned home it was half-past five. Peter and his mother were already taking tea. He said, 'Hello!' and passed through into the lobby, where he hung up his hat and coat. Then he joined them at the table.

'You're late,' said Mrs Fury. 'Where on earth did you get to?'

'Oh! I got half-way down with Possie, and I changed my mind. That man is the lousiest and most uninteresting fellow I ever met.'

'H'm!' Peter looked at his mother. Then he averted her sudden glance and looked at his father.

'Aye. So I walked slowly back. I went to have a look at what's on at the Lyric next week,' he went on. 'A good show. I came back through the Park. It's a miserable-looking part of the city that, and no mistake.'

'Have you heard about Mr Postlethwaite?' exclaimed Peter excitedly, unable to keep back the startling news any longer. Mr Fury, still thinking of the dreary appearance of the Avon Park, replied, 'What . . . ? You what? Possie?'

'He's in hospital,' remarked Mrs Fury. 'And a good job it is you didn't go with him to that meeting . . .' Peter interrupted with 'Yes. He got his head bashed in by the police.' 'Aye!' Mr Fury sat back. Sunday could be a most exciting day. There was no longer any doubt of that.

'How'd it happen?' he asked.

'You can well imagine,' remarked Mrs Fury. Now she repeated her question, revealing that her curiosity had not been satisfied.

'But what a place to go! All the old rips of the day are to be found there,' she said. She pushed away her cup and saucer and got up. 'Avon Park's got quite a bad name. On Sunday nights it's just disgraceful.'

Mr Fury was no longer interested.

'Suppose it's no better or worse than any other Park,' he said. 'Anyhow, it's the first time I ever went to it. Who told you about Possie?'

'Everybody knows,' said Mrs Fury. 'I believe the city is like a madhouse. The police used their batons on the crowd.'

'Oh aye.' Pause. 'H'm! Wouldn't be them if they didn't,' said Mr Fury. 'Did Possie get a blow, then?'

'Yes. He's in the Manton Hospital now, with a terrible gash in his head.'

'Oh dear! That is bad. I suppose Mrs Postlethwaite has gone down there?' Mr Fury got up from the table. Then he said laughingly, 'No wonder! No bloody wonder! That damned suit he's wearing is enough to get anybody's goat.'

Mrs Fury began clearing the table. As she passed to and from the kitchen she kept up a running commentary. Peter went into the yard. 'It's most dangerous to go near the town,' she said. 'I hope you'll stay clear of it. They are just a lot of roughs, that's all, just out for mischief. And the time that's wasted! They ought to be working.'

'Aw – forget it, for the Lord's sake,' said Mr Fury. 'You don't understand anything about the strike.'

The woman laughed. Indeed, she was quite sure she did. She had seen strikes before – not with Denny out, of course – but the children. Desmond and Maureen and John.

'I've just been telling Peter,' she said, 'that he must keep away from town.'

'Yes! Of course!' thought Mr Fury. 'Easier said than done.' He would like to know the name of the lad who could be kept from going into the city.

He sat down on the cane chair by the window. 'Him' was fast asleep in his chair, head thrown back in the attitude of the utmost abandon, whilst round his open mouth a lone fly circled flirtatiously. For a long time Dennis Fury watched the fly, momentarily expecting it to fall into Mr Mangan's mouth.

'You can't keep the lad tied up like a house dog,' Mr Fury said. The table had now been cleared. Mrs Fury sat down, spread her arms crosswise upon the cheap American table-cloth, and looked across at her husband. Mr Fury knew this attitude well. It was inquisitional. His mind seemed to prepare itself, the whole mental arsenal to become alert. He thought ... 'Well?'

'Have you seen Brigid today?' asked the woman. Peter came in. He stood leaning on the dresser looking at his father.

'No, I didn't see Brigid,' said Mr Fury. He leaned forward and spat into the grate.

'I saw her,' remarked Peter. 'Just after eight o'clock.'

'Oh! Was she alone?'

'Yes. Miss Pettigrew can't go out now,' went on Peter. 'The doctor won't allow her.' He began drumming upon the dresser with his fingers.

'Oh!' She hadn't heard about that. 'Stop that row when I'm talking.' The drumming noise ceased. 'Go outside,' said Mrs Fury. 'I want to talk to your father.'

'Yes, Mother.' Peter went into the parlour.

'About tomorrow,' began Mrs Fury. She paused, as though to give weight to her words, to allow them to sink into her husband's mind.

'Well? What about tomorrow?' Mr Fury rose to his feet and approached the table. He leaned on it with his hands, and repeated, 'What about tomorrow?'

'There will only be your strike-pay next week, and Anthony's money,' said Mrs Fury.

'Of course,' replied Mr Fury. 'I know about that already. But you've got *his* pension,' he added, and pointed to Mr Mangan, still snoring contentedly in his chair.

'Father's money only keeps himself,' said the woman. 'Do you think the strike is a joke? Seems you do.'

'Don't be so silly,' he said. 'Last thing I ever thought of, that it's a joke. It isn't a joke, Fanny. I know it isn't.'

209

'Then try and be a little more interested,' said the woman. 'I have a lot to do.'

'I know that,' he said. 'What do you want me to do?'

'I want you to go and see Mr Lake about Anthony's money. Can't you draw your strike-pay at the same time?' She drew her arms in from the table and settled them in her lap. As Mr Fury looked at his wife, he thought, 'Aye, you seem to have aged suddenly.' A tenderness woke in him. He leaned over the table and placed one arm round her neck.

'Well, old girl, we've come through worse times than this, haven't we? I know I skitted about this strike all along. But blame Possie for that. I tell you I heard nothing from that big ... I mean, day after day it was nothing but "By God, Fury, it's looking bad. These miners coming out an' all! We'll be in it." I had that sort of thing shoved down my neck for six solid weeks. So I turned round and just sat on the fellow. It just got my goat.'

'Now he's flat on his back,' remarked Mrs Fury.

'Serve him right! Serve him right! He wouldn't think twice of putting one of us flat on our backs on the twelfth of July. Sometimes I think I was the biggest man in the world to go in with him. Anyhow, no use talking about that ...'

'No. Not at all. We have something else to think about.'

'Of course.'

'Plans to make.'

'Yes. Brigid's not in any of them, is she?' asked Mr Fury.

'Don't you get worrying about Brigid, for you can be sure she isn't worrying over us. She'll be quite set up with Miss Pettigrew. And I'm glad. Yes, I'm glad.'

'Aye. We're all glad.' Mr Fury turned, looked at Mr Mangan, and said to himself, 'Even Slobberer's glad. First time I've seen him sleep in the day-time.'

Mrs Fury got up and said, 'Put some coal on the fire.' Then she went into the parlour. Peter was sitting in the arm-chair reading a book. The woman did not even glance at him. She took a seat by the window. Like the other inhabitants of Hatfields, Mrs Fury took up duty at the observation post – excepting that she confined her duty to the evening. As she looked out of the window a man and woman had come to a halt outside Mrs Postlethwaite's door. 'Oh,' thought Mrs Fury, 'it's George and his wife. How fat Anne is getting!' Mr Postlethwaite junior had a small terrier on a leash, which now frisked about the young woman's skirts. 'George always has an animal of some kind with him,' she was thinking. She heard the front door open. Mr and Mrs Postlethwaite passed into the house.

She could hear the loud-voiced woman talking in the lobby. Mrs Fury felt that she ought really to have knocked at the back door and sympathized with Mrs Postlethwaite, but pride and a stern sense of duty kept her back. Her relations with the woman were distant, almost frigid. The stumbling-block was colour. Mrs Fury's was green – Mrs Postlethwaite's orange. When she had first come in live in Hatfields there were a great many Irish people living there. Now things had changed. Half of Hatfields were Billies, and their allegiance to Prince William was strikingly manifested in the colour of their curtains. Even the children going to school were affected. They wore bright orange ribbons in their hair. On the twelfth of July orange ran riot. Mr Fury came into the parlour.

'George and his wife have just gone in next door,' said Mrs Fury.

'Oh yes.' Mr Fury stood looking out of the window. From the kitchen there came a fit of coughing, followed by a strange choking sound.

'Peter!' called Mrs Fury, without taking her eyes from the window. 'Peter! Run to your grand-dad.'

The boy put down his book and went to attend to Mr Mangan.

'By the way,' began Mr Fury, sitting down in the chair just vacated by his son, and flinging aside the book he had been reading, 'by the way, it looks as though that chap Mulcare won't come now. It's a pity, really. He could have got Peter a job as easy as winking.'

'It's quite unnecessary now,' remarked Mrs Fury. 'Peter has got a job.'

'He's got a job! When? Who with? Aye, you're a peculiar woman. You never said a word about this to me,' he concluded.

'All that doesn't matter,' replied the woman. 'I got the boy work. I saw Father Moynihan myself.'

'And what's the job?' asked Mr Fury.

'I don't really know yet. He's going to work for Mr Sweeney. He's starting on Monday. The pay is small, but it'll help to keep him in clothes.'

'Oh! Well, I'm glad. Right glad. It doesn't do for young lads to be hanging round like he is.'

'No. I told him that.'

'There's George now! And his wife. Oh! I think they must be going to the hospital to see him. Poor Mr Postlethwaite!' Then, to her husband's complete surprise, she dashed out of the parlour into the lobby and opened the door just as Mrs Postlethwaite, accompanied by her son and daughter-in-law, made to move off down the street.

'Oh! I say, Mrs Postlethwaite!' she called out. 'I'm so sorry to hear about Mr Postlethwaite. I hope he isn't badly injured. It's disgraceful. It is really.'

211

The barrel-like Mrs Postlethwaite looked at her son, then at her daughter-in-law, as though to say, '*This*, for the first time in eighteen years, is surely phenomenal.'

'Yes,' Mrs Postlethwaite said. 'Poor Andrew! They tell me he's got a fractured skull.' She put a handkerchief to her face.

'Da's always in trouble,' remarked George in a voice loud enough for the whole of Hatfields to hear. 'I told him many a time, "Keep out of it. You'll get one on the napper one of these days." Come along, Ma,' he said, putting a hand through his mother's arm. Anne put her arm through the other.

'It's terrible having to go all that way to hospital,' said Mrs Fury. 'Why not try Mr Hobhouse? He might get you a cab.' Mr Fury had followed his wife into the lobby, but the Postlethwaite family had not seen him. He was hidden behind his wife.

'But we couldn't get a cab through, Mrs – what's this,' said George, the name Fury having momentarily escaped his memory. 'Quite impossible to get a cab through those crowds.'

'Oh dear me! It's really awful,' Mrs Fury wound up. Anne smiled at Mrs Fury, saying, 'Thank you – thank you.'

Then the procession moved slowly down Hatfields. The whole street now knew that Mr Andrew Postlethwaite lay hovering between life and death as the result of a baton blow on his head.

The Furys returned to the parlour. Peter, having attended to his grandfather, came in again. He was going out, he said. The mother sat up. 'Where are you going?'

'I don't know,' replied Peter. He looked almost appealingly at his father.

'You keep away from the town, my lad, or you'll be finding yourself alongside Mr Postlethwaite.'

'You must know where you're going,' said Mrs Fury.

Peter said he was going for a walk on the road. The mother looked at her husband.

'Why don't you go too?' she said.

'But I've been out all day. The lad is old enough to look after himself.'

Peter stood there waiting.

'Oh, run off, for Christ's sake,' growled Mr Fury. 'You're not a convict.'

As soon as the boy went out, the woman turned upon her husband.

'You know right well why I wanted you to go out,' she began. 'I can't trust that boy, and never will again.'

'Oh, I know what you're frightened of,' said Mr Fury, 'but that doesn't matter. If Peter wants to see his brother, nothing will stop him.'

The woman leaned her head on her hands. Of course. It was true. She couldn't stop him. And Desmond, that reprobate, would simply poison his mind. Yes, she *was* afraid. She looked up at her husband.

'I asked him on his honour not to go.'

'Well, then, he *won't* go. Peter *won't* go. He's a lad like that. He'll keep his word. But sooner or later he'll see him, somewhere, some time, sooner the better maybe. Postlethwaite was telling me the other day that they're out a lot lately . . .'

'I'm not interested. I have something else to think about.'

Dennis Fury began to pace the room. Quite right, she had something to think about. So had he. The home. Yes, the home. Well . . . Suddenly he looked at his wife.

'Don't worry, Fanny, we'll pull through. And there's my little bit.' He stopped, staring open-mouthed at his wife. Mrs Fury lay back in the chair. She had turned suddenly pale.

CHAPTER X

I

'A Mr Fury to see you,' said the secretary, and stood waiting at Mr Lake's desk. Mr Lake was a tall, corpulent gentleman with a very red face. His neck appeared to ooze over the stiff linen collar. The collar seemed to serve one purpose only – to hold his head on his shoulders. He now looked up at the girl and said brusquely: 'Show the man in.'

He sat back in his chair, folded his arms, and waited. When Dennis Fury knocked, he called out, 'Come in,' and immediately changed his position, dropping his arms to the desk, pushing papers here and there. Mr Fury said, 'Good morning, Mr Lake,' and stood, hat in hand, in the middle of the room. Mr Lake, without looking at the man, said, 'Well, Fury, what can I do for you?'

Mr Lake and Mr Fury knew each other well. Mr Fury had once upon a time worked under Mr Lake. Mr Thomas Lake had risen much bigger now. He had a private office of his own – 'Marine Superintendent'.

'Sit down,' commanded Mr Lake, and Mr Fury sat down.

'Looking for a job?' asked Mr Lake. Then their eyes met. Mr Fury slowly shook his head. No, he wasn't looking for a job, he said – whilst he thought, 'Christ! here's my chance. Maybe get that damned ship I've wanted so long.' But now the thought froze as Mr Lake said, 'I'm glad to see you're so comfortable, Fury,' and he studied the colour and cut of Dennis Fury's suit, the well-brushed bowler that lay on his knee, even the polished black boots.

'I came about my son Anthony,' began Mr Fury, making himself more comfortable in the chair. He stroked the crown of his bowler with his fingers as he made a sweeping survey of the room. 'Indeed,' he thought, 'Thomas bloody Lake has made a quick ascent.' Mr Lake said, 'Ah! ...' paused, and then added quickly, 'That's different. Draw your chair in here, Fury,' he concluded.

'Yes, thanks,' replied Mr Fury. How the fellow had changed! Getting almost sociable now. But perhaps there was something in it.

'Have a cigarette,' said Mr Lake. He flicked open a case and reached across to Mr Fury.

'No thanks, never smoke them.' What the hell was this? Better get down to brass tacks. He looked Mr Lake straight in the eye.

'It's about my son,' he said. 'They've stopped his allotment money. They've refused it on the ground floor.'

'That, of course, is customary,' remarked Mr Lake. 'Its stoppage would date from the day of the accident. Have you heard from the lad? I'm surprised he didn't mention it when he wrote.'

'I know nothing about that. The lad wrote to his mother saying he would be home this week.'

'Yes, yes. Of course. I understand. But he won't be home yet awhile,' went on Mr Lake. 'We have heard from our agents in New York. This stoppage will prevent that. You understand?'

Mr Fury did not reply. He was thinking furiously, 'Can they stop it?'

'I suppose you know it's a compensation case,' said Mr Fury. Mr Lake smiled. 'That remains to be seen, Fury,' he said. 'The action on your son's part was purely voluntary . . .'

'Then why stop his money?' asked Mr Fury. What the devil was the fellow getting at? Doubted the lad's claim to compensation, and yet stopped his money! He looked angry now, and Mr Lake was quick to notice it. He said casually, 'We must consider the matter carefully. All information and documents relevant to the case are in the hands of our solicitors. Perhaps you would like to have a talk with our Mr Devereaux?' Mr Lake sat back in his chair.

'No,' said Mr Fury. 'I'm afraid I couldn't do that now.' He could hear his wife speaking into his ear, 'Answer no questions.'

'I can't see why his money should be stopped, Mr Lake,' continued Dennis Fury. 'The accident happened on board that boat, and he was carrying out his duties as a sailor for the company. Isn't that correct?'

'No. Not quite,' said Mr Lake. 'Be careful what you say, Fury . . .'

'But you know, Mr Lake,' said Mr Fury heatedly, 'you know as well as I do that that ship couldn't leave the quay in New York without her wireless was rigged up.' He stopped suddenly. Ought he to have put that remark like that? Ought he to have even mentioned compensation? He had better be wary. Perhaps it were best left alone. Better talk it over with Fanny. If he made a mess of this, she would never forgive him. He had never been involved in an accident. No. He wouldn't say another word.

'Yes,' continued Mr Lake. 'But, you haven't got the gist of the thing, Fury. You must understand this. Your son was not compelled to go up that mast. He was not even on duty, as a matter of fact. It was a purely voluntary act. If you were a wise man you would let me introduce you to Mr Devereaux. He could explain everything.'

'I don't want to see any solicitor,' replied Mr Fury. 'That's quite definite. I only want to know why you've stopped his money like this.'

'And I've already told you,' replied the impatient gentleman. This fellow was an ignoramus. He understood nothing. He had known Fury a long time now. He hadn't changed much. Hardly at all.

'Perhaps you can tell me when the lad will be coming home?' said Mr Fury.

'Yes, I can tell you that, Fury. Not under a month. This strike has thrown all our plans into the air. As soon as we hear from our agents in New York we will write to you.'

'Plans! Their plans!' Mr Fury was saying to himself. But what about *his* plans? What about Fanny? The lad himself? 'I can't see how you can stop his money,' Mr Fury blurted out. He was desperate now. To have to go back to Hatfields without that allotment money was more than he could bear. If it hadn't been bad enough even getting down to the office! This Mr bloody Lake was just the same. No change.

'You must see Mr Devereaux,' Mr Lake said.

'Good enough!' Mr Fury rose to his feet. 'I won't see him. I've already told you that. I'll see somebody else.' His face had gone red. Mr Fury felt he would like to drive his fist into the fat gentleman's face.

'Of course, Mr Devereaux will be pleased to see anybody you nominate,' remarked Mr Lake. He too rose to his feet. He pulled out his gold watch and looked at it, and from it to the window, a pensive expression upon his red face. 'Yes, of course, always be glad to do that.'

'Well,' thought Mr Fury, 'that's jiggered it. Mr Lake does not intend to be obliging.' He crossed to the door. As he opened it Mr Lake called out:

'What are you doing these days, Fury?'

'Railways,' Dennis Fury said. His hand gripped the door knob more firmly.

'Very glad to hear it. Not much in your line these days,' said Mr Lake. Then he completely surprised Dennis Fury by adding, 'Family well?'

'So-so,' replied Mr Fury. 'Good morning.' The door banged. Mr Lake returned to his desk and sat down. He could hear Mr Fury swearing as he tramped down the corridor. Mr Lake smiled.

'All that journey for nothing!' exclaimed Mr Fury. He went down in the lift. For a moment he stood contemplating in the spacious hall of the building, his eyes taking in the many improvements and alterations that had been made since last he had visited the office of the Torsa Line Steamers. 'Swell beggars now,' he said to himself. Then he passed through the swing-doors into the street. He looked up and down the street. Crowds everywhere. Marching in every direction. Police at every corner. And what was that by the Front? Soldiers. 'By Christ!' exclaimed Mr Fury. He set off for home at a sharp pace. Well, things seemed to be getting worse. Nobody was working.

People were coming out all over the country. Suddenly he stopped. 'Why not go and see Possie?' he thought. 'Poor beggar!' A crowd came out of a side street shouting and laughing. Somebody called out, 'The butchers are coming.' The crowd rushed up the street in the direction of the railway station. Mr Fury found himself caught in the crowd. Where were they rushing off to? He dodged back to the side-walk again. Not much use going back up Mile Hill. Best take the bottom road. He turned back again, and as he passed the Torsa Line offices he spat as though in a sudden fit of contempt. 'Lousy swine!' He reached the dark road. Here the roads were not entirely impassable. Every dark gate had its pickets, its police, its soldiers. 'H'm! Looks like a damned siege. Where have the khaki chaps come from? And when?' Outside the Branston Dock he stopped to watch a scuffle between half a dozen beshawled women and two policemen. It was half-past eleven in the morning. The six women had just emerged from the dock carrying rolls of cloth, hams, tins of food. They were promptly stopped. Where had they got this stuff from? Mr Fury thought, 'Pinched it.' Suddenly he laughed. One of the women struck a policeman with a ham, and the officer fell back against the wall. He walked on. Near the Branston goods station another crowd blocked his path. This was quite different to anything he had seen that morning. Everybody was laughing, and a man kept shouting, 'Go it, Roger! Go it, Roger!' Mr Fury craned his neck. The crowd was ringed round two coupled dogs. Mr Fury continued on his way. 'That's all they have to worry about. H'm!' Near the Garton Dock things were quieter. Mr Fury had not seen a quieter group of people gathered round the dock gate. The road was almost deserted. Further up, just at the corner of Bank Street, there was an unoccupied wooden bench. Mr Fury increased his pace. Then he sat down on the bench.

He felt hot, and he felt miserable. All that way for nothing. How was any-body to get down there tomorrow – or the next day – or next week? And the company were bound to write. But how was it going to be done? Already rumours were flying about that every pedestrian going citywards was being stopped and questioned by the police. Looting was taking place at night. The shops in Hurst Street and Andrew Street had had all their windows smashed. The iron gate had been pulled down at the entrance to the railway station. The Castle Hotel was boarded up. Its few guests, caught by the sudden stoppage, had to content themselves with passing their time in the billiard- and smoke-rooms. Some of these people had booked for America. Now shipping was held up. So they must wait. Occasionally, fugitive ex-cursions were made into the city via the rear entrance of the hotel. The authorities had taken a serious view of the situation. Specials were enrolled, outside police were being called in, and already a draft of soldiers had come from the neighbouring barracks. The facts were now occupying Dennis Fury's mind. The situation *was* bad. He had laughed at the idea of the strike. But he wasn't laughing now.

He got up from the bench. 'Oh well. We'll pull through all right,' he told himself.

He turned up Bank Street, and at the top found himself on Mile Road again. Now he was beginning to feel hungry. He crossed Price Street without even glancing at the Kilkeys' front window, and eventually passed into the entry at the rear of Hatfields. As he came to the back door Mrs Fury came out. They stared at each other for a moment, unable to speak. They were like two thieves who have just discovered each other's presence in the same building. Mr Fury was the first to speak.

'Where are you going?' he asked.

'Out. Can't you see?' she said. She was caught out. She was between two fires. She wanted to go and she didn't want to go. Mr Fury did not understand.

'Can't you say where you're going?' he asked her.

'To Maureen's,' she said.

'Oh! I see. All right. Don't you want to know what Lake said?'

'No. I have no time.' She had made her decision. She would not back out. She simply could not afford to.

'What's the matter, Fanny?' asked Mr Fury. He became anxious now.

'Nothing. Your dinner's on the hob,' she replied. Then she hurried up the entry. Mr Fury stood watching her go. This was queer. Something funny indeed. Didn't even wait to hear about the lad's money. He went into the house. Another surprise. 'Him' was still in bed. Peter had started work at his new job. Ten shillings a week. Mr Fury got his dinner and sat down. But he couldn't enjoy it. His favourite dish. He pushed the plate aside and went upstairs. Mr Mangan was asleep in bed. It was the first time he had ever seen 'him' sleeping at that time of day. He made to descend the stairs again, but suddenly an idea occurred to him. He went into Peter's room. He looked at the unmade bed, the clothes tossed into a bundle at its foot. He went to the fire-grate and stood there, leaning his hands upon the mantelshelf. Then he smiled. Well – after all, there was this little bit he had hidden away. He knelt down and looked up the chimney. He recalled now how each week he had put two shillings up the back of the chimney. Nobody had known. Nobody could know. The room was unoccupied since Desmond had left it. He put up his hand, and a shower of dust and soot came down the chimney. His smile vanished. He thought he heard the door move, and looked round. But the door was closed. His face was black with soot. He put his hand up again and began to grope about the brick shelving. 'H'm! Funny!' he thought, as he groped. 'Funny!' His other hand gripped the mantelshelf. Again he ran his hand along the shelving. Then he loosened his grip upon the mantelshelf. 'Good God!' The money was gone! Gone! Nearly twelve pounds. That he had saved week by week, and nobody had known. His face went white, his eyes closed, whilst he thought, 'Gone! But where? Who knew?' Then he opened his eyes again and stared frantically at the chimney. It couldn't be! Impossible! Perhaps it had blown down. The grate in the room was full of paper, as there had never been any fire in the room excepting once when Desmond had been ill. Now with feverous fingers he tore the paper out, shook it, shot it into the air, tore it, rolled it into balls, and in his haste and extreme excitement shot the rolled balls of paper all over the room. No! 'Good Christ!' Perhaps the draught had blown it higher up. Again he shot up his hand, grasping frantically, higher, higher, then changing hands. This procedure sent down shower upon shower of soot. The room was now covered with it. 'Damn!' he cried aloud, unable to control himself any longer. It had gone; there was no doubt of it, that twelve pounds of his had vanished. He staggered to his feet, and without considering his now blackened clothes, sat down on the bed and placed his head in his hands. Continually he cried in his mind, 'Who? Who? How long ago?' He jumped to his feet, and turning round looked at the grate. Then he shouted, 'It's that fellow Peter. That's who it is. But why should he take it? What has he done with it?'

And he had meant to surprise Fanny. Yes. He had meant to surprise her. Of course she knew, but she didn't know how much. She didn't think where he had hidden it. Now he couldn't surprise her. No. He could only stand there, staring, cursing the empty grate. Whoever had taken it was mean. Mean! He wanted to cry, to shout out there and then his anger, his disappointment, the very pain that had seized him as he made the discovery. But perhaps, one never knew, there might be ... He knelt down. 'Please, St Anthony, help me to find this money.' As though fortified by this very utterance, he once more knelt down and put his hand up the chimney. But a quite different hand, a trembling and knowledgeable hand. It touched nothing but brick, it disturbed nothing but cloud upon cloud of soot. It was useless. He looked up the chimney. If only he could seize the grate, tear it to pieces, crush it beneath his feet! As he looked up into the black hole he seemed to trace upon the darkness his very despair. He sat down, his arms to his sides, and continued to stare bewilderedly at the grate. Perhaps the money would suddenly blow down. Perhaps the brickwork would give way and reveal the secret at last. Perhaps ...

He swung his body round and sat on the floor, facing the door. He looked at the sooted bed, the floor, the furniture, and at the paper scattered about the room. Light dawned suddenly. Of course, only last night he had mentioned this, and Fanny, yes, Fanny had seemed surprised. 'I wonder, wonder,' he thought, hardly daring to believe it, and then: 'Peter. Perhaps it is that fellow.' As though the thought had given him some reassurance, he began to clean up the room as best he could. He gathered up the paper, swept it into the grate again, and then went downstairs, returning with shovel and brush. He swept the floor. Then he took the bed-clothes on to the landing and shook them. He flung them on the bed, picked up shovel and brush, and went below again. Fanny had gone to Maureen. What for? Why the sudden rushing off like that? Gradually confusion gave place to ordered thought. Surely, surely she hadn't sensed anything, hadn't expected him to go looking for that money there and then. But if she had taken it, why hadn't she mentioned it to him? It seemed so silly, childish. But why? What could she want it for? She had his wages, Anthony's allotment money, 'him's' pension. No. He couldn't understand it. He went out into the yard. He felt he wanted air, fresh air, after that encounter with the grate. A face appeared over the wall. A voice called, 'Hello, Mr Fury!' The man looked up.

'Hello, George!' he said, and crossed over to him. George Postlethwaite jumped up and sat down on the wall.

'How's your dad?' asked Mr Fury.

'Oh, he's not too bad. Mother and I and Anne went to see him last night. Aye, Da's a caution. I told him; I said, "Dad, you're a bloody old fool, going and getting that head on you size of a football." Yes. They put twelve stitches in it, and I said to him, "Serves you right. Oughtn't to have gone down like that. It was asking for it." That's what I say. What d'you think?'

Dennis Fury wanted to laugh. There was something about Andrew Postlethwaite's son that made him want to laugh. George was really funny.

'Nice way to talk about your dad,' remarked Mr Fury. 'Suppose he'd pegged out?' Mr Fury leaned against the wall and looked up at Mr George Postlethwaite's good-humoured face.

'Ah!' said George. 'It would have served him right an' all. So it would. What's he want going on strike at his age? Da won't say Whoa yet, not for a heck of a time. I don't see anything in this strike stuff,' he went on. 'What you reckon you get out of it? Cracked heads is all I can see. I said to Desmond yesterday, I said, "There's so many bloody rights being fought for, that a man doesn't know whether he's on his head or his arse" – 'scuse me – and that's the solemn truth.'

'Yes – oh yes. How's Desmond getting on?' asked Mr Fury. 'I haven't seen him for a solid month.'

'Oh, he's getting on all right. He was in that baton charge yesterday. Da told me about it. Your Desmond pulled down one of those mounted policemen and knocked all his teeth out. But as I say, What do you get out of it?'

'Oh well,' replied Mr Fury, 'I don't know. Mind you, I don't agree with this particular strike.'

'All the same,' interrupted George; 'every bloody one on 'em.'

'Oh well, I expect you get a bit of fun out of them too.'

'Maybe. Not much fun in getting twelve stitches from lug to lug.'

'So Desmond's getting on all right. Glad to hear that.'

'Yes. So's that missus of his,' said George. 'She's out all the while now.'

'Oh aye!' Mr Fury was getting interested now. He climbed the wall and sat down alongside George.

'Have a cig.'

'Never smoke those things,' said Mr Fury. He continued the conversation.

'So she's out all the while?'

'Yes. So's Desmond. Only yesterday we went for a walk to the beach. Anne didn't notice at first. But I did. We saw a woman sitting on a huge stone staring out over the sea. Seemed so strange. Wasn't a summer's day yesterday, was it?'

'No,' replied Mr Fury, all ears now, and keenly excited at the turn which the conversation was taking. No doubt about it. George was in every way as proficient as his father.

'Anyhow it looked funny, this woman all by herself looking out to sea. We were sitting on an old boat just opposite the Marine Parade. Guess who it was. I went up close's I could. She didn't see me.'

'Who?'

'Your Desmond's missus,' said George. 'She's a queer un, isn't she?'

'Indeed!' Mr Fury could hardly conceal his surprise. Was George fishing, he wondered. He couldn't tell him anything, for he knew nothing about the woman. He looked at George and replied slowly, 'Maybe she went out for a walk, just like Anne and yourself.'

'Maybe,' said George. Then the conversation ended as abruptly as it had begun. Mrs Postlethwaite from the kitchen called, 'George! George!'

'Yes, Mother! Coming,' and George jumped down from the wall. Mr Fury did not move. Mrs Postlethwaite looked out of the door and said, 'Nice day,' to which Mr Fury replied that it was, in a rather absent-minded way. Mrs Postlethwaite went on, 'Wife out?'

Mr Fury turned round. 'Yes – went out a while ago,' he replied.

How sociable the Postlethwaites were today, he thought. Time to jump off the wall and return indoors. He would cut a figure before Fanny, sitting on the wall like that. Just as he swung round to lower himself into the yard, George came out again.

'That aunt of yours was up there last night' – but it was now too late. Mr Fury had dropped into the yard. He went into the house.

'What a time she is!' he said to himself. 'What can she be doing at Maureen's all this while?'

One thought capitulated to another. So many different thoughts had never before played havoc with Dennis Fury's mind. They'd stopped Anthony's allotment money. Fanny rushed out, not even waiting to hear that it had been stopped. Desmond Fury was in the baton charge, and Sheila Fury was always out. And on top of that, his money – his hard-earned savings – was gone. If Fanny wasn't such a one for secrets, for keeping things to herself, everything would be quite different.

He couldn't sit down now. Couldn't rest. Impossible. Why didn't Fanny come back? Five hours away now. Well, he was going to have it out with her as soon as ever she got back. He could stand a lot. But this – the stealing of his money – it was just mean. Dirty and mean. He wouldn't have minded at any other time. But just now, when things *were* a bit below the level, well, it was a caution. He knew she had a lot to do. He had never denied it. Hadn't he put the money away for such a very purpose as this? Saving it for a rainy day. Cutting himself short of things, never breathing a word to his wife. Now he hadn't even the satisfaction of being able to surprise her, of being able to say, 'Here you are, Fanny. I saved this up on the Q.T. It'll help out.' He paced up and down the kitchen. For the first time he seemed to notice the empty high-backed chair. 'His' chair. With 'him' in it he would hardly have noticed it. Now, with 'him' out of it, it was full of significance. Why hadn't Fanny got her father up? What was up with the woman at all? The more he thought of that visit to Maureen, the more mysterious the atmosphere became. Had she given the girl the money? Fancy her going round like that! So suddenly. If he remembered rightly, she had only crossed the doorstep of thirty-five Price Street twice since the girl got married. Tired of the kitchen, feeling as though it were too small, suffocating him, he went out into the yard again. But it was only cold and miserable there too. He had a good mind to go out. He looked at the clock. Then he swore and sat down again. No, he would wait, hang on until she came back. She couldn't be away for ever. And as soon as ever she put her head in the door he would ask her straight out. After all, he had a right. It was his money. At that moment Mrs Fury appeared. Mr Fury got up as she came in.

Mrs Fury, without looking at her husband, passed across the kitchen and sat down in the high-backed chair. She was flushed and excited. She began fidgeting with her hat.

'Still got that damned old hat on,' he said. 'And after me going and getting you one at Hobhouse's!'

'Oh, shut up!' The woman turned her head round and stared up at the clock.

'What's up?' asked Mr Fury.

'Nothing.'

'Oh!' said Mr Fury. He went over to her. 'Something wrong,' he went on. 'You rushing off like that.' They faced each other now.

'What did they say at the office?'

'Say! They said lots, and stopped his money into the bargain.'

'Stopped it? What for?' Mrs Fury pulled the pin from her hat. She held it so tightly clenched in her hand that for a moment Mr Fury imagined she meant to run it through him. He had never seen her so excited before. 'What did they say?' She took off her hat and threw it on the table.

'They said that when a man met with an accident at sea his allotment note was cancelled from the day of the accident. I said ...'

'Yes? What did you say? How wide did you open your mouth? Remember last time?' The woman rose to her feet and stood looking at Mr Fury. There was something hard and bitter in the expression on her face, as though a kind of malignant rage had suddenly flashed itself there.

'This woman,' Mr Fury was thinking, 'this woman is beside herself about something.' And as he traced the bitterness in her expression he felt he would like to crush it, to wipe it out with the question, 'Where's my money gone to?' He drew back and leaned against the mantelshelf. 'What are you being nasty about?' he asked her. 'Have I done anything?'

'Nasty!' The woman laughed. 'Nasty!' Then she went upstairs. Mr Fury followed. Hearing him coming behind her, she banged the door and cried, 'Go away! Please leave me alone.' Then silence. The man stood outside the room door listening. He could hear her quick breathing. Once she walked across the room. Whenever she became excited it seemed that the whole house echoed to her anger, her restlessness. The very air harboured it. What was all this about? Not a word about his money. Not a word. Slowly a bitterness seemed to grow upon him too as he stood there, hidden in the darkness of the landing. Why wasn't the woman straightforward? What was worrying her? Why couldn't she tell him? Why didn't she tell him everything? Everything – and clear the air, for good and all. The house might settle itself down to a little peace. She would keep things to herself; then, when she could no longer hold herself in control, she exploded. Mr Fury called softly, 'Fanny!'

He hardly expected it, but the door opened. She was looking at him now. Here was resignation, surrender. The bitterness, the hardness had gone. Mr Fury succumbed to it at once.

Was it mere subterfuge? Was she planning something fresh?

'I'm sorry,' Mrs Fury said slowly. 'I'm sorry. Sometimes one can't stand it.'

'If only you wouldn't keep things to yourself!' He thought, 'To ask about my money now is out of the question.'

'Here,' he said. 'I got this this morning. It's the strike-pay.' He handed her the five shillings. 'I kept the odd coppers for tobacco.'

'Thank you.' She went into the room again, Mr Fury at her heels.

'What did they say at the office, Denny?' she asked. She was standing by the window arranging the curtains. At the same time her eyes swept Hatfields. Children were playing in the street. At some of the doors men sat smoking, women talking.

'They said lots, and stopped his money into the bargain,' said the man. He was leaning on the iron rail of the bed. 'If you hadn't rushed off like you did, I could have told you that hours ago.'

'But they can't stop it.'

'Oh yes. Yes, they can. Lake told me. Some technicality. They reckon Anthony wasn't on duty at the time. He was purely a volunteer. I argued their rights to stop it, but Lake wanted to refer me to their Devereaux. I wasn't having any. Another thing is that they don't even know when the lad will get home. Shipping companies' plans are all to hell with this stoppage on. Boats held up in New York. Lake was quite sociable this time. Getting real swell – big office of his own – even offered me a cigarette.' Mr Fury laughed now as he recalled the incident.

'All of which means that I shall have to see them myself,' said Mrs Fury, still looking up Hatfields.

'That's it! Best to see them yourself. I quite agree.'

Suddenly the woman beckoned. 'Who is this man?' she asked. 'He's just stopped outside our door.' She drew back the curtain and her husband looked down.

'Well, I never!' he exclaimed, his expression revealing a pleasurable anticipation. 'Why, it's that young chap Mulcare I was telling you about. This is a surprise.'

'Will he come in?'

Mr Fury said, 'Of course. Of course he'll come in,' and made towards the door.

'I shall be down in a few minutes,' Mrs Fury said. 'I have to attend to Father.'

'Yes, yes.' Mr Fury was hurrying down the stairs. This was a surprise. He opened the front door.

'Hello, Mike!' he called out boisterously. 'Glad to see you. Come in. Thought you'd sailed long ago.'

Mr Mulcare smiled, and followed Mr Fury into the kitchen. 'Sit down here.' Mr Fury cleared the sofa of hats and coats and newspapers.

'Well, well! I'm glad you came,' he said. 'Where's your boat?'

'She's across at Manchester,' replied Mulcare. 'She came down there with a scab crew, and is loading now.'

'Oh aye.' Mr Fury sat down. 'The wife will be down in a tick. So she's really going, then?'

'Yes,' Mr Mulcare said. He made himself comfortable on the sofa. He was wearing a light grey suit, white collar and blue tie, and soft peaked cap of a material similar to the suit. He wore black block-toed shoes and grey socks. Mr Fury was lost in admiration. What a fine, well-set-up young man he looked! Suddenly Peter came into his mind. Peter wearing a light grey suit and soft cap. 'Why,' he thought, 'that lad of mine dressed up like this – he'd knock socks off Mulcare.' He already visualized Peter sitting alongside Mr Mulcare.

'You're looking grand. Oh, here's the wife.' Mrs Fury had come into the kitchen. Mulcare at once rose to his feet, and said, 'Good evening, Mrs Fury.' The woman made a step forward, then stopped and subjected Mulcare to a scrutinizing glance. Her head was bent forward. She seemed to survey his person from beneath her eyelids. 'How are you?' She shook hands with the young man and sat down by the table.

'Are you the young man Mr Fury was telling me about?' Again her eyes fastened upon his person. They rested first upon his grey silk socks, then slowly climbed until they came to rest upon his face.

'A fine, strong, healthy young fellow,' she thought. So this was the young man who would get Peter away. This was the Mr Mulcare who had left his father in Ireland. Whilst her husband talked and the young man listened, Mrs Fury set to studying him. Rather well dressed. A sailor? What kind of a sailor?

Mr Fury looked across at his wife. 'Would you make a drink of tea, Fanny?' he asked.

'Yes, of course.' She got up and went outside. Mr Mulcare seemed to follow the woman with his eyes. He half turned his head and looked at the alarm-clock.

'Would you like a drink, Fury?'

'Not now. Not now. I hope you'll wait. I was sorry I missed you last time. The lad will be in soon. He started work today. Some sort of errand-boy's job. I don't know what it is exactly.'

'Does his mother want him to go to sea?' asked Mr Mulcare.

'Oh yes, I think so. If you could get him a job, certainly. He's at a very impressionable age, really,' continued Mr Fury. 'He ought to go away. Pull him out a bit. But mind you, I don't want him to go below.'

'No, of course not,' replied Mulcare, laughing. 'On the bridge, eh?'

Mr Fury said, 'Anywhere excepting down below. I had thirty years of it.'

'So one can see,' replied the young man.

'Why, here he is now,' said Mr Fury, jumping up as he heard the back door latch lifted. Peter came into the kitchen.

2

He was wearing a dungaree suit of his father's. His face and hands were dirty, on his head he wore a light tweed cap, pulled hard down over one eye. When he removed it, his hair, imprisoned all day, and quite unused to head-covering, shot up in obvious rebellion.

'Go and clean yourself up,' cried his mother. 'You're a sight.'

'Half a minute,' said Mr Fury. He turned to his son and caught his arm.

'This is Mr Mulcare. Remember me telling you about him?' At which announcement Mr Mulcare rose from the sofa and shook hands with Peter.

'Pleased to see you,' he said.

Peter stood head and shoulders over the man. They seemed to take stock of each other. There was something about the grip of the man's hand that established a confidence at once.

'Well! You're a fine big lad,' said Mr Mulcare. He turned to Mr Fury, 'Isn't he now?'

Mr Fury laughed. Peter was beaming at the compliment.

'Yes,' Mr Fury said. Mr Mulcare sat down again.

'Take your coat off, man,' said Mr Fury. 'Fanny's making some tea.'

'I can't stay, Fury,' replied the man. 'I only called here on chance. I am on my way down to meet a friend.'

'Oh!' It was obvious that Mr Fury was keenly disappointed. He had spoken to Fanny so often of Mr Mulcare, praising his qualities, his abilities, and now he wasn't even going to stay. Peter had gone out to wash himself.

'I am sorry you're not going to stay, Mike,' said Mr Fury.

'I only wanted to have a look at your boy, Fury,' replied Mr Mulcare.

At that moment Mr Mulcare's eyes alighted upon a spider climbing the wainscoting. He lay back and followed its erratic course. Now it stopped. Mr Fury kept looking at Mr Mulcare with rapt attention. The spider proceeded up the green-painted wood, and the young man's eyes followed. Suddenly it disappeared. The man's eyes seemed glued to the spot. He was lost in thought. Still studying Mr Mulcare, Mr Fury's ears attuned themselves to the running commentary in the back kitchen. Mrs Fury was busy at the stove. Peter was drying himself with the roller towel.

'But I don't understand,' Mrs Fury was saying. 'You've finished there?'

'Don't you see?' Peter replied. 'The job's a scab one, and it is no use going down again. Mr Sweeney told me. I went out for a load to the North Market today, and never got back with it. Half-way home a crowd of nearly two hundred people upturned the whole cart-load of potatoes. I was lucky to get horse and lorry back to the stable.'

'Oh!' said Mrs Fury. She had been thinking of something else, the scene at Maureen's house. She said brusquely, 'Better get your tea.' The clatter of the cups aroused Mr Mulcare from his reverie, and he sat up suddenly on the sofa. Mr Fury had not spoken a word. Peter sat at the top of the table near the door. Mr Fury and the visitor sat on the sofa, against which the table had been pushed. Mrs Fury sat opposite them. She now poured out the tea.

'What a fine-looking woman!' Mr Mulcare was saying to himself as he watched her fill the cups. There was something fascinating in watching her. He looked from the mother to the son. This dual admiration in watching her left Mr Dennis Fury derelict. He wasn't even on the map. As the woman handed Mulcare the tea, she subjected him to a penetrating stare, as she remarked in a casual way, 'Sorry you have to go.'

Mr Mulcare smiled. He looked up at Peter.

'So this young chap wants to go to sea?'

'That's it,' remarked Mr Fury, now on the map again. 'That's it. Can you get him a job? He wants to go. Don't you, Peter?'

For a moment the boy did not reply. He was looking at his mother.

'Yes,' he said. 'Yes, I want to go.' There was something venomous in the woman's glance. So that was it. He did want to go. This was the end, the very end of her idea. She could hear her daughter now. She seemed to pass out of the kitchen into number thirty-five Price Street. 'You've sacrificed everything for an idea. You have made your own life like a prison.' When she looked at her son again, he was smiling. She would have liked to strike him. 'Yes, he wants to go.'

'Well, then,' said Mr Fury, 'that's settled.'

'On the other hand,' said the visitor, 'he can only lie low until this strike clears up.'

'What do you think of this business, Mr Mulcare?' asked Mrs Fury, as she began to gather the cups together on the tray.

'I think it is a nuisance,' he said, and moved forward on the sofa.

'I quite agree with you. It's a disgrace. Nobody gains anything by it.' She pulled out the table to let him get free. Mr Fury also got up. Peter remained seated. If that strong grip of Mr Mulcare's hand had created a confidence in him, it was wavering now. There was something about the man Peter did not like. His calm self-assurance, the way he looked at people as though from some lofty height, and his smile that seemed forced. There was something cold, dispassionate, about him. Who was the man? How did his father know him?

'I must go,' said Mr Mulcare. 'Excuse me.' Mrs Fury moved aside to let him pass. With four in the kitchen, space was cramped.

'I am going down your way,' said Mr Fury. The woman had not expected this.

'Going to see Possie next door,' he added quickly, seeing surprise in his wife's quick glance.

'Can I go?' asked Peter. He got up from the table.

The woman did not reply immediately. Had this been arranged? It certainly looked as though it had. 'I don't know. It rests with your father.' Then she said hurriedly, 'Oh yes, go if you wish.' She wanted to be alone. She wanted to be quiet, to think, and also she wanted to study Mr Mulcare. She had pinned the man down in a corner of her mind. And when they had gone – when they had left her alone – she would indulge herself. She would place Mr Mulcare in a corner and look at him.

Peter was already dressed. Mr Mulcare stood, hat in hand, waiting. Mr Fury came in from the lobby.

'I'm going your way,' said Mr Fury. Mrs Fury stood underneath the mantelshelf. Surely this manoeuvre had been planned. They wanted to talk. But not in the house. And then Peter's asking to join them. Surely it had been arranged.

'Well, hope to see you again soon,' remarked the visitor. He shook hands with Mrs Fury. 'I like your boy.' Then turned towards the door.

All three passed out into the street. Mrs Fury called, 'Denny.' The man came back.

'Don't go sitting in pubs with that boy.'

'No, I'm going straight to Manton Hospital.'

'All right.' She followed his figure until he caught up with Peter and Mulcare, now carrying on an animated conversation. She shut the door and sat down.

There was something disarming about the sudden silence of the house. She took out her work-basket and placed it on the sofa beside her. She took out one of Mr Fury's shirts and began to sew.

'I never saw such a man before,' she was telling herself. It wasn't his manner or his person, or indeed his dress. It was just his hurry to be off. One might have thought that the kitchen of number three Hatfields had had a suffocating effect upon him. The something disarming about the silence was the fact that one's thoughts came trooping out. They confronted one. Silence endowed them with a life of their own. They became living beings. They stood in rows, pointing and gesticulating. They accused, reminded, goaded, warned. It was inevitable that she should take down that work-basket and begin to sew. The act of sewing, the steady movement of the hand, the even rhythm of the needle as it passed to and fro, in and out, acted as a kind of gentle drug. It spun a web about these thoughts and imprisoned them. But as the silence grew, broken only by the steady breathing of the woman and the periodic click of needle against thimble, the figure of Mulcare emerged and stood before her. As she raised her eyes, the figure moved towards Mr Mangan's chair and sat in it. Suddenly Mrs Fury turned her head and looked away towards the window. At the same time she drew back in her chair. It was as if she herself had risen and pushed him into that chair; as if she had said, 'In one moment I shall attend to you,' and then had pushed him beyond actuality itself. The web she had spun about her thoughts began to give way. Maureen confronted her and spoke a woman's name. Ragner, the name was. Anna Ragner. Mr Michael Mulcare had sunk into oblivion. As she pictured him in her mind, an inner voice seemed to say, 'There are other things to attend to.'

Maureen seemed to whisper through the wall, 'You have sacrificed every-thing for your idea.' As she said this, Peter came running in. The figure of Mulcare rose in the chair, stretched out a hand, and clasped it over her son's mouth. Then Maureen laughed. Silence again. Mrs Fury shuddered in the chair.

'What on earth am I thinking about?' she exclaimed. She picked up her sewing again.

'You are thinking about the college authorities.'

'And my knock. A most peculiar knock,' said the landlord.

'And my scratching,' commented the butcher.

'And that matter of the loan.' Mrs Ragner's thick lips parted in a smile.

Mrs Fury's head began to nod. She let fall the shirt she had been sewing. There rose a sound, a kind of warning gong – it sounded in her own mind. It seemed to rise from some unfathomable depth of her being, after she had sat alone in that kitchen, and the sound seemed to ring in her ears. It was as though the bricks and mortar of number three Hatfields had become humanized. The house had a tale to tell. She was alone at last. The walls, the kitchen, the rooms, the grate, each endowed with a voice of its own, began to tell the woman their tales. Endeavours, hopes, promises broken and fulfilled, lies, cheating. Limned in those very walls was the story of her own life. Mrs Fury had fallen asleep.

When she awoke it was already dark. How could she have fallen asleep like that? She looked at the shirt upon the floor, the scattered contents of the basket. The fire had burnt low. She was shivering. She got up, and having flung some coal upon the fire, put up the tin blower. Opening the window for draught, she then crossed to the lobby and stood listening at the foot of the stairs. Anthony Mangan was snoring. He hadn't been too well today. She went upstairs to look at him. Lighting a candle, she held it high over the old man's head. 'Poor Dad,' she thought, as she went into her own room. She put down the candle on the dressing-table, and from a drawer took out a long official-looking letter. She sat down on the bed and began to go through the papers. The fees must be paid. Must be paid. She would never rest. Then as she flung the papers from her as though they burned her fingers, as though they harboured some foul poison, the whole scene with her daughter rose crystal-clear in her mind. Yes, she was determined to do it. Yes. Even if she starved. There was no doubt of that. She would see this through to the end. She, *she* had taken Denny's money.

'I am being pressed by the authorities,' she had said. It's not enough that one should see the idea blown sky-high. But there must be a settling up also. Principle! Must be done.

'Of course. Of course. But what can I do? Nothing. Except take you to Mrs Ragner,' Maureen had said.

'Ragner. Anna Ragner?'

'That's it,' Maureen had said.

'But surely – surely – are you in with this woman too?'

Maureen had laughed. 'Certainly! How do you think we live? On twenty shillings a week?'

Her laugh had frightened Mrs Fury. Was that why she was so determined to go back to the factory? Had she seen the man Sharples? Yes, of course, that was the very reason. Yes, she had seen Sharples. She was starting work soon. 'Oh! Indeed!' That had surprised the mother.

'Aren't you happy?' she had asked her daughter. 'Besides, what about the child?' Maureen's coolness had only increased her astonishment.

'I shall see to that too,' Maureen said.

'You seem to have changed,' remarked the mother.

Yes, she had. Marriage had given her the dignity of a human being. Mrs Fury had cried. It had been bad enough to have to go, to explain everything, but to have to listen to this. It was more than she could bear.

'Insulting!' she had cried.

'Nonsense!' said Maureen. 'We're no longer children. We're human beings.'

And yet she had to bow down. There was no escape. There was no way out excepting through that woman. Ragner. Anna Ragner. Mrs Fury kept repeating the name under her breath as she went downstairs again.

'No!' she cried in her mind. 'It is useless. I *must, must* give it up. It is too late.' This flirting with the matter, this dalliance, this faint, faint hope. It was too late. Had he not said 'Yes'?

She would have liked to have struck him. That word revealed his very falsity. The idea was sunk into the abyss. Never again. Never. She lighted the gas. What time would they be back?

Seven o'clock. She got dressed and went out. She would go to chapel. She locked the front door. Then she went upstairs. She put a chair on each side of the old man's bed and thought, 'That will be all right till I come back.' She left the house by the back door. She hurried down the back entry, crossed the main road, walked by her daughter's house, which was in complete darkness, and turned into Ash Walk. A few minutes later she was kneeling in the chapel of St Sebastian. Father Moynihan had seen her coming. He was standing outside his confessional box when Mrs Fury entered. Save for these two, the place was empty. He stood looking at the woman, her head bowed down. She was completely alone in that island of benches. He went up the middle aisle and knelt down behind her. After a while he touched her arm, and she turned quickly, exclaiming, 'What is that?'

'Good evening, Mrs Fury,' said the priest. 'I saw you come in. Will you come into the house?'

She rose to her feet and followed Father Moynihan through the vestry. 'Sit here,' he said, and drew a chair towards his study table.

'Well, Mrs Fury,' he began, and the expression upon his face seemed to add – 'and tell me *everything, everything.*'

'There is nothing to say, Father,' said the woman. 'Except that I am ashamed. I am not disappointed. Only ashamed. I would not have minded anything else but this. I . . .'

'Yes, I know,' said Father Moynihan. 'It is disappointing. Father Doyle and I have every sympathy with you. Let me assure you of that. Yes. We are sorry. He was a real nice boy. Now he has changed. He lacks what you have got, Mrs Fury. What is going to become of him?'

The woman slowly raised her face until it almost touched that of the priest. 'That I do not know, I do not know.' There was a weariness in her voice.

'It's a great pity. A great pity. And the unfortunate part about it is that there is so little doing now. This strike has affected hundreds of my parishioners.'

'His father,' began Mrs Fury, 'his father is trying to get him away to sea.'

Father Moynihan's expression underwent a lightning-like change, and raising his two hands he brushed one against the other with a light quick movement, as if to say, 'Well, that's the end of the matter. I wash my hands clear of it.' He got up from his chair and began walking up and down the room.

'It's tragic,' he said. 'When one comes to think of all the fine women who have left home and come here! Here to this city. Tragic.' He looked at the woman. 'Tragic,' he said again.

'Yes, Father. I know, I know.'

'How is the old man getting on?' He sat down on the chair again.

'Well, Father,' said Mrs Fury, 'he's really very low. He doesn't speak at all now.'

'Oh! Dear me! And that eldest boy of yours?'

'I never see him, Father. I only saw him once with his wife. We never go there.'

'That was strange,' continued the priest. 'Father Doyle and I have often talked about it.'

Mrs Fury fidgeted in the chair. Was it impossible even to secure peace in the chapel, to hide oneself, to forget? It seemed so. Here was Father Moynihan, feeling in the best of spirits, and asking all kinds of questions.

'I have nothing whatever to do with them, Father! I know nothing.'

'But you know who his wife is, surely,' said the priest. He rested his hand on the back of Mrs Fury's chair.

'No, Father! I don't even know that. And if I know anything, my son knows even less.'

'Well, she's the daughter of a North Country clergyman,' replied Father Moynihan. He got up from his chair again, this time to indicate that her time was up. He placed the chair against the wall.

'Well, Mrs Fury, you have my best wishes. I . . .'

The woman took a small gold cross from her pocket. 'Will you bless this, Father?'

'Certainly.' Father Moynihan blessed the cross and returned it.

'Well, good-bye now. Come and see me again some time. By the way, how did the boy get on?'

'Oh, Mr Sweeney sent him home, Father. The boy couldn't work. The crowds in the street called him a scab.'

'Oh! Dear me! Dear me!' This was sailing too near reality. He showed the woman to the door. 'Good-bye now.'

'Good-bye, Father! Thank you.' The door closed. The darkness swallowed her up. The trees flanking the path to the gate soughed in the wind.

Peter now sat between Mr Mulcare and his father in the back parlour of the Pitchpine. Mr Mulcare had ordered a small whisky, Mr Fury took plain beer, whilst Peter had a bottle of mineral water in front of him. This was real adventure. He had never been in a public-house before. He was content to sit and listen to their conversation. They were talking of his father's old ship, the *Ballisa*. In the opposite corner a man and woman attracted the boy's attention. The woman had approached the man from a lone seat up the back of the bar. She now subjected the gentleman to some good-natured badinage. The man was quite indifferent to it all. He sipped his beer contentedly, whilst his eyes roamed along the shelf above his head, filled with brightly coloured bottles. The woman was slightly tipsy, and swayed to and fro. Once she spat. The action disgusted the boy. It might have been a man who had spat upon that sawdust-covered floor. The man now put down his glass, and said in a rude manner, 'Are you going to clear out or not – you poxy-faced-looking bitch?' Mr Fury stopped speaking and looked across at the couple. Then he looked at Peter. Mulcare seemed oblivious of the incident.

'They're making a damned mistake, Fury. That's what I think,' said Mr Mulcare suddenly. 'Every time it's the same. One wonders sometimes what they are really trying to get at.'

'Get at! I suppose they're going to kick against their wages being lowered.'

'Aw! ... You're making a mistake, Fury. And is that the basis of the strike, the cutting of wages? Think again.' He laughed loudly.

Mr Fury exclaimed, 'Well, I know! They've cut the bloody miners' wages to nothing. You have some high ideas of your own, young man. But they don't get you anywhere.'

Peter was staring at Mr Mulcare.

In the opposite corner the lady had refused to budge. Her expression was that of a lady whose dignity had been questioned. Mulcare suddenly asked, 'Is she soliciting?'

Mr Fury scratched his head. He hadn't caught the word, and he did not want to ask a question. He was thinking of Peter.

'One of those old bag-women,' he said quickly. 'They're always about.' He drained his glass, got up from the table and said, 'Excuse me! Won't be a tick! Going out to pump.'

Mulcare turned to Peter. 'Your father was telling me you were at college for seven years,' he said.

'Yes,' replied Peter.

'Didn't you like it?' asked Mulcare.

'Only at first,' replied the boy.

'Why only at first?' questioned Mulcare. He leaned his head in his hand and looked closely at Peter.

'Well, it was all a cod,' blurted Peter, as though he had been saving up this effort. And it was an effort. But it seemed that with Mr Mulcare it was different. He liked the man now. His confidence was returning. He hadn't liked him in the house. He had detected a sort of arrogance in him. The way he had looked at his mother. He hadn't liked that.

'A cod! You mean you made a mistake,' said Mr Mulcare. 'One doesn't have to spend seven years in a college in order to discover that it was all a cod.' He had an idea that the boy was lying. He began to finger the empty glass. 'Barman,' he called, 'come here.' The barman came hurrying forward. 'Same!' said Mulcare. He turned to Peter. 'I once went to college too,' he said, and a smile appeared.

'You did?' Peter was surprised.

'Yes, but I didn't stay seven years like you. Only two years, Peter.'

The boy smiled. It was the first time the man had called him by his Christian name.

'I hated it,' said Peter. He had warmed to the man, and was becoming more expansive. 'It was like gaol.'

'Gaol! What were you training for? Priesthood?'

'Yes,' replied Peter.

'I am sure your mother was disappointed,' said Mr Mulcare. Peter remained silent. After a while Mulcare added, 'I like your mother.' Then he turned round and looked towards the door. 'What a time your father is!' he said.

So this man had been at college, and now he was a sailor. Peter wanted to know more. 'What college were you at, Mr Mulcare?' he asked.

'It's such a while ago that I've forgotten. I wish your father would hurry.' He turned to look at the door again. Peter looked at the man in the corner. The woman was now sitting on his knee. The man kept saying, 'Drink it, dearie. Get it down your gul. You'll need it.' With a none too steady hand he forced the glass to the woman's mouth. She laughed into it so that the spirit splashed about her face. 'Clumsy! Clumsy!'

Mulcare placed a hand upon the boy's arm. 'You want to go to sea. Why?' There was something so direct about the question that Peter, his thoughts momentarily absorbed by the actions of the man and woman in the corner, from which pair it seemed he could not now take his eyes, that he replied without turning his head, 'Because I want to see the world. To see life!' The man and the woman suddenly looked his way, tittered, and then to the boy's complete surprise drank his health from the same glass.

'Good luck to the laddie. All the best, Softy.'

Mulcare laughed. Peter blushed and looked down at his half-empty glass of lemonade. 'What a time your father is,' said Mulcare. 'Hasn't fallen down, I hope.'

'Yes. Your mother is a fine woman,' said Mr Mulcare. He picked up his glass and looked over its brim at the boy as he added, 'Well, good luck to you, boy!' He drained his glass and put it down on the table. Where the devil had Mr Fury got to? Surely he hadn't gone out for any special reason. He looked at Peter, who was still watching the antics of the inebriated lady and gentleman in the corner.

'Did you ever come across a chap named Logan?' he asked.

Peter appeared thoughtful for a moment. 'No,' he said, 'I can't say that I have.'

'I know the Principal,' said Mulcare. 'He taught me once. But that was before he went to Cork at all. A most ambitious gentleman.'

'You mean Brother Geraghty,' said Peter.

'That's the man.'

The door opened, and Mr Fury came in. He sat down and looked at his son. 'Where the hell did you put yourself, old man?' asked Mr Mulcare.

'Oh,' he said quietly, 'I met a chap in the passage there whom I haven't seen for years. It's funny, wherever I go I'm always bumping up against people whom I sailed with at one time or other.' He began to play with his lad's watch-chain. Now he pulled out the watch and said, 'It's getting late. I must go. I promised a friend of mine who is in hospital to go and see him.'

'Have a short one?' asked Mr Mulcare. It seemed this friend of his whom he was going to meet was a gentleman of great patience, for it was now nearly eight o'clock, and he had promised to meet his friend at a quarter past seven. Now Mr Fury reminded him of his obligation.

'What about that friend of yours?' he asked.

'He's all right! You'll like him! Well – a short one? Don't know when I shall see you again.' He looked at Peter. 'And this lad is going aboard my ship soon, aren't you?'

'Yes,' replied Peter. 'Yes.'

'I've had enough,' said Mr Fury. 'I must go, and I don't know whether I shall get into that hospital at this hour, either.'

All three rose to their feet. The inebriated pair now focused their attention upon the trio moving away from the table.

'Night!' said the gentleman.

'Hee ... eee,' the woman said.

'That's a bitch all right,' remarked Mr Mulcare. They passed out into the street. They stood on the kerb talking for a few minutes.

'I suppose you'll go and see the fireworks on your way back,' Mr Mulcare remarked. He began to settle his tie.

'Fireworks? What fireworks?'

Mr Mulcare laughed and slapped Dennis Fury heartily on the back. 'Why, they're having fireworks every night in town,' he said.

Well, he, Mr Fury, wasn't interested in those kind of fireworks. He shook hands with Mr Mulcare. Peter shook hands.

'So long now,' said Mr Fury. 'Take care of yourself.'

'I'll take care of myself,' replied Mr Mulcare. 'And I'll be seeing you again soon, won't I?' The remark was obviously addressed to Peter.

'Yes. This strike will soon be over,' said the boy. He stood down off the kerb.

'Good for you, prophet!' said Mulcare. Then he waved his arm and was gone. Peter stood looking after him. Now his father pulled his arm.

'Come along,' he said. 'That man would talk all night if one let him.'

They hurried down the road. After a long silence, Mr Fury exclaimed, 'He's a nice fellow, isn't he?'

'Yes. I like him,' Peter said. He nearly added, 'He knew Brother Geraghty,' but saved himself in time. He didn't want to go back to that subject. He only wanted to forget it. A bad chapter. He must wipe that from his mind.

'He'll look after you,' continued Mr Fury. 'He's a good sailor. Knows his job. And above all, he is respectable. And anyhow,' he added, looking Peter full in the face, 'it'll do you good. Every lad should do a couple of years at sea. Even those lads in the colleges.'

They turned into Lyons Street. Then they came to a halt. At the bottom of this street a crowd was gathered. Save for the sickly yellow light from two distant lamps, the street was shrouded in darkness. They moved on again. They could hear somebody shouting. They stopped again.

'I was going to go through here,' said Mr Fury, 'it's a short cut to the hospital. Now it seems we can't.' They were standing on the fringe of the crowd. Every door in Lyons Street was open. Men in their shirt-sleeves stood about on the doorsteps, whilst women leaned over their shoulders. They were listening to the harangue of a gentleman in the crowd.

'Yes. That's what they do. Shoot you down. Are you going to allow these people to shoot you down?' The question seemed to be addressed not to the crowd gathered about him, but to the street and the streets beyond. His question was flung to the whole city. 'Are you?' he was shouting. Mr Fury and his son stood listening. Someone shouted 'Specials!' and the whole crowd seemed to sway. 'Specials!' the voice repeated. Peter looked up and down. 'Specials.' he was thinking. Then he went down before a wave of rushing bodies. The crowd had made a sudden rush up the street towards the main road. The Specials had worked their way up from the bottom. Peter struggled to his feet. His father was not there. He looked round, dazed – where had his father gone? Mr Fury had been pushed up the street by the crowd. Doors banged. Out of the darkness figures emerged. They carried batons, and on their right arms they wore blue armlets. One of these men came up to Peter. He raised his arm. The boy cried, 'What's the matter?' He was frightened now. 'Clear to hell out of it.' the man cried. Peter stared at him. He was standing in the middle of the street. The street was a wilderness, all doors had closed. A moment ago it had teemed with life. There was something nightmarish about the sudden change. 'Where am I?' the boy was thinking. Then he ran. The man who had threatened to strike him now laughed. Peter had fled. At the top of the street he stopped for a moment to look down. There was nothing to see save the skulking figures in the darkness.

Peter was too bewildered to realize that the fireworks had already begun. He had only once ventured near the town. That was in broad daylight, when he had driven Mr Sweeney's lorry to the North Market. He had cursed Father Moynihan then. The crowd had called him a scab. He walked slowly down the main road. Then he stopped and stood in the shelter of a shop door. His father must have got mixed up in the crowd. As he looked up and down the road, he saw crowds of people emerging from the many side streets. 'Where are all these people going?' thought the boy. Should he go home? It was useless looking for his father now. Suddenly he darted out of the doorway, and stopped a man hurrying towards town.

'Can you tell me where the Manton Hospital is?' he asked. The man, who stood over six feet in height and was almost as broad as he was long, now looked down at Peter, at the same time increasing his pace. Peter kept pace with him.

'I was going there with my father, but I lost him in a crowd,' said the boy. The man seemed not to hear. His eyes were fixed upon a crowd of people in the distance. This crowd was now turning towards Mile Hill.

'Manton Hospital,' said the man. 'Oh! – I'm going your way. Step out.'

'Thanks,' said Peter. He buttoned his coat and began to swing his arms. This man could certainly walk fast. It was taking Peter all his time to keep up with him.

'Got somebody in there?' asked the man.

'No,' said Peter. 'No one belonging to my family. Friend of my father's.'

'Oh, I see,' said the man. He screwed his face up into a kind of monkeyish grimace.

'Not bad case, is it?'

'No,' Peter said. 'What a peculiar-looking man!' thought the boy. He was dressed in a tail-coat, grey trousers, and wore elastic-sided boots. On his head he wore a deerstalker cap. He was without collar or tie, and his shirt was open at the neck. As they passed under a lamp, Peter saw his hairy chest, and also noticed that down the right side of his face the man had a long scar.

'What is your name, anyway?' asked the strange-looking man.

'My name is Fury,' replied Peter.

The man pulled up. He laid a heavy hand upon the boy's shoulders. 'Good!' he said. 'I'm Professor Titmouse.' Peter laughed. But the man to his surprise did not return it. He frowned.

'Don't laugh!' he said. 'Please don't laugh!' They moved on again.

'Am I walking in a dream?' Peter began to ask himself as he stared at the man. They had reached the top of the hill, and were about to descend, when the man stopped.

'You strike me as being a very irresponsible person,' said Professor Titmouse. 'I happen to be going to Manton Hospital too. I hope you will not carry it beyond the doors. I have a son there.'

As he said this, he drew a black rag from his pocket and wiped his eyes.

'Oh!' said Peter. 'Forgive me. I'm sorry.'

'Carry it beyond the doors!' Peter was saying to himself. Carry what beyond the doors? His irresponsible spirit? What was the fellow talking about, at all? They were now catching up with the crowd. The man put the rag back in his pocket.

'I hope your son is all right,' said Peter. 'I didn't know. I'm sorry.'

Professor Titmouse grimaced. 'All right,' he said. 'All right. I'm a peculiar fellow. Yes. He's all right. My son's all right. He's safe. Secure. Do you work in the city?'

'No,' said Peter. 'I'm going to sea soon. I was at a college in Ireland.'

'Oh! Dear me!' The man's figure seemed to shake, as though he had been overcome by emotion. He stopped again. 'Life is strange,' he said. Peter did not reply. He was lost in contemplation. Who was Professor Titmouse? Where had he come from? It took the boy all his time to prevent himself from laughing. Professor Titmouse reminded him of a Provincial Comedian.

'I must rest a minute,' said the professor. 'Please wait for me.' The man stepped into the shelter of an emporium. He sat down on the stone floor and stretched out his legs.

'Sit down, my boy,' he said, and Peter sat down beside him. The man's face was lost to view. The darkness of the shelter had obliterated it. The boy could only hear his heavy breathing. 'Yes, I have a son,' said the professor. The black rag came out of his pocket once more. 'Funny how we should meet. Both going to the same place. Dear me!' He blew his nose with great vigour, an action that seemed to shake his whole body. The boy was feeling cold. The professor replaced the rag in his pocket. Peter felt the man's hand on his shoulder again. 'And now we must be off.' He struggled to his feet. His deerstalker hat fell off. The boy picked it up and handed it to him. 'Thank you,' he said. 'Strange that you have never heard of me,' he continued. 'Everybody knows Professor Titmouse. Aye. Dear, dear!' He sighed. 'I was young like you once upon a time.'

'Yes,' Peter said. He was at a loss for words. 'Yes.'

'And I had ideals. But there, that is silly of me, to talk like that.' And for the first time the man laughed. It was the most peculiar laugh that Peter had ever heard. It seemed to rise, a kind of dull roar, from the depths of his huge body, a full throaty laugh, almost like the croak of a frog. But it had been an effort. He now began to spit violently into the road, his mouth made the most fantastic movements. And he continued to expel mucous matter from his throat.

'Ha ha! Ideals! Illusions, my boy. Illusions. I lost mine very quickly.'

Peter looked at the man as he spoke, noting the big teeth in the top part of his mouth. They reminded him of horses' teeth. At the same time he was visualizing Mr Mulcare and hearing him say, 'But one does not find one's ideal behind the four walls of a college.'

It started up a train of thought in the boy's mind, a train of thought that was not allowed to suffer interruption, for Professor Titmouse had once more fastened his eyes upon the heels of the crowd. He had forgotten the boy. His thoughts were taking flight again, winging far ahead of the crowd, far ahead of the city. Peter was getting tired of the rapid pace. To slacken down meant an impromptu departure. He began to wonder what time it was. As though the professor had divined his thoughts, he drew from his vest pocket a solid gold hunter attached to a piece of string. 'Nine,' he said. 'Quite early yet. The rats never appear before half-past ten.' Peter stared at the man. Was the fellow drunk, or was he a little light-headed? When he surveyed the figure and its fantastic dress he was rather inclined to the latter theory. The bottom of the hill was reached. They stood on the edge of the crowd. Professor Titmouse turned to the boy.

'If you turn right, and cut across Dacre Road, then turn left at the bottom, you will come out into Elston Street. The hospital is there.'

'But aren't you going?' asked Peter. 'I thought you were going to see your

239

son,' he said. He put his hands in his pockets, and looked right into the professor's eyes. The man must be mad.

'You can go, or you can stay with me,' remarked Professor Titmouse. 'I do not think my son will be in too great a hurry to see me,' he went on. For the third time the black rag came out of his capacious tail-pocket.

'Oh!' said Peter. 'Oh! ...'

'Yes. I have a little business on hand.'

'I'll wait, if you like,' said Peter, hardly knowing why he had said it.

'It's better for the dead to wait,' said Professor Titmouse. 'My son will be in no great hurry.' He raised his hand and swung it in the air towards the crowd. 'Look!' he said. 'The rats are coming out. The fun will soon begin. Excuse my habiliments,' continued the professor. 'I shall shortly change them.' Suddenly a voice that seemed to come from the far corner of the Square cried out, 'Kick his nose! Kick his bloody nose!'

'There!' said the professor. 'The fun has begun. And everything is free. Free!' He grasped the boy's arm, and with a strength that surprised the boy pushed him forward into the crowd.

3

'Right through!' said the professor. He bent down and spoke into Peter's ear. It was almost a hiss.

'If we get through here, we can make our way to the back of the Forester Hall. Then we can work our way into the lions. I always manage to get a good view from there.' His grip tightened upon the boy's arm. 'Evidently,' thought Peter, 'this strange gentleman makes a hobby of it.' An obstacle arose. A fractious group refused to move. The professor pleaded, cajoled, then finally swore. 'Make way, please.' A passage was made, if only for the satisfaction of seeing this strangely dressed figure pass. Everybody stared at Peter.

'Brownie!' shouted a voice. The professor swung round. 'Pshaw! ...' As they pushed on, the lane seemed to grow longer. The boy was beginning to feel ashamed. He could feel the thousands of eyes upon him, and at times hands reached out, touching him. Once he felt a hand go into his pocket. At once he stopped, caught the hand, then struck out at the man. A scuffle ensued. Professor Titmouse was pulling hard. 'Come! Let them amuse themselves,' he said. 'He was picking my pockets,' shouted Peter angrily. He got no further; a huge man turned round, and driving his rump into Peter's back, catapulted him headlong down the lane. Professor Titmouse swore.

'Disgraceful! Another halt!' It didn't seem so easy after all. The lane closed up. Human bodies cemented themselves once more. At the north end of the Square rope barriers had been erected. In the middle of the road corporation water-carts had been lined up behind the ropes. The police were massed alongside the Castle Hotel, the railway station, and the Forum Theatre. This long line of authority shifted from end to end of the Square. Then it swerved off diagonally, fringing the Forester Hall. The setting reminded one of the overnight preparations for a public execution. But this was a new game. A waiting game. The tocsin had not yet sounded. Three times, between half-past five and seven o'clock, the police had charged the crowds. Now they seemed to be increasing. The authorities were perturbed at the sudden turn in the situation. It was not enough that the whole life of the city should be threatened by the sudden strike, but in the evening people began to congregate in the main streets. The suburbs supplied their quota. From north, south, east, and west the people came. The centre of the city had reached suffocating-point. These crowds had gathered for many reasons. They were there to protest against the butchery of the police on the previous Sunday, against the importing of foreign police. But it seemed that anger had been chiefly aroused by the arrival of a military force from the neighbouring barracks. The air itself was electric, charged with every sort of possibility. The authorities were taking no chances. Some in the crowd had come to loot, and others, like Professor Titmouse and Peter, had come to see the fun. It was fun to stand and watch the police, bored, angry, bursting to let loose, to fly among this mob and scatter them. Occasionally fusillades of bricks, bottles, stones were flung. 'Butchers!' the people shouted. 'Swine! swine!' The police stood still. Outside the railway station the horses of the mounted police stamped impatiently upon the stones. From over the river there came a biting icy wind. The mass of bodies seemed to draw closer together for warmth, for security, for moral strength. The police were patient. Their time would come. They were there to stop looting, to clear the streets. At half-past three in the afternoon the Riot Act had been read out. In a large room in a house situated in the south end of the city the industrial leaders were in conference, to deal with the situation. Mr John Williams had twice interviewed the chief constable. He had protested against Sunday's sabotage, the breaking up of a peaceful meeting. Hundreds were in hospital. Individual acts of terrorism were taking place daily, day and night. The authorities held they were doing no more than their duty. Their sense of fear seemed greater than their sense of duty. There were not enough police to deal with the situation. The Government were apprehensive of unbridled licence. Orders were given for a detachment of Hussars to make immediate departure for the city.

Professor Titmouse wiped the sweat from his forehead.

'Well, my boy. Here we are. Do you think that you can get under that stone belly?' The professor waved his hand towards the lion.

'Think so,' Peter said. He stood looking up at the lion as though at any moment it might come to life and spring upon him. They had managed to work their way behind the Forester Hall. This was accomplished by passing through a urinal and climbing over its wall. Peter still held the sourish, acrid smell in his nostrils. When the wall had been climbed, they had to force their way through an aperture between the wall-top and the roof. They had thus reached the top of the steps. As they hung suspended there for a moment, the boy's eyes wandered over the sea of heads. Professor Titmouse had said, 'Be careful, my boy!' So they had reached the plateau. More pushing and struggling. The clock of the Forester Hall struck half-past nine.

'Here!' said Professor Titmouse. 'Just in time.'

Peter looked from the stone lion to his companion. 'Yes, I can get up there.'

'Good! Then go ahead.' The crowd's attention was now turned to the two figures climbing the great stone lion. Peter paused.

'Go ahead. Never mind the crowd,' entreated Professor Titmouse. 'They'll forget you in one single second. That is one of the virtues of crowds. They can forget instantly. They will be looking across the street at that ferocious-looking inspector in a moment.' He climbed up. Peter had now seated himself astride the animal. The professor sat behind him. Immediately Peter shifted his position so that he could sit facing the man. He was the sort of person he did not like to turn his back upon. He was becoming suspicious already. At any moment the strange man might fling him off. At the same time he was enjoying it. This was certainly the biggest adventure of his life. All thought of his father had now vanished. The crowd below had started to shout. Professor Titmouse chuckled. He laid his hand on Peter's shoulders.

'Now! We are here. We can now proceed to enjoy the spectacle. In two minutes something will happen. I say that because I know.' The boy did not hear. He was looking in the direction of the Castle Hotel. Here a disturbance had already taken place. A brick had been flung at the hoardings, and in their frantic efforts to dodge this hefty missile three or four policemen had fallen in a heap. Peter was surveying the situation. His eyes wandered slowly along, rested on the Forum Theatre, then his head turned and he took stock of the crowds massed about the steps of the Forester Hall.

'Ah, my boy,' said the professor, 'I can see that you are interested already. Are you a sociological student, by the way? If you are, then I give you my hand. I am very interested. But these, of course, are not revolutionary tactics, merely sporadic pricks of authority.'

'Yes,' replied Peter. 'I understand,' and his voice seemed to come from far away.

'Crowds always attract me,' continued Professor Titmouse. 'Ah!' he exclaimed suddenly. 'Look at that!' He raised his hairy hand and pointed in the direction of a large tailor's shop standing midway between the Castle Hotel and the railway station. Peter strained his eyes. At what was the man staring? At the same time he was saying to himself, 'If they suddenly charge this crowd, we are safe.' Crouched on the stone lion, it was impossible to see them.

'There!' said the professor, as the crashing of glass in the roadway caused the whole mass of bodies to sway forward as though some huge hand had risen out of the earth and pushed them towards the road. 'Keep quite still,' the professor whispered in Peter's ear. 'The psychological moment has not yet arrived. Those gentlemen in blue yonder have a sense of proportion. They know when to be quiet, when to make a noise; meanwhile, this little diversion is interesting. Observe.' He pointed with a long forefinger towards a section of the crowd. 'Now,' continued Professor Titmouse, 'if you will look just below you, you will notice the extraordinary effect that has taken place. But perhaps you have already done so.' He was now leaning on the boy, his two hands upon Peter's shoulders. Gripping the lion's mane more firmly, Peter looked down.

'It begins with a minute wriggling. Some sort of current has passed through them. The current makes them restless. It says in effect, "Something is happening in front." But damn it, they can't see. They fret, press forward, their pupils dilate, their heads are raised, they stand on tiptoe, and they are all asking themselves the same question, "What is happening?" Ha ha! There we have the advantage, my boy; we stride the heights, we look down into the pit. Tell me,' he went on, 'have these people any interest for you? Do you attach any significance to their presence? Who are they? What are they here for?' He suddenly arched his back. Peter laughed. There was a sort of tensity in the professor's expression. 'Looks like a monkey endeavouring to solve a conundrum.' Now he stroked his cheek with his left hand.

'They are here to protest against the brutality of the authorities,' said Peter.

'What?' Professor Titmouse sat back so suddenly that, but for Peter gripping his arm, he might have fallen from the lion. 'Fiddlesticks! To protest! That is wrong, my boy. They do not know why they are here. Understand me. They are a lot of sheep. Look!' he said. 'Would you say that action constituted a protest against brutality? Brutality. They do not know what the word means. Look!' he repeated. 'Just below you. There is brutality. Real brutality. Wicked. Look at the child! She is crying. She is being crushed. Her mother holds her to her breast, but she is being crushed by the crowd. What right has that woman to bring her child here? To stew for hours, suffocated by sheer weight, by the smell of sweating bodies, of mouldy clothes. Does that constitute a protest against brutality? No, my boy.'

Peter, looking down, saw the woman. She was easily distinguishable by her white blouse. She was bareheaded. She had a tiny girl in her arms. The child gave vent to periodic bursts of weeping, which the woman countered by swears, by occasional slaps on the child's legs. The pressure of the bodies against her had partly loosened the woman's clothing. Her blouse was open, and the boy could clearly see her breasts. Their whiteness stood out boldly in the darkness. He looked at the man on the lion.

'I quite agree with you,' he said. 'The woman should not be here.'

'No,' said the professor. 'And pretty soon those gentlemen over there are going to clear this rabble out. That woman will fall. It is inevitable. Tomorrow the air will ring with protests against brutality. Has it any redeeming feature? Yes. It is unconscious brutality. A crowd has no focal point, for the simple reason that it has no head. It has only a body. Well, well, enough of these deliberations. If you look towards that shop now, you will see something interesting. A gentleman – I presume it is a gentleman – from pure generousness of spirit has decided to entertain a section of the crowd with a performance. On the other hand, I may be quite wrong. It may be that he is the direct manifestation of a certain spurious philosophy. You know the word "get" has almost philosophical significance. The gentleman is going to get something. If he did not get it for nothing, it would not be philosophic. Do you understand? Well, he has decided to get something. He has not gone into that shop window for nothing. No, sir! Why do not the police prevent him? Are they afraid of him? Well, he is of small and of slight build. No, my boy; as I say, the psychological moment has not yet arrived. Excuse my continually speaking into your ear, but I could not make you hear clearly if I did not bend closely to you. The noise is deafening. The noise of people breathing, talking, coughing, laughing, swearing. They are waiting for a cue. Possibly that little gentleman has supplied it. There! He has disappeared into the hole in the window ... Notice the restlessness of the people below us. They know something interesting is going to happen. But they can't see. If one cannot see a thing, one tries to imagine it. Alas! Crowds have no imagination.' Professor Titmouse had raised his head and appeared to be speaking to the empty air.

A light had suddenly appeared in the window of the tailor's shop. It came from a candle-stand in which burned five candles. The slightly built man, who had crushed his way to the front and climbed through the hole in the window, was now standing holding the candle above his head. He seemed to be surveying the contents of the window. Professor Titmouse suddenly put his hand in his pocket and took out his spectacles. Peter watched him put them on.

'Cheap,' said the professor, 'but they suit me admirably.' Authority on crowds as he was, he found something significant enough in the action of the little man in the window and concentrated his attention there. Peter he had forgotten altogether.

The man in the window had quite coolly begun to undress himself. There were cries of 'Ooe! . . .' from the crowd in front of the shop. A great shout went up as he removed his trousers. He then approached a wax gentleman wearing 'Our latest Winter Style', and proceeded to divest it of its apparel.

'Look at him! He's a cool'n!' somebody shouted, as the man began to dress. Suddenly the man paused . . . then disappeared again. When he came out he had a new bowler hat in his hand. He blew out the candles, crawled out through the hole in the window, dressed in 'Our latest Winter Style', and with a sweep of the hand bowed to the crowd and put on the new bowler hat. The crowd moved forward. The newly clothed gentleman disappeared in the gathering as quickly and mysteriously as he had emerged.

'There,' said the professor, turning his attention to Peter once more. 'Observe, such actions are propitious. The little man has new-clothed himself at the expense of some poor shopkeeper. But is that honest? I ask you?' He put his face close to Peter, and added in a sort of half-frightened whisper, 'Is it?' as though the very action of the man in the window had involved him in some kind of moral problem, as though the action were portentous and his very fate had been caught in it. But the boy only laughed.

'Don't you see?' continued the professor. 'That action was backed up by the moral force of the crowd. No. Immoral force. But is it fair? Is it honest? Is this a peaceful gathering? Is it a fair protest against brutality? You are laughing at me. Well! I said this evening that I thought you were irresponsible. Curb it, my boy. It is dangerous unless one can temper and control it. However, I shall not disturb your enjoyment of the fun. But the man's action is a bad one. It harbours frightful possibilities. Do you condone such actions, young man, or does your very irresponsibleness whirl you clear of questioning its morality? However, I can see at once that you are not greatly interested. I shall not indulge in ethical deliberations, set your mind at rest upon that. Propel your spirit forward, sit straight up upon that lion's back, and prepare to enjoy yourself. Satiate yourself. Yes, enjoy yourself not by a profound contemplation of this assembly, of the social fabric, but physically, my boy. Lose yourself in this mass. Become part and parcel of it. Absorb its blind strength, its dull rage, its very breath, the multifarious smells that arise from their bodies. Allow your eyes to wander here and there, in and about, up and down. That is what you are sitting upon that lion's back for. You did not set out to study, not this evening. I could tell that as soon as I looked on you. I am a good judge of faces. No, my dear boy. The thing to do is to lose oneself, to surrender oneself to its intoxicating, I will not say toxic, qualities. Not I. But you. I withdraw. I stand outside of that now. You are young. Life holds out delicious flavours. Ha ha! What does one require to live? To enjoy life? Not much. From what you tell me, you set out to acquire knowledge. You were at college, so you informed me. Well, at a college one learns. Learning is knowledge. But be careful. Be careful. A little is enough. Too much is rank poison. It destroys one's simplicity, my boy. A little, and consume that little. Well, that's enough. Content yourself. Don't mind me. Watch the crowd. Watch the crowd. Watch the down-trodden workers. See them move forwards and backwards, sway, rise, fall. Look at the faces. The map of life. By a single stretch of the imagination this lion can become the very empyrean heights. One moment!'

Professor Titmouse opened wide his mouth, as though he were going to yawn. Peter moved away from him.

'Ha ha!' Professor Titmouse laughed. 'Did you think I was going to eat you?'

What are all these people here for? And what are they waiting for? Nobody is going to address them. And why those great rope barriers? Those corporation water-carts strung across the north end of the Square? And why is the Forum Theatre boarded up, the railway station, the Castle Hotel? The professor put his hand on his head.

'Fancy!' he said. 'I entirely forgot to give you my card. Here you are.' He pulled from his pocket a heavily thumb-marked card and handed it to Peter. The boy took the card. He read it. 'R. H. Titmouse. Professor of Anthropology.' Smilingly he placed the card in his pocket. In a moment he had forgotten it. Well, why was he sitting here? Who on earth was this strange man sitting opposite him?

Suddenly the professor exclaimed: 'Have you ever studied crowds, my boy? The tantalizing qualities inherent in them. What are crowds? A mixture of cowardice and impudence.' Then he clapped his hands in the manner of an excited child. His eyes appeared to dance in his head, his hands trembled; it was as though the intoxicating atmosphere had caught him too. His mouth opened and closed. 'Ah!' he said, and became suddenly rigid.

'Is the fellow really mad?' thought the boy. He had gradually made the distance between his companion and himself greater by moving further up. And now he sat precariously balanced upon the lion's head.

'I have never studied crowds,' said Peter, 'though I am sure you are right. It is getting late. I must go. My father will be wondering where I have got to.' He made a movement, but Professor Titmouse caught his leg.

'One moment, my young friend,' he said. Then he raised his head, and his eyes searched the vast Square.

'I will tell you what those people are here for, my boy,' he continued. 'They are here to loot! They are here to get something for nothing. But where are the men who could send these people home about their business? I will tell you. They are in a large and resplendent hotel higher up the road, and they are endeavouring to put the world to rights. Ha ha! And why don't the police move? Why don't they clear the Square? Because they are waiting for provocation. Our little friend who stole the suit would not actuate it. It requires something bigger, something symbolical. They are waiting for a growl, a murmur, to rise from its depths. Then they will set about their lawful duty.'

'I am not concerned with all that,' remarked Peter. 'There! Listen!'

The clock of the Forester Hall struck ten. 'It is late. I have to go.'

He made another move, but the professor's hold upon his leg only tightened. 'Please!' Peter said. He leaned forward and stared boldly into the man's face. But the professor only laughed. He saw the fear skulking behind this apparent boldness. 'Be patient, my boy. Keep cool.'

He caught his nose between two long fingers and blew vigorously.

'Have you ever noticed – the almost pestiferous odour that crowds exhale? Ha! Something is happening over there. Stand up, my boy. Look! There, stand erect. I shall hold your legs.'

'I am not interested,' said Peter. 'It is late. I must go now. I have a long way to go.' He tried to free his leg from the professor's grip, but the man's fingers were like steel.

'Come,' said the professor. 'Stand up and look into the seething abyss. Behold those who have risen from ten thousand stinking mattresses, who have emerged from their rat-holes. Look at them! Bury your nose in that stinking heap. Can you see perfectly?'

'Please leave go my leg,' said Peter sharply. 'I am going.'

'Going!' The expression upon Professor Titmouse's face revealed both surprise and annoyance. 'Go! Where will you go, my boy? Where? Why? Tell me. Have you ever indulged in the delights of mathematical calculations?'

'This man,' thought Peter, 'must be mad.' He was smiling at the boy. It seemed to endow the man's face with an expression of vileness. He began rubbing his mouth with his index finger.

'I must go,' said Peter furiously. 'My father . . .'

'Your father! Late. The Manton Hospital is closed. What are you talking

247

about, my boy? Or is it that you are quite unused to such exhilarating adventure? Well, well! Surely you would not desert me! I have enjoyed your company. Pardon me if I say that your physical presence has had a most extraordinary – I might even go further and say a most profound – effect upon me. Mentally you bore me! Understand? You are naïve, untutored in certain niceties, polish, decorum. In brief, you are ... well, no, I shall not say that. But I think you are a little sly – a little callous, I mean. Please excuse me. I am rather prone to adopt the cold, ice-like precision of a surgeon. It's a weakness of mine. Tell me! Where is your home?'

Peter, his eyes fastened upon the man's face, seemed unconscious of the scene taking place below him. As for Professor Titmouse, the crowd, the Square, the police, they no longer existed. Hidden in shadow, these figures upon the lion could not be seen. And the people below, like some vast silent river, flowed slowly past. The police were pressing them backwards towards the long Mile Hill.

'I confess I rather like you,' continued the tall man sitting astride the lion. 'I experience the most extraordinary feelings in your company. I too had a son once! Dear me! Dear me!'

Peter lowered his eyes. They rested for a moment upon the professor's elastic-sided boots, then slowly climbed until they came to rest upon his face. 'I'm going now,' he said.

If the man prevented him, he would shout; then they would be discovered, and the professor's 'pestiferous crowd' would know how to deal with the matter.

'Come, my young friend,' said the professor. His tone was wheedlingly affectionate. 'Come! You do me an injustice. Perhaps my directness has rather puzzled, rather frightened you. Don't be afraid, my boy. I am only another human being like yourself.' He laughed again, that strange throaty laugh, so that for the second time Peter visioned his horse-like teeth, blackened and rotten. And again he proceeded to expel, with much effort, a mucous substance from his mouth, though this time he used his black rag, having in mind no doubt, the great number of heads below him. This rag was part of the sleeve of a woman's satin blouse. The lower part of the face was hidden by the rag, which he held tightly to his mouth. Peter turned his head away. The peculiar noise the man made, almost like the gobble of a turkey, the click of his tongue, made him feel physically sick, as the other evening his grandfather's slobbering had done when he had had to feed him. Now he wanted to vomit. He closed his eyes. The professor had leaned forward again, so that the boy could feel his breath upon his face.

'On the other hand,' said Professor Titmouse, 'we could in a single moment

248

tumble from this stone animal into the maelstrom. But why do that? Let us look down. The scene is changing. The crowd are cowed. They are moving quickly away. That can only mean one thing. They will break out somewhere else. Very soon you will be able to descend and walk freely across the Square.'

'Close your eyes again, my boy,' said Professor Titmouse. Now his protruding lips appeared to touch Peter's face. 'Close your eyes. The sky is leaden, oppressive. One might expect rain, even thunder. The moon has come riding up, a little shyly, and its pale light has touched those towering masses of masonry, that we call tall buildings, that oppress and suffocate. Its light has also fallen upon a young girl who is leaning out of the top window of a house just opposite where we sit. It seems to have caught her hair, now glistening like silver. Her hands are gripping the window-pane. She is looking down upon the Square. There is nothing inquisitive or searching in her glance. She may have come to the window for a breath of air. But see! She has retired. The window has been closed. The air has become infected with a pestilential odour. It rises up from the Square. The moon's light is gradually revealing dark corners. There are people crouching there. They look like so many terrified animals. This mass of brick and mortar seems to suffer change under the almost miraculous white light that floods it. Did you hear that sudden cry, my boy? Our friend from the tailor's shop has committed hari-kari in the Square. There! The police are putting him in an ambulance. What can that mean, my young friend, that sudden surrendering of life before these crowds beneath that moon's light? There! It has passed again, and the towering buildings are lost in the darkness once more. Have you ever noticed the extraordinary effect that light can have upon certain objects? The Square. The play of the lights against the walls gives the impression that the oppressive mass of masonry has become humanized and appears to perform the most fantastic-like movements. The height seems to increase, so that looking up from the Square one has the impression of being imprisoned between two walls, which for some strange reason have drawn closer together. Now! The people have begun to move. The police have charged them. Some hand has thrown a lighted paper into a shop. Listen to their shouting. The flames are rising. Arms ride the air, sticks, stones, and bottles fly, batons whizz past one's head. As the flames spread from shop to shop, flames which no mortal hand can now put out, those towering walls are thrown clear, one can see them perfectly. One can see them for what they are. Prisons, my boy. And who are these running people, these swearing crowds? Look! The light of the fires has caught them. Goblins from the Inferno! Ha ha!' The professor suddenly gripped Peter's body and embraced him. The boy struggled.

'You swine!' The bodies seemed to sway, then fell clear into the Square. They held together for a moment, then the boy lunged and broke free. Professor Titmouse's legs seemed to shoot into the air. This was a nightmare! This was no dream! A huge face seemed to thrust itself at Peter, the boy ducked. Horses were coming up at the gallop. The boy gave one look at the man struggling upon the ground.

'Have you got my card?' shouted the professor. 'Come and see me some time! I am so lonely.' But Peter was already running; his hand shot out, grasped a coat, and now he was carried along. This avalanche of flying bodies frightened him. If he didn't look out he would be trampled to death. He screamed as he heard troops thundering past. He did not know that Professor Titmouse had been laid suddenly low by a blow from a baton. He ran on. Sweat broke out upon his forehead. Where was he running? Was it really a dream? Then he heard a scream behind him. A man had fallen under a horse. By God! This was no dream! Far ahead he could see lights. He still hung desperately to the tail of the brown tweed coat. The man in front seemed quite unconscious of the weight behind him. He tore on, possessed with one idea, one desire, to get free of the oncoming horses. At the end of the Square the crowd broke. Some turned up John Street, others turned down towards the Front. At last! With a sort of final and desperate lunge the man in the brown suit broke free and tore up London Street. Peter followed the crowd that now streamed downhill. If he could get to the Front he was safe. There was the dark road, a two-mile walk, and then he would be home. He pulled out his handkerchief and began wiping his face, though he never slackened in his mad dash down the hill. He could see the long narrow street, and at the bottom a light. The light became a beacon, a goal. He increased his speed. He left crowds running behind him. He knocked a child down, but did not stop. He heard its scream.

When he thought of the mad professor his blood ran cold. There was something about the man's figure, the touch of his hand, his almost pesty breath, that made Peter shudder. The impression remained vivid in his mind. A madman! A madman! And that sudden embrace. He stopped for a single moment and spat. He must. If he did not stop he would be sick at once. He must spit it out, the disgust, the pure disgust he felt. 'Where is Dad?' He began to run again. For fifty yards he ran free; now he was on the fringe of yet another crowd, running towards the long narrow street with that beckoning light at its bottom. This, then, was the firework display Mulcare had remarked upon! 'Poor man!' said Peter, 'he said he was lonely. Poor man!' They had entered the long narrow street. Peter now saw for the first time that there were a good many women in the crowd.

Ahead there were sudden cries. The crowd pulled up. Somebody shouted, 'Specials! Specials!' More people came running down. Peter was in the middle of the crowd. The police were running down, batons raised. The Specials had emerged from the darkness, they closed the approach at the bottom. The people were hemmed in. Peter kept his eyes upon the light. It was the lamp above the gate entrance of the Moreston Dock. 'Make way! Make way!' The people appeared to swim round him, he himself floated in the air. 'Make way!' Then silence again. The crowd moved towards the bottom of the street. Peter went with them. There was no escape. He wanted to turn round and run back. But that was impossible. He could not move. They were hemmed in by the high walls of a cotton warehouse. Old rope, heaps of damp cotton, pieces of corrugated iron, waste-paper, rags, and tins littered the street. Each time Peter moved, the man on his left swore. 'Where the devil do you think you are going to?' Peter threw his hands in the air.

'I want to get out,' he shouted. 'I want to get out.'

'Then get out, you bastard!' shouted a woman, who promptly butted him forward with her backside. 'Get out.' He was feeling sick again. The whole atmosphere seemed to take on that nightmarish quality which he associated with the crowd in the Square when, in company with Professor Titmouse, he had sat astride the stone lion. The stale breaths, the smell of garbage, of cheap shag, of grease, of steam rose all around him. 'Keep quiet!' shouted the big woman. 'Don't you know those swine are hiding at the bottom?' She struck the boy in the back with her fist. Temporarily thrown off his balance, the boy shot forward again and fell into a group of women. As he fell among them, he spat. He could not help it. A hand struck him in the face. 'Beast! Beast!'

It was so dark in the street that he could not see. The faces about him bobbed up and down, in and out, like a sea of splashing light. He was trapped. Whichever way he turned, the crowd hemmed him in. Suddenly he drew himself up to his full height, and shouting 'Make way!' hurled himself forward. If he remained in this crowd a minute longer he would smother. To his complete surprise the crowd fell away and he went hurling down an avenue of human bodies, to come to rest against the wall of the cotton warehouse. He put out his hands and felt the wall. Here it was even darker. He groped his way slowly along. He would soon come to one of the hoist doors. He stopped. This was one. He stepped into it for shelter and leaned against the wooden door. Before him a bleak mass, out of which rose the many lights, the lights that were human faces, upon which there was limned a terror and desperation. Above the sea of faces, the foul smells. 'If I can get down to that light,' thought Peter, 'I am free!'

There was something delicious and exciting about the very idea. His whole body trembled at the thought. He felt he had been flung into a stinking pit, that he had lain there for many hours, imprisoned by bodies, many bodies, and crowned by the hoarse laugh of Professor Titmouse. He could see his huge rotten teeth again as the man opened his mouth to emit that slow strange croak. A human toad. A lonely human toad. The professor was right. The atmosphere, the scene was spectral. The air was filled with sudden yells. The crowds were running up the street again. Beasts at bay. Rats caught in the trap. Peter shuddered and crouched against the wall. 'By a single stretch of the imagination,' the professor had said, 'you can now sit on empyrean heights.' And by a single stretch of the imagination he could be roaming those broad green fields of the college in Cork. The air was humming again. Sticks rose and fell. The crowd struck out as the Specials came up to them. 'God!' cried Peter, and clutched at the chain guard that swung across the hoist door. Now the crowd had vanished. Dark forms were running in pursuit. The Specials. The air seemed suddenly filled with clouds of blue armlets. The shouting ceased. Peter clung tight to the chain, so that he felt its great weight about his body. Here in the protecting darkness of the great iron door he was safe. He poked his head out, and looked up and down the street. Then he crept out, and still keeping close to the wall, walked slowly down the street. At that moment the clock of the Forester Hall struck eleven. 'Good heavens!' exclaimed the boy under his breath. He stopped. Three dark forms loomed up. Peter turned on his heel and made his way back again. Perhaps he could get out the other way.

At the top of the street other forms flittered about in the darkness. He made a decision. 'I can't stay here any longer.' What had he done? Why should he be afraid to go down? Filled with determination now, he walked boldly back again. At the bottom of the street he was pulled up. Where was he going to? Peter held his breath; then he stammered, 'I'm going home,' and stared angrily at the man in front of him. He was wearing a high collar and pince-nez. The blue band on his arm reminded Peter that the gentleman was a Special – probably an opportunist, certainly a patriot.

'Home!' said the man. 'Where the hell is that?' He subjected Peter to a minute scrutiny.

'I live in Hatfields,' stammered Peter.

'Then get to hell out of it!' shouted the man, and lifted his arm threateningly. The boy turned and fled. How many miles had he run tonight? Ah! There was the light. At last! He was safe. He was on the Dock Road. Now it was easy. He knew his way back to Hatfields. The road, unlike the street, was badly lighted. The dimmest of lamps shone feebly, but bravely, every seven or eight hundred yards. The boy walked along under the shadow of the sheds. Here the atmosphere was different. From the quays and warehouses came the smells of raw tobacco, of ripe fruits, of seeds, of rope and oils. Suddenly he started to run again. A man had loomed up out of the shadows. 'Some drunken man returning to his ship,' thought the boy. He had reached Brook Street now. He stopped to get his breath. Before he was aware of it, the man had caught up with him. The boy, seeing him, again drew into the wall and attempted to make himself as small and insignificant as possible. But, as the man hurried past, something about him caused Peter to start. It reminded him of ... of ... He dashed away from the wall and ran after the man. 'Desmond!' he shouted. 'Desmond!' Then he burst out laughing. It was Desmond. It couldn't be anybody else but his brother. He put his hands on his hips, spread his legs apart, and shouted, 'Desmond! Desmond!'

The man had stopped. He appeared to be uncertain as to where the call had come from. Then he espied the tall figure standing on the kerb, ankle-deep in rubbish. He came hurrying up.

'Desmond! Desmond!'

The man stood hesitant. 'I ... who ... ?'

'I'm Peter. Don't you know me?'

'Good God! You! What are you doing here?' The two brothers stood staring at each other, lost for words. Then Desmond rushed up to Peter and gripped both his hands.

'Peter!' he said. 'Peter! Well, by God! But tell me – tell me ...'

They began to walk along towards Bank Street.

'I was with Dad,' said Peter. 'I lost him in a crowd. We were going to see Mr Postlethwaite at the Manton Hospital. But we lost each other. And then I met a man, a most impossible person. I have his card in my pocket – look!' He pulled the professor's card from his pocket. 'Look!' He was excited. His face was very red.

'Yes. I know. But what are you doing here? I thought you were in Ireland!'

'No. I've left now. I gave it up. It was a pure cod. I'm going to sea next week.'

Desmond Fury was dumbfounded. He was quite unable to speak. It was extraordinary enough to meet his brother in that way, but to hear that he had left the college, was actually going to sea! Well ... he must collect himself. He must get his breath. It was all too surprising. George Postlethwaite was right after all. And he, Desmond, had lightly dismissed it as one of George's tall yarns. They covered the distance up Bank Street, Peter talking excitedly, Desmond listening attentively but maintaining a silence that astonished the boy. But he did not know that such news had taken Desmond's breath away. At the top of the street they pulled up. Desmond put a hand on his brother's arm. 'Now I must go. It is getting late. Come and see me tomorrow.'

'Where? What time?'

'Do you know the Blue Bird Café at the back of Lewis's yard?'

'Blue Bird Café, Blue Bird Café,' muttered the boy. 'Oh yes, yes, I know.' He was growing excited again. 'What time?'

'About seven,' said Desmond. 'By God, you've grown! Well, good-night. You must hurry,' he continued; 'nearly twelve.'

'Yes. Good-night, Desmond. Good-night.'

They parted. In a few minutes they had disappeared, Peter round one corner, Desmond round the other. A fog-horn began to blow. A fog was rising over the river.

CHAPTER XI

I

Mr Fury was tired. He yawned, stretched himself out in bed, and rolled over. Mrs Fury was already up and dressing. The man closed his eyes. When he opened them again, he hoped to find her gone. Then he would lie at his ease. He yawned again. He wanted to ask her where she was hurrying off to, but something warned him not to question. Her manner. He hadn't slept a wink all night. The woman had been so restless. Her movements, her quick breathing, were enough to make Mr Fury cover his head with the clothes.

In the back room Peter was snoring so loudly that Mr Mangan's feeble efforts were put to shame. Peter had had a nightmare. He had been riding pick-a-back with Professor Titmouse round and round Powell Square. The sun was shining down on them. After a while, the professor collapsed. Peter woke up, stared bewilderedly about the room, then fell asleep.

His mother was now dressing herself in front of the dressing-mirror. She looked at the still figure in the bed. It seemed to increase her own vitality. Now she stood fully dressed. She was wearing the same clothes as she had done on the occasion of her visit to the shipping office to see Mr Lake. On every occasion that necessitated a trip to town Mrs Fury wore the same clothes. They might well have had a label attached to them as they hung in the cheap ply-wood wardrobe: 'Mr Lake!'

She crossed to the window and looked out. The air was damp and the streets covered with a thin film of rain. Nobody about. Hatfields had not yet come to life. The circumstances and the occasion made it possible for the men-folk to lie back at their ease. The women could do the worrying for a change. She opened the bottom window. In addition to the stale smell from the near-by yard there now rose the smell of frying bacon, of grease, of frying meat. People were getting breakfast ready.

Ten minutes past eight. The woman left the room, closed the door silently behind her, and passed downstairs. She stirred the slack in the grate, put up the tin blower and then opened the kitchen window for draught. The fire was soon blazing. She started to make breakfast. At the same time she was forming plans. Should she see Mr Lake first, or should she go at once with Maureen to see this Mrs Anna Ragner?

She sat down to think it over whilst the kettle boiled. Then she got up and went into the back kitchen to get the tea.

She had decided that Mrs Ragner could wait. Anthony was more important. He had been much in her thoughts lately, and she hadn't had a letter from him since the one she received the day after Peter's return. No. They could not stop the boy's money like that. It was a mistake, and it was more necessary than ever. Her husband's five and threepence was nothing, Mr Mangan's pension a pittance. The allotment money was far more important.

Having poured the tea, she poured out a cup, drinking it standing at the table. She did not want anything to eat. She wasn't hungry, and besides, there wasn't time. She put on her hat (the one from Hobhouse's had been carefully wrapped in tissue paper). This new hat came into her mind now. She would wear that hat on some more auspicious occasion. But nothing warranted her wearing it today. For one thing, it required a decent costume to go with it.

Mrs Fury was now ready. There was only one thing to do. Go upstairs and tell Denny she was going to town, leave orders with him, have him see to Mr Mangan and get his own and the boy's meals ready.

As she opened the door of the room, the man, who had been lying awake under the bed-clothes indulging in the wildest day-dreams, sat up. Better that than to be called. Better to show anticipation than annoyance. The door closed. Mrs Fury stood at the foot of the bed.

'I'm going now,' she said quietly. She looked back at the door, and as though Peter's snores had prompted it, said quickly, 'And get that boy up too. He would lie there all day, snoring like a pig, if you let him.'

'Where are you going?' asked Mr Fury. He rubbed his eyes, blinked, then opened them wide. He leaned forward in the bed and looked, not at the woman's face, but at her hands. The grip upon the bed-rail accentuated their whiteness, their slimness. They seemed to stand out, things apart from her person.

'That's all,' said Mrs Fury. 'Oh, and see to Dad,' she added quickly.

'But where are you going to at this time of the morning?' asked Mr Fury.

'I'm going to see Mr Lake,' she replied sharply. 'I thought you knew that already.'

'How did I know? You never said anything to me about it. But look here. I don't think you'll get down there,' went on Mr Fury. 'Do you know the whole bloody city is in a state of siege? You can't get near Mile Hill now. They stop everybody. Just turn them back without any questions. Not police this time, but soldiers. If it hadn't been for last night's silly business it would have been all right. But those crowds of Buckos from John's Road have got the authorities' goat. Apart from that, it's dangerous.' Mr Fury worked his way slowly down the bed, clothes and all, and caught his wife's hands. 'It's true,' he said.

'Well!' exclaimed Mrs Fury. Slowly she withdrew her hands from the bed-rail. The word 'Well', and the manner of its utterance, seemed to mock her husband's apprehension and concern. This concern now manifested itself very forcibly, for Mr Fury climbed out of bed and hurriedly dressed. As he threw his braces over his shoulders, he said quickly:

'It's no joke! You can't just trot off to town as though you were going on a picnic. It's too serious. The authorities are angry and they'll stop at nothing. Haven't you heard about the curfew? You can't get into the street after ten. Believe me, Fanny, you don't know how bad it is. You haven't been to town. I have, and I know.'

He was now dressed. He went up to his wife.

'Look here! I'll go. Just say what you want doing, and I'll go like a shot. If you went off now, I'd never rest. I wouldn't know what to do. I'd just be worrying all the time. Now then! You get that coat and hat off, Fanny.' His eyes rested on the straw hat and he said petulantly, 'Aye, woman, you're a caution. D'you know, that morning we went down with your sister to look for the boat, d'you know, Fanny, I didn't mind anything except you wearing that bloody old hat? And after me getting you one at Hobhouse's!'

'Listen to me,' said Mrs Fury. 'What would this Mr Lake do for you? Nothing. Well, please understand that I intend to see Mr Lake myself. They are not going to do just as they like with Anthony's money.' Mr Fury resigned himself. They could go on talking all morning, but that woman would never alter her mind. He knew it only too well.

'All right, woman! You go ahead. If you see Lake I'll raise a cheer. I'll even put a long chalk-mark on this here ceiling. I've told you. You'll get turned back. Why walk six miles for nothing?'

'Don't be so ridiculous! How do you think we're going to live? I ...' Mrs Fury stopped. Mr Fury was looking at her in a peculiar way. They stood facing each other outside the front room door. The combined snores of Peter and his grandfather rose, cutting the silence.

'If you had not used up that money, and I *know* you have,' Mr Fury's eyes seemed to say.

'And I have,' Mrs Fury's changing expression supplied the answer.

'All right, then. Off you pop,' said Dennis Fury.

She'd be back in half an hour, fretting and scolding, if he knew anything.

'Dad must go downstairs today. See you give him the milk pudding I have just put in the oven. And I have left everything in the kitchen for you. You have nothing to do but light the gas and put the pans out.' She made a move towards the stairs. 'And keep your eye on that boy,' she added quickly, and her voice seemed to convey a warning note.

'Yes, yes. Of course. All right. Ta-ta.' Mrs Fury had gone out the back way. Dennis Fury thought, 'Silly woman. Just won't be told. Won't be told. Determined! Determined! And she knows I know about my money. Aye. My own bloody money that I saved. No need to ask where that went. Well, must go and wake him up.' He stood on the landing and shouted, 'Peter! Peter! Seven bells. Seven bloody ringing bells,' he said. 'Get up.' Then he went into Peter's room.

'Yes, coming!' Peter had shouted, and immediately buried himself in the clothes again.

'Come on!' said Mr Fury, as he opened the back room door. 'Your mother's gone to town on business. We have to look after the house today.' He sat down on the bed.

The boy sat up. 'What time is she coming back, Dad?' he asked. Then he got out of bed and began to dress. He was thinking of Desmond now. Seven o'clock at the Blue Bird Café. He'd manage it somehow or other.

His father was busy filling his pipe. 'I don't know,' he said. 'I never asked your mother what time.'

'Oh!' Peter carefully folded the blue pyjamas he had received from Aunt Brigid. 'How is Mr Postlethwaite?' he asked. He stood against the table looking at his father. How old he seemed to be getting, and even smaller each day! A little old man.

'Oh, he's all right. Silly old beggar,' replied Mr Fury. 'Well, better get below and see what's doing. I asked your mother three times if she had had any breakfast. "Yes," she said, "I had breakfast." But she only lies, Peter. Only lies. The woman eats nothing, and I know it. She's gone down to town to see Mr Lake! That's where she's gone. Sometimes I think your mother is a trump. You ought to be proud of her. The best woman in this street. I was a fool once. She ought never to have come to Hatfields.' They went downstairs.

'Did you ever find your money, Dad?' asked Peter.

'Oh yes! I found that. That's all right. Now better get some breakfast.'

'Yes.' Father and son began to lay the table. Mr Fury sat down to bread and butter, Peter to some fried bread.

'Where did you get to last night?' asked Mr Fury. He paused, hand in the air, holding the bread as though the question could allow of no delay. 'Yes. Where did you get to?' Then he put the bread in his mouth.

'After I lost you, I started off in the direction of the hospital. Then on the way I met a most peculiar person. I asked him the way to the hospital. He said he was going there too. Had a son lying ill.'

Oh aye.'

'Then we got involved with another crowd near Powell Square. We couldn't get out.'

'Yes – were you there when they cleared the Square?' asked Mr Fury.

'Oh yes, Dad. But I was sheltering on one of the lions. This man said he was a professor. He *was* funny. Look! He gave me his card.' The boy got up from the table and ran into the lobby. He came back flourishing the card, which he handed to his father.

Mr Fury read it. 'R. H. Titmouse. Professor of Anthropology.' He put his finger and thumb against it and flicked it across the table. 'Never heard of him,' said Mr Fury. 'There's your grand-dad!' he exclaimed, and jumped up from the table. He stood listening at the bottom of the stairs. Yes. It was 'him'. He was coughing and choking. 'Aye! You're a bloody old nuisance,' he growled under his breath. 'Peter!' he called. 'Hurry up there! I want you to help me get your grand-dad downstairs. Your mother says he must go into his chair today.' Mr Fury slowly climbed the stairs.

'Yes, Dad! All right! Coming,' shouted the boy, and began to gulp his tea. As Mr Fury climbed, the choking sounds became more audible. Mr Fury's apprehension increased. He went into the room. Mr Mangan had slipped off his pillow. For a moment Dennis Fury turned his head away. There was something about the position in which the old man was lying that reminded him of a young baby. His shirt had ridden up over his rear owing to his exertions. His face was a livid red, and the blood seemed to have flooded that big bald head, giving it the appearance of a great beetroot!

'Aye, slobberer!' said Mr Fury. He sat the old man up and patted him on the back. Gradually his face resumed its former colour. The blood flowed away from his head, the livid red gave place to the parchment-like colour. He was breathing quickly. Peter came up. 'Best get your grand-dad downstairs,' he said.

Anthony Mangan must have his breakfast. Then he must be washed, dressed, and carried downstairs. Then he must be tied in with the piece of belting. Mr Fury was nonplussed. He looked at Peter. 'Should we get him his breakfast now?' asked Mr Fury. He shifted his glance to 'him'.

'That would be best,' said Peter, hoping his father would oblige.

'Then go downstairs and get his pobs. You'll find it on the hob. It's all ready.'

The boy went down for the pobs. Mr Fury again patted the old man on the back. 'Aye, slobberer,' he said, 'you can hear every word we say, with those big ears of yours – aye, and you can see everything. But you never open your gob. Do you? Aren't afraid of us, are you, eh?' He smiled, looking down on the man's bald head. A lump of dead ivory. Nothing more. Peter came up with the pobs. He stood holding the plate in one hand, the spoon in the other, whilst he watched his father take from his pocket a large red handkerchief and place it under Mr Mangan's chin.

'I've just been telling your grand-dad how mean he is, taking advantage of eyes and ears and never obliging with that mouth of his,' said Mr Fury to the boy. He placed one hand flat upon Mr Mangan's head, and as though the action itself had momentarily spirited away the old man in the bed, he turned again to Peter, and said in a whisper: 'Your mother was a fool ever to take him from Ireland. It was real cruel to take him away from his own home. He was a fine old man one time, your grand-dad was. I got nothing against him, except his mumblings, and he doesn't talk about Belfast any more. Your Aunt Brigid just planted him on your mother. That's what she did. Same as all her other bloody relations, when they were hard up, planted themselves on us. Aye. I wasn't here, or it wouldn't have happened. Lived on her. Then when they got their belly full, just cleared out. Just look at your Aunt Brigid. Treats your mother like a piece of dirt. Gone off to stay with that hump-backed old bitch Pettigrew! She never even asks your mother how she's getting on. Not a word. Well, Peter, my lad, for so many reasons, I like your mother. She's proud. I like her for it. You take my word for it, soon as ever there's a boat back to Cork, Brigid will be back to her stuffy old house in the Mall, and you won't hear any more from her. Nobody will. After a while she'll get hungry again. She'll get desperately hungry for another glance at her relations. Then she'll arrive like a bloody old dowager and just look us over. Your mother is worth ten of her, any day. Here! Get me that spoon and plate. I'm standing here talking to you, and your grand-dad waiting for his breakfast. Go down and get his chair ready.'

Mr Fury, having delivered himself of this oration, now sat down on the bed, and began to feed Mr Mangan, whilst he thought, 'Lord, fancy having this every day for years, and not getting a word of thanks!' It was like piling stuff into a hungry and insatiable pig, a pig that had no head, only a belly and a mouth. A great open mouth like a crocodile. He laughed then, so that the spoon trembled in his hand and he upset some of the bread and milk on the bed. Yes, he knew all along Fanny had taken that money. And he knew why – aye, he knew why. Spent on the lad below-stairs. Well, he wouldn't say a word. Not a single word. He understood.

The room door opened again, and Peter came in. He sat down and watched Mr Mangan being fed. Those small bead-like eyes, cupped and almost hidden by the shaggy brows, had they always been small like that? They were open now. Those eyes were resting upon his face. Why didn't he speak? What did those eyes appear to say? Did they say: 'Look! Look at me! I am a person. I am imprisoned by my years, by ageing and helpless flesh. Once I was young like you.' Did those eyes harbour hatred, maliciousness? In fact, did those eyes really see, and what did they see? Peter now looked at his grandfather's hands. Large, fleshy hands, lying upon the bed, the fingers crooked up, the nails long, bluish, spotted, the palms of the hands hard, much lined, the skin like leather. And that mouth, that helpless mouth. The mouth that hung loosely like an old, empty and useless pouch, the spittle settling about his lips and chin. The mouth which in sleep lay open and gaping. Peter looked suddenly at his father. There was something in his manner, in the way he held the spoon, that seemed to mirror the gentle tenderness he now felt. Yes. His father cursed Mr Mangan, but he knew also that he pitied him too.

'Well, that's done!' said Mr Fury. He put down the plate and spoon. Then he said to his son, 'Give me a hand here; I'm going to dress slobberer now.'

Between them they managed to get Mr Mangan's heavy tweed trousers on. Peter thought, 'How many years has he been wearing these trousers?'

'Now his woollen vest,' said Mr Fury. They put the woollen vest on.

'There are still two waistcoats,' remarked Mr Fury; 'will you get them?'

'Yes, Dad,' replied the boy, already visualizing their surface, filmed by grease, food stains, and saliva. As he picked them up from the chair he felt that sickly feeling again. They seemed cold, clammy to the touch. At last! They had put his two vests on. There was only his coat.

'That can go on when we stand him up,' said Mr Fury. 'Where's his socks?'

'Here,' replied Peter.

'Good! You put one boot on, I'll put the other.'

Anthony Mangan, like some wax figure, was now fully dressed.

'Hold him,' said Peter, and went for his grandfather's coat, which hung behind the door. This coat, like the vests, had a greasy and food-stained frontage. It was green with age. They managed to put this on, during which time Mr Mangan swayed from side to side like a drunken man. The swaying movements were accompanied by deep grunts.

'How Mother manages him I don't really know,' remarked Peter.

'*Your* mother,' replied Mr Fury slowly, and laying great emphasis upon his words, '*your* mother can manage anything. *Anything*. There! All set.' He laughed. Peter laughed. Mr Mangan did look so funny, balancing so precariously.

'Your grand-dad's getting positively ugly,' said Mr Fury. But the boy made no reply to the remark. For the first time he appeared to have divined the callousness of his father, but it was an unconscious callousness, the callousness of a child who sticks a pin in a kitten. They took Mr Mangan by his arms and got him outside the door. They paused at the top of the stairs.

'I can carry him down on my back, Dad,' said Peter.

'Don't worry. Just keep tight hold of his arm. Ready!'

They began to descend. Every second stair they stopped. The stairway was so narrow that all three men were jammed together. They seemed to force themselves down. Another pause. This time, a rest for 'him'. The bottom of the stairs had been reached.

'Easy!' cried Mr Fury. 'Easy! Your grand-dad's no feather, and he isn't a block of wood either.'

They got him into the kitchen. Peter drew the chair near to the fire. Mr Mangan having been placed in the chair, Peter wound the belt round. Then father and son sat down on the sofa to survey the now secured figure. Also Mr Fury wanted to get his breath. As he lay back on the sofa, Peter exclaimed, 'We haven't washed him, Dad.' Mr Fury, as though overcome with a sudden weariness, closed his eyes. 'Let him be!' he said. 'He can get a wash tomorrow.'

Peter glanced up at the clock. Half-past eleven. Mr Fury seemed to have fallen asleep again. The boy bent down to fasten his bootlace. His father, disturbed, sat up.

'What are you doing?' he asked.

'Fastening my bootlace,' replied Peter. He sat up again. 'Tell me, Dad,' he said, and he leaned his hands on his father's knees. 'Tell me, is it true that Joe Kilkey is twenty years older than Maureen, and that she had to marry him?'

'What's that?' Mr Fury was thoroughly awake now. 'Who told you that?'

'I just heard it,' said Peter.

'Well, it's a damned lie. I'll bet you any money it was your Aunt Brigid. Any money you like. Maureen's all right. So's Joe Kilkey. All they want is to be left alone. She's got a quiet, decent man for a husband. That's what your mother wants, Peter. A quiet, decent man like Joe Kilkey. She ought never to have married me. I'm too harum-scarum. I can't settle down in any one place for long.'

'Are you going to sea again, Dad?' asked the boy.

'I don't know,' replied Mr Fury. This was a question he wasn't in the mood for answering.

'I hope your mother's all right,' he said. He had been thinking of her all the morning.

Peter thought, 'Mother's out! We're alone. The time for asking questions has come.'

He looked at his father and said, 'The other night I called to see Maureen, and she never opened the door for me.'

'Perhaps she didn't hear you,' said Mr Fury. He got up from the sofa.

'Maureen wouldn't do a thing like that,' he went on. He took a spill from the mantelshelf and lit his pipe. He puffed frenziedly at the pipe.

'Hang it!' he exclaimed. He sat down and began to clean the pipe.

'If Maureen saw you and didn't open the door, maybe she had a reason. Your sister, like the rest of the family, contributed to your keep at the college. Also, like the rest of us, she goes to chapel. Well, I don't exactly know — but I hope she does. She'll hear things. By now your Aunt Brigid will have met everybody in the parish! But now that you're asking questions, perhaps I, as your father, can return the compliment. Just what happened that you had to leave Ireland? I know, mind you! And it's not inquisitiveness on my part, let me assure you of that, Peter, but just that to hear it from your own lips is better. You understand?' He crossed to the sofa and looked down at his son. 'You're no child now. Your mother thinks so. Well, that suits her. I won't interfere. Why did you have to go?'

The boy looked up at his father. 'This little old man has slaved all his life. Can I begrudge him an answer?'

'I went with another fellow named Carlow to a house,' said Peter. 'There were other lads from the college there as well as me. There were women there, about ten of them. There was an old woman too. It was her house. She used to stand outside the college gates. Whenever the fellows were coming out she used to sell things to us. One day Carlow and I bought a little rubber boy from her. She said it came from Italy. The rubber boy was full of water. She showed us how to work it. When we went back that night, Carlow said to me, "That's Judy Scanlon, old Judy Scanlon! She's one of these." At first I didn't know what he meant. Later I found out. Carlow was testing this rubber boy under the tap. It wouldn't work. It was blocked up. There was paper inside. It was a note: "Come to see me one day. I'll give you a good time." Carlow begged me to go with him. "It's no secret," he said. "Everybody goes. The Brothers know. They close their eyes to it. It can't be helped."'

During this recital Mr Fury had assumed a hunched position. He had bent right over, as though engaged in a minute scrutiny of his son, as though he were asking himself, 'What is this? What is it all about? Is this the little boy upon whose head the bishop placed his aged hand; in whose coat Father Moynihan pinned the silver medal?'

'And did you go?' An involuntary utterance. He was hardly aware that he had asked the question. He knelt down. 'Look at me,' he said. 'Look at your father.' Peter raised his head.

'Did you go with Carlow?' asked Mr Fury. Peter could see the feverish workings of the muscles in his face; his hands trembled by his side.

'Yes, Father! I went with him.' The man clenched his two hands. 'Went with him – went with him'; he kept repeating the phrase until it tapered to a mere whisper. Then he rose to his feet.

'Well,' he said. 'That's honest, anyway. I won't say any more than this. I am indeed both sorry and glad. Sorry and glad. Funny to say that, isn't it? Well' – he passed his hands across his face. 'Enough, I'm not going to go into that business again. But you take my advice and steer clear of all that. If this man gets you to sea, then it's a heaven-sent opportunity. You're the only one in this family who has never ailed like this. Shake hands,' he said, 'shake hands. I'm glad you told me. Your mother swore she would tell me nothing. There! It's all forgotten. I only want you to remember that your mother did much for you. Much! And you've got to do something to help her now.'

'Yes, Dad,' said Peter.

'All right.' Mr Fury pulled out his watch. 'I wonder where your mother has got to? Listen! Can I leave you here to look after your grand-dad? I'm really worried about your mother. I ought never to have let her go.'

'Yes,' said Peter. 'I'll stay with him.'

Mr Fury put his coat and hat on and went out by the back door. Yes, he was really worried about Fanny. 'Going off like that without a bite in her belly. Already twelve! H'm! Too far for Fanny to go. But she *will* do these things. Then she takes it out of me later.'

At the bottom of the entry he stood for a moment. Suddenly he thought, 'Such coolness! Such coolness! And I was like a cucumber myself. Wonder I never struck him down.' H'm! Tasting fruit early, he thought. Was that all college life could do? Whip up the dirt in one? He turned into Price Street. Ah! That reminded him. What was this about Maureen refusing to open the door to her brother? *She* must have heard too. Then it *must* be that confounded sister-in-law of his. If this very minute he should bump into her, he would put the question to her fair and square: 'What are all these yarns you are spreading about my children?' Children! He repeated the word. Then he laughed. Children! He thought of Peter and the rubber boy. Passers-by hailed him. Workmates on the shelf just the same as himself. 'How do, Fury!' 'How do, Denny!'

He hailed them in response. 'Hello, Jack.' 'Fine day, Ned.'

He turned out of Price Street, then stopped again. Where was he really going? What the devil was he thinking about? About Professor Titmouse juggling with the rubber boy; and that leprous-looking woman dancing a bacchanal in the pub? Across the road from where he stood there was a small garden. This miniature park named Eldon Gardens was the resort of children, tramps, out-of-work men and women, decrepit gentlemen down on their luck. Housewives from the neighbouring streets generally made use of its six brightly painted green benches. It was an escape, an asylum from the slaving of the kitchen and the table. Price Street's young offspring learned to walk on its gravel paths; old men with sticks, looking lecherous and suspicious, sat watching young children playing, the while they poked their walking-sticks savagely into the gravel, as though the free and light movement of these children, their innocent smiles and laughs, struck a blow at their own lecherous spirits. On one of these benches Maureen was sitting sewing when her father stepped into the garden.

'Why, Maureen!' said Mr Fury, affecting an astonishment the very falsity of which struck Mrs Kilkey at once. 'Why,' he said, 'what brings you here? Is this a new rendezvous?' The young woman countered him.

'This place! Why, Dad, I have been here many a time. It's I who should be surprised, not you. It's the first time I have ever seen you here.' Mr Fury sat down. The search for Fanny must wait just a while. This was a piece of luck. Couldn't have been better. Maureen put down her sewing.

'Seen your mother lately?' asked Mr Fury. He dug his heels into the gravel.

'Yes, I saw her yesterday. She came round.'

'Oh! Fancy! Of course, your mother does a lot of things that I know nothing about,' said her father. 'Was it anything particular?' he asked.

'She looked rather worried,' said Mrs Kilkey, whose eyes were resting upon her father's hands. Each time she met her father, her eyes, for some reason or other, wandered to his hands. She noticed their thinness, their whiteness, and above all she noticed their hard scaly appearance. Her father's hands were mirrors, into which she could look and see reflected all his working years. All his years at sea, in the stokeholds of ships. The hands seemed to cry out, 'We have done our work! We have done our duty! If you would know this man, then look at these hands.' So she looked at them now, and at the tattoo marks higher up upon the wrists. Those wrists were like steel. And from his hands her eyes wandered to his face. 'Poor Dad!' she thought. 'Poor Dad!' Mr Fury took out his clay pipe. When he felt it between his teeth he was content. A pipe offered peace, security. Now he began rubbing up Mr Mulcare's 'hard stuff'. Again Maureen looked at her father's hands. They assumed significance of another kind. It was as though the hands were now happy, feeling that strong sweet-smelling tobacco being vigorously rubbed upon their palms. Had they been endowed with a voice, those hands would have laughed to express their joy in feeling that pipe, that tobacco upon them.

'No. It wasn't anything very particular,' said Maureen. She picked up her sewing again.

'Joe all right?' asked her father. He blew the initial cloud of smoke into the air with a flourish, a sort of abandonment, like a man who has blown all his troubles behind him.

'Oh yes,' replied Mrs Kilkey with a casualness that seemed to reveal her indifference to the question. 'Yes, he's all right.'

'What does he do with himself?' asked Mr Fury. 'Joe's never seen anywhere.'

'You'll always find him playing billiards,' said Maureen. 'That is Joe's main pastime. He's there most evenings. When he isn't there, you'll find him with his feet on the fender and a paper on his knee. The man is the greatest reader I ever came across.'

Dennis Fury eyed his daughter up and down. 'How she's growing!' he thought, and seeing her swelling breasts said to himself, 'Aunt Brigid to a T.' Well, that was something of an event. Something to look forward to. Mr Fury put a question. There was a certain delicacy about it. Now he felt sorry he had asked it. He saw Maureen blush.

'If it's a boy, I'll make him work,' said Mrs Kilkey, 'and if it's a girl, the same applies. It's the best cure that I know of every kind of weakness, bodily and mental.'

'Um!' Her father smiled.

'Listen!' he said. 'Why didn't you see the boy the other night? He was very much hurt, Maureen. You never opened the door to him. Why was that? You seem to be changing.'

The colour rose to Mrs Kilkey's cheeks. 'Why *should* I have opened the door to him?' she asked. 'Only yesterday Mother came running round to me! Crying! Quite a scene! Joe fortunately wasn't there. And all over Peter! Why should I want to see him?'

'He's your brother,' said Mr Fury, completely taken aback by his daughter's manner. 'He's only a boy, after all.'

'He drove everybody from the house. Now, why don't you admit it, Dad?' She put down her sewing, and gripped the bench tightly.

'Drove everybody from the house! Don't be silly, girl. Desmond wasn't driven from the house. He had a perfect right to do as he likes. And if it comes to that, you married Kilkey to get out of that other devil's clutches, didn't you now? Tell the truth. It's all very well putting on the airs of a martyr, making people feel your dignity has been offended. Tommy-rot. Christ! Your mother is a woman. Aye, she is in fact a real woman. Worth every one of her damned children. And the like of you closing your door on the boy! God almighty, what he did, thousands have done, millions have done, since the world began, and will go on doing. Now you close your door. Have you any feeling left at all? Or has marriage just destroyed it? Maureen, I think you're just in a bad temper today. That boy feels ashamed enough. Your mother was hurt. Let me tell you that. She cried. And I know why. She doesn't want Peter going round to Desmond's house. But he *will* go! He will *go*! The lad has no friends. Everybody he used to know, the boys in the Guild – aye, the holy Chapel Guild – they all cut him. But Peter's going to sea.'

'He should have gone long ago,' snapped Maureen.

Mr Fury laughed. 'Aye,' he said, 'you're jealous, Maureen, jealous.'

He flung up his hand as though to ward off an imaginary blow. 'No,' he said. 'That's all right. You needn't even tell me about it. I know what you are going to say. But I know all about it.'

'What was I going to say?' asked Mrs Kilkey. It was one of the rare occasions when she found her father in a bad temper. Something must have happened, to have upset him like this. What could it be?

Her father caught hold of her hands. 'Listen to me, Maureen. I know your mother took my money. And even when I asked the boy if he had taken it, I even knew then. I only wanted to see what the boy would say. Yes. Your mother took my money, and she used it up.'

'On Peter.'

'Well! I suppose so,' said Mr Fury. 'But I wouldn't begrudge the money.'

'And now she's looking for more,' Maureen fired at him. 'Isn't that the truth?'

'I know nothing about that. I hardly know anything. She tells me nothing. But that's an old habit. And I can well understand it, when I have been away at sea most of my life. Perhaps if I had worked ashore all my life you would have been different children. Ah well!' He sighed, raised his head, and his eyes appeared to ransack the sky, against which there now appeared a great line of rolling black clouds.

'I think it's going to rain,' he said, though his mind was a complete blank. It seemed to have sunk, collapsed. He lowered his head. 'Ah, Maureen,' he said, 'I wish I had my time all over again.' His voice was filled with a passionate tenderness as he looked up at the sky; he might have visioned some world of pure fancy, into the calm and peace of which his spirit might have slipped quietly, gently, leaving behind it upon the green bench of the park his tired body.

'Everyone says that,' remarked Maureen, 'when it's too late.' She put the sewing in her bag, and made preparation to go.

'Funny!' he said. 'Funny! I never had the pleasure of seeing any of you children grow up, never had the pleasure of saying good-night, of cuddling you in the blankets, of taking you out for walks. Aye! I would have loved that. But perhaps I was a silly old beggar. Oh well ...'

'Yes, Dad. You're getting sentimental and silly.'

'Yes,' said Mr Fury. And at that moment he bowed his head, and a single tear-drop splashed upon his gnarled and crooked fist. 'Yes,' he said. 'Yes.'

Maureen had risen to her feet. She was looking towards the park gates, unconscious of the fact that her father had suddenly given vent to his feelings. The man rubbed his eyes, feeling ashamed, thinking Maureen was looking at him, but Mrs Kilkey seemed indifferent to all that.

'I'm going now, Dad,' she said. 'I shall see you again soon.'

'Yes. Yes of course, ta-ta, good-bye,' he said, without glancing up at his daughter.

'Dear me! Dear me!'

He laid his head in his hands and cried like a child.

2

Peter had just fed Mr Mangan. He had woke suddenly and yawned, so that the boy, who had been reading on the sofa, let fall the book and looked across at the figure in the chair. Peter laughed. There was something so comical about his grandfather. And that mouth which opened and closed, it reminded him of a duck fishing in the mud for food. He had given him his milk pudding, exercising the greatest patience in doing so. Where on earth had his father got to? From three till four the boy had spent time sitting on the wall watching the wizened little woman from number nine wash her clothes at the dolly-tub standing in the middle of the yard. Then he had gone in, made some tea, cut bread and butter, and so appeased his growing hunger. Mr Mangan was still asleep. He had been snoring some seven hours now. Peter wandered up and down stairs, bored, disconsolate. Well, it would soon be half-past seven. At half-past six he had given up all hope of meeting his brother at the Blue Bird Café, but just as it struck the half-hour his father came up the yard. Peter went and unlocked the back door.

'Hello, Dad!' said the boy, but Mr Fury did not reply. He pushed roughly past his son, and went into the kitchen. He sat down on the sofa.

'Oh!' he exclaimed.

He looked hot and tired. An unsuccessful journey. He had walked the six miles to town and back again. He looked at his son.

'Hanged if I know where your mother has got to! I knew right well she'd meet difficulties going down there. But she never will listen to me. Have you had your tea?'

'Yes, Dad. There's tea in the pot now.'

'Has slobberer had anything?'

Peter picked up the pudding dish. 'Just had this,' he said. 'He was asleep all the afternoon.' He put the basin back on the table.

'Looks as if you are waiting to go out,' Mr Fury said. 'Where are you going?'

'A walk,' Peter replied.

Mr Fury got up and took off his coat. Then he rolled up his sleeves and went to the fire. 'You let this go out,' he said.

Peter said nothing.

Mr Fury put the blower up. 'Light the gas,' he growled. 'The bloody house looks like a railway station.' The boy lit the gas, then he stood waiting.

'All right. You go ahead and do whatever you want to do,' said his father. 'I know you want to go out. You've been stuck with "him" all day, so I suppose you can go out. But don't you be late! Understand? If you are, then look out.'

'Yes, Dad.'

This warning had a double meaning. He could look out for his father, and he could look out for his own head, for after ten o'clock the military cleared the streets. Soldiers and Specials were gradually encroaching upon the neighbourhood of Hatfields. Apart from the mob violence and sporadic looting, the authorities were afraid of the different religious factions coming to blows. A rather ugly little incident on the King's Road the previous night had made them unduly apprehensive. So after ten Peter was to look out for his head. Peter had promised that he would. At twenty minutes to eight he left the house. Mrs Fury had not then returned. The boy was looking forward to this meeting with his brother. For one thing, he would be different from the others. Maureen didn't even want to see him. He still felt uncomfortable. That sudden return from Cork had upset everything. He couldn't feel at ease in the house. The distance between his parents appeared to grow. Well, Desmond at any rate wouldn't start piling it on. And there was nowhere else to go. The boys in the neighbourhood with whom he had first gone to school openly snubbed him. These boys had now left school and were working in shop and factory. He had met two of them. They had called him 'snob'. When Maureen refused to open the door to him, Peter felt more wretched still. Now his spirits had risen. He liked his elder brother. They had spent much of their time together on fishing excursions. As he turned out of Hatfields into the King's Road he thought, 'Poor Mother! Out all day.' Where had she got to? Why hadn't she let him go to town to interview this Mr Lake? He felt quite capable of doing so.

Groups of men stood on the corners, and in the middle of the road. The boy hurried on. 'Blue Bird Café,' he kept saying under his breath. 'That must be the big wooden hut on the plot of waste ground behind the tramway sheds.' It was. There was no other café of that name in the whole city. Peter used to play on the ground where the rough dining-rooms now stood. As he came in sight of it, it began to rain.

The Blue Bird Café was an ordinary workmen's dining-room. It was mostly frequented by the men from the tramway and loco sheds. Here one could bring one's own meals, and obtain hot tea or cocoa from the counter. Coffee seemed never to have been heard of. For those who preferred the Blue Bird Café's bill of fare, there were hot-pots, soups, tea and cakes. Most customers, however, brought their own food. The proprietress of this dining-room was a woman named Clara Lynch. To her customers she was simply 'Clara', though the local police had added to that the title of 'The Amazon'. This had come about by reason of the prowess she had revealed on several occasions in dealing with unruly customers.

When Peter reached his café, he stood outside the half-open door. There were about a dozen customers there at the time. Mrs Lynch did not confine her clientele to loco workers or the tram-men. The Blue Bird Café welcomed everybody. Down-and-outs, tramps, occasional bookmakers' touts, and more than one lady from the beat. Through the half-open door there now issued great clouds of steam that came from the three large urns on the marble counter. The dozen or so tables were equally marble-topped. Peter stood looking in. Conversation filled the long, low room, punctuated now and then by a sudden burst of laughter. What struck Peter most was the spitting. Everybody spat in the most audible manner. He could see Mrs Lynch, a tall woman with red hair, standing behind the counter. She leaned forward on folded arms. Peter went up to the window and looked in. A film of grease and steam covered it. The whole atmosphere reeked of steam. Maybe Clara's customers felt themselves compelled to spit. He went to the door again and looked in. The sound of frying fat now appeared to overwhelm all ordinary conversation, as though at the moment the morsel of 'best hake' had been put into the pan everybody had ceased talking to hear the noise the fat made. Fried fish and chips was really an 'occasional', and only for special customers. Peter thought, 'I wonder if he's coming?' There was something chilly and miserable about standing outside this long wooden hut. At that moment two things happened. Desmond arrived. And this time he did not shake hands, and Peter noticed it at once.

'Hello!' he said. 'Been waiting long?' He opened his blue overcoat and shook it vigorously, and a shower of rain-drops shot out. He wore a light grey cap. Around his neck was tied a white silk scarf. Desmond Fury never wore anything but a cap. Peter was without headwear, nor did he have an overcoat.

'About twenty minutes,' he was saying, when the noise of the sizzling fat itself was drowned by a stentorian voice calling out from within the hut:

'I asked for China tea, and I'm going to bloody well get China tea.'

'Let's go in,' said Desmond, and caught his brother's arm. 'I'm in a hurry.'

Desmond was always in a hurry to get off to some meeting or other. This was a purely imaginary meeting. Only habit made him say it.

They went into the café. Their entrance was not without significance, for a most delicate situation had arisen. The two brothers chose a table near the door.

'Evening, Mr Fury,' called out Clara from the counter. 'Dirty, isn't it?'

Desmond was an old customer. She had recognized him as he came in at the door. This she was able to do by looking through a hole in the brown curtain that hid the administrative side of the café from the customers. She now pulled the curtain back to extend her compliment to the customer and to see him comfortably seated. She did not seem to be interested in Peter. Mrs Lynch, however, did not pull the curtain right back, as this would have upset the delicate negotiations now going on between herself and a client. Judging by the state of the atmosphere, it would have been a feat in itself to sit down to a full meal. The air was thick with smoke, the steam rose triumphantly from the urns, and everybody talked. The fried fish and chips had now been served. Desmond made a hurried survey of the customers at the various tables. Nobody there whom he knew.

'Well,' he said, 'we'll have some tea, and talk.' He raised his hand in the air and called 'Hilda! Tea and cakes for two,' to which came a reply in a thin cracked voice, 'Coming.' Although he did not know it, Desmond had put a momentary spoke in the easy-running wheel.

Hilda was Mrs Lynch's help. She was a young woman of twenty-eight. She was plain, modest, a good worker, and had a generous, willing spirit. Hilda lived always in the present. The future was something that did not interest her. It had no significance. She had no relations. She was without ambition. She now appeared with a tray which she laid on the table.

'Evening,' said Desmond. 'How are you feeling now?'

'Same,' Hilda said, and smiled. She looked at Peter but her expression changed.

'That's hard lines, then,' said Desmond, and as the young woman turned away he raised his hand and gave her a resounding clout on the rump. Her laughter increased. Then she vanished behind the counter.

'Good girl, Hilda,' said Desmond. 'Do anything for a fellow.' He began filling Peter's cup. 'You can always tell when Clara's gay,' he said.

Peter stared at his brother. 'No,' he thought. 'He doesn't look a bit different.

Just as Mother said. A boor.' How tall he was! And what hands! There was something aggressive about his very physicalness.

'Let's talk,' said Desmond. He placed his elbows on the table and took stock of his brother.

Whilst they talked, negotiations had come to a head behind the counter. Hilda had gone into the back room. Hidden behind the curtain was a seedy-looking clerk named Mr Sandys. Mr Sandys was feeling passionate. Mrs Lynch wished to direct this into the right channels for a certain financial consideration. Mr Sandys had done his part. Hilda was willing to oblige, and at this very moment had put her head out of the back room and beckoned. Mr Sandys, highly excited and now visibly trembling at the very thought of a possible excursion to Nirvana, had taken off his coat and was ready to go forward, when the whole café seemed to quake as the burly-looking tram-driver who had a few minutes ago vociferously demanded China tea now woke up from his doze and repeated his request. He was about fifty years of age. His face had that puce-like colour that one comes to associate with tram-drivers. 'Where's that China tea?'

Everybody looked at him. Even Desmond and Peter stopped talking and turned round in their chairs. At the same time the curtain behind the counter was quickly pulled back to reveal Mr Sandys going forward holding up his trousers. Attention was immediately diverted from the tram-driver to Mr Sandys. But he had passed into the back room. The curtain rolled back. Everybody remained silent. Now the curtain was flung back again and Clara appeared. She made a rush towards the table where the man sat thumping its marble top and still loudly demanding China tea, which the Blue Bird Café did not stock. When Mrs Lynch seized the man by the back of his collar and dragged him to his feet, there was only one surprised person in the café. That was Peter. And his surprise increased when without any hesitation Mrs Lynch dragged the half-tipsy tram-driver to the door. She let him fall to the floor whilst she opened wide the door. Peter laughed. A moment later the awkward customer found himself sitting on the grass verge outside the café. Mrs Lynch by this feat seemed to have consolidated the title which the police had given her. She banged the door to, and once more vanished behind the curtain. Order had been restored. Everybody settled themselves down again. Peter thought, 'Yes, Hilda is a good girl. Most obliging.' Suddenly he laughed.

'What are you laughing at?' asked Desmond. He lit a cigarette.

'Nothing,' he said. He fixed his eyes upon his brother's face.

'Have a cake?'

'No, thanks,' replied Peter. He was content to take his tea, to stir it slowly, and to stare at his brother. He now felt like a truant schoolboy who, prior to being taken to the Reformatory, is being given a little refreshment by his generous escort.

'I'm surprised to see you,' exclaimed Desmond. 'Never thought I would see you back. However – how's Mother?' Then he leaned back in the chair and assumed a contemplative attitude. It gave him a rather comical appearance, for when lost in thought he had a habit of caressing his upper lip with his tongue.

'Mother is out,' replied Peter. 'She had to go to town to the shipping office. She's been out all day.' He never took his eyes from Desmond's face. It seemed to him a hard, brutal face. It lacked refinement, sensibility.

'Poor Mother!' Desmond said. 'Always out. Always trapesing somewhere. Never seems to get tired. We don't get on together now. But I dare say she has told you.' He threw the cigarette away. 'Aren't you having a cake?' he asked.

Peter gave one look at the cakes. Mrs Lynch had retrieved them from the window, where they had lain all day. 'No, thanks,' Peter said.

Desmond laughed. He picked up a scone and tore it in two. In that little action Peter had seen mirrored the difference between them. He looked at Desmond's hands. There had always been a difference between Desmond and the rest of the family. He saw it now. Slowly his eyes travelled up his brother's body and came to rest upon his face. Now he nodded his head.

'Yes,' he said, 'I already know about that. About everything.' He had drunk his tea, and now pushed the cup to one side. His hands rested on the table. The difference in their hands seemed to cry aloud to each other. Suddenly he drew them from the table. He felt they should not be there. Those huge hands seemed to threaten. At any moment they might dart forward and grip his own. They challenged one's right to the table. As Desmond ate, Peter watched the muscles of his jaw move. When he drank tea he made a peculiar sucking sound with his mouth. Yes. Desmond was different. But he hadn't changed. Not a bit in all those seven years.

'And what about you?' asked Desmond, thinking, 'Nearly as tall as me – and the dead spit of Mother.'

'About me!' The boy paused as though considering the matter. 'Oh well! As I told you last night, I ran away from the place. I got fed up with it – I . . .'

'I did hear from Postlethwaite's son that you had come home, but I never believed it. And now he tells me Aunt Brigid came over with you. What brought her over? I thought she and Mother were through with each other.'

'She came over to see Grand-dad, I suppose,' replied Peter. 'She isn't with us now.'

'Oh!' Exclamation of surprise from Desmond.

'She's with Miss Pettigrew. We had no room for her,' said the boy. And now he didn't want to talk about himself any more. He wanted to talk of other things. The strike, how Desmond liked his new job, and Mr Kilkey and Mrs Fury. A tall order. That other thing was a pure cod. Worse than gaol. Desmond leaned forward in his chair, and gripped the boy's arm. Slowly his hand worked its way down to his brother's, which it now gripped and held.

'Yes,' he said. 'A cod! A bloody cod! A cod for your mother too. Crucifying herself for a cod! That's how it is, isn't it?' He smiled, so that for a second the boy glimpsed the two rows of strong, almost perfect teeth. 'What does she think of it?'

Peter coloured up. 'Are you another?' he asked. 'Is one never to hear the last of it?'

'What!' said Desmond. 'What's that, little boy? Has seven years of college taught you nothing? Are you still suffering from your sensibilities? You had no right to go. I said so long ago. I had three years of it in Hatfields. I thought your mother was light in the head. Anyway I got out. So did Maureen. It was just impossible to live there any longer. And anyhow I had to go some time or other. But I'm not going to preach. I'm not one of those sort. You take my advice. Go and work. Finest thing you ever did in your life. It cures everything, and besides, just think of it. As you went up, higher, higher, another went down. Understand that. *Down*. What does Dad know? Nothing. He never did know anything – always at sea. But I knew, and your sister knew. Some day you'll hear that story. Aye, and Mother knows. I never in all my life saw anything like it. She would have given her blood for you – and Christ – Christ – it was tragic, because we knew it *was* a cod. I don't blame you, Peter. Not a bit. You took a chance. It's only a chance that any boy would take to get away from this bastard place. No. I'm with you there. I remember when I was at school I wanted to be something. But I couldn't do anything. I was building castles in the air, for nothing. You wanted to get away. Oh, I know! And hundreds, thousands of women like Mother are doing the same, hoping, clinging like leeches, bitten with this crazy idea of giving sons to God! I don't believe in all that rot. Not a bit. You know I don't. But even worse, your mother wouldn't even be told. It was wicked – really lousy – it was madness. Poor Mother! Only one thing worries her. Heaven –' Desmond laughed. 'Heaven!' he said. His whole body shook, his laughter increased, he couldn't stop laughing. Customers were staring at him. Suddenly he got up. 'Come,' he said. Peter got up and followed his brother to the counter, where he paid his bill. Mrs Lynch looked curiously at Peter. 'My brother,' Desmond said, and gave Peter a pat on the back. 'Nice lad. Just home from college.'

*

274

They left the café and stood on the edge of the grass plot.

'What a lousy night!' said Desmond. 'This way,' he said. Peter thought there was something peculiarly off-hand about his brother's manner. They walked down behind the tramway sheds.

'Who was the man who went down under that goods train the other night?'

Desmond pulled up. 'Were you there?' he asked.

'No. I was watching them from the wall at the back of Maureen's house.'

'Oh, that silly swine! He'll get killed one of these days,' Desmond replied.

'How long do you think this strike will last?' asked Peter. He took a cigarette from his brother.

'Months.'

'Months! All that time?'

'Why not?'

They passed through Price Street, turned left, and pulled up outside Desmond's home. The man took a key from his pocket and opened the front door. They passed into the house.

'Shut the door,' Desmond said. He hurried into the kitchen to light the gas.

'Ah!' thought Peter. 'At last! Mother will never know.'

Desmond had lit the gas. Peter went into the kitchen, pausing for a moment to look round. The houses in Vulcan Street were no different from the houses in Hatfields. They had six rooms. Although the kitchen in which he stood looked larger, it was purely because of the way its furniture had been arranged. The fire was low in the grate.

'Sit down,' said his brother, and went out to get coal for the fire.

The boy sat down. He looked round. The walls were bare. There was a table in the centre of the floor, covered with cheap American oilcloth. Four chairs lay against the wall. At one side of the kitchen stood an oak dresser upon which were two green vases, a dog of the same colour, and a small cabinet-box which Mr Fury had brought from Japan at one time. The dresser was now littered with newspapers, letters, typed documents, the pages of which were covered with tea-stains. Hairpins, feminine combs, and powder-boxes lay scattered about. Upon the top shelf some loose coins lay as though hastily thrown there. Peter now looked up at the mantelshelf. Excepting for two tea-caddies, it was bare. Above it there hung a framed photograph of Keir Hardie. Mr Hardie was wearing his cap. Desmond having refuelled the fire began to poke it.

'You ought to get Dad to make you a blower like ours,' said Peter.

'Yes,' said Desmond.

He seemed particularly keen to get a blaze into the grate. He was in his shirt-sleeves, which he had rolled up to the elbow. He put the poker down, sat back in the chair and sighed. It was the sigh of a man who is glad to get his great bulk comfortably fixed in a chair. This armchair creaked beneath the weight. His shirt was open at the neck.

'Well,' he said at last. 'Here we are! Tell us something about yourself. What did you do all those seven years?' He looked at the boy.

'Oh!' he said. 'I'm sick of that. Everybody knows why I left there.'

'I should have thought you would have thought twice about seeing me,' remarked Desmond with a loud laugh.

'I came to see how you were getting on,' said Peter.

'Oh! I'm getting on all right now,' replied Desmond. 'Somehow,' he was telling himself, 'somehow there's a mistake here! Yes, I'm sure there is.' He slapped his hand on his knee. 'What were you expecting to see? A palace? Tell me. You look a bit disappointed about something.'

Peter moved forward in the chair. 'What on earth is at the back of Desmond's mind?' he asked himself.

'I'm not disappointed,' replied Peter. 'Why should I be? It's the silly attitude you adopt. You're no different from the others.'

'What! What are you talking about?'

'I'm no small boy now,' continued Peter. 'Am I?'

He rose to his feet and stood looking down at the big man in the chair.

'Remember when we used to go fishing down at Antree,' began Peter, 'and I used to do all your worming for you? And I asked you to let me hold the line. And you wouldn't. D'you remember that? I was a little boy then. But all that has altered. And when I come to see you I don't want you to adopt the attitude of a hurt but forgiving brother.'

'Oh aye! And do you think I am worrying about you? Or about any of the family? No, by God! No. I pitched all that behind me long, long ago. Mother never comes. None of the family. They're ashamed.'

He got up and stood in front of Peter. 'Tell me,' he said. 'Does Mother know you have come here?' His whole manner had changed, and the boy saw it at once.

'No, she doesn't know. Did you think she sent me here to spy?' he asked heatedly.

'Now, listen to me, Peter. I'm your brother. I'm older than you, though I'm not as clever. See! I admit that. Because of this I am rather suspicious. That's all. I thought Mother might know you were coming round. Mother would do anything to break my home up. Do you understand? And I won't let them. Does she know you met me on the Dock Road?'

'No,' said the boy. 'And what's more, I shan't tell her I've been here either.'

'All right, then. We won't argue about that. I'm glad you're not being a priest. Yes, I am glad. All priests should be burnt. That's my opinion. And if I had my way I would burn Father Moynihan tomorrow. He is the one who put those crazy ideas into your mother's head. But tell me, can people like Mother afford it? They can't. Nor can anybody else. And there's no return for it, is there, only a sure place in Heaven.'

He smiled and waved his hand towards an imaginary heaven.

'I'm not thick, Peter. Don't think that. I kept that house going for years — you included — when Dad decided to do a walking tour through the States. Your mother never said nothing. Everything was going on in the same old monotonous way. I wasn't blind, mind you. No doubt she thought I would never marry. H'm! Then I decided to get out. Yes, and I'm going to get out of here soon. Your thick brother has ambitions. He's going to walk out of this stinking muck-heap, and on somebody's back too. Doesn't matter whose.' He patted his chest. 'Just consider,' he went on, 'just consider the number of people who squeeze their guts out for nothing.'

'Well,' said Peter, 'that's honest. Is that why you joined the Labour Party?'

'Yes,' he said. 'When I first went into it I did the dirty, mucky work. Out night after night, in all kinds of weather. Standing on street corners, ringing a bell, looking very much like a lunatic, and considering myself lucky if I got an audience of three people. But there was always a dog. Yes. Plenty of damned dogs. Seemed more intelligent than the duds I spoke to. Talk about cabbages! Christ! They weren't even *good* cabbages. Yes. I did that for weeks, months, years. Getting the mucky end of the stick all the while. Do you think these people are interested in bettering themselves, in improving their conditions? No, sir! You do a couple of years on the parade ground and you'll see the truth of the matter. Let the bastards vegetate, let them lie in their own muck. They're not interested. No, sir! Just not interested.'

After this flow of oratory Desmond sat down.

'But I am sorry for the women,' he said. 'Aye, I am sorry for the women.'

'That reminds me,' said Peter. 'I was in town the other night sitting on one of those lions in Powell Square watching the fun. I met a most comical man named Professor Titmouse. Have you ever heard of him?'

'Never heard of him.'

Peter noticed that his brother kept looking at the clock. Perhaps he wanted him to go. Funny that he hadn't mentioned a word about Sheila!

In a corner of the kitchen there stood a tool-box. On this tool-box there stood a large draught-board. As soon as Peter saw this he exclaimed, 'Let's play a game.'

'Yes.'

Desmond got the draught-board and laid it out on the table.

277

'White or black?' he asked.

He looked up at the clock again. His mind wasn't on the draught-board. He was thinking of something else, whilst at the same time he looked forward to the game with his brother with almost boyish excitement.

'Black,' Peter said.

They arranged their men. Suddenly a key turned in the lock. Peter sat up and looked towards the door.

'What's the matter?' asked Desmond. 'Move. Why don't you move?'

'Yes. I was moving. Who was that?' He looked questioningly at his brother.

'That's Mrs Fury,' replied Desmond. 'My move.'

Peter heard somebody walking along the lobby. Now the person climbed the stairs.

'What the hell's wrong with you?' growled Desmond. 'I've been waiting for you to move.' His tongue began stroking his upper lip.

Desmond was thinking hard. He put his face close to Peter's, and his eyes seemed to dart forward as he asked in a whisper, 'Have you been drinking?'

Peter laughed.

'Drinking! What makes you think that?' he asked. He could no longer conceal his astonishment. What was Desmond thinking about? Was the fellow mad? Peter moved. Desmond moved. A silence grew between them. Peter was listening to footsteps in the room above his head. 'That must be Sheila,' he was thinking. What a funny way to come home! To go right upstairs without looking in. Did she always do that? Were they always out? Where did she go? And who was she? How had his brother come to marry this Protestant woman? And was she really what his mother had said? No. His mother had said that in a moment of rage. Of course, his mother hated her. How long had they been married? These thoughts began to race round Peter's brain. Suddenly he took two men from Desmond.

'You know I don't drink, Desmond,' he repeated. 'Perhaps you've had one or two.'

Desmond made no reply – he was too busy. He was studying the boy. Was this his brother? Little Peter? Of course not. This was a man. A complete stranger. It seemed only to occur to him now. The fire had burnt up. Desmond got up to put a penny in the gas-meter. Peter was unconscious of everything except the sound of the feet upstairs. What a strange house! What a peculiar life to lead! And how changed his brother was! He was glad he had not asked after his sister-in-law – that would have been most unfortunate. No doubt about it. Desmond seemed loath to talk about his wife. Perhaps he was ashamed. He heard the door bang. Desmond had come in again. As he looked at the huge man Peter thought, 'No. I'm wrong. He wouldn't be ashamed. He doesn't understand the meaning of the word. He's too thick.

He looks like a big butcher.' Desmond sat down again. The game was resumed, but they could take no interest in it. It seemed as if the sudden arrival of Mrs Fury had charged the atmosphere with a kind of light that threw into forms the hidden thoughts of one and the other.

The one thought, 'He seems very restless. I wonder why? He is not thinking of the game at all,' whilst the other was thinking, 'He is worrying because she was out when he arrived home.'

Desmond was now studying a problem. It affected three white men and one black. His eyes were fixed upon the board, whilst Peter's were fixed upon the kitchen door, which had opened, slowly and silently, as though the intruder were apologizing for her entrance and did not wish to interrupt their game of draughts. Peter sat quite still. There was something furtive about his manner; he was watching the door and at the same time watching the board. A hand appeared. It moved slowly round the door.

The hand seemed to be endeavouring to unhook a black satin dress which hung upon a nail behind the kitchen door. The nail had caught in one of the threads of the torn bodice. It searched about, trying to find the nail.

'How silly!' Peter was thinking. 'Why doesn't she open the door and take it off the nail in the ordinary way?' The hand became an arm. A woman's bare arm right to the shoulder had appeared behind the door. There was something about the arm which sent the blood mounting to Peter's forehead. In its frantic endeavours to retrieve the dress from the nail it had only served to make it more secure than ever, for several threads of the torn bodice had wound themselves round the nail; and in addition to that, the movements it made seemed to Peter beckoning movements. The long white arm, clearly lined against the black varnished door, seemed to call. To call to Peter as he sat there, his whole body tensed, his mind confused by a swift panorama of pictures that not even Professor Titmouse could have conjured in his wildest moments.

The hand, as though severed from the body to which it belonged, had now been endowed with a life of its own. The hand spoke. The hand spoke to Peter sitting in the chair. 'Behind this door,' it seemed to say, 'is a body, to which I am attached. This body is now naked. And I am endeavouring to get this dress from the nail in order to clothe it. But if you should suddenly dash forward and open the kitchen door, be sure you will see something to start the eyes in your head, to send your blood mounting higher and higher.' There could not be any doubt about it. That hand seemed to beckon. Desmond moved his man, but now to his great astonishment Peter shot out his hand and shouted, 'My move! It's my move!' and pushed the man to the floor.

Desmond sat up. 'Here! For Christ's sake!' he said. He seemed suspicious now. 'Have you got the jim-jams?' Peter was trembling like a leaf. Desmond caught his brother's arms, and forcing him towards himself, looked into the boy's eyes. 'What's the matter?' he said. 'What's the matter with you? Has seven years of college heightened your sensibilities? What are you staring at?'

'Nothing! Nothing! It's all right. Let go my arm. I'm sorry I spoiled your game. I don't know what was the matter with me.' He laughed a curious high-pitched laugh. 'I was dreaming,' he said. 'I could see a man committing hari-kari in Powell Square, and some Goblins clothed in Pentecostal flames came and carried him away. I . . .'

The door opened, Mrs Fury came in.

Desmond got up. 'Hello, darling!' he said. 'Got back? This is Peter. This is my brother Peter . . .' He looked from one to the other. He didn't seem sure of himself. What was all this blather about Goblins? Was the boy ill?

'Pleased to meet you,' Mrs Fury said. She gave him her hand. The boy shook it. And now he held it, thinking, 'This is the hand – this is the hand that crept round that door.'

The woman was smiling at him. She could feel him trembling. She loosed her hold. Turning to Desmond she said, 'About supper?'

Desmond was sitting in the chair. For a moment he did not speak. He kept staring at Peter, then at his wife. 'Is there anything in it?' his eyes seemed to say. 'Hang it! I can't understand.'

'It's getting late,' he said.

He looked directly at his brother. Peter did not move. He kept glancing at the woman, at her hand, her arm, her breast, her long body, now hidden behind the black dress. But he had seen it. Yes. He had seen that naked body. He had stripped her at a glance.

Sheila Fury thought, 'What a funny boy!' She stood, her body hard pressed against the table so that her dress tightened beneath the pressure, and the clear outline of her body was there to see, and Peter had seen it. From her white neck to her firm and supple breasts, and lower. But Desmond too had seen it. He looked at the clock.

'Too late for supper.'

He was abrupt, and he was now determined. Whilst that woman stood there, her body clearly lined in the light, his own seemed to sing, to cry out, to protest. So he looked at Peter.

'It is late,' he said. 'Hadn't you better go? You must come and see us some time. You will, won't you?'

Peter got up. 'Yes,' he said. 'I shall,' and looked, not at his brother, but directly into the eyes of the woman. In a flash she had divined the position.

280

Her expression changed. Her eyes seemed to ransack Peter as he stood there, whilst the snub that had parted her red lips seemed to say, 'Well, yes, come. You are so funny. Yes. Do come.'

For Peter the woman did not exist. She had vanished. Through a sort of haze he could see a naked arm floating in the air. And then the arm made short circling movements, as though it wanted to grasp something, to hold it, to embrace it.

'Surely,' said Sheila, 'there is time for supper.'

'And I say there isn't,' replied Desmond. He had moved towards the door.

'What is all the excitement about?' said Sheila. 'Cool yourself, man! We can offer your brother a cup of tea, surely.'

'It's nearly ten o'clock,' said Desmond. 'Can't you hear those swine outside?'

'Swine? What swine?' She had fixed her eyes upon her husband, upon his large, brutal-looking mouth, as though the very force of her glance might close it and hold it fast. Desmond caught her arm.

'Listen!' he said. 'Listen!'

All three stood listening. From the street came the sound of hoofs. The soldiers had arrived. The woman went into the parlour and looked out through the window.

'Yes,' she called out. 'It's those Hussars again.'

Desmond followed his wife into the parlour. Peter remained standing at the kitchen door. The long lobby was in darkness. He too had heard the sound of horses passing down the street. But he was holding on to the kitchen door, looking at the nail to which adhered some threads from Sheila Fury's black dress. He picked these threads off, and stood looking at them. Desmond came in again. Peter hastily dropped the threads and looked at his brother.

'I must go,' he said, essaying a smile, a smile that he knew well could not conceal his agitation.

'Yes, of course.' They walked down the lobby.

Sheila Fury came and joined them at the door. Peter, his hand upon the brass knob, turned and looked at the woman. There was nothing to see now, only her white face and those burning eyes.

'Well, good-night, Peter,' she said. She did not offer him her hand.

Peter opened the door and stood out on the step. Mrs Fury had gone into the parlour again. A mounted soldier drew rein outside the Furys' door.

'Where is that man going?' The question was addressed to Desmond Fury.

'Going. He's going home. Where the hell d'you think he's going? To commit suicide or assassinate the King?' He cleared the step at a bound and went up to the soldier.

'Our orders are to question anybody in the streets, and to arrest where no satisfactory explanation is forthcoming,' the soldier said. He looked down at Desmond Fury.

'Thank you. We are well aware of that.' He called to his wife. 'Sheila! Bring out that iron bar.' Mrs Fury came running out with an iron bar in her hand. This bar was an inch thick and three feet long. It had apparently been a railing forced from a gate. Desmond Fury, in full sight of the soldier, handed this bar to Peter. 'Here!' he said. 'Now go. If you find any obstacles barring your path you know what to do with it.' He looked up at the soldier. 'This boy lives only a few streets away,' he said.

The soldier looked at the iron bar. Desmond took the bar from his brother.

'It's all right,' he said. 'Beat it now! Our friend has given me his word. In fact, he informs me that nobody is beat up excepting under the greatest provocation. Isn't that so?' But the horse had begun to move. At the top of Vulcan Street there were other horses drawn across the street. Now it wanted to join them. The darkness swallowed it up.

'Good-night.' Desmond shook hands with Peter. Something made the boy turn his head. Mrs Fury was looking at him from the parlour window.

'Good-night.' The hand holding his own squeezed tighter so that he almost winced with the pain.

Feeling the woman's eyes upon him, he leaned on to the door and said laughingly, 'What's the matter with you, Desmond? Are you afraid of me?' In a moment he was pulled forward. He was looking at two rows of teeth. The rest of the face seemed to be hidden in the darkness of the lobby.

'Afraid? No. But I'm jealous.'

Peter could feel his brother's hot breath upon his face. Ah! So he had suspicions, had even guessed. 'I'm not clever,' he could hear his brother saying, 'but I'm not thick either.'

The door banged. Peter was standing in the street. A single lamp shone. The other had been blown out by the wind. He stood looking at the door. In the next house the parlour was lighted up. He heard a man singing. He recognized the voice at once. It was George Postlethwaite. He looked at the window of number seven again. Was she still standing there? No. She had gone.

Then he heard a step in the lobby. He put his ear to the keyhole. Raised voices broke the silence. Mr and Mrs Fury were arguing in the lobby.

'Now!' Desmond was saying. 'Now, have you been on that bloody shore again? Where is this shore? What is it? What's there to attract? – or is it some other shore?'

There was no reply from the woman.

'You were there last Sunday. The people next door saw you. Tell me, for

Christ's sake, have you got some holy itch for the sea? What is it? Out! God! You're never in!'

The woman was speaking.

'Out! What are you talking about? You're never in yourself. Mind your own business.'

'I am.' Desmond shouted. 'I am minding my own business. One can't get a word out of you. Where do you go running off to at night? Everybody is talking about it.'

'Don't press on my arm. It hurts.'

'Her arm! Oh, that arm,' thought Peter. 'He's pressing that arm that came round the door. The long white arm.'

'I'll kill you one of these days, you bitch,' Desmond said.

Peter walked away. Now he knew. Before he had only guessed, groped in the darkness. Now he understood everything. Well, he would see that white arm again soon. 'Yes. By God, I will!' He was in a ferment. He started to run, stopped. Hang it! What was wrong with him? 'Keep cool, you fool, Mother will notice. Yes, Mother will notice.'

He pulled his handkerchief out and wiped his face. He felt hot all over. His tongue was dry. At the corner of Price Street he was stopped by the military. Where was he going? What was he so excited about? Why, the fellow was trembling. The soldiers barred his path.

'What have you done? Murdered somebody?' One soldier poked Peter in the ribs with his finger.

'Been following one of those bag-women,' another soldier said.

'I'm going home. Just there. See!' He pointed in the direction of Hatfields.
'Scoot!'

Peter ran. He knocked at the door. Was he all right? Did he look all right? That fellow had said he was trembling. The door opened.

'Late,' Mr Fury said. He drew back the door. Peter entered the house, his father following into the kitchen. Mrs Fury was sitting at the table. She did not look at Peter nor her husband. She looked directly in front of her. She looked at nothing. There was nothing to see. Her mind was a complete blank. Peter wanted to say 'Hello, Mother,' but the look upon Mrs Fury's face prevented it. Mr Fury tapped him on the shoulder.

'Get your supper and get to bed,' said his father. He too sat down.

Not once during his hurried meal did the woman move. She seemed glued to her chair, that hopeless, almost frozen look upon her face. Mr Fury picked his teeth with one of his wife's hatpins.

Peter, having finished his meal, rose from the table.

'Good-night, Mother – good-night, Dad.'

Nobody replied to him. He went upstairs. The moment he reached his room he pushed the catch back. Then he opened the drawers. He was searching for an envelope. That long envelope with something hard in it. Ah! Here it was! The very thing. Feverishly he pulled out the photograph of Desmond and his wife. As he tore off that of the woman, he thought, 'How did it come here?' But perhaps Desmond had given it secretly to his father. He flung the other half, from the glossed surface of which Desmond's hard face looked out – though it had seemed to soften a little as for the occasion – into the grate. Then he set fire to it. He had torn it in two. He had freed the one from the other. He undressed and climbed into bed. Then he lighted the lamp, lay back and held the photograph of Sheila Fury in front of him. He knew then that it had been worth it. Those seven years at college – that accidental meeting. He kissed the face that looked out at him from the cardboard. 'There can't be any mistake about it,' he thought. Then he hurriedly placed the photograph under the pillow, blew out the lamp and stretched himself in the bed.

Mr Fury passed the door. He was going to bed. Below, tired of silence, of the spectacle of his wife sitting frozen and dumb at the table, he had said, 'I'm going to bed, Fanny.' She did not answer. Just looked ahead at nothing in particular. In his room, Peter had begun an excursion into a new, strange, and wonderful world.

The gas burned low, finally went out. But Mrs Fury was still sitting at the table. There seemed nothing else to do but sit there, staring at the wall.

3

Hatfields, like its neighbours, Vulcan Street and Price Street, abutted on to the main King's Road. King's Road was about a mile in length. It ran parallel with Harbour Road, at the end of which stood Mile Hill. When one had descended Mile Hill, flanked on either side by shops, public houses, and occasional waste ground, occupied at week-ends by travellers in linoleum, one had reached the city. Hatfields also ran flush into Dacre Road. At the bottom of Dacre Road there were the docks. Eleven and a half miles of them. This Dock Road ran right into the city and beyond it. Mrs Fury was now debating in her mind which way she should go. The top road seemed the more favourable, but it had its disadvantages. It was heavily patrolled. From Harbour Road came the looters and the roughs. It was not advisable to go that way. One was bound to be held up.

On the other hand, to go along Dock Road was to invite attentions of a disagreeable kind. One never knew from what dark hole or corner a man would emerge, a most repulsive sort of person who made a habit of accosting women, old and young.

There were a number of these men always frequenting that area. They were mostly tramps. At night they slept out on the shore. Here their instincts seemed to have full rein, and more than one woman taking a morning walk along the shore was surprised when from behind some sand-hill there suddenly emerged one of these species, entirely naked.

As the woman stood, hesitating, at the corner of Hatfields, these things passed across her mind. In a series of pictures she could see them. But the Dock Road would be patrolled too. Her husband was right. Still, she was out now, and besides, it just had to be done.

Mr Lake sat in that office of his for no other purpose than to be seen, to be interviewed upon the vital matter of her son. The fact that she had not had any recent letter from him only served to make her more determined than ever. After all, it was important. She could not see why or how she should be stopped by anybody. This proposed journey was nothing new to Mrs Fury. She was used to it. It wasn't so much the having to walk, that was nothing – she could walk miles – no, it was all the obstacles placed in one's path by these disputes. The merest loafer at the street corner felt it to be his shining hour. He stepped out into the road and asked people where they were going. To town! H'm! Then he pulled his cap down hard over his eyes.

'Can't go that way, ma'am.'

'Why?' the person would ask. 'Why not?'

'Dangerous!' He was a well-informed fellow, he knew. But if the person liked, he would take her another way. In brief, for a small financial consideration, he would free her path of all obstacles. The pedestrian generally fell for it. Yes. One's path was barred by obstacles. Those obstacles were explanations. Explanations all the way there and all the way back.

'Where are you going? Why? What is that you are carrying?'

Tiring, irritating. It made one's walk a veritable torture.

'I'll call into the chapel on my way,' she said to herself, and immediately turned towards Ash Walk. The streets were deserted. Only smoke pouring out from the forest of chimneys indicated that behind the bricks and mortar people lived, that these people were now rising, washing, dressing, making breakfast.

She went into the chapel and knelt down. There were about twenty people scattered amongst the benches. Father Doyle was celebrating half-past eight Mass. Before her she saw a stout woman who had just sat back after receiving Communion. That head and that hat meant only one thing, Aunt Brigid. She was more certain than ever that it was her sister when her eyes alighted on a small bent figure next to her. This small figure was wearing a poke-bonnet. The bonnet seemed to sway, to bob up and down.

That could only be Miss Pettigrew. None but Miss Pettigrew wore a bonnet like that. She must have dragged herself out to Communion in defiance of Dr Dunfrey's orders. Mrs Fury made the sign of the Cross, rose to her feet, and hurried from the chapel. She had made her decision. She would go the top road. It was quicker, in spite of the hill climb on the return journey. She straightened her hat. Then she bent down against the railings and tightened her shoelaces. She turned out of Ash Walk, passed down Price Street at a sharp pace, glancing hurriedly at the Kilkeys' window, and found herself on the main road. She felt better, more confidence in herself, as though she had imbibed a little strength from that visit to the chapel. A quarter to nine. With luck she should be there by half-past nine.

She reached the top of Bank Street without any difficulty, but when she came to Hotspur Road a minor disturbance had taken place. In Hotspur Road there was a bag factory. Around its red wooden gate a group of about fifty women wearing shawls had congregated. One of their number, a very stout woman, whose face was covered with running sores, was loudly proclaiming that the gate should be opened.

The police were there in full force. They could deal easily with these irate women, but that would not solve the problem. The foreman of the bag factory lived in a small house adjoining it. He had now come out, and was endeavouring to pacify the angry women. What was the matter? Everybody shouted at once. They wanted the gates open. What for? To go to work. The manager laughed. That was impossible. What was the use of making bags when there weren't any orders? Everybody was on strike. When their husbands and brothers decided to go back to work, the gates would open. Not before.

The manager disappeared into his house again. As he closed the front door he caught the eye of the police inspector. It was a well-meaning glance. The door closed. The manager took the precaution to lock it. The bolt shot back. The police went over to the women. They must go home. The women refused to move. Yes, the situation was dangerous. The sudden arrival of angry men-folk was the danger.

All this had no interest for Mrs Fury, whose path was blocked by a crowd that had swiftly gathered at the top of the street, and gathering force, now flowed into the road.

Mrs Fury looked ahead. She must either go right through or make a wide detour. She decided to go through. She began to push. People turned to look at her, more than one elbow jabbed roughly against her. A policeman saw her pushing through.

The first of the obstacles had arrived, not in the form of a crowd of decrepit-looking people, half-washed and half-dressed, but in the form of a policeman's eye.

As he approached, the crowd, from pure habit, fell away, so that Mrs Fury, now isolated, standing in a cleared space of at least six feet, became the attention of everybody. There was something deferential about the manner of this policeman as he went up to the tall woman and asked:

'Where are you going, Missus?'

'To town,' said Mrs Fury. She looked straight at the man. 'To town,' she said, 'on business.'

'Is it important?'

'Yes! Very important.'

'You understand the state of things in the city?'

'I do.'

'Where are you going?'

'To the Torsa Line Shipping Office for my son's allotment money.'

'Oh!' said the officer. 'I see!' He walked away.

Mrs Fury passed on. When she reached Harbour Road another obstacle arose, more formidable. She stopped. For the first time she saw people running. Saw batons raised, heard frightful screams. In the middle of the road lay a number of pianos, which an angry crowd of people, mostly women, had dragged out of the piano warehouse near by. Not content with that, they had begun to smash them with hatchets, whilst some young men had come out of a chewing-gum factory higher up the road, and were, at the time the police decided to clear the road, busily engaged in pouring fluid gum down into the framework of the pianos.

Mrs Fury saw none of these things. She saw only raised batons, heard screams, saw the terrified crowd darting back into their houses. She leaned against an empty shop door. She felt sick. There was still a mile to go. She ought to have taken something besides a cup of tea. Men, women, and children were flying past. The police came on at a run. She crouched against the woodwork. As the first policeman passed she screamed, 'My Jesus!' But they had not seen her. She was trembling all over. Perhaps she ought never to have come. She looked up and down.

These sporadic outbursts on the part of the inhabitants of Harbour Road and its adjacent streets occurred at regular intervals, almost, one might say, as though they had been planned overnight. These were no spontaneous kicks at authority, but calculated. Periodically some shop or factory was raided. The whole length of the road gave one the impression that gigantic building operations were afoot, for every shop had boarded its windows.

Mrs Fury moved away from the shop doorway and continued her journey.

She wanted to sit down somewhere. She felt her shoes pinching again, and a blister had come on her heel. As she drew near Mile Hill, the streets became more crowded, the scene more animated. Here a squadron of troops was drawn up, there a detachment of mounted police. Could she get through? Suddenly she exclaimed aloud, 'I wish I had asked Denny to come with me. Peter could have well looked after Father.' But it was too late now. In any case, if she kept on walking she could be there in twenty minutes. Yes. She *must* keep on. She wanted to sit down. The very thought of being able to rest her feet only increased her determination. Of a sudden she stopped, thinking, 'My God! Supposing that Mr Lake isn't there, after all! All this for nothing. No. Impossible! Just impossible!'

Twice in her quick walk down Mile Hill she had been stopped and questioned. At the bottom of the hill another kind of authority asserted itself. Federation delegates were everywhere. They swarmed like flies.

'Where are you going, Missus?'

The woman's path was closed by a burly-looking man. He was dressed in a blue serge suit and wore a collar and tie, though this seemed to make him feel uncomfortable, for he repeatedly tugged at the collar as he eyed the tall woman up and down.

'Who are you?' asked Mrs Fury. This was something new.

'I'm a delegate,' he said. 'Don't you know it's dangerous hereabouts? Listen to me, Missus. In a few days' time Mr John Williams will be the only authority in this city.'

'I'm not interested in Mr Williams,' replied the woman. She drew herself up to her full height and looked down at this red-faced individual, still tugging at his collar.

'No? Oh aye! You're one of those women who try to break the strike, eh? Well, I'm interested in you, see!' He gripped Mrs Fury's arm, and pulled her behind the shelter of a disused tram-men's hut.

'Yes,' he said.

Mrs Fury struck him in the face with her fist. She shouted, 'If my husband were here he'd break your neck, you insolent swine.'

She tore loose from the man and began to run. But again her path was blocked right across Powell Square. The Hussars were lined up. They had piled arms and were now standing at ease.

Mrs Fury was given to understand that from this point any further progress was impossible. That was definite. Final. The woman turned pale. As she looked across the Square she saw the doors, the great swing-doors, of the shipping office's high building. It seemed to call to her, to inform her that somewhere beneath its great dome Mr Lake was sitting, Mr Lake was waiting. The officer looked at the woman.

'I'm sorry,' he said. 'It's in the interest of your own safety.'

'But I must go,' Mrs Fury pleaded. 'I have to get my son's money.'

'Is it very important?'

The woman said, 'Yes. I depend on it.'

'People come down here for all kinds of reasons.'

'Please!' Mrs Fury said. She wanted to add, 'My feet are paining. I want to sit down.' She listened to the questions. Questions! Questions! Questions! Soon it would be impossible to breathe.

'But other people are walking about,' said Mrs Fury. 'I must go! I must go!'

At last! Well, here she was! There in front of her was the building. And there were the police, the soldiers, the Specials. When in Heaven's name was the strike going to end? It was like a war. It was bad enough going out in order to buy some food, but this – this questioning was far worse. She looked at the note in her hand. Then up at the great swing-doors. Here was something that the strike had not affected. Clerks, she told herself, never went out on strike. No. They were busy over their desks. Mr Lake, of course, would never think of going out on strike. She approached the swing-doors and handed in her note. She passed inside. Then she stood looking about. This wilderness of marble again. Those great flights of stairs. More marble. Those long windows. Those lines of pictures, the polished woodwork. The ascent and descent of the lifts, noiseless save for a low humming sound that reverberated through the building and came to an end with the sudden click of the gate. Yes. Here everybody was working. Everybody attending to his business. Here was order, efficiency. Occasionally people hurried past her, mostly typists and secretaries from the lower floors. To the right, a long highly polished bench. Mrs Fury sat down. 'Oh!' she said, 'the relief! Away from those crowds, the dust, the questioning, that beastly man calling himself a delegate.' She looked at her hand. Yes. The skin on her knuckle was broken. Well – she could not have done anything else. As soon as she had rested her feet, she would go up in the lift and sit in the corridor. 'At half-past three I must go and interview that woman,' she said under her breath. Now she must see Mr Lake. She settled her long coat, brushed the dust off its hem with her hand, and as she passed a long mirror set in the buff-coloured wall, she paused to examine herself. She straightened her hat. Then she walked to the first lift that came down. It was rather a slack day for the lift attendants. The gate clicked and shot back. The woman stepped in. The man shut the gate and pressed the switch. Mrs Fury ascended. The attendant did not even look at her. She might not have been there. Top floor! The gate clicked again. Mrs Fury stepped out. She smiled now. She *was* really here. She walked along the corridor, and when she reached Mr Lake's office stood outside for a moment contemplating. Yes. She felt better now. She was quite ready to talk to the gentleman. She opened the door and passed in. She rang the bell. The window shot up. Yes. This was the same girl as last time.

'Mrs Fury to see Mr Lake!' she said. Then she sat down.

'Oh! I'm sorry, Mr Lake isn't in yet,' replied the girl. 'Can you wait? He's never here before eleven, you know.' She smiled at Mrs Fury.

'What a nice girl!' the woman was thinking. Then she exclaimed, 'Oh!' and her face fell. 'Oh dear me! Very well, I'll wait.' Of course she could wait. Then she added, 'I wonder if you would be kind enough to get me a glass of water. I've had to walk all the way from Hatfields.' She leaned back and rested her head against the wooden partition.

'Certainly!' said the girl, and she hurried away to get the water.

'Thank you,' Mrs Fury said. She drank the water quickly, at a single gulp. 'Thanks very much.' She handed the glass to the girl and smiled at her. 'I'll wait here,' she said. 'Will that be all right?'

'Oh yes.' The girl went away. The window shot down. Mrs Fury was alone. 'How quiet and peaceful it is here!' she thought. She stretched out her legs. 'Oh!' she said. If only she could take that shoe off! But she couldn't do that. She leaned her head against the wood again. The silence itself appeared to close the woman's eyes.

Twice the door opened and two gentlemen passed through. The woman did not move. One of them stood looking at her in a curious sort of way. Then he too passed into the office. Mrs Fury had fallen asleep. As the time passed, more people arrived. Telephones began to ring, typewriters kept up a steady tattoo, broken periodically by a swishing of papers. The woman did not move. Her bosom rose and fell. She was fast asleep. Sleeping had changed her. That tensive, agitated expression upon her face had given place to a calmness and serenity. Her finely moulded face was dead white. Wisps of black hair about her ears accentuated it. It was in this state that Mr Lake found her when he arrived at the office. As he came in he paused, seeing the sleeping woman on the bench. Then he closed the door silently and stood looking down at her. Yes, he knew the woman at once. He could tell that face anywhere, pick it out of any crowd. Hundreds of women came to see Mr Lake in the course of his duties, but he could never form pictures of them in his mind. They were simply faces. Mrs Fury seemed different. Of course! She had come to see him recently about her son. He recalled the incident at once. She had had a faint in his office. But he had never expected to see her here now, at this time – and certainly not sleeping soundly on the office bench. He passed through to his inner office, and sat down. How on earth had the woman managed to get down to the office? Of course she must have walked, but how did she manage it? He rang his bell, and the window attendant answered it. 'How long has that woman been here?' he asked.

He began arranging papers on his desk.

'She's been here since a quarter to ten, Mr Lake,' the girl replied. She stood waiting, her hand playing with the knob of the door. Mr Lake looked up from his desk.

'Well, you say I'm here, then, and will see her,' he announced.

'Yes, Mr Lake.' The girl closed the door and went away. She raised the window and looked out. Now she smiled, for Mrs Fury had commenced to snore. She lowered the window, and went out through the door. Gently she took the woman's arm, and said in a whisper, as though Mr Lake might be listening, 'Excuse me, lady – Mr Lake is here now. Will you come this way, please?'

The woman sat up as though shot. 'Oh!' she exclaimed. 'I'm sorry! Imagine my falling asleep.' She laughed. She felt foolish, highly embarrassed. 'I . . .'

'Will you come this way, please?'

'Yes. Of course. Thank you.' She followed the girl through the outer office, and now she experienced afresh that feeling of age. Typists and clerks looked at her as she passed through. Were they looking at her hat, at her swollen ankles, at her worn shoes – the only ones she could walk in, the others pinched so much – or were they looking at her long serge coat? She could feel their eyes upon her. They stopped outside the office, on the glazed window of which she read in bold black lettering, 'Mr Lake, Private'. 'Thank you,' she said. The girl had gone, the door was open – Mr Lake had raised his head – he was looking at her and saying, 'Come in, please! Come in!'

Mrs Fury entered and closed the door behind her. This time, and she noticed it at once, the gentleman did not rise.

'Good morning, Mrs Fury,' he said. 'Will you take a chair?'

As the woman seated herself he said, 'Thank you,' and immediately proceeded to forget that she existed, for at that moment the telephone bell rang and he picked up the receiver – 'Hello! – Yes.' He hung on waiting, whilst his eyes began roaming about the desk, alighting on this and that paper. 'Yes – No – I have altered that! But ring me again. Engaged. Good-bye.' He put down the receiver and looked across at Mrs Fury. She was sitting straight up in the chair, her hands lying idly in her lap.

'Well, Mrs Fury,' he said, 'and what can I do for you?'

He leaned forward, resting his arms on the desk, so that a goodly portion of his white cuffs were exposed to view. Mr Lake, who always looked hale and hearty, seemed to have excelled himself today, or perhaps it was only the tall pale-faced woman sitting frigidly upon the leather-cushioned chair that served to heighten this unusual appearance and manner of the stout man behind the desk. His large head somehow seemed a little uncertain of itself, as though at any moment its position would be threatened by the collapse of those layers of fat that hung over his collar. This large cut-away collar served a single purpose, in that it formed the foundations for the security of the large head. He was wearing a grey suit today, a light grey tweed suit, as though optimistic that the fine weather might oblige by arriving before its time. He also wore fawn spats. Mrs Fury saw them now, as she lowered her eyes and peeped a little furtively under the table. These were buttoned about a pair of fine black shoes, with very pointed toes. The woman now raised her eyes and looked at Mr Lake's face. Yes. This was the gentleman who had said. 'Bring this lady a glass of water.' It had touched her deeply. It struck some hidden chord in her being, and now, looking at the man's large blue eyes, she experienced it again. To hear it had been like music, it had been more, it had touched the woman's heart. In Hatfields nobody said 'lady'. This was altogether a different world. Quiet, peaceful, inhabited by men with clean faces, grey suits, and white collars. So different from that other world. Yes. So different. How could Denny talk so insolently of this man, who now stroked his chin and said suavely, 'Now, Mrs Fury'?

'I have come to see you about my son. It seems that my husband could get no satisfactory explanation from you. He said my boy's money had been stopped. I have come down for some explanation of this matter.' She moved her right hand and raised it in the air for no other purpose than to touch her straw hat, which she seemed to have imagined had moved to an awkward angle. But there was nothing wrong with her hat. It sat secure upon her head. Mr Lake lowered his hand and laid it on the table.

'I see!' he said – pushed some papers to one side and said again, 'I see.' Perhaps he was considering the matter. He looked away towards the window.

'Yes. I see no reason why any money should be stopped,' continued Mrs Fury, 'at least not until satisfactory reason is given. I have not walked four miles for nothing. All this apart from the fact that my boy is lying in hospital. I know nothing beyond the facts he gave me himself. My husband told me that he was not coming home under a month.' Mr Lake had lowered his head. Now he raised it to find himself subjected to the woman's penetrating glance.

'That is quite true,' he replied. 'I can tell you that your son is doing well, and if he continues to progress, I see no reason why he should not rejoin the *Turcoman* at his old job – that is, after the usual annual overhaul. The

292

Turcoman will sail again in January, Mrs Fury. As I told your husband when he called, this stoppage has upset the Company's plans, so that some ships, booked for home, have been ordered to refuel and take stores aboard from New York, and proceed further. The ship your son was due to sail on has already left that port. But we have a ship scheduled to leave New York for Liverpool on the twenty-eighth. Your son will sail on that ship. With regard to the allotment note, that is entering another matter.' Mr Lake's expression changed. He sat back in his chair, and allowed his eyes to wander round the room. Then they alighted on Mrs Fury's straw hat. He smiled. 'Yes. What is the explanation you require, Mrs Fury?' he asked quickly. His manner was now that of a gentleman upon whom time is pressing, and who desires to bring the matter in hand to a close as soon as possible.

'I do not think you have offered the explanation I have come for,' began Mrs Fury. 'As you know, my son met with his accident the day after his allotment was due, so that you must know I am entitled to that. What is more, Mr Lake, I require that money now. It is needed. I cannot see why you should stop it. I have never heard of this being done before. When Mrs Ferris's son met with that accident aboard the *Amilian*, his money was not stopped.' She stopped suddenly. Mr Lake had risen to his feet.

'I quite understand,' he said. 'Quite understand. Is your husband out?'

'Yes.'

'Oh! Dear me! What do you think about the dispute, Mrs Fury?'

'Nothing. You are getting away from the point. Shall I go to the office on the ground floor for the one pound thirteen and eightpence that is due to me, or do you simply refuse to pay this money?' She too had risen and now stood facing the stout gentleman, whose corporation, as though resenting the position it had been forced into, rested heavily against the mahogany desk. 'Well?' she said. Why was he evading the point? Good God! To think of the sum under dispute, to think of it, and then to see that great building, those marble stairs and floors, those polished woods, those carpeted offices, this well-dressed gentleman with white cuffs. Yes. When she thought of it, she didn't feel tired now, not even hungry – necessity like some willing hand had appeased, necessity had obliterated these feelings. It had forced her to her feet. Mr Lake and Mrs Fury stared at each other.

'Tell me,' said Mr Lake, more suavely than ever, 'tell me, Mrs Fury, are you intending to make this a compensation case?'

'You asked my husband the same question, and you got your answer. But that isn't the point, Mr Lake.' She seemed to thrust her white face so close to Mr Lake's highly coloured one that the gentleman started back. 'That isn't the point, Mr Lake!' she shouted. 'The point is that we have to live.' In that moment when she leaned towards him, as though necessity's hand had pushed her forward, Mr Lake saw only her open mouth and some broken teeth. He sat down.

'I wish you to understand, Mrs Fury,' said the gentleman, 'I wish you to understand that this matter is out of my hands. Has the money been refused you?' Mr Lake was cold, indifferent. He only wanted this woman to go. But, judging by the determination with which she planted herself in the chair again, it was obviously going to be difficult.

'But you yourself refused it,' she said sharply. 'You refused my husband. As for compensation, that is another matter and has nothing to do with my money.'

'There must be some mistake, then,' said Mr Lake. 'In any case, this matter is not in my hands any longer. I think you had better see Mr Short.'

What? The matter was not in his hands? Had she come all that way for nothing?

'But you have always dealt with allotment notes, Mr Lake,' said the woman.

'I don't deal with them now,' said Mr Lake. He rose to his feet and crossed to the door, saying as he placed his soft fleshy hand upon the door handle, 'I thought you had come to me for advice of some kind. Very sorry! Some mistake has been made. The department is not in my hands now, Mrs Fury. You had best see Mr Short. Corridor two. Fourth floor. Room fifty-eight.' He turned the handle of the door. The woman rose to her feet. Now that sickly feeling *had* returned again. All this for nothing. Why hadn't he explained?

'Miss Green,' called Mr Lake.

'Please show this lady to Mr Short's office. Say Mr Lake sent her down.'

'Yes, sir.'

Mr Lake now smiled at Mrs Fury. 'I hope you find this rather urgent matter dealt with to your satisfaction,' he said. 'Obviously there is a mistake somewhere.' The woman had gone. Mr Lake seemed to be talking into air. he could see the woman quite clearly, not with her passionate face and open mouth, glimpsing her broken teeth, but sleeping – leaning against the buff wall of the small waiting-room, her mouth a little open, snoring. Mr Lake smiled. He closed the door of his office and returned to his desk.

'Will you wait here, please? Mr Short has gone out to have coffee,' said the boy who had raised the window of the inquiry office in room fifty-eight. He looked at Mrs Fury, smiling. 'Yes,' the woman said. Still smiling, the boy shut the window. Wait! Of course she could wait. She was used to waiting. She could wait until the very earth cracked, exploded, blew out, disappeared into space. Of course. She sat down on a chair and looked at the little glazed window – 'Inquiries', she read. 'Inquiries', she said to herself. And the word became imprinted upon her mind. Inquiries regarding the sum of one pound thirteen and eight. 'My Christ!' she shouted, and paused, mouth open, as though the very words had stuck there, holding her mouth in this peculiar position, like a fish with a hook in its mouth. Then she laughed. Her eyes focused themselves upon the glass window again. The lettering moved. The lettering began to dance. First one was stripped naked and laid on the table. Then gentlemen began to dissect the body. And now were exposed to view the various organs – heart, brain, lungs, spleen, stomach, bowels. The inquiries were beginning. First survey not entirely satisfactory. Something else. Ah! There! Feelings, thoughts. The gentlemen became more inquisitive. Well, that was enough! Everything had been revealed. Anything else? Yes, this woman is not satisfied. She is waiting outside. The matter is one of great urgency. The sum of one pound thirteen and eightpence is involved.

'Mr Short won't be long now, madam.' The window shot up and down again. The lettering ceased to dance. It was still now. 'Inquiries', her eyes read again, and the lettering was dancing round her brain. The door opened. Two gentlemen came in, one small, bearded, about sixty years of age. The other taller, thin, aesthetic-looking. They carried tightly rolled umbrellas.

'Haw haw! Yes, I remember that. That was when Jones upset his wine in the lady's lap. Yes. Haw haw!'

They passed through without seeing the woman sitting on the seat. 'Mr Short will see you in a few minutes,' said the boy.

'Thank you,' Mrs Fury said. The door opened, and a man came in from an outside café, bearing a tray. On the tray were poached eggs on toast, tea for one, rolls. The waiter looked at Mrs Fury. As he lowered the tray in order to open the door, the woman had full view of its contents.

'Dirty day, isn't it?'

'Yes,' Mrs Fury said, 'filthy.'

The man disappeared into the office. For the fourth time the window shot up. The boy closed it again. He had merely wished to ascertain whether the woman was still waiting. Now he came out to her and exclaimed brusquely, 'This way, please!'

Mrs Fury knew at once that she liked the girl in Mr Lake's office much better. She passed down a narrow corridor.

'In there,' said the boy, and disappeared as though by magic. Mrs Fury saw a large clock over Mr Short's door. A quarter to twelve. How time seemed to fly! Even when one had to wait. She opened the door.

'Yes, come in!'

This was a larger office than that of Mr Lake. It had a long low desk of rosewood. On the wall there hung framed pictures of the Company's steamers. These were displayed proudly flying the International flags. Mrs Fury noticed at once that the windows were clear, and that heavy blue curtains hung on each side of them. The floor was covered with a pile carpet, which made her feel more conscious than ever of her shoes. The carpet was light green, a darker green bordering it. Mr Short's brown boots, spatless, rested on a little red foot carpet. Mr Short was the gentleman with the beard. She recognized him, having seen him pass through, and his boisterous 'Haw haws' rang fresh in her ears. He was bent almost double over the roll-topped desk. He was endeavouring to pin some papers together. The small thin hands trembled as he pinned them.

'Sit down, Mrs – er –' he said.

But this time Mrs Fury politely ignored the invitation. This time she would stand. When she sat she was too conscious of having to wait, and of feeling hungry. No. She felt better standing up.

Mr Short repeated his request. 'Please sit down!' Well, at least courtesy wasn't at a premium in the offices of the Torsa Line.

Mrs Fury said, 'Thank you, I prefer to stand.' She looked down at the little man's carefully oiled grey hairs, and she could not help smiling.

'Yes?' said Mr Short. He knew perfectly well what Mrs Fury wanted. But one could not part from tradition. All inquiries were prefaced with an inquisitive and at the same time an arrogant 'Yes?' Any departure from custom would be disastrous.

'I have come for my son's allotment money,' said Mrs Fury. 'Perhaps Mr Lake mentioned this to you on the telephone.' The woman had an idea that Mr Lake had already informed Mr Short that she was coming down.

'Oh yes,' said Mr Short. 'What is all this about your son's allotment? Hasn't he had his money? Dear me!' He turned his attention to some papers. 'I find that the sum of two pounds became due on the third, but from that date the money automatically ceases. No doubt you will see our Mr Devereaux in the matter.' He began writing. He blotted the chit and handed it to the woman. 'Some mistake must have been made,' he said. 'Good-day,' he concluded.

Mrs Fury did not answer; she was too full. She felt she wanted to burst, to cry out that she had been right, that if she hadn't come down herself she would never had got it. She rushed out of the office, almost knocking the boy over as she went. Well, she had got it. No, she hadn't minded waiting at all. She wasn't even hungry. She took the lift to the ground floor. There she found a queue of nearly a hundred people lined up in the corridor. It was paying-out day for the *Aurelian*. She saw this at once by the large notice which hung in front of the crowd. It read: '*Aurelian*. Half-past one to four o'clock.' What time was it now? Twenty minutes to one. Well, that wouldn't be long to wait. She had been waiting since twenty minutes to ten. She took her place at the end of the queue and leaned heavily against the long low window. She didn't mind anything now. Even the walk back. It was nothing. Two pounds would lighten her steps. Denny would be surprised. Suddenly she struck the window-pane and said to herself, 'That woman! Of course. I must see her at half-past three.' The sudden bang on the window attracted everybody's attention, but the woman seemed not to notice. In any case she wasn't even there. That two pounds, like a magic carpet, had already carried her home.

A continuous hum filled the corridor. Everybody talked, laughed. They all seemed to know each other. They talked about their husbands, sons, brothers, and how lucky they were to have got away before the strike began. It was dreadful. A young man shot dead by the soldiers last night. Two dray-loads of beer upset on Harbour Road. An old man in Keeper's Hill beaten up by the Orange band. Three hundred people in hospital with head wounds. All the police from Babbinton had great spikes in their hats. Cruel bastards. They had knocked down cripples who were waiting to go to a concert. Disgraceful. They say you won't be able to get in or out of the city tomorrow without you have a pass from Mr Williams. Dreadful. They were glad their men-folk had got away. The steady hum reminded Mrs Fury of the peculiar low noise of the lift dynamos. Beyond a hum it was nothing. The air seemed electric with words, disjointed phrases, giggles, and laughs. Some youths in the queue were indulging in horse-play. The clerk put his head out. He looked very important and greatly bored. 'Keep quiet! How do you people expect to be paid if you make all that noise?' Yes; how were they? How was he, in fact, to carry out his important duties at two pounds a week with such a racket going on about his ears? Mrs Fury stood at the glass window, thinking, 'Soon be time.' The first thing she must do when she got home would be to get those shoes mended and get them stretched. For two pins she would fall flat now. Her feet were aching again. The irate clerk came out into the corridor this time, giving the waiting queue a full view of his person. They noticed he wore spats, similar to his superiors, and black coat and pin-stripe trousers. Mr Coats seemed to manage very well on two pounds a week, and without losing any of his importance. Then he disappeared again, and the most striking thing about him as he made his hurried return to the office was his spindle legs. Mr Coats was well known. Mrs Fury knew him too. She had taken her husband's and her son's money from his parchment-coloured, sweaty hands many times. At last the queue began to move. Mrs Fury looked at the clock. She began to count, add, subtract, multiply. It passed the time away. At the same time she leaned on one foot, then on the other. These alternate movements seemed to ease the pain in her feet. At last she was at the window. Mr Coats took the chit without looking at her, placed it on the desk in front of him. Then he read it. He then went to a drawer and drew out another chit. He placed it alongside the first one, then buried his hands in a perfect mountain of silver, and the very feel of the coins seemed to impress upon him the importance of his position.

'Fury! *Turcoman!* One pound,' he said. He flicked a pound-note from the drawer, put the chit with it and flicked it under the grill.

Mrs Fury almost fell. 'It's two pounds,' she said. 'Two!' she shouted. She was angry – obstacle after obstacle.

Mr Coats was equal to the occasion. 'One pound,' he said. 'Look at your slip. "One pound tobacco and slops." Next.'

Mrs Fury turned away from the window. Her hand shook. She walked slowly down the corridor. When she came into the daylight she read the white slip of paper. 'Contra account. Slops fifteen shillings, cigarettes five.'

Yes. Of course. It was right. The *Turcoman* pay-lists had been sent to the office. Yes. No doubt whatever. She was disappointed. A whole pound. And it meant such a lot. She thought of her shoes. 'Have to leave them now.' She found herself in the street. She was confused, excited, as though she had been imprisoned in some dark pit and had just emerged into the daylight. She stood hesitant, looking round her. Well! Here she was! She had been waiting in that building so long that she had forgotten a great many things. There was a strike after all, and Anthony was in hospital, Brigid was with Miss Pettigrew, and Peter was hoping to get away to sea.

Gradually confusion drifted away, and her world was set to rights again. 'I'll go home the bottom road,' she told herself, and started to cross the Square.

Now she was home again. Would she have some tea? Mr Fury said. 'I've just made it, Fanny.' She shook her head. Mr Fury protested. Ridiculous. She hadn't had a bite all day. How had she got on? Had she seen Lake?

'Yes! I saw him.' She flung the pound-note on the table, looked at it for a moment, and then pushed it away from her as though it were dirt, something foul and contagious. 'There it is,' she said, and thought, 'Yes! There it is! Out all day for that!'

'Well! That's better than nothing,' Mr Fury said. Yes. It was. Better than waiting. She looked at her father in the chair. Had Dad been fed? Mr Fury nodded his head.

'Is the boy out?'

'Yes. He's gone for a walk,' replied Mr Fury. 'I couldn't say no to the lad. Been in all day.'

'Of course! Have you had something to eat?' she asked.

'Yes. Look here, Fanny,' said Mr Fury. 'You look tired and done up. Go to bed.'

'You go,' the woman replied. She sat down at the table and looked at the pound-note. A knock at the door. Mr Fury opened it. Peter followed his father into the kitchen. He sat down in his old chair near the fire. Peter said nothing. He ate some supper and went to bed. There was something in the expression upon the woman's face that frightened him. It seemed like a warning. He finished his supper, got up, said 'Good-night,' and went upstairs.

'Go to bed, Fanny! Go to bed!'

'You go! I'm all right.'

'This is silly,' Mr Fury said. He got up and left the kitchen. As the man ascended the stairs his heavy tread seemed like giant hammers, and with each tread of his feet he seemed to stamp upon the woman's brain. She could feel them. The door closed. The light was getting low.

They had left her with Dad! The woman got up and went into the back kitchen. In the darkness her hand groped along the shelves. She was searching for a little butter, a quarter pound of best butter she had put away. Her little luxury. She groped, thinking, 'I left it behind that pan.'

She struck a match. No. The butter had gone. Her little luxury had disappeared. Well, she didn't want to eat, after all. She wasn't hungry, merely deluding herself. She returned to the kitchen and sat down at the table again. Mr Mangan grunted. She raised her eyes slowly and looked at the wall in front of her. Well, there was nothing else to do but sit staring at that wall.

CHAPTER XII

Mr Fury woke up, thinking, 'Ought to be a good show at the Lyric this week.' He turned over in the bed.

'I'll be hanged!' he exclaimed. 'What time is it?' Had he slept on? And where was Fanny? He jumped out of bed. How long had she been up? He slipped on his trousers and tiptoed to Peter's room. The bed was empty. Must be late! Slept in! Yawning, he returned to the front room. His mind was befogged. He went to the window and looked out. Children were playing in the street. Then he heard St Sebastian's Chapel bell ring. Half-past nine. That must be the elevation bell at the nine o'clock Mass. Now dressed, but wearing his rope slippers, he went to Anthony Mangan's room. The old man too was up.

'I'll be hanged!' he said again, and left the room. He stood for a moment on the landing. How silent the house was! He went downstairs. Mr Mangan was sitting in his chair; a big fire blazed in the grate. Peter had gone out. Mrs Fury was sitting at the table, her arms folded.

Looking at her, Mr Fury thought, 'She was sitting like that last night. What's the matter with the woman?' He sat down opposite her at the table.

'You were up early,' he said.

'Yes.'

She had not been to bed, but had remained sitting in the kitchen. She had kept the fire going, made some tea about half-past three. Now she was sitting in exactly the same position as when her husband last saw her, the same expression upon her face. She reminded Mr Fury of a certain wax figure of a well-dressed lady that, standing too long in the window under a hot sun, had begun to melt. Looking at his wife, it came back to his mind vividly. Hardly any difference. Fanny was just like that wax figure.

'What's the matter?'

'Nothing.'

'Has Peter gone out?'

'Yes.'

She changed arms, now resting the left upon the right.

'What in the name of Christ are you staring at?' shouted Mr Fury. 'Surely you haven't been sitting like that all night! Strike me lucky, but it's enough to give anybody the pip.' He darted a glance at his father-in-law. 'Him too,' he thought.

Had she had any breakfast? The table was bare, even the cheap American oilcloth had vanished. Or was he just dreaming? Had the hands of the clock, tired of their even beat, broken loose and raced round their clock face? And what in the name of Christ was she looking at? He turned his head round quickly and looked at the wall. Had she seen a bug crawling up it, or, like Mr Mulcare, had she just sat there fascinated by a slow-moving spider? Anyhow, he, Denny Fury, could see nothing to look at. Or had his wife had a dream like that famous saint who, returning from a visit to Hell, and in order to prove the fierceness of the fires thereof, had burnt a hole in the wall with her foot? If not, then what on earth was she thinking about? He raised his head and looked at Mrs Fury again. 'Ah!' he thought, 'she's been in Peter's room, and she's seen that mess-up. She must have guessed! She knows I know all about the money. She took it.'

'I wish you'd tell me what you have on your mind,' he said.

Suddenly Mrs Fury's face changed colour, the muscles worked convulsively. It was as though her husband's words had started some atrophied organism working in her body. Mrs Fury heard sounds in her head. It was as though her mind were singing. She put her hand to her head and laughed. She imagined that somebody had made a hole in her head, and that a great number of people went tramping past, pressing down her brain as they went by. And they were singing. She laughed again. Dennis Fury was stricken with fear. He gripped the table and stared at her more raptly than ever. What was she thinking about?

'Listen,' he began, then stopped. The woman had begun to smile. 'Yes. No doubt about it,' thought Mr Fury, 'her and that wax figure might be sisters.'

'What about breakfast?' he asked.

'Yes. Of course,' the woman said.

She rose to her feet, looked at Mr Fury, then disappeared into the back kitchen. Aunt Brigid was doing a highland fling on top of Mrs Fury's head.

'Oh Jesus Christ!' she said, and dropped the cup she held in her hand. Mr Fury jumped up.

'What's that?'

'Nothing,' she said.

Peter came in, his hair blown over his face by the wind. He swept it back with his hand.

'Where have you been?' Mr Fury said. It was a growl.

'Half-past eight Mass,' Peter said.

301

'Oh!' his father exclaimed.

He went into the parlour thinking, 'Fanny must be going balmy.' He stood by the window. Looking out he saw – just nothing. Peter was now standing behind him. He touched his father on the shoulder.

'Dad!' he said. 'Dad!'

The man turned round. 'What – what's the matter?' He was thinking of his wife.

'Grand-dad has to go for his pension,' Peter said. He began tugging at the curtains.

'Today? Forget it,' his father said. 'Today? It's Friday. Today's only Wednesday.'

'Yes, I know. But the time is changed now,' the boy went on. 'Mother had it altered at the Post Office.'

'But all pensions are paid on certain days of the week, you know that as well as I do, or at least you ought to know. Where were you last night?'

'Out,' Peter said.

'Yes, I know you were out.' Mr Fury raised his voice. 'We know you were out. But where? And don't you talk to me like that, you young pup, or I'll flatten you! See!'

'Sorry, Dad. Mother says we must take Grand-dad to the Post Office.'

'Oh! Oh!' Dennis Fury plumped himself in the chair. 'Your mother says, does she? Listen to me' – the sudden change in his voice startled Peter. 'Listen to me! Your mother is all wrong. When did she tell you that? D'you know your mother's going out of her mind? Do you? You bastard! Where were you last night?'

'Dad! Dad!' The boy gripped his father's knees. He could feel them trembling under his touch. 'Dad!' he said. 'Dad!'

'Yes! Yes! It's all right. Sorry, laddie,' he said. 'I didn't know what I was saying.'

He wiped his face with a large red handkerchief covered with great white dots.

'Sorry, Peter! Sorry!' The man seemed confused, bewildered. 'Must be getting light in the head,' he said. He laughed then. 'Your mother must have made a mistake,' he said. 'It's Friday when "him" goes down.' Peter could not understand his father.

'No. It's today. Mother just said.'

'Just said! But I can't get a word out of your mother. I asked her if she'd been to bed. She said "Yes," but it's a bloody lie. She's been sitting at the table all night, staring at the damned wall. I *knew* it!' Mr Fury said. 'I *knew* it. I know your mother better than anybody. Out all day yesterday. *All* day. How she got to town and back, God only knows. But she did. Aye, Peter, you ought to be proud of your mother, lad. Aye! She got Anthony's money. She did that. I couldn't get it. That swine Lake and me don't get on well together.' He leaned towards his son and added in a whisper, 'And your mother didn't have a bite of food the whole day. Of course she said "Yes" when I asked her. But your mother's like that. Wouldn't complain. Never says a damned word. You never know when her belly's empty.' He suddenly brought his hand down heavily on Peter's shoulders. 'Aye! She's like that. If ever you do anything on your mother I'll break your neck. Yes, I will that!'

Breakfast was laid. Bacon for Mr Fury, bread fried in the gravy for Peter. They sat down. This time the American oilcloth had appeared. It was newly scrubbed. Mr Fury deliberately changed his seat, and said to Peter authoritatively, 'You sit there.' Yes, if Fanny looked at that wall once more he'd jump out, get the hatchet from the coal-house, and smash it down. That's what he would do. Getting on his nerves. Couldn't stand it any longer. Not a word was spoken during the meal, until Peter pushed away his plate.

'What's the matter with you?' said Mr Fury, thinking of his wife's silence. 'I say, what's the matter with you?' He put down some bacon rind from his fork.

'Nothing,' Peter said, looking somewhat distractedly at his mother. 'I'm not hungry.' He sat back in his chair.

'Oh! You're getting very particular. One of these days you will be hungry, and you won't stick your nose up at fried bread.'

'I'm not sticking up my nose at it,' replied Peter. 'It's only what we got at college, anyhow.'

'Fried bread!' cried Mrs Fury in her mind. 'Fried bread!' She thought of the school fees.

'You're turning into a little snob,' Mr Fury said. 'The bloody seven years' holiday has turned your head! That's what I think! Your mother doesn't agree, of course. Fanny,' he said, turning to Mrs Fury, 'Why don't you eat something?'

'In a minute,' she replied.

Her husband got up. In a minute. That might mean tomorrow or next year. He went out to the closet and sat on the seat. He lighted his pipe. Soon great clouds of smoke came out through the space between the door top and the roof.

'Sitting there like a dummy,' Mr Fury thought. 'Almost as bad as "him".' Hang the confounded strike!' He couldn't see what anybody was getting out of it, except a few lucky ones like Mr Postlethwaite, who got a clout on the head. No. They wouldn't get anything. And that son of his, here, there, everywhere, talking a lot of bull about workers' rights. Now he came to think of it, that George Postlethwaite was right. Nobody got anything out of it except a cracked head. You couldn't beat those bosses. They had all kinds of plans up their sleeves, every kind of help at their hand. Soldiers, police, mounted and on foot. Specials, toffs from the colleges and universities wearing blue armlets. A lot of tommy-rot. As the smoke filled the small closet, Mr Fury thought, 'Aye. All their damned promises will go up in smoke.' He could see Mr Postlethwaite lying in that hospital ward, his head heavily bandaged. He could hear George saying, 'Trouble with these fellers, Dad, is they never know when to say "Whoa!" That's a fact. An' all you got for your trouble was a fat head.' Mr Fury suddenly laughed. 'Yes,' he thought, 'George is right.' Well, he never wanted the confounded strike. It just came. And there was Fanny sitting there like somebody daft. He knew what was the matter. Of course he did. And her own sister kept clear now. Might be asked to help a bit. Mean bastard. That's what she was. Her and her blasted father. The house had never been right since he came, anyhow. Now he was too old to go back.

'Belfast!' he exclaimed. 'The old man'll never see Belfast.' He spat on the floor. 'No. Just kick the bucket in his chair. Ought to bury the chair with him when he dies.' Yes. Everything seemed to have gone topsy-turvy all of a sudden. He thought of his daughter. 'Aye. I used to like Maureen – but I'm damned if I do now. Never comes near to see her mother. Wouldn't even see the boy. Too independent.' Stuck up all of a sudden. Well, he would never ask her for anything, not even for a pinch of tobacco. Certainly Fanny wouldn't. He'd swear his solemn oath on that. The water made a gurgling sound in the bowl. He banged the door, but it came open again. Blast! One would think the landlord would put a latch on it. He returned to the kitchen again. Mrs Fury was busy in the back kitchen.

'Can I do anything?' he asked. He could see how worried she was. What was on her mind? She hadn't cleaned up for days. 'Can I help with anything, Fanny?'

'No.' She swept the dishes into the sink. Mr Fury stood watching her wash them. 'I said No,' the woman shouted. The man leaned back against the mangle.

'All right,' he said. 'Don't get your shirt out about it. I'll go out.'

'Go out,' Mrs Fury said. Dennis Fury took her at her word. In two minutes he was hurrying down Hatfields. He was like a man who has suddenly remembered an important engagement. But his destination was nowhere in particular. Simply 'out'. As soon as the back door closed, Mrs Fury called to her son:

'Did you leave that note at Price Street?'

'Yes, Mother.' He heard her washing down the drainboard.

'You put it under the door as I said?' She was wringing out the cloth into the sink.

'Yes, Mother,' Peter called back.

'Did you wait until Mr Kilkey had gone out?'

'Yes.'

Mr Joseph Kilkey, when not working, always went out to the half-past eight Mass at St Sebastian's.

The house was silent again. The woman came into the kitchen. Her sleeves were rolled up beyond the elbow.

'Has your father gone?' she asked. She had actually seen her husband pass down the back yard as she stood behind the window, washing up, but now she seemed to have completely forgotten it.

'He's gone, Mother.'

'Then you go too,' she said. 'You can easily catch your father up. Go for a walk with him.'

The boy seemed not to comprehend.

'I said, Go out,' replied Mrs Fury. 'You're in the way here.'

'Yes. All right. I'll go out,' Peter said. He put his coat on and went out.

The woman sat down. She was alone at last. They had gone out. She felt the air was clearer. Now she could get on with her job. She got up and threw the window open. That was better. Now she could begin. She stood by the window contemplating. Should she begin at the top or at the bottom. The whole house was a disgrace. Suddenly she said, 'I'll begin at the top.' She went into the back kitchen, armed herself with bucket, cloths, soap, and scrubbing-brushes. Yes, the place was like a pigsty. She filled the bucket and went straight upstairs. She went into Mr Mangan's room. She would do his first, then the boy's. After dinner she would do her own room and the kitchen and back kitchen. She began to clear the clothes from her father's bed.

Anthony Mangan's room contained a large iron bedstead, a cane chair, and a table. The floor was covered with oilcloth, now almost worn bare. Two rusty laths from the bed trailed upon the floor, so that each time the bed was moved to be made up the laths scraped the cloth. This continuous scraping soon trod great holes in the oilcloth. Mrs Fury now removed the bed from the wall. The bed consisted of straw mattress, sheet, blanket, and two over-coats. The sheet was stained with slobber. The woman flung the bed-clothes on to a chair, turned the mattress up, and then flung up the window. She carried the bucket to the corner, knelt down and began to scrub. When the oilcloth was wetted it threw up an odour, partly the smell of its own cloth,

305

partly from a kind of staleness that lay hidden beneath it, and that rose up each time the woman scrubbed the floor. Each scrubbing was a revelation. It revealed more clearly how worn the cloth was, and there was always that thin film of mould between it and the floor. At one time this sheet of oilcloth had been lifted and the wooden floor thoroughly scrubbed; now it was impossible. The oilcloth if lifted would come to pieces. Only its own rot seemed to hold it together. Moreover, it was practically glued to the floor. As she scrubbed with great circular movements of her right hand, which movements she changed alternately, the circular movements had a peculiar effect upon her. They made her dizzy. Sometimes her hand made sweeping circles long after the desire to scrub had left her, as though through long habit she had become a slave to its rhythm, a rhythm that pulled one to the floor, that held one's knees in a vice-like grip. She experienced this dizziness now. She was kneeling just at the end of the bed. The strong smell of carbolic soap filled the room. She had finished scrubbing a patch of the oilcloth to her satisfaction, but somehow her arm, as though controlled by some force outside her own body, continued to make these rotary movements. At such times she instinctively put her hand out and caught the leg of the bed, or the chair, or the corner of the table. It had a steadying effect. The other arm stopped moving. Mrs Fury caught the rail of Mr Mangan's bed, and rested back on her heels. After she had rested a while she began again. Mr Mangan's room was even dirtier than she had thought. She had now reached the door. Outside of this was a clean white patch of boarding from which she had taken a small green carpet upon which to kneel. The smell of carbolic came through to the nostrils, as though it rose vaporous from some hidden cavity of the boarding. The woman rose to her feet and surveyed the room.

'Well, that's better!' she thought. 'Smells cleaner, and the wind coming through the window will soon dry the floor.' Oilcloth seemed to imprison and hold water; it never dried as quickly as the boards, she was telling herself as she put the bucket down on the landing and went into the room again. She began to make Mr Mangan's bed. She paused, holding the sheet in her hand, staring at her father's expectorations patterning it. Should she wash it? No. Not today. She couldn't do everything in one day. She went to the door again and stood surveying the floor. 'That's done with,' she said aloud, 'and it wanted it.' Yes. And thank God she was able to do it. She thought of Mrs Postlethwaite and her rheumatics, of Mrs Barroise with her water on the knee. Yes, thank God she was able to do it. She picked up the bucket and went into Peter's room. She sat down on the bed, thinking, 'This was Desmond's room.'

*

Well, really, now she came to think of it, it was disgraceful. That boy had had everything. Everything. And it had only ruined him, swelled his head. She looked at Peter's bed. Peter's bed, also of iron, was smaller. Instead of a straw mattress it had a flock bed, two sheets, a blanket, and an overcoat. The overcoat had at one time been worn by Mr Mangan himself. But Dad was younger then, even hale and hearty. In addition to the iron bed, Peter's room contained a dressing-table. It was very old, its oak polish almost worn away. The back of the dressing-table was made of stout unpolished ply-wood. This dressing-table served two purposes. Everything in the Fury household seemed destined to serve two purposes. Peter's dressing-table hid a huge hole in the wall. The paper had rotted. Mrs Fury had covered it time and time again with fresh paper. The paper became damp, and finally fell from the wall. Undaunted, Mrs Fury bought a tea-chest, took off the lid, and decided to nail it over the hole in the wall, which was now growing bigger. At that time the dressing-table stood against the window. With the first stroke of the hammer the nail bent, the plaster came away. The wall must be rotten, she thought. Perhaps the landlord would see to it. But that gentleman had somehow forgotten the matter. Mrs Fury decided to move the dressing-table, no feat in itself, but one which caused her endless labour. Desmond had tried again with the tea-chest top. The wall protested – there was a great hole there now! If one cared, one might put one's head through and look fifteen feet down into the back yard. As she sat on the bed she cast her eyes under this table. Just as she expected. A small pool of water was lodging on the floor. This slowly trickled through and made stains that turned a rich brown upon the ceiling beneath. She stripped Peter's bed, and as with her father's room, flung up the window to let the air in. There was a three-legged table, on which stood a small brass oil-lamp. In the corner and nailed to the wall was a shelf containing books. This was always on the point of collapsing. The damp was creeping along the whole wall. Having cleared the room, Mrs Fury went below to get fresh water. She threw a glance at her father as she passed through the kitchen. Mr Mangan sat, both hands on his knees; to Mrs Fury's great surprise he seemed to be smiling. She was inclined to stop, to see how long that smile would last. But she merely refilled the bucket and returned upstairs again. At half-past eleven she would go down and have a cup of tea. As she knelt down and began to sweep under the bed she noticed soot. Now, as she swept, it rose in clouds. What was this? And here was the strip of carpet all marked with somebody's feet. Under it more soot. The sheet on the bed was marked too, but she had noticed it in rolling back the bed-clothes. Then he knew! Now she understood his remark: 'My little bit,' he had said. Denny must have gone to the chimney for it. And she had taken

307

it. She had taken it for that young devil Peter. Yes. And it had gone. But there were still fees to be paid. She hadn't seen the end of that yet.

Half-way through the scrubbing of Peter's room she stopped for a rest. She rested standing, leaning against the wall, one hand holding on to the bookshelf. It began to shake, and she loosed her hold of it. She looked at the books on the shelf. A French Primer! Bio-chemistry. History of the World. *Les Misérables* – in French. *Handy Andy*, by Lever. She was reading the titles of the books. 'H'm,' she muttered. 'H'm. A lot of rot! Waste!'

Having finished the floor, she remade his bed, dusted the table and dressing-table, and went downstairs. She paused on the bottom stair, as though a sudden thought had arrested her progress, but she only stopped to get breath. She placed the bucket and cloth away. She made some tea, which she drank in the back kitchen, sitting down before the mangle, using the cloth-board as table. Yes. The house must get a real clean-down. It was simply filthy. 'I wonder?' she exclaimed. 'I wonder?' and rising to her feet began to search the shelves. She lifted the pans and looked underneath. She ran her hand behind them. 'No. Of course not. That hungry boy must have found it.'

She sat down again. Mrs Fury's one luxury was a quarter pound of best butter, which she bought each Friday out of her father's pension from Mr Potts, the grocer. This butter she generally placed under one of the iron pans. It was better than roast beef, better than chicken, it was everything to the woman. To Mrs Fury a cup of tea with a slice of bread and best butter was a feast. Now it had gone. Sometimes she went a whole day without anything but this butter on her mind, her thought continually turning to the quiet meal when the others had gone to bed. At one time Brigid Mangan used to send her weekly supplies. That had stopped long ago. Miss Mangan was so busy seeing that the priests' bread was buttered that she had no time to think of sending anything. 'I wonder where Denny's got to?' she said aloud. 'I wonder?'

Time to feed Mr Mangan. She heated his milk, put a small drop of brandy into it from the bottle in the cupboard, and went to her father. She was certain that it could only be the brandy that was keeping the old man alive.

Having seen to 'him', Mrs Fury once more refilled the bucket and went upstairs, this time to her own room. The front room of the house in Hatfields was larger than any of the other rooms, and its window looked out on the front street. It was oblong in shape. In the corner where the big iron bed stood there was a high shelf, a fixture in the room. All the houses in Hatfields had a high shelf let into the wall of the front room. Here Mrs Fury had erected an altar. It was covered with a white strip of cloth. Upon it there stood a small statue of the Sacred Heart, and two vases containing artificial flowers. When fresh flowers were obtainable, the artificial ones were placed to one side. In front of the statue itself there stood a small red glass lamp, in which a night-light burned. Owing to the semi-darkness of this corner of the room, the light from the lamp threw a rich red glow upon a part of the wall, as well as sending this glow upwards like a sort of halo that hung above the altar itself. The lamp had been burning in Hatfields for seventeen years and had never gone out. Not for one single moment had this light been extinguished. When the night-light had burned through, another was already lighted, waiting to take its place. This everlasting illumination seemed almost symbolic. It was like the woman's own faith, to which she had clung passionately, and which had never wavered. Against the amorphous mass of everyday urgencies, against these the light threw itself forward like a bright burning shield. She never entered the room without going to this altar. And when-ever she stood in front of it, she felt calm and peaceful, as though the tragic face of the figure in front of her had moved, had put out its holed hand and touched her gently upon the shoulder. Her whole soul seemed to rise, her spirit cling to this face and to the light that glowed so redly and softly upon it. Dirt was nothing, filth was nothing, lies, insult, cheating, all these things were only sores that one reflection from that glow could obliterate. Mrs Fury, having scrubbed white the wooden flooring beneath this altar, now rose on her knees, closed her eyes and prayed. And with this closing of the eyes Hatfields had disappeared, its walls crumbled to dust; its dirt, its sameness, its monotony, its people too, had gone as if with a single flash some heavenly fire from the lamp, like a monstrous sun, had burnt and dried it up. And before it had knelt her children, and now she named them: Desmond, John, Anthony, Peter, her daughter Maureen. Naming them, she raised her right hand, making a sort of half-circle, held it for a moment in the air, then made the sign of the Cross. 'In the name of the Father, and of the Son, and of the Holy Ghost. Amen.'

She lowered her head, her arms had fallen limp to her sides, and she remained thus. It was as though the life in her had suddenly gone out, and thought itself had been drawn up by the red glow towards that face. After a while she got to her feet and continued her work.

She pulled the huge bed from the wall, and two dead flies fell into the film of dust that had collected behind the bed. She picked up a mouldy half-penny, some rusty nails, an old holed glove. These she placed on the mantel-shelf. Then she knelt down and began to scrub. Suddenly she stopped. The hand with the brush stretched out towards the window, the other rested on the iron bucket. She was staring at the wooden floor. For some reason or other the room had seemed to expand, to extend, so that she imagined she knelt on the brink of a veritable wooden desert, that she must scrub to the very end of it, pausing here and there for a rest. It was as though she had seen mirrored there her own life, as though those occasional pauses were merely magic moments stolen from time, from the long day itself. She looked up at the altar again. There was the early rising, the cleaning, the cooking, washing, mending, Mr Mangan, his comfort, the comfort of others. She saw them all now crystal-clear. These things seemed to rise from the wood and confront her. And when they were seen to, there was that quietness and peace, in the corner, where the ceiling glowed red. Everything was worth it. She began to scrub again. Below, somebody had come in. It was Mr Fury. She heard him climbing the stairs, pause outside the room door.

'Are you there, Fanny?'

'Yes. What is it?' she asked, her mind wholly upon other things. 'What is it?'

'Are you busy?' asked Dennis Fury. He was leaning on the landing, smoking his pipe.

'Yes. I am.' And the tone in which it was conveyed seemed to leave no doubt but that she was. 'Did you see Peter? I sent him after you.' Hearing a step, she added loudly, 'Don't come in! I'm busy. I left your dinners in the oven. Peter's plate is on the top shelf, yours on the bottom.'

'Oh! Righto! Righto!' Mr Fury replied. He went downstairs thinking, 'What's she doing?'

Then he heard the sound of the brush upon the floor. Mrs Fury had begun again. Having scrubbed beneath the bed, she began to push it back against the wall. But for some reason it would not budge. One of its castorless legs had become stuck in the wooden floor. She looked into the bed. She went to the top of the bed and, placing her hands underneath, began to lift. But the bed was stubborn and refused to move, as though it were angry at being disturbed, as though it had resented those festoons of fluff being brushed away from its rusty legs. Mrs Fury went to the door and called, 'Denny! Denny!' She sat down on the bed. The effort had been too much for her. Mr Fury came running upstairs.

'What's up?' He burst into the room. He looked at Fanny. She was hot, her face was livid, smudged here and there by dust marks, and a stray feather or two from the pillow had planted themselves on her hair. Her long arms were bare, almost to the shoulder.

'What?' he asked again.

'Will you lift this bed?' she said. 'It's got stuck in the floor. It's really a nuisance. I do wish I could get another castor for it. I have this trouble every time.'

'Why don't you leave it against the wall?' Mr Fury suggested. He lifted the bed up. 'There!'

Well, that was done, and there wasn't a word more to be said. When Fanny's spring cleaning began – he called it spring cleaning though it was the woman's weekly job – it was best to get out.

'You look hot,' he said, and went out of the room.

He tramped heavily down the stairs. 'Ah!' thought Mrs Fury. 'Those stairs! I knew there was something.'

Although the man had lifted the bed clear from the patch where the wood was brown-stained and rotted, it had not occurred to him to push it back against the wall. 'His dinner would get cold,' Mrs Fury thought. 'Wonderful creatures, men.' She pushed the bed back to the wall. It made a harsh scraping sound. The twenty-five-year-old iron bed was feeling the passage of time. It hated being moved at all. As she scrubbed the last patch near the door she heard Peter coming in. After a while he called up, 'Dad says what about your dinner, Mother?'

'Yes! What about it? Have you had yours?' she called downstairs. One hand lay immersed in the dirty black water, the other held the loose knob of the front room door. The boy shouted up:

'Yes. I'm going to get mine now.'

'Well, that's good,' the mother called out.

Silence again. She heard the kitchen door close. 'As long as they have theirs, everything is all right,' she thought.

She got to her feet, surveying the newly cleaned front room. That was done. What was next? Of course. The landing and the stairs. The landing was dark and smelt musty, probably from the damp film of mould that clung to the bare red-distempered walls. Here and there the plaster had given way. Every time a person ascended the stairs, a shower of dust fell from some new part of the wall that had surrendered to the damp. This dust was now an inch thick upon that part of the floor behind the banisters. The floor was bare. Here and there rusty nails protruded, showing where oilcloth had once been.

The woman went downstairs to refill her bucket. She never glanced at Mr Fury or her son as she passed through the kitchen, though the usual cautionary look was extended to her father. Mr Mangan, however, was quite safe, the great belt lashed round his chair. She emptied the bucket and refilled it with clean hot water from the boiler in the back kitchen. The mice that nightly ran along the shelves of the back kitchens of the houses in Hatfields had a habit of falling into the boilers, and as Mrs Fury ladled the water into the bucket she saw two dead mice. She called to Peter, 'Come here a minute, Peter!'

'Take these things out and throw them in the bin. It's a disgrace. One can't keep a single bit of food in the house with these mice!'

Peter carried them away. The woman went upstairs, placed her bucket on the floor, and sat down on the huge tin band-box that lay in the corner of the landing. It had just occurred to her that she had to see her daughter at half-past six. She thought of this, endeavouring to draw a picture in her mind of the whole proceedings. She could see Mrs Anna Ragner quite clearly now.

No! She had better not think about it. Just forget it. Her mind had a habit of conjuring up the most weird trains of thought. They seemed to take wing, to encircle and carry her away. She knelt down and began to scrub. During a momentary pause she heard her husband say, 'Well – I suppose we'd better go out. Best to keep clear when your mother's working.' He was talking to Peter. She heard them moving about the kitchen. She seemed to divine their thoughts from their movements. She could mirror her husband's irritation, his restlessness. He was like a ship anchorless in a storm.

The other! Peter! Well, he was an unknown quantity, a mystery. The boy seemed not to know what to do with himself. Such were Mrs Fury's thoughts, when the back kitchen catch was lifted and they went out again. Where were they going? What did they do with themselves when they went out? Her thoughts seemed to synchronize with the circular movements of her scrubbing-brush. 'What a job!' she exclaimed. She didn't mind anything excepting the landing. Now she came to think of it, Maureen had been a help. She pushed back the tin box that contained nothing but a set of broken venetian blinds. Then she renewed her scrubbing. She had reached the end of the landing, and was on the point of taking out the stair-rods, when she heard a noise in the kitchen. Only one thing could make that noise, her father's high-backed chair. She must attend to him at once. This was Mr Mangan's signal that he was hungry. She wrung out the cloths, flung them to the floor, and for the fifth time went into the back kitchen with her bucket. She left it in the sink and went in to her father. She tied an apron round his shoulders, tucked it beneath his chin, and then got his milk pudding from the oven. Milk puddings and pobs were Mr Mangan's only food.

She began to feed him. Those small bright eyes seemed to say, 'I can see you, Fanny. I can see you looking hot and tired. I'm sorry for you. I can see you raising that spoon up and down.' The woman wiped her father's mouth after each spoonful. Once she was sure he smiled, and she said in a sort of confiding whisper, 'Dad! You look almost bonny today!'

There, that was done. A quarter past two. How time flew when one worked! She made some tea, made toast at the fire, and sat herself down.

There was something significant in the way the woman approached the square table set in the centre of the kitchen. She seemed not to walk to it, but to be drawn towards it by some magnetic power. And the act of sitting at it seemed a kind of blind obeisance to the slavery of this dead wood. The table was a throne, a cage, a cell, a refuge, a lighthouse. Everything, thought, word and deed, seemed centred about this four-legged table. Her family had sat at it, as children, as men. Plans had been made there – even John's dead body had been laid upon it. The wood seemed to have drawn into it something of their very spirit.

The woman ate hurriedly, as though there were not a minute to be wasted. Now to the stairs. Would she get the stairs and lobby finished by half-past three? Would she have time to do the two kitchens? Having filled her bucket, she ascended the stairs once more.

Somebody knocked at the door. Mrs Fury ran downstairs. 'Oh!' she said. 'Mr Swift, I'll send it down.' She looked at the man with the soft hat. He seemed very disgruntled. 'But you always say that, Mrs Fury,' he said, putting his foot on the top step. Instinctively Mrs Fury moved the door. 'Do you think I'm going to run away with your damned money?' she said. 'I said it'll be sent down, and it *will* be. I promise that.' She shut the door and started on the stairs again. Half an hour later she heard another knock. Apparently this visitor was expected, for she went downstairs, took an account-book from the dresser drawer, and picked up her purse.

'Good afternoon.'

'Oh yes. Rent.' She opened the purse, then suddenly her mouth twitched. In it lay the pound-note she had obtained from the shipping office. There was no other money but this pound. And how she hated to give this pound! She wouldn't get any change out of it, for there were arrears to be paid. Why hadn't she thought to change that pound-note? She could have given him the bare rent. The shillings she wanted so much! She bit her lip in her anger. It was too late now. The man had seen the pound. Quickly he had receipted the woman's book and marked off her arrears.

'Thank you,' he said, handing Mrs Fury the book, and reached his hand out for the money.

'Do you mind if I leave the arrears till next week? I'm really short,' Mrs Fury said. She kept putting her hand to her face as though she imagined the collector were staring at the smut marks upon her nose and cheek.

'Sorry!' the man said. 'I've already ticked it off. *Thank you.*' He raised his voice as he said 'Thank you' – adding in an undertone, 'Eightpence change. Good-day.'

He was gone; the door was shut; she was standing in the dark lobby looking at the coppers in her hand. 'Eightpence change! Eightpence change!' she could hear the collector say. Well, she had been a fool to let him get off with that pound-note. As she began scrubbing the lower stairs she became conscious of the draught coming in under the door and blowing along the lobby floor. It was late afternoon, it had grown suddenly dark. The atmosphere became cold and bleak. The very oilcloth upon the lobby floor, that was continually lifted up by the draught, accentuated this bleakness. Having finished the stairs, she thought, 'Well, it is early yet. I might do the lobby as well.' She knelt down and gave it a rough scrub. She would have liked to have given it a thorough clean, but time was pressing now. She would do the kitchen and then finish for the day. There was no doubt about it, the place *was* dirty. This last week or two had been like some fantastic dream.

As she approached the corner to wash under Mr Mangan's chair she exclaimed, 'Dumb! Dumb!' as she pushed the old man in his chair further towards the cupboard. She had almost finished the kitchen when she felt a pain shoot across her back. She looked at the clean red tiles, and then at that patch by the back kitchen door. It was black, and it seemed to proclaim its dirtiness, to cry out to be washed. But no – she couldn't do it. Not another single stroke! She was done up. She wanted to lie there, now, this very minute, on the damp kitchen floor and fall asleep. As she leaned over the iron bucket her head did begin to nod. Now she squirmed, for the pain had shot across her back again. No. She must get up at once, or she would fall into the bucket. The floorcloth, water-soaked, lay on the floor. As she rose to her feet she trod upon the cloth, and a stream of dirty black water oozed out and flowed across her newly scrubbed tiles. She didn't even notice this, but walked to the sofa, and seemed to fling her body upon it, a dead weight. So she fell asleep, her head laid on the sofa arm, her two long arms hanging over it, so that it gave the impression of a person who has been struck down by a blow, who has lain on his face, and flung his arms past his head, encircling it as for protection. And upon this stretched-out figure the bead-like eyes of Mr Mangan seemed to fall, and to lie there too, as though he too knew her weariness, and shared it in spirit. Only the clock ticked, the fire gave out its murmurous noises from between the bars, like a sort of consolatory song. Half-past five. Neither Mr Fury nor his son had returned.

Darkness came suddenly, so that the walls of the kitchen now mirrored the dancing flames of the fire. With the growth of darkness the light spread further and further until it embraced the full walls of the kitchen. It caught a part of Mrs Fury's black hair, and gave it the appearance of glistening pitch. Her hands hung limp, the fingers bent, as if the scrubbing-brush had patterned their position so, had taken their due toll. The woman slept. The

314

water from the floorcloth had now trickled right across the clean red tiles, and had made a little pool under Mr Mangan's chair. The light from the fire caught this too. There seemed nothing that could escape its devouring eye. The bucket lay by the door. The unscrubbed patch looked cold and uninviting. The walls seemed to throb under the fantastic movements of the ever-climbing flames. She had taken the tin blower down and laid it inside the fender. The silence was punctuated by the monotonous tick of the alarm-clock, the occasional dropping of live coals upon the tin blower, and by Mrs Fury's laboured breathing. Anthony Mangan seemed not to breathe. He was like one dead. Those bright eyes, still focused upon his daughter, had vied with the brighter light of the fire, but the fire had conquered. When the flames died down, when that dull red glow took the place of the yellow flames, then his eyes would shine – 'like a cat's when the darkness comes', as Peter had once said.

The woman woke to the sound of their coming. They were actually in the kitchen, Peter lighting the gas, Mr Fury laying the table. Mrs Fury's head felt heavy. What was the time? Good Lord! She got up, hurried into the back kitchen, and washed herself. Then she went upstairs, changed and dressed, and came down again.

'Are you going out, then?'

Yes. She was going out. She had business to do. Had she had her tea? Yes, she had had her tea. She was standing by the lobby door. Peter and his father were in the act of sitting at the table, when the man's eyes fell upon his wife's hat.

'Fanny,' he said, 'you're a caution! I bought you a nice hat at Hobhouse's, and now you never wear it. Dear me! You're a caution!' He sat down and began to eat.

'Tut! Tut!' Mrs Fury said, and in a moment she was gone.

PART THREE

PART THREE

CHAPTER XIII

I

Price Street was in darkness save for the path of light that came from the open door of number thirty-five, where Maureen Kilkey stood waiting for her mother. Its two lamps had been blown out by the high wind. The tall figure of Mrs Fury now loomed up out of the darkness. The filtering light from the kitchen gas caught her face.

'You look tired, Mother,' said Maureen, as she looked at her mother. 'You are tired, aren't you?' she asked. She had her left hand upon the front door knob, her right was drawn up and covering her breast.

Mrs Fury smiled. 'I'm not tired,' she replied.

'Of course, my mother all over,' thought Maureen. 'She would say that, even if she was ready to drop.'

Seeing the attitude of the young woman on the step, and the now questioning glance she received, Mrs Fury repeated, 'I'm not tired, what makes you think so?'

'Nothing,' Maureen replied. She closed the door. They linked arms and walked slowly down the street. Not a word passed between them until they turned into the main road, when they increased their pace. The very movements of Mrs Fury betrayed an anxiety that could only be appeased when the large gloomy-looking house in Banfield Road was reached. At last Maureen spoke.

'It's a long way, Mother, and all uphill. But you know that already.' She suddenly pulled up and looked at her mother. This pause only served to steel Mrs Fury to her purpose. What was her daughter dallying about? Didn't she want to go now?

'Please, don't be worrying about me, Maureen,' she said reassuringly. 'I am used to climbing. Was your husband in when I called?' she asked. They had moved on again, as though the purpose itself had pushed them forward.

'No,' said Maureen. 'He wasn't in. He's been out since half-past ten this morning at the Moreston Dock, doing picket duty.'

'But isn't that dangerous, child? Some man called for your father to go picketing at a railway station, but I wouldn't let him go. It's a disgraceful state of affairs. I never thought the stoppage would turn out like this. The few devils who are working are finding it takes them all their time to get home safely with their wages. And as for food, it's getting difficult. How are you managing?'

'Oh, I'm managing all right,' replied Maureen. 'Are you?'

'Oh yes. Quite well. I can see your father is sick of it already. The poor man doesn't know what to do with himself. I shall be glad when he goes back to work.' She clung more tightly to her daughter's arm. They had now reached the end of King's Road. Here they stopped to rest for a moment.

Their way now lay along Harbour Road until Bellman's Theatre was reached. Here they would turn left, along Aston Road for nearly five hundred yards, when they would cross the lines into Instone Road. Here, the first hill began. Having reached the top of Instone Road, one stopped for a moment to contemplate, before an even steeper hill was climbed. This was Causeway. At the top was Banfield Road. They would turn right along this road until they reached a pickle factory. At the back of the factory, standing detached on a small piece of waste land, stood Anna Ragner's house. From Hatfields the distance was five miles. Mrs Fury had never been in this, the highest part of the city, during her long life in Hatfields. For one thing, there was no business that would take her there. And again, it was inhabited by people of a different religious persuasion to Mrs Fury. Here the Billies lived. In the neighbourhood of Hatfields it was not much different. She knew everybody, and most neighbours, except for a sprinkling of families like the Ferrises, were stalwarts of the Prince of Orange. The few Catholics whom circumstance had compelled to live here were considered to be most unfortunately placed, for on the twelfth of July the people proceeded to reveal their loyalty to Prince William in as blatant and bloody a manner as possible. It was a miniature Vesuvius, for every spouting lava of a most vicious and filthy kind. Mrs Fury's devotion and faith impelled her in every way to steer clear of such a place. Now, for the first time, she was going into the stronghold. It was to her an excursion into the unknown. In the present circumstances it was more than an excursion, it was a real adventure. Maureen had nothing much to say. Maybe she was preparing herself for the interview with the lady in Banfield Road. As for her mother, she had already conjured up visions of this woman and of her house. She had already climbed the hill, passed through the street, and entered the house. The lights of Bellman's Theatre proclaimed to all and sundry that inside its doors the show of the century was about to open. That inside one might sit down and forget about strikes, hold-ups, baton charges, the persistency with which landlords and creditors knocked at the doors. In brief, for the sum of one and threepence – Gallery sixpence – one could shut out all reality and lose oneself in a pleasant dream, the ears attuning themselves to the ribaldries of the low comedian, the senses teased and excited by a row of legs in tights. The lights from the theatre threw a sort of halo over great piles of timber, oak and ash, teak and pine, that towered above the wall of the timber yard on the opposite side. A small queue of people were lined up outside the Gallery entrance to the theatre when Mrs Fury and her daughter came in sight of its doors, and finally under the gleam of its lights. The two doors leading to Pit and Stalls had now been closed. Obviously that select clientele had already taken their seats. Mrs Fury turned suddenly and smiled at Maureen. 'That reminds me,' she said. 'Your father has actually asked me to go to the Lyric this week. How he imagines we are going to go, heaven knows. His five and threepence won't help.' She laughed, but Mrs Kilkey did not share it, she rather resented this remark about Dad. Dad was always being made to look a perfect fool. At the kerb they pulled up. Here they would turn again. Adjoining Bellman's Theatre was a large public-house called the Travellers' Arms, and right opposite this, near the tram stop, there was situated a large public convenience. Just outside of it these stood four iron benches, painted a vivid green. Maureen was pointing at them.

'Let's sit down here for a rest,' she said, and pulled at her mother's arm.

'I'm not tired, Maureen,' said Mrs Fury quickly. She did not know that her daughter, heavy with child, was feeling very tired herself. She saw these occasional rests as nothing but obstacles. Would she never get there? When were they going to arrive? She was sick now. She wished she had wings so that she could fly to Banfield Road and back again to Hatfields.

'But I'm tired,' Maureen said sharply. '*I* want to sit down here.' She pulled her mother towards the vacant iron bench. Was her mother the only tired person in the city?

But again the woman drew back, exclaiming, 'Surely, Maureen! Those benches are right alongside those lavatories!'

'What does that matter?' Another hand was pulling Mrs Kilkey towards the bench. An invisible and impatient hand. Mrs Fury allowed herself to be drawn slowly along. They sat down. The silence of Price Street seemed to envelop them again. They were like two strangers who have suddenly met one another in an even stranger world, and who for some reason or other have been struck dumb. Mrs Fury, her arms resting by her sides, looked in the direction of the town. Maureen was looking the other way, up the hill, and now wondered whether even *she* could really climb it.

Mrs Kilkey was now feeling sorry she had come. A strange feeling had come over her. She had felt it before. Yesterday she had been having breakfast with her husband. They had gone into the back kitchen, she to wash up, Joseph

Kilkey to dry the dishes. For some reason this strange feeling had arisen at a moment when her husband was seized with an ardent desire to kiss her. But her whole nature had revolted. She could not understand. The very sight of his face so near to her own only filled her with paroxysms of blind rage. She was beside herself. She had struck him in the face and run upstairs to her own room. There she had bolted her door against him, and had lain on the bed, her whole body bathed in sweat, surrendering to the peculiar flood of feeling that had taken her. And again, as she had sat quietly and peacefully sewing in the garden, she had been overcome by it. And her father had seemed to wilt before her uncontrollable wrath. So it had come again to her as she sat on the iron bench. She had sensed its coming. It was not *her* hand that had dragged the reluctant Mrs Fury to join her on that bench. No! It was another hand, that invisible hand that seemed to push itself up ruthlessly from some hidden depths of her own being, and now it caught and held her. It was in such moments, when the tide of feeling overwhelmed, that she seemed most conscious, and most sensitive to the life she carried within her. The hand had risen as from the very root of her being, and now sought to drag her down. Down and further down. Seated upon the iron bench, she had huddled her figure, her head was lowered upon her breast, her two hands clenched, and she was surrendering herself. She wanted this hand to hold her, to pull her down, to sink lower and lower, beyond consciousness itself. The desire to sink was a hunger in itself. She was naked upon that bench, for the hand had stripped her. She willed herself to it and was dragged down, yet she wanted to hide, to shield herself, to clothe her nakedness. At first Maureen could not understand these feelings. They bewildered. She thought, almost with horror, 'I ought not to have come! I must go! I will be caught out, taken unawares.' Yes, she only wished to hide herself now – to be alone – absolutely alone with the quickening life within her. To shut everything out, as yesterday she had shut her husband out and locked her door. The woman beside her on the bench was only something black, a heap of clothes, and finally nothing. She felt a swimming sensation in her head, and the blood seemed to race madly through her veins. The swimming sensation produced dizziness, and she experienced that feeling of a person who under an anaesthetic hangs suspended for a moment between the abyss of reality and unconsciousness. Now she was actually floating. The world had collapsed. She was floating in the air and she was crying. She shivered violently, so that Mrs Fury, lost in her own thoughts, turned round and said, 'What is the matter?' She leaned towards Maureen, then suddenly drew back, as she exclaimed under her breath, 'My Jesus! Her time has come.' What was she to do? She stared abstractedly at her daughter. It *was* Maureen and it wasn't Maureen. It wasn't a real face – only a quasi-human one. She clutched her daughter's arm.

'Maureen! Are you ill? Tell me, for Christ's sake.'

'I'm all right now,' Maureen said. She rose to her feet. But Mrs Fury remained seated. She had momentarily forgotten Maureen. Her thoughts had carried her back to Hatfields. She was thinking of the kitchen floor, and of the bucket she had left unemptied; of the floorcloth; of the little pool of water beneath Anthony Mangan's chair. She had been too tired to shift them. Perhaps Denny would clear them away. Maureen had sat down again. There came to Mrs Fury's ears a sound, the quick intake of a breath. It was Maureen. She turned quickly. That sudden inhalation was like a warning.

'Maureen! Maureen! Tell me. I . . .'

'I'm all right, I told you,' said Maureen, almost angrily. She stamped her foot. 'Haven't I told you I'm all right?' She drove her hands into her coat pockets. Mrs Fury slowly raised her head and looked at the woman in front of her. In that semi-darkness, for even Mr Bellman's bright lights did not illuminate the benches, she could see her daugher, heavy with child. She rose to her feet and linked arms with Maureen. They set off towards the hill.

'Maureen,' said Mrs Fury. There was kindness and gentleness in the woman's voice. it was unlike the harsh rasping voice that Dennis Fury knew. Perhaps in the street one's whole life changed; perhaps that flight from the Hatfields kitchen, from that square wooden table, awoke long-buried feelings. 'Maureen, if you don't feel well, please say and I'll go back home.'

She found a smile. 'I'm all right now, Mother,' said Maureen. 'Don't be worrying about *me*.'

'But do tell me! Please! and I will go back.'

Mrs Fury stopped, open-mouthed, looking away up the hill. It was as if her very desperateness had put a hand across her mouth.

'I'm all right! Isn't that enough for you? Why talk like this when you know we have to go? You want this money, don't you?'

How quickly Maureen could change, thought the mother. She felt her words now, she felt their cruelty, that joined forces with her own bitterness, her own helplessness. Yes, she must go. She must climb that hill. She must go right on. There could be no pause – she just must. If she had to crawl on her knees. She felt the blood slowly drain from her face, she could even see that white face, as though her desperateness had placed a mirror in front of her. 'Oh!' she exclaimed. 'Oh!' Did she ever imagine that she would be walking up this hill, her daughter at her side and carrying child? No. This was like stepping from light into darkness, and she dared not say a word, not a single word. Everything depended on this woman now. She was filled with dread lest Maureen should stop again, should change her

323

mind. That seizure upon the iron bench had lost its tragic force for Mrs Fury. It had only been one other obstacle. At any moment Mrs Kilkey might say 'No!' She might even shout aloud in that very street, 'No! You're a fool! You've been a fool all your life and will continue to be one until you drop.' She must keep silent. This silence was agony. There was so much to say, her heart was full, was choked. She wanted to open out, to empty herself, but she must guard her silence. She stopped again, leaning against a shop doorway. 'What is the matter now? Don't you want to go? Don't you want the money, then?' She dared not speak. 'If only we had reached the top of the hill,' Mrs Fury was thinking. If only her feet didn't begin to pain, everything would be all right.

'I do not think we can get that way,' remarked Maureen. She had already seen a crowd gathering at the top of the street. At the corners of the different streets, police and soldiers stood about. Excited groups of people were now marching up and down Instone Road. Some youths and girls were indulging in horse-play in the darkness of shop doors. Mrs Fury watched the soldiers send them about their business. Then they took up their positions again at the corner of the road. They looked very bored. Occasional threats, accompanied by much swearing, came floating down to them from the top windows of neighbouring houses. Maureen again exclaimed, 'I don't think we can get up that road. We had better make a detour round.'

'Why?' asked Mrs Fury. She stood erect, almost martial-looking, looking at Maureen, occasionally glancing up Instone Road, where it seemed that the people were only waiting for a chance-thrown brick to open the gates to them.

'It's not wise,' Maureen said.

They turned down a side street. This meant that when the bottom was reached they must begin the climb all over again. 'God!' thought the woman; 'when are we ever going to get there?'

'Do you think we can get back before half-past nine?'

'Certainly, if you hurry.' Maureen stepped out, saying, 'Come along, then.'

Here it was at last! Banfield Road. Mrs Fury stood panting after the long hill-climb. Banfield Road might well have been Banfield Forest, a jungle.

'Ready now?' Maureen was pulling on her arm again. One stopped for a moment to get one's breath – but it was impossible. This hand kept pulling at her arm. 'There it is!' said Maureen. 'That big house over the way. Can you see it?'

'Yes,' replied Mrs Fury, 'I can see it,' though she was actually looking back down the steep hill she had climbed.

They heard a great crash of glass, and without waiting to see what had happened, both women began to run. They had reached Banfield Road. Mrs Ragner's house made up Banfield Road. The large stone house was in utter darkness, save for the faint reflection of the red lamp that hung in the hall; the light came through the fanlight and illuminated a patch of gravel just below the step. Maureen and her mother almost ran up the long path; Mrs Kilkey pulled on the bell. In the darkness Mrs Fury clung tightly to her daughter's arm. The door opened. A tall thin man, wearing a blue sailor's jersey and rope shoes, stood looking at the two women silhouetted in the doorway. His thinning yellow hair was brushed down neatly on his head, and he wore a fringe over his forehead; his eyes were so small that for a moment the observer took him to be eyeless, until he spoke, when he opened them wide and looked at you in a most distrusting manner. As he stood looking at the two women his eyes were half-closed, he seemed to see a person more clearly in this way. His long arms were bared to the shoulder, for the sleeves of the jersey had been cut off. He had one hand on the door, one foot, its toe catching the light. His attitude was that of a person who is not at all certain as to his position. Who were these women? What did they want? It was getting late. He turned round and looked up the hall. Mrs Fury saw stitched in white thread across the back of the jersey 'Allan Line'. Obviously he had been a sailor. His weather-beaten features, and that almost knowledgeable air that one comes to associate with seafarers, were enough to stamp him as a person who has seen a good deal of the planet upon which he is placed. The tall man now asked in a wheezy voice:

'Who are you? What is it you want?' At the same time he took the liberty to lower his head and to stare impudently at Mrs Fury and her daughter.

Maureen drew back, saying, 'The name is Kilkey. I have already arranged to see Mrs Ragner.'

Was it that he didn't like them, or was it that he was merely tired of opening that door? Certainly this tall woman was different to anybody he had seen. Was it a new client? Possibly. How tall she was! He studied Mrs Fury's face for a moment. 'You had better come inside,' he remarked at length, 'though I don't suppose Mrs Ragner will see you.' He said this very slowly, as though he begrudged the utterance, as though he had sensed the urgency of the matter. Mrs Fury and Maureen stepped into the long hall. Its ceiling was low, much stained, and, like the walls, needed cleaning. As they stepped inside, the man closed the door. This was done so quickly and silently that neither woman was aware that it had closed. In addition, the man with the jersey had vanished as though spirited away into the air. Mrs Fury would have liked to sit down on the chair in the hall, but she leaned against the hat-rack instead.

'Who is that man, Maureen?' she asked.

'That's Mr Corkran,' replied Maureen. 'He lives in the top of the house. He is Mrs Ragner's handy-man. He cleans up, does all the messages, answers the door, even audits her books, and when necessary he throws troublesome people outside.'

'Here he is now,' said Mrs Fury.

The door at the end of the hall had opened, and Mr Corkran, with raised hand, was beckoning them to come up. He rarely spoke, as though a premium had been put upon his tongue. Instead, by gesture he conducted his business, and with the utmost satisfaction. His right hand was raised in the air, and the long forefinger moved backwards and forwards. 'Come up!' the finger said. When they stood before him, Mr Corkran, through his half-closed eyes, seemed to intimate that, though eminently respectable-looking – and indeed that older lady was rather striking-looking – he was not yet quite sure of them. The expression upon his lean face manifested this distrust. Suddenly he moved aside, saying, 'In there.' The door closed. He was gone again, and the two women were standing in the room. Mrs Fury caught her daughter's hand and gripped it tight.

Like the hall outside, the front sitting-room of Anna Ragner's house was long and low-ceilinged. At first glance this room seemed to convey to one the impression that it had at one time been furnished on a grand scale. Here, on the now bared walls, were great patches, from which heavy furniture had been dragged, and higher one saw where large pictures had once hung. The great chandelier in the middle of the room was now but a shadow of its former self. The room had been turned into an office and reception-room. The floor was quite bare. At the bottom end, near the window, across which hung velvet curtains, there were four rows of chairs, six in a row, and at the rear a long wooden bench. Mrs Fury and her daughter walked down the room, hardly noticed the dozen people seated on the chairs, and sat down on the wooden bench. At the top of the room, and about a chair's space from the wall, there stood a trestle-board which served as a desk. This, too, was bare of covering. On it lay a large account-book, an ink-pot, and by its side a yellow-handled pen, with a much-corroded nib. To the right lay a litter of papers, mostly letters, their envelopes keeping them company. Behind the desk sat a plump middle-aged woman. She wore a black serge dress, that served to throw up more strongly the pallor of her skin, and whenever the light above her head moved, it gave one the impression of dead ivory flushing into life. Around her neck she wore a gold chain, and at her breast was pinned a single pearl brooch. The black head of hair was done up neatly, and in it was fixed a comb whose brilliants from time to time flashed fire as they were caught by the swinging light overhead. At one moment they lay dull, at another they flashed with great brilliance. It was as if they were feeding from this light above. It swung, by reason of a strong draught that came through the partly open door just behind the woman. She made no attempt to close it, as though she were conscious that the swinging bulb threw her face into light and shadows. It pleased her to think that the score of eyes at the bottom of the room remained unsatisfied. Until one walked up to the table, she could not be seen. She was not there to see. There was only the light. Mrs Fury had been staring at this woman for some time, and Mrs Ragner had seen Mrs Fury. She had seen her in much the same way as Mr Corkran, through lowered eyes, almost as if she were sleeping. Her feet were shod in tan shoes, and rested upon a small black carpet. It kept them warm. To her left there burned an oil-stove, that filled the room with a pungent odour of paraffin oil. The large open grate was bleak and bare. Anna Ragner did not provide warmth for her clients. She provided nothing but money. Apparently the entrance of Maureen and her mother had put a spoke in the business wheel. She was like a school-mistress waiting for a pupil to settle down and be quiet. Apart from the whisperings amongst her clientele, the room was silent. She now pulled the large black account-book forward, opened it, and turned over the pages. Then she called out in a loud voice, 'Hanrahan!' Immediately the whispering ceased. Business had begun. From the group on the chairs a little woman rose and walked quickly up the room. She wore a plaid skirt, and over her head and shoulders a large black woollen shawl. One hand clutched nervously at the shawl, the other held an envelope containing money. As she reached the table she let the shawl fall from her head and lie loosely across her shoulders. She was about fifty years of age, with a small wizened face that looked as though at one time some great iron hand had caught and crushed it. Her hair was grey and sat untidily upon her head. 'Hanrahan,' Mrs Ragner said, and the little woman placed the envelope upon the table. It was dirty with finger-marks, and damp with the woman's own sweat, for she had been sitting with it tightly clutched in her hand for an hour and a quarter. Mrs Ragner emptied the coins from the envelope and counted them. She appeared to do this quickly, and without even touching the sticky dirty paper that contained them.

'This is wrong,' she said. She did not look at the woman. Mrs Ragner preferred to study her clients from a distance. She pressed on a bell. A moment later Mr Corkran appeared, again as though by magic. He might have been actually standing outside the door, waiting for this summons, so quickly did he answer it.

'Yes,' he said.

'Will you look in the other ledger, Corkran? This woman has made a mistake. The name is Hanrahan. The loan ten pounds. The principal and interest weekly is twenty-five shillings. There is only seventeen and sixpence here.' She did not raise her head at all. Mr Corkran, like her client, did not exist. Only the money existed. The door closed. Mr Corkran had gone away to 'his little office'. Meanwhile, the beshawled woman had begun to drum her red hands upon the trestle-boards. She seemed not to know that her fingers were moving, she could not hear the sounds.

'I know the amount is not right, Mrs Ragner, but I can't bring more because the matter is out of my hands. My husband would not give me more.'

'How is that?' Pause. 'Please don't make that noise, it irritates.'

'He did not like you applying to the works for the statement about his wages.'

'Oh! Didn't you understand this when the loan was contracted, or have you just forgotten the conditions covering the loan? Is your husband working?'

'Yes,' Mrs Hanrahan said.

Mr Corkran had returned. He stood looking at Mrs Hanrahan, and then said, 'The figures you mention are right. The principal weekly is seven and sixpence, the interest seventeen and sixpence. There was a default in the payment. In four weeks only the interest was received.'

'How have I forgotten this matter?' Mrs Ragner said.

'There is still three pounds of the loan to be paid,' Mr Corkran remarked.

'And the amount already paid?' asked Mrs Ragner.

'Twenty-seven pounds two and sixpence.'

'Thank you.'

Mrs Ragner turned to the woman again.

'I suppose you know that the paying-in of interest only does not help you to clear the principal.'

'But we can't do it,' Mrs Hanrahan said. 'My husband is on short time, and my eldest son is out on strike.'

'These circumstances are no part of the agreement, surely,' said Mrs Ragner. Again, as if the limbs themselves lived a life apart from the woman's body, the fingers began to drum upon the table. 'Stop that, please! Will you give me that address again?'

'Foulkes and Foulkes, Ship Repairers, Greasly Street North.'

'Thank you. That is all.'

The book closed. The seven half-crowns were swept into a leather bag that lay open on the chair beside her. Mrs Hanrahan closed the door. Mr Corkran showed the little woman to the door, and said quite cheerily, 'Good-night, Mrs Hanrahan,' but the woman made no reply to him.

*

Who was that tall woman sitting on the bench? Mrs Ragner concentrated herself once more. And the young woman beside her? Ah! she had seen the young woman before – of course! A client. Then the tall woman must be her mother. Looks rather proud, independent. What a hat she has on! She pressed the bell again; her interest in the tall woman had grown to the extent that she decided to allow her other customers to wait. She turned quickly and looked up at the man in the jersey. Would Mr Corkran tell that tall woman to come up? Yes, the one wearing the black straw hat. She followed him with her eyes as he hurried down the room. Now she saw Mrs Fury rise to her feet, and the younger woman. They were coming up the room. Oh, of course. She knew the young woman quite well. She couldn't remember the name very well. 'She's very big with child,' she was thinking as the two women approached the table. She did not look at Maureen's mother, and seemed to get some satisfaction from the woman's embarrassment. She did not have to look for it. It came instinctively. It emanated from Mrs Fury and touched her.

Maureen said, 'My name is Kilkey! I am already dealing with you. This is my mother. We came about a matter of a loan, Mrs Ragner.' Having said this, the young woman turned round and looked at her mother as though to say, 'Well! Here she is! Now begin.'

Anna Ragner leaned lazily upon the table. Her hands lay together, and now she looked at them. There was a ruby ring upon the third finger of the left hand, and two simple gold bands upon the fourth finger of her right one. Mrs Fury did not look at her hands, but straight into her face. She said to herself at once, 'A Jewess!' But she was wrong, as Maureen later told her. The woman was English, though of German descent on the father's side. Mrs Fury glanced once or twice towards the door. Maureen pressed forward against the trestle-board, as though endeavouring to lighten her weight. Her coat was open. Mrs Ragner's sleepy eyes took stock of the swollen belly, then they travelled slowly up Maureen's body until they rested on her face. 'Of course!' she said. 'Kilkey! That's it.' Then she lowered her eyes again, opened her account-book, and proceeded to forget that Mrs Fury and daughter existed. She turned the pages over, pored over a page, then repeated the process. She was looking for nothing in particular. She was only conscious that the tall woman, so proud seemingly, and so embarrassed, was still waiting. Well, that was good. That was discipline. Let the woman wait. She would attend to her in a minute. She looked under the table, and noticed with some curiosity that the tall woman was wearing odd shoes, and this curiosity was increased when the woman began to lift up, first one foot and then the other. She rested now on her right leg, now on her left. How fidgety the tall woman was! And the younger woman. She stood stock-still, her shoes gripping the floor. At last Mrs Ragner exclaimed in a hard voice:

'Kilkey! Yes. What is it?' Again she looked at Mrs Kilkey, ignoring the mother. She could attend to her later.

'It's about a loan,' began Maureen. 'My mother wishes the loan of twenty pounds.'

'Yes! I see.' This in a slow drawl. 'Yes. Have you security?'

'Oh yes. My husband will sign the promissory note.'

Mrs Fury now pressed her hands upon the table, and looking at Anna Ragner unflinchingly, exclaimed, 'I am quite honest, Mrs Ragner.'

'Ha ha!' Mrs Ragner laughed. 'Well! Well! Yes, I do not doubt it for a moment, Mrs – er – er – Fury. But it's no good as security, is it?' her smiling face, with its thick parted lips, seemed to rise in the air and almost touch Mrs Fury's own.

'I quite understand,' Mrs Fury said. She wished the floor would open up and swallow her.

'Would you mind waiting in the next room, Mrs Fury? – thank you.'

The word 'thank you' uttered so casually was like the closing of a door. Mrs Fury and Maureen, like Mrs Hanrahan, had passed outside the circle of Mrs Ragner's vision. Mr Corkran now showed them into another room. As they sat down Mrs Fury laughed. She had to laugh. She couldn't help it. She must laugh or burst.

'Mother, Mother! Please don't be so ridiculous. What is the matter with you?'

'Are you ashamed?' asked Mrs Fury.

'Never mind! Stop laughing. The whole house can hear it. Please! Please!'

'But I can't! I can't!'

The door opened again. Mr Corkran said, 'Quiet, please.'

'I hope she comes soon,' Mrs Fury said. 'It's awful – this waiting. These unending questions.' At that moment Mrs Ragner entered the room. She had disposed of her other clients. She sat down at a table. 'Sit here, please.' She looked at Maureen. 'This is your mother?'

'Yes,' Maureen said.

'Well, Mrs Fury, I shall be quite pleased to accommodate you with a loan if your daughter's husband will sign the promissory note.' She did not ask Maureen if her husband was working. She seemed to take Mr Joseph Kilkey for granted. 'Now there are one or two questions,' went on Mrs Ragner. Her fingers fidgeted with her pearl brooch, her lips had parted again, as though for a smile.

'Yes,' Mrs Fury said.

330

'What is your husband's name? Where does he work? What are his wages?' She spread out the fingers of her left hand and seemed to breathe on them.

'My husband's name is Dennis Fury. He works on the Lanton Railway as a loco-man. His wages are twenty-two and sixpence a week.' Mrs Fury looked away towards the tall bookcase that stood against the wall near the window.

'I see,' said Mrs Ragner. 'Have you any children working?' she asked.

'No,' replied Mrs Fury, 'excepting one at sea, and at the moment he is not bringing money in.' Beneath the table Mrs Fury's fingers had gripped her knees. Her eyes rested upon Mrs Ragner's pearl brooch.

Maureen now took up the conversation. It was quite all right, she said, her husband would sign the note. 'It's a question of what the repayments are and the interest.'

'Of course I should want this weekly,' said Mrs Ragner. She lay back in the chair, stretched her arms, and yawned. Mrs Fury thought she looked a very common person. 'The repayments can be at fifteen shillings or a pound per week,' began Mrs Ragner. 'One could not accept less weekly for such a sum. I am sure you will understand. Any default in payment would send the interest up. You see, I have other people wanting money. The payments must be made each Friday, promptly. I am here between five and seven, and eight and ten.' Mrs Ragner did not see clients in the daytime excepting at her small office in town, which consisted of a single room. 'I am sure,' Mrs Ragner was telling herself, 'I am sure this woman is feeling her position very keenly.' Once more she smiled at Mrs Fury, but the tall woman on the chair did not respond. Her expression was beginning to affect the lady opposite. There were some more questions to ask. She began stroking her hair, looking directly at Mrs Fury, as though putting her under a sort of final survey. This woman had a fine face, and in addition she wore a hat. And now she didn't like that face, she was even jealous of it. Nature had been unkind to her. It had given this begging woman something she could never have. No. All her clients wore shawls, this one opposite wore a hat. Well, from now on she would proceed to forget that the woman was there. She would ignore her. She turned to Maureen, leaning over the table, her hands clasped together:

'Supposing for some reason your husband's position as guarantor should fail. Have you any furniture that would cover the amount advanced to your mother, that is to say, have you furniture of the value of this loan and entirely your own? Or, on the other hand, have you valuables of any kind, Insurance Policies? You see, it is necessary to ask you these questions. I have to accept your husband's signature for the twenty pounds, or I have to refuse it. I do not wish to do that, however.'

Her figure swayed in the chair. Now the time had come to recognize that

Mrs Fury, 'a tall striking woman', was also in the room. And it seemed that the only preliminary necessary was another smile. That fixed expression, that tense passionate face, called for one. She turned her head and looked at Mrs Fury. Smiling, she asked in a low voice, 'Are you in great need of the money?'

Mrs Fury did not move. Something like a bell seemed to strike in her mind. More questions. When would it end? 'Yes,' she said, 'I am in need of it.'

'Very much?'

'Yes.' The woman placed her hands on the table and repeated her reply. 'Yes,' she said.

Maureen had suddenly placed her hands on her stomach. She felt a pain coming. She seemed to crouch in her chair. She could see neither Mrs Ragner nor her mother. She thought, 'Serve her right. She comes here and expects the money to be put into her hand right away.' Mrs Anna Ragner now leaned so close over the table that Mrs Fury drew back in her chair. It wasn't the woman's face that made her do it, only her breath. It smelt strongly of onions. 'Would it be too much if I asked why you require the money?'

'To pay bills,' Mrs Fury said. 'God!' she cried in her mind. 'Even Aunt Brigid would have been better than this.' But it was no use refusing now. She daren't. Her whole soul thrilled to the possibility of paying those Authorities.

'I see,' Mrs Ragner said.

She got up from the table. Maureen got up too. Mrs Fury remained seated. 'Will that be all? I shall give you this note. If Mr Kilkey will sign it I shall be pleased to accommodate your mother with the loan.' She saw Mrs Fury's lips begin to tremble, and made sure she was going to speak, but she only turned away towards the door, seeing nothing now save Mr Joseph Kilkey's big hand wielding a pen as long as himself, and scratching his name on the document. 'Perhaps you could bring me the note tomorrow,' Mrs Ragner said.

They had passed out of the room, and were standing in the hall. Mr Corkran had now appeared. He stood looking at them, one hand holding the banister. His half-closed eyes rested on Mrs Fury's face. They said, 'Who are you? Where have you come from? You do not belong to these parts. I would like to know more about you.' Mrs Fury, quite unconscious of these eyes staring at her, was measuring the hall with her eye and thinking that the paper which covered it was disgracefully dirty. A rather peculiar sort of house.

'Corkran,' Mrs Ragner said, 'see these people out.' She motioned to the door. Mr Corkran, in opening it, had pressed his face close to Mrs Fury's. The woman shut her eyes. 'It's a dirty night, ma'am,' Mr Corkran said. But Mrs Fury made no reply. She was putting her foot on the step when her daughter ran back up the hall and caught Mrs Ragner's arm.

'Please, Mrs Ragner,' she said, 'my mother is ill. Would it be all right if she sends my brother up for the money?' For the first time she seemed to see in this figure dressed in a serge costume a living woman.

'Provided your husband signs this note, and that your mother understands that the principal to be repaid must be at the rate of one pound per week, the interest two and sixpence. That is to say, the weekly payments will be twenty-two and sixpence. Where the principal returned is at the rate of fifteen shillings weekly, this interest will be three shillings a week.'

'Yes, yes! I understand. Thank you, Mrs Ragner.'

Maureen felt that pain again. The hall was deserted. For some reason or other Mr Corkran had struck a match and was guiding her mother down the long gravel path. Mrs Ragner had gone into her room. The young woman bent down and held her stomach, saying, 'Oh! Oh!' Then she went out into the path. She hurried down to the gate and joined her mother. The tall man passed her.

'Good-night,' he said, but Maureen did not answer him. She caught her mother's arm, saying:

'Let us hurry. It is late, Mother.'

'Maureen, you have been kind, coming all this way with me. And I don't know how to thank Joe for his kindness. I really don't.'

'We mustn't talk about it any more,' Maureen said.

Mrs Fury had been glad of the rest. Once she had actually fallen asleep, to wake up at the sound of Mrs Ragner's rings scraping the table. Well, it was over, thank heaven. She looked at her daughter and said:

'Will there be any more questions to answer?'

'No, no! No more questions to answer.' Mrs Kilkey wanted to fall down again, to grip her body, to roll from side to side; anything to appease these pains.

'Are you all right, child?'

'Yes! Here's the hill. The rest is easy.'

They did not speak to each other until they came in sight of Bellman's Theatre. A troop of soldiers were galloping along the main Harbour Road.

'How late it is, Maureen!'

'Then hurry!' Maureen cried. She was feeling desperate. She only wanted to get home, to undress, to lie on her bed. To be alone.

She felt her mother's arm glide round her waist.

'I know you're not well, Maureen. I shall never forgive myself if anything happens.'

'Oh! Don't start that, please! For God's sake! You'll get your money. Don't worry,' said Maureen. She was angry. It was the pain, and not her spirit, that had spoken.

'Here we are!' Mrs Fury said. 'King's Road.'

She felt as if a weight had been lifted from her. In a few minutes she would be in Hatfields. She hadn't minded the walk, the questions. It had been worth it. She hoped Denny would have some tea ready when she got in. This nearness to home made her feel drowsy again. She had been on her feet since seven o'clock that morning.

Maureen was almost panting now. They had reached Price Street.

'At last,' she said. 'Good-night, Mother! Don't stop. The soldiers are out, and it's not wise to stay out at this time of night. I have a key, and in any case Joe will be in.'

'Good-night.' Mrs Fury kissed her daughter. 'Good-night.' Then they went their ways, Maureen down Price Street, Mrs Fury across the road and round to Hatfields. When she reached the house she put her hand in the hole of the wall to get the key, but already the door was open. Mr Fury had placed a mat behind it.

'He must have gone to bed,' she thought. But Dennis Fury was sitting in the kitchen when she went in.

'Oh! Hello! Here you are! I thought you were never coming,' Mr Fury said. He was sitting in front of the fire, and he did not turn his head when he spoke.

'You needn't have waited for me,' she said. 'You could have gone to bed.'

'I wasn't waiting for you,' replied Mr Fury. 'I'm waiting for the lad to come in.'

'What! He isn't in! How long has he been out?' she asked. 'Denny, you ought to know it's dangerous for the boy to be out at this time of night – what with these soldiers riding about the streets ... A man was shot dead in the Instone district tonight!' She took off her coat and flung it on the sofa.

'I got some supper ready,' Mr Fury said.

She couldn't eat it now. She only wanted a cup of tea. She was worried about Peter.

'He may have gone to the show,' Mr Fury said.

'Show! What show? He hasn't money for shows.'

'How do you know? Suppose his Aunt Brigid gave him something for his pocket. Always does. Lousy old devil! There she is stuck in old Petti-grew's, and never even came round to see how you were getting on.' He poked the fire into flame.

'You left the bucket in the middle of the floor,' he went on. 'Fell over the bloody thing. Spent half an hour mopping it up.

'Peter is late, wherever he's gone! I wish you would speak to him about this. I'm going to bed.'

'Then go,' said Mrs Fury. 'Go! You must be tired, I'm sure.' She laughed, seeing him go through the kitchen door. Yes. He must be tired. Then she leaned on the table, her fingers still holding the cup. Her head dropped. She was fast asleep. The front door was pushed in, but she did not hear it. Now it closed – the mat was being straightened out in the lobby. Peter came in. He sat down and looked at his mother.

'Poor Mother!' he said. Mrs Fury was snoring softly over her tea-cup.

2

At seven o'clock in the morning Desmond Fury had got up and dressed. He had slept badly; he went below and lit the gas, then he put the kettle on and decided to shave whilst it boiled. He stood in the middle of the kitchen rubbing his huge head; he would like to have gone back to bed again, but he could not very well do that. He had a most important engagement. His mind was befogged, he had the heavy head of a man who has spent a rather bibulous night. But Desmond Fury did not drink. He was in a bad temper, he was in a desperate hurry, and he was suspicious. He felt exasperated, this suspicion had come so suddenly. What was he suspicious about? He did not really know. 'Hang it all!' he exclaimed under his breath; 'people only talk, people are really bastards!' Upstairs his wife was peacefully sleeping. He looked at his watch. H'm! He must be at the corner of Ash Walk by half-past eight in order to join three other delegates from the branch, Mr O'Hare, Mr Cruickshank, and Mr Stevens. They had to be in Garton by eleven; would they manage it? He began to shave, whistling a popular tune as he applied the lather. When he finished, the kettle was boiling madly on the stove. He made some tea, then some toast over the stove. He carried the things to the table and sat down to breakfast. In his hurry he had cut his chin. Now the blood dripped on the toast, and he flung it into the grate, cursing. He looked at the cold grate. This morning she could light the fire for a change. Usually before he went out to work he took Sheila a cup of tea. This morning it never occurred to him to do so. His thoughts were occupied with but one thing. The journey to Garton. The situation was getting worse, so it seemed to Desmond. Was all his work just running to waste? Night after night spent at the branch rooms, arranging meetings, canvassings, keeping the books, collecting the subs. Was this a waste of time? No. It was worth it. As he supped his tea he counted the days and the months and the years he had spent in the cause. Yes, sometimes he did think it was all hopeless. However, he had set his mind upon this thing and he was not going to lose his chance. By God, no! This strike was his opportunity, it might not come again. 'I'll fling the damned hammer into the Augth. To hell with it! Yes, and Vulcan Street can go to hell. For all I care, Vulcan Street can sink into the earth.' He had served his apprenticeship. Others could pick up plums, why should not he? He pushed away his cup and began pacing up and down the kitchen. He was dressed in his Sunday clothes; his blue overcoat, well brushed, lay over the arm of the chair. 'I must think about it,' he said suddenly, then sat down again. He poured out some tea, holding the cup firmly in his strong fingers.

'They want gingering up,' he said aloud. 'Yes, they want gingering up.'

There came to his mind a perfect picture of that Sunday meeting – a fiasco, a disaster. The word 'Solidarity' began to ring loudly in his ears. He laughed. Solidarity! They didn't seem to know what the word meant. What use asking for solidarity – when one half of the workers were in disagreement with the other half? Yes, they *had* been fools. Was there no way of controlling the element that hung leech-like to their tails, that caused dissension, that thought of nothing but destruction, of acts of sabotage, of looting? Of course, they had walked right into the trap. Right into the damned trap. And now they were dribbling back to work in ones and twos. The miners were standing fast – they always did – but the others, the railmen, the trammen, the factory workers – here they were slinking back to work. What was one to make of the damned business? Who was to blame for all this? He laughed aloud. A pretty question. The more he thought about it, the more urgent that journey to Garton was.

Here was a powerful limb of the city, a veritable stronghold, beginning to crack up. If they lose this strike, all his years of work were wasted. No. It won't be lost. They just daren't lose it. Throw them back years. Good God! Were they to continue building this foundation without effect, without reward? It was like trying to build a castle on sand. He wiped his mouth with his hand and got up from the table. Ten minutes to eight. Plenty of time. Now he must go upstairs. He filled a cup with tea, and suddenly thought, 'What the devil?' and poured it back into the pot. He sat down and began lacing his boots. 'Huh!' he said aloud, and rising to his feet left the kitchen. He climbed the stairs, making a great noise with his heavy boots. He stood outside the bedroom door. The house was wrapped in silence. 'Of course!' he said, turned the knob of the door and silently entered the room. He closed it, and stood looking towards the bed. Yes. In that bed lay the cause of his suspicion. Was it a joke? People tell tales, of course. Or had this business just begun since the strike? He smiled. 'I won't believe it!

I won't even harbour the thought.' He tiptoed to the bed and stood looking down at the sleeping woman. Desmond Fury, looking at his wife, now forgot Mr O'Hare and Co. They had faded out. The word 'Solidarity' no longer rang in his ears, nor the three hoots upon Mr O'Hare's motor-horn. He heard nothing but the gentle breathing of this woman. Here was something that stood outside strikes – outside of the world itself. Here in bed was something dream-like. He bent down and looked into her face. It was calm and peaceful, like that of a child. 'Yes. People are bastards! They only talk.' Smiling, he placed a hand upon her shoulder, and said, 'Wake up.'

Mrs Fury lay diagonally across the bed, her long hair billowing up like foam at one side of the pillow. Her mouth was partly open, so that he glimpsed her small teeth. One long arm hung over the side of the bed, the other rested with a sort of protecting gesture against her breast. The bed-clothes were drawn up to her neck. There was something languorous and provocative about her as she lay there, unconscious of the presence of her husband, that huge man now bent over the bed and seeming to ransack her inert body by the intensity of his gaze. He shook her gently again, saying:

'Wake up, Sheila! It's me! I'm going away now. Come! Wake up!' As she opened her eyes she saw this huge face close to her own, and she saw a mouth. She opened wide her eyes. Now that face appeared to be all mouth, and it looked as though it were ready to swallow her. When Desmond said softly, 'How nice you are!' she saw his big teeth quite clearly. He put out his tongue and licked her lips. 'How nice you are!' he repeated. The woman immediately turned over on her side, saying scoldingly:

'Please don't do that! I have asked you not to. I hate it!' She buried her face in the clothes.

'I'm going to Garton,' Desmond said. 'Have you any money? Say three shillings?' Again he put out his tongue, and as she turned over he caught her head with his right hand, drew it to his arm, and stroked her half-open mouth with his tongue.

'Don't!' the woman said. She sat up in the bed. He saw the pear-shaped breasts bulging against her night-dress. 'When are you going to Garton?' she asked. She gathered up her hair and added, 'Get me some pins from the table, please.' Her eyes rested for a moment upon his broad back as he bent over the table, searching for pins. He picked them up, and as he straightened up looked at himself in the glass.

'You look very nice,' Sheila said; 'now give me the pins.' Desmond was looking at his wife through the mirror. His own face seemed not to interest him. He handed the hairpins to his wife. 'Thank you!' Sheila said, and pinned her hair.

'I'm going in ten minutes,' Desmond said. He sat down on the bed,

337

and placed one of his large hands at the back of the woman's neck. She moved her head, saying, 'Why?' Then she pushed his hand away. Desmond put it back again, saying, 'You mustn't push it away like that, Sheila. It's mine; and I don't like it.' He smiled. The clock in the kitchen struck eight. He looked at his watch. 'Fast,' he said. He leaned nearer the woman in the bed, and allowed his eyes to rest upon her parted lips. 'On the other hand, I don't think I *shall* go,' he said quickly, and studied her face. But it registered nothing. Neither surprise nor disappointment. 'Pure imagination,' thought Desmond. The face revealed nothing. Yes. People only talked. What would they do if they couldn't talk? Go mad, he supposed.

'What will you do when I go?' he asked. 'I know it's useless asking you to come with me.'

'Of course. I wouldn't be interested,' Sheila replied. The man suddenly changed his position so that his body lay slantingly across the bed, its bulk resting upon the woman's legs. He lay on his back, his face upturned, so that it lay just beneath that of his wife. He could see her white neck, with the delicate blue veins patterning its cream-like surface. He could see her chin, her parted lips that reminded him of a flower petal. Above this he saw the delicate line of her nose. Her nostrils seemed to quiver. The breast rose and fell to her quiet breathing. He saw her eyes, and above them the forehead. She was lovely to look at.

Sheila Fury, having arranged her hair, lay back against the bed-rail. As she did so, Desmond Fury moved his head forward as though he would kiss her, but he did not. He resumed his old position, the eyes again fastening upon the upward sweep of her beauty. He liked looking at her like that. The woman put her hands behind her head. 'What do you expect I shall do?' she asked petulantly. 'Throw a fit?'.

'No!' It was almost a snarl. 'You certainly won't do that,' he said. 'You'll go out instead.'

'Well?' She stroked his face with her right hand. 'Well?' she asked.

'What else!' he growled. 'You'll go out! But that isn't the question though, is it?'

He had raised his face, and because he knew it irritated her, and because he derived a certain pleasure from it, he stuck out his tongue and stroked her chin with the tip of it. Mrs Fury smiled. She could not help it, feeling this great dog's hot tongue licking about her chin. But with the smile Desmond drew it in again, closed his mouth, and raised his head still higher. In this position he could see into his wife's nostrils. She felt his hot breath upon her face.

'Yes!' he said, suddenly sitting up. 'Yes, where do you go off to?' He caught her hands and squeezed them, drawing them down from behind her head. 'Aye,' he added. 'Aye. Where do you?'

'You know where I go. You know what I do,' she said. 'I'm honest enough to say so.'

Then he dropped her hands. He tore open her dress-body, and said sharply, 'Yes, where?'

'What about it?'

Mrs Fury did not lose her smile. She remained cool, calm, collected. She began stroking the back of her husband's hand. The hairs tickled her flesh.

'You still love me?' she said.

'Never mind that! Answer my question.' Desmond began to shout. He drew up his knees.

'I go out to see my friends,' Sheila said. She began feeling his chin, and rested her fingers on the spot of plaster. 'Darling, you've cut yourself.' She bent her head and kissed his cut chin. Her lips seemed like silk rubbing against his hard face.

'Who are these friends?' he asked heatedly.

'Who are yours?' came the reply. '*You* are never in. Your ambition has gone to your head.' She burst out laughing. 'What is the matter with you, darling?' she said softly. She leaned heavily on him.

'Nothing,' he growled. 'Nothing.' He appeared like a sulky schoolboy. His mood had changed. Thoughts sank, suspicion was clouded out. He saw only a woman lying in the bed. His woman. A body. His body.

'Then, why wait? You'll be late,' said Sheila sharply. She pouted her lips, then stuck out her tongue and made a noise at him. 'Yes! You'll be late. Mustn't be late.'

Desmond gripped her hair and drew her head down upon his knee. He pressed her face to her breast. 'I never ask you questions, do I, Sheila?'

The woman shook her head. No, he never asked her any questions.

'I never asked you where you came from. Who you were. I just took you. You know why.'

He kissed her passionately. The woman closed her eyes.

He blew gently upon her face. 'Open them,' he said. 'Open them and look at me. I never asked you about the past, did I?'

'No,' she said. She raised her arms and clasped them around his neck.

'It doesn't interest me. Understand?' He laughed, saying, 'Darling, what do you do when I go out? Please tell me. I love you! Please tell me.'

'Whilst you spend your energy at street corners?' she questioned him.

'Well?'

'I spend my time just thinking how foolish you are.' She laughed again. She knew her husband so well. She knew him inside out. Now, she was telling herself, her big dog was beginning to get annoyed. She could almost feel the rage stirring in him.

'Never mind that. I married you. You're my wife. 'Where do you go at night?'

'Nowhere.'

'Do you want me to believe that?' he growled. His face wore a sullen expression, an expression that seemed momentarily to darken the texture of his skin.

'Don't pinch my arm, you fool!' she shouted at him. What was it that she could fling against this strength? What was it she could use against this huge dog, this sullen brute? What weapon?

She raised herself up. 'What is the matter with Desmond, I wonder? I wonder? But perhaps he wants something. Is that it?' She stroked his hair with her hands.

'I only want to know where you go. People are talking. I don't want to know anything of what you used to do; only what you do now.

'Sheila!' He flung her back upon the bed and knelt over her. 'Sheila! I love you madly. Forgive me. I won't ask you any more questions. I love you madly.'

'How nice!' she said, opening her arms to him. 'How nice, big dog!'

'But no matter where you go, you're my wife, eh?' he said, grinning at her. He pulled open her gown and cupped her breasts in the hollow of his huge hand. 'Christ!' he said. 'I love you. A minute.'

She drew the gown over her head and lay back staring up at her husband.

'Yes, I love you.'

The woman drew his head down, and whispered into his ear, 'Darling — do you? But isn't my big Desmond silly asking all these questions? Isn't he a funny boy? Come, you know what you want. Are you still ambitious, darling?' Her mouth tickled his ear, but he did not feel it. He heard nothing but the breathing of the woman on the bed. The spout of desire sucked up his thought. His blood sang. Feeling his body grow limp, she said softly, 'Get up! You know you'll be late.'

The man raised his head. Already she was pushing him away. 'You love me, don't you, Sheila?' he said. The expression upon his face was bovine, his thick lips were parted, he breathed heavily.

'Stay!' she said. 'The cause of the workers is going to your head.'

She knew he would rise from the bed, and go downstairs, and hurry out. She knew this as well as she knew her own finger.

Desmond Fury had got off the bed. He stood in a corner of the room dressing.

'I'm going now,' he said. He walked back to the bed, leaned down and said, 'Kiss me.' There was something bestial and cunning about his grin. His grin said, 'You are mine. I love you. When I come back your body will still be here. It will always be here. That maddening, everlasting flesh.'

Below in the kitchen the clock struck the half-hour.

'I'll be late!' he shouted, and rushed from the room. His heavy tread made the stairs creak. He drew on his overcoat. He felt happy, exhilarated. Then he laughed. 'Ha ha! People are only bastards. They're only jealous.' That experience had been ecstatic. It clouded out those tormenting thoughts of his. She still loved him. Ah! Now he could conquer everything. What had been worrying him? A little boy wearing a nice clean collar. 'Huh!' he said. 'Huh!' and began flinging some things into his cheap attaché-case. No! The wise thing was never to ask questions. It was silly. He loved her too much, and by God! if he kept asking them she might go away. He mustn't. People only talk. Nothing mattered but that he loved her – now – his wife. His slow ponderous mind harboured suspicion no longer. Let her go out! It only harboured a dread fear that she might cease to love him. 'To hell with people!' he cried in his mind. Why set in motion the wheel of the past? He had taken her from the strand in Ireland because he loved her. No. He didn't care if she came from Hell itself. And she would be there when he got back. He laughed as he closed his attaché-case. 'People are bastards,' he muttered. 'But they're only jealous of her loveliness, that's all. Yes, she is lovely to me, and, by Christ, I shall kill anybody who comes between us.' The door banged. He hurried down Vulcan Street whistling loudly. Mrs Fury could hear him as he went down the street. She lay back in the bed, and covered her head with the clothes. She began to cry. In the night she had been dreaming of her father, and another man who wore a beard. She fell asleep stroking this beard. Number seven Vulcan Street was wrapped in silence.

'Will I be in time?' Desmond was asking himself as he turned the corner into King's Road. He looked at his gun-metal watch again. Mustn't be late. Mustn't disappoint them. That would upset his plans. He hoped they would get Williams down to Garton. That was very important indeed. Already he could see himself on the Executive Committee, saying good-bye to duties at the branch rooms. Desmond was smiling. There was an optimistic spring in his very step. 'You are a happy man,' his body appeared to say. Funny that, seeing these soldiers returning to barracks from a night patrol of the streets, he should think of that hammer. 'Ah! I'll fling that to hell,' he said. He had now reached Ash Walk, in which stood the chapel of St Sebastian. Ash Walk was a small street, containing but a dozen houses, St Sebastian's taking up the opposite side. Well, the car wasn't there. He had better wait. Impossible for them to have been and gone. Mr O'Hare was no such punctual gentleman. As he came slowly down the Walk two old women came out of the chapel and passed him. He knew them. They turned their heads away. Desmond sat down on a doorstep. They wouldn't be long now. He looked across at the sleepy-looking chapel, with its comical steeple. Once on a time he had rung the Angelus in that belfry. But that was a long time ago. He had given up all that sort of thing. Fairy tales. He smiled. He folded his arms and leaned back against the door. His eyes followed the line of the steeple until they reached the weather-vane. But his thoughts had gone further. They had passed over the roof, dragging Desmond Fury in their wake. He could see himself a small boy at school, singing in the choir, going collecting with Father Coghlan. 'Ah!' he thought. 'What times those were!' His father was at sea. He used to go to the shipping office once a month with his mother. He had wanted to stay on at school. But that couldn't be. His mother had stood by him, but his father was adamant. It couldn't be done. Then he had wanted to go to his grandfather in Ireland, and again to Ohio to his uncle. Childish ambitions. Silly. Yes, he remembered those times. 'I liked those times,' Desmond thought. 'We were happy.' The family income was twelve and sixpence a week. He remembered leaving school and going to work in a timber yard for six shillings a week, hours six to six. He bought his first fishing-rod. Maureen went to work in a draper's shop. The family income increased to twenty-three and sixpence a week. 'Happy times,' he was thinking. Suddenly, for no reason whatever, his father had deserted his ship and gone tramping in a large continent called the United States of America. He remembered exactly just how his mother had looked when at the shipping office they told her there was no money for her. He used to read the letters sent to his father.

'Dear Denny, – We are very happy. We get your two pounds ten each month. It's wonderful. I only hope the work isn't too hard.'

'And his father's reply, 'Not a bit – but the grub's lousy.'

'Yes, that tramp in the States,' Desmond was thinking, 'that tramp was the beginning of it all.' Maureen went to work at a jute works. He, Desmond, had got sacked from his job. They were living on five and fourpence a week, but they were happy. His mother went out to work. It helped. Not a line from Mr Fury. And she had always kept them fed, clothed them. Kept them clean. Ah! through all that time his mother had never lost faith. Never lost faith! It shone brightly over the house. And John was coming along. 'Poor Mother!' Desmond said. Then a letter had come out of the blue. It was from Mr Fury. He was working in a rigging gang in one of the big Ohio yards. Not a penny came with the letter. 'I'm on the ice,' he wrote. Desmond rose to his feet, and began walking up and down the walk. On the ice. Aye, his father had been a real harum-scarum and no mistake.

They had come through. Mother had sailed them along splendidly. The man gave a sigh, and his large brutal face took on an expression of tenderness and compassion, as though the thought itself had patterned it. 'Poor Mother!' he said. He thought of his sister, of her awakening nature, and he thought of the man at the jute factory. 'The Beast' they called him. 'Well, that was over and done with. 'Dear me!' he exclaimed aloud. 'Dear me! How one's mind can carry one away!' He looked down the Walk. Not a soul in sight. 'Aye! And here we are!' He spoke aloud, as though addressing the chapel. 'Here we are! Still in the same old place.' Why had he come out so early? Now he came to think of it, he needn't have hurried. Peter came to his mind. 'How right I was! Mother backed a loser once again.' He had expected to see a rosy-cheeked boy wearing a nice Eton collar, and he had discovered a man almost as big as himself. 'Well, well, he must be getting very fond of me all of a sudden. I must get him to bring my rods from Hatfields. Yes. We must go fishing together again.' He walked to the top of the Walk and looked up and down the road. Were they coming? Nearly nine o'clock. Surely they hadn't been and left? If they were to be at Garton by noon they would have to get a move on, always assuming that Mr O'Hare's bone-rattler would be equal to the task. Mr O'Hare's broken-down old motor had materialized out of the subs from funds. The branch was growing. They decided to buy this derelict car and use it in the furtherance of their work. The only person capable of driving it was Mr O'Hare. His mind became occupied now by the events of the past few days. The possibilities were that this stoppage might break up all of a sudden. 'They want gingering up,' he said to himself, 'gingering up.' But where on earth was the car? Had they cancelled the plans? Had the motor broken down? He became worried. Nine o'clock. He sat down on the step again, pulled a note-book and pencil from his pocket and began to write.

Father Richard Moynihan was fifty-five years of age. Tall, thin, with steel-blue eyes and thin grey hair, he looked exactly what he was, a priest of God. The lean nervous face marked the ascetic in him, whilst the smiling blue eyes informed all who came in contact with him that though a priest of God, he had a sense of humour. He had been parish priest at St Sebastian's for nineteen years. The Furys were already installed in number three Hatfields when he came over from Ireland. He had christened Peter, confirmed John, and married Maureen. He had a warm regard for Mrs Fury, whom he looked upon as a clean, honest, and hard-working woman. Father Moynihan's congregation numbered some eight hundred souls. They were made up entirely of working people, with here and there a shopkeeper or merchant thrown in. By his very nature he had soon created a bond of sympathy and confidence between his parishioners and himself. Whilst looking after their spiritual welfare, he never forgot that they were human beings. He visited them in their homes at least once every three months. He interested himself in their welfare. He took part in their pleasure and hobbies. He organized outings for them, arranging everything himself. He had built a new hall for the young men of his congregation, and had put a billiard-table and games into it. He appointed Joseph Kilkey to look after it. He never lost touch with the people. Already he was arranging an outing to take place in July for the old members of his flock. At the moment he was worried. The strike had put a brake upon his enthusiasm, for nearly all the men in his congregation were out. Day after day the wives of these men came to him; he was kept busy day and night listening, advising. Only this morning Mr Ferris, who looked after the St Vincent de Paul funds, had come to tell him that they were exhausted. 'Then something must be done, Ferris,' Father Moynihan said. 'I'll see to it.'

He was now sitting in his study, leaning over his desk, his long fingers pressed against his cheeks. Before him lay a blank sheet of paper and a pencil. The intensity with which he looked at this paper might imply that he momentarily expected some words to write themselves upon it as though by magic. The priest was in fact studying a problem. He had been studying it for some months. When the strike came he gave it up. He turned a key in his brain and said, 'Well, there! Some other time I will attend to you.' Here was the problem again. And not his hand, but Miss Brigid Mangan's hand, had turned that key and let it out again. That visit from Aunt Brigid had been a little disturbing. Peter Fury, a boy for whom he still had a high regard, in spite of his misdeed, he, the last child of the family, was going about with Desmond Fury's wife. Was this true? He closed his eyes, and the whole interview came clearly before him. He could see Miss Mangan, expansive of bosom and wearing a grey dress, standing in the vestry, her face with its heavy flush, no longer smiling, but deadly serious. He smiled, thinking how she would still call him Richard. He had known Miss Mangan before his ordination. A nice problem, and one that whetted his appetite. 'You must promise me, Brigid, that you will breathe a word to *nobody*, not even your sister.'

'Yes, Richard,' Miss Mangan had replied, and he had respected her sincerity. But would she keep silent? Surely Mrs Fury had enough to do.

'I shall see to this,' he had said.

'A pretty problem,' he said to himself, and opening his eyes, stared at the paper again. He rather prided himself not only upon his ability to solve problems, but also upon his unerring eye in spotting them. He picked up the pencil and wrote upon the piece of paper, 'Downey'. Then he uttered the word aloud, repeating it as though by sheer repetition he could disentangle it from a certain web in his mind. If he kept this name before him long enough, something would be bound to happen. Nobody had been more surprised than Father Moynihan when Desmond Fury had brought this woman back from Ireland. And from what little he had heard of the event he had endeavoured to erect some sort of mental scaffolding upon which he might peg from time to time such ideas as occurred to him. But the surprise was not so much in Desmond's marrying (he had never thought the man would commit himself to matrimony), no, the surprise lay in the fact that Desmond Fury had married the woman without any knowledge of her past, her home, or her people. To have met an obviously distressed woman on the banks of a river where he was angling one hot July morning, and to have accepted her there and then, no questions asked, only served to deepen the mystery. It seemed destined that he should fish in that river, that she should be there, that he should pack up his belongings there and then and return to Gelton. A man of Father Moynihan's ability was not going to accept a situation like that without a strong pinch of salt. What had been the reason? What force had driven the thing to its conclusion? Was it that the attraction was purely physical? Was it his sheer physicalness that had been the key to the bargain? He had seen this woman once. A rather striking creature. But nobody was going to tell him, Father Richard Moynihan, that this union was ideal, even though its consummation might be founded upon a psychological theory. The more he thought over the matter, the more whetted became his appetite. He had known Mrs Fury's eldest son long enough to discover that he was a simple, honest man. He did not credit him with any intellect, beyond the ordinary common sense that told a man his right hand from his left. He even smiled at his radicalism. He would be foolish, however, to pretend that the man's marriage outside the chapel was no surprise to him. It *was*, considering the woman who had reared him. It was an action that had caused the first rift in the Fury household.

He now asked himself a question. He looked at the sheet of paper. 'What has most surprised me?' He tapped his pencil sharply upon the oak desk, as if he were summonsing the answer to appear at once. Yes! What was it? He leaned further over the desk. Was it the difference in types? She, at one glance, seemed to stamp her mental superiority over her husband. Was it the mere fact that Desmond had married at all? No. It was the obscurity. That was it. This woman had just arrived from nowhere. They were now installed in Vulcan Street, their lives wrapped in the same mystery. But – and Father Moynihan tapped again with his pencil. But now they both went out. They were never in. And they were hardly ever seen together. He knew what kept the man out. But what was *she* up to? He questioned Mrs Fury one day. 'I know nothing about this woman,' Mrs Fury replied, 'except that her name is Downey.' All that meant nothing. Ireland was full of Downeys. Whichever way he looked at it, it seemed to mirror a fascination. He had only seen Desmond once since his marriage. Desmond and his wife had been standing waiting for a car. He retained a perfect picture of her in his mind. There was something about her that had struck him very forcibly. She had the forehead and eyes of a striking, even noble woman. But the lower part of the face seemed to mock that which crowned it. It was as though Nature had played a trick upon this woman. She was two persons in one, as if Nature had given her two forces, one which climbed and one which descended. Which of these two sides of Sheila Fury's nature was destined to conquer? That was another problem which he, Father Moynihan, had registered in his mind. Some time he would sit down and ponder upon the matter. At the moment it could wait. It interested him, psychologically and physiologically. He looked at the name Downey which he had written on the half-sheet of paper. The interest now was sociological. What did this woman do with herself? Where did she go at night? Who were her friends? Perhaps she had relations in the country. Was her continuous absence from the house a demonstration of her husband's utter blindness? No, he would not say that. Was it merely a demonstration of his simplicity? To ask no questions? To say nothing at all? What, then, was the basis of their union? Were they happy? He leaned back in his chair. Desmond was here, there, and everywhere. Yes, he had ambitions. Where did they lie? Father Moynihan's inquisitiveness would have set him making some tacit inquiries, but Vulcan Street was a stronghold of people holding different religious views to his. Only this had caused him to abandon the project. But his mind remained full of the subject, and Aunt Brigid's visit had shot it to the surface again. He got up from the desk. Half-past nine. Now he must go. From eight to half-past eight Father Moynihan said his Office, then he had breakfast, unless he was saying the nine o'clock Mass. At half-past he started out on his usual round of visits. Each day he took a different street, as each Sunday of the month he took a different street for the collection. He pushed the chair to the wall, left the room, and stood for a moment in the vestry corridor, his finger to his chin, as though indulging in a rapid mental survey of the morning's work. He went up to his bedroom and changed. He rang the bell, and stood waiting for the housekeeper. 'Tell Father Heraghty I shall join him at lunch at half-past one.' Then he went down to the vestry, picked up his hat and stick and went out. As he walked slowly down the gravel path that led to the road he paused to look at the desolate appearance that winter's hand had given the garden. The trees were bare, the sparse, sourish winter grass looked bleak and uninviting.

From the middle of this path Father Moynihan had a good survey of the Walk. He saw a tall man hurrying down it. He was carrying an attaché-case, and his big overcoat was buttoned up to the neck. The priest walked to the gate, turned for a moment to glance at the garden from the other side of the railings, then passed into the road. As he did so, the man with the attaché-case seemed to increase his pace. Then the sound of a motor came to his ears.

'Ah!' exclaimed Father Moynihan, 'the very man.' He stepped quietly in front of the hurrying man. There was no doubt whatever in his mind. He completely blocked his path.

'Ah, Mr Fury!' he exclaimed with a jolly laugh. 'Here you are at last!' He laughed again. He had consolidated himself there. That half-hour's meditation seemed to have fortified him. The very way in which he said 'at last', left no room for doubt. 'Well!' he said. 'Well, Desmond, where are you hurrying to?' He offered the man his hand, and the other replied by keeping his own in his pocket. 'At least,' thought Father Moynihan, 'we know where we are.' Desmond Fury, wont at one time in his life to raise his cap to a priest, now showed by a quick movement of the hand, and pulling his cap down tighter upon his head, that the raising of it to a priest was a courtesy in which he no longer indulged. Whilst he stared at the priest, two different expressions seemed to fight for a place upon his big face. He wanted to be bold, but he felt a little bewildered. The appearance was too sudden. Besides, he had never expected it. The result was an expression that revealed at once to Father Moynihan the man's embarrassment. Desmond Fury shifted first one leg, then the other. He wanted to be off. He was in a great hurry. The obvious sang-froid of the priest only served to increase his desire to be off. Apart from that, the car, which must be Mr O'Hare's, was tooting again. Round the corner of Ash Walk, and abutting on to the King's Road, there stood a motor, a very old and dilapidated-looking affair, in which sat three men. Father Moynihan could hear its noisy engine quite distinctly. To Desmond it was an urgent summons, to the other merely a slight irritant. The priest looked Desmond up and down. Most extraordinary, that on this very morning when he had been studying that little problem, and reviewing in retrospect Miss Mangan's visit, one of the people of the problem should now stand in front of him. Desmond Fury kept opening and shutting his hands, digging them into his pocket and pulling them out again. He reminded Father Moynihan of the great inn-keeper at Fermonteil whose name was Raoul. 'Excuse me' (the 'Father' had been left out). 'Excuse me,' Desmond said, 'I'm in a hurry.' Yes, he is in a hurry. He is very embarrassed, and the priest's laughing eyes seemed to reply, 'Yes, one can see that, but I, Father Moynihan, am not.'

'Tell me,' said the priest; he paused, looked away for a moment, as if beckoning a thought that had suddenly taken flight. 'Do not be afraid. I am not going to ask you if you have been to your Easter duties this year, my good man. Oh no! I have enough sense to know just what kind of gentleman I am talking to.' He smiled at Desmond, and placed his hand on his shoulder. 'No. That is truly a matter for your own conscience. I do not consider myself your spiritual guide any longer. You are no child. You are a grown man. I have had too much experience of the world, Mr Fury.' He laughed. These laughs irritated Desmond. He felt as if somebody were pricking him with a pin. He made a move, but Father Moynihan moved also, and the expression upon his face seemed to hold Desmond there, as if his two feet were rooted in Ash Walk. Desmond Fury thought, 'This fellow intends to hold me up. What the hell does he want?' He connected the priest's sudden appearance with his mother. But he was wrong.

'I'm going to Garton,' he said quickly, in the manner of a person who simply *must* be off, whose whole life depends upon his immediate departure for Garton.

'How is your wife?' This question was asked coldly, as though the person had hated to ask the question. The smile had vanished.

'Quite well,' replied Desmond. 'I don't know what you really want, but can't you see I have to go now?' He moved forward, his hands seemed to sweep the air. The motor-horn was tooting madly. 'I wish to say that I am in a hurry.'

'I only wanted to ask you a question,' said Father Moynihan. He laughed again. 'Surely those spoliated people from the abyss can spare you a few minutes. I haven't stopped you for a joke. Tell me, have you any sense of responsibility? And further, understand that your mother is not behind this. Your mother has enough to look after. You say you are going to Garton. What are you leaving behind?'

'I don't understand you.'

'Does your wife know?'

'You leave that woman out of it,' Desmond said rudely.

Father Moynihan felt that now the barriers were down.

'Does your wife know?' he asked again, in a casual, indifferent manner.

'Of course she knows! What do you take me for? A fool? And anyhow, what business is it of yours?' He pushed past the priest to one side.

'Don't be so surly,' the priest said. He caught Desmond's arm. 'I hope, when the millennium comes, that you will instruct the saved in the principles that you lack. That is to say, courtesy and respect. I have no wish to pry into your affairs. I have something else to do. There are no two points upon which we, as men, could agree. I am not interested in your socialism, or your wife, or your home, or yourself. Having thus established my disinterestedness, may I repeat my question? Have you any sense of responsibility?' He looked at Desmond's large hands, now pulling at the pockets of his coat. There was another hoot from the motor. Father Moynihan turned his head in the direction of the sound. 'Who is blowing that horn?' he asked.

'How inquisitive this fellow is!' thought Desmond.

'My friends are waiting for me,' he replied. He would like to have shot out one of his long arms and pushed the priest to one side, but staring at the imperturbable figure only weakened his resolve, Father Moynihan could disarm him with a single glance. The priest said to himself, 'This fellow is beside himself with rage.' He began banging his walking-stick against his leg. Once the horn tooted, a veritable fusillade that seemed to say, 'We are going ... NOW.' At the same time a man appeared round the corner, waving his hand. He had recognized Desmond Fury talking to the priest.

'What is it you want to know?' It was almost a growl that came from Desmond.

'Nothing, beyond answering of my question,' replied Father Moynihan. His imperturbability was utterly beyond Desmond Fury.

'Then why hold up traffic?' said Desmond. He had raised his voice. He had grown red in the face. 'Coming!' he shouted to the man at the bottom of the street.

'Yes, of course I have. I have to be at Garton by noon,' said Desmond. 'Do you think I'm a fool?'

'I don't really know,' said Father Moynihan, 'except, of course, that people are talking.'

'That's enough!' Desmond Fury shot up his big hand and flicked his fingers in the other's face. 'I don't listen to tales.' Then he ran down the street.

Father Moynihan stood looking after the running figure. 'A boor,' he said. 'A boor.' Yes indeed, he was that huge inn-keeper of Fermonteil to the life. He dusted his coat down with his hands and continued on his way down the Walk. 'One would get nothing from *him*.' That was obvious. Well, he would see. He began swinging his cane as he increased his pace. At the bottom of the Walk he stopped to look up and down the road. He then turned into Price Street. At thirty-five he stopped and knocked at the door. There was no answer. He knocked again. Mrs Kilkey herself came to the door. She threw it wide at once.

'Why, Father Moynihan!' she said. 'You are about early today. Please come in.'

'I wanted to see Joseph. I hope he is in.' He sat down on the chair by the dresser.

'Of course. Yes.' She called up the stairs, 'Joe! Joe! Here's the priest to see you.'

'Coming! Coming right away,' called down Mr Kilkey. Maureen sat down.

'Well, Maureen,' said the priest.

'Here he is now,' she said.

3

'You were late,' the little red-faced man said as he moved up and made room for Desmond Fury in the car. This second-hand and worn-looking motor now began to creak under the weight of the four men. Desmond's fifteen stone and a half was indeed something to creak under.

'Late! Blast it!' he said, as he made himself comfortable. 'I was early. If you had arrived here at half-past eight as I did, it would have saved me a lot of trouble.'

'Who was the fellow you were arguing with?' asked Mr O'Hare, whose straggling moustaches seemed to mock the serious expression upon his lantern-jawed face as he made a frantic endeavour to get the car going.

'A black crow,' Desmond said. Then he shouted 'Wait,' and jumped out of the car. 'Thank you, Stevens,' he said. He put one hand on the bonnet, and with the other gave a quick and vigorous turn to the starting-handle. The engine started again. The noise it now made sounded like a large number of nuts and screws being rattled in a tool-box. A cloud of smoke gushed out from the exhaust-pipe. When Desmond seated himself, the smoke ceased to gush, as though he had sat directly upon its source and quashed it. After a series of rattling sounds, as though the engine's heart were summoning up its best efforts, the car bounded forward, with another cloud of thick bluish smoke gushing from the exhaust. Mr O'Hare, with both hands on the wheel, now concentrated upon the task in hand. They should be at Garton by noon, providing nothing happened. But at a time when *everything* was happening in the city the possibility of a smooth passage seemed somewhat remote. The three men at the back of the car, in spite of much crowding, had managed to make themselves comfortable. Mr O'Hare remained alone and aloof, his long greying moustaches blowing in the breeze. There was a vacant seat by him, but in spite of the crowding in the back it had been decided for some strange reason or other to leave it so. Perhaps they expected to pick somebody up. Mr Stevens and Co. were in the back of the car for conference. They had taken note-books from their pockets. Desmond was vigorously sharpening his pencil. He had forgotten his tussle with Father Moynihan, and he had forgotten Sheila. Even Peter's peculiar manner on the night of his visit was a thing of the past. There was only the matter in hand, and this, by its very nature, clouded all other things out. Mr Stevens began to talk. He had a volubility of which even Mr Williams might be envious, and accompanied his speeches with certain dramatic mannerisms that not only pleased his audience but pleased Mr Charles Stevens himself. He was about five foot ten, so thin as to look almost haggard, though, in spite of this, he had a cheery nature. He was a checker at a goods station. He was happily married and had eight children. He began making wavy lines with his pencil as he spoke.

'The trouble is,' he said, 'and it's been the trouble all along – the trouble is, our organization is simply lousy. These bloody Capitalists, however, are so well organized that they can enlist the aid of the armed forces, to say nothing of the police. And who are the armed forces? Our own lads, of course! Our own bloody lads. The miners are bloody stickers, and what we have to do when we get to Garton is to ginger the bastards up.'

'I think it's a failure,' commented Mr O'Hare from the front.

Desmond joined in: 'Our real enemies are our own people. Never mind these bloody Capitalists. Our own people. My own father is just a damned scab. He would go to work this minute if he got his chance. You don't have to go any further than the street you live in. You'll see there, and quite plainly too, the very things that break up and ruin these strikes. It seems to me that when we call our men out, we leave out of all consideration another class of people.'

'What class?' asked Mr Stevens.

'Our class,' said Desmond, 'the tail end of it. These bastards who go looting and give the police and the soldiery their opportunity. Look at that Sunday afternoon meeting! It was completely ruined by a section of the crowd who are not interested in anything but getting something for nothing. So they loot and go mad, and fill their guts. "Let's have a smack at the bastards," they say, and at the first move of the police they show them their behinds. If one could get hold of them, if one could control them, it would be all right. The difficulty is that you can't get the workers to keep together. If I know anything, I've been speaking myself hoarse, winter and summer, at the meetings of the Party, in committee, in the streets, everywhere, in fact, and I know that is the obstacle. And again, this blasted religion is used. The authorities know their cue all right. The man next door to me belongs to a lodge. He's a working man, a nice decent chap, but he won't join a Union. Won't join anything. No. He bangs a big drum in some band or other, and that's all he cares about. And the women are no different. You can't get them to hold an opinion two minutes on end, and they do just as much looting as anybody. If this strike collapses, then only one thing has ruined it, the workers themselves. Oh yes' – Desmond became quite caustic – 'oh yes. They come forward and take the benefits we have won for them.' He lighted a cigarette and blew out a cloud of smoke with great violence, as though he were blowing away all these obstacles that kept the workers tied to the wheel.

'They want edicatin', that's what they want, edicatin'. Fury's quite right. I live in Hally Street,' interrupted Mr Cruickshank, a very little man dressed in clerical grey, with a horse-like face covered with freckles. Mr Cruickshank was a plater. 'I live in this street where nobody but dock labourers live. A few are in the Federation, but most of them are in nothing. If they have any brains, then they just piss them against the walls of the pubs. That's all I got to say. They want edicatin'.' He sat up suddenly and burst into a violent fit of coughing. He took out a dirty white handkerchief and wiped the bloody spume from his mouth.

'What are we going to do? What are the plans?' asked Desmond. 'Did they get that hall?' The car stopped so suddenly that all three men catapulted forward, and three pairs of hands grasped the woodwork. What was the matter?

'Nothing,' replied Mr O'Hare. He had taken his hands from the wheel and had turned round. 'Nothing,' he said, stroking first one moustache, then the other with his long fingers.

'Now we're stopped,' said Mr Cruickshank, 'I think I'll nip over yonder for a pump.' He rose to his feet. Desmond Fury made way for him.

'Me too!' said Mr Stevens. The two men hurried across to the urinal.

'Fury's quite right, you know,' remarked Mr Cruickshank, feeling much relieved.

'Yes. Have you met his missus?' asked Mr Stevens. His eyes narrowed as they ran up the white-tiled wall. Mr Cruickshank remarked that he hadn't, whereon Mr Stevens demonstrated his ability to glide from one subject to another. The position was serious, but he could enjoy a joke. 'I saw her once, and by God! she's a corker. And a bottom ...' he sighed, as though the instantaneous picture had afforded him much pleasure.

'Fancy!' Mr Cruickshank said. They hurried back to the waiting car. The car moved off. Desmond suggested they should lower the hood.

'There is no time for that,' announced Mr O'Hare. He increased his speed.

The position, then, was as follows. Desmond lay back on his seat. They must hold as many meetings as they could in the street. If the owner of the hall had suddenly changed his mind, that could not be helped. Were the dockers standing fast? Yes. The dockers were standing fast. Who, then, were the most unreliable? The railwaymen. Precisely. In some stations and yards they were dribbling back to work in ones and twos, also the tramwaymen were going in. Hang it! They had better have a general meeting. Where was Williams? Where was White? They had better get them. In Arnton!

Then they must get them. What was to be done? The three heads moved as one. They were thinking deeply. 'Nobody on my section has scabbed, anyhow,' Desmond said. He began tapping his pencil on his thumb-nail. Mr Stevens began to speak, but Desmond was now so lost in thought that he did not hear him. The events of the past three weeks began to pass kaleidoscopically across his mind. First the rumour, then the coming out. More rumours, ebbing and flowing over their heads for a week. Then the decision to support the miners. The mass meeting calling for solidarity. Its breaking up. When Desmond thought of that fiasco, he could have cried. Nothing worse could have happened. It played right into the bosses' hands. It seemed to have been created specially for the occasion. Yes, there was no doubt about it whatever. The workers had spoiled it themselves. After all the careful planning, the warning, even the pleading with them, 'Stand fast! Stand fast!' If they only had! But they hadn't. They had gone past themselves. Could he blame them? That was a hard question to answer. Well, they had sailed nicely into the trap. They had simply gone mad. Shops looted, factories turned upside down, even food destroyed. A mad riot. The police were equal to the occasion. The Capitalists were ready for them. Hundreds of batoned people were still in hospital. A state almost of siege existed. One could not put one's head out of the house after ten. 'Yes,' he thought, 'the position is very serious.' He looked at his companions. Mr Stevens was beginning to nod his head, whilst Mr Cruickshank contented himself with staring at Mr O'Hare's broad back, and occasionally at his flying moustaches. 'No doubt about it,' thought Desmond, 'the workers are mugs, bloody mugs. They could hold the town, aye, even the country, if they liked.' It wasn't that they didn't like – no, he knew that well enough – it was because they didn't know how. If he wasn't speaking gospel truth, then he would kick his own behind. What was he to do? Well, what he meant to do was to get out. Yes. Get out of that damned length. Almost time he got promotion. He wouldn't ask for it either. No. He would just take it. Push himself up higher and higher, and then – Exby. Yes. Exby. No more hammers, no more lengths. In brief, no more dirty work. Others had done it. He would do the same. If he didn't grasp his chance now, it might not come again. Yes, somebody else could call meetings, somebody else could read the minutes, and ring that damned bell too. He had rung it into ears long enough. Into ears that seemed to Desmond Fury to be stuffed, blocked up. Obstinate, ignorant clods who closed their ears to everything. He shook Mr Stevens by the arm.

'Hello!'

'Will we get back tonight?' Desmond asked.

Mr Stevens rubbed his eyes, and then with his left hand his chin, covered with three days' stubble. 'Hope so!' he said, looking at his companion on the left, but Mr Cruickshank was deeply absorbed in endeavouring to bite off a ragged bit of stubborn thumb-nail. He had his thumb-tip in his mouth and was pulling at the nail with his teeth.

Without moving his big thumb, he managed to say, 'I don't think so.'

'Oh, blast it! We can't be at Garton all day,' said Desmond.

'What's your bag doing here, then?' called Mr O'Hare from the front seat.

'Yes, I know,' replied Desmond, 'but now I think I must get back.'

'We may not get back until Saturday,' announced Mr Stevens. He removed his bowler hat and scratched his head. Then he began twiddling it between his fingers.

'What! Stop this car!' said Desmond.

'We're almost at Garton,' said Mr O'Hare. The engine rattled suddenly, as though the glad news had served to make it throw every ounce of energy behind the wheels.

The car was now on the outskirts of Garton. Garton was another industrial centre. It was one of Arnton's limbs. Seventy miles beyond Garton lay the mining country, now derelict, but Mr O'Hare and Co. were not proceeding so far. Their business lay in Garton. The streets were crowded with people. Mr O'Hare slackened the speed. Groups of people stared at this broken-down car, the first of any vehicular traffic they had seen for nearly three weeks. It became obvious to them at once that the four gentlemen in it, workers dressed in their Sunday best, must be Federation officials of some kind or other. A cheer was raised. Somebody flung a stone. Desmond suggested that the hood should be lowered and the car stopped. They ought to speak there and then. 'Impossible!' said Mr Cruickshank. 'apart from that, I'm hungry.' Desmond, looking at this wizened little man, now smiled and said to himself, 'Quite true! Even to look at you makes me hungry myself.' Mr Stevens also was against such a thing. They must get to the branch rooms and meet the other delegates. No doubt some sort of meal would be available. The car moved on. As they progressed the crowds increased. They turned round the corner where the Halton Arms stood, and opposite which there stood a large shop, empty save for the huge poster in bright red lettering which announced to an indifferent populace that 'Christ would save the world', under which somebody had written in chalk a foul word of derision. Mr O'Hare as he turned this corner actually smiled. It was the first time he had smiled that day. He was feeling highly pleased, not only with himself, but with the car that had peformed its task, if not feat, splendidly. It pulled up, its wheels gripping the kerbstone as though it meant to stay there for ever. As the four men climbed out, its stature

354

seemed to increase with the removal of the fifty-odd stone it had carried for thirty-three miles.

The rooms of the Federation, number thirty-one Branch, were situated over a tailor's shop, now empty, its owner having gone bankrupt. Already the committee were considering the renting of this shop for the coming municipal elections. Desmond, followed by Mr O'Hare, Mr Stevens, and Mr Cruickshank, now climbed the stairs. The branch rented two rooms; one was used for the meetings, the other was used for a dining-room. The door leading to the dining-room was now open, and as the party passed into the committee-room they saw a stout little man at the table. He was eating bread and cheese, and from a blue mug he occasionally supped beer. Desmond Fury did not know this man. He had never seen him. Mr Johns, however, for that was the gentleman's name, knew not only Desmond Fury, but almost every man in the Federation. Mr Johns was a crane-driver at one of the large northern goods wharfs. He worked devotedly for the cause. All his spare time was taken up by street meetings, by personal canvassing. He had a large family of nine children. His wife was paralysed. He was a man of cheery disposition, he was generous of spirit, he believed in Socialism. It was his ideal. He lived and worked for it. Unlike many more in the movement, he was unobtrusive, he worked quietly, he stole nobody's thunder. He had no personal ambitions. He wanted to see all workers' conditions improved. He was now having dinner. He had just come in from the tram terminus, where he had been speaking. He knew better than any man what the conditions were. He knew what caused strikes. He knew the fear and terror that they spread, and he knew the secret silent suffering that went on all the while. Everybody liked Mr Johns. He was a member of the Council at Garton. Even his worst political opponents liked him. He pushed away the remains of his meal and took out his pipe. He could hear a lot of talking going on in the next room. He had better go in as soon as he had taken a fill for his pipe. He did not recognize the voice. Desmond Fury was speaking. Suddenly the voice ceased, and he heard chairs being moved about. The door opened and Mr O'Hare and Mr Stevens came in.

'Hello, Johns!' said O'Hare. 'How are things?' He sat down. Mr Johns shook hands with Mr Stevens. Desmond Fury came in with Mr Cruickshank. Mr Johns' eyes met Mr Fury's. 'We don't know each other,' they seemed to say. Mr Cruickshank seemed to shiver in his clothes, standing head and shoulders below Desmond Fury, who had now gone up to the table where Mr Johns sat. Mr O'Hare and Mr Stevens were engaged in high conversation. Mr Cruickshank sat down to burst into another fit of coughing. Desmond Fury looked at Mr Johns. 'Who is the fellow?' he thought. He smilingly offered his hand to Mr Johns. 'Who are you?' he asked. 'I don't know you.'

Mr Cruickshank's handkerchief came out again, and he wiped his mouth. 'He's an honest man,' said Mr Cruickshank, and he looked directly into Desmond's eyes. 'He's an honest man, Fury.'

CHAPTER XIV

I

Anthony Mangan, sitting belted in his chair, seemed to be taking an unusual interest in Mrs Fury. She had brought in from the front parlour two chairs belonging to the parlour suite. These were now standing in the middle of the kitchen floor. The kitchen table had been pushed back to the wall. One of the chairs had been varnished. Mrs Fury, kneeling on the floor, was busy varnishing the other. Every now and then she stopped to loosen the brush, which stuck to her fingers. Her face had two varnish smears on it. It was half-past four and the kitchen was growing dark. She must light the gas. The old man never took his eyes off the woman, he seemed to follow her every movement. For the past hour the house had resounded to hammerings, for Peter had been busy fixing up the bookshelf in his room, which had collapsed that morning from the rottenness of the wall and the weight of books upon it.

He came downstairs and passed through the kitchen. He did not see his mother kneeling at her task. He did not see Mr Mangan, the silent witness of the procedure. He saw something else – a sort of beckoning light in the distance which drew him on. Mrs Fury did not even raise her head as her son passed through. Peter was glad of this, and yet her silence made him pause at the back kitchen door. Funny that she had never even asked him where he was going. He glanced back at the kneeling woman, then, lifting the latch, he went out. It did not matter, anyhow. That light was beckoning to him. He didn't want any tea, he wasn't hungry. He closed the door and went down the yard. Then he passed into the entry and began to run, and did not stop until he had reached the main King's Road. Here he hesitated, looking up and down the road. His manner was furtive, he seemed undecided. First he walked in the direction of town, then he retraced his steps, stopping again outside a boot-shop, now closed and boarded up, for its windows had been smashed in. Whichever way he turned he saw this light. Filled with a sudden resolution, he made straight for number seven Vulcan Street. Well, she said he could come, and they were going to go out together. He did not stop again until he reached his brother's door. He raised his hand to knock, but again hesitated. '*I am not looking,*' a voice seemed to whisper into his ears. '*I am not even interested in your fugitive passions, my boy. As*

I told you before, I am only interested in sociology, and in the various phenomena that human activities throw up. Ha ha!' He could hear this harsh croaking laugh ringing in his ears. Peter looked up and down the street. Then he knocked at the door and waited. There was no reply. He looked up at the bedroom window, then through the parlour one. Yes, there was a light in the kitchen. He could see its reflection in the lobby. He knocked again. 'Surely, surely,' he was saying, when to his surprise Mr George Postlethwaite put his head out of the door of number nine, and looking at the boy said, 'Hello, there! Desmond's away. Aye. He's been away two days now. Up beyond Garton.'

Peter replied, 'Hello, George! Thanks. I ...' he almost said, 'I know all about it,' but saved himself in time. The door in front of him opened. The person must have been standing behind this door, for Peter could not see anybody. The door opened slowly and a woman's voice said, 'Come in.'

Peter entered the lobby. The door closed. George Postlethwaite continued to stare.

In the dark lobby he touched the woman's hand. This was the light, this was the beckoning light that wiped out the vision of his kneeling mother, of his father reading upstairs, of his ugly grandfather. This light swept everything away.

'Hello!' he said, and touched Sheila's arm.

'Come,' Mrs Fury said. They went into the kitchen. She drew out a chair for Peter, saying, 'Wait, I shan't be long.'

Then she went upstairs. Peter sat straddled upon the chair. He looked round the kitchen. Yes. There was the draught-board that he had upset, there the table against which her body had leaned, there the patch on the floor where she had broken the mantle, and she had leaned heavily against him as she put a fresh one on. He felt a strange sensation as he recalled the pressure of her body and how he had felt its bulk. As he closed his eyes, the whole thing came to him again, crystal-clear. Sheila's feigned surprise on that first morning he had called. He had divined it at once. And of course he had said, 'Is Desmond in?' And the woman, laughing, had replied, 'He isn't in.'

She knew that too. She knew he had come to see her. At first he had been shy and embarrassed. He remembered how he had first walked along the dark lobby to emerge into the lighted kitchen and see her standing under the gas. He had felt like a person who is walking barefooted along a lengthy carpet in the darkness, whose knowledgeable feet have told him that further and still further there is more carpet. Then suddenly he steps into a pool of icy water. Yes, that was how he had felt at first. He had sat straddled upon this same chair, content to sit looking at her, caring not whether she

358

ever spoke, as long as she remained there and he could sit looking at her. She was wearing a long velvet dress, her throat was bare, and her mouth was partly open. The camera had lied to him, for he saw that her mouth was bigger than it appeared to him on the photo which he had torn from the card. She had a broad forehead, and her large eyes were set well apart. But the mouth seemed to upset the harmony of the features. She had small teeth and her lips were red and full. He remembered studying them, thinking of his sister's coarseness. No. Maureen was not like that. Perhaps the jute factory had made her so. Sheila Fury showed up Maureen more clearly than a microscope. Once Sheila had leaned towards him, saying, 'You are funny.' And then she had asked him why he left school in Ireland. Yes, she had caught him out. He hadn't known what to say. Just the same old thing, 'I didn't like it. All a cod.' A screen for his dirtiness. Yes, a screen for his dirtiness. They had had breakfast together.

'I like you,' he had said, and Sheila had smiled. He sat upright in the chair and exclaimed aloud, 'And I do like her.' He put his hand to his mouth. *'Why not love me? I am so lonely. Have you got my card? Do come and see me some time!'* Then he burst out laughing.

Sheila Fury came into the kitchen. She was dressed for going out. Her lips had framed a question, but she said nothing, just stood at the expression on Peter's face.

'What are you laughing at?' she asked.

'Nothing. Nothing, Sheila,' replied Peter, and he waved his hand in the air, as though he were casting out from his mind the vision of his strange companion on that memorable Monday night. He got up from the chair and smoothed his coat and trousers with his hand. 'Ready,' he said. 'Which way?' He stood, hands in his pockets, looking at the woman. 'This way,' she said quickly, and they went out by the rear entrance. The entry was narrow, so that they pressed against each other as they walked. When they came out into the street, they increased their pace, slowing down to a rambling gait when they reached the main road. They were obviously two persons wholly undecided what to do or where to go. They stopped again, and in the dark shelter of a shop doorway Sheila asked, 'Does your mother know you have been to see me' – she paused – 'three times?' She did not look at him, but away up the street.

'No. That doesn't matter, anyhow.'

'I know where we'll go,' Sheila said. 'Come.' She caught Peter's arm. He felt the softness of her arm against his own, and her action was significant. If he had not been sure before, he was sure now. He was certain. It was the breaking down of the barrier. Shyness and embarrassment fled from him. He kept looking up into her face.

359

'Where are we going?' he asked, not caring whether she replied or not, not caring what she said. That arm that had crept round the door was through his own. Yes, he even had some of those threads from the black bodice in his pocket.

'To have tea,' Sheila replied. They passed four streets without speaking. Sheila Fury then said, 'We turn this way.' She intended to go to a café situated at the bottom of Circular Road, but now as they came in sight of it she realized at once that they ought to have gone the other way. A crowd of people was standing at the top of the road. It was a silent crowd, and it seemed to be waiting for something. Peter had seen it too.

'There must be something up here,' he said. 'Shall we go and see?'

'Yes.' The woman's voice seemed to come from far away. 'Yes,' she repeated. 'We ought to have gone the other way. It's difficult to get through crowds like this.' As they came up to its fringe, the whole body of people seemed to turn their heads. They were looking down the Circular Road.

'It's soldiers!' cried Peter. He pulled roughly on Sheila's arm. 'Soldiers!' he said.

The crowd were waiting to see these mounted troops pass by. A detachment of thirty Hussars were coming up the hill at a walking pace, headed by an officer. Sheila and Peter stood a little away from the road, and waited. Just beside Sheila a young man was standing. He was about nineteen years of age. He was in his shirt-sleeves. Hearing the noise outside, he had come out of the house. The soldiers were drawing nearer. The crowd began talking loudly. Here they were – the Hussars, who two nights ago had galloped off to Mile Hill to break up a disturbance that had broken out between two sets of strikers and their families. A religious feud. Yes. Here they were – the fellows who had gone forward with fixed bayonets and dragged people from their beds, who had shot dead an elderly man for no other reason than that he had been standing in the line of fire. The angry murmur rose in the air.

'Here's the bastards!' shouted a voice, as the mounted men drew nearer.

'Yes! Here they are, the dirty swines!'

Sheila held on to Peter's arm. 'Yes, here they are!' shouted a woman's voice in the crowd. 'Give them a gutful, the swines!'

'I'm going,' announced Sheila, but Peter held on, saying, 'Wait, Sheila! Please wait!' The crowd had begun to move forward in a body towards the troops, who had now reached the top of Circular Road. As if from nowhere, police appeared and began to drive them back towards the kerb. 'Please wait!' Peter said.

There could be no doubt about the ugly temper of this crowd. They pressed forward. 'Halt!' cried the officer. The troop halted. 'About turn!' he cried out, his eyes surveying the crowd. Hands were raised. 'Give it to the bastards!' From an upraised arm a glass beer-bottle flew. It struck a horse, that reared, almost throwing clear its rider. At the same time the crowd rushed forward on the smashing of the glass. The troops had levelled their rifles.

'Stand back!' The crowd pressed on.

'Fire!' shouted the officer, now red in the face. 'Ugh!' the crowd stood cowed. They made a wild rush for the kerb.

Peter screamed. 'Sheila! Sheila! Oh Christ Almighty!' The young man on her left had fallen. From his breast there rose a veritable fountain of blood. 'Sheila!' screamed Peter. The woman had collapsed in his arms. Then she fell. She fell, seeing nothing, hearing nothing, conscious only that her face was wet. The boy's hands were trembling. He knelt down, wiping her face. He could hear somebody shouting, 'Stand back! This woman is dead. Stand back!' Peter began shaking, his hand dropped the bloody handkerchief. 'Is she hurt? She has fainted.' A great noise flooded Peter's ears. Then somebody was saying, 'Fainted! It's blood-splashes.' And the speaker was looking into the boy's white face. 'Are you with her?'

'Yes, yes!' His eyes were full of tears. 'Yes! Is she dead? Please!' He began shouting, wildly, incoherently, but the same calm voice now said:

'It's only the splash of blood from that man. See!' And he pointed to the dead youth, now covered by a soldier's overcoat.

'Take the woman home.'

Sheila Fury had opened her eyes and looked into Peter's face.

'Let me help you,' the man said. Somebody was holding water to her mouth. 'There! There!' A space had been cleared. Everybody seemed to be yelling, shouting, swearing.

'Take her out of this,' the quiet-voiced man said.

'Are you all right, Sheila?' Peter stammered. He trembled violently, holding her hand.

'There, go now.' The boy put his arm round the woman and they pushed their way through the crowd. A lump had come into his throat, he could not speak. Through dark passages, through entries, he hurried with Sheila. Yes, they had better go back. 'Home!' Peter was saying. 'Home!'

They entered the house by the back door. Peter could not drive out that flood of sound in his ears. He saw Sheila sit down on the sofa and rest her head against the wall. The fire burned low in the grate. He said, 'Shall I light the gas?' but the woman said, 'Sit down.' He sat down by her side. Sheila seemed unable to speak. Her face was pale. She breathed quickly, holding her hands to her side. The boy looked into her face.

'Oh! The blood!' Sheila said under her breath. 'The blood!' Peter did not hear her. He was deaf, and he was blind. He did not see the fountain of blood spurt from the youth's chest, he heard no cries. He saw only this face in front of him. This face had looked out at him from its welter of blood, and he wanted to fling himself upon her body. He gripped Sheila Fury's hands.

'Sheila!' he said. 'Oh, Sheila!' Her face was expressionless. 'Sheila!' cried Peter, pressing her hands. Then he leaned forward and kissed her. She sat motionless.

'Did you not see me behind you? You are *callous, my boy. Your mother cannot come. She is chained to some heavy wood. She cannot come. But I shall not spoil your dish. Ha ha!'* Sheila Fury leaned towards the boy.

'Peter! Peter!'

'Are you all right, Sheila? Please tell me!' His hand were trembling.

'What is the matter with you?' she asked faintly. 'What is the matter?'

'Nothing! Nothing!'

He buried his head on her breast. He could feel the woman's heart beating against his head. He burst out laughing now.

'I thought somebody was shouting into my ear,' he said.

'Please!' the woman said.

She rose to her feet, and drew her hand slowly across her forehead.

That incident in the Circular Road had had a peculiar effect upon her.

'Well!' she said.

Then she pushed him away with her hand. He stood, watching her go, and as she closed the kitchen door she slid her white hand up and down.

She went upstairs. The boy stood looking at the door. Then he sat down on the chair and laid his head on the table.

'What is the matter with me?' The feelings that ran riot in him were strange and terrifying.

'You are a young fool,' said Professor Titmouse.

Yes, that was who it was. That was the voice always raging in his ears. That was the person he had dreamed about.

'It is just that she cannot help it. Go up. She is waiting for you. Do not hesitate.' And, as though the man in the deerstalker hat had lifted him from the chair, Peter rose to his feet, opened the kitchen door and went upstairs.

Professor Titmouse seemed to tramp behind him.

'Here vanity has flowered anew, my young friend. Her fastidiousness will excite you tremendously. I should call this social cowardice, but then, you are not interested. You are too young. Besides, that chained woman can wait . . . Horrid? . . . Life holds out many delicious flavours!'

The black satin rag seemed to wave in front of Peter's face.

'Yes! That was a phenomenon. I myself was there. That bright fountain of blood, my friend, was a gleaming sword. But whose hand will hold it? Away! Up you

362

go! She is waiting for you. You tickle her vanity. You stir her latent maternal feelings, and of course that Black Bull is at present in Garton.' The man seemed to look into the boy's face. *'I wish I could share your feast, but all that is too late. It is a good feast, a rare feast. It shall blot everything out. And now, good-bye.'* Peter stood outside the door of the bedroom. 'Come in.' He opened the door, closed it silently behind him and stood looking down at the woman. Sheila Fury was naked. She was lying on her side in the bed. *'Go forward. Why hesitate?'* croaked the voice in his ears. He walked up to the bed and stood looking down at the woman. Yes, this was the light, the bright beckoning light. *'A single flash. No more,'* croaked the voice. *'That soft flesh is not soft. It is steel. Many a man breaks his head against it.'* The boy knelt down at the side of the bed and looked into the woman's face. Where and when had he knelt like this before? Ah yes! When he received his first Communion.

'Well!' said the woman, laughing. 'You are a funny boy. Come here.'

He climbed on to her bed, and gripped her arms. 'Sheila!' he said. 'I love you.'

'How much? How much do you love me?' She turned over and lay looking at him. He only smiled, the while his eyes roamed over her naked body. Her very skin seemed to shimmer in the candle-light, whilst her hair, which she had let down, clouded the pillow.

'Are you afraid?'

'No.'

'Not even of Desmond?'

'No.'

'Come, then,' she said, and drew his head down upon her breast. She kissed him. Her blood quickened. It pleased her to see this boy's head upon her breast. She liked the feel of it, as she liked the feeling of his hot and clumsy hands. The candle burned low, gave a final splutter, then went out. This sudden darkness seemed to accentuate their heavy breathing, just as the air around them seemed to throb to the desires that filled and held them fast, flesh to flesh.

Peter felt as though rivulets of flame were sweeping across his body. He felt the woman's hot breath upon his face. And he was actually floating in the air, bathed in the light of her body. Suddenly he began to sing. His clear alto filled the darkened room.

'Ssh!' the woman whispered in his ear. 'Ssh! . . .' But he only sang louder. 'Ssh!' she said. 'Tell me what you are singing.' She crushed his face against her own so that their eyes seemed to meet, and Peter was gazing as he sang, gazing into two deep pools of living water. He stopped singing.

'I was singing a song about an Irish King,' he whispered in her ear. He

363

heard her laugh, and it seemed to violate the silence of the room, that now harboured the lovely tones of Peter's voice.

'But I couldn't understand you.'

'I was singing it in Erse,' Peter said. He lay limp across her body. He felt as though some great weight had been lifted from his own, and those pools of water into which he rapturously gazed scintillated, seemed to whirl round in one luminous circle. Against this vision there sounded from below the sharp chiming of a clock.

'Get up now,' Sheila said. 'Get up.' The clock had struck in the kitchen. But Peter did not move. He lay heavily upon her; seeming to draw, as though by a peculiar magnetic power, a sort of vapour from those depthless pools, a vapour that clouded all about him. It was as if he had been drugged. The woman pushed him away and sat up. For the first time he seemed to see her smiling face. Before, it had been nothing but those dancing waters. Yes, she was smiling, and he had turned away his head. 'Look at me,' she called to him. 'Peter! Look at me.' But he only turned his head further away from her. She caught his arm and pulled him towards her. 'What is the matter, darling?' she said. 'What is the matter? You are crying.'

'It's nothing!' He shouted this, wiping his eyes with the back of his hand. 'Nothing.' He felt like a small child now, ashamed and angry in her presence. He experienced a feeling of revulsion. He could almost feel, with a sudden fear, that old sliminess creeping upon him. 'Nothing,' he said.

This time the woman did not answer him. She was dressing quickly. 'Light a candle, Peter,' she said. 'I can't see.'

He struck a match and began to search about for a candle. He found a stub on the mantelshelf and lighted it. 'What time is it?' he asked, and crossing the room, stood behind her, watching her tie up her hair. She smiled at him through the mirror. Again he was looking at her heavy mouth, that mouth which seemed to everlastingly mock the upper part of her face. Where did she come from? He didn't care. Who was she? He didn't want to know. Where did she go every night, and why did she always sit by herself on the shore? He didn't know, and he didn't care. He placed his arms on her shoulders and drew her head back. 'Kiss me,' he said.

But the woman only put out her tongue. 'Funny boy!' she said.

Now he felt hurt. He said, 'I'm not a boy, Sheila. They all think that.' He relaxed his hold on her.

'Who are all?' She placed a comb in her hair. 'Who are all?' she asked again.

'Everybody.'

'Oh!' She turned round and flung her arms about him. 'Well, you are funny,' she said. Peter laughed.

They went downstairs. Sheila was going out again. Where was she going? He didn't care. He was happy now. He watched her make up the fire. He wanted to say, 'When is Desmond coming home?' Instead, he merely said, 'Can I come again, Sheila?'

The woman went up to him, and placing her fingers under his chin said, 'Not when Desmond is here.'

'Well, then.' He looked appealingly at her, and now she realized why he had come. Her intuition told her with a flash.

'We will go out on Sunday. Will that do?'

'Yes,' he said. 'On Sunday, on Sunday.'

'Unless Desmond stays in.'

'That doesn't matter,' he shouted. He caught her in his arms. 'I love you, Sheila,' he whispered in her ear. Then he shouted again, 'All that doesn't matter.'

'Be quiet! What is the matter with you? Don't you know there are people next door?' She put her hand over his mouth.

'I don't care!' he shouted through her spread fingers.

'If you love me, you must,' she said quietly. 'Now, you had better go.' She stood by the door, as if waiting for him to go. For nearly a minute they were silent, the woman leaning against the dresser, the boy standing under the gas-bracket. There was the door, and there was Sheila. And beyond it there was the street, and darkness. He didn't want to go. He didn't want to lose sight of her for a moment. He made a quick rush to the dresser.

'Let me go with you, please.'

'Are you mad?' She pushed him away, and going to the kitchen door said, 'Please go. This way. Do you love me or not?'

'Yes, yes. But can't I go with you?'

She pushed Peter towards the door. 'Peter, go now. Only until Sunday. Please!' The situation seemed to have taken a ludicrous turn. She burst into a fit of laughter. Then she gave his mouth a fleeting kiss. 'Sunday. At the bottom of Dacre Road. About half-past six.'

'You promise?'

'Yes.'

'Honest and truly?'

'Yes, funny boy. Now go.' She watched his tall form go down the yard. As soon as the back door closed she went down the yard and bolted it. Then she returned to the kitchen, turned low the gas, and went out by the front door. This she closed silently behind her, by turning the key in the lock. A moment later she had been swallowed up in the darkness.

Outside the back door Peter was still standing. He felt as though his feet were rooted to the ground. He shivered with cold, the darkness only appeared to clothe him, for that experience in the bedroom seemed to have left him naked. This curious feeling of being unclothed grew stronger as he walked, so that once he actually felt his body in order to make sure about it. He stood for a while in the bottom of the entry. Then he went along and into the street. And now he didn't care. He knew she loved him. She must love him to have done that. He leaned against a wall, and caressed its cold surface with his hot hand. 'Damn!' he cried. 'Damn!' *'Well, it has only begun, my boy, it has only begun. It's a long journey, and educating all the way. You will go again and again. She can't help it. But come and see me some time too. In your presence I experienced the most extraordinary feelings. I . . .'* Peter started to run, but the voice sounded louder in his ears. *'What did I tell you? That flashing light, eh? It clouds out everything. Ha ha! Yes, it clouds out everything. I am tremendously interested in social rottenness, my boy. Yes, run! Run for your life. You haven't the lovely light to hide behind now. And that fountain of blood keeps bursting up, taking fire, that burning sword. Have you learned nothing from that act, my boy? Ah! . . .'*

At the corner of Hatfields Peter stopped. *'There is no need to run, my friend, she is in no hurry. Besides, she is very busy. Yes, she is varnishing those chairs.'* Peter took out his handkerchief and wiped his face. He was sweating. 'Damn!' he cried into the darkness. It was as though this man had come alive, had emerged from the web of his dream, and now rode him pick-a-back, driving him on. 'Go away!' he cried. 'God! Go away. Leave me alone.'

'Ha ha! The first reaction is always one of revulsion, my boy. But you'll overcome that. I still look askance at your callousness, but you are young. Your ideals are stinking in the heap. No matter, you can still laugh, and that Black Bull will bellow later on. Ah, my boy, you have been educated the wrong way round, but as I say, you are young.'

Peter remained standing at the bottom of Hatfields. He heard the tramway clock strike. 'Shall I go in?' he was thinking. 'No.' He walked back down Hatfields, and turning into Price Street, walked slowly up, stopping to look at the darkened number thirty-five. Maureen didn't matter anyhow. He didn't care if he never saw her any more. And Sheila was nicer. His sister was hardened, coarse, and she was having a baby. He laughed, thinking, 'Soon I shall be an uncle.' Somebody had stopped in front of him. 'Hello!' the man said.

The boy looked up. At first he could not distinguish the figure in the darkened street. Then the man laughed. Why! Of course! It was George Postlethwaite. Dapper little George Postlethwaite with whom he had used to play 'tally-ho'. Like Peter, George was bareheaded.

'Well, did you find anybody in?' asked George. He noticed that Peter was trembling.

'Yes, oh yes. I – I'm just going home. Which way are you going?'

George turned his head, and pointing with his finger said, 'I'm just going down to the stables to see my horse. Doin' anything? Would you like to come?'

'Oh yes!' Peter said. 'I'll go. Which way?'

They moved off, George looking into the other's face, saying, 'Aye, laddie, it seems a long time since my old man chased you up Hatfields with that brass rod of his. And those games of "tally-ho". Ever remember them?'

Peter's face became wreathed in smiles. 'Yes,' he said. 'It only seems like yesterday, doesn't it?'

'Yes,' said George. 'And aye, but you've grown a rare wopper, Peter my lad. D'you like being home again?' He adjusted the chain that hung over his shoulders.

'Not much,' Peter said.

They turned into Ash Walk, and walked its length without speaking. Then George said, 'Just at the back of those houses.' He slackened his pace. 'How's yer dad an' yer mam? All right?'

'Yes, thanks – oh, listen!'

George laughed. 'Aye, the old un knows when I'm coming. You bet. It's been a bit of a mucksweat what with this 'ere strike and those bloody balm-pots going off the top. Silly sods! Here we are.'

They stopped in front of a big red gate, and George took from his pocket a large key, to which was attached a square of wood. 'Got any matches?' He unlocked the gate. Peter followed him into the yard. He searched for matches, but George shouted, as from far away, 'Got mine – it's all right.' He struck a match, and the yard revealed itself for a moment. Then the match went out. Mr Postlethwaite was unlocking another door. 'Here we are,' he said. Peter followed him inside. The smell of hay and horse-stole filled the air. In the darkness he could not see the great roan mare, but he sensed her, he could almost swear he was touching her. George lighted a hurricane lamp and hung it on the nail. 'There she is! Hey, Nabob, old girl.' The mare was lying down, but as George approached her she struggled to her feet. 'Isn't she great?' he said. The roan had turned round and put her head against George's shoulder. Her large gentle eyes looked out at Peter, questioning, as though she were asking, 'Who are you?' 'Come over,' George said. Peter stroked her head and then her nose. He could feel her warmth against his body. 'Best roan mare in the country,' George said. 'Mr Dimmock, by gosh, he isn't half proud of her. Taking prizes all the year round, and gettin' any price for her foals. You're a beauty, aren't you, Nabob?' Nabob's ears seemed to dance about on her head. 'Get that stool, laddie, and sit down,' said George. 'Just behind you.' Peter sat down on the stool. He looked at

George standing there, the roan's head resting over his shoulder. There was something in the attitude of both man and beast that touched him. The lamp shone down upon them. 'Aye,' said George, as he began stroking the roan again. 'Ever you want a real friend, Peter, you just take a horse. Better'n any human being. And I know. Me and Nabob's been together for years now. Haven't we, Nabob?' The mare put her mouth to George's head, and began rubbing his hair, and there seemed something mischievous in those large eyes. Nabob was indeed enjoying herself. She was having an enforced holiday. Outside in the big yard stood the lorry she pulled, its wheels rusted from recent rains. George let go his hold of the mare and went up and looked into her manger. 'This holiday isn't doing you much good, old girl,' he said. 'You're getting too fat.' He drew some hay down from the loft, and put it into the rack.

'Does she stay here all the time?' asked Peter.

'Oh aye,' replied George, 'but every morning I take her out, not in the shafts, of course. I take her out for a little walk. I come down twice a day.' He had turned his back on the mare, who was now feeding contentedly. He drew a box from the wall and sat down on it, so that the light from the lantern shone full in his face. 'What a funny little fellow George is!' Peter was thinking, as he looked into Mr Postlethwaite's weather-beaten face. One had only to look at him once to realize that George was a contented man who had no responsibilities and no worries, beyond Anne at home and the roan. 'Why don't you come and see us some time?' began George. 'Mother was only saying the other day, "What a size Peter Fury's got!" You must come and see us. You know where I live, anyhow. Next to Desmond. Aye, he's a mad un, your brother is.' He began drumming on the box with his stubby fingers.

Peter sat up. 'How d'you mean, he's a mad un?' he asked.

'Well, look at him. Out all the while. Gone to Garton now. Speaking there. Aye, every day he is out. And when he's working on the length he goes out in the evening. But I never did see anything in all this blather about socialism. Workers are only bloody mugs, I know, but when a fellow starts going off his onion about socialism, well ... ever heard your brother speaking?'

'No,' said Peter. He made himself comfortable on the stool.

'And his missus is never in, either. Funny pair. Still, when a fellow goes off like that, what can you expect any woman to do? I used to hear them arguing the fat at night. Sometimes Anne and me couldn't get to sleep for it.'

'Where does she go to, then?' asked Peter, and there was no doubt whatever by the way he looked at Mr Postlethwaite that he expected to hear

368

something which might whet his curiosity. But George was non-committal.

'Don't know,' he said. 'People talk, of course. I heard somebody say the other day that she goes to a house in town every night. Reckon your Desmond picked up a tartar when he married her. Your mam was in a way. Aye, no mistake about it. They had a fine row. I was at Mother's that day. You never heard anything like it. Carried on like billy-o. I like your mam,' he went on. 'And Mother does too, but somehow they always steer clear of each other. Suppose you know why?'

'Yes,' Peter replied, 'but I think it's silly.'

'Must go now,' said George. He got up from the box and kicked it back to the wall. He went up to the mare, who seemed to have sensed his imminent departure, for she had turned her head round and looked at Peter. Peter was taking George away. Peter was taking this man away who came twice a day to see her.

'Is she all right there?' asked Peter, as they went out into the yard.

'Right as rain. There's nine o'clock struck. I was late this evening.'

Peter looked back at the now darkened stable, then he followed George across the yard. He helped him slide back the big red gate. Having locked it, they set off towards home.

'Wouldn't like to come up to the house?' George said. 'Only nine o'clock.'

Peter hesitated. Mention of the house made him think of Sheila again. 'I don't know, it's late, really.' No, *she* wouldn't be there. He would go if *she* was there. 'I had better go home,' he said, and he thought, 'This man knows. This funny little man knows all about me.' They parted company at the corner of Hatfields.

'Good-night. You come up and see us some time, laddie,' said George. 'Ta-ta now.' He left Peter standing at the corner of the dark and deserted street.

Now that George had gone, the boy became aware of his loneliness. He felt isolated. He had better go home. Yes, he could have his supper and go to bed. He could lie quietly in bed and think of all that had happened. Tonight he could fall asleep thinking of Sheila. Thinking of her would cast out his loneliness. Yes, he was lonely. Nowhere to go. His father always growled, and his mother ignored him. His sister wouldn't see him, and Desmond – yes, Desmond didn't like him either. He felt certain of that. When he went to the billiard-room nobody spoke to him, because they had heard about his failure at the college. Yes, he hated them. But on Sunday, on Sunday at half-past six ... He began running up the back entry. Outside the door he stopped. 'Yes – on Sunday. I shall see her on Sunday.' And nothing else mattered.

When he entered the kitchen he was surprised to find the gas turned low, and the high-backed chair was empty. He went to the foot of the stairs and called, 'Anybody in?' The echo of his own voice seemed to float down from the darkened landing. 'H'm!' he exclaimed. 'Funny nobody here.' He turned up the gas, then went into the back kitchen. He was feeling hungry. In a brown mug he found a quarter loaf, which he cut in slices. He looked for butter, but this time his search behind the pans was unsuccessful. He put some marmalade on the bread and went back to the kitchen. There was tea in the pot. In the Fury household this pot, like the proverbial Russian samovar, was never empty. He sat down and had his supper. When he had finished, he went to the foot of the stairs and called again, 'Anybody in?'

She had knelt there varnishing those chairs. And she hadn't seen him. And the other night when he had come in she had been sitting at the table, fast asleep, her fingers holding the cup. His mother had been fast asleep. He had been able to look fully into her face, and he had seen the lines about her eyes, which, when closed, seemed to reveal even more clearly those lines which at first he only noticed upon her forehead. Perhaps the lines crept down from the forehead and so spread about one's face. And the fringes of her black hair touched the white of the table. As he sat looking at the deserted table it seemed she had come to it, and was now sitting there. He could even hear her breathing. He took off his shoes and tiptoed across the kitchen. He looked at the table again. Then he went upstairs. Outside his room door he paused. They must all be out. He turned the knob and entered the room. It was pitch dark. The window was open from the bottom. He put his shoes on the floor. Then he sat down on the bed. 'Oh!' he said, and jumped up again. His father was sitting on that bed.

Mr Fury, dressed in shirt and drawers, had heard his son come in. He had got out of bed and stolen quickly into Peter's room. He would wait for him. He sat quietly in the darkness, hardly breathing. He had heard his son call up the stairs, 'Anybody in?' but he had not made any reply. He was content to sit as quietly as a mouse and wait there. He would catch the boy out. He would surprise him. 'Light the lamp,' he said. Peter struck a match and looked at his father. 'Light it,' his father said, but he only dropped the match in his confusion. He struck another one and lit the lamp. He placed it on the table so that his father's face was framed in the light and his own was in the shadow. 'Sit down here,' Mr Fury said, 'I want to talk to you.' How frail his father looked in shirt and drawers! A little old man. He sat down by his side. The man folded his arms and looked across at the bare wall. 'What's up with you?'

'Nothing, Dad,' replied Peter. 'Nothing.' And his eyes, falling upon the tattooed star upon his father's wrist, remained there. 'Nothing, Dad,' he repeated, with downcast head. His head began to throb, and he felt once more that burning, scalding sensation in his blood, as there loomed up for a moment a picture of Sheila Fury. Sheila Fury standing by the door and saying 'Go. Go now.'

His father shouted, 'What is the matter with you lately? You go about half goopy. And you don't eat anything. No, by God! you turn your damned nose up at what your mother and I are glad to eat.' He leaned his elbow on the table and rested his head upon it. Now his face was in shadow, and the light had flung his shadow upon the bare wall, giving Mr Fury a monstrous head and long lean body. And the figure trembled on the wall. Suddenly he jumped up from the bed saying, 'Wait a minute! Don't you turn in yet. I'll be back in a second.' He turned towards the door.

'Mother's out,' Peter said, but his father did not hear him. Mr Fury banged the door and now stood on the dark landing. What did it matter? He would still go down; she had gone out, but what of that? Dennis Fury held firmly in his mind a picture of his wife. He would go down. He would see her again, sitting at the table looking at her father. Yes, he would see her, the boy's mother, just for a moment. He only wanted to hold this picture of her secure, then he would go back upstairs again. Peter stood listening. Mr Fury was creeping downstairs as though he might wake his wife, who an hour ago had gone out to see her daughter.

A minute later Mr Fury came back. 'Well!' he said to himself. 'That's strange! I never heard her go out.' He entered the room and banged the door. He was like a man who has made a sudden decision, and now wishes to sit down and reflect upon it. He closed the door. Peter was sitting on the bed. He did not see his father standing in front of him, he heard no door shut, no bolt shot back. He did not even hear his grandfather's loud snores that seemed to waft under his door. He saw nothing but this woman. She filled the room, he could put out his hand and touch her, he could smell her body, feel her breath. To Peter the very air in the room was charged with her spirit, her loveliness, her half-open mouth seemed to tremble in the air, to laugh at him, to smile, to speak. He wanted to burst out singing, to smash down those dismal walls with his voice, he wanted to burst.

'What is wrong with you? You were out all day. Where were you?' Mr Fury was shaking his son by the shoulder. 'Wake up! You're falling asleep.' He gripped his son by the hair, and forcing his head back made to speak again, but now he dropped his hand and drew back. 'Have you been drinking?'

Peter burst out laughing. He continued to laugh, his whole frame seemed to shake beneath this prolonged laughter.

'But you're sweating,' his father said, and he watched his son pull a handkerchief from his pocket and wipe his face. Then he said heatedly, 'I

371

don't give a confounded hang what you've been doing. But I want to talk to you. Understand? Stand up,' he said. Mr Fury did not look at Peter. He was looking at the door; he was looking through and beyond it; he was looking at his wife sitting in the kitchen.

'You were out all yesterday, and the day before, and again today. Where do you put yourself?' The boy began fumbling with his tie. It was a new one which yesterday his mother had bought him. 'And last night, and every bloody night this week? And you don't eat. Tell me, surely you're not eating outside? Insulting us. Turning your nose up at what your mother struggles to get. Aye. By Christ, you've changed, sonny! Look here, if I thought you were eating outside this house and insulting your mother, I'd break your confounded neck. We are glad to get it. You stick your nose up at it. Well?'

Peter remained silent. 'I came up to bed,' went on Mr Fury, 'leaving your mother down there, and she's off again. Then I went to bed, but I couldn't sleep a wink. So I came in here and waited to see you. See? I *want* to have this talk with you. Where do you go? Have you been at Kilkey's? Or at the Pettigrews'? Have you been up at Vulcan Street? You have money in your pocket. Who gave it to you? How much have you got?'

Peter replied, 'I have two shillings. I've had it two days now. Aunt Brigid gave it to me. I met her going home from Mass.'

'Oh aye. Very nice of her, I'm sure. Strike me lucky. I've worked for nearly forty years, and I can't even get two-pence from your mother for a fill of twist. She's been out half the day and nearly broke her back varnishing those chairs. D'you see? Aren't you ashamed of yourself? Don't you think you're selfish? If I saw you turning round to give your mother a hand in the house, by God I would like you for it. Instead of that you clear out. You never say where you are going. Not a word. But that isn't the point. No. That isn't the point.' The man caught his son by his shoulders and pushed him against the wall. In the light of the lamp it seemed to Peter that his father's face was clouded with blood. 'No. That isn't the point,' he shouted. 'Aye! You stick up your nose at the grub, hang you. That's what college has done for you. Ruined you.'

'But I can't eat it, Dad,' Peter said, and he thought, 'What is the matter with him?' He was frightened now. It was the first time he had ever seen his father like this.

'Your mother and I are *glad* to eat it.'

They stared at each other, and a silence came between them, punctured by Mr Mangan's deep snores.

'Well?'

'I went with George Postlethwaite to the stables.'

'Aye! Where'd you meet him? Vulcan Street?'

'No. I met him in Price Street.'

'Did you see your sister?'

'No, Dad.'

'Who've you seen, then? You've seen somebody. You've seen somebody who has made you go a little off the rocker. What are you shaking for? Stop it. Stop it, or I'll knock you down. D'you hear?' he shouted.

'I've seen nobody.' Mr Fury dropped his hands. He went and leaned over the table. He turned the wick down, as the lamp was smoking. His face had resumed its former expression, and the boy saw the sallow, sunken cheeks of a man who has spent his lifetime feeding fires.

'I know you think I'm always growling. Sometimes I'm a bit bad-tempered, but not always. In fact, your mother says I'm soft. H'm! A lot of growling I do! But by the living Christ, when I see your mother sitting down there ... Oh! ... Well – I don't know *what* to make of you. The other night you were so hungry that you pinched that little bit of best butter that your mother had on the shelf. Yes. She put it behind the pans, and you took it. Mean! That's what I call it. Bloody mean! I've been hungry many a time. D'you think I'd pinch it? By gosh, no! I wouldn't be so mean. The one luxury your mother has. Just think, she did nothing but walk all that day, and she never got back till after ten at night. She made herself a cup of tea, and when she went to the shelf for the bit of butter, it wasn't there. No. You took it. Rather than deny that woman her little pleasure I would sooner eat ... But you're a curious unfeeling lad, and I can't make you out. You're not like anybody else in our family. Well, let me tell you that though you may look upon me as a sort of old fogy, I'm not so dense. I don't cut a line alongside you young fellers, but what matter? I've always tried to do the right thing. It costs nothing, after all. I've seen a few things since I've been home. I don't go about with my eyes shut, believe me. You've been spoiled, ruined. That's what's wrong with you. And now listen ...' For the second time Mr Fury gripped his son by the shoulders. 'And now listen to this. When you go to sea – clear out. Do you understand? Clear to hell out of it, and don't come back. Your mother and I will probably get a little peace. We can get on very well together. Your mother and I have been married over thirty years, and everybody was happy until you came along.'

'Dad! Dad! What's the matter, please?' He staggered back against the bed, and finally sat on it, looking up into Mr Fury's white face.

'Go downstairs and see,' said Mr Fury. Banging the door behind him, he went out.

'Dad!' called Peter. There was no reply. He went to the front room door and stood there listening, his hand fumbling the knob. 'Dad!' he called, 'Dad!' Peter's bare feet were trapped in the shaft of light that crossed the landing-

373

floor from the open door of his room. 'Can I come in? What is the matter, Dad?'

Mr Fury did not answer. He was standing by the window looking down into the bone yard. One night he had not been able to sleep and he had walked out. He had stood in that yard, and his son had followed him there, and he had refused to listen to the boy. He drew the curtains back across the window. There seemed to be no point in staring into that yard now. He could hear Peter's bare feet pattering about the dark landing, from the floor of which there still rose the smell of soda and carbolic. 'You get to bed!' he shouted. Then he lit the candle. The silence was broken by a loud laugh on the landing.

'I don't want to go to sea! I'm not going to sea! I'm going to work with Desmond on the railway.' Then Peter rushed into his room, shouting, 'I'm not going to sea!'

There was a crash in the boy's room. Mr Fury dropped the candle and rushed to the room. He could see Peter standing against the bed-rail. The floor was covered with glass. 'Peter! Peter! What's the matter? By Christ, you have been drinking. Oh! A mere boy! Stop laughing when I tell you, or I'll fling you down those stairs.' He clapped his hand over his son's mouth. 'Ssh!' he said, 'Ssh! Your mother has come back. Ssh!'

He held on to his son. Below, a key turned in the lock.

Peter burst into tears. 'Ssh!' his father said. 'Ssh! Here's your mother coming up now.'

2

Mrs Fury was shaking Peter roughly by the shoulder and saying, 'Get up! Get up at once. I have something for you to do.' The boy sat up, grinning. Who was the person pulling him about? 'And you have caught a cold, you fool. You're sweating like a horse. Get up! Get up!' She began shaking him again. Peter sat up.

'Yes, all right, Mother. Coming.' He sat with his knees drawn up, waiting for her to be gone.

'Your father's gone off in a great temper, Heaven knows where. Now, don't you lie down again.' Then she was gone, the door creaked on its hinges.

Peter got up and dressed, and hurried downstairs. What did she want? 'God!' he thought. 'She must have found out.' But, while he was sitting at the table dipping his bread in the tea, she told him what she wanted him to do. Peter's eyes had already noticed the absence of two chairs from the parlour suite. Here they were in the kitchen, right at his hand. Mrs Fury said, 'As soon as you are ready, I want you to take these chairs down to McIntyre's, understand?'

Peter looked at the chairs again. Yes, these were the chairs she had been varnishing. He didn't know what to say. Had he to carry these chairs all the way to McIntyre's? He hated the idea, and as though his mother had divined his thoughts she shouted:

'Come along now. Hurry up. I can see at once that you don't want to go. Do you expect me to take them, or your father, when we have a great hulking son doing nothing but filling his belly and galavanting around the place?'

The boy went red in the face. He got up from the table and stood looking at the chairs. He said gruffly, 'What am I to do when I get there?'

Mrs Fury went up to her son, and looking him straight in the face said, 'Do I have to explain to you that I am selling them? Do I have to explain to you that we have to live? Get out. Here, take these chairs and be off. Are you ashamed to carry them through the streets? Leave them at the shop. Your mother has done the dirty work. All you have to do is leave them there. Mr McIntyre will pay you.' She watched her son pick up the chairs, and now he stood hesitating in the kitchen. Which way should he go? Better go out the back way. He put them down again, then carried one at a time down the yard. 'And don't be long,' Mrs Fury cautioned him. She followed her son down the yard.

'I shall give you a couple of coppers for your pocket,' she said. Peter, without making any reply, went off down the entry. As she closed and locked the back door she heard him laugh. Peter had stopped in the entry and was sitting on one of the chairs. He pulled out the two-shilling piece his aunt had given him. Well, she could keep her coppers. He didn't want them, and why was his mother selling these chairs? Yes, why was she selling them? Were they so badly off, after all? His father had been saving money up for a long time, and now they were selling chairs. He got up and continued his way down the entry. At the bottom he stopped again. He hated to go into the street. Everybody would stare. Why had his father gone off in such a bad temper? Ah, he thought, he must have found out who took his money. Leaning on the chairs he looked back up the entry. Then his mother had lied to him. She had told him everything was all right. All those years he had been away. They were really poor. Selling their furniture. He picked up the chairs and went out into the street. But passers-by saw nothing unusual in a boy carrying two chairs through the street. 'McIntyre's is over a mile away,' he said to himself. Periodically he stopped and sat down. The chairs were not heavy, but awkward to carry. He could see a man coming along the road, carrying a large brown parcel. The man seemed to be walking straight towards him. Peter started to move on again. As he picked up the chairs the man came up, looked curiously at him for a moment, and then passed on. He stopped again, looking after the boy. Then he ran back to Peter and caught him by the tail of the coat.

'Excuse me!' he said. Peter dropped the chairs and swung round. 'Excuse me!' he said. 'Is your name Fury?'

'Yes, my name is Fury,' replied the boy, staring curiously at the man with the parcel.

'Is it Peter Fury?'

The boy smiled. 'My name is Peter Fury,' replied the boy. He sat down on one of the chairs.

'Hang it all!' exclaimed the man. He put down the parcel and sat on the other chair. 'Well, my name is Kilkey,' he said, laughing. 'Joseph Kilkey, and by all the rules I am your brother-in-law. Pleased to meet you, my boy. How are you?' He shook hands with Peter. The boy seemed unconcerned. Then he burst out laughing.

'Well, I never,' he said. 'How are you, Joe?' So this was his sister's husband. Aunt Brigid had told him all about Mr Kilkey. How old he looked! He patted his knees with his hands.

'I'm just going round to see your mother,' Mr Kilkey said. 'When are you coming to see us?' he asked.

Peter at once got up and picked up the chair. 'I don't know,' he said. 'I went round twice to see Maureen, but she wouldn't open the door, so I don't think I shall go again.'

Mr Kilkey sat fast in the chair. 'Ah!' he said, 'you mustn't say that! Your sister wasn't very well that night. You must come.' Joseph Kilkey got up. 'Yes, you must come round and see us. Maureen will be right glad to see you, laddie.' He picked up his parcel. 'Well, so long,' he said, and went off down the street, leaving Peter staring after him, chairs in hand.

Well, well! That was Maureen's husband. She wanted him to go round there now. 'That is very nice of her,' thought Peter, 'but I shan't go.' He disappeared round the corner.

Mrs Fury had just made her father fast in the chair when the knock came to the door. At first she did not open it, but went into the parlour, and peeping through the curtains saw a man standing at the door. She could see the large parcel he carried, but she could see nothing of the man except the back of his head. She went back into the kitchen and sat down. It was somebody selling things. She well knew those timid knocks, as though the person was ashamed to offer his goods, or feared to burst his knuckles on the wood. But the knock was repeated, very loudly. The gentleman at the door was very insistent. 'Let him knock,' she thought. Again she went into the parlour and looked out. 'Heavens!' she said, catching sight of the man's

376

face. Then she rushed into the lobby. She stood holding the door knob in her hand. This was a surprise. Why had he come? She opened the door.

'Good morning, Mrs Fury. Can I come in?' He saw at once how astonished the woman was. He stood there smiling.

'Well, Mr Kilkey! I never expected you. Never. You're the last person I ever thought I should see at my door.' The woman laughed. 'Please come in.' She pulled back the door. She was surprised, she was truly astonished, and she could not hide it. Here was a man whom she had never had in her house but once. She didn't like him. She distrusted him. Like her sister, she thought Mr Kilkey an ugly old man, and her dislike of him was merely occasioned by the fact that Maureen had married him. Of Mr Joseph Kilkey she knew nothing, beyond the fact that he lived in Price Street, that he was a stevedore at the docks, and that he attended to his duties at the chapel regularly. She also knew that he was the caretaker of the new hall which Father Moynihan had built, in order, as he had said in the pulpit, 'to keep the young men of his congregation off the streets'. Here was this man in her own kitchen.

'Sit down, Mr Kilkey,' she said, and watched him put the large brown paper parcel on the floor and kick it under the table.

Mr Kilkey looked at 'Dad'. 'How is the old man these days, Mrs Fury?' he asked.

'Oh, Dad! He's just the same, Mr Kilkey. The stroke has had a terrible effect upon him. Please excuse me for a moment,' she added quickly, and went off upstairs, leaving Joseph Kilkey still looking at Mr Mangan belted in his chair. 'Poor old man!' he said.

Mrs Fury was standing on the landing. With her fingers she was scratching on the banister. Had Maureen sent him round? Good God! What could the girl have meant by that? Was she to go through the same old thing over again? It must be about the loan. It couldn't be anything else. This was too much. She had never liked the man, and yet, yes – she must admit it – the fellow was decent – what other man but Joseph Kilkey would put his hand to such a thing? No. She had nothing against him at all. But Maureen! How mean of her! To send him round like this. To ask questions. More questions. The man was smoking, she could smell it coming up the stairs.

As she stood there upon the dark landing she was filled with a desperate longing to fly – to fly away from Hatfields. She went slowly down the stairs. Through the kitchen door she saw Mr Kilkey leaning on the table. He had taken off his cap. As she came in, Mr Kilkey drew his pipe from his mouth.

'That's a fine boy you have, Mrs Fury,' he said. 'I met him coming up.'

The woman did not speak. He had met Peter with those chairs. He had met Peter carrying those chairs. She turned and looked at her father. 'He has met Peter on his way to sell those chairs to Mr McIntyre,' her eyes seemed to say. Well, she had better sit down. She crossed to the sofa. She could not take her eyes off Mr Kilkey's bald patch.

'Did Maureen send you round?' she asked, her eyes still fixed upon the bald spot.

Joseph Kilkey smiled. 'Oh no, Mrs Fury. She didn't even know I was coming,' he replied. 'I thought I would come round myself. I hope you won't mind my taking this liberty.' He had turned round and was now facing the woman on the sofa. He was looking at her shoes, at her dress, at her hair. He was looking into her face and thinking, 'I am glad I came. I am so glad I came. And I shall come again. I like this woman.' He pulled his chair out from the table, crossed one leg over the other, and leaning over in his chair continued: 'Yes, I thought I would come round and see you. You are no doubt wondering why. It isn't that matter of my signature, Mrs Fury. No, that is quite all right, I can assure you. I was only too glad to do that for you.' He paused again.

'Here,' thought Mrs Fury, 'here is this ugly person sitting in my chair and telling me it's all right! And I have never liked him.' She lowered her head upon her breast. For the first time she felt she had been wrong. She felt ashamed, she did not want to look at him. What could she say to this? Mr Kilkey got up from the chair, and sat down beside the woman.

'I would like to do something for you, Mrs Fury,' said Mr Kilkey. He took out his pipe and relighted it. 'Mr Fury out?' he asked, and he looked around the kitchen.

'My husband has gone out,' replied the woman. 'I think he went about his strike-pay, Joe.' She had never called Mr Kilkey 'Joe' until now, but the man's earnestness, his simple, honest approach, had touched her. And yet, she wanted to laugh. What could this man do? What help could he offer? Nothing, so far as she knew. With his signature, yes, but then Mrs Anna Ragner and herself would finally settle that matter. She became suddenly cautious. Even now she might withdraw. She had best consider her position. This strike might go on for a while yet. And her son's allotment money was held up. She had that to attend to. She could foresee even now what this stoppage involved. Any decision she had contemplated taking was now out of her reach, for Mr Kilkey said, 'Oh! That note is all right, Mrs Fury. I saw to that. Maureen will go up with you.' After a while, as though he had learned her position from Mrs Fury's expression, he added quietly, 'I quite understand! And now I want to do something,' he said again.

'I am sure that is very nice of you, Mr Kilkey,' replied the woman.

Mr Kilkey reached down for his brown paper parcel and said, 'I got your boy a rig-out. Maureen was telling me that Peter is going away. I hope you will accept these with my best wishes.'

The woman was so taken aback that she could hardly speak.

'Joe!' she said. 'Really! I hardly know what to say. It is most kind of you. I . . .'

Words failed her. She could only sit looking at this man, and if she had distrusted, if she had never liked him, she liked him now. There was a loving, generous spirit hidden within that man. It seemed to shine out from beneath his ugliness, it beautified his person. 'Thank you! Thank you!' She placed her hand on the man's arm.

Mr Kilkey's parcel lay spread open upon the red tiled floor. And there was a full outfit. Shirts, trousers, dungarees, jerseys, sea-boots, white canvas bag and lanyard, even soap and matches, tin plate, cup and spoon. A sailor's full bag. The sight of these articles upon the floor only served to convince the woman that it was all too true, all too real. Her son had shut one door, and was opening another. And she herself must see it closed. She mustn't think about it any longer.

'We're none of us perfect, Mrs Fury,' Mr Kilkey was saying. 'I quite under-stand. I talked to Maureen about it. You take my advice, my good woman, and let Peter go. He could never do anything much here now, and it's for his own good. I mind how hurt he felt that night he came down to the hall. Nobody would speak to him. I was there at the time, but it never struck me at the moment that it could have been your son. Well, well,' he went on, 'I hope you'll let him go.'

'The boy never breathed a word to me about that,' said Mrs Fury. 'I had wondered why he would not go near the schoolrooms. Now I can understand. Still, it will do him good. It will be a lesson to him, Mr Kilkey. A lesson. Tell me, do you think this strike will go on much longer?' She looked almost pathetic as she asked this, as though the man at her side was going to solve the dread problem for her there and then.

'They'll all be back at work next week, Mrs Fury. You take it from me.' His eyes seemed to wander up and down the woman's face. 'You've reared a big family,' he said, 'but you look well on it.' They smiled at each other now. There were no more barriers, no more distrust, no more dislike. They might have been friends for years.

'What a good man he is,' thought Mrs Fury, 'a quiet, steady, sober man. I feel I ought to take back all that I have ever said against him.' Ah! If Peter had had this man's companionship, how different everything would have been! To think that he, a comparative stranger to her, should come round to her house and do this generous thing, whilst her own sister kept clear of the place. Mr Kilkey was no rich man. He must have done without something to get these clothes. Here her thoughts came to a halt. To have been inquisitive on the matter would have taken away the kindness that had prompted it. She began to gather up the clothes, looking carefully at each article as she dumped it into the bag. Then she carried the bag out to the back kitchen.

Mr Kilkey sat silent and thoughtful. Here was a woman who, if his wife was right, was at the moment tormented and distracted, and yet was able to hide it behind a calm and unruffled exterior. He did not know what worried her, but he guessed it must be the failure of her young son, and the callous indifference of her eldest one. 'What she wants,' thought Mr Kilkey, 'is a long holiday – a holiday away from Hatfields, away from the city.' Yes, Mrs Fury wanted a holiday. He would like to do something. He heard her pattering about in the back kitchen, and called out, 'I hope you are not getting anything for me, Mrs Fury,' to which the woman replied, 'No, no . . .'

The more he looked at the woman, the more firmly convinced he became that the piece of orange cardboard in his pocket had been a good idea on his part. He pulled out the orange ticket from his pocket, and subjected it to a minute inspection. It was like the three hundred other tickets that Father Moynihan had had printed, but now, as he held it in his hands, it was different, it was significant. He got up and went into the back kitchen. Mrs Fury was standing looking out of the window, and she was holding the white lanyard belonging to the canvas bag. She turned on hearing the man behind her. The man stood near the mangling-machine. He seemed awkward, hard put to it to know how to begin. He had sold tickets to many women, but not to Mrs Fury, and besides, this was not a ticket he wanted her to buy. He had bought it, and he only wanted her to accept it. He started to laugh. It seemed the best way to begin. 'I'm sure you'll think I'm a nuisance, Mrs Fury,' he began, 'but there's just one other thing to do, and then I'll go away.' She looked at the ticket in his hand. 'I want you to accept this ticket, Mrs Fury. Maureen bought it for you, and nothing could please her or myself more than for you to have it.' After a while he stammered out, 'You deserve it.'

'But what is it for?' the woman's questioning glance seemed to ask.

'It's for a week's retreat to an Ursuline convent, Mrs Fury. The whole of the Third Order are going there for a week. I don't know anything about the place, mind you, but from what I've been told it's really beautiful. It's a great manor house in its own grounds in the country which the Ursulines have taken over. Father Doyle and Father Heraghty are going as well. Please take this' – he held out the ticket. 'I am sure you'll like it.' Seeing the woman's hesitation he went on quickly. 'You know right well, Mrs Fury, that you deserve this week's holiday. And you ought to go. Don't begrudge yourself a quiet week in the country. I don't want to be poking into your affairs. Sometimes Maureen and I talk things over, you see.' He became confident. 'You'll get your lad off to sea, Mrs Fury. Let him go! It's your duty to him and to yourself.' He stopped suddenly. He felt he had overshot the mark.

Mrs Fury held the ticket in her hand. Who was this man offering her a ticket? Who was this fellow who insisted on her going, who advised her about her children? She let the piece of cardboard fall from her fingers.

'But how could I go, Mr Kilkey? That's impossible! What would Denny do? And Dad?'

'Maureen and I have arranged all that,' said the indefatigable Mr Kilkey. 'There's no need to worry.'

Mrs Fury became seated and dropped the lanyard on the floor. Then she said, 'I must think about it,' whilst Mr Kilkey hoped his plan had worked. Maureen had arranged nothing, but he, Mr Joseph Kilkey, would see to that, and as soon as he got home. He followed the woman into the kitchen again. He did not sit down, but stood leaning on the dresser.

'Maureen will come round and cook and look after Mr Fury and your father. Do go,' he urged. 'The change will do you good.'

The tears that came from Mrs Fury's eyes surprised him, though it was nothing but his own fondness that had drawn them out. 'Cheer up, Mrs Fury,' he said.

'Mr Kilkey,' she blurted out, lifting her apron to her face. 'What am I to say to all this? Your kindness astonishes me. How could I be other than honest with you? When you married my daughter I hated you. I never forgave Maureen for it. I wouldn't have you near the house. I didn't like you. There! Now you know. Forgive me.'

Joseph Kilkey smiled. 'Well,' he said. 'Let's forget all that. I only wish I could have done more for you. I like you, Mrs Fury.'

Well! What more was there to say excepting, 'Thanks! Thanks!' and to take the piece of coloured cardboard that had the power to carry her out of Hatfields for a whole week? She was too full. 'Thanks! Thanks! Please go now, Mr Kilkey.' She shielded her face with her coarse apron and watched Joseph Kilkey put on his cap. She followed him to the back door and let him out. She remained standing there until he disappeared round the corner of the entry. Then she went back into the house. She picked up the ticket, looked at it for a moment, and casually dropped it into the big green vase upon the dresser. It was as though, looking at it a second time, she had doubted its power, mistrusted that man's kindness. But why should she do that? 'It is so unusual,' she was thinking. Between smiles and exclamations of astonishment that nobody save Mr Mangan witnessed she went about her work, and only fell back into her old state when she stood in the parlour looking at the vacant places near the wall where the chairs had stood. She must sit down. That visitation had been almost overwhelming. Everything was so uncertain. Even her son's going to sea, the strike, Mr Mangan's health, Anthony's return. One made a decision today, and tomorrow it was altered. One could be sure of nothing. She laid her head on the arm of the rocking-chair. How kind that man was! She could never have believed it. Never! And how splendid it would be to get to the country for a whole week. Perhaps by that time the strike would be over. But now – well, one's every step was aimless.

A series of sharp coughs from the occupant of the high-backed chair reminded her that she must be up and doing. Reality was pressing in, breaking down the texture of her dreams.

Mrs Fury was busy washing in the back kitchen when the back door resounded to a series of kicks. She let fall the sheet she held in her hand and stared down the yard. Who could this be? Peter, of course. She had locked the back door after Mr Kilkey. She hurried down the yard. When she pulled back the door Aunt Brigid and Miss Pettigrew were standing in the entry. 'Well!' she said. She drew back into the yard, holding the latch in one hand, the other she held to her apron. Miss Mangan was wearing a new grey dress. She looked anything but pleased.

'I'm surprised you never heard us, Fanny,' she said coldly. 'Miss Pettigrew and I have been knocking at the front door for nearly five minutes.' She advanced into the yard, followed by the hobbling old woman of eighty-two, whose guest she had been for the past three weeks.

'Well!' said Mrs Fury. 'Well! Come in.' She preceded them up the yard. 'I thought it was the boy,' she said, turning round to her sister. 'He is out.' Miss Pettigrew came up haltingly, banging her stick on the stones. The little old woman was smiling. 'Well,' she was thinking, 'it's been worth it.' She had shamed Miss Mangan into coming. The three women entered the kitchen. Mrs Fury became flurried. She stared from one to the other. Miss Pettigrew sat on the sofa and gave a sigh. She felt done up. Aunt Brigid, prior to sitting down, placed her parcel on the table and remarked, 'I have brought a bottle of port for Dad. It's the best port that Mr Dingle has in the shop.' She sat down and threw open her coat. Her grey gloves, one of which was fast becoming holed, she now drew off and laid on the table. She looked across at Mr Mangan. 'I'm sure that port will do him good,' she said. She made herself comfortable. Mrs Fury did not sit down. She was too surprised to move. So she had come now! H'm! But she didn't want her here at all. And as for the old woman on the sofa, she did not want her either.

'How are you, Fanny?' asked the old woman, looking across at Brigid as though to say, 'How slow you are, Brigid! Well, I have done it instead.' Her poke-bonnet with its single red rose bobbed up and down.

'Quite well,' replied Mrs Fury. 'I hope you are the same.' She leaned against the side of the grate. 'No. I shall not sit down,' she said to herself. 'At least they will know that I don't want them here.' To see her own sister sitting there, and sporting her new costume, only increased her admiration for Mr Joseph Kilkey.

'How are things?' asked Aunt Brigid suddenly. She did not look at Mrs Fury, but at the ornaments on the mantelshelf above her head.

'One can't complain,' replied Mrs Fury. She looked at the bottle of port on the table.

'Did you hear about the celebrations in honour of Father Coghlan?' asked Miss Pettigrew. 'He's turned ninety-four yesterday.' She said this as though her own eighty-two years were a mere nothing.

'No,' Mrs Fury said, looking anywhere but at this talkative old woman.

'Fancy!' said Miss Pettigrew. 'I thought you would have heard. How is everybody?' She turned her head and looked away through the window. Miss Mangan looked glum.

The oldest parishioner of St Sebastian's, who had made such a quick recovery from her illness, due no doubt to Dr Dunfrey's unfailing skill, now drew from her skirt pocket a small bottle of sweets. Miss Pettigrew always carried this small bottle of sweets wherever she went. She unscrewed the lid, and holding out the bottle in her trembling hand said in a wheezy voice, 'Have a jujube, Fanny!'

Mrs Fury looked at the woman and then at the bottle. 'I never eat them, Miss Pettigrew,' she replied, 'thanks all the same.' To be offered a jujube in the middle of a busy morning was something really phenomenal to Mrs Fury.

Undaunted, the old woman turned to Aunt Brigid. 'Have a jujube, Brigid,' she said almost pleadingly.

Miss Mangan leaned forward in her chair. 'Thank you, Biddy,' she said, and looked straight at her sister as if to say, 'I shall certainly take one because you refused.' She smiled now, not at the situation, but at her own inability to extract a confection from the narrow bottle, for her plump fingers could not reach them, whereon Miss Pettigrew, with a vigorous shake of the hand, shook a red jujube upon Aunt Brigid's lap, remarking between loud sucking sounds, for she had taken one herself, 'I find them excellent for colds, Brigid, excellent! Dr Dunfrey thinks they are too highly acidized, whatever that may mean, but I think he's wrong.' She said this with the ardent conviction of a person who had put down her recovery to the return to the jujube bottle rather than to Dr Dunfrey's unfailing attention.

'Thanks,' repeated Aunt Brigid, picking up the jujube and putting it into her mouth. The silence of the kitchen was broken now by the twin sucking sounds of Miss Mangan and Miss Pettigrew. Mrs Fury did not move. 'I don't want them here! What have they come for?' she was thinking.

'How are the children?' asked Aunt Brigid. 'Has Peter got anything to do yet?'

'Not yet.'

Miss Pettigrew raised her head and looked at Mr Mangan. 'How is your father, Fanny?' she asked between audible sucks.

'Just the same,' Mrs Fury replied, and she glanced at the old man.

'Fanny!' said Aunt Brigid. 'Why don't you sit down? Do please sit down. It makes me feel uncomfortable seeing you stand like that.' She made a violent move in her chair.

'Yes, sit down, Fanny,' advised Miss Pettigrew. With her figure in profile, Miss Pettigrew looked just bonnet and nose. The veins in her thin neck stood out as she talked. Her skin was yellow, and had an almost scaly appearance.

Mrs Fury went into the parlour. She came back with a chair and sat down.

'They say now that everybody will be back at work next week,' began Aunt Brigid. 'I do hope it's true. I *shall* be glad to get back to Ireland.'

'Yes, I'm sure you will,' replied Mrs Fury. She was surprised at her own calm. These two women bored her. Bored her to distraction. What could have brought her sister here? Had she something unpleasant to say?

Miss Pettigrew took another jujube from her bottle. 'Fanny,' she said, 'are you coming with the Order to the Ursuline Convent?'

'I don't know.' She got up again from the chair. She couldn't sit down. She was restless. There was that journey again to Banfield Road. Why didn't these people go away? She picked up the wine-bottle from the table.

'What is this, Brigid?' she asked. Miss Mangan was too astonished to reply. What was that? Why, the port wine she had bought for her father. As she held the bottle in her hand the kitchen door was thrown violently open, and Dennis Fury, followed by Michael Mulcare, came into the kitchen.

'Hello!' he said. It was almost a growl. 'Sit down, Mike,' he added, 'if you can find room.' Then he surveyed the gathering.

Mr Fury took one glance at Miss Mangan and went out. 'Fanny!' he called. 'Fanny!' Mr Mulcare was smiling at Miss Pettigrew. 'Have a jujube, young sir,' she said. Mrs Fury went into the back kitchen. 'Listen,' said Mr Fury, 'where's that boy?'

'Peter? He's gone out!' She stood staring at her husband.

'Where? Where's he gone?' demanded the man. 'He ought to be here – now.'

'He's gone to McIntyre's with a message for me. What is the matter?'

'Matter!' shouted Mr Fury. 'Matter! That lad ought to be here. Mr Mulcare's ship is sailing on the next tide. He wants to get out. D'you understand me?' The bewildered woman understood nothing. Mr Fury rushed into the kitchen. He stood looking at Miss Mangan. 'What do you want?' he asked angrily.

Aunt Brigid had not expected this. 'What on earth is the matter with you, Denny?' she said. Her face had grown pale.

Mr Fury wanted to dive at her. 'Matter! I'll tell you what's the matter!' he shouted. 'You clear to hell out of this. Understand? You mean —, that's what you are. You never put your face near here all the time you've been at her house.' He pointed at Miss Pettigrew. 'And take her to the devil too. Get that? Go ahead!' His eyes fell on the bottle. 'What's this?' he growled.

Mrs Fury came rushing in from the back kitchen. 'Denny! Denny! Have you lost your head? Such language! Brigid brought that port for Father.' She gripped her husband by the coat and tried to push him back to the sofa.

'Leave me alone!' shouted Mr Fury. 'I know what I'm doing. I want this sister of yours to go. Right away. The old devil! She only comes round here to insult you.' He pushed his wife away. 'Come along, Miss Mangan! You get to hell out of it.' He stood in the middle of the kitchen, red-faced, swinging his arms. 'Where is that lad?'

Mrs Fury shouted, 'Haven't I told you? He's out.'

'Then he must be found! Mulcare's ship is sailing with the next tide, and if I know anything he's going with him. Are you getting out?' he shouted. 'You pair of hags. You do nothing but insult this woman, hang you! She's worth ten of you.' He picked up the bottle. 'And take this too. If the old man drank it he'd choke out of sheer protest against your generosity.' Whilst he stood there, livid with anger, Miss Pettigrew from sheer fright dropped her bottle, and the kitchen floor was covered with red confections. Mr Mulcare began to gather them together.

'But, Denny! For God's sake control yourself. What is all this talk?' said Mrs Fury.

The man ignored her. 'Are you going ...?' He said no more, for Miss Mangan had already risen to her feet. She could not speak. Miss Pettigrew, having put her jujubes in her pocket, followed Aunt Brigid to the door.

'Keep away from here!' shouted Mr Fury. He banged the door in their faces. Then he looked at his wife. 'Fanny,' he said, 'where is that lad?'

'I told you.' She turned to Mr Mulcare. 'Mr Mulcare,' she said, 'please excuse my husband. I ...'

She sat down near the table. What was all this excitement about?

'Well, I'm going to find him,' said Mr Fury. 'Yes. By God, I'm going to trim his sails.' He looked at Mulcare. 'Wait,' he said. 'Please wait here.' Then he rushed out of the house.

Mr Mulcare now removed his cap. He went up to the table, and leaning one hand upon it said, 'Mrs Fury, I have a job for your son on my boat, and I make you this promise, that I shall look after him. That is, if you want him to go.' He stood looking down at the woman's crumpled hair. 'By sheer accident I met your husband this morning as he was coming out of the Federation offices. Well, my ship is going, for this strike is finished. Do you want your son to go?' he asked. Then he went back to the sofa and sat down.

Mrs Fury, without a word, went up to her room. She sat down on the bed. She felt as though a wheel were turning in her head. First Mr Kilkey, then her sister and Miss Pettigrew, and now Mr Mulcare and her husband. There wasn't even time to think. She could only sit there, numb. What should she do?

Whilst she sat there, dazed, unable to make any decision, her husband came into the room. 'Hang it!' he said, 'where is the lad? If he misses this ship I . . .'

'Denny! Denny! Please! Control yourself. Will you at least let me be quiet for a moment?'

He sat down by her side and put his hand on her shoulder. 'Let him go! Let him go, Fanny! I don't care if I never see one of my children again. I only want peace. And we ought to be on our own. Understand? Let him go! Mulcare is a good man. He'll look after him.'

Even now she hedged. She hated to see him go. It was like turning the last page of a book. She hesitated. The man pulled out his watch. Then he went downstairs again. Mulcare was walking up and down the kitchen. Mr Fury said, 'It's a caution. I'll . . . if he misses this chance . . . I . . .'

'There isn't much time, Fury,' remarked Mr Mulcare. 'I don't think your wife wants him to go.'

Mr Fury whispered into the man's ear. 'That's the kind of woman she is.' He seemed to hold his breath for a moment. 'She still wants her son – in spite of everything. She hates to let him go.'

Mulcare made no reply. Then he said casually, 'I've got an hour. No more.'

'If I was his age,' said Mr Fury, 'I would go like a shot! By God I would! Aye, Mike, and if I could get a job I would go now.' There was something almost desperate in his utterance, as though in that very moment his being hungered to be free, his spirit longed for the sea again.

'You must be content. All you have to do is to be content,' remarked Mulcare. 'Your time's up, Fury. Isn't that it?' He watched this old man sit down on the sofa.

'Aye, I suppose so. I suppose so,' Mr Fury replied.

The other man continued his pacing of the kitchen. Once he looked at the figure of Mr Mangan. Then he stood to listen to somebody moving above-stairs. Somebody up there was pacing the floor too. When Mr Fury looked up at the clock he felt certain that its face had grinned at him. So sure was he of this that he got up and turned its face to the wall. 'Of course!' he cried in his mind. 'Of course she would send him out. She's a caution.' Well, he couldn't sit down. No. He got up again and went upstairs. Mrs Fury was kneeling in front of the altar. The man closed the door quickly and stood at the top of the stairs. He pulled the five and threepence from his pocket and looked at it. That could wait. He would give it to her later on. He sat down on the stairs. He could hear Mulcare walking up and down the kitchen. Extraordinary! Extraordinary! That he should have met him at that very fortunate moment. It had been like the solving of a problem, a problem which had kept him awake the whole night. By heavens! he had seen nothing like Peter. Not for many a day. He was certain the lad was drinking – and then smashing that glass vase in his room!

Mulcare had stopped by the window. Suddenly he went to the kitchen door and shouted, 'Here's your boy now!'

'What!' Mr Fury almost overbalanced as he ran down the stairs.

The front room door opened. Mrs Fury called after him, 'Denny! Denny!'

'What?' shouted Mr Fury.

'Is that Peter?' she asked.

'Yes. It is,' replied Mr Fury, 'and only just in time too.'

'I want him to come up here at once.' she said. Then she went back into the room and shut the door.

She could hear shouting below-stairs. 'You don't want to go? Why? You said that last night too. Tell us why? There must be some reason for it. Is it your mother? Then, by Christ! if you don't, I do! D'you hear me?'

Mrs Fury stood listening on the dark landing. She heard Mulcare say, 'If he doesn't want to go, Fury, that's the end of the matter.'

'Then I'll go!' shouted Mr Fury. The woman on the landing gripped the banister.

'Denny! Denny! Come here!'

She put her hand to her forehead and held it there for a moment.

'Your wife's calling you,' she heard Mulcare say, and now she saw her husband climbing the stairs. As soon as he reached the top she gripped him by both arms, saying, 'Denny, dear Denny! Do you mean that? Do you mean that?'

'Of course I do! Him or me. I've had enough.'

387

The woman, filled with dread, leaned on him and asked, 'Do you mean it?'

Then she became excited and pushed her husband into the room. She clung to him.

'Denny! Don't be foolish. Stay here. Stay with me. I *don't* want you to go. Let Peter go. I don't care now, only about you.'

'All right!' There was no doubt about Mr Fury's determination. He went to the landing and shouted:

'Peter, come up here at once!'

He stood waiting for him.

'Go in!' he said. 'Your mother wants you.'

Peter went into the room. The man went out, hearing her say, 'Come here! Please kneel down.'

Mulcare began his pacing of the kitchen again.

'Everything's here, Mike! She's got a full bag for the lad.' He pulled out his watch.

'What time's the tide?' he asked. It was now ten to twelve.

'Three thirty-five.'

'Bags of time,' said Mr Fury.

He stood looking at the man. This continual walking up and down began to get on his nerves.

'So you lost sight of Hagan,' Mr Fury said.

He began cleaning his pipe. He was calm again, as though no such things as Brigid and Miss Pettigrew, Peter and his mother, had turned the house topsy-turvy.

When Mulcare sat down Mr Fury smiled. What a relief! The fellow seemed to him to be restless. Hang it! there was plenty of time.

'Oh! I don't know where the hell he went. We went to a house last night,' said Mulcare, 'and I'm afraid one of the ladies turned his head completely. I haven't seen him since he retired with her.' He lit a cigarette.

'I want you to look after our lad,' Mr Fury said. 'Of course, I know you will. Tell me, how did they manage to get the ship down the canal to the Moreston? Has she got all her crew?'

'Yes,' replied Mulcare. 'She's got all she wants. They were a deck-hand short, and I told the bo'sun I was bringing a boy along. Anyhow, your damned strike is finished.' He laughed now and began scratching his neck. He was wearing a blue suit and a jersey and his Australian hat.

'I'll show you his rig-out,' said Mr Fury. 'That woman has more foresight than ten thousand.'

He went into the back kitchen and brought back the sea-bag, into which Mrs Fury had put all the clothes Mr Kilkey had brought.

'Splendid!' Mulcare said. 'Even matches and his plate and spoon.'

'Well, Fanny's packed my bag for thirty years,' said Dennis Fury, 'so she's no amateur, is she? Look here,' he said suddenly, 'will you have a drink? I can give you a drop of brandy and plain water.'

'No, sir, thank you.'

'Have a cup of tea, then?'

'No,' replied Mulcare. They were silent for a moment as though they had both stopped to listen to the speakers in the room above.

'Would you take a jump, Fury, if she turned out to be short-handed?'

'No, I wouldn't,' said Mr Fury. 'I wouldn't leave my missus for twenty quid a week. And that's that.' Then he said, 'Ssh! Ssh! She's coming down.'

Without looking at her son, Mrs Fury said, 'Come here. Kneel down.' She was herself kneeling in front of this altar in the front room. As he knelt down he said, 'I don't want to go to sea, Mother. I could get a job on the railway.'

She seemed not to hear. She lifted her head high and looked at the lamp.

'Bless yourself,' she said. Peter made the sign of the Cross.

'I want you to go away now, Peter, for your own good and my peace. I sent you to college years ago. Now you are back again. I ought to have let your father take you to sea long ago. I can see now how foolish I was. But I have no more regrets. All that is wiped out. I have forgotten it. My own life has flashed by, and I've hardly noticed it. I have done everything I could. And your father wants you to go. Your father and I have talked about it, night after night. We have watched you about the place. We know you feel your position. From now on you owe it to yourself.' She turned her head so that the red glow from the lamp fell upon it. 'Are you listening?'

'Yes, Mother.'

'All I ask of you is this. I ask you to be clean, to be honest and upright, to hold your faith. Will you swear that now?' Her eyes rested upon his face. 'Will you at least promise that?'

Peter looked at his mother's face. Then he whispered, 'Yes, Mother.'

She caught his hand and raised it in the air. With her right hand she blessed herself.

'You swear that now you will be clean, decent and honest, and that you will hold your faith.'

She threw her arms round him and continued: 'You are my son, Peter, and I still love you. No matter what my family has done, I have never forgotten that. You have had your chance. A chance that the others never had. They have seen things you will never see. Whether I see eye to eye with my married children or not, I know this, that they worked hard, that

389

we managed to keep our family together in good times and bad times. Your father has done his share. Well, there, I shan't say any more.'

She loosed her hold upon him and rose to her feet. But Peter remained kneeling. All her words were nothing, he had not even heard them. She had lifted his hand towards the lamp, but he could not remember. He knew he was kneeling, but there was no altar there. There was a bed, and a woman upon that bed. And he was kneeling in front of her.

The door closed. His mother had gone downstairs, but he did not hear her go. He did not pray. He only tormented himself with questions, with vague hopes. How could he see Sheila now? How could he go? He got up and went to the window. 'Poor Mother!' he said. 'She still believes in me. And I do not want to go. I only want to work ashore so that I can see Sheila. I love her. No. I don't want to go!'

Whilst he stood there his father came into the room. 'All right, Peter,' he said. 'You come downstairs and get a bite to eat before you go.' Then he went out again. His father had not come near him. He had not even talked to him. Then his father must hate him. He closed his eyes and saw again the face of Mulcare in the window as he came up the yard. He had gone into the kitchen, and the first thing his father had said was, 'Well! Get your things ready. Mr Mulcare's ship sails at half-past three, and you're going on it.' Yes, his father had finished with him. He had flung himself upon the sofa, saying, 'I don't want to go! I can get a job on the railway with Desmond. I can get a cleaner's job.'

'It's either you or me!' his father had shouted, and he had caught him by the hair. 'You or me!' Then his father must know. He went slowly downstairs. There was the bag, already packed and secured by the lanyard, and there was the man with whom he was going away and with whom he would share his life. There was his mother. She looked as though she had been crying. And his father, standing by the mantelshelf, hands behind his back. He would not look at him, but continued to stare at the carpet. He looked angry. And there was his grandfather, huddled in the chair, mouth wide open, staring at nothing in particular. They seemed to him like the figures from a dream. He stood in the middle of the floor, and they all looked at him. He could feel their eyes, as though they were ransacking him, searching for his thoughts. Nobody spoke. He wanted to shout, 'Stop looking at me! Stop looking at me! It's all right. I'll go.' Then his father drew himself up, and put out his hand, saying, 'Well, there is only one other thing.' He pulled him by the arm and they went into the back kitchen. Mr Fury closed the door. 'There is only one other thing. Where have you been all morning?'

Peter replied, 'That doesn't matter now,' and stood back, thinking his father would strike him.

390

'It's time to go now,' Mulcare said. He picked up his slouch hat and swung it in his hand. 'Come on, my boy, slip to it.'

'Yes, he's really going,' said Mrs Fury to herself. 'He's really going. Another to the sea,' as she watched her son pick up the canvas bag and place it upon his shoulder.

Mr Fury was standing by the mantelshelf.

'Your cap,' he said.

'Let him take this one,' replied the woman.

'Ready, Fury?' said Mulcare; and immediately Mrs Fury went up to the man by the door.

'*He's* not going down,' she said. 'I'm going.' Her smile was brave as she added, 'That man would take a jump this minute. I know it.' Her husband grinned at her. 'Please wait,' she said quickly, and hurried upstairs. In a few minutes she was down again.

'I'm ready now.' She wore the same clothes as she had put on for the visit to Mr Lake.

Peter stood, now, looking at his mother. He had dropped the bag between his knees. Mr Fury crossed over to him and put out his hand – he did look at his son. His attitude was, 'Here's my hand – take it or leave it.' 'Good-bye,' he said, 'good luck.' Peter did not answer him. He put the bag on his shoulder again. Then he turned round and looked at his grandfather.

'Where'll you be when I come back again?' he was saying to himself. 'Staring in the grave?'

'Kiss your grandfather,' said his mother. Behind her Mulcare smiled. Peter bent down and kissed Mr Mangan on the forehead. Then they went out, leaving Mr Fury sitting by the fire. He was thinking of Mulcare's words: 'Your time's finished, Fury.' Yes, no doubt about it, his time was finished. He would never get another boat. Strike him pink, he had had his last bout with the sea. Again he could hear his wife saying, 'Denny, don't go! Stay with me.' He could see her face now, as she had stood under the altar in the front room: 'Please don't go!' Yes, it had touched him. And he wouldn't go. He would stay with his wife. Soon they would have the place to themselves. Then they would have a little peace. He got up and picked from the floor a piece of orange-coloured cardboard. Mrs Fury had dropped it from the vase as she searched the dresser for a pin.

'Kilkey!' said Mr Fury. 'That's Kilkey, or I'll eat my hat. Good old Joe!'

Mulcare was talking to his mother, but Peter did not hear what they said.

They were walking by his side, but somehow he himself was alone – intensely alone. The world around him seemed to have drawn down its shutters, and now, even as he walked, he knew, he could feel and see them, there were two figures, one each side of him. The street had changed. There were three long ladders, and he was on the middle one. He climbed warily. Sometimes he missed his footing and the woman said, 'Take my arm'; and just as he was about to catch hold, the man with a deerstalker hat leaned forward, leered in his face and said, 'Take mine.'

'You mustn't stand like this,' said Mulcare. 'We have to hurry,' and Mr Mulcare put a hand upon his shoulder. Peter jumped, then shot forward, almost overbalancing the white bag from his shoulders.

'Yes. All right! I am hurrying.' And the ladders had flashed from sight, and he was crossing the bottom of Hatfields. The world about him took shape again. He could see the black shutters being rolled up.

'You need never worry on that score,' Mr Mulcare was saying. 'I shall look after Peter. In six months you won't know him.' She felt no qualms about letting Peter go now. Then Mulcare asked:

'Did you really think your husband would have gone?'

'Gone!' The woman burst out laughing. 'He would have gone like a shot. I know him too well.'

'How foolish that would have been!' he said, and looked at her passionate face. Peter walked along as though they did not exist. Only when his mother said sharply, 'Turn here,' did he realize where he was. From time to time he had stopped, looking distractedly about him, as though in a moment the smiling face of Sheila Fury might penetrate the brickwork at which he stared, or from some hole in the pavement Professor Titmouse might emerge, put his spectacles on, and, leering at him, say, 'I think you are a little sly – even callous. Ha ha!'

'Don't stand like this!' Mrs Fury had raised her voice. Peter was now in the middle. His mother walked near the wall, Mulcare on the outside. They turned from Dacre Road, and Mulcare, catching the boy by the arm, said:

'Can't you hear her winches? She's just finishing loading. Look!' All three stopped. Yes, there was the ship, sure enough, there her towering masts, her sleek funnels painted blue, and that delicate white band encircling them. There she was, her stern facing them. Actually on the street. And as the winches sang and the cargo rose high from the sheds and whirred dizzily down her holds, the water rose. As the water rose, the ship sank. The roofs seemed to rise higher even as they stood looking at her. It was as if the street itself had imprisoned her, had flooded her with its bricks and masonry.

Peter looked at the stern, and read her name in gold lettering. The ship was loading, she was waiting for him, for Mulcare.

'It's a big ship,' said Mrs Fury as they continued their way down the street. As they came nearer the woman said:

'Fancy! There are men actually working down here. I thought ...'

'But they're all going back to work,' Mulcare replied.

'Thank God!' she said. 'Thank God!'

'We better go down through the shed,' said Mr Mulcare. They crossed the road and passed under the wall of the grain warehouse. Well, there they were at last. Along the shed there lay an old discarded chute. On this they sat.

The woman raised her head and looked at the masts. To her they seemed to touch the sky. Men were loading her for'ard hatches. The others were being covered up. The network of falls that hung from her derricks was being taken down, the blocks unshipped. A quartermaster was standing behind the binnacle on the monkey-bridge. In the air there rose the smell of old rope, of pitch, of meat and fruit. Had she ever dreamed that she would sit on an old cargo chute and see her last child follow the same path as her husband? Had she ever dreamed that she would sit by this other man, Mr Mulcare? Some men with bags had arrived and were now climbing her gangway. Mulcare got up.

'Excuse me.' Then he went away behind a meat waggon. It was as if his going had loosened their tongues at last.

'Peter! I am sure you will be glad you went. Mr Mulcare will look to you. He has promised me that. He is an old friend of your father.' She looked earnestly at her son, as though by her very look she might draw words from him. But Peter merely looked at the ship and said nothing. His bag had fallen from the chute to the ground. He did not pick it up, but sat swinging his legs. His mother was there, sitting by him, and before his eyes were mirrored all the energy and activity which one sees in a departing ship. He saw the crew go aboard, he saw the dockers shouting and laughing, joking with each other as they battened down their hatches. He saw the white burst from the funnel as they tested her whistle. 'You have changed so much, Peter,' his mother said. She looked away then, knowing he did not care what she said.

Mulcare came back and sat on the chute. The sun came out. Under it the whole scene seemed to change. The dreary atmosphere was gone. In that paradisial moment the ship itself had appeared to move from the quay as though, feeling its warmth, she were straining to be free, to be free from those roofs from those towering cranes, that imprisoned and held her fast. It was as if she had smelt the ocean again, her spirit touched its unfathomable depths.

'We must go aboard soon,' Mulcare said, and looked away up the shed. How quiet this boy was! Saying nothing, and yet about to tread for the first time upon a long and adventurous road. He looked at Peter. The boy was looking up, higher than the roof, higher than the cranes, higher than any mast, as though thought itself were endeavouring to free his feet from the ground, to drag his body from the dead wood. 'Cheer up!' Mulcare said. Now he smiled. 'It's no holiday, of course,' added Mulcare. 'You'll have to work.'

It was the end. So the woman thought as she looked from one to the other. She felt calm and peaceful. She had only to hear the man say, 'We must go now.' She had only to rise and kiss this boy, and turn away, and she would have turned that last page of the book. She would begin again. After all, she loved him, in spite of everything. He was only young. He could try again. She was glad, glad in her heart that it had all been so. Perhaps it was God's good will. This man would take her son. The sea would do him good. It was all for the best. The end of the page. She turned to Mulcare.
   'I know you will look after him,' she said, sensing the man's desire to be off. More men were climbing her gangway.
   'Don't you worry, Mrs Fury.' He turned to Peter. 'Pick up your bag.'
   The woman caught hold of Peter and embraced him. 'Remember what I said to you.' That was all. Then she kissed him. 'Good-bye! God bless you.'
   Mulcare looked away up the shed. Peter bent down to pick up his bag. As he swung it from the ground the contents of his inside pocket fell out. 'Wait, Peter!' Mrs Fury stooped down to pick them up. As she did so, she saw on the ground in front of her two photographs. As she stared at these she knelt down upon the ground. She continued to stare at them. Then she struggled to her feet. Her face went white. She held the photographs of Sheila Fury in her hand. She reached out to Mulcare. 'Take these,' she said. 'Take them away,' as though they burned her hand, as though, touching them, they befouled. Mulcare took them from her.
   She stood in front of her son, a helpless rage seized her, fleshed itself upon her features. 'Where did you get them? Have you been with that woman?' she asked.
   'Who is this?' asked Mulcare, quite unaware of the rage that spread like fire across Mrs Fury's face.
   Peter said quietly, 'It's my brother's wife.'
   'What?' said Mulcare. Then he looked at the woman, and he closed his mouth like a trap.

'His brother's wife! His brother's wife!' the man was saying. 'But where have I seen her?' The photographs seemed to say, 'You saw me a little while ago. Your friend and I retired together.' The face seemed to smile out at him.

'Have you been with that woman?' Mrs Fury seemed ready to explode. Her whole body became tensed, she leaned forward and almost touched her son's face. 'Have you been with that woman?'

Mulcare dropped the photographs to the ground and stared at Peter.

'Yes, I have. I have been with her many times,' Peter said.

'What!' Then she raised her clenched fists and struck her son between the eyes. 'What!' she screamed. 'What!'

Peter drew back, but she moved with him. Her rage, fleshed upon her wild and agitated face, pushed her forward. She struck him again, and saw blood run down her son's face. Again she struck, this time with both fists together. A cloud seemed to blot out everything but this face. Peter was laughing. She struck him again. She felt the soft flesh give way beneath her blows. There was nothing in front of her now save his face. The face of her son who that morning had knelt with her before the altar. The face seemed to grow bigger, to grin at her. And as she struck she shouted. The world disappeared in this great white cloud, and she struck not Peter but everybody. They seemed to float past and receive her cruel blows – one long procession. 'My God! I thought it had ended,' she was crying in her mind, 'but it is only beginning.' Again and again she struck, not Peter, not a man, but all men, all those who had cheated and insulted her. Somebody was dragging her back, but her clenched fists, as though now freed from her body, continued to strike. 'Damn you! Damn you!' she began to scream.

'Mrs Fury! Mrs Fury!' somebody was whispering in her ear.

'Damn you! Damn you!' She continued to strike at her son's face.

'Take that madwoman out of this!' shouted a voice from the gangway.

Blinded by her own tears, she made one last strike at Peter's face. But Mulcare was already dragging the boy up the gangway. Men were waiting to unship it. Somebody had picked up Peter's bag and had carried it on board.

Mrs Fury struck nothing but the empty air.

'Take that madwoman away!' shouted a man at the top of the gangway. The woman stood still. Looking up, she saw him, her son, Peter, with his bloody face, just as he disappeared round the gangway head. Then she walked back to the house.

FIND OUT MORE ABOUT PENGUIN BOOKS

We publish the largest range of titles of any English language paper-back publisher. As well as novels, crime and science fiction, humour, biography and large-format illustrated books, Penguin series include *Pelican Books* (on the arts, sciences and current affairs), *Penguin Reference Books, Penguin Classics, Penguin Modern Classics, Penguin English Library* and *Penguin Handbooks* (on subjects from cookery and gardening to sport), as well as *Puffin Books* for children. Other series cover a wide variety of interests from poetry to crosswords, and there are also several newly formed series – *King Penguin, Penguin American Library, Penguin Diaries and Letters* and *Penguin Travel Library*.

We are an international publishing house, but for copyright reasons not every Penguin title is available in every country. To find out more about the Penguins available in your country please write to our U.K. office – Dept EP, Penguin Books Ltd, Harmondsworth, Middlesex UB7 0DA – unless you live in one of the following areas:

In the U.S.A.: Dept DG, Penguin Books, 299 Murray Hill Parkway, East Rutherford, New Jersey 07073.

In Canada: Penguin Books Canada Ltd, 2801 John Street, Markham, Ontario L3R 1B4.

In Australia: Marketing Department, Penguin Books Australia Ltd, P.O. Box 257, Ringwood, Victoria 3134.

In New Zealand: Marketing Department, Penguin Books (N.Z.) Ltd, P.O. Box 4019, Auckland 10.

In India: Penguin Overseas Ltd, 706 Eros Apartments, 56 Nehru Place, New Delhi 110019.

Jocelyn Brooke

THE ORCHID TRILOGY
The Military Orchid/A Mine of Serpents
The Goose Cathedral

The themes of orchids and fireworks, lifelong obsessions, run parallel throughout this trilogy, and in his exploration of these Brooke distils a vision of himself – early childhood, schooldays, life at Oxford and in the army. A kaleidoscope of memories which ultimately fuses into an image of his own personal reality that remains firmly rooted in the Kentish countryside of his childhood.

'One of the notable writers to have surfaced after the war' – from the Introduction by Anthony Powell

'He has an ear for talk; an eye for the beautiful and a sense of the comic. He writes simply and never shows off. Yet he is as subtle as the devil' – Sir John Betjeman

THE IMAGE OF A DRAWN SWORD

The Image of a Drawn Sword is Jocelyn Brooke's only true novel. Yet in this exploration of friendship, sexuality, guilt, alienation and power, he reveals an underlying autobiographical element in which his own physical experiences in the army are translated into a Kafkaesque vision where fantasy and reality are disturbingly blurred.

'The skill and intensity of the writing make peculiarly haunting this cry of complaint on behalf of bewildered Man' – Pamela Hansford Johnson

'Seldom have naturalism and fantasy been more strangely merged. Mr Brooke is a great writer' – Elizabeth Bowen

KING PENGUIN

R. C. Hutchinson

TESTAMENT

Writers, critics and his vast reading public agreed that the novels of R. C. Hutchinson would remain among the enduring classics of the thirties and forties. Rediscovered and restored to print, *Testament*, his finest novel, portrays life in Russia at the time of the Revolution.

Narrated by his friend, the soldier and painter Alexei Otraveskov, the story of Count Anton Scheffler opens in 1917, in Russia mutilated by war and poised for revolution. In scenes of magnificent and vivid realism – on crowded streets and railway platforms, in prison camps and society drawing-rooms – Hutchinson paints an epic canvas and, in the figure of Anton, gives us a rare and unsentimental portrait of greatness, and a masterly study of the mentality of heroism.

RISING

R. C. Hutchinson was writing the final pages of this novel on the day of his death in 1975. The study of an episode of South American history, *Rising* develops into a profound examination of racial and other human relationships, and of the eternal problem of evil. The central figure in the story is Sabino, the outcast member of a rich mine-owning family, who leads a military expedition to safeguard a railway line from saboteurs. Sabino's men are virtually slaves – half-starved miners pressed into unwilling service. With a realism that is all but physically shared by the reader, R. C. Hutchinson shows his characters growing and changing against an almost biblical background of harsh trials and illuminating incidents.

'Genius is impossible to define, and the word has become tarnished by exposure, but I believe that R. C. Hutchinson had it, and that future generations will think likewise' – Rupert Hart-Davis